LESSEK'S KEY

The Eldarn Sequence Book 2

Also by Robert Scott & Jay Gordon from Gollancz:

The Hickory Staff

LESSEK'S KEY

The Eldarn Sequence Book 2

Robert Scott
and Jay Gordon

Copyright © Robert Scott 2006

The right of Robert Scott to be identified as the author
of this work has been asserted by him in accordance
with the Copyright, Designs and Patents Act 1988.

First published in Great Britain in 2006
by Gollancz
An imprint of the Orion Publishing Group
Orion House, 5 Upper St Martin's Lane,
London WC2H 9EA

This edition published in Great Brtain in 2007 by Gollancz

1 3 5 7 9 10 8 6 4 2

A CIP catalogue record for this book
is available from the British Library.

ISBN-13 978 0 57507 952 6
ISBN-10 0 57507 952 5

Typeset by Deltatype Ltd, Birkenhead, Merseyside

Printed and bound in Great Britain by
Mackays of Chatham plc, Chatham, Kent

The Orion Publishing Group's policy is to use papers that
are natural, renewable and recyclable products and made
from wood grown in sustainable forests. The logging and
manufacturing processes are expected to conform to the
environmental regulations of the country of origin.

www.orionbooks.co.uk

In memory:

Jay Mark Gordon

(1944 – 2005)

ACKNOWLEDGEMENTS

Last year, while Jay and I were busy telling Steven Taylor's story, there were many people who took time to tell Jay's. His family and I are indebted to all of them but my sincere appreciation goes to Heather Nicholson, Tali Israeli, Sam Altman, and Richard Marcus. I know Jay appreciated their efforts as well. I would be remiss if I did not mention the staff of caring people who helped Jay remain comfortable in the last months of his life. Ardent supporters of his writing, Jay's nurses took time from a gruelling daily regimen to celebrate every bit of good news he received about the Eldarn books. Speaking for Susan, Stacy and Karen we cannot thank all of you enough.

I owe thanks to Bill Bixby, Jamie Addington and the staff at Bull Run for their ongoing support and flexibility. Thanks Gena Doyle and Uncle G for reading, asking questions and calculating irritating math problems. If reading chapter drafts wasn't enough, Pam Widmann was invariably willing to drive around Idaho Springs with a cell phone and a camera, snapping pictures of roadside ditches, empty lots, alleyways and even the city landfill. Thanks Pam. Thanks to everyone at Caribou Coffee for the 239 gallons of free refills, and thanks to Mr Macbeth and the Gypsyman for their efforts to rouse the cheering section around the world.

As ever, I owe sincere thanks to Jo Fletcher and the staff and writers at Victor Gollancz. Jo herself has given countless hours to these books – weekends, late nights, vacations, even commuter time. My gratitude also goes to Gillian Redfearn, Jonathan Weir, Sara Mulryan, Simon Spanton, and James Lovegrove for making a fledgling writer's introduction to this industry painless and enjoyable.

Finally, thanks to Kage, Sam and Hadley for their love and support.

CONTENTS

BOOK III *The Wolfhound*

BOOK IV *The Hickory Staff*

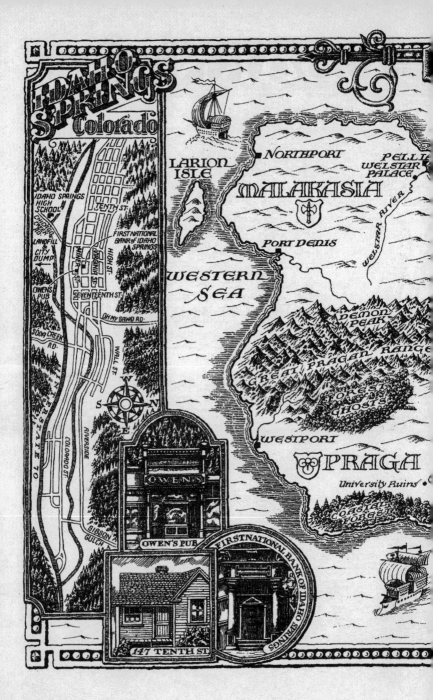

ORINDALE HARBOUR

The creature huddles in the recessed doorway of a waterfront tavern. Closed now, and empty, the windows look in on an abyss, a room so shrouded in middlenight that the glass might mark the entrance to the Fold itself. Light from sporadic sentinel torches left burning along the Orindale waterfront reflect off the windows, but, ignoring the laws of physics, their glow doesn't bring any illumination to the darkened tavern; the diffuse glow merely bounces back.

The creature knows well that places exist where nothing matters, where light cannot penetrate, where the absence of perception provides for the absence of reality. The Fold. Isn't that how the old man described it? It's worse than death, because death, like life or love, is held so close. Death has meaning; it's a profound event, feared above most horrors, but meaningful nevertheless. This place is worse, more tragic: the Fold embodied. This is a place so devoid of colour and touch, scent and sound, that nothing can survive. This is the place mothers go after the broken bodies of their children are found washed up on a beach or lying in pieces across a field. It's the end of all things, the event horizon.

Nothing can remain here long – except for the creature. Stooped and broken, hunched at the waist and dragging much of its torso like a disintegrating appendage, the thing in the doorway resembles a tree that has lived too long, the victim of too many woodsmen hacking deep, disfiguring scars. It can stand upright, but that's painful, that requires effort, and hope, and the creature refuses to have hope. Instead, it waits. Fortified by its ability to see and understand its own condition, as if seeing itself from above, the creature becomes the darkness, dragging it along as it drags its own body. It sees the mossy nubs that work their way through the rotting planks of the waterfront walkways. It steps in the puddles of piss and vomit that surround the taverns. It watches rats battling over half-stripped chicken bones tossed from windows two and three floors

3

up, and insects devouring half-digested bits of venison regurgitated by drunks reeling towards home, their ships, maybe, or the downy beds of the local whores.

One night it finds a finger, lost in a bar fight and on another, a portion of someone's ear, which it turns over and over in its fingers, trying to imagine the whole from which this bit was severed. Finally, it stashes the lobe in its robes, tucked beside the finger, the chicken bones and the bits of venison, before starting out again.

This wretched thing would be willing to die if it were willing to allow itself an experience so meaningful. Its pallid flesh is hidden beneath the folds of a stolen cloak as it stares out at the Orindale night, listening, waiting and planning. It does have a mission: it is driven by its desire to hunt and kill the black and gold soldiers. There are so many; thousands have come here, and it kills one, two, sometimes five in a night. Men or women, it doesn't care. It doesn't dismember them, or eat them – not much of them anyway, there is plenty of food along the waterfront – and nor does it perform deviant acts with their corpses. Instead, the creature slices them open: through the neck is quiet, but the gullet works well, too. It finds some strange satisfaction watching the young Malakasians struggling to replace handfuls of innards, as if packing lengths of moist summer sausage into a torn canvas sack. From some come moist clouds of exsanguinous fog, particularly when they are gutted in the early morning.

The creature's pain comes and goes, but when it strikes it is searing, nearly unbearable. Beginning in its neck and shoulders, the fire bolts across its back, paralysing its legs and forcing it ever deeper into its crouch. Though it cannot remember the past very well, it knows that it has brought this upon itself. There are hazy recollections of a frigid river, a flat rock, and an aborted attempt to straighten itself, to regain its previous form, but it did great damage that day, hurling itself repeatedly against the unforgiving stone. Then the pain was glorious, making it see things, hallucinations, nearly translucent lights like wraiths scurrying over hillsides and flitting between sap-stained pine trunks. Now it salves its wounds with the black and gold soldiers.

They'll never capture it. They've tried. It outsmarts them easily; it avoids their snares, because it lives among the things that crawl and slither on the ground, safely beneath the gaze of the Malakasian occupation army.

A stray dog happens by, a filthy, disagreeable mutt with mangy fur, a pronounced limp and a broken canine uselessly askew in its lower jaw. The dog gives the creature a low growl, a warning, more out of fear than any real threat. But it's too late. Brandishing a long knife, the creature pounces. Cat-quick and deadly, it buries its knife in the dog's throat and twists with such force the stray can do little more than yelp before dying on the cobblestones.

The hood of its cloak falls across its shoulders, revealing an ashen face, a man's face, sickly-white like the colour of spoiled milk. His eyes focus on nothing. Though bent, he is a big man, and powerful. He doesn't feel remorse: the animal will make a tasty breakfast and, if he rations the meat, lunch too.

The creature – the man – is distracted by something. Licking at the bloody knife, he peers into the darkness hovering over the harbour. He can make out flames, watch-fires, he assumes, that burn on bowsprits, jib-booms, and stern rails though they appear to float above the water. He closes his eyes and listens: something has happened. One of the ships is coming apart; even from this distance, he can hear beams splintering, masts collapsing and planks pulling free and snapping like hickory knots in a bonfire. He judges the distance at well over a thousand paces and decides it can be only one ship. Hazy recollections taunt from just beyond the periphery of his consciousness, and a feeling: this is good, this vessel snapping in two and sinking to the bottom of Orindale Harbour – but he can't recall why.

Without warning, and surprising himself, he speaks. 'They must have made it.' Then he looks around in terror. 'What does that mean? Who said that?'

'They must have made it,' he repeats and this time realises *he* has spoken. He is hearing his own voice. It's as if he hid part of himself, enough to preserve the integrity of who he was ... hid it far enough away to allow himself ... the creature, that is ... to eat things like discarded fish innards, severed ears or vomited venison bits. But he is close enough to hear when his *doppelgänger* speaks.

'Say that again.' He is looking anxiously about the abandoned waterfront, still aware of the cataclysm taking place in the harbour, but ignoring it for the moment. 'Say that again.'

'The ship, the *Prince Marek*, they must have reached it.'

Bending slowly, an indistinct blur in the darkness, the hunched creature sheaths his long knife. He peers side to side, aware there are things he doesn't understand, and mumbles, 'Good then ... back to the hunt.'

Sallax Farro of Estrad tucks the dog's limp form beneath his cloak, pulls his hood up and hurries south along the wharf.

A tangible silence like a spectre creeps across the countryside. Trees ignore the wind and stand upright; leaves quiet their rustle as onshore breezes fade to a whisper. Waves lapping against the shoreline flatten to nearly indiscernible ripples; seabirds land and nest, their heads tucked protectively beneath wings. Even the northern Twinmoon appears to dim, as if unwilling to illuminate Nerak's disappearance.

All of southern Falkan draws its shades, closes its doors and waits. Nerak is gone, and Eldarn has not yet decided how it will respond. Like a battered child finally witnessing her father's arrest, the very fabric holding this strange and beautiful land together rumbles with a growing desire to scream out *We are free!*, but those screams emerge as a nearly inaudible whimper. Many feel the dark prince's exit, shuddering for a moment, and then returning to the business of their lives. There is a status quo to be maintained. There are expectations and accountability because, of course, the dark prince may return.

South of the city is a meadow, just above the inter-tidal zone: more of an upland bog, rife with sedge, rushes and coarse coastal grass. The meadow, flanked on three sides by the scrub-oak and heavy needle pines that mark the sandy edge of the Ravenian Sea, is an anomaly. The expanse of thick foliage and dense fertile soil, thanks to a narrow stream rushing by just out of sight behind a stand of pines, form an unexpected oasis trapped between the intimidating Blackstone peaks to the east and the cold salt waters to the west.

On this night, the meadow grasses are brushed back and forth by Twinmoon breezes charging unchecked north and south along the narrow channel. Painted pale Twinmoon white, the grasses glow with the muted brilliance of a snowfield at midday.

Gabriel O'Reilly appears, interrupting the ghostly surface, a blurry cloud of spectral smoke. His battle with the almor has taken him across the Fold, through the great emptiness and within a breath of the evil force lying restlessly inside. He has seen the centre of the world, has passed through the dead of the Northern Forest and through the great cataclysm that pushes the edges of the universe ever outwards. It is all he can do to maintain his sanity as he looks into the face of a god – it *must* be a god, for nothing else could generate such beauty, such destruction and such pure, uncomplicated power. But this isn't his God; he's not home yet.

Gabriel O'Reilly has felt the fires of the demon lands, smelled their putrid stench and sensed their inhabitants: legions of creatures marshalling their resources in an effort to weaken his resolve and purloin his very essence. At times, he has seen home, Virginia, and though he doubts any of it is real, he imagines he can smell it, touch it, feel those lush rolling hills beneath his bare feet. Slamming through forests and burrowing through mountains, O'Reilly and the almor careen, a tangle of demon limbs in a ghostly fog across time and worlds. As they pass through the pristine wilderness of his home, he checks beyond the rise of each hill, hoping for just one glimpse of a Confederate brigade marching to face the Army of Northeastern Virginia.

And all the while he holds on to the demon almor, the one sent to take Versen and Brexan, the only friends he's made in five lifetimes, forcing himself to remember why he grips the creature so hard, hanging on despite the drain on his sanity.

Now the almor is gone. O'Reilly has no idea how long they have battled, but suddenly the demon vanishes, falling away into the burned over wastelands of a distant world. It is as if its will to engage him has run dry.

Has it been days? Years? O'Reilly doesn't care. Instead, he casts his senses about the meadow, detecting no sign of Brexan, Versen or the scarred Seron they fought together. As much as he can remember of disappointment, the spirit feels it now. He had hoped that beating the almor would have given him a way home: the path to heaven, the right to look upon the face of his own God.

But it hasn't happened, and he is still here in Eldarn. O'Reilly floats above the meadow another moment, his indistinct face a mask of loneliness; then without a sound he slips between the trees and disappears into the forest.

He is not gone a moment when others appear along the edge of the meadow, following O'Reilly through the trees, hunting him. One, the leader, pauses to stare across the Ravenian Sea. It has been many years since William Higgins has seen the sea, long before his daughter was born, before he left his family in St Louis to seek his fortune in the mountains above Oro City, Colorado. He turns after the others; they are close behind O'Reilly now. As the cavalry soldier-turned-miner fades from view, his ghostly white boots pass through a fallen cottonwood tree. The sound of a spur, chiming through the ages, rings once above the din of the onshore breeze.

*

Although the sounds of the *Prince Marek* shattering in the harbour do not reach her, Brexan Carderic is unable to sleep. Moving north, she is less than a day outside Orindale, expecting to reach the outskirts of the Falkan capital before dawn. She doesn't hear the *Prince Marek* coming apart, but the stillness that follows in the wake of the ship's death reaches her. She makes her barefoot way slowly along the shore, recalling the loss of her boots, discarded in the Ravenian Sea after she cut Versen loose from the stern rail of the fat merchant's ship. With every step towards the city, the Malakasian imagines first how she will find this man and second how she will torture him when she does. Burning Versen's body was the most difficult thing she'd ever done, yet she did it meticulously, thinking she will have one chance to get something right, but she will live with its memory for ever. She chose every branch carefully, avoiding green wood so her fire would blaze quickly into a fury. Even as the flames claimed Versen's body, Brexan sat, imagining the horror of failing to get that first spark to kindle.

She cries as she remembers that day, sitting by his side, rising only to find a piece of scrub-oak, a pine bough or a thatch of cedar brambles. She didn't speak to him, or kiss him goodbye, nor did she take any of his scant belongings as keepsakes. Instead, she sat with him, watching as his pyre burned down and eventually out.

Mark Jenkins stands on the forward bench of a small skiff borrowed from an elderly fisherman he believes now to be the Larion Senator, Gilmour Stow of Estrad. He has a half-moon gash above one eye, and blood clouds his vision. Mark thinks he must have been hit by a splinter of glass when what was left of the aft end of the *Prince Marek* began breaking apart; he ignores the bleeding and, screaming out her name, searches the wreckage for any sign of Brynne. He scans the castaway spars, rails, barrels, beams and sections of sailcloth that have begun floating away. He has given up hope that the Pragan woman will appear alongside the skiff, offer him an alluring grin and ask if she might come aboard. He tries to spot a pale upper arm, a bare cheek, temple or even a supple leg in the light cast across Orindale Harbour by the northern Twinmoon.

Before him, the great sailing vessel sinks away. Apart from avoiding the undertow as the tons of metal, wood and tar careen towards the bottom, Mark doesn't give the remains of the *Prince Marek* more than a glance. He is shouting Brynne's name, but it fails to occur to him that Steven and Gilmour might be lost as well.

Then a thought nudges him. There's something … he has seen something, something he can't remember at the moment, but even that is enough to give him pause, to turn him around stiffly, a mannequin on a rotating pedestal. The last few minutes have been too traumatic; his search for Brynne has distracted him. There are other problems, other threats.

Where's Garec?

They left him sleeping in the catboat. That isn't it. There's something more.

Versen? No.

Mark's voice fades until he can barely hear himself whisper the Ronan woman's name.

The clouds. Those clouds of mist. Where are they?

He saw one; it had been coming out over the harbour, right before the ship shattered in two. He searches the night, rubbing a sleeve across his face to wipe the blood from his eyes. *There it is.* It's as if a black fogbank has blown west to hover over the harbour. Despite Mark's certainty that he witnessed the cloud moving away from shore, towards the *Prince Marek*, not ten minutes earlier, now it looks to have stopped – not retreated; rather, it remains stolidly in place, about two hundred yards off the waterfront. But it's frozen there, impervious to the efforts of the onshore breeze to carry it back into town, thicker than any normal cloud and heavier than fog ought to be. Like a column of ethereal soldiers poised to charge, the mist looks as though it is awaiting its next set of orders: *fall on the partisans and kill them all*, or perhaps, *return to the city and await further instructions*.

If the cloud advances, he'll swamp the skiff, turn it over and hide in the air pocket below, praying the thin boards of the fisherman's boat will be enough to stave off the deadly fumes. Mark clears his throat and begins shouting again for Brynne.

Gilmour Stow allows himself to be pulled beneath the surface as the colossal ship sinks by the bow, then, opening his eyes, mumbles a quick spell in a cloud of bubbles, and his underwater vision improves. Brighter, nearly in focus now, the *Prince Marek* floats effortlessly towards the bottom, picking up speed and casting off loose cargo, rigging and more than a few bodies. It's a beautiful sight; ironic and tragic that such a ship would look most glorious when wrapped jib to spanker in the very water that buoyed her for so many Twinmoons. He watches until it disappears from view.

In one hand, Gilmour clasps Steven Taylor's hickory staff and in the other, the only existing copy of Lessek's spells, notes and reflections on the nature of magic and the Larion spell table. He had been so certain the book had been lost a thousand Twinmoons earlier; he curses himself for not realising Nerak had it all along. He is a powerful foe. Thinking back to their battle just moments earlier, Gilmour wonders if the fallen Larion magician had given his best: granted, it had been a titanic blow, and it had required all of Gilmour's concentration to keep from being pulverised. But had it been Nerak's *best*? Had he really felt the sum force of the dark prince's power? Kicking towards the surface, he wonders if Nerak was telling the truth: *That was naught but the tiniest of tastes, Fantus, a minuscule sample drawn from the very furthest reaches of my power.*

The only blow Nerak had an opportunity to land: had it been a feint, a flick of the wrist? Would a focused spell, carefully woven over time, tear Gilmour to ribbons or reduce him to dust? He hopes he will be in possession of Lessek's key and in control of the spell table before he has to discover the full extent of Nerak's power.

Clutching the staff close, Gilmour emerges from the depths and immediately forgets the dark prince. Fear and regret seize him as he hears Mark Jenkins, nearby but invisible in the darkness, screaming Brynne's name.

'Rutters!' the older man murmurs, realising Brynne is lost.

It's not the crashing and snapping of beams in the *Prince Marek* that finally wakes Garec Haile of Estrad, but the faint sound of shouting. His gaze slowly focuses on the heavy weave of a blanket he borrowed from his sister's room the previous Twinmoon. The archer wriggles to a sitting position, shrugging off layers of wool, draws a few stabilising breaths and feels the gentle undulating rhythm of the harbour tide. 'I'm on the boat,' he says out loud.

In a rush, the events of the past avens return; he jerks himself upright. 'Steven! I've been shot. Oh, gods, I've been shot!' He reaches for the arrow, the black Malakasian arrow he knows he will find jutting crookedly from his ribs – but despite the recollection of an intense burning pain as the polished shale pierced his skin, the young freedom fighter can find no sign of injury. 'Gone,' he says, feeling nothing but a tear in his tunic and the sticky remnants of blood drying on his clothing. 'How can this be?'

Wishing for more light to conduct a thorough examination, Garec takes a deep breath. There is no rattle, no telltale vibration of fluid pooling in his lungs. He places a hand over his heart; it, too, seems strong, thrumming beneath his fingers.

Standing, Garec's legs falter for a moment and he nearly topples headfirst into Orindale Harbour. Balancing, he stretches and cautiously considers his apparent good health. 'I'm all right,' he whispers and only then realises he is alone on the catboat. 'Where is everybody?'

Garec's question is answered with another cry, faint but urgent. He feels his stomach roil as it comes again: *'Brynne!'*, a sob recognisable in the distant voice. Instinctively, Garec reaches for his bow.

It's not there.

For a moment, he feels a nearly overwhelming sense of relief. He hoists the vessel's small sail and almost immediately it is captured by the onshore breeze; the keel turns lazily in a loping circle towards the wharf. 'Rutting boats,' he grumbles, picking his way aft to the tiller. 'I'll be out here for the next Twinmoon.'

'Brynne!' The hopeless cry resonates through his bones; Garec guesses that his friend is dead. What happened? How long had he slept? Had they tried to take the *Prince Marek* without him? Awkwardly, he pulls the sail taut and gropes for a wooden stanchion along the starboard gunwale; failing to find one, he hangs on to the line in one hand while wresting the tiller with the other to bring the boat about. Navigating as best he can in the moonlit darkness, he sets a course for the sound of the distraught voice.

Carpello Jax shifts three candles closer to the polished looking-glass propped above his fireplace mantel. His beard is coming on nicely: step one in his transformation.

Sweat dampens his face and neck despite the evening breeze. He drags a ruffled linen sleeve across his forehead, a frequent move over the past several days. Not that it has been warm in Orindale; rather, Carpello sweats because he is grossly overweight, and because he anticipates his audience with Prince Malagon. He is sure the dark one knows Carpello's schooner is moored in the harbour; it won't be much longer before he's summoned to the royal residence to present his report. Carpello has prepared a convoluted tangle of lies and remains confident he can sell his story to Prince Malagon: he is a businessman, and he lies for a living.

Through the open windows, Carpello hears the sounds of a cataclysm unfolding in the harbour, but for the moment he doesn't move to investigate. He is nervous, and that has awakened a handful of sublimated memories. The most tenacious this evening is Versen, the woodsman. Carpello runs a hand across the ample hillock of his abdomen, touching the wound dealt him by the woman just before she went overboard in an effort to free the troublesome Ronan. Carpello had meant to interrogate the girl and then to give her to his crew as a diversion, but things had gone terribly wrong. By the end of that day, he had lost both prisoners and his Seron escort.

Carpello grimaces. It will be a difficult tale to weave for the prince; he reviews his own version once again, to ensure all the details are committed to memory, as if they had actually occurred. The sweaty businessman knows the secret to successful lying is believing one's own fabrications; Prince Malagon will be Carpello's most challenging audience yet.

Outside, there is another explosion, but Carpello's thoughts are still with the woodsman. Even facing torture and death, the young man had surprised him: 'A very good friend of mine looks forward to meeting you,' he had said. 'If I were you, I would take my own life rather than ever run into her again.'

'A woman? I shall be enchanted, I'm sure,' Carpello had responded.

'You'll be dead,' the Ronan had answered flatly, 'and she'll make it last for Twinmoons ... a grisly death is on its way to Orindale right now.'

Had Versen been bluffing? Carpello wipes the sweat from around his eyes once more. He doesn't believe so. Versen had sounded convincing: a specific woman wanted to find and kill him. But why? Carpello feigns ignorance for a moment, trying out his 'innocent' face in the candlelit looking-glass. He watches it fall away. He knows why.

Reaching into his belt, he withdraws a thin fillet knife with a tapered point and a polished edge. Wiping it on a chamois, he leans in close to the mirror and, with a steady hand, slices the bulbous mole from the side of his disfigured nose: step two.

Blood blooms from the wound, dripping from Carpello's sagging jowls to stain the frilly ruffles of his linen shirt. He sways unsteadily, feeling faint. His vision tunnelling, he staggers backwards to sit with a groan in a nearby chair. Carpello Jax begins to cry as Versen's voice echoes grimly in his head: You'll be dead ... and she will make it last for Twinmoons.

Alen Jasper wakes, groans, rolls to one side and vomits repeatedly into a ceramic pot beside his bed. *Too much wine tonight. Too much wine every night.* Spitting between dry heaves, the former Larion Senator runs a wrist over his mouth and then his forehead: cold sweats; he might be sick.

'Nonsense,' the old man tells his darkened room. 'You haven't been sick in eighteen hundred Twinmoons. You drink too rutting much. That's all, no need to lie about it now.' He's interrupted by the need to retch, but this time Alen vomits on the floor; the contents of the ceramic pot are too foul for a second round. Collapsing onto his back, he stares at the ceiling and feels the tremors begin. 'Pissing demons, you can't need a drink already.' With a frustrated curse, he promises to deny himself another drop until after sunset the following day. 'Suffer, you drunk fool. Go ahead and shake.' The sweat rolls from his forehead, tickling the sensitive skin behind his ears and staining his already damp pillow grey.

Alen breathes shallowly in an effort to ease the pain in his head and calm the angry waste churning in his stomach. He reaches for a cloth draped across a bedside chair. It's a gesture he has perfected over hundreds of evenings similar to this, but tonight something is different. The cloth feels odd in his hands, as if his fingers, deadened from Twinmoons of drinking and malnutrition, have suddenly rejuvenated themselves. The cloth is softer; he can feel wrinkles, tiny imperfections in the weave that he has not noticed before. He catches the fleeting aroma of beeswax from a taper burning on his mantel.

He stops wiping his face and inhales deeply. Behind the grim flavour of his vomit and beyond the sharp tang of the candle, he finds it: roast gansel. Churn prepared the meal two nights ago, and the smell is still hanging about his house. He hasn't been able to detect aromas like this in fifty Twinmoons.

Alen swings his feet over the edge of the bed, outside the splatter of this evening's meal – he can't recall what it was – and onto the floor. He runs a hand through sweaty hair and whispers, 'What's happened to me?'

Moving to an armoire near the window, Alen splashes generous handfuls of cold water on his face and feels the familiar sensation as it trickles beneath his tunic to dribble down his back. The cold slaps him awake and he shivers, a genuine shiver rather than the all-too-common drink-shakes that generally visit him in the pre-dawn aven. He pulls off his rank clothes and considers himself in the glass.

'Fat, you rutter.' Alen purses his lips disgustedly. 'How did you get here?'

He is unaware that a Twinmoon's travel to the east, Prince Malagon's flagship is sinking, nor does he realise that a Larion far portal has been opened and that Steven Taylor and the dark prince have both crossed the Fold in search of Lessek's key. Alen is powerful enough to have detected the brief but powerful battle between Fantus and Nerak only a half aven earlier, but Alen's senses were dulled, from apathy, alcohol and grief. He stands naked, reflecting on the Twinmoons that have turned him into this reprehensible, out-of-shape creature that stares back at him from the looking-glass.

Not many people can stand to look at themselves naked for too long: most are too critical, pining for something – more muscle, less paunch, more hair, bigger breasts ... Alen's assessment of himself goes beyond superficial disgust as he delves more deeply into his own cowardice, his grief and his fear.

Hiding in his specially-designed house where no one in Eldarn can find him, he pines for everything he wanted to do, the leader he wanted to become, and for the things he wanted for his children. Though they had become interesting and engaging adults, and Alen remains proud of them all, there could have been more, if only he had done something: stood his ground, defended the Larion Senate, killed Nerak, and travelled to Durham to find his daughter, Reia. He should have brought her home to assume her place in the Senate; she would have been a powerful sorcerer. His daughter – *Pikan's* daughter would have stood toe-to-toe with the world's most powerful magicians, scholars and leaders, even with Nerak.

But Alen had not done any of those things. Instead, he had come to Middle Fork to wait, to lose hope and to drink. He had certainly come to do that.

But this evening something has changed. The pallid whiteness of his flesh has faded to a healthier pink. He can smell again, and feel. His fingers caress the fabric of his bedside cloth: Alen feels himself rejuvenating from within. The cold fear and stolid grief slip away, as if someone has pulled a stopper and allowed his essence to drain out. He is no happier with himself – he isn't pleased with the bandy arms, the bony legs or the bulging pot-belly hanging over the shrivelled penis he has not used for more than pissing – too often red – for more than five hundred Twinmoons. But this evening, with the stench of his vomit still heavy on the air, Alen senses a change; it skips across his skin and for a moment, the old Larion researcher feels the atrophied member stir between his legs.

Alen watches his stomach tighten, slimming his figure, as he stands up straight. Dropping the cloth, he brings his hands together, fingertip-to-fingertip, and feels the magic pass. His head clears as he turns away from the glass, intrigued by his regained strength.

'Why tonight?' he asks. The room is empty, but he knows to whom he has really addressed the question. 'Why now, you whoring bastard? Why now, when I'm this old, this tired, and a rutting dog-faced drunk?'

Lessek doesn't answer, and Alen shifts uneasily towards the armoire, wanting clean clothes. He tries to avoid looking back at the glass, but as he reaches for the cabinet door it's unavoidable and he is forced to look himself squarely in the face.

He realises what has happened.

The wrinkles at the corners of his eyes are not as deep as usual, and the grim creases in his forehead not as pronounced. He quickly dons a clean tunic and hose, mumbling as he does, 'Can't be ... where would he go? ... They haven't let up in so long ...' Hastily knotting a leather thong at his neck, he picks up the basin and tosses the remaining water across the puddle of vomit. With a thought, he casts a simple spell and watches as the water carries the spoiled vestiges of his dinner away, leaving a spotlessly clean floor in its wake.

Magic surges through him, and Alen is tempted to let go with a thunderclap, something that will shatter the windows and scare the dog-piss out of his neighbors. But he decides first to experiment, to be absolutely certain the changes that woke him from his stupor are lasting. Grabbing a cloak and a pair of worn leather boots, the former Larion Senator kicks open his chamber door and bellows, 'Wake up, my friends! It's time to get going!'

SILVERTHORN, COLORADO

'I think I'll go tomorrow,' Jennifer Sorenson says, unaware that, a world away, Malakasia's flagship is shattering into black shards and sinking into Orindale Harbour.

'No, stay the weekend,' Bryan encourages. 'They're predicting fresh snow Thursday night. We'll ski the powder for a couple of days, and you can drive back to the city on Saturday, or even Sunday if you don't mind traffic going down the mountain.'

'Please stay,' Meg adds, 'and if you don't want to ski, we'll go shopping. The antiques shops in town are terrific.'

Jennifer forces a smile, appreciating everything they have done to help her cope with Hannah's disappearance, but shopping for antiques and skiing in the Rocky Mountains remain low on her list of priorities. 'Thank you both. I really mean it, but with all the antiques I've sold in the past few months, I don't think I even want to look at another one for a very long time. And Bryan, I just don't know that I can go up there without—' Jennifer coughs, covering a sob.

She has been at her brother's for the past eight days: reading, writing letters and sharing walks with Bryan and Meg, but she has not been skiing, not one run. She hasn't even looked up at the mountain; raw emotion is just too near the surface. There has been no news of Hannah since the Idaho Springs police told her the search and rescue efforts underway on Decatur Peak would be suspended until spring. 'The snow is too deep for an effective search, Mrs Sorenson. I'm sorry,' the detective had said, coolly, *professionally* sympathetic. She had not moved as the numb realisation washed over her: Hannah was lost, presumed dead.

Wrapping an arm around her shoulders, her brother says, 'I'm sorry, Jenny, I didn't— But stay anyway. We'll, I don't know, cook gourmet food and drink too much expensive wine.'

'No.' It's a genuine chuckle this time as she reflects on her brother's sometimes curious endeavours in the kitchen. She wipes her eyes. 'Look at me. I'm a mess. You don't need me hanging around here.'

'Don't be silly,' Meg says. 'It'll be better here than at home. The store's finally empty, so you're spending too much time at the house. Just take a few more days to regroup.'

They don't understand.

'There's no place,' Jennifer begins falling apart again. 'There's no place to hide. There's no safe place. I can't get away from her. She's everywhere. Don't you see? I can't stand it. One minute she was there on her bike. I made her put her helmet on as if she was a ten-year-old, and then she was gone. I can't just sit around waiting until spring for some hiker to—' Jennifer collapses to the floor; Bryan kneels to take her in his arms.

'Just a few more days,' he whispers. 'I'll go back with you on Sunday, and we can take care of a few things there.'

'No!' Jennifer shouts. 'We won't. I won't clean out her room. I won't do it. She is not … she's not gone, Bryan.'

'Jenny, please.'

'No,' she shakes her head too hard, causing her vision to tunnel. 'You tell me how they got to the trailhead, Bryan. How did they get there? All three cars were at the house. Hannah's climbing gear was at our house. She wore running shoes up there that night. She knew it had snowed.'

Standing, Jennifer breathes deeply in an effort to calm down; it doesn't help. 'I'm sorry, but you climbed with her, Bryan, she wouldn't go up there in running shoes. She isn't on that mountain. I won't believe it, and I won't clean out her room. I won't cancel her insurance. I won't take her fucking messages off the answering machine. I'm sorry, but there is nothing like this. This would have been easier if they had just told me she was—' Jennifer wails, a cry that breaks her brother's heart.

'Please don't apologise,' says Meg. Uncertain what to do with her hands, she alternates between clutching at the crew neck of her sweater and rubbing her palms along the outer seams of her jeans. Feeling useless, she moves into the kitchen for some water.

Bryan takes his sister by the shoulders as the *Prince Marek* hoists her broken transom to the Falkan night and begins sinking into the harbour. He takes a breath, bracing himself just enough to say, 'A few more days, okay?'

Defeated, Jennifer finally nods. 'Okay.'

'Great.' He makes an attempt at levity. 'What shall we cook? Grilled elephant balls?'

'Sounds lovely,' Jenny can't stifle a giggle. 'I'll rent *Casablanca*, and we'll make an evening of it.' She sees the relief in his face; her heart lightens. Bryan will always be her little brother.

'Make it *Victor Victoria*; I'm in the mood for a cross-dressing soprano,' he grins at her.

'I'm afraid Meg will have to help you there, Bryan.'

'Nah, she's an alto,' he whispers, and together the siblings laugh, holding one another, waiting for the comforting predictability of everyday life, absent since Hannah's disappearance, to return.

THE JOURNEY WEST

The silver charter bus cast a tapered shadow across the concrete wall of the Morrison K-Mart. The sun was coming up behind them, and Steven turned to look out the back window in an effort to see how far above the prairie it had risen. He must have fallen asleep. It had been dark when they left the bus station downtown.

Morrison. The milk run was all he could get out of Denver at this hour. They had one more stop in town, then on to Golden; there was a stop outside City Hall, one near the brewery and then finally out Interstate 70 to Idaho Springs. He would be home in less than an hour.

'Excuse me.' Steven turned to the man sitting across the aisle, a thin, reedy character with a series of piercings in his ears, chin, tongue and nose. 'Do you know what time it is?'

The emaciated stranger slid his left sleeve halfway up his forearm, exposing a tattoo of a naked woman with gargantuan breasts, no waist, and a tremendous backside. About her flying tresses were the words *Born to*, scripted in traditional olive drab. Steven didn't know what the woman was born to do, because the operative verb in the phrase was covered by the heavy face of the young man's wristwatch.

'It's six-thirty.'

'Thanks.' He needed a watch. Mark and Gilmour would have closed the portal over an hour ago. Steven hoped to get home, find Lessek's key and to be back in Eldarn by evening: ten and a half hours. Assuming all went well, that would be plenty of time; he couldn't check in on his parents, or on Myrna and Howard at the bank, but Hannah – he had to know; it was the only way. He would dial her house, let her answer the phone, and then hang up. No one could know he was in Colorado: they would delay him too long, maybe try to keep him here, talk him out of going back. He might peek through a window to see if his mother was there, look to see how worried she might be, or if she had moved on by now. He hoped she had; he hoped they all had.

He sighed. He and Mark hadn't discussed how they would explain their sudden disappearance back in October. So, he would call to hear her voice, just to confirm that Malagon had been lying, that night in the Blackstones, and that Hannah had been here, safe at home all along.

The three days since the explosion at the airport were a bit of a blur; now Steven closed his eyes in an effort to forget the devastation on the tarmac. The distant hum of the bus tyres and the soothing rhythm of the highway lulled him, a momentary respite from the horrors he had faced, but all too soon his thoughts returned to Express Airlines flight 182 and his desperate race across the country.

He had known, somehow, that the young woman carrying the baby on the plane was Nerak. Maybe it was the staff's power keeping him safe, or maybe it was just luck, but the moment he caught the woman staring dead at him despite the fact that her baby was screaming, Steven knew he had to get off that aeroplane.

He would remember her, and that baby, for the rest of his life. She had carried the infant like she was heading for a touchdown. Steven guessed that she kept her hand in her pocket to cover the dark circular wound Gilmour had told them marked Nerak's victims. And she had not pre-boarded the plane and that was strange: a young mother with a child, travelling alone, who waited to board with the mass of fleshy businessmen and pushy suburbanites heading to DC for the weekend. *Jesus, that baby was dead now.*

When the plane exploded, Steven was already running up the jetway. The force of the blast threw him across the concourse and headlong into the check-in desk at the opposite gate. He suffered a serious gash across his right shoulder, and a large purple bruise welled up on his cheek. His clothes were on fire, and he had to roll around for a few seconds to smother the flames; his ears rang, and his hearing had not returned until later that evening, but otherwise, miraculously, he had been spared serious injury.

Although the airports reopened the following day, he couldn't risk purchasing another ticket: his name would appear on their *this-guy-is-supposed-to-be-dead* list. The FBI would spend six weeks asking him where he had been for the past several months and why, when he had finally returned, aeroplanes had started exploding all around him.

So he drove Arthur Mikelson's car, a Lexus with leather interior

– the nicest car he had ever been in – and he cried as he listened to radio reports of faulty ignition systems and gas fumes from the fuel truck, and he burned with an intense desire to tear Nerak's decomposing black heart out and feel the dark prince's demonic blood drip from his fingers.

The Charleston Airport parking lot had been mayhem, too, but he had his first stroke of luck when he reached the booth beside the parking garage, for there was no one inside to collect his fee. The toll collectors were standing on top of a grassy rise, watching the burning terminal. Steven squeezed the Lexus between the toll gate and the row of hedges marking the edge of the soft shoulder, scratching the rear panel. No matter; it was a day for ignoring minor injuries.

His second stroke of luck was managing to bypass any roadblocks: he had no idea where the city police were, other than a few cruisers, lights ablaze, which escorted ambulances and fire trucks into the airport. Maybe it took the locals a while to respond in the wake of such a disaster, but whatever the reason, he thanked God.

He didn't stop again until Knoxville. The Lexus was running on empty, and Steven needed food and a few minutes' rest. He used some of Arthur Mikelson's money to buy new clothes: jeans, underwear and socks, a heavy cotton shirt, and a sweater, beige, so as not to stand out as Mark had when they had first arrived in Estrad Village. He wanted a lined Gore-tex jacket, but he was nervous about using his credit card, and he wanted to conserve as much of Mikelson's $400 cash as possible. As he planned to be in the car until he reached home, Steven decided against the jacket; he could collect his own before returning to Eldarn. He flipped the car's dashboard heater to 'full', turned west and pressed on.

If he drove five or ten miles above the speed limit, Steven estimated the trip would take around thirty hours, but soon he began to worry that Nerak would somehow find a way to reach Idaho Springs before him. Outside Nashville, he pulled over to buy a box of crackers, a half gallon of orange juice, and a crescent wrench. Sitting in the parking lot, he broke down – despite his promise to himself to be strong – and sobbed like a frightened child. *We might not make it.* Then he gritted his teeth, wiped his face and drove on.

Early the following morning Steven detoured six hours to St Louis and used the wrench to steal a set of Missouri licence plates from an old pick-up truck parked behind a motel. The truck didn't look like it was used often; he hoped to be in Colorado before anyone noticed the tags were missing. He was back on the highway before the sun broke the horizon.

In Boonville, he threw Arthur Mikelson's South Carolina licence plates into the Missouri River, purchased a box of doughnuts, a couple of apples, a very large cup of coffee and a padded envelope. In Blue Springs, he tried to sleep for a bit, but nightmares of the baby – *was it a boy or a girl?* – haunted him after only a few minutes' rest. Waking with a start, Steven rubbed his eyes, ate an apple and several doughnuts, and started driving again.

His second night out from Charleston found him in central Kansas, the prairie rolling past in a seamless dirge of muted winter colour, and he had nearly driven off the highway twice in a losing battle to stay awake. Trying to keep himself alert, he began singing in the numbingly repetitive tradition of 'Ninety-nine bottles of beer on the wall',

Put up a sign, put up a sign, put up a goddamned sign . . . oh . . . put up a sign, put up a sign, Governor, won't you put up a fucking sign when you're halfway across this boring state.

Finally, too tired to continue, he gave up, parked the Lexus across the street from a motel and, using more of Mikelson's cash, registered for a room.

Two cheeseburgers with extra tomato, onion and mayo, two orders of crispy French fries with extra ketchup and a large vanilla milkshake later, Steven walked across the street to the motel and punched in a 3.30 a.m. wake-up call. With any luck, he would be in Denver by late the following morning. He turned on his television and ran through the cable channels until he found a 24-hour news programme, then emptied his pockets onto the bedside table: $123.00 and some change, a black leather wallet that had been soaked and dried out so many times it was barely recognisable, his Visa card, receipts and the crescent wrench.

He was half-listening to the report of the on-going investigation into the Charleston tragedy—

Medical examiner reports more than 215 lost—

He pulls off the sweater and cotton T-shirt; he is too thin.

—still making contact with victims' families—

The cheeseburgers roll in his stomach, summer thunder.

—FBI is cross-checking manifests for evidence of—

Steven freezes. His Visa card rests in the stark light of a cheap high wattage bulb in the bedside lamp. The FBI.

Slowly, he reaches for the remote and turns off the television. 'They will know I wasn't on the plane. They will know where I used this card.'

For a few moments Steven paced around the room in a desultory fashion. The bathroom. No help there. The door. Nothing outside. The FBI could be out there right now. The TV. No, leave it off. What to do now, goddamnit, what to do? He turned a complete circle, reached for the phone, then the remote, and finally for the Visa card. Sitting heavily on the bed he held the card up close to his face, as if directions how to proceed might be scribbled there in exceedingly small type.

'I can't use this anymore,' he whispered. 'They'll be looking for me. I'm a fugitive. At least, I will be when the medical examiner confirms I wasn't on that plane. Shit.'

He rubbed his temples and glanced at the bedside clock. 8.17 p.m. 'They'll think I was away all that time preparing the attack. They'll think I'm a terrorist.' For a moment he reconsidered making contact with his parents, then, shaking his head, discounted the notion. 'Time to get going,' he murmured and pulled the T-shirt and sweater back over his head.

Outside, it had begun to snow.

Driving through a winter storm in Kansas made Steven feel as though snow fell horizontally, and that all the news reports showing flakes falling from above had been fabricated in a great communications conspiracy. Westerly winds off the Rocky Mountains caught up with clouds of dry billowy snow and blew them in wild torrents until they slammed headlong into the Appalachian Mountains a thousand miles away. By the time the snow reached central Kansas, it appeared to be travelling at just shy of the speed of sound. At any minute Steven felt his car would be lifted, nose-first, and thrown backwards into rural Missouri.

An hour west of Salina, Steven calmed enough to think through his options. He was driving a stolen car that had probably been photographed leaving the scene of a devastating aeroplane tragedy. He had been issued a boarding pass and would be assumed dead, but before long, an especially thorough forensic pathologist would realise he had not been on the plane. *How long might that be? Five days? Six?* At that moment, every FBI agent, state trooper, town cop and tenacious Boy Scout in America would be searching for him. Thankfully, he had not used his credit card since purchasing the plane ticket, but that would have been enough. Buying the ticket ensured that the FBI, perhaps even the local Idaho Springs cops, would confirm that Steven Taylor of #147 Tenth Street, missing since last October, had surfaced again, just in time to participate in a terrorist attack on a passenger jet. Again, great shit.

In Hays, Steven pulled into an all-night Wal-Mart and used more of Arthur Mikelson's cash to buy a book of stamps, a wool cap, a heavy-knit scarf and a black magic marker. In a motel car park just off the exit ramp, he used the crescent wrench to remove licence plates from an Illinois SUV loaded with ski equipment. He placed those tags on a pick-up truck from Michigan. The Michigan plates he traded with a Pontiac from New Jersey with a guitar in the back seat and gave the Jersey plates to an old Cadillac from Nebraska, then put the Nebraska tags on the Lexus and tossed the Missouri plates into a nearby dumpster. He hoped the morning confusion over who had whose licence plates would buy him an additional few hours' travel time and perhaps even be discounted as a group of local boys having late night fun.

Outside Colby he pulled off the highway, gassed up the Lexus for the final time, placed the entire book of stamps on the padded envelope and, with the car running, fell asleep in a brambly draw between two corn fields.

Steven cried when the Denver skyline came into view late the following afternoon. With the sun drifting west over Mt Evans, it was hard to look at the city without hurting his eyes, but he didn't care. Whether the tears came for joy at finding his way home, for the tragedy in South Carolina, or for the grim, seething hatred he held for Nerak, it didn't make any difference. Overwhelmed, he forced himself to keep both hands on the wheel, letting go only once to flip to his favourite radio station. Second nature, even after all these months. Bruce Springsteen was singing about red-heads, and Steven Taylor rolled down the window, despite the cold, and sang along.

Later that evening, he drove north along Broadway, past Meyers Antiques. The store was boarded up, with large *This Space Available for Purchase or Lease* signs posted on the showroom windows. Turning east, then taking a left, he rolled slowly past Hannah Sorenson's house. He had no intention of making contact with her, but hoped she might wander past a window, or even be outside shovelling snow. *Get lucky.*

But he *had* been lucky so far on this trip. Maybe he would find one last measure of good fortune before stepping on the far portal again. He slowed to a crawl, passed the house at less than five miles an hour, and willed Hannah to appear. The Sorenson home, a 1920s row house with a small porch and a bay window, was a red-brick clone of every other house in Grant Street. A naked light bulb illuminated the front lawn in a pallid smear, and a haphazard collection of unread newspapers dotted the stairs, the stoop, and the snowy grass. Steven sighed. No one had been home for some time – he counted the papers – at least twelve days. No sign of Hannah.

Driving through town, he was slowed by rush-hour traffic, and in his distraction at failing to spot Hannah he almost missed the afternoon DJ crying out, 'Hey Denver, it's finally five o'clock on this chilly Thursday. So, if you haven't left work yet, get going! Go ahead, just leave! Here's a classic from Zeppelin to help blow you out the door.'

Five o'clock already. Mark would be opening the far portal right now. He hoped they still had it – although since Nerak was hot on *his* heels, there was no reason why they wouldn't. Gilmour would keep them safe, and as long as Nerak was on this side of the Fold, there would be little to threaten the company of Ronan partisans.

Right now he had to decide whether or not to drive the Lexus into Idaho Springs. If he did, he might be able to find Lessek's key, open the portal and be back in Eldarn by five-fifteen the following morning. But if he ditched the car in Denver, he could take an early bus and be in Idaho Springs by late morning, giving him the time to hide his tracks a little. If he left the car in Denver, they might not trace it to him.

'Bullshit,' he said out loud, 'you bought the damned plane ticket, stupid – you might as well be wearing a radar beacon. Anyway, forget the police. Concentrate on Nerak.' Steven focused: the shutdown of the airports would have delayed him for a day, so he might have driven, or maybe taken a train. Maybe he just waited for the next flight anyway. If he'd driven, he would have made up time when Steven had been forced to sleep. A train would be slower – but that was assuming Nerak had allowed it to run on schedule. He shuddered. Who knew how quickly the dark prince could be in Denver with a runaway Amtrak? If he'd waited one day for the airports to reopen, Nerak would have picked up a two-day lead.

'Shit. Why didn't I think of that?' Steven nearly drove into the guardrail in his frustration: this race was so mismatched that there was no way he could win it. Nerak would be there – how could he not? But if he had beaten Steven to Idaho Springs and retrieved Lessek's key, then surely he would be gone by now. He hadn't come through the portal to kill Steven – although that might have been a welcome side-effect – he'd come because he was afraid the Ronans would regain possession of the stone. If he had the key and the portal, he wouldn't hang around. He would skip back to Eldarn, turn his wagon towards Sandcliff Palace and begin working with the spell table.

Steven made his mind up: he would spend the night in Denver and take the first bus to Idaho Springs in the morning. He pulled a U-turn and headed back towards Hannah Sorenson's house. It might be a long night, but he would stand vigil. Phoning was not enough; he wanted to see her.

Around midnight, Steven went to find a drink, smiling wanly to himself when he realised he actually missed Garec's tecan. How bizarre was that, after spending months pining for good coffee! He yawned despite the caffeine, then took out a piece of notepaper and scratched a letter to Arthur Mikelson.

> Arthur,
> Thank you for the use of your car. I hope you find it in good condition other than the scratch on the side. Although, I did throw your licence plates in the Missouri River. Sorry. It is parked in the stadium lot between 23rd Avenue and Union Station in Denver, Colorado. If you are unable to pick it up soon, I am sure it will be towed, but there are signs in the parking lot telling you how to get in touch with the towing company. I owe you $400, and when my circumstances change, I will get that to you, plus something for your trouble. You will find the contents of your wallet intact. I did not use your ID or attempt to use your credit cards. Your T-shirt and exercise clothes are in the trunk. I have kept your address and will get the money back to you as soon as possible.
> Thanks.

Steven didn't sign the note, but folded the paper around the wallet and tucked it into the padded envelope. He'd add the keys once he'd parked the car, then mail it back to Charleston at the bus station.

That done, Steven turned his attention back to Hannah's house. He looked at the array of newspapers lying forlornly on the porch. 'She's not coming,' he heard himself say. 'She's there. The black-hearted bastard was telling the truth.' He would wait another two hours, just in case. Two hours – and then he would go back, and he would take up the hickory staff, and he would face Nerak. He had spent three days trying to forget the screaming baby on board Express Airlines flight 182 and the carnage that had unfolded behind him that day, but now he allowed those images back. He could almost feel them seep into his bone marrow and fester there like an infection. He might regret it later, but he wanted to hear that baby screaming when he finally gutted Nerak and sent what passed for his soul in pieces to the furthest corner of Eldarn's hell.

THE FJORD

Mark Jenkins awakened to the sound of a gull squawking at the passing boat. The high-pitched caws reminded him of summers at Jones Beach. For a moment he thought there was something significant he was supposed to remember, something about the beach, or Long Island, then he let the notion fade. There would be time later to dwell on it.

He lay back in the narrow bow of the sailing vessel he had stolen for their covert attack on the *Prince Marek*, his head on Brynne's folded blanket, ignoring everyone else. Above, the single sail was taut, but apart from the salty tang of organic decay drifting out from the inter-tidal zone – he didn't need to look up to know that they were near the shore – he couldn't feel the breeze which pushed the boat along. The sun was bright and warm, too warm for autumn, and as it fell across his face, Mark wished that sleep would take him again. There was perhaps no more perfectly innocent time than the few seconds after waking, when, for three or four breaths, there would be no pain, no stress, no nothing. In that brief space of time Mark sometimes forgot where he was, even *who* he was.

And today's awakening would be the worst, for Brynne was gone.

Mark gazed into the near-cloudless pale-blue sky, staring at nothing, until he was jolted from his introspection by two stony cliffs coming into view. The gigantic granite gateposts stood nearly two hundred feet high, towering over the sailboat as it passed between them. Mark watched the sail flutter and collapse as the light wind was cut off and the boat slowed nearly to a stop. As the cliffs swallowed him up they cropped the expanse of cloudless sky into a thin ribbon, reminding him of an arroyo near Idaho Springs, a narrow canyon – a killing field for Clint Eastwood, Gary Cooper or John Wayne in the closing minutes of any one of hundreds of westerns he had watched as a boy. He imagined this view, the stony walls, the powder-blue stripe, was one dozens of C-list actors had enjoyed moments after being thrown from the saddle with the hero's .45 slugs buried in their chests. But that was home; out here it wasn't an arroyo, or a box canyon: here, it would be … what? A fjord? Good enough, he supposed, not really caring, a fjord.

Brynne was dead. *Missing*, Garec said, but Mark knew better. The explosion as the great ship blew across Orindale Harbour had been devastating. Gilmour hadn't seen her on the main deck, and Mark knew she was on board – he had let her go. There was nowhere else she could have been except on the quarterdeck, stalking some unsuspecting guard, or throttling the life out of a Malakasian sailor. She would have had no chance as the planks beneath her feet dis-integrated into splinters – one of which had become lodged in his own neck. Gilmour had yanked it out later; Mark had it wrapped in a piece of cloth and shoved into his pocket: a grisly souvenir.

'I love you,' Brynne had whispered in almost comic mimicry of Mark's clumsy profession only minutes earlier. He had laughed at her accent: she had sounded like a German tourist. But she was perfect, for him, and for his world. They were supposed to be together. Looking down at him from the aft rail, she had looked like any other woman – any other *perfect* woman, a doctor or teacher, an accountant, even. That was from the shoulders up, away from the bristling array of daggers, dirks and blades she wore across her chest and at her hips, the weapons that marked her as a doomed revolutionary fighting an unbeatable enemy. It would be a long time before Mark recovered.

He ignored the looming cliffs, wrapped himself in Brynne's blan-ket and ran a finger over his cracked lips. He felt his neck, where Gilmour had removed the black splinter. The wound was infected, seeping pus, and as Mark poked the swelling, discoloured fluid spurted out. He found a piece of stained sailcloth and dipped it into the salt water, then dabbed gingerly at the jagged tear. He folded the cloth into a small square, pressed it against the wound and left it there, its coolness comforting.

His wound attended to, Mark buried his nose in the blanket and inhaled, hoping to catch her aroma, but all he could smell was pungent woodsmoke. He felt tears come again and stared up between the cliffs, Heaven's granite gate, trying to control himself. Weeping wouldn't bring her back, and he didn't want the others to see his weakness. The grey and white gull drifted overhead, cawing a warning. Mark felt as though he had been switched off, paralysed by grief. Would he die here? That question had bothered him for weeks, but now it no longer mattered.

Listlessness and rage warred inside his head, making him feel nauseous and exhausted. Only by shortening his breath, taking gulps of air, could he keep from vomiting all over himself. Finally, as he regained his equilibrium, he sat up and reached for a skin of water. He focused his eyes on Garec and Gilmour, who were talking quietly in the stern.

'I wonder how far in it goes.' Though still too pale, Garec had been getting stronger since Steven had pulled the arrow from his lung, but his face looked haunted. His cheeks were sunken, and his eyes darted nervously from left to right.

'We should continue on.' Gilmour looked distrustful of the granite gates, as if he feared Eldarn's own Gary Cooper might be up there, taking aim over the open sights of a lever-action rifle. 'This fjord will shelter us while we find someplace to put ashore.'

Garec looked around. 'There's nowhere to land here; we'll have to go further in,' he said. It was the midday aven, three days since Nerak had blown the *Prince Marek* out of the water. Now they needed a flat bit of ground before Steven's watch read five o'clock, for it was almost time to open the portal. 'But we've lost our tailwind.' He nodded towards the sail, hanging flaccid from the single spar. 'We won't get far at this rate.'

Humming softly, Gilmour traced a weaving pattern through the air; with a turn of his hand, a gentle breeze snaked into the fjord, caught itself up in the limp sailcloth and began pushing the stolen vessel inland. With a satisfied look he asked, 'What time is it?'

Garec looked at Steven's watch in consternation. 'Um, three and— let's see, the rune four represents a twenty, doesn't it, so three and twenty. We have almost two full revolutions of the long stalk before we have to open the portal.'

'Two hours. Less than an aven,' Gilmour confirmed. 'That's not much time.' With another gesture he increased the wind thrumming through the narrow canyon. 'We'll give it an hour. If we haven't found level ground by then, I'll swim the portal over and scale the cliff face. I'm sure I can open it up there.' The Larion Senator, still using the emaciated body of Caddoc Weston, the Orindale fisherman, pointed towards the top of the fjord.

'All right.' Garec knew better than to doubt Gilmour's abilities – he might look like a frail old man, but Garec was quite certain he would scamper up the stone cliffs with all the agility of a mountain goat. 'I hope we find someplace soon. Mark needs a break, some hot food ... gods, Gilmour, he needs *any* food. Have you seen his neck?'

'He'll be fine. There are things no sorcery or wisdom can change, and he is in the throes of one such thing right now. Time is the only thing we can give him.'

'And what of Steven? What if he fails to come through again today?'

Gilmour heard the growing agitation in Garec's voice. 'Then we will wait until his watch reads 5.00 again and we will open the portal. Each time we do, we will be closer to Sandcliff Palace, of course.'

'What if he's not coming back?'

'He'll be back.'

'But you said if the portal in Steven and Mark's house was closed, he could fall anywhere in their world. Is that right?' Garec tried to remember what Gilmour had told them about the Larion Senate's far portal system.

'Yes.'

'So, what if he was dropped someplace ... I don't know ... in-hospitable?'

'Inhospitable?'

'Right. Someplace frozen solid, or filled with molten rock, or rife with angry marsh adders— you know, inhospitable. You heard them: it's a place with flying machines and self-propelled car-wagons. Why would it take him this long to get here?' Garec's anxiety was almost tangible.

'I'm not sure, Garec, but I do know that it's too early to give up hope, or to start doubting him.'

'I am not doubting *him*, Gilmour, I am worried that something has happened to him.' He sighed, and brought up the subject he knew the old man had been avoiding. 'And Nerak went through right after him ...'

'It was perhaps five or six breaths later.' Gilmour had obviously been pondering this question himself. 'About as long as it would take him to get up off the deck, cast his final spell and then leap the three or four paces to the far portal.' It had been longer than that – not much longer, just a moment or two, but time enough for the dark prince to make eye-contact with his former colleague. '*Well done, Fantus*,' Nerak had whispered, a concession of one round lost. *We'll play again later*, Nerak's eyes had said, and in them, Gilmour had seen the end. He was not powerful enough, and failing to kill Nerak that night – *Nerak could not be killed* – had cost him dearly, for now Nerak knew the extent of Gilmour's power. He had felt it in the mystical blows the old man had landed.

'I barely slowed him down,' Gilmour muttered.

'What's that?'

'What—? Oh, nothing. What were we talking about?' The man seemed to age before Garec's eyes. 'Oh, yes, Steven. It wasn't much time, but as long as Steven remembered to close the portal as soon as he passed across the Fold, he'll be fine. There was ample time to shut the other end down before Nerak disappeared.'

'So, in Steven's prolonged absence, we must assume that the portal in his home was already closed and that wherever he fell is closer to Idahocolorado than wherever Nerak fell. Because if Nerak reaches Steven and Mark's home first …' He hesitated.

'Then all here is lost.'

'What about those?' Garec motioned towards the hickory staff and the wool-wrapped leather-bound book Gilmour had tossed into the sailboat three nights earlier.

The old man sighed and took out his pipe, then felt through his pockets for a pouch of tobacco. 'They represent great power; that's true, but only Steven can wield the hickory staff.'

Garec reached tentatively for the length of wood; for a moment he looked like a child caught stealing a pastry through an open bakery window. 'Why?' He released the tiller and took up the staff in both hands. 'Why won't it work for you or—' He looked over at Mark. 'Perhaps for him?' He didn't even consider that the staff might respond to his own commands.

'That's a mystery to me, Garec.' Gilmour abandoned his quest for tobacco and took hold of the tiller. 'I believe Mark is correct in his assumption that Nerak has no idea what force is hidden within it, and that alone has given the dark prince reason to fear it. However, Nerak is not accustomed to fearing very much and he is … I suppose it's best to say he is out of practice at fearing anything.'

'So, in Nerak's mind, the staff is something *you* have constructed for Steven, and therefore it falls within the expectations he has for the limits of your power?'

'Right. Something he supposes is of little threat to him.' Gilmour looked over at the stark granite cliff. *Well done, Fantus.* Nerak's ironic words chilled his skin; he shook his head in an effort to focus on the conversation.

'And the book?' Garec made no move to reach for the ancient tome. 'Can you use it?'

'That we'll find out soon enough.' Gilmour pressed his lips together in a tight smile. 'I may have made a grave mistake there.'

'How do you mean?'

'The night I fled Sandcliff Palace, I left everything – all the writings, books, scrolls, everything. I just fled as fast as I could, with my shoulder hanging useless and my ankle flopping back and forth. I was numb, and far too scared to consider that one day I might need Lessek's library.' He adjusted their heading to move the little catboat around a tight bend in the fjord. 'This book tells me that Nerak has done much more than reflect on his studies.'

'I don't understand.'

'I have always known that Nerak spends most of his time sequestered in Welstar Palace working through spells, memorising incantations, trying to weave together all the threads he needs to operate the spell table – so he can rend a sizeable gate in the Fold ...'

Garec finished his friend's thought, 'But you never imagined he would use Lessek's journals to speed up the process.'

'I thought it had all been destroyed.' Gilmour shook his head despondently. 'I was there: it was a massive explosion; most everything in the library was reduced to rubble.'

'Yet Lessek himself has sent you back—'

'For the Windscrolls, yes. If Pikan was right that night, we'll need the third Windscroll.'

'So that one wasn't destroyed?'

'I don't know, Garec. I honestly don't. I thought the entire collection was lost, but when I saw this book on the *Prince Marek* I realised that Nerak went back and retrieved—'

'At least this one,' Garec broke in. 'He went back to get *this* book.' He started to point at it with the hickory staff but recoiled at the thought of the two magical artefacts coming in contact with one another.

Gilmour chuckled wryly. 'Yes, at least this one, but I have to assume the Windscrolls are still there and that the secret to Nerak's weakness is in their text.'

'Nerak's weakness lies elsewhere.' Garec echoed Lessek's cryptic statement. 'It must be in the Windscrolls.'

'It might.' He spotted a satchel tucked beneath the transom and a real smile crossed his face as he pulled out a leather pouch of tobacco. 'That's where we'll start, anyway.'

'Mark seems to think *this* has something to do with it.' Garec returned the hickory staff to its place beside the book.

'We can hope, Garec. And if Steven retrieves Lessek's key and returns here safely, we will have several very powerful allies.' Gilmour decided it was time to change the subject. 'What does the watch say now?'

Steven's watch showed both the stalks on the five rune as Garec charted Gilmour's progress down the precipitous cliff, the curiously small tapestry that was the far portal folded beneath one arm. The sorcerous breeze was stilled to a whisper and Garec had little trouble keeping the boat steady against the fjord's southern wall. Its bow nestled snugly in a crack between two boulders and the wooden hull thunked gently against the stone in perfect time with the gentle rise and fall of the water. That drum-like beat was the only sound in the fjord and the silence weighed heavily on Garec. He felt uncomfortably warm, despite the sun dropping steadily in the distance.

Garec could make out Mark Jenkins' lumpy form, now bundled inside several blankets, but in the shadows he couldn't see if Mark was asleep. When the foreigner rasped at him from the semi-darkness, Garec jumped, shouting in surprise and nearly tumbling overboard.

'Is he back?'

'Rutting lords! You scared me!' Garec sat back down clumsily.

Without moving, Mark asked again, 'Is he back? Is Steven here?'

Garec frowned. 'Sorry. Not yet.'

'Where are we?'

'My guess is that we're at least two days' ride north of Orindale. I've heard of these cliffs, but have never travelled far enough up the coast to see them before. We came into the fjord hoping to find someplace to put ashore and roll out the far portal – we couldn't see anything particularly promising north along the coast, and we didn't want to risk Steven's return through an unopened port, so it made sense to find a beach or a flat rock before the watch said five o'clock.' Now his eyes had grown used to the dim light, Garec could see Mark peering up the craggy wall in an effort to spot Gilmour.

'But there was nothing?'

'No.' Garec shook his head. 'So Gilmour scaled the wall and opened the portal up there.'

'How far have we come into the fjord?' Mark made no effort to lift his head; Garec could give him an accurate synopsis of their progress.

'Not far ... maybe a morning's ride. Gilmour is helping out with a breeze, but it's slow going, lots of twists and turns, too many submerged rocks.' He peered up at Gilmour himself, then asked, 'Are you hungry, Mark? There's still plenty of food from Orindale: wine, beer, smoked gansel, anything.'

'Not now, thanks.' Mark sounded genuinely appreciative. 'Maybe later.'

'Right. That's fine, later. Just let me know.'

'Garec?'

'What?' He took several steps towards the bow, then, not wanting to intrude, sat on his haunches and stared into the shadows. 'What can I do?'

Mark whispered, but Garec heard the question with no difficulty. 'Did it hurt?'

Recalling the fiery pain that had slithered and scratched its way across his side, gnawing through his flesh like a subterranean creature armed with spindles of needle teeth, Garec was forced to take a moment before answering. 'Yes, it did. It was much worse than I would ever have imagined.'

'I want you to teach me to shoot, Garec. I want to get good at it – maybe I'll not ever be as good as you or Versen, but I want to hit what I choose. Maybe it won't be in the heart every time, but as long as it hurts, I don't mind.' Mark made a shuffling sound, shifting his position and leaning forward in earnest. 'Will you teach me to shoot?'

'I don't know if I can,' the Ronan bowman said.

'What do you mean?' Mark was indignant. 'You're the best archer in Eldarn. You might be the best archer anywhere, my world included.'

'I don't know if I can pick it up again ... if I can do it anymore.'

'You can, Garec,' Mark murmured. 'I'm not asking you to kill anyone. I just want you to teach *me* how.' There was a long pause and Mark added, 'I will take care of the killing.'

'I don't know how to explain it, but once you do it, kill someone, they never leave you alone. Each of them – and I have killed many, Mark, I regret that I have – they never leave you.' He struggled for the right words. 'I think that's why, when I finally took one, right in the ribs, it was a perfect shot. I should have died. If it hadn't been for Steven, I *would* have died. I feel like I've been given a second chance. Does that make sense? And with my second chance, I'm not going to be a killer. I can't do it anymore.'

'You've chosen a bad time to grow a conscience, Garec.' Mark untangled the blankets and hauled himself to his feet. He looked dreadful. His sweater was stained a deeper red where his neck had bled, and he had a dirty piece of cloth pressed against the wound; a bloody circle marked the centre of the patch like the perfect-score zone on an archery target.

Mark grabbed Garec's arm. 'I am going to kill them, as many as we encounter, until one of them manages to kill me or until I go home to Colorado for ever,' he said quietly, firmly. 'Now, you don't *have* to do anything, I am not demanding, but I am asking, as one who loved her, that you help me extract a bit of vengeance for her.'

'You will regret it.'

'I already regret it.' With that Mark managed a smile, and Garec was truly afraid.

'All right then. We'll begin as soon as we put to shore. You can have my bow.'

'I want to make my own.'

'I'll teach you how.'

Brexan Carderic clung to an oak log, her improvised life preserver, and allowed the tide to drag her north through the Ravenian Sea. She had taken to the water after coming upon Malakasian pickets around their watch-fires, burning vivid orange against the steel-grey of the gathering dawn. Turning back to keep from being seen, the former soldier had dragged the lump of wood into the water and began swimming with it, hoping to pick up some sort of current that would take her far enough to avoid detection from the beach.

The Twinmoon had passed, but Brexan, preoccupied with thoughts of Versen, the scarred Seron and the bloated merchant from Orindale, had no idea how long ago: though both moons still hung in the northern sky, they were obviously on their way south again. Now the twin orbs pulled the waters of the Ravenian Sea along fiercely enough that Brexan had to hold hard to the log. She stopped kicking, saving her strength for the long swim back to shore.

Once the pickets were far behind her, she steered the log towards the beach, watching as several large warehouses came into view. Feeling confident as the shoreline grew closer, Brexan let go of the log and began swimming towards a patch of swampy rushes bent with the morning tide. It was a mistake. She had underestimated both the distance, and the toll the cold water had taken on her. The log was already out of reach.

Brexan's limbs felt heavy, useless; to counter the shivering she started treading water. 'Stupid, stupid fool,' she scolded herself, 'you had to go and make this so much harder than it needed to be, didn't you?' She hadn't eaten in days; only the sheer tenacity of her will had kept her moving so far. She hadn't exactly determined to live yet, but there was Versen to be avenged. She had no idea how she would clothe and feed herself once she arrived in Orindale ... maybe a little prostitution – though she would need to improve her appearance. She couldn't see people paying good silver for an emaciated, sunken-eyed, starving deserter in rotting clothing and no shoes.

No, it would have to be theft: she would steal what she needed to get herself aright and after she had avenged Versen – killed, and killed again the fat businessman who had been the cause of her grief – she would try to find Versen's group, Gilmour and Steven, Mark and the Ronan woman, Brynne. Joining their fight would bring her closer to Versen; that way she might find friendship, even if his death had denied her love.

But that was for the future: now, she needed to get to shore.

Brexan focused her fast-dwindling strength on moving east, towards the swampy area south of the wharf. She distracted herself from the encroaching cold by watching Orindale's waterfront day begin. Military and merchant vessels moved through the harbour in an oddly regimented pattern; on the wooden wharf stevedores hauled nets and worked block-and-tackle cranes. Pilot boats bustled about, while sailing vessels and heavy barges moored up, reefed sheets and either took on or began unloading cargo.

As she drew slowly closer, she caught sight of a familiar vessel, anchored offshore: the schooner she and Versen had escaped from, the *Falkan Dancer*. With its sails neatly reefed, its rigging taut and its brass polished, the ship didn't look like a death ship, a slaver, a traitor's vessel. With sunshine on her spars and the vestiges of morning fog billowing across the waterline, the schooner seemed almost mystical, a vessel on which to escape with a lover for a Moon's passage through the northern archipelago or a holiday cruise to Markon Isle, maybe.

But Brexan knew better, and warmth spread through her as she growled, 'I am going to gut you, you rutter.'

The swim ashore suddenly felt manageable, but even so, it was a long time before she reached the protective cover of the rushes and collapsed in the foetid mud. Just a few paces up the eroded bank Brexan spotted what looked like a dry patch of ferns rimmed by a thick circlet of brambly ground cover, looking soft and safe: a place to rest for an eternity. But Brexan didn't have the strength to heave even her tiny frame up the muddy slope; instead, she used the rushes to pull herself out of the water, peered around to be certain no one had seen her, and fell into a deep, exhausted sleep.

She woke to feel the prickle of cedar twigs alongside her face; twitching her nose, Brexan recoiled at the smell and sat up with a start. The sun had dried the exposed layers of her clothing, but she was lying on wet homespun and several handfuls of marsh mud had turned her hair into a stinking clay sculpture. Brexan braced herself with one hand and winced.

'Oh, pissing demons, that hurt,' she swore as she found several cedar thorns lodged in her palm. She pulled them out, looked around, and realised to her surprise that she had somehow moved up the muddy slope and into the fern bed. 'How did I get up here?' She searched the forest, then looked down the short hill to the marshy area where she had come ashore.

'I guess I must have—' she started, then stopped. There was a rustling below; and she saw a shadow, furtive and quick, moving to the shelter of a nearby evergreen bush.

'Who's that?' Brexan called as she sprang to her feet, trying not to groan as over-used muscles protested. She reached for the knife she had last used to kill the scarred Seron, but it wasn't there. She looked about on the ground, but she couldn't see it there either.

She turned back to the stranger and, emboldened by fear and anger, shouted, 'Come out here, right now. I appreciate the lift out of the mud, but I am in no mood to deal with this nonsense.'

Shaking, Brexan forced her hands into her tunic belt, hoping to steady her fingers. 'Come out, now!'

A low growl emanated from the bushes and Brexan felt her stomach turn. She thought for a moment of fleeing, trying for the Ravenian Sea: few pursuers would follow her there. Instead, she thought of Versen, felt for the warm strength of his hand in hers. She almost reached for him, before recalling that she was on her own these days. She took a determined step towards the bush, picking up a tree branch as she moved. It was too long and too bulky to be much use, but it might keep her anonymous assailant from tackling her to the ground.

'Are you one of Malagon's men?' she called again.

A second growl preceded another rustling of leaves and Brexan watched in horror as a hideous man took shape before her, stooped at the waist and covered head to heels in a torn and stained cloak. The stranger didn't make eye contact at first. Instead, brandishing Brexan's knife, he looked all around, assessing both her and the surrounding forest. His face was contorted by pain or rage – Brexan couldn't decide which – and his clothes, splattered with mud and blood, were apparently rotting off his body. Bits of food of some sort congealed at the corners of his mouth; his fingernails were blackened and broken.

His stoop appeared to be the result of a back injury or a damaged shoulder, for though he pulled himself upright for a few moments, towering over Brexan, he soon returned to his crouch with a grunt of relief.

Brexan leaned forward, too terrified to move any closer, but still determined to get a clear view of the foul-smelling stranger. 'Do I know you?' she asked, timidly, her voice cracking in fear.

He looked into her face, just for a passing moment – but it was enough.

'Sallax?' Brexan whispered. 'Sallax Farro? Is that you?'

A look of genuine surprise passed across his face, then, slipping Brexan's knife inside his cloak, he was gone.

'Wait,' Brexan shouted, 'come back here! You have my knife! *Sallax!*' Putting fear to one side, she chased after him, pulling up short when she passed by the bush where he had been hiding. She was immediately assailed by an amalgam of smells left in the former partisan leader's wake: sweat and swamp mud, tangy rotten meat and spoiled milk hit Brexan's empty stomach and sent her reeling. The former soldier almost fainted, overbalancing into a soft fern-covered depression.

When the nausea wore off, she decided clothing, boots and something substantial to eat were urgent, then she could track Sallax and find out what had happened. The sweet aroma of broken ferns washed away the lingering traces of Sallax and she took a moment to savour the fresh scent, wondering why he appeared to have been so horribly afflicted – and why he seemed to be carrying the contents of a compost heap around in his cloak. Questions for later: he must be in disguise, perhaps working his way into the city via some trash barge along the river.

Less than two avens later, Brexan was pulling on a pair of polished leather boots and tucking the flared ends of her new leggings in. She used a piece of sack-cloth to dry her hair, though not very successfully, so she decided to spend the remainder of the day eating and drinking, as close to a tavern fire as she could get without melting.

Outfitting herself had been easier than she had expected; lined with waterfront pubs and shops, the Orindale wharf was such a hive of activity that few people took notice as she made her way along the plank walkway into the city. She had straightened her clothes and cleaned off as much of the mud as possible. And while it would have taken no more than a cursory look to detect the miserable condition of her tunic and hose, no one was interested.

It hadn't taken long to find a likely victim: the number of ships moving in and out of Orindale meant finding a seaman, roughly Brexan's size, was an easy task. The youngster Brexan chose had made his way straight into the nearest tavern, dropped his sea-bag beneath the bar and ordered a bottle of beer, a pot of breakfast stew that had smelled so good Brexan wondered if she might steal that as well, and a loaf of freshly baked bread.

After he had finished his third bottle of the cheap Falkan brew, Brexan, watching from the corner where she'd slumped in an apparent doze, decided it was time to strike. She made her way confidently through the tavern's front room, lifted an empty tray from the mantel and collected up a number of empty bottles and mugs. As she slid the full tray onto the bar, she quietly hefted the bag from its place on the floor and moved quickly through the kitchen as if she had every right to be there.

Without slowing her pace, she hurried out the back, through the alley and back into the forest, where she stripped off the clothes she had stolen in Estrad and ran down to the sea.

While she scrubbed the dirt from her face and hair, Brexan wept. Any memory of Versen, any lasting impression from his touch, or his lips against her skin, was gone now, scrubbed clean in the bitter salt water. Finally she climbed from the sea, pale and shivering, and donned her stolen clothes, clothes not stained with Seron blood, but also with no trace of Versen's distinctive scent of woodsmoke and herbs.

Now Brexan said out loud, firmly, 'He's gone. Let him go. You have things to do.' She slumped as choking sobs took her again. It would be a long time before she could follow her own advice. For now, though, safe in the coastal forest south of Orindale, Brexan let the sadness overwhelm her again.

*

Later, Brexan sat near the fire at a tavern several streets back from the waterfront. The front room began to fill as the dinner aven approached, but Brexan barely heard the rise in chatter; it was toneless background noise. Instead, she stared into the fire, the low embers casting a glow across her table that reminded her of Pellia and her family. What would they have thought of Versen? A Ronan, a freedom fighter, he might not have made a good first impression, but the big man's curious sense of humour and stalwart commitment to his values would have won over her family as they had her.

Behind her, a musician began strumming a few chords on a bellamir and Brexan woke from her reverie. She gnawed at a gansel bone, more for something to do than hunger. A bowl of stew and bread had preceded a brace of roast gansel legs, washed down with a bottle of good Falkan wine and followed by cheese. It had been too long since she had eaten: feeling stuffed to bursting with hot food and good wine was a feeling she had almost forgotten.

Whenever the fire died down, she summoned the barman. She was tired of being cold too.

As she took a long draught from her wine goblet, Brexan felt the warm, dizzy sensation of incipient drunkenness wash over her. Her vision blurred and tunnelled pleasantly as she stretched her feet out towards the fire, warming the soles of the seaman's boots, padded with handfuls of sack-cloth to fit her small feet. The sailor had been paid three silver pieces for his last voyage: he had made the fortuitous – for Brexan – mistake of tucking the coins into his sea bag. With that much silver, Brexan would be able to live comfortably in Orindale for the next Twinmoon, with coin enough for a room and a new pair of boots from a real cobbler, not just some street vendor with lengths of tanned hide and a sewing needle.

Slowly, a plan began to emerge through the comfortable stupor: she would find lodgings; she needed to do that tonight, but there would be plenty of choice. Tomorrow, boots, her first pair since enlisting in the Malakasian Army ... and a skirt, a heavy wool skirt, loomed wool, not the ratty homespun she had been wearing for the past Twinmoon. She would linger over the process, trying whatever caught her fancy, and then buying real women's clothes, from a high-class city shop. If it took all day, that would be fine. She would shop and she would think of Versen and she would end the day here again, here beside this same fire.

And tomorrow evening, she would work out how to find Sallax, and the owner of the merchant schooner moored out in the harbour.

IDAHO SPRINGS

Steven pulled the cap down over his ears and wrapped his face and neck in the scarf. Bright sunshine and dry mountain air gave the illusion of unseasonable warmth, and to passersby the hat-and-scarf combination might look a bit excessive, but he had to ensure he was not recognised by anyone. The bus had dropped him off, the only passenger exiting in Idaho Springs, on the east side of town, and there was no way to avoid using main roads.

With nine blocks to go, he crossed a road to avoid a family dressed in matching ski-jackets, then, anticipating a straight shot home through the relatively quiet residential part of town, he nearly ran over Mrs Winter, the elderly woman who owned the pastry shop next to the bank.

'Oh, geez. Sorry, Mrs W,' Steven said before he could stop himself, grabbing the surprised older woman by the shoulders in a clumsy effort to keep her from falling to the snowy sidewalk.

Thankfully, Mrs Winter didn't hear very well. 'You should watch where you're going young man,' she scolded, but Steven was already hurrying away at a run. 'Young man!' Mrs Winter cried at his back, 'young man, that was very rude of you!'

'Sorry, Mrs W,' Steven murmured to himself as he paused to catch his breath. He looked up the hillside to where Oh My Gawd Road ran, hundreds of feet above the floor of Virginia Canyon. It was named for the reaction of most travellers: Oh My Gawd Road was still dirt for much of its length, and there were no barriers along the circuitous route to the old mining town of Central City. He and Mark had cycled it once; Steven remembered fondly Mark groaning his displeasure at the gruelling climb to eleven thousand feet. 'Just for the record,' he'd rattled through shallow gulps of thin air, 'I think this form of travel sucks. Next time, we're taking the bus or a plane or a frigging space shuttle; I don't care.'

Steven smiled at the irony: if only his roommate had known that day the various forms of travel he would be using in the coming months, he might have allowed himself to enjoy the bike trip. Who knew the pair would be travelling across the Fold, whatever that was, on horseback through the coastal forests of Rona to Seer's Peak, on foot through the Blackstones, and then drifting through Meyers' Vale on the *Capina Fair*?

He grinned. One day he would drag Mark back up that canyon and into Central City to celebrate with a night at the tables, the city's main attraction. As his thoughts drifted, he slowed to a distracted walk. Something was tickling at the back of his mind: something was wrong. *Travel. What about travel?* He turned and stared back up Virginia Street. Mrs Winter was gone, most likely sweeping the snow from the steps in front of her shop by now. Travel. He had travelled; he had come a great distance, though he had no idea how far he was from Eldarn now – a million miles? A few inches?

That wasn't it, it wasn't Eldarn. It was South Carolina: he had come from South Carolina and the trip, without real sleep and only a few stops for gas and food, had been as gruelling a journey as the bike ride through Virginia Canyon last July.

What was it? Steven unwrapped the scarf from around his face and drew his first unfiltered breath of Idaho Springs air.

The Larion far portal in his house was closed. Steven stopped dead. He had been so distracted by events at the airport, and hurrying so fast across the United States that he hadn't thought about *where* he had arrived: the far portal had to be closed, otherwise he would have come from Eldarn straight to his living room. Someone – and much as he hated the idea, he had to accept it was someone after Hannah, as she was obviously there now – but someone had come into his house and closed the portal. Who would that have been? Her mother, Jennifer? But there had been a pile of unread newspapers on her front lawn; maybe Jennifer Sorenson was in Eldarn too?

But someone had been in 147 Tenth Street after Hannah, because someone had closed the portal, probably by folding up the tapestry. The police? Investigators would have been called, he guessed, maybe several days after the roommates' disappearance: one of them might have inadvertently closed the portal. Even worse, what if they'd detected the tapestry's power and taken it away, shipped it to Washington, DC, or to some research facility in Boulder?

He started to run again, breaking out into a cold sweat. Ignoring the chance he might be seen, he pulled the watch-cap from his head

48

and ran a hand through his hair to free the matted strands.

And there it was: 147 Tenth Street – and what Steven saw was far worse than his most hopeless nightmares. The portal had not been taken by the Idaho Springs Police; it had not been checked into evidence and locked in a room in the town hall basement, or shipped to DC, or even sealed in a container and hidden far below ground level in a subterranean basement of a top secret radiation centre in Nevada.

This *was* worse. Standing on the icy sidewalk in front of 147 Tenth Street, Steven was struck dumb, completely devoid of any idea as to what he should do now.

His house, the small yard at the back, the two-car garage and the fence separating 147 from Dave and Cindy's place next door were gone.

'Oh, great pissing demons, Churn, it's not that high up.' An exasperated Hoyt patted Churn's saddle encouragingly.

Churn replied with a series of tentative hand gestures, embarrassment clearly evident in his face.

'Do you expect us to walk all the way to Welstar Palace?'

With no trace of humour, the burly mute nodded.

'No,' Hoyt said, 'you are getting up there and you are going to ride this horse. Churn, I have seen you overcome obstacles that would kill any normal person. You can't tell me that riding a horse is going to get the better of you. You, the man who took six Malakasian guards outside that arms warehouse ... alone ... you are going to give in to a child's fear of – of what? Heights? Big animals?'

'Heights,' Churn signed. 'And it was seven guards.' The Pragan rebel tugged distractedly at a leather strap hanging from the open neck of his tunic.

'There you have it, seven,' Hoyt said, 'fixed their rutting hides with your bare hands. This horse should be a red cinch. Now, chop chop, let's ride.'

'No. I'll walk.'

'What is it?' Hannah asked. 'Is he afraid of horses?'

Hoyt turned to her with a frustrated grimace and said, 'No. Not anything that complicated. Our intimidating hulk of walking granite here is afraid of high places. High places! Can you believe it? He'll take on the entire Malakasian Army by himself while suffering a head cold and holding a frothy tankard in one hairy paw, but he won't look out the upstairs window of his own house.'

'Vertigo,' Hannah said. 'I understand it can be crippling.'

'I don't know what that word means, ver—'

'Vertigo.'

'Vertigo.' Hoyt nodded. 'Well, if it means high places turn him into a whining, wet-nosed infant, then you're dead on with your diagnosis.'

'It's a serious condition, Hoyt and you, as a healer, should know that.' Hannah glanced at Churn, who nodded his agreement.

'Oh, stop it, Hannah,' Hoyt argued, 'it's a long way from his vital organs, knocking around in that cavernous tank he calls a brain. And if it's so crippling, how is he able to run and jump from rooftop to rooftop when we're dodging arrows and other Malakasian toys?'

'We're only up there at night,' Churn signed. 'I don't see down.'

'You are a god-rutting cat up there,' Hoyt said crossly.

'When running for my life – I don't think about it. This is different. I'll be up there looking down at everything all day – it's just too high, Hoyt. I can't do it.' Churn's hand moved with fluid grace in the longest monologue Hannah had yet heard from the silent giant.

'So if we're riding for our lives, you won't mind being in the saddle?' Hoyt pressed. 'But out for a pleasant morning canter, a nice jaunt through the forest and up over the hills into Malakasia, you won't go, because the horse is too tall? Gods rest us; I need to find a shorter horse.'

'It's not the horse. It is that my feet won't be on the ground – and I will have time to think about it.'

Hoyt shook his head. 'So, I need to find an exceedingly short horse, one short enough for your feet to drag? That won't slow us down a bit, Churn. Nah, we'll be at Welstar Palace in no time … thirty-five Twinmoons from now! We could crawl there faster.'

'I'm not getting on the rutting horse!'

'All right! All right! No need to yell!'

Hannah grinned at the interchange. 'Maybe we can—'

Hoyt interrupted, mumbling to himself, 'Whole idea is bad … Malakasia … get ourselves killed … take a lot longer dragging … Alen is going to be furious—'

Hannah touched the wiry Pragan on the shoulder. 'I have an idea.' They were standing outside a small mercantile shop at a crossroads northwest of Middle Fork, a place too small to have a name, but where the purchase of four horses and saddlery would not arouse suspicion or start any unwanted rumours. It had taken a day, and a good deal of careful questioning and monetary encouragement before the locals cooperated, but the two thieves had finally located a horse farm willing to deal. Now Alen was inside the mercantile, gathering supplies they would need for their journey into Malakasia.

For three days they had walked north and west, leaving Alen Jasper's home in the pre-dawn aven and before most of Middle Fork was awake. Alen had shouted until the others roused themselves, insisting they pack just what they could carry and leave immediately: Nerak was gone and Welstar Palace was undefended.

Hannah was certain the former Larion Senator had originally planned to take her to Welstar Palace so that he might commit an elaborate suicide at the hands of his former nemesis; now she had no idea what was happening, if sending her home to Colorado was even an option. And she had not yet summoned up the courage to ask. Hoyt said the trip north would take them well into the next Twinmoon, so Hannah figured that with at least sixty days at her disposal, she had time to persuade him.

She had been so worried about the old man's health: Alen drank far too much – she was worried sick that one day she would find him lying dead beside a pile of empty bottles. Though she doubted Alen's ability to get her home, she'd never doubted his willingness to make the effort. *We shall both get what we want, Hannah Sorenson*: she recalled the eerie voice through the locked door of her bedchamber. His English was flawless. He had obviously been across the Fold or through the Fold or whatever it was she had done to get to Eldarn from Colorado.

And he had changed, sobered up in a moment – with a little help from Churn and a trough of cold water – after he met her. It had obviously been a significant moment in the old man's life, meeting her, and even though his mystical resources had obviously not been taken off the shelf in years, discovering that someone other than Nerak controlled the Colorado end of the Larion far portals had made a marked impression. So Hannah had believed that Alen – or Kantu, as he insisted on being called when he was drunk – was committed to finding and using the Malakasian version of the ugly carpet that had dropped her in Southport.

Now Hannah was no longer sure what he was planning. Everything had gone by her in a blur that morning, from hearing him yelling to grabbing her few clothes and hurriedly stuffing bread, cheese and wineskins into a bag.

Even Alen's home remained an enigma. The many hallways, rooms and fireplaces seemed to exist only inside, while outside, a single chimney jutted from the roof of the small structure visible from the street. Hannah had been perplexed by the way the house, whether blocked by the rising or setting sun, obscured by surrounding buildings or draped in fog, was nearly impossible to see clearly. She had it fixed in her head – though not without some difficulty, for even in her imagination the shape was fluid – that the place was tiny, unexceptional ... but inside, it was massive, with twisting hallways, rooms off rooms off rooms, and staircases leading upwards and down at random intervals. Fires burned merrily in fireplaces all over the place.

As they left quietly, unobtrusively, Hannah turned briefly – but the house was different, no longer the unassuming little building Hannah usually saw. Now Alen's house looked like something out of a gothic horror novel, a meandering mansion several storeys high, with exposed beams and mortar walls set with latticed windows and heavy oak doors. On the roof, the single chimney had been joined by a bevy of smokestacks. Hannah almost expected clouds of dark smoke to start billowing skywards.

'How is that possible?' she whispered, hefting her bag onto her shoulder. 'What the hell is happening?'

'I had to remain hidden,' Alen said, hearing her. 'Fantus, my friend and colleague, took on strange professions and hobbies to obscure himself from Nerak's view. He avoided magic so Nerak could not pinpoint his location. Me? I hid right here, right where I was when I heard ... well, when I heard that the world had ended.'

'Nerak looked for you all this time?'

'No. Nerak knew my magic posed little threat. He was more interested in Fantus.'

'So why the camouflaged home?'

'There are others in Welstar Palace, Hannah.'

'Other what?'

'Magicians. Sorcerers. The sort of talented young people Pikan and Nerak sought throughout Eldarn to recruit for the Larion Senate. In the old days they would have been brought to Sandcliff to study.' Alen turned away from the house and set off down the road.

Hannah scurried to catch up with him. 'But with Sandcliff over-run—' she began.

'Nerak brought them to Welstar Palace and started them on a variety of unsavoury undertakings. One of their tasks was to find me. It was fairly simple to mask my comings and goings, especially this far away, but inside this house, I could relax, turn things off for a while.'

'Good Christ. All this time?'

'All this time, Hannah, but this morning, right now, they have stopped seeking me. So it will probably terrify the people of Middle Fork, but I am releasing my old house – and I do love this house – to stand here in all her British glory. You know, they'll probably think it cursed and burn it down.' Alen looked back at her for a moment. 'Come. Let's get going.'

Hannah ignored his order. 'That's right. You said you had been in … where was it?'

'Durham,' Alen answered, without emotion. 'It's where we left Reia.'

'What do you mean by stopped?' Hannah asked. 'How do you know?'

With a sigh, Alen said, 'I can feel it. Actually, I *can't* feel it.'

'It?'

'It – them – looking for me. They've kept it up eight avens a day, sixty days a Twinmoon, for the past nine hundred Twinmoons. About an aven ago, they stopped, and I haven't felt anything from Nerak himself since last Twinmoon.'

'Felt him?' Hannah jogged to catch up with Alen again.

'Not too long ago, the Malakasian city of Port Denis was wiped away, levelled. I couldn't see it as clearly as I might have before I started dri— well, you know … but I don't believe he left anyone alive.'

'And you are able to feel that? See it? How do you know it was that particular city?' Hannah asked.

'It was bigger than most spells. Magic ripples through existence, usually tightening skin into gooseflesh or tickling the hairs on the back of one's neck. It's easy to detect, and with training, one can use those warnings to follow them back to their point of origin.' Alen stopped and faced her; Hannah glimpsed Hoyt and Churn in the distance as they disappeared around a corner.

'So, the Port Denis spell was—' She was fascinated and horrified at the same time.

'Like getting hit in the stomach with a log.' He considered this analogy for a moment, then added, 'I felt it in my bone marrow, like a disease that strikes in an instant, every symptom, every pain, all condensed into one blast, and then passes just as quickly as it came.

You might live for a long time afterwards, but those few moments will stay with you for ever.

'But now the sun is coming up. We need to get away from here before the locals discover that they can't quite remember what my house used to look like.' And with that, Alen of Middle Fork hiked his pack higher on his back and left his home of over nine hundred Twinmoons without a second glance.

Hannah followed, oblivious to the large dog, a wolfhound, maybe, that slipped out of the shadows and kept pace behind her as she trudged through the Middle Fork mud.

Hannah was about to lose her temper. Alen was still inside the store, and it was beginning to look as if Hoyt and Churn were going to sort out Churn's phobia in an unpleasantly physical fashion.

She started to pound Hoyt's back, shouting 'Shut up, shut *up*!' until, in surprise, the two men fell silent.

'Thank you,' she said grimly. 'You're worse than bloody children! Now, listen: I've had an idea.'

'That we club him over the head and strap him to the saddle like a late-autumn deer?' Hoyt muttered. 'Excellent notion, Hannah, very creative. I agree wholeheartedly.' Hoyt grinned then, and winked at Churn, who signed something he obviously didn't feel comfortable translating.

'I said shut up and listen,' Hannah said firmly. 'Hand me that axe.'

'Ah, even better,' Hoyt said as he tugged the weapon from Churn's saddlebag and passed it over. 'Let's just cut his head off. And you need not worry about getting messy. I'll carry it in my bag.'

Churn cuffed Hoyt on the back of his head, nearly knocking him to the ground.

'Rutting lords,' Hoyt protested, 'not so hard.'

Hannah glared and the two of them looked chastened. 'Sadly, it's nothing that grisly – although I could always change my mind. I'll be right back.'

As she walked off into the woods behind the mercantile, Alen came out carrying several bulky canvas bags. 'Here,' he said, 'divide this lot between the horses. If we run out of room, let me know and I'll take care of it.'

'Right,' Churn signed and moved off towards the tree they had been using as a hitching post.

Hoyt turned to Alen. 'You know we can't travel north along the road; we'll have to go through the forest.'

'Have you used that route before?' Alen asked.

Hoyt had travelled to many places, and had seen more strange and wonderful things than most people imagined existed. Work and study had taken him to the distant corners of Eldarn: he had run, crawled, or fought his way out of trouble in as many cities in the Eastlands as any Ronan or Falkan partisan – but he had never travelled through the forest of ghosts. He had always believed that he would have to be fleeing for his life before he entered those enchanted woods. He sighed. 'No,' he said, 'I haven't. I hear it's terrible. I guess I'm about to find out.'

'It can be,' Alen said unhelpfully, 'but there are some who pass through with no trouble at all.' He didn't sound convinced that their passage would be easy. He looked around and shrugged. 'You're right, of course, we can't use this road, and if we try any of the mountain routes we'll certainly encounter border guards.'

'And I would just as soon not have to fight our way *into* Malakasia – bad enough we'll most likely have to fight our way *out* once we get there.'

'And if we do get away, we will need to find a place to—'

Hoyt interrupted, 'If we *do* get away, we will need to come up with a good story as to why we went in at all, because we both know creeping around under cover of darkness is something people do to get *out* of Welstar Palace, not in. *If* we get back to Southport alive, Branag and the boys'll never let me forget this one. A bad idea, my old friend, this is a very bad idea.'

'You'll be fine; I'm certain of it.'

'And you? And Hannah and Churn?' Hoyt asked.

'If we do things right, we'll all get what we need from this journey,' Alen said reassuringly.

'That's cryptic. Am I supposed to be just fine with the idea that you want to kill yourself?' Hoyt asked. 'Still thinking you lived too long?'

'I *have* lived too long, Hoyt, let there be no mistake about that, and I will welcome death when it comes looking for me. But if Nerak is gone from Welstar Palace and his magicians have stopped their search for me, I would like a chance to get in there and – while sending Hannah home – disturb things a bit.'

'*Disturb?* Odd choice of words.'

'It's the best I can come up with.' Though he sounded light-hearted, Hoyt recognised that he was deadly serious. 'Nerak has a team of magicians in there, powerful magicians, who would – *should*

55

– have been Larion Senators. I want them dead. They have been serving evil for so long, and if I have a chance to break down their operation, I will.'

'And?'

'And what?'

'There was something else after that, wasn't there? Something you left out?'

'He has a daughter too.' Anger washed over Alen's face, masking for a moment his pain, loneliness and loss. 'I have waited my whole life for this.'

'Have you?' Hoyt pressed. 'I thought you never killed yourself because Lessek wouldn't let you.'

'Perhaps. And your point?'

'You think this is why he forced you to keep living all this time – to go to Welstar Palace and kill Malagon's daughter?'

'No—' Alen started, but stopped as Hannah appeared with a solid length of wood in one hand and Churn's axe in the other.

She smiled at them. 'My idea: If Churn sits in the saddle and uses this stick to keep in contact with the ground ... well, maybe he won't struggle so much with the height.' Neither man answered; worry creased Hannah's forehead. 'What is it?' she asked anxiously.

Alen looked at Hoyt, his countenance grim, and finished his sentence. 'No. There is something else.'

'What was that?' Hannah joined them 'Is something wrong?'

Hoyt smiled at her. 'No, no. Things are fine and I bet you're right. If we can get that hulking tree-trunk in the saddle without killing him or his horse, I bet this stick idea will work.'

CHICAGO CREEK ROAD

'Nerak, you sonofabitch!' Steven shouted at the empty lot, 'did you have to flatten my house?' He was turning in circles, one way and the other, trying to take in the enormity of what had happened to 147 Tenth Street.

To the right, Dave and Cindy Siegfried's yellow-sided, split-level place sat quietly against the hillside as usual. Their cars were missing from the driveway; Steven assumed they were already at work, unharmed and completely unaware of the Eldarni dictator's foul presence in the Rocky Mountain foothills.

The morning sun reflected off the recent snow, almost blinding Steven as he paced furiously. His gaze fell on the winter-thin hedgerow that separated 147 Tenth from the corner of Tenth and Virginia and his attention shifted: without the end wall of the front room, here was a completely different view of Idaho Springs. Down there were Abe's Liquor Store, the 24-hour convenience place, and the ten-minute Oil & Lube he ignored until his car was four or five thousand miles late for a change.

He shuddered, an involuntary response to the chilly air against the layer of sweat that had broken out on his face and neck, then realised it was something more. He felt the familiar crackle of magic, the hickory staff's magic, as it rippled across his shoulders, between his ribs and down his thighs into his very bones.

He felt calmer now. The far portal was gone, and that meant Lessek's key was gone also, but now was not the time to collapse in despair. Years ago, his cross-country coach, claiming it to be Buddhist philosophy, announced, 'Men, when you are running, run.' It took years for Steven to understand what his coach meant, but the coach's words came back to him now.

'When you are looking, Taylor, look,' he chided himself, and drew a deep breath of home.

Almost immediately, he saw it, bent askew, a small sign pegged into the ground near the sidewalk that had been almost covered by snow. Brushing it clean, Steven read aloud, 'Lot for sale. Call Trevor Hadley at—' He crouched and considered the sign. 'Lot for sale,' he repeated. 'But that's not right ... *Trevor Hadley*.' The phone number was someplace up the canyon in Georgetown, he thought.

Steven shook his head and tossed the sign aside, watching as it disappeared into a snow bank. 'Not right,' he mumbled again, and took several steps back towards the centre of the vacant lot.

He looked again at Dave and Cindy's house, and this time he noticed something he'd missed earlier: the bright yellow siding was darker along the bottom edge. Trudging over, he scratched the discoloured area and peered at his finger.

'Soot,' he said, sniffing it. 'Smoke, creosote, some damned thing. Fire. Goddamnit, our place burned down. And maybe—' Steven rushed back to the expanse of flat ground that had been his front room. 'There's nothing here now, no debris. It *was* a fire. It burned. Maybe it happened a month ago, two months ago.' The excitement in his voice grew. 'Nerak might have got here first, but there's *nothing* here. The house burned down!'

He turned in a circle again, getting more excited as he continued, 'Look, it's flat – too damned flat. It was never this flat. They brought in a bulldozer, bulldozed the place level.' He was running now, small laps around the property, taking in the boring emptiness from every angle. 'Nerak!' he shouted, not caring that someone might see him raving like a madman, 'Nerak, you don't have anything! You might have been here, but you don't have the key or the portal, you arrogant bastard. Didn't expect this did you? Well, what are you going to do now, you invisible prick? Freeze your spirit nuts off out here, I'll bet!'

Reality caught up with Steven so suddenly that he slipped and fell headlong into the snow. The key and the portal *were* gone. That much was obvious. But where would they be? Where would a load of fire debris be taken in Idaho Springs?

He retrieved his watch-cap and scarf and began sprinting along Tenth Street towards town. If he knew where to look next, he had to assume Nerak would take someone, kill them – Cindy or Dave, maybe – and come to the same conclusion. *Didn't they usually drive to work together? Why were both cars gone this morning?*

Steven didn't spare more than a glance at Abe in the window of his liquor store, or the mechanics working in the open pits at the Oil & Lube. Nor did he notice the neon signs blinking their ceaseless messages across the intersection at Tenth and Virginia, COLD BEER westward towards the mountains and OIL CHANGE $26.99 east across the foothills.

Myrna Kessler glanced at the digital display on the clock radio she kept tuned to her favourite Denver station. 9.04 a.m. Eight hours to go and she would be on her way up the canyon and over Loveland Pass to meet friends at a restaurant in Frisco. From there they'd spend the evening in Breckenridge, then she'd find someplace to crash until morning and get a few runs in before the tourists battled through their hangovers or the locals made their way up from the city.

Her car was packed; she had $108 in her pocket and about enough wiggle room left on her Visa card for an inexpensive dinner and a couple of drinks during happy hour. Myrna was attractive; she never had any problem finding men to buy her drinks, but setting out deliberately to do that, shaving off thirty IQ points and wrestling herself into a Wonderbra, always left her feeling as though she was on stage in some outdated farce. What was the point? $25 would cover her drinks, and Howard's if necessary, and she could wear whatever she wanted. Anyway, she could be bumming around in her oldest sweatshirt and she was still noticed: men paid attention to women who had a pulse.

There had been a few customers, but the weekend rush wouldn't hit until 11.30, when most of the town, Friday paycheques in hand, started their lunch break. Myrna and Howard would work the windows together until 1.00 p.m., when, as quickly as it had started, the queue would be gone. Then Howard would trundle sadly across Miner Street to Owen's Pub and she would be left to close the bank at five o'clock, locking the doors and shutting off the lights.

Howard had been depressed since Steven and Mark's disappearance. He had refused to fill the assistant manager's position, even with a temporary employee, and he followed the investigations assiduously every day. Word around town was that he had climbed as far up the Decatur Peak trail as he could before the snow grew too deep for him to go any further. Myrna didn't like to think of her boss up there, battling through thigh-deep snow and shouting for Steven and Mark until his voice gave out.

The police had been little help and Howard would never forgive them for it; he didn't think the local authorities had done a comprehensive investigation into the mysterious disappearance of his friends.

It didn't help that the roommates' house at 147 Tenth Street had burned to the ground the day they had gone missing – a highly suspicious *accident*. No remains had been discovered in the ashes, and the fire marshal believed one of them had left the gas stove burning. Apart from the cars parked out front – Hannah Sorenson's car was there, too – there was no evidence to show where the trio might have gone. Because of the snow, the police couldn't even determine when Hannah's car had arrived, or if Steven or Mark's cars had been moved since that Friday afternoon. It hadn't been a good day for climbing, and no one could work out how the trio had reached the trailhead unless someone else had come by to pick them up before dawn Saturday morning.

Both Myrna and Howard had been interviewed three or four times during the investigation, by local police, a city detective and then by members of a state police missing persons team. Each time the procedure had been the same: the officers arrived and had asked to speak with Howard; Myrna had shown them to the manager's office. And after an hour or two, one or more of them had come back to the lobby and invited her to join them. Howard always shot her a glance as he sidled past to take up her position at the teller window. Invariably, Myrna was offered Howard's chair and made comfortable before the interrogation began. Always the same questions:

Had Steven ever spoken of enemies, people who disliked him or those from whom he had borrowed money?

No.

Had Steven changed dramatically after meeting Hannah Sorenson?

No more than any twenty-eight-year old who finds someone he cares about.

Hadn't Myrna studied in Mark Jenkins' class at Idaho Springs High School?

Yes, history.

Had he ever given her the impression that he had extreme political beliefs?

No.

Had Steven?

Steven didn't have political beliefs.

What did Steven and Mark do in their free time?

Climbed, went biking, they did some distance running, and Mr Jenkins was a swimmer.

Did Steven swim, too?

Do you really think he might be off swimming somewhere? All this time?

Just answer the question, please.

No, Steven was not a swimmer.

Was Mark Jenkins in love with Hannah Sorenson?

I don't know.

Could there have been bad blood between them after Hannah came into Steven's life?

They went climbing that Saturday. It snowed that day.

Were they gay?

Why are you talking about them in the past tense and how is their sexual preference going to help you find them?

Just answer the question, please.

No.

Have you climbed Decatur Peak?

No.

Have you climbed with Mark and Steven?

No.

The questions had gone on, a rhythmless poem of point and counterpoint, until one of the officers had thanked Myrna for her time and encouraged her to call if she thought of something or remembered something, as if Steven's political beliefs or his preference for peanut butter over cream cheese or Mark's swimming in the town pool would help locate them under seventeen feet of mountain snow.

Now Myrna wasn't sure which was worse: the fact that the police had asked the same pointless questions so often, or that they had stopped entirely. She remembered the morning the *Clear Creek County Gazette* quoted state officials saying the search along the Decatur Peak trail would be suspended until spring. If they were up there, they were dead. Howard had given a cry, a muted bark that had been half frustration and half rage before running, his squat form at once both comical and tragic, to the town office of the local paper. He had been gone for thirty minutes before Myrna watched him sulk back down Miner Street to Owen's. Finding it locked, at 8.50 in the morning, he had turned and walked home, never sparing the First National Bank of Idaho Springs a second glance.

This morning, Howard was in his office. He was in a foul mood again and Myrna needed a break; she had been running the bank on her own for the past month and she refused to allow his depression to ruin her anticipation. It was a special day, not just because of her planned weekend, but because she had received her federal financial aid forms. She could finally get to college, leave the canyon and move to Fort Collins. She felt a sudden pang of guilt that Mr Jenkins – after all this time she still struggled to call him Mark – was not around to help her with the application and grant forms. He had promised he would talk her through the paperwork. Myrna said a quiet prayer that the boys would be found before she left for university.

As she started on the forms – her social security number, her income, her mother's maiden name, and so on – Myrna was distracted for a moment by the piece of paper she kept safe under the glass sheet across her desk. On it was drawn a series of circles in different coloured ink, measuring diameter lengths around each circumference. *Pi.* Steven had caught her drawing the sketches the afternoon he had first met Hannah Sorenson. Myrna had never taken the time to ask him how he knew that Egyptian architects—

The small bell above the lobby door rang, waking Myrna from her daydream; she quickly shuffled her financial aid paperwork to one side.

A police officer crossed the lobby with a purposeful stride: *not here to open an account*, she thought. *More questions, terrific.* Perhaps he would start with Howard and she could get a few pages done.

'Good morning,' she said, not really surprised to be ignored. When he reached the old pine countertop, Myrna realised he wasn't from Idaho Springs. The patch stitched across his shoulder read *Charleston City Police.* Unnerved at his silence, and somewhat disturbed by what appeared to be dry blood caked in his ear and across the lobe, Myrna nevertheless offered her most hospitable smile.

'A bit out of your jurisdiction this morning, aren't you, Officer?' *Men pay attention to women who have a pulse*, she thought, and waited for the young man to respond.

A distressing feeling, like sudden tunnel vision, overtook Myrna Kessler. Still trying to be polite, she tried to discreetly shake the weird feeling, closing her eyes and tossing her head sharply. She didn't want to embarrass herself further in front of the out-of-town police officer – he might have news of Steven and Mark – Myrna ignored the sudden itch on her left wrist. She swallowed hard, trying, with her last breath, to maintain the professional integrity of the First National Bank of Idaho Springs.

'Officer? Can I help—?'

'I want Steven Taylor,' the policeman said before crumpling to the floor. He struck his chin on the countertop hard enough to split the wood.

Myrna reached through the slatted window and ran her fingers along the fissure. A black, festering wound opened on her left wrist and without even trying to scream, she let herself go. The splintered edge of the broken countertop was the last sensation she felt before spiralling away.

Myrna stood up, stepped into the bank lobby and crossed to David Mantegna's discarded form lying on the floor. With an unexpectedly vicious kick to the ribs she turned Mantegna's body over, then bent down and withdrew the officer's 9mm pistol from the leather holster in his belt. She rooted around in his pockets until she found a pouch of chewing tobacco, which she stuffed into her blazer pocket.

Without looking back she walked out into Miner Street and the brilliant, snow-blinding morning.

'Myrna?' Howard called from his office. He leaned to one side to see if he could catch a glimpse of the young teller without getting out of his chair. 'Myrna?' he shouted again, listening in vain for the sound of her footsteps, or the soft hum of a receipt gliding through her desktop computer. Nothing.

'Shit, Myrna, you're supposed to tell me before you go to the can.' As he got up to attend the teller window he glanced along the narrow hall, past Steven's silent office. The bathroom door was open and the light switched off. 'Where the hell did she go?' he growled. 'Goddamnit, if I've told—'

Howard's gaze fell on the broken section of pine countertop outside Myrna's slatted window. Reaching through to feel the fractured edge, he felt wetness: a shallow pool of what appeared to be dark blood.

'Oh, shit,' he breathed, and hustled through the connecting door, stopping abruptly as the sight of the dead body of the Charleston City Police Officer. Kneeling beside the young man, Howard searched for a pulse, and, feeling nothing, tried a few uncertain thumps where he thought the breastbone was. Still nothing.

He looked up and screamed through the empty bank, 'Myrna!'

Steven picked his way hurriedly to Howard Griffin's house on Fourteenth Street, north of Miner, but close to the city centre and the First National Bank of Idaho Springs. He estimated the time at nearly 9.00 a.m. on Friday; even at his most tardy, Howard would be at the bank by now. Avoiding the front door he made his way to the back and used the spare key stashed beneath a loose plank in the deck to open the patio door. Cautiously, he stepped in.

He waited a full minute, counting down the seconds while listening for sounds: his boss preparing breakfast, or showering, or hefting his not inconsiderable bulk up the Mt Griffin Stairmaster. After sixty seconds or so he moved quickly through the laundry alcove and into the old bachelor's rarely used kitchen. There, taped to the refrigerator like a gallery of child's art, were a series of newspaper articles chronicling the story of Steven and Mark's disappearance and the ensuing weeks of investigation and recovery efforts along the Decatur Peak trail. He stood transfixed by the headlines. The *Denver Post, Rocky Mountain News, Clear Creek County Gazette* – even the *Washington Post* and *New York Times* – there were cuttings from all of these, affixed to Howard's refrigerator, a yellowing testament to the missing roommates. Steven collected them all and folded them carefully in his back pocket. Right now he didn't care that Howard would know someone had been in his house: he and Mark needed to know what had gone on.

The house was well-heated, even with Howard out at work all day, and Steven was finding it too hot to breathe. He unravelled the wool scarf from around his face and as he tossed it over the back of a chair he noticed a small cork board hanging on the wall in the breakfast nook. More newspaper features were displayed there, and Steven hastened around the table to retrieve these as well.

He unpinned the first and glanced at the headline. These were different. The first, clipped from an October issue of the *Rocky Mountain News*, was headlined *Denver Woman Listed Among Springs Missing*. His hands began to shake and he rubbed his palms roughly against his denimed thigh. He was certain he could feel the staff's magic again, that familiar slowing of time and the tickling sensation of its power dancing along beneath his skin.

Shaking his head, he said, 'No. No. Stop it. It's too far away. You're just upset. Get hold of yourself. This just confirms it. That's all. This is nothing new.' He sat down, his heart racing, until his pulse slowed and the dizziness passed.

Upstairs, he stole a nylon backpack from the hallway closet. In the bedroom, he took several pairs of wool socks, two neutral-coloured sweaters, as many pairs of gloves as he could find, two cigarette lighters from the bedside table and a lined Gore-tex jacket. Over one arm he carried a second jacket for Mark. They had used their stolen silver to outfit themselves in Orindale, and the sailboat Mark and Brynne had repaired was well stocked with essentials, but socks and coats from home would be welcome, for Mark too.

He struggled into the backpack and ran down the stairs, stopping short at the bottom. 'A watch, damn it,' he cursed and pushed past the door into the living room. Apart from a large recliner that Howard always treated with all the deference of a holy relic, the room looked like a bomb had hit it. Books, newspapers, dirty dishes, an errant shoe, orphan socks – even a pair of forgotten boxer shorts – lay scattered about. There was a teetering pile of out-of-date *TV Guides* against one wall. Steven whistled. 'Holy Vicksburg,' he said, 'Howard, how the hell do you live in this?'

Ignoring the mess, Steven bravely ploughed his way towards the baby grand piano, which was decorated with a half-empty bottle of beer and a gnawed pizza crust atop a wrinkled dishcloth. Behind, on the large bookshelf, was Steven's prize: an old wristwatch lying forgotten on a pile of creased paperbacks.

He grabbed it: off by an hour, so it had obviously been up there since before the clocks had gone back some months before, but the second hand was sweeping round inexorably. 'Okay, 9.22,' he said, adjusting the watch back sixty minutes. 'Now it really is time to get going—' He stopped, remembering a promise he had made months earlier, then peered around, grinning as he appropriated one final item from Howard Griffin's living room. 'Vicksburg,' he said softly.

His stomach growled, but Howard's refrigerator offered only beer, a suspicious-smelling bottle of milk and a box of muesli bars. Howard was the only person Steven knew who would follow a healthy breakfast of orange juice, dry wheat toast and a healthy grain and dried fruit bar with a three-beer-grilled-beef-and-onion-ring lunch and think he was eating well. He grinned in remembrance as he stuffed a handful of the bars into his pack, followed by several cans of beer. In the freezer he found a full can of ground French roast coffee, which he appropriated, together with a packet of filters lying on the counter.

'That ought to do it,' he murmured. 'Thanks, Howard. I'll pay you back.' Steven carefully wrapped the scarf around his face, pulled up his collar and left the house, relocking the door and stashing the key where he'd found it.

The city dump was a long way out, so Steven decided to borrow Howard's dilapidated 1977 Thunderbird, a powder-blue, long-nosed sedan the size of a small whale. It sat rusting in the driveway with the keys dangling from the ignition, exactly where he expected them to be.

'No one's going to steal my car, are they?' Howard had laughed when Steven had borrowed the behemoth once before, 'their family and friends might see them in it!'

And now, a year or more later, there they still were, hanging by the steering wheel. Steven was almost shocked when the engine immediately roared into life. *Thank you, Howard,* he thought as he backed out of the drive. *I really will pay you back one day.*

He turned towards Chicago Creek Road and the Idaho Springs City Dump.

Nerak tossed the gun onto the passenger seat of David Mantegna's car, then extracted a large pinch of chewing tobacco from the red, white and blue packet and pushed it into his mouth – and gagged violently, spitting the wad onto the floor. He swore: the girl had apparently not developed any taste for tobacco.

'Too bad, my dear,' Nerak said silkily, his voice a sinister echo in Myrna's dying mind. 'You'll just have to get used to it.' He retrieved the clump of tobacco, then, ignoring the bits of dirt that had stuck to it, popped it back into his – Myrna's – mouth. 'I love this stuff,' he told the dying spirit, glad of Mantegna's nicotine addiction; he so enjoyed that warm buzz. 'If I had more time in this tired old world, I might harvest a season's worth.'

He glanced over at the pistol and grinned. He had enjoyed that too – in fact, the carnage had almost made this annoying side-trip worthwhile.

Nerak could have made Idaho Springs from Charleston in eighteen hours if he had driven Mantegna's Mustang nonstop at top speed, but he had taken some unplanned – most entertaining – detours. Somewhere in Kentucky he had stopped to refuel and to satisfy his – and Mantegna's – craving for tobacco. When the hapless clerk demanded payment for the fuel and the distinctively coloured pouches of *Confederate Son*, Mantegna's favourite, Nerak shot him. What an ingenious invention, Nerak told Mantegna; much easier to handle than his first guns, more than a hundred years before, and so much more efficient than the unwieldy weapons in Eldarn.

He turned from the bloody remains of the clerk and squeezed the trigger again, this time firing into the glass doors of the cool cabinets, and bottles shattered, spilling multi-coloured liquids onto the floor. The cash register was next, then a beer advertisement hanging on the back wall, where several half-naked women were playing a game in the sand – *volleyball*, the word appeared in his mind. Nerak fired once through the ball and once through the broad forehead of a muscular young man watching, a beer bottle dangling from one hand.

Finally, curious, Nerak fired into Mantegna's hand, his *own* hand, just to experience the weapon himself – and as the bullet blew most of it off, an excruciating arrow of white-hot pain raced up his arm. 'Outstanding!' Nerak screamed as his ruined hand dripped gore.

Nerak collected his chewing tobacco, stopped the blood spurting from his wound with a thought and stepped outside to continue his journey. Three fingers and half of his palm lay abandoned on the floor behind him.

As he crossed the parking lot, the dark prince waved his hand and changed the car from blue to red, jumped in and sped off, laughing hysterically. He drove at breakneck speed through Missouri, chasing the fleeing sun and taking pot-shots out the window at anything that took his fancy – passing cars, livestock, backpackers he spotted outside St Louis. The police officer had been an enthusiastic member of the NRA and Nerak found three boxes of ammunition beneath the front seat. He turned the car yellow, the colour of pus, to celebrate.

Kansas had been the highlight of his journey as he'd cruised across the flatlands at one hundred and thirty miles per hour, pursued by the regional militia, or *state troopers*, in Mantegna's lexicon of law enforcement. They had come after him on two-wheeled motorised vehicles of some sort – *motorcycles*, Mantegna interjected dully – and two-tone, heavy-bodied sedans with clamorous sirens and sparkling red and blue lights whirling about overhead. Best of all, they had tracked him with a wonderful flying *helichopper-copter-whirlybird* thing. Mantegna had so many words for this glorious contraption that Nerak was not sure which was the common term.

With a wave of his hand he had flattened the front tyres of the motorised cycles, chuckling in high good humour as the riders had spun off into the air.

The helichopper-copter had reacted aggressively, dropping from the sky to force Nerak off the road. It scraped the side of the Mustang with one of its landing rails, and though he could have crashed the whirlybird with a gesture, instead, relishing the challenge, he had taken aim and fired Mantegna's weapon several times into the shining belly. The helichopper-copter reeled away, banking like a frightened plover in a gale and Nerak watched the man inside wrestling with some sort of control, trying to save the giant bird's life.

It was too low, though, and the great blades slashed the ground, sending up sparks as the metal hit the roadway's stone surface. One of the chasing sedans was caught by the whirling scimitars, which sliced off the car's nose and sent the helichopper-copter spinning over a harvested corn field where it crashed, tail-first, and exploded so powerfully that it almost drove Nerak's car into a ditch.

Kansas had been enjoyable.

Nerak slipped a fresh clip into the 9mm and returned the weapon to his waistband, then grinned and spat a mouthful of foul brown juice out the window. He wasn't surprised to find the house he was seeking had been razed to the ground: Myrna had known, so Nerak learned of the disaster moments after taking the young woman's soul. But it wasn't the house he was interested in; he got out and strode confidently across the vacant lot, casting a magic net aloft to search for the stone. He was a few paces across the level expanse of frozen ground that had been Steven and Mark's front porch before he saw footprints in the snow.

Nerak bent to touch a print. Splaying Myrna's fingers, he murmured, 'You have been here this morning, Steven Taylor.' He closed the woman's eyes and reached out again for the stone key. Nothing. It was gone.

'Where is he?' he asked Myrna, but she was dead now and didn't respond – no matter, the Eldarni dictator knew everything she had ever known. He concentrated for a moment, then smiled. 'The city dump. Won't that be lovely this morning?' He shook his head, a gesture that was faintly reminiscent of Myrna. For a minute he considered incinerating the rest of Idaho Springs, sending a tidal wave of fire rolling from peak to peak across the canyon. That would teach the meddling foreigner a lesson.

'Anyone you love live here, Steven Taylor?' Nerak spat a stream of tobacco juice at a grey squirrel that had wandered too close and added, 'No ... no need. I know where you've gone.'

Instead of returning to Mantegna's battered car, Nerak sat down, cross-legged, on the snow, facing south through Clear Creek Canyon. He pulled out the pistol and placed it at his side. 'Are you up there, my young sorcerer? Digging in the mud and shit for my keystone?

68

Gilmour is far away, Steven, and you will spend a very long time regretting this little journey.' The dark prince closed his eyes and began searching the distant canyon.

The Idaho Springs City Dump was located south of town on Chicago Creek Road, a two-lane highway that wound its leisurely course through the Arapahoe National Forest towards Juniper Pass and the Mt Evans Wilderness. Steven looked up at Devil's Nose on his left and Alps Mountain on his right, feeling intimidated, as though he were driving beneath the twin shoulder blades of a sleeping god.

He parked Howard's Thunderbird beside a chain-link fence with a large green sign on the locked gate reading:

> City of Idaho Springs Landfill and Recycle Facility
> Hours of operation: Tues. – Thurs. 6 a.m. – 6 p.m.
> Sat. & Sun. 6 a.m. – 12 noon.
> Or by Appointment

A phone number at the bottom had the words *leave message* after it in small block capitals crookedly affixed, the kind often stuck onto mailboxes.

Steven looked around to make sure he was alone, then leaped as high as he could and grabbed the chain-link fence. He hung there for a moment, then pulled himself up and over, landing hard on the other side. Huffing from the exertion, he muttered, 'Man, you need to get back into shape!' He brushed the snow off his legs and started up the unmade road to the landfill site, checking signposted turnings to the right and left: *Plastic Recyclables*, *Aluminium Recyclables* and *Paper Recyclables* respectively. As he jogged past *Appliances And Used Tyres* he saw a rickety overhead arch bearing the words *Idaho Springs City Dump* – obviously erected in less politically correct times, he grinned to himself.

He stepped over a knee-high chain that ran across the road and heard the thin wail of a siren echoing up the canyon. 'God, I hope I'm right,' he said under his breath. The dump stretched out before him: a mountainous landscape in miniature. The rolling hills of rubbish might have looked tiny next to the Rockies that towered overhead, but Steven felt his heart sink: the tapestry – and Lessek's key, of course – could be *anywhere* ... and there was a hell of a lot of *anywhere* to search.

He needed a strategy. Mel Fisher's discovery of the treasure ship *Atocha* in the 1970s had fascinated him: Fisher had used a grid to map the ocean floor around the wreck ... the mathematician in Steven took over and he altered his perspective, looking at the garbage hills as a topographical calculus problem.

There were three hummocks in the foreground about thirty feet shorter than the six or seven hills flanking them. This dump had served Idaho Springs for as long as he could remember, and the fact that there were only ten or eleven hills in the entire valley meant either the landfill was much deeper than it looked, or it took the city a long time to generate a two-hundred-foot-high mountain of trash. But whichever assumption was true, the end result was the same: something dumped as recently as October would be close by.

'*Close by* is, of course, entirely relative,' he grumbled. 'I bet everything else since October is sitting on top of my house right now and I'm about to spend the better part of the next five years digging around in here looking for a rock. And I didn't even have the sense to steal a shovel. Am I quite mad? There has to be a better way.'

Nothing immediately sprang to mind so he decided to root around until he found some dates: franked letters, maybe, or old utility bills. Using those as a guide, he could chart a rudimentary map through the mountains based on the passage of time. If he ignored areas where the rubbish came from before October 15, or after the previous week, he hoped to zero in on the final resting place of his and Mark's charred possessions.

'Let's get going!' Steven said briskly. He took a few steps towards the hill on his left when his toe caught on something solid beneath the snow and he cursed and flailed his arms in a desperate effort to regain his balance. 'Speed bumps?' he yelled, 'Why the hell do we need speed bumps at the damned—' As his foot landed he felt a shock of pain fire through his leg and he tumbled to the ground. 'Ah, shit, my knee,' he groaned, and rolled onto his back, clutching it with both hands.

Anticipating the dull throb of soft tissue damage, he sat up and gingerly straightened his right leg, the one that had nearly been bitten off by the injured grettan in the Blackstone Mountains south of Meyers' Vale. But though he expected another blast of pain, Steven found to his surprise that he was able to flex and extend his leg with no problem.

'Huh,' he said, his voice bright with relief, 'I must have come down on it crooked or something.' He stood up carefully, putting a little weight through the leg until he was certain there were no injuries. 'Thank God! I'd be flat-out screwed, trapped here with a blown knee.'

Below, the siren's cry came again, and as Steven stepped over the disfigured snow angel he had made another explosion lanced through his leg, spilling him to the ground once more. 'What the hell *is* this?' he shouted up towards Alps Mountain. 'What's wrong with me?' He clutched at his knee with one hand and rolled into a sitting position. Grimacing, he started to straighten the leg – and once again, it was as if nothing had happened. Swearing, he took off his gloves and stuffed them in a pocket, then carefully rolled his trouser leg above the knee so he could see if it had swelled up – maybe he had torn a ligament or something and the cold was numbing it.

'I'll bet it was coming over that rutting fence,' he said, not noticing the Eldarni profanity. 'Just my bloody luck.' But the leg looked perfectly healthy. Steven, at a loss, put his clothes to rights and heaved himself back on his feet. He tested the leg again, gingerly at first, then stamping both feet hard, but it felt fine.

Still swearing under his breath, Steven turned back towards the hills of rubbish. This time he stopped dead, his foot in mid-air: when he looked down, he saw he was about to put his boot on exactly the spot where his knee had twice buckled beneath him.

Standing upright, one foot suspended several inches above the ground, he waited until he felt it: a muted sensation, like the soft rubbing of fingertips against an unfinished pine tabletop or the coarse skin of a callused palm. 'Gilmour?' Steven whispered, then stepped back, planting his foot away from the impacted snow where he had fallen. It was an urge now, like something – some*one* – was guiding him; he reached out, palms forward, as if to feel the air before him. He tried to recall how he'd felt all those months ago, when he was so determined to break into the bank safe and see what William Higgins had deposited there a century and a half earlier – he remembered feeling driven as he hurried home to see what was so important it had merited an eternity in a safe-deposit box.

He recognised that feeling; it was back: Lessek's key and the Larion far portal were here, close by. He was not too late; not yet.

Steven covered his eyes: they were deceiving him, telling him there were acres of garbage to consider. There were not. Now, when he removed his hand, the landfill was gone, blurred into a waxy backdrop of beige, green and white. In its place were three tears, like irregular gashes on an oil canvas. The rips separated the landscape, pulling and tugging at the wash of colour that had been the valley below.

Steven's breathing slowed as he understood what he was seeing; he had experienced something like this before, when he had touched the leather binding of Lessek's spell book that night on the *Prince Marek*. He was overwhelmed with a monumental sense of power, as vast as the Midwest he had crossed just days before. Closing his eyes again, he reached into the air; it was tangible, malleable. *When you are running, run, Steven.* The way to win the battle was not to battle. The way to win the battle was to *create*. Ideas and algorithms swirled around him, and for a moment everything that ever was or would be was spread before him: opportunities won and lost, all was clear. It was maths. Maths could do anything, even the Fold could ...

When Steven broke free from the magic, he found himself struggling to breathe, as if unseen arms encircled his chest. He cursed the altitude, rubbed his eyes and zipped his jacket up under his chin. It had grown colder; around him, the valley seemed darker.

Delicately, carefully, Steven edged the toe of his boot forward until it reached the point where he had fallen twice that morning. Nothing. No shock of Larion magic this time. He cautiously inched forward; now he knew what he was looking for. 'A speed bump,' he said, 'a speed bump in a city dump. Who would have thought—?'

He walked to the snow bank towering above the road and began kicking at the base of the five-month accumulation of ploughed snow and ice. It was there; he was certain – just a foot or so away from where his legs had given way: a small granite stone, irregular and nondescript. Lessek's key.

'A speed bump.' He shook his head and laughed out loud. 'It bounced off the truck when it hit the speed bump.' Steven turned the stone over in his hands, then slipped it into the pocket of his stolen jacket. The distant scream of sirens carried up the valley from Clear Creek Canyon.

He slipped several times on his way up the north face and some twelve feet down the other side of the middle mound of garbage, making him bitterly regret his lack of clean clothing. Wiping off a lump of what he was hoped was only rancid beef, he began digging through the layers of snow, frozen mud and damp rubbish. Three feet of mouldy food, rotten newspapers and dirty diapers later, his torn gloves came away thick with black, smoky mud. Paydirt: the remains of 147 Tenth Street.

Ten minutes later found Steven pulling out a wrinkled, sodden, almost unrecognisable Larion far portal. Though it looked – and felt – disgusting, as he tossed it over his shoulder, he noticed its fragrance, a hint of lilac, Hannah's perfume. Its energy, the force that had driven him to rob his own bank, hadn't waned. He could feel it pulsing through the muscles of his shoulder like a second cousin to the hickory staff. He glanced at the stolen watch, 10.54 a.m., six hours until he could get it back again. He hadn't expected to miss it so much.

As he came down from the trash mountain, Steven wore a look of grim confidence. Lessek's Larion portal was his; this time all the trepidation and terror he had experienced the night he followed Mark to Estrad were gone. In six hours he would step back into Eldarn, this time without fear, but he would carry with him sadness for Versen's loss, loneliness without Hannah, and slow-boiling hatred for Nerak.

From the trees to the north came yet another wailing siren. As if he had suddenly heard it for the first time, Steven snapped his attention towards the sound. He swore, and began sprinting towards Howard's car. Nerak was in Idaho Springs.

CASKS ON THE QUAY

On the north bank of the Medera River, where it spilled out into Orindale Harbour, there was an alehouse, bigger than most along the waterfront, catering to a mixed clientele of sailors, stevedores and merchants, and even a few Malakasian soldiers. It was a positive hive of revelry, from early morning until late each night, with fights tending to be little more than angry shoving matches as no one wanted to bring the full scrutiny of the local occupation force onto the establishment. Going too far would raise concern among the officers, and risk them closing the tavern, or, worse, having it burned to the ground.

Periodically someone would drink too much, talk too much, grope too much, or spout one too many unwise remarks about Prince Malagon, the occupation generals or even the wife or mistress of a good friend, and fists would grasp knives, blood would spill and bodies would be carried out a side entrance and unobtrusively tossed into the river.

The tavern owner kept a massive barrel filled with sawdust and it was the scullery boy's job to scamper across the floor, dodging kicks and comatose drinkers, and ladle a few scoops onto whatever was pooled on the stained planks underfoot. The process generally took a few moments, and then noise level would rise again and things would return to normal.

In the predawn avens, violence was overcome by sex – or at least what might pass for sex in the grey time before sunrise. Sailors on leave, often just returned from long Twinmoons at sea, would spend the early part of the evening puffing out their chests shouting bold, if idiotic, platitudes about bravery and the sea, and fighting one another. By the middlenight aven, their thoughts turned as they grew desperate to find a warm woman in a warm bed. There were rare nights when full-on sex could be had on a table, behind the bar, or on a burlap sack out the back, and there were nights when a woman or two – periodically, even a bright young man – would take a knee and in front of the gods of the Northern Forest offer oral entertainments.

But with relatively few women willing to kneel down and service a crowd of healthy, if dog-piss-drunk sailors, the men were left to get creative, or to rely on the *grippers*, those females (generally), not all of them whores, who would make the late rounds, collecting coins and leaving a trail of comparatively satisfied young men in their wake, often while chatting with companions or enjoying a beer themselves. Evenings when the beer had flowed particularly deep and when women were particularly scarce, some men, desperate as they were, would come to agreeable terms and perform the service for one another.

And in the moments before dawn, to the sound of heavy boots shuffling over patches of sawdust, the place would empty.

The alehouse was less than a stone's throw from the bridge that spanned the Medera, connecting Orindale's northern and southern districts. It was here that Garec and Steven had first spotted the *Prince Marek*. Most harbour traffic passed over its narrow span, and the bridge provided an excellent vantage point from which to assess local activity.

During the morning aven, anyone standing on the bridge would have been able to watch as the tavern's scullery boy made several trips out of the side entrance with a wooden bucket. From the bridge, one could observe as the boy scooped sawdust from a huge wooden barrel that could easily have accommodated him and a handful of his friends to boot. The cask was filled with fine brown sawdust, and there was no reason to believe the seven or eight other barrels arranged in a confused pattern along the riverside held anything else.

Yet one did.

While the bridge provided an unobstructed view of the alehouse, and the unsavoury (usually unmoving) characters periodically disgorged into the river, the haphazard maze of barrels was perhaps the best place in the city from which to observe traffic across the bridge, and provided the perfect cover for one observer's stealthy comings and goings.

The morning visitor to Orindale's harbour bridge would not have seen the cowled inhabitant of the cask forest, no matter how closely he observed, as daylight was time for sleeping, for eating whatever had been scavenged the previous evening, or for watching platoons of soldiers, Seron, or merchants with carts and wagons.

A thin peephole, broken through one of the cask slats with an awl, was also invisible from the bridge, and it was through this fracture that the creature took in Orindale's rhythms and patterns: who came and went? Which merchants received shipments and at which piers? Who might be addled enough to leave part of their cargo unprotected, or, even better, sparsely guarded on one of the piers overnight?

The creature was always hungry, but death was more important: countless numbers of the black and gold soldiers had fallen, and no one had been able to ascertain more than the fact that he worked alone, stalking his victims, two or three at a time, slashing them to death. If they cared, it was always a near-perfect display of hand-to-hand skills.

He had even killed several of the Seron monsters; they had put up a far greater fight and the hooded assassin had learned that if he failed to strike the fatal blow with his first lunge, his life was in very grave danger. The Seron were strong and conscienceless; killing one of them was more akin to taking out a grettan: dangerous and exhilarating all at once.

He had fading recollections of a Seron in the Blackstone Mountains. That one was different, tame, almost – more like a broad-shouldered farm animal than a soulless Malakasian killer. But this was the Seron who had thrown something at him, a rock, maybe, or a log: it had shattered his shoulder, forcing Sallax to throw himself onto a rock in an effort to set the joint aright. He couldn't recall how he knew to try that, but it hadn't worked, and now he seethed with hatred for the Seron, all Seron, most of all every time he was forced to hunch over to alleviate the throbbing pain.

There *were* good things about the pain, though: generally it was steady, but when it grew excruciating, as if the tissues were tearing anew, the rolling socket joint forcing its crooked way forward, driving his upper arm nearly around behind his back, then his thoughts left him alone. When the pain exploded, his mind went blank, abandoning any attempt to bring foggy memories of past Twinmoons into focus. Then, things fell away and any thoughts of Sallax Farro of Estrad were lost in a flare of white fire. That was when things were easy. Hunting made sense; eating anything he could find became second nature and living in an empty barrel was not an inconvenience at all.

This evening, Sallax was hungry. He had eaten the last of the dog before crawling from his cask in the pre-dawn aven. It had been good meat, but after three days it was growing rancid. He needed to find another source of food – he had hoped for another stray, for they often hung around the warehouses on the southern wharf – and he would have found one if it had not been for that woman. *She had called him Sallax, as if she knew him.* He was unsettled at the memory of her reprimanding him – him! He could snap her neck with two fingers.

He had dragged her from the mud. It had been cold there, and the fern bed was dry, and warm in the morning sun. She ought to have thanked him, but instead she had been angry. That had interrupted his plans; instead, distracted, he had wandered through the side streets, where he at least found some discarded bread, a half-full bottle of beer and some mouldy cheese thrown through a window. Why they didn't want it he couldn't imagine.

Now he kept an eye on the bridge, lit by torches in sconces. He would hunt again this night, and perhaps take another Seron – the monsters were particularly on his mind. *Something to do with that woman? She had called him Sallax.* But he was hungry and wanted real food, another dog – or maybe even a gansel, or a beef tenderloin, something cooked, or something he could hastily char over one of the fires the lost men kindled down alongside the river.

Sallax had been hesitant to leave his barrel this evening; his foggy mind was in turmoil. The woman was no threat to him; there was no need to kill her – so why was he panting here like a rutting dog after a bitch? He could kill her if he chose, or he might let her live … but that wasn't what was causing his chest to tighten.

She had known Sallax … she had known *him*. Was she the one to help him? Could she wrench his shoulder back into place? Maybe she could flesh out the half-seen images in his memory. Perhaps he might even speak with her about them, these people, the old man especially. He knew they were strong, and committed, and he wanted to see them – but they stayed at the back of his mind, the rutters, and he couldn't see their faces.

His shoulder ached and he growled in fury, slamming against the side of the barrel until he was sure it would topple into the Medera River.

Hearing that name, *his* name, that morning had changed things. She – the barefoot, muddy woman – hadn't come by, she hadn't crossed the bridge. She was still in the southern part of the city, so that's where he would go. It would be cold, but that was fine; the cold soothed his shoulder, cleared his head.

The cowled killer that had haunted the Orindale waterfront for the past Twinmoon slipped without a sound from inside his hiding place and moved into the shadows of the alehouse just as the side door flew open with a crash. Three men emerged, two in the unmistakable black and gold livery of the Malakasian Army, between them a drunk, sopping wet, sporting a breastplate of regurgitated supper and cheap wine.

'You seem a nice enough fellow,' said the taller soldier, 'and I'm about sure you'd have no problem making the swim to shore, even as drunk as you are. So, let's complicate things a bit, shall we?' He turned to his colleague, who drew a dirk and slid it into the drunk's belly.

Blood spurted from the deep puncture wound. The drunk screamed, and cried out again as they tossed his body into the water.

The hooded man lurking in the shadows frowned when he heard the cry and the splash. It was not that he cared that these soldiers executed a drunk, but he was surprised that he couldn't hear the victim's shouts from beneath the surface of the water.

'Have a nice swim, boy,' the tall soldier shouted, then, clapping a hand on his compatriot's shoulder, said, 'Come on, Reg, I'll buy you a beer.'

'Hold on.' Reg paused and peered between the barrels.

'What is it?'

'Nothing. You need a gripper?'

'Sure. You?'

'Back here. Let's be quick about it.'

With a grin, a wraith shrouded in death was upon them, materialising out of the shadows. *He would find the woman*, he thought as he hacked viciously at the soldiers until their bodies lay twitching in a puddle of congealing blood. *She would help him*. He cleaned off the knife he had taken from her. *And if the pain grew too great, he would give up and kill her as well*. He pulled the lid from the cask nearest the door and poured several shovelfuls of sawdust over the bodies. One, still fighting for life, coughed, then fell silent.

Sallax was already gone.

THE CANYON

Steven executed a three-point turn that would have had his driving licence revoked, the rear end fishtailing across the road as the tyres shrieked. He pulled out of the skid and pointed the snout of the powder-blue Thunderbird back towards Idaho Springs. Once safely in the northbound lane, he hit the accelerator and grinned as the mighty V-8 engine roared in response. The car almost took flight, leaving the city dump in a cloud of exhaust as he raced recklessly towards town.

The big car careened over the icy road, but Steven held on, even when a great brown ram emerged from the woods on his right, cream-coloured nostrils flaring. The bighorn was heavy-bodied and rippling with muscle, three hundred pounds or more, Steven thought, and moving at nearly thirty miles an hour. It burst from the trees and thoughts of Nerak vanished for a moment as Steven took in the raw beauty of the animal – until it swerved at the last possible moment and pointed its huge curled horns straight at Howard's car.

It took a second or two to filter through, but as soon as he realised the ram was coming for him Steven hit the brakes, nearly sliding into the gully. He managed to get the car's rear wheels to grip, despite the slushy mud on the hard shoulder, but by swerving all he achieved was to provide the beast with a naked broadside.

'Shit,' Steven shouted an instant before impact, but there was no time to do anything – not even fasten his seatbelt; there were none. He braced himself for the impact: at least it wasn't his side facing the furious beast. When it hit, it was terrifying; far worse than he'd expected. The passenger-side door crumpled in and the windows shattered. Steven's head bounced off his side window, cracking the glass, and his head; blood started to mat his hair.

He brushed away shards of glass, hoping he would still be able to drive into Idaho Springs. 'Or anywhere,' he groaned, feeling for the edges of the gash on his head. 'Oh God—'

The force of the ram's attack had shifted the car on the slippery surface and now Steven was facing south towards the dump once again. The engine sputtered into silence. Outside he heard a braying cough, the bighorn sheep, dying. He winced and watched in horror as the once-graceful creature struggled to rise from the ground, one leg dragging uselessly, another twitching. It appeared to have broken one shoulder in the attack, and dark blood flowed from the lower curl of one horn which had been ripped away. It reminded Steven of the grettan that had attacked and nearly killed him in the Blackstone Mountains. Even before the ram turned towards him, Steven knew he would see amber eyes.

'Hello, Steven,' Nerak's voice rang in his head. 'I'm coming for you.' The voice was matter-of-fact, and Steven felt his bowels contract with fear. No magical field emerged to protect him, no supernatural current beneath his skin warded him. The broken ram made a futile, final attempt to crash through Howard's Thunderbird, but this time the possessed bighorn glanced off the side of the car and tumbled to the road in a heap.

Steven fumbled for the ignition, watching the backs of his wrists, waiting for the telltale sign of Nerak's attack. Would the wound just open in a circle, or would it begin as an irritation? He panicked for a second: where was Lessek's key? No, it was safe – at least for the moment … maybe he should throw it out the window and try to lose it in the snow? No, just drive away: north, south, wherever.

He tried the engine, cursing furiously when it sputtered and died, then bellowing his approval when, on the third attempt, the engine caught and sprang to life. He heard the ram die, braying miserably before it fell silent.

'Thank Christ,' Steven said, willing his heart to slow down now. He caught a whiff of foul rotten eggs and rancid beef emanating from his clothes and recoiled, nearly retching into his lap. He grabbed for the door, but it was stuck. *Air*, he thought, *must get some air in here. Then head down the hill. Nerak is in the city, but I've got a few minutes.*

Confident the dark prince wasn't on hand to take his soul, he pushed again at the door before realising he had locked it earlier. 'Can't even get myself out of the damned car,' he chided with a thin smile and flipped the locks up with a bruised thumb. 'Just a couple minutes to get—'

The ram gave a cry and leaped onto the hood of Howard's car. Rearing back on its haunches, the huge beast towered over the windshield, blocking the sun for a moment before crashing its hooves down through the glass and into the front seat.

Only blind, heaven-sent luck saved Steven's life as one of the ram's hooves split the cracked leather between his knees and the other missed the outside edge of his thigh by less than two inches. As the windshield shattered, the ram's head slammed down; it would have crushed Steven's chest, had the great curls not caught on the roof. Only the creature's lifeless face, blood dripping from each nostril, stared down at him. Mucus and saliva dripped from the ram's lips onto Steven's thighs and, weirdly, he thought he detected a faint hint of tobacco.

Repulsed and terrified, Steven squirmed back into the seat, but the ram's forelimbs held him trapped and all he could do was sit there and stare up into the haunted visage. Less than a foot away, its glowing yellow eyes peered back at him in hatred.

'Give me back my key!' the animal roared, its great chest pressing against the pillars of the windshield.

Steven said nothing but, thanking God he'd got the engine going, pulled the car into gear – any gear, he didn't care – and stomped down on the accelerator. He could think of no other way to shake off the three-hundred-pound hood ornament before the dead creature managed to reach him.

The demon ram's lifeless lips opened in a maniacal grin and it snapped at Steven's face, missing his cheek by inches. 'My key, Taylor. I want it now.'

The sound of Nerak's voice booming out was horribly unnerving, especially as there was no breath, only flat teeth, snapping and clicking together like the jaws of a wolverine trap. Steven tried to ignore it as the car bucked, spun its wheels and finally gripped the road with a screech, tearing backwards down the valley towards Idaho Springs.

Nerak, though still some miles away, was using all the power at his disposal to end any opposition right here and reclaim the talismans for ever. Steven braked hard and turned the wheel towards Alps Mountain, barely managing to duck a vicious snap as the force of the turn shoved the ram's snout even further inside the car. The old car spun, and Steven realised he had only the illusion of control on these snowy roads, but still he rammed his foot on the accelerator, turned back towards Devil's Nose and shouted, 'Get off my god-damned car, you prick!'

Steven was deafened by the V-8's engine screaming; the oil light flashed a warning and the speedometer dial showed red. He was dangerously close to sliding headlong into the ponderosa pines that lined the road, but once again he slammed on the brakes. This time he pushed the gear shift into park, letting forward momentum drag the ram's dead body from the hood. There was a loud crumpling thud as the beast hit the road, but without waiting to see if the animal would spring up again, he wrenched the gear shift back into drive and stood on the gas, praying out loud that the Thunderbird wouldn't give up yet.

The powerful engine roared and the car bounced clumsily over the devil ram's carcase.

Several hundred feet beyond the body, Steven checked the rearview mirror. The ram, broken and bloodied, hadn't moved. He swallowed hard, fighting the revulsion he felt at the sight of the beast lying there, mutilated by a monster. He glanced into the back seat, saw the far portal and the stone and breathed a heavy sigh. 'Round one,' he croaked, 'that was round—'

The car bounced hard over something in the road and Steven rammed his head into the roof, bouncing again when the rear wheels cleared the obstacle. In the mirror he saw a ponderosa pine, perhaps eighty feet long, had fallen across the northbound lane of Chicago Creek Road. 'Sonofabitch, that hurt,' he said, slowing down. He felt the gash on his head, bleeding badly now.

'I don't remember that—' Steven's voice trailed away as he watched, further ahead, as another pine pulled up from its roots and fell across the road.

He swerved around the second tree and avoided a third, slowing again another hundred yards along as a boulder, as large as a cement truck, crashed through the forest, bounded across the road and into the pines on the opposite side. As he drove down the twisting curves, rocks and trees came at him from all angles, some blocking his passage, others attempting to crush the car, heading for the outskirts of town and the Interstate 70 ramp.

Steven grinned as he dodged Nerak's attacks: this he had mastered; it was predictable. He twisted and turned the Thunderbird, alternating between accelerator and brakes as he wound his way to freedom. The bighorn had been terrifying, but this wasn't so bad.

'Keep them coming, Nerak,' he shouted. A cold wind blew through the broken windshield to numb his face. 'I've got your number now, you motherhumper.' He was less than a mile from home when, second nature, he checked the rear view mirror.

Terror gripped him and Steven froze, though the car continued at a steady fifty miles an hour. With his eyes fixed in the mirror, he inadvertently drove over the thick brambly limbs of a fallen pine and bashed his head against the roof a second time. He snapped his attention back to the road and braked hard, skidding to a sideways stop. He needed to see for real.

There, in the great draw between Devil's Nose and Alps Mountain: an avalanche of flame was cascading downhill towards Steven Taylor and the resilient old T-Bird. Nerak hadn't wanted to crush him with the pines and the boulders; he had slowed Steven's escape long enough to bring all the fires of Hell roaring through the valley. The two million pines that had melted together to show him the three tears in God's canvas were all in flames.

Steven watched, truly horror-stricken, as thousands of acres of forest were engulfed, then, screaming obscenities at the inferno rolling down on him, put the car in gear – just as a Ponderosa crashed down on the back of the Thunderbird, flattening both rear tyres.

So that was that. Steven reached into the back and grabbed the tapestry and stone, ramming the far portal into Howard's backpack and the key into his pocket, then saluted the fallen Thunderbird and set off at a run down Chicago Creek Road. Behind him, the fire raged on. His only hope was to run as fast and as far as he could.

Coming into the outskirts now, he ran past the high school, recalling the rules his running coach had pounded into them twelve years earlier. *Drop your forearms and bring them up until they are parallel with the ground.* Done. Not fast enough. He could feel the heat tickling at the hairs on the back of his neck. Exploding trees were hurling bits of flaming bark and fiery brambles past him. *Keep your head up and your hips forward.* Done. Still not fast enough. Steven heard the Thunderbird explode with a devastating crash. *Get up on the balls of your feet.* Tough to do in Garec's boots, but he tried.

Then he saw the bridge, a short span over Clear Creek that separated the city in the north from the high school in the south, the same span every high school student in Idaho Springs crossed every morning and every afternoon from September to June. How many times had he crossed that bridge in his lifetime? Ten thousand? Fifty thousand? And yet, at the moment, he couldn't remember what the stream looked like beneath the concrete structure. How far down was it to the water? Far. Maybe twenty-five feet? How deep was the water down there? Not deep enough. *You'll break your legs. Don't do it.*

The first flames passed on either side of the road, taking trees six and seven at a time, moving faster than any forest fire he had ever seen. Clear Creek was his only option. *Don't think about it. Just get there.* He had less than a hundred yards to go, but his back and legs felt as though they were already on fire and he thought he could smell melting synthetic fibres. Was he already burning? No, not yet. The aroma wasn't that strong, like the faint scent of tobacco in the demon ram's saliva.

To his left, a pine tree exploded, and a moment later Steven felt boiling sap and burning needles slam into him, knocking him to the pavement. He fell hard, tearing the skin from both palms, rolled over and bounded to his feet once again. A droplet of boiling sap stuck to the side of his face and he felt it boring into his skin. In pounding agony now, he ripped at the sap droplet with bloody fingertips until he had rubbed it off his face.

'Don't think about it,' he shouted between coarse, shallow breaths. 'When you are running, run.' And he did, covering the last fifty yards and throwing himself bodily over the guardrail at the edge of the narrow bridge. As he leaped, he tried to twist in the air so his feet were down, and in the long fall he prayed he would find a pool free from jagged rocks.

Steven struck the water with a bone-jarring splash as the roiling flames passed overhead.

Gilmour gazed across the Falkan fjord; the glassy surface reflected a canvas of black, white and grey. There was no whisper of wind this far inland and the water looked as though it had frozen over in the half aven since the three companions had pulled their boat beneath the trees. The Northern Twinmoon had broken days ago and now two glowing white orbs illuminated the former Larion Senator.

He stretched the old fisherman's legs towards the campfire, soothing the weary tissues with a thought. If he were like Nerak, he would be enjoying a more youthful body, but Gilmour had only ever taken those in the last few moments of life or the first few moments of death, and although young people died as well, in recent times he had been guided to elderly men. The first had been the logger Gilmour, who stripped and rode naked pine trunks downriver. He'd been called upon to free an especially disagreeable trunk that had become lodged between two submerged rocks. The river had been running low that season, lower than any of them could recall, and none of the woodsmen working the drive had seen the hidden trap before, but the jam it caused stretched upriver for nearly half an aven's ride. Hundreds of thousands of logs were crushed against the stubborn singleton, enough potential energy to level a small town. Gilmour had been quick about his duties, but as he moved lightly across the jam he caught the toe of his boot on a tiny pine knot, scarcely bigger than a thumbnail, and fell just as the mass of trees broke free.

Finding the old man's body tumbling along, Fantus had taken him, then clawed his way out from under the logs and, for the benefit of his new colleagues, cursed like a madman at the entire logging industry. As surprised as they were to see him alive, they never doubted it was their longtime friend: they never had any idea Gilmour had died on the river bottom.

He had enjoyed being Gilmour the logger, and had stayed on, riding trees with all the skill and balance of a court dancer. The forest had been a good place to hide from Nerak and his hunters; Gilmour suspected that was why Lessek had led him to the river that morning.

He had been in the logger's body for nearly eight hundred Twin-moons and Gilmour – Fantus – had nearly forgotten what he had originally looked like before becoming the wiry old man. He shook his head and shrugged at the frozen sea. 'What does it matter, anyway?'

Now he was getting used to the body of the fisherman, Caddoc Weston. He had been inhabiting it for days now, but had not taken to the new name; he preferred Gilmour. It suited him, even more than Fantus, his own Larion label – what sort of name was that? His mother had certainly never given him that name ... for a moment, Gilmour tried to recall his mother. He grimaced with the effort, but a faint swishing sound and a glimpse of a yellow dress was all he could bring back from those days. Two thousand Twinmoons – most of the current Era. He had lived it all, and for his troubles the swishing sound of fabric and a fleeting image of a woman's yellow skirt were all he had left of his mother.

Caddoc Weston had fallen face-first into a slimy haul of jemma fish while drifting in a skiff, several days south of Orindale, though he died from some sort of respiratory ailment – ironic given his workplace. Gilmour assumed the dampness of the Ravenian Sea had finally caught up with the old fellow. When he arrived, led once again by Lessek, Gilmour, like Versen and Brexan before him, had wondered how such a frail man had found the strength to haul jemma nets alone.

Gilmour had tossed most of the fish overboard, hoisted the skiff's tiny sail and caught the breezes north into Orindale. Luck and a bit of nefarious espionage had reunited him with his Ronan partisan friends.

As he tried to make his new body more comfortable, he wondered how long he would be in it – and if it would be his last; after all, he and Nerak were moving at a breakneck pace towards their final confrontation. He tossed a log onto the campfire, watched as flames began slowly to devour it and decided that if this was to be the last body he would inhabit in his lifetime, he would make some improvements. With a gesture, he toughened the muscles in the old man's legs, strengthening the ligaments and tendons. He coated the vertebrae in the scrawny man's back with a fresh calcium shell and he breathed thick, healthy blood into the worn disks between them. He straightened the fisherman's posture, healing a tear in the labrum of his right shoulder and curing the arthritis that swelled his joints and made tying his pack painful. Finally, Gilmour sharpened his sight. Now, when he looked across the fjord, he could make out the nearly invisible rise and fall of the sea as it breathed slowly, asleep beneath the twin moons' nightly vigil.

He adjusted his position against the boat's unyielding transom, wedging his pack between the small of his back and the sandy ground. Their stolen vessel was tucked under a stand of oak and maple, camouflaged in case the partisans needed to reclaim it. He didn't imagine their travels would bring them back this way, but knowing there was one exit route left open gave him some comfort. Gilmour enjoyed the feeling of renewed strength in his muscles and stretched out to catch the fire's warmth on his feet.

Garec and Mark slept. The young foreigner had returned to his position in the bow, despite the fact that the vessel, now beached, was listing precariously to port. Garec had rolled into his blankets and jammed his own pack up against an exposed maple root near the fire. Gilmour had not slept since Nerak had followed Steven through the far portal and into the foreign world, three days past – it didn't trouble the old sorcerer; he didn't need that much sleep, but he would have liked to doze here tonight, where there was a feel of autumn further inland.

He shivered involuntarily. Winter would be upon them soon, even here in the flatlands; he didn't look forward to crossing the Falkan plain with freezing rain and snow at their backs.

He drew thoughtfully on his pipe, dragging the acrid cloud into his lungs; he was waiting for the tobacco to numb his senses and blur his vision. Caddoc Weston had not used tobacco much, but like it or not, he was a smoker now. One little vice wouldn't kill him, after all. Gilmour clucked; the poor fellow was already dead. It was well worth the headache he knew he would have in the morning. 'And no magical cures,' the old sorcerer scolded himself with a cough. 'You'll pay for this one just like any hundred-Twinmooner with his father's pouch.' Puffing again, Gilmour felt the smoke's warm caress tickling the back of his throat and he coughed violently. 'Rutting mothers,' he grunted, 'that was a bad one.'

He reached for a wineskin. They didn't have much left, three or four skins of the Falkan red, that was all. Gilmour promised himself a few sips from this one would be his last for the evening. His throat hurt and his mouth tasted like a sheep-herder's ash pouch; a few swallows were all he would need. Then he would try to sleep.

As he rooted around behind the transom, his hand brushed across the wool blanket wrapped around the book of Lessek's writings. He recoiled with a start, then peered around until he found a full wineskin. Why had he left the book there? He hadn't thought of it, that's why: the library had been in ruins. Scrolls had been torn to pieces, or burned to ash; others had still been in flames when he woke. His vision had been clouded, and the smoke from Pikan's explosion had burned his throat.

The pipe smoke drifting lazily into the sky now tasted like that night, acrid yet sweet, the flavour of burned corpses and plague. Gilmour told himself it was just a mistake, though he had known the book was there, and he had the spell to release it. He could have taken the book – forget the Windscrolls – but he could have taken the book, studied its secrets and crushed Nerak's bones with it. But he had not. He had dropped his broadsword in terror and run screaming and crying until he had struck the frozen ground outside Sandcliff's ballroom window. And then he had kept running.

For the next nine hundred and eighty Twinmoons Gilmour had run away. For a time he had harvested tobacco in Falkan. He had been a teacher, a logger, a chef and now he was a freedom fighter – but none of that would have been necessary had he thought to take the book with him when he fled.

He reached over the stern rail for the woollen cloak: he just wanted a peek at the book the founder of the Larion Senate had used to fashion the spell table and tap into magics of worlds beyond the Fold. It was near the start of the Second Age; Lessek had been a young man when he had hewn the granite disk from the mountains of northern Gorsk and carried it to Sandcliff Palace. And Nerak had used this same book to learn everything he needed to know about how to defeat Gilmour, to open the Fold and to allow his evil master to ascend into Eldarn.

Gilmour sighed: he had to learn this book too; it would take hundreds of Twinmoons … He had two, perhaps three, and it wasn't enough. The old Larion Senator felt a weight pressing against his chest. He drank deep from the wineskin, until he felt he had the strength to stand.

The woollen cloak started to fall away with little coaxing, but as Gilmour gave it a final tug, a corner of the material caught and toppled the book end-over-end onto the deck. 'Demonpiss!' Gilmour muttered angrily, 'Just when I get up the lordsforsaken nerve—' He bit off the end of his rant and checked furtively to be certain Garec and Mark were still sleeping. The leather covers of the spell book were opened wide, the heavy pages splayed. He had no choice now; he had to pick it up.

Gilmour reached into the boat, grasped the spell book gently by the front cover and returned it to its place on the bench – and nothing happened, there was no magical reaction at all. Tentatively he flipped open the front cover, to read what Lessek had written on the opening folio, but though he strained, he could make nothing out, even after he snapped his fingers to provide a little light. The page was blank.

'Lessek, you are going kill me,' the old man muttered and reached out to turn the page. He brought his sorcerous light in closer. 'The ash dream,' he read aloud. That was it. He took a moment to admire Lessek's fine script. The characters were delicately scratched with a sharp quill; smooth and even. Gilmour sighed again; he realised at once that not one page would stand out; there would be no single spell with which to rule worlds beyond the Fold. Each page would be part of a whole, but useless by itself. There would be no scribbles in the margins leading to sudden magical discoveries. This book was one man's masterwork, and only when read cover to cover, and understood as a whole, would it show how to unleash the force used to create the spell table thousands of Twinmoons ago.

So that's what he had to do, read Lessek's book, beginning right here at the birthplace of Falkan's greatest fjord, a fractured bit of Eldarn itself. *Nerak's weakness lies elsewhere*, he thought, *it lies in the Windscrolls*. That night Gilmour had gone to retrieve the third

Windscroll for Pikan; in his haste, he had overlooked Lessek's desk – and this book.

Gilmour remembered his dream as he slept on top of Seer's Peak: Nerak and Pikan, with Kantu lagging behind with an injured ankle … they had discovered something, discussed something; he didn't know what. Had they tried something creative with the Larion magic? It didn't matter; what mattered tonight was that Nerak had a weakness. He might have had a thousand weaknesses nine hundred Twinmoons ago, but tonight, he had at least one and Gilmour knew where to find it.

He would study the book until he understood Lessek's magic, and he would protect himself and his friends from Nerak until he had the third Windscroll in his possession. He was one of the last Larion Senators – only Kantu remained, somewhere in Praga – and protecting Eldarn was their responsibility. *Nerak's weakness lies elsewhere*: yes, but his *strength* lies here in this book.

Gilmour thought again of Seer's Peak. Garec and Steven had dreamed too. Garec had seen wraiths moving through Rona's forbidden forest, mobilising for an attack, and had been able to use Steven's magic to ward off the spirit army. That had turned out to be a true foreseeing: Lessek had shown them real images of their journey, things they would need to address if they were to survive. What had Lessek meant them to learn from the dead, arid land that had once been lush Ronan forests? He wondered if saving Rona was going to fall to Garec – if Rona was even particularly at risk. 'It was King Remond's home,' Gilmour murmured, 'Markon Grayslip's home too – he called himself a prince to avoid upsetting his family, but Markon was Eldarn's rightful king.'

And what of Steven Taylor? He had dreamed of a maths problem, of calculus machines and telephone speaking devices – and had he not, he would never have been able to crack the code and open Prince Malagon's lock-box, his Malakasian safe-deposit box.

So Gilmour's mission was clear: find the third Windscroll and use it to banish Nerak for ever. It was probably buried under a thousand Twinmoons of debris, but it would be there – and if Nerak had read and understood it, his weakness would no longer exist. 'Stop procrastinating,' Gilmour said out loud. 'Read the rutting book and you will be as strong as Nerak. Stop running and face him.'

The old man took a last swallow from the wineskin, corked it and dropped it to the sand. 'The ash dream,' he whispered. 'Let's see what's on the next page.'

Gilmour took the blow on his chest. Sharp and bright, striking brutally hard, like lightning through a rip in the Fold, it pushed him backwards and he felt ribs snap. He struck his head on the ground, and just before he passed out he saw Lessek's spell book slam shut, seemingly of its own will.

THE REDSTONE TAVERN

Brexan was drunk again, enjoying her second evening beside the fire at the Redstone Tavern. Tonight's gansel leg – they roasted them perfectly here – the potatoes, bread and glorious cheese (she had eaten another half-block today), combined with the wine to warm her from within, while the fire blazing away ensured there was no trace left of the Ravenian Sea.

The Redstone Tavern was the sort of place Brexan enjoyed; with friends from home, she would be drinking, carousing, making jokes about sundry sailors, stevedores, maybe even a few of the Malakasian officers. But now she ignored the other patrons, a cross-section of Orindale society as, blanketed in sweet tobacco smoke, they yammered loudly to be heard above the din. Periodically they abandoned their conversations to bellow the refrain of some popular song or roar their appreciation of a well-told joke.

Crossing her legs beneath the heavy woollen folds of her new skirt, Brexan sipped at the last of her wine and considered ordering another half-bottle. She had spent her first free day since conscripting herself into the Malakasian Army strolling idly through the city, wandering into shops near the old imperial palace. One wing of the building had been demolished in an unexplained explosion several nights earlier, but the crumbling walls and shattered stained-glass windows didn't mitigate the beauty of the surrounding boulevards.

She had found her skirt before the end of the midday aven, in a shop several streets away from the waterfront, though it hadn't been her first choice. A delicate flowing skirt with an embroidered floral pattern and a hem of lace had caught her eye, and, tempted for a moment, she had held the skirt up against her body, against the sailor's ill-fitting clothes. It was the most feminine article of clothing she had ever seen, let alone worn, and in the middle of a pirouette she had thought of Versen – not that she had forgotten him for a moment, for he was always there, if not in the forefront of her mind. Sometimes he would interrupt her thoughts, cause her to stare distractedly for a moment or two, maybe even make her stumble. Brexan couldn't decide whether she wanted to live the rest of her life with such a boldly intrusive apparition haunting her, but whenever she thought it might be less unsettling if he were simply to fade away, she found herself reaching out as if to retrieve him, bring him closer.

Versen had been with her that morning, but not until she had twirled the pretentious skirt about the shop had he made his presence felt.

It's lovely.

'It's not me, though,' she had answered in a whisper, fearing the shopkeeper might overhear the one-sided conversation and toss her into the street.

No matter ... things are different now. You should buy it. Versen's voice had been comforting as she fingered the luxurious fabric.

'You think so?'

I would love to see you in it – the murmur not of a voyeur, but a lover.

'But you can't, can you?'

I can't. No.

Brexan stood still, hoping that if she remained motionless she would be able to hold him a moment longer. She didn't have to get back to work yet. This day, the whole day, was for her. It was the midday aven now and she didn't have to be back on Sallax's trail until tomorrow. She didn't have to track down and kill the fat merchant until tomorrow. Today was supposed to have been a gift, a moment's grace, and the fact that Versen had come was all the more reason to make it last as long as possible.

Pressure built up behind Brexan's eyes and her head started throbbing. She pinched the bridge of her nose and felt a tear on her wrist. The skirt dangled limply from her hand.

Now, as she leaned into the fire's warmth, Brexan flinched when she recalled what had happened next.

Standing in the shop, a handful of fabric clutched close to her face, she had suddenly become revolted: the print was unnecessary, the lace hem too feminine – it was all too vulnerable. Her knees threatened to buckle and she had dropped the garment as if it had been on fire.

'Hey, pick that up,' the shopkeeper shouted, already on his way across the front room.

Ignoring him, she had reached for a utilitarian garment hanging on a rail: the woollen skirt she wore now.

'Get out of here. I don't have time for your nonsense. These pieces are expensive—' His voice faded as he caught sight of the sailor's silver piece Brexan was displaying. She gave the coin a flip, a gesture that might have said, *go scratch yourself, horsecock*.

In a breath, the shopkeeper's demeanour had changed, switching to grovelling obsequiousness as if a second personality had unexpectedly elbowed its way into his head. 'Sorry, ma'am. It's just that sometimes ... well, you know ... with the Occupation—'

Brexan cut him off. 'I'll take this one.' Rubbing the thick fabric across her cheek, she fought to clear the image of Versen from her mind.

'But that's just a skirt. Wouldn't you rather—?'

She cut him off again. 'This one – and some leggings, something tough, woollen, I think.'

The shopkeeper gave up. 'Fine, wool.' The floral print hung over his arm and he waved her towards a shelf.

'And I need some shoes.'

'Shoes?'

'No.' She changed her mind. Her one day of freedom ended there. 'Boots. I need boots.'

She paid for her purchases and changed into them before leaving the shop, making the merchant a gift of the sailor's stolen garments. At the Redstone Tavern, Brexan slept until the aroma of grilling meat and simmering stew woke her for dinner beside the fire.

Now she tossed her head, shifting her too-long hair away from her face. The strange pain had returned, pressing against her sinuses; she felt like a tempine fruit squeezed too hard. She allowed her vision to blur as she looked into the fire, trying to relax.

The clatter of tankards roused her and she held a hand aloft to get the attention of the serving boy; he finally looked over, his eyebrows arching in a nonverbal enquiry, *What would you like?*

She picked up the empty bottle and he nodded in understanding. *I'll be right there.*

Brexan half-smiled. *I'll be waiting.*

She had lost enjoyment of her day to memories of Versen, the wrong memories, but she had to take the bad with the good; she couldn't just have the disarming look of his green eyes, the feel of his legs against hers when they were imprisoned in the darkness of the schooner's hold, or the way he had dropped his weapons to take her hand when the Seron were upon them: she had to remember his shattered image as vividly as she recalled the brightness of his smile.

In the vertiginous recesses of her mind, the cordoned-off section that remained sensible regardless of how much she managed to drink, Brexan promised not to drown her sorrows every time the anguish grew too grim to face head-on; in return, she silently agreed to get back to the business of hunting and killing at first light the following day.

With her decision, knowing she was not going to spiral into an alcoholic coma every time she felt sad, the weight seemed to ease. She would pick herself up at first light and get back on track – but this evening she would let herself fall apart. The second bottle of wine seemed as good a place as any to get started.

Morning arrived with all the delicacy of a battering ram assault on a stone keep. Brexan made an effort to get up, felt her vision tunnel and fell back into the expensive feather mattress, one of the Redstone's more luxurious features. When she realised the incessant pounding was going on inside her head, not outside, she rolled to the edge of the bed, hung the offending appendage over the side and waited – when nothing happened, she drew herself into a foetal ball and tried to go back to sleep – but the throbbing pain was too much.

Brexan, realising she would need to extricate herself from the bed, make her way across the room and drink the contents of her water pitcher dry if she hoped to quiet the band hammering away inside her skull, threw back the coverlet – and discovered that she was naked. The events of the previous evening came back to her in a flood of embarrassment: awkward invitations and clumsy drunken sex with the young man from the kitchen. 'Oh, you whoring rutter,' she groaned and looked back at the bed, begging him to be gone. Thankfully, all that remained was a lingering aroma of beef and gansel stew. She wrestled her aching body into a sitting position and dropped her head down to her knees until she felt she could breathe without vomiting.

She dragged herself across the room to the armoire and grimaced as she caught a glimpse of herself in the glass: skin the colour of city snow, and her mouth hanging open. Her breasts seemed to sag more than they had the last time she had seen them so thoroughly exposed. Brexan stood up straight, despite the cramp in her lower back, but it didn't help as much as she'd hoped. Her eyes looked like she'd been punched.

'You did this to yourself, young lady,' she said in a hoarse whisper, regretting her decision to engage in improvisational alcohol therapy.

Stepping closer to the glass, Brexan examined herself. Although still sore and discoloured from the deep tissue bruising, her ribs appeared to be healing slowly. Her cheek worried her more; the Seron, Lahp, had cracked it with a vicious punch and then the scarred Seron, the horsecock with the ruined face, had re-broken it, knocking her unconscious and leaving Versen to battle him alone. Brexan hadn't been anywhere near a mirror in the past Twinmoon, so this was the first time she had seen how crookedly it had knitted together.

'Damaged goods. No matter.' She shrugged at the worn figure in the mirror. 'You were never much to look at, anyway.' She rubbed her throbbing temples and considered her options. She had new clothes, a pocketful of money and a warm, safe place to sleep; that was a good start. Despite the hangover, she shot herself a grin. 'Next time try to stay sober enough to have more than just a fuzzy recollection, my little slut. What's the point of having an encounter if all you remember is falling over while trying to get out of your leggings?'

The morning was bright, filled with the telltale aromas of low tide: the tang of seagull guano, tidal rot and decomposing fish innards. Brexan left the Redstone for some fresh air and shortly afterwards found herself spilling the contents of her stomach into a muddy alley running from the street down to the river. It wasn't the foetid smells of the wharf blowing in on the morning breeze, but the fierce early-aven sunlight that pushed her over the edge.

Once she'd finished heaving, she went to find water, stepping across the threshold of a nearby cheese shop. Almost immediately, she regretted her course of action. 'Demonpiss,' she muttered as the pungent smell hit her, and backed out as quickly as she could. Mould cheeses of varying shapes and sizes dominated the wooden shelves and as she started dry-heaving, she wondered who in all Eldarn would pay money to eat spoiled cream with plants growing out of it. She cursed, spat out a mouthful of discoloured saliva and grumbled, 'Everything in this town makes me puke. I've got to do something about this. The other day it was Sallax and this morning, it's the slobbering cheese.'

She stumbled back towards the waterfront, searching for a tavern, a produce stand, any place where she might get something to quiet her raging stomach. She felt the ground shifting beneath her feet as sweat dampened her forehead, armpits and back. Several streets later she came to a boarding house with a large tavern downstairs. She pushed her way through the door and squinted while her eyes grew accustomed to the semi-darkness.

As she bumped and shuffled towards the bar, a gruff voice asked, 'You all right?' With her eyes still not focused, Brexan wasn't sure if the bald man had an open sore on his forehead or if he had been injured in a fight.

'Fine. It's just a bit bright out this morning.' Brexan tried not to sound like a woman on the verge of collapse. 'I'd like some water, please.' No sooner were the words out of her mouth than she regretted making the request.

'Water?' the bartender squinted at her.

'And a beer,' Brexan added quickly, 'in a tankard, please.' She dropped several copper coins on the bar, unconvinced she would be able to smell the beer without retching right there onto the man's boots. Pretty sure her stomach wouldn't be able to handle even the smallest sip of the local brew, she leaned against the bar, her back to the tankard, while waiting for the barman to bring her water. Brexan rubbed her eyes, but when she tried to focus on the tavern's sprawling front room, she saw stars, tiny sunbursts of yellow, red and white.

Then she saw him.

He was sitting alone near the window; he hadn't seen her come in, or if he had, he hadn't recognised her. He certainly hadn't marked her as the soldier he'd spoken with in Estrad Village, more than a Twinmoon ago. Lafrent, Jacrys— whatever his name was, he was a Malakasian spy and Lieutenant Bronfio's murderer – and there he sat, enjoying a mug of tecan and a loaf of what smelled like fresh-baked bread. The well-dressed man appeared to be watching the street.

Brexan blessed her good luck – *one stroke this morning, anyway* – that the killer had not been facing in the other direction.

'Your water,' the barman said sarcastically, placing the goblet next to the untouched tankard of beer.

Brexan turned back to the bar and emptied the goblet, then lifted the tankard, grimacing at the thought of more alcohol – but it was the excuse she needed. She turned back to the window, leaned against the bar and watched Jacrys.

Jacrys Marseth tore off a chunk of bread, dripped it into his tecan and savoured the flavours: a reminder of home. He didn't actually miss home, but by having the same breakfast every day, he was able to bring some predictability to his life in the Eastlands. No matter where he woke, whether it was in a feather-lined bed or behind a stack of crates, breakfast was Jacrys' daily offering to himself. Bread and tecan was spy food, quick, sustaining and readily available.

As he watched the street outside, Jacrys thought of his home. He had not been back to Malakasia in thirty Twinmoons or more; he didn't even know if his father was still alive. His mother had died long ago – Jacrys remembered his father's clumsy attempts at baking bread and the discarded loaves – some overdone, some undercooked, some not risen, emerging as hard as logs. Growing up without a mother had been difficult, made worse by his father's frequent absences – a tradesman in search of a trade, the old man had travelled from town to town throughout northern Malakasia, sometimes going as far as Port Denis to take work on the docks. There had never been much money in the house and Jacrys was often left alone to fend for himself. He had learned to fight among Pellia's street people, how to use a knife without flinching, and he even picked up a few spells from a conjuror living below a brothel. The magician had been young, but sickly; it was much later that Jacrys realised the sorcerer-turned-carnival trickster had been so ruined on Falkan fennaroot that he was surprised any of the spells worked at all.

Jacrys had found the magician's decomposing corpse one summer's day, and in return for disposing of the stinking body off the Pellia wharf, the madame who operated the whorehouse upstairs had given him the dead man's apartment. Jacrys ran errands for the women, sometimes fetching a particular vial of perfume, sometimes slinking through dark alleys to slip a dirk between a stranger's ribs. The madame, while open-minded about sexual engagements, did not tolerate violence or abuse to her girls. Jacrys, although younger than most of the men frequenting the brothel overhead, had grown skilled in hand-to-hand combat, and was even more deft at moving through Pellia undetected; he was the perfect errand boy for the whorehouse. From time to time one or more of the girls came to thank him personally for his services.

At the age of one hundred and thirty Twinmoons, Jacrys had been badly wounded, stabbed twice and slashed across the abdomen by an angry customer who was just as skilled with a short blade. Jacrys was nursed back to health by the whores, then packed quietly one evening and slipped away. He had realised that although talented, he would not last long here; no matter how deliciously the girls rewarded him, it was time to go.

He had enlisted in the Malakasian Army, being promoted to sergeant after only eleven Twinmoons in the Prince's service and making master sergeant before turning one hundred and fifty. One night, while patrolling the border between Averil and Landry, Jacrys' platoon had been attacked by a crowd mostly of Pragan students. The angry, inebriated mob had decided that together they could march, unarmed, through Averil and north all the way to Welstar Palace. Strengthened by too much Pragan wine and fennaroot, the mob had taken a border station, killed several guards and begun moving through a residential area of southern Averil, lighting fires and attacking Malakasian citizens as they went.

Jacrys' platoon, one of three, had been ordered to show no mercy, and to send a powerful message by bringing back prisoners for a public display of Prince Malagon's disapproval. His lieutenant had ordered Jacrys to move his squad into position alongside the mob's exposed flank, using the narrow alleys as cover. Anticipating a quick – and bloody – victory, his soldiers had hurried into the fray, in their eagerness breaking formation. Screaming orders, Jacrys had tried to keep his squad together, but the scent of blood and the promise of carnage was too much. Though unorganised, drunk and disorderly, there were now hundreds of Pragans: they had taken heavy losses, with scores of them dead or dying, hacked down, knifed, some even set alight with torches – but they had not retreated.

A gang of the rebels had rushed Jacrys' position, killing or maiming several of his men and effectively cutting them off. The lieutenant ordered a charge through the enraged revellers to rejoin the remainder of their platoon, and with a shout, the handful of Malakasian soldiers had brandished their weapons and charged.

Less than a third of the way through the crowd, Jacrys had realised that he and his lieutenant were alone, the soldiers with them were missing, killed or injured. Knowing he was about to die, the young master sergeant had grown furious at the notion of dying under the boots of a band of drunken students, and the weight of his anger lent weight to his arms: Jacrys, swearing like the proverbial trooper, cut a swathe through the crowd, pulling his lieutenant with him – until the man had stumbled, felled by a sword stroke below the knee, and crashed to the ground. Jacrys hadn't hesitated: he rushed to the lieutenant's side, threw himself over the man and summoned one of the spells he had learned from the fennaroot addict in the whorehouse basement, praying this one would work.

Jacrys knew their lives had been saved when the mob's collective attention shifted away from the two forms huddled quietly in the dirt. Jacrys once again thanked the dead sorcerer for teaching him the simplest of magic, for it had taken only a moment to utter the curious, ancient words, then the mob eddied and swelled around the two men. His little suggestive spell had them convinced that he and the lieutenant were already dead.

Much later, Prince Malagon's magicians had helped Jacrys refine this spell; he used it to keep from being detected even by the great Gilmour, the Larion Senator, who had periodically searched for him, casting his gaze back over the partisans' trail with irritating unpredictability.

Returning to save his lieutenant's life – only Jacrys knew it had been an act of rage rather than compassion – earned him the respect of the officers and the ambitious master sergeant took advantage of his elevated status in Prince Malagon's army, however temporary, to secure himself a transfer to the Eastlands and a chance to train with a covert corps of Malagon's personal spies and information specialists. One hundred and sixty Twinmoons later, Jacrys was a master of intelligence and espionage.

The prince himself called upon Jacrys for some of his most nefarious plans, and the spy had never disappointed – not until now. He dipped the last of the bread and pushed aside the empty mug. There was work to be done today – although he was not looking forward to another five avens roaming through Orindale searching for Steven Taylor, the foreigner with the stone key Malagon wanted so badly. With Gilmour dead and the bowman, Garec, badly injured, Jacrys thought it would be relatively easy to retrieve the key from Steven – if only he could track the partisans down. He was fairly certain he had not killed Garec, so they must have gone underground.

It had been days since he had seen any sign of them and he was beginning to grow frustrated with his lack of progress, particularly as this group was about broken: their leader was dead; Sallax, the traitor with an axe to grind, was either missing, found out, or killed, and Garec had at least a few cracked ribs, maybe even a punctured lung.

He muttered a curse, recalling the night he had been forced to choose between Garec and Steven. Jacrys had been huddled in the shadows behind the warehouse for over an aven waiting for the two so-called freedom fighters to return. Then when they came, their cloaks had been pulled closed and their hoods lifted to cover their heads. There had been rats, lots of the ugly little demons, scratching about at his feet – ironically, it had been the rodents that had given him the answer: the boots. Steven Taylor's boots looked like nothing Jacrys had ever seen; it was easy to spot them, heavy with leather and silly crisscrossing bits of twine holding them together.

But the horsecock archer had been wearing them.

For days Jacrys had wondered why the two men had exchanged boots – were they a disguise? Or were the two men softies, sneaking away to exchange who knew what else? Yet again he felt anger welling at his wretched luck. If only he had chosen right, he could have killed the staff-wielding foreigner, then retrieving the stone would have been so much easier.

Now they were *all* missing and he had to brace himself for another futile day of asking questions and paying off Orindale whores, barmen and criminals for any information leading to the Ronans' hiding place. He didn't know how they had managed to make their way into the city, given the array of forces blockading Orindale from Falkan and Rona, but Jacrys was certain they had managed to spirit themselves past the Malakasian picket lines and that they were still in the city. With Garec injured, they would not have risked a retreat through enemy lines; it would have been too dangerous. They had to be inside city limits, and Jacrys would continue searching until he found them.

The one piece of good news was that the dark prince hadn't appeared, even after the explosion at the old imperial palace and the unexpected sinking of the *Prince Marek* in Orindale Harbour. His carriage hadn't been moved and there was no talk of anyone coming or going from the Falkan ancestral residence. The army remained entrenched and no one moved in or out of the city without attracting Malakasian scrutiny. Without Prince Malagon seeking him, Jacrys was free to move through Orindale as he pleased.

These things, considered together, gave Jacrys hope. 'It's just a matter of time,' he said quietly. 'I *will* get that key and the dark prince will owe me – well, whatever I wish.' He chuckled, stood up and tossed a coin on the table, then stepped out into the brilliant morning sunlight.

He didn't notice the young woman, white as a corpse, pay her own tab at the bar and unobtrusively follow him out.

DENVER

Freezing cold and sodden through, Steven broke into Howard Griffin's house for the second time that day. He took a change of clothes and grimaced at how the older man's jeans hung about his narrow hips for a moment before falling off like a collapsing circus tent. 'This won't do,' he said, looking to find a pair that came within four inches of his waist size.

In the end, he decided it was quicker and easier to dry his own clothes and, stripping to his boxers, tumbled everything he had bought or stolen in the past three days, including Garec's borrowed boots, into Howard's clothes dryer and set the timer. Returning to the kitchen, he made two roast beef sandwiches, careful – despite his harrowing morning – to smell both the meat and the mayonnaise. With his mouth full, Steven gingerly slid aside the curtains of Howard's kitchen window and waited for Nerak to show himself again.

Outside, Idaho Springs had come to a sudden, unexpected halt. Except for the intermittent wail of fire alarms, ambulances and police sirens, the town was silent. From Howard's kitchen Steven could see Miner Street, and in the first fifteen minutes, he saw three police cruisers, two fire trucks, their lights ablaze, and the red pick-up their town fire marshal used when making inspections or running back and forth between Idaho Springs and the surrounding observation towers. All of the emergency vehicles had been going dangerously fast, as if the fire might somehow burn itself out if help didn't arrive as quickly as possible. From somewhere east of Howard's home, a hollow voice with too much reverb warbled out half-comprehensible instructions through twenty-five-year-old speakers mounted on lamp-posts and rooftops throughout the city.

That was it; no civilian vehicles passed. He spotted no SUVs loaded with school children, no tourist cars ornamented with three thousand dollars-worth of ski equipment, no big yellow buses hauling the middle school basketball team to Georgetown or Golden. He wasn't really surprised; he knew what everyone in town would be doing. The fire fighters would either be battling the flames near the high school and the few homes and businesses on the south side of the creek, or they would be hustling to make their way across town to assist those who had been at the firehouse, gearing up for another Friday night of poker and college basketball.

Like voyeurs at a fatal traffic accident, the citizens of Idaho Springs were outside, lining the streets and sidewalks to watch, in stunned silence, as the hillside blaze made its way inexorably towards them. As he stared out of Howard's kitchen window, Garec's boots clumping and banging inside the clothes dryer, Steven felt a cold sense of dread begin to creep across his naked flesh. Blaming his time in the creek and the burgeoning lump on his head, he took a blanket from the back of the couch, wrapped it around his shoulders and returned to the window to watch as the fire, now several miles across and at least three miles deep, cast a false sunset over Idaho Springs. Deep orange smeared through the sky in broad strokes, seeping into warm violet, as forbidding as it was beautiful. If it had not been for the clouds of black and grey smoke roiling east towards Floyd Hill, Steven might have believed that the sun was setting in the south, somewhere behind the Mt Evans wilderness.

Outside, people were standing shoulder-to-shoulder, lining the streets. Some had taken to the rooftops to improve their view; others climbed up into truck beds or onto park benches for a better view of the devastation. They talked in whispers, because speaking in a normal tone was somehow inappropriate in the wake of such a disaster. They were standing silently, reverently watching as the fire claimed the hillside along Chicago Creek Road. It wasn't the right season for this; the hills were wet with snow and there had not been a significant fire in January for as long as anyone could remember – yet a blaze of epic proportions threatened the canyon, threatened the entire city ...

Twelve minutes after pushing the start button on Howard's old dryer, the spell was broken. It started as a scream, a lone voice piercing the morning with what sounded like *Sandy!* or *Mandy!* – then slowly, like a rollercoaster starting down its initial hill, the people of Idaho Springs began to move, as if time had caught up with them, starting now to hurry, in an effort to retrieve the minutes they had lost. It was Friday and school was in session; there were nearly five hundred students at the high school across the river and the citizens of Idaho Springs, slapped awake from their twelve-minute reverie by the sound of someone screaming for Sandy or Mandy, began mobilising to get the children to safety.

Mayhem ensued and Steven decided that, dry or not, he would take advantage of the clamour to get into the bank. He dressed quickly, jammed half a sandwich into his mouth and the leftovers into his pocket next to Lessek's key. He didn't worry about the students; the path of the burning avalanche had followed him when he turned east to get across the Clear Creek bridge and although three exit routes would be blocked by the conflagration and cars were most likely exploding in the faculty lot, Steven's lazy right turn would have left open a path from the school down to the river. Any student who had ever sneaked out of lunch to smoke would be able, like the Pied Smoker of Hamelin, to lead the others to safety through the streambed and north into town.

When he reached the bank, Steven scanned both sides of the street, hoping to spot Howard and Myrna; he looked up to find his old boss standing on the roof of Owen's Pub. 'Figures,' Steven said with a smile. 'Probably enjoying a beer with the show.' He shook his head wryly and peeked through the lobby window for some sign of Myrna Kessler. She wasn't in her usual perch behind the teller window and Steven waited a couple of minutes to ensure she wasn't going to emerge from one of the rear offices.

It wasn't like Howard to leave the bank unattended, even on those periodic occasions when everyone would file into the street to chart the progress of a smaller fire somewhere in the hills above town. But this was different; it was January and the fire burning along the canyon wall was an anomaly, a potentially deadly anomaly. Perhaps Howard had asked Myrna to work the window and answer the phones. Instead she'd stepped out to watch from the front step.

Steven leaned back and peered through the front windows to see if she was standing outside, but instead of Myrna, he saw, crisscrossing the bank's front door, a crooked row of crosses made of yellow police tape.

Alarm bells ringing, Steven turned the corner, ducked beneath the bottom cross and pushed open the front door. He spotted an Idaho Springs police detective standing on the hood of a rusty old Chevrolet Caprice Classic, the town's answer to an unmarked vehicle, parked across the street – Steven had met the young cop once at the pub and remembered him as a witty guy with a penchant for pistachio nuts and Irish jokes. Like the rest of the city, the officer had fallen prey to the overwhelming urge to watch as the fire, no longer falling down the hillside with unnatural speed, but inching its way ever closer with grim certainty.

The lump had been invisible from the street, but inside it was obviously a large body, probably a man, draped with a white sheet – awaiting the arrival of the Clear Creek County coroner, Steven guessed. He stepped over the corpse, reached through Myrna's window for her bag and as soon as his fingers closed around her car keys he quickly moved towards the side exit, away from the detective who was still gazing towards Chicago Creek Road.

His hand on the doorknob, Steven hesitated, looked back into the lobby and sighed. He had to know.

He peeked out the glass door: the detective was swapping between hand-held radio and cell phone, apparently unconcerned that he had left a dead body lying on the floor of the town bank while he watched a forest fire consume a high school car park. Steven considered snaking his way across the lobby on his belly, then shrugged. No one was interested in the bank right now. He walked across the floor and crouched beside the corpse. He didn't recognise the man beneath the sheet – death changed facial features – he did recognise the uniform. This man, *D. Mantegna*, from his breast plate, must have been one of the officers working at Charleston Airport three days earlier. Steven turned away from D. Mantegna's sallow, sunken visage and looked down at the man's left wrist. There, a black circle that looked like a third-degree burn, was Nerak's calling card, the same entry wound the young mother must have been hiding when she boarded the plane with the baby held in the crook of her arm like a football.

The Idaho Springs Police were not waiting for the county coroner. With a dead body in a Charleston International Airport security uniform turning up in a bank eighteen hundred miles from the scene of an apparent terrorist attack, the detective outside would be waiting for the FBI.

Steven stood up and hurried out the side entrance towards Myrna Kessler's car.

Twilight fell as the four riders carefully navigated the dirt road between vast fields of potatoes, greenroot, onions, carrots and pepper weed. Hannah tried to make out individual smells, but the onion and pepper weed were too flamboyantly aromatic to separate.

She slouched in the saddle, resting her back, and waited for Alen to halt them for the dinner aven.

Pacing them were a brigade of horse and mule-drawn flatbed and slat-sided farm carts, dozens of them, stretching from either side of the road. Teams of harvesters, farmhands and children alike, trudged slowly behind the carts, tossing in vegetables in slow rhythm. The scene looked to Hannah like a sweeping Hollywood epic where, as the sun fades to red, the camera pulls back from one toiling child to capture the masses, stretched out to the horizon ...

When the wind died for a moment, she could hear their cries: *Potato ... ho! Carrot and pea ... hee! Onion or greenroot ... come harvest with me!* At first, she thought the cries were filled with sorrow, suffering, as if these people had been enslaved by some heavy-handed plantation owner with a team of whip-wielding overseers, but after several stanzas, Hannah realised the calls and responses were changing, the words moving through a variety of activities: leisure time, cool beer, sex, the coming winter. After a particularly flirtatious verse about women and men, Hannah heard laughter, scattered giggling at the crudity of the text. It was improvisation; they were making it up, keeping the rhythm steady to match the slow gait of their horses. Leaning in the saddle, she tried to make out another verse, but the breeze returned and drowned them in a swirl of onion and pepper weed. Stillness fell over the fields once again; the riders had moved on ahead. Hannah turned to watch the harvesters until they faded from view.

Churn had been doing relatively well most of the day. His first moments in the saddle had been difficult; Hoyt was nursing a painfully bruised shoulder and a ringing ear, the price for keeping the bigger man aloft long enough for him to experiment with Hannah's sapling strategy. At first, Churn had gripped his friend hard, as if clinging onto life itself, until Hoyt had shrieked for mercy.

Finally Alen and Hannah calmed Churn enough to try the cane idea, and Churn had released Hoyt only when he had the stick in one muscular paw and the pommel grasped with the other. Wide-eyed with terror, the mute had only released the saddle-horn long enough to berate his companions with economic but vituperative insults.

'Would you look at that?' Hoyt teased. 'Which one is the horse?'

With inhuman quickness, Churn cupped his hand for maximum pain and boxed one side of the smaller man's head, landing a direct hit over Hoyt's ear and sending his friend reeling to the ground.

Hoyt rolled over in the dirt and shouted, 'I told you not too hard, you slack-jawed oaf!'

It took a good three avens, but eventually Churn started to relax in the saddle. He was not yet a horseman, but he had not yet fallen either. He jabbed at the ground with Hannah's cane, and clung hard to both pommel and bridle. They didn't make particularly good time, but if it took Churn several days to feel comfortable in the saddle, then that's what it took. Riding was still quicker than walking.

By the dinner aven, Churn had mastered a three-step survival technique. Feeling the rhythm of his horse's gait, he would use his powerful legs to lift himself in the saddle, step one. Next, he would await the appropriate moment and release his not inconsiderable bulk back into the saddle, step two. Finally, in the beat between sitting and rising again, he would lift and plant his sapling cane, preserving a tenuous connection with the dusty Pragan road, step three.

It wasn't pretty, but it worked. With darkness closing in about them, Alen quickened the pace slightly in hopes of reaching the edge of the current vegetable farm and finding a grove of trees or perhaps a forest where they could camp. He didn't relish the notion of sleeping in one of the fields – though he hadn't detected Malagon's magicians in three days, the idea of being so vulnerable, especially at night, was too unsettling.

In time, he guessed, he would overcome his fear of sleeping outside, but like Churn, it would not be tonight. He spotted an indistinct blur on the horizon and said, 'Is that a grove of trees or just a stand of bushes over there?'

'Trees,' Hoyt said. 'It looks like a good place to spend the night – and there's plenty of food scattered about as well.'

'Good,' Alen said. 'Churn! We're about done for the day. Congratulations, my old friend. You survived.'

Churn, busy gripping his pommel and sapling, didn't answer.

After a dinner of fresh vegetable and venison stew, Churn and Hannah moved through the grove collecting enough wood to keep their fire kindled for the night. Hoyt used a whetstone to polish the thin surgical knife he carried and Alen sipped from a wineskin while scraping stew from dirty trenchers.

'I hate to be the one to bring up another sore issue,' Hoyt began.

'But you will,' Alen could sense a thorough chastising on the horizon.

'Someone has to,' Hoyt said, 'and I've known you longest.'

'And I need to cut back on the wine, right?' There was no irritation in Alen's voice.

'Think about where we're going. How much confidence would *you* have if the person to whom you looked for guidance and leadership was ass-over-hill each night?'

'You're right,' Alen said.

Hoyt went on, 'And where we're going – Churn and I might be the only two people in Eldarn willing to tag along on this journey. I mean, Hannah *has* to go, and you have your— your *problems* to work out, but if you're getting kicked in the head every night, it won't bode well for—'

'I said, you're right,' Alen said, a hint of irritation appearing now. 'I will cut back – some.'

'Oh.' Hoyt was genuinely surprised; he had been expecting a harder fight. 'Oh, well, uh, good. I'm glad to hear that … and I don't know that you have to quit entirely.'

'I should,' Alen said. 'It's the only way to be certain it won't raise its cadaverous head looking for me, especially when things get difficult later on.'

Hoyt had what he wanted: Alen's commitment. Now it was up to the former Larion Senator. 'Well, you can address those details as they – sorry – arise. But either way, I'm glad to hear that and I know Hannah will appreciate seeing less of that kind of behaviour as well.'

'I'm sure she will.' In a display of good faith, Alen handed the wineskin over.

Hoyt wasn't sure what to do with it, so he jostled it back and forth between his hands for a few moments, drank a quick slurp as if to say *See? This won't be awkward at all* and then set the skin aside, wishing Hannah and Churn would return. 'Does it affect your abilities?' he asked.

'You mean being drunk? Does it impact my ability to work Larion magic? I should say so; although I'm not entirely sure, because I have used so little magic in the last—' He stopped and thought for a while. 'I don't know how many Twinmoons it's been. I don't know how many have passed. Isn't that funny? One can actually drink enough to lose whole Twinmoons. Pissing demons, but I am a sorry sop.'

'So, it does,' Hoyt confirmed.

'Oh, yes.'

'Will you be able to get us inside?'

'I don't know,' Alen answered honestly. 'I haven't been to Welstar Palace. I have seen it in visions, when Nerak's worked various unholy spells, but I didn't watch with the eye of one planning a covert assault. And to answer your next question, no, I don't know if I have enough magic left to keep us safe, especially once we get inside. There was – is – a whole team of magicians looking for me and who knows how many more doing other work for our dark prince. It will be my final test, of that I am confident.'

'But your house,' Hoyt said, 'how did you keep your house hidden for so long?'

'I cast that spell long before your great grandparents were born, Hoyt. If I hadn't released it on purpose, it would have stayed that way until I died, maybe even longer.'

'Didn't that drain you, keeping it going that long?'

'Not really. You see, magic is kind of like physics: once something gets going, it actually takes more to stop it than to keep it moving. Look at our twin moons. Those two hunks of rock have been spinning around this world since the beginning of the first Age, longer than that. And they are about perfect, meeting in the northern and southern skies with such predictability that we know the day and time, within an aven, when they will align. It's amazing. Something got them here; something got them started and even something as huge as our own sun, gigantic in the distance, can't pull them away from each other and from us.'

'So, the magic keeping your house hidden—'

'Except for the occasional flicker when a bird would slam into it and perish right there in the sky – that took some quick explaining – but apart from that, my house would have remained camouflaged, people on the street finding it curious but difficult to recall, possibly for ever.'

Hoyt smiled, but his eyes betrayed his trepidation.

'You don't have to come along, Hoyt,' Alen said. 'Actually, I don't know why you're here at all. What have you got to gain by going into Welstar Palace?'

'I don't know,' he said. 'Maybe I won't go in. Maybe just Churn will go with you. He's wanted to get his hands on Malagon for a long time.'

'Malagon won't be there. Of that I *am* confident.'

'Well, anyone, anything, then. Churn has his own ideas for *disturbing* Prince Malagon's happy existence,' Hoyt said.

'Good. Then he will be welcome to come along – and Hoyt,

should you decide to join us, I promise I will keep a clear head and I will use whatever power still remains in this disintegrating old body to see Hannah home, and to see you and Churn safe out again.'

'Thanks,' Hoyt said, genuinely relieved. He could ask nothing more. He had the option of abandoning this quest, so it would be his decision, and whatever he decided, Alen would not judge him.

'Regardless,' Alen added, 'we might not make it that far.'

'Hey, don't joke. That's not funny,' Hoyt said.

'But it is true.' Alen pulled a thin scroll from his saddlebag and unrolled a parchment map of northern Praga and the Great Range bordering Malakasia. 'We have to get through the forest of ghosts, and apart from you leading us, I don't know how we'll make it.'

'Me?' Hoyt was dubious. 'Why me?'

'Because the rest of us have something at stake in this journey. Granted, you hate Prince Malagon and Nerak as much as any free-dom fighter, but you participate as you see fit, or as your fortunes guide you. You are a thief, my boy, and I am fiercely proud of you for that. You fight when it's convenient and sometimes you run. You don't have to come to Welstar Palace, and perhaps you will decide in the next Twinmoon – or the next aven – that you don't want to go on, and you won't. You have no stake in this.' Alen's eyes reflecting the firelight gave Hoyt a disconcerting feeling.

'What does that have to do with the forest of ghosts?'

'Maybe nothing.'

'Grand,' the young healer sighed. 'Alen, please try to make some sense. If I have to do this and I don't know how or what to expect, I might lose all of you in there—'

The older man interrupted, 'And maybe everything.'

'Go on.'

'If the forest of ghosts actually works as legends claim, then Hannah, Churn and I will all experience visions. We all have a critical emotional stake in this journey. If the forest targets those who traverse the northern wilderness pursuing their heartfelt dreams, the three of us will be set upon as soon as we breach the first row of trees.'

'I don't understand.'

'You aren't on your life's journey, Hoyt. You are out for a stroll, ac-companying friends north to Malakasia. And why? Because there's nothing more appetising on the Hoyt agenda this Twinmoon. Churn and I are dead set on revenge. We might actually fight each other over who gets to suck the marrow from Malagon's bones. And

Hannah has to get home. If the forest actually assails us – and given the number of travellers who have never made it through those foothills, I believe it will – then Churn, Hannah and I will need you to guide us through.'

'I don't know how.' Hoyt picked up the wineskin again. He wanted something to occupy his hands. 'I don't have any magic.'

'I'm going to try and give you some.'

Hoyt drank deeply and coughed as the bitter tang of a cheap Pragan burned the back of his throat. His mind raced for an alternative to bringing helpless friends into a haunted forest. 'Maybe we can take one of the western roads. Won't there be something out that way with a light patrol, something we can handle in a straight fight?'

'If there was, I would be the first to suggest we go in that direction.' Alen reached over and took the skin. Corking it, he added, 'But if even one of those sentries managed to escape, every soldier in southern Malakasia would know in an aven.'

Hoyt nodded disconsolately. 'You're right. At least this way, we have an honest shot.' He sighed. 'How much time do I have?'

'At the rate Churn is letting us ride – five or six days before we get there.'

'All right,' Hoyt said, determination in his voice overcoming the trepidation, 'what do I have to do?'

'Ms Sorenson,' Steven said, 'I need your help.'

Jennifer Sorenson's washing machine churned away downstairs as she browsed the entertainment pages of one of the dozen or more newspapers that had piled up on the steps and lawn in front of her house. She never read headlines since the one had noted, in a good bold font, that the search for her daughter had been postponed until spring due to prohibitively heavy snow in the mountains. So now Jennifer scanned for book and film reviews or even a recipe for those periodic nights when she felt like cooking for one.

When the doorbell rang, she noted her place and went to the door, expecting a mailman burdened with two weeks of letters, bills and junk mail. 'Just a minute,' she called and, not bothering to check through the peep hole, she slid the bolt back and opened the door – and there he was, standing face to face with her, the monster who had taken her daughter. It had taken her a moment to recognise him: he had lost weight, and his last shower wasn't recent – but it was him, Steven Taylor.

'Ms Sorenson,' he looked at her expectantly, 'I need your help.'

Rage flooded through her, warming her skin and numbing her senses, a mother's fury: she would beat this man to death, ravage him as every mother who had ever lost a child to a kidnapper or a paedophile dreamed of doing.

Jennifer leaped at him with a growl as adrenalin-fuelled hatred flooded into her bloodstream. She kicked, bit and punched all at once, a wild woman with flailing fists, fingernails, booted feet and teeth. She had dreamed of ripping this man apart and painting her face with his blood, of chaining him in her basement and keeping him there, barely alive, for the next thirty years. She had dreamed of beating him to death with a metal pipe until his body was reduced to bone shards and jelly – but each of those scenarios had required some planning. She had never expected him to come to her; yet here he was, Steven Taylor in person, and all the rage she could summon, all the hatred and fear she had felt from the first time she had ever watched Hannah get into a car and drive off with a young man – Edward Coopersmith, in high school – was focused on him now.

'I am going to kill you,' she screamed and managed to get a handful of his hair and the Gore-tex collar of his coat.

'No – wait – Ms Sorenson, please,' Steven cried, backing away and bringing his hands up in self defence, 'I can take—'

Jennifer held onto Steven's hair as if it were her only link to Hannah, a greasy, wiry hank that would somehow bring her daughter home if only she pulled hard enough. 'I knew you weren't on that hill, you fucker. Where did you take her?' Not waiting for an answer, Jennifer spun around; Steven fell to his right as she, her hand still entangled in his hair, stumbled to her left and brought her elbow around in a wide arc that took the young kidnapper squarely beneath the chin, snapping his head back. Stunned, Steven fell down the concrete steps. Jennifer leaped down beside him and landed several brutal kicks to his ribs and stomach, hoping to hear his last breath, his death rattle – until she suddenly realised what he had been trying to say. *She's alive . . .*

The last kick was little more than a token, then she crouched down beside him.

'She's alive, she's okay . . . I know where—' Steven's voice *was* a rattle, wet and hoarse, she could barely hear it above the noise of the traffic.

But Jennifer had been listening for him to beg, to cry out that he was dying. 'Where is she? Where? Did you bury her body, you bastard?' She forced down the glimmer of hope; rage would comfort her until Hannah was home or until Steven Taylor was dead. She bounced the back of his head off the concrete and watched as his eyes rolled back. 'Speak up, young man – where is she?'

Jennifer realised she was panting, barely sucking in enough air to keep her vision in focus. Steven interrupted with a whisper. 'Praga.'

'Prague? Did you say Prague?' She needed him conscious now, and shook him roughly. 'Shitty guess; her passport is upstairs.'

'Not Prague.' Steven looked like a cadaver, his cheeks sunk in and his eyes staring at points in the distance. 'Praga – I have been trying for two months to get to her – I need your help.'

Jennifer began to soften as the hope, locked in her mind in an iron strongbox, began clawing its way out. Her hands shaking with adrenalin, she gripped Steven's collar and heaved the young man's face up until it was inches from her own. Shaking all over now, she warned him, 'If you are lying to me, I promise you months of unholy agony before you die, Steven Taylor.'

'We have three hours,' Steven said, his eyes finally focusing on hers with surprising clarity.

'What do you mean?'

'Three hours and I'll go get her.'

Brexan stumbled, toppling a stack of wooden crates with a clatter she was certain could be heard over the Blackstones. 'Mother of a cloven-hoofed whore—' Her curses would have embarrassed a docker, but she cut herself short as she lost sight of Jacrys. She was tired, dehydrated, and quite unable to keep up with the indefatigable Malakasian spy. 'Drank too rutting much last night, you fool,' she said softly. 'What were you thinking?'

Brexan had been chiding herself all day for the embarrassing lack of control, not just the drinking, but the casual, if unmemorable, sex. She was still dehydrated after vomiting up her breakfast, and it was making her joints ache and her head feel as though it had been cracked by a passing blacksmith. Several times she had been convinced the spy had detected her as she tracked his circuitous path through the city, but Jacrys had continued on his way, talking with locals and peering into windows. He had eaten some fruit and a piece of dried meat with another small loaf of bread during the midday aven. Brexan, still unable to eat, had taken advantage of the break to guzzle a beer and a mug of water in a tavern across the street.

An aven later, that had been a mistake. The alcohol had made her sleepy and nearly bursting with a need to relieve herself. When Jacrys had stopped to engage in an animated discussion with a stevedore, Brexan had sneaked behind a row of juniper bushes, hastily hiked her new skirt above her thighs and pissed. She ignored the puddle of acrid fluid with a sigh and an embarrassed shake of her head.

She needed rest, food and then more rest, and unless Jacrys stopped soon for the night, she would be forced to abandon her surveillance and attempt to find the traitorous murderer the following day. 'Why don't you go back to your inn?' she muttered. 'Aren't you hungry? Don't you want to take a break for food? It's well past the dinner aven now. Don't you want to sit for a while? Maybe a day or two?'

Two small boys with dirty faces, soiled tunics and irretrievably black fingernails passed her, carrying an old chainball between them, but they stopped long enough to take a wide-eyed look at the odd woman talking aloud to no one.

'There's nobody there, lady,' one of the youngsters said in a small but amused voice.

Brexan whirled on them. 'Yes, you wretched little rutters. I am a full-gone lunatic with a cracking nasty headache and a tendency to talk out loud to phantoms right before I kidnap, kill, cook and eat annoying little boys!'

The two children screamed and ran, their chainball forgotten, as fast as they could to get away from the homicidal woman with the drawn face and the deathly-pale skin.

Brexan winced at their cries, whispering, 'Yes. That's grand. Alert the entire city.'

Hustling along the side street, she was careful not to make any additional noise but assumed, for the fourth or fifth time that day, that she had already created such a clamour that Jacrys would be waiting for her at the next corner, knife drawn and ready to pierce her ribs – but when she reached the main thoroughfare, the well-dressed man was working his way along the river towards a tavern near the waterfront, apparently oblivious to the racket. Jacrys paused at the tavern door and looked left then right, as though the person or people for whom he had been searching all day would somehow appear, then gave up and entered the inn with a dismissive shrug.

'Thank the gods,' Brexan said. 'Have five courses, six if you want them. I'll pay. Just give me a few moments to catch my breath and get some water.' There was an alehouse conveniently across the way; with any luck she could get a table near the window so she could keep a close watch on the main boulevard while choking down a hasty dinner and drinking an ocean of cold water.

She crossed the street, pausing to allow a mule-drawn wagon to pass, then fell in behind the cart before stepping onto the plank walkway lining the muddy road that wound its way to the northern wharf. She stopped long enough to stomp the mud from her boots and checked angles of sight from the various windows in the alehouse; she didn't want to lose Jacrys if he were only visiting the tavern to ask more questions. Worried he might slip past her in the darkness, Brexan decided to look around for a better place to sit, one without an obstructed view of the waterfront.

She rounded the corner and disappeared into the darkness of the alley, but she had not taken five steps before she sensed another presence: someone backed against the wall to her left. Something was wrong. She took one or two awkward, lunging steps back towards the main street before feeling a hand clamp down on her shoulder and then around her throat. Brexan strained against the grip until she lost her balance and then the stranger heaved her off her feet and slammed her into the alehouse wall.

The force of the blow knocked the air from her lungs and Brexan, too weak to fight back now, gasped for air and looked longingly towards the relative safety of the waterfront boulevard. The grip on her throat made regaining her breath all the more difficult. Light streaming through the alehouse windows was only a few paces away, but it might as well have been a Moon's ride, for the alley darkness had swallowed them.

'Tell me who you are and do not lie. I have some respect for spies, even hideously inadequate spies like you, but I have no patience for liars. So be quick about it and don't lie, because I will know.' The man's voice was difficult to hear over the rushing blood and raspy inhalations echoing in Brexan's head, but she knew who it was. *Well, you knew you had been too rutting noisy, you stupid fool,* she thought, disgusted with herself.

Her vision tunnelled as consciousness closed in, then she regained control. Her vision was blurry, but she could see the cut of his cloak, the broad shoulders, the frilly edge sewn onto his hood and the white lace collar. He *was* a good dresser. 'I'm—' Brexan coughed and spat in an effort to draw breath, but the spy didn't seem to care that her spittle dribbled across her chin and dripped onto his wrist.

'You're …?' he prompted, loosening his grip just enough for Brexan to wheeze audibly.

'My name—' She took quick breaths; they were coming somewhat easier now. She forced herself to make eye contact with the Malakasian killer, knowing if she looked him in the face, he would be prone to believe what she said. 'My name is Brexan. I was sent here by General Oaklen to—'

'To what?' Jacrys asked, his dirk drawn now and pressed against her ribs. Brexan could feel its tip against the bruise where the scarred Seron had elbowed her.

To what? To what? To what, you idiot, a Malakasian general sent you here to do what?

'To get the stone key, the talisman … he told me you were looking for it as well and …' She hesitated, forcing her gaze back up to his face.

'You're lying, Brexan, or whoever you are.' He pressed the dirk a little harder between two of her ribs. 'How could you have known who I am?'

Brexan took the risk of her life and prayed it would create enough credible confusion that the spy would spare her. 'I met you once in Estrad.'

Jacrys paused at that, loosened his grip and even withdrew the dirk's point. 'Go on.'

Heartened by this measure of good luck, Brexan said, 'I met you and after Bronfio was killed – I don't know if you had heard, but he died in the assault on Riverend Palace, just a few days after you had visited him in our camp—'

Now it was Jacrys' turn to lie. 'I hadn't heard. Pity. He was a promising officer.'

Brexan tasted a sour tang in her throat. 'Anyway, when he died, I was one of the only ones who knew what you looked like and Oaklen, sorry, General Oaklen sent me to get the stone. He said Prince Malagon wants that stone as soon as possible and that you had failed to—' She paused in her story for effect, looked down at her boots again and waited.

Jacrys was angry, but he did not return the dirk to her ribs. 'Failed to do what? Failed to do what? Tell me!'

'You know – failed to get it back.'

'That is none of your concern. How did you know where to find me? I came across the Blackstones. It nearly killed me. Did you manage that, Brexan?'

Jacrys was off balance and she decided to confuse things further, hoping to weave such a tangled web of nonsense that the spy would let her go, if only for an instant. She would make a quick dash for the street and disappear into the crowds along the wharf. 'Oaklen sent me to Strandson. There was a merchant. He never told me his name. But he had one of them, Versil, Versec— something like that. He, the merchant, had Seron with him. They had caught this fellow, Versil and they were bringing him here. It was a schooner, a fast ship. The merchant, the fat man with the mole on his face right here,' Brexan indicated the side of her nose with one finger, 'he told me where to start looking for you.' She held her breath, hoping to the gods of the Northern Forest that the Malakasian spy had worked with the Falkan merchant. This was it; this was the moment – there'd been just enough accurate information to be believable, but if Jacrys had never met the fat traitor, Brexan was about to die.

Jacrys relaxed his stranglehold on the young woman and muttered, 'Carpello, I am going to kill you.'

Carpello! That's his name. Thank you, Jacrys. And no, I am going to kill him.

The spy looked back at her. 'Well, my darling. I must say you aren't much for espionage, are you? And although I believe you are telling me the truth, I cannot have you meddling in my affairs, Oaklen or no Oaklen.' He raised the dirk to her throat. 'Goodbye, Brexan.'

'No! Wait!' she pleaded. 'I know where they are, where they're hiding.' Brexan assumed he'd been looking for the Ronan partisans; it was them he had followed north from Estrad. Gabriel O'Reilly had told them about the wraith army descending on the Ronans in the Blackstone forest, but the ghost had known nothing more. She took another risk. 'The Ronans,' she said finally. 'I know where they are.'

She was about to name them, hoping it would add more credibility to her claim, when she caught herself – if any of them had been killed and Jacrys knew it, she would be caught.

'No you don't. It was a good try, though,' Jacrys said.

'But I do,' she answered. *Keep him talking. Keep him talking.*

'Then why did you follow me all day?'

'Because I don't believe they have the stone.' *What are you saying, Brexan? Think of something else, anything else. What if he knows the stone is back in Colorado?*

'Really? And why is that?' He was getting bored, she could tell.

'Because if they had it, Gilmour would have taken it to Sandcliff Palace, right?'

Jacrys, in control now, prepared his bait. 'Why don't you tell me where they are?'

'Take your knife away from my throat and perhaps I will,' she said firmly. Despite the cold, Brexan could feel sweat breaking out on her forehead. 'I saw them just the other day, two days ago – no, three days ago.'

'Really? Gilmour and the others?' The master spy set the hook. 'You saw Gilmour and the Ronan partisans, here in Orindale?'

'Yes,' Brexan sighed, 'Gilmour and the others. They are south of the imperial palace, hiding in an old wine shop. It looks closed, as if the merchant is only there for the warm season.'

Jacrys moved in close. Brexan could feel his breath on her face, the warm, damp feel of Estrad. Had it all begun in Estrad? Had she really come this far, only to be killed by the man who had started her on this journey?

Pressing his cheek against hers, the spy renewed his grip around her throat. 'Gilmour is dead, my dear. I killed him last Twinmoon. Goodbye.'

With Jacrys' cheek caressing hers, Brexan remembered Versen, lashed to the bulkhead in the schooner's hold, and how he had manipulated his bonds so that he could lie flat on his back. When she did the same, their cheeks had touched in the darkness. Brexan thought it was the most intimate thing she had ever done with another person. Waiting to feel the sharp pain of the blade pierce her ribs, she tried with all her might to remember every detail of Versen's stubbly cheek coming to a gentle rest against hers. *Goodbye, Versen,* she thought and waited to feel her life drain away.

Then there was someone else with them. Mercurial-quick, the cloaked intruder dropped down on them from above. *He must have been on the roof,* Brexan thought in the instant before Jacrys, as startled as she, was pulled away from her and tugged roughly down the alley. Brexan didn't wait to see what happened; she took to her heels and ran into the street, about to escape into the anonymous throngs moving along the wharf, when she stopped. 'Sallax!'

She almost knocked over an elderly couple walking hand-in-hand along the pier and she reversed direction, shouting, 'Sallax!' as she ran back towards the alleyway.

THE FAR PORTAL

'I can't open it until five o'clock.' Steven suppressed his irritation. Jennifer Sorenson was upset, and even he had to admit his story didn't sound especially convincing.

'Five o'clock, because that's when your roommate will lay out *his* charred, egg-stained rug, and you'll land right in his lap?' Her scepticism was salt rubbed in his wounds – wounds that Hannah's mother was responsible for; he felt as though he had been in a car accident. His ribs and abdomen throbbed furiously from her kicks and his head was about to break open. He felt certain the roadmap of cuts and bruises across his head would never heal.

They sat together in front of the television, watching the coverage of the unprecedented winter firestorm that had already claimed eight square miles along Chicago Creek Road. Between interviews with townspeople and firefighters, the square-jawed anchorman spoke to a helicopter pilot who was monitoring the damage from above. The arrhythmic jouncing of the picture as the helicopter navigated the tricky thermals along Clear Creek Canyon made Steven feel even more nauseous.

It was 4.10 p.m. and it had taken two hours to recount his tale. He left out the part about being able to work magic with the hickory staff. If there was a slim chance that Jennifer Sorenson didn't already believe he was insane; *that*, he was quite sure, would have her calling the local psychiatric hospital. She had stopped him several times, throwing up her hands and shouting, 'That's enough, Steven, I'm calling the police.' So far he had persuaded her to let him continue, begging her to wait until five o'clock, when he could prove he was telling the truth.

In the past fifteen minutes the conversation had taken a turn for the worse and Steven knew Hannah's mother wouldn't make it through the hour.

'All right, I'll do it, but we can only leave it open for a second,' he agreed reluctantly.

'Why? Why not leave it open until Hannah comes back, or until Mark finds her?' Jennifer's tone was half disbelief and half sarcasm.

Steven, for all his sympathy for the woman, began to get angry. 'You're not helping,' he said. 'I have been in Hell. I have had my life threatened every day for two months, and I am telling you that, regardless of whether you believe me, you need to have a little faith for forty-five more minutes.'

'No. Do it now.' Jennifer's eyes were hard.

'Fine, but if Nerak finds us because I open this now, I – *we* – may have to escape through it, and that means we might be dropped on top of a glacier, or at the bottom of a river, or anywhere. There is nothing I can do about that. Do you understand?'

'Oh, sure. The demon creature trying to release all the hounds of Hell onto the funny little world you discovered will be right here in the next ten minutes, because you took two seconds to show me a carpet? You are mad, Steven Taylor, mad and dangerous, and I want to know what you have done with my daughter.'

Without another word, Steven took a book from the coffee table, something big with black and white photos on the cover, and handed it to her. He rolled out the Larion far portal, holding one corner, and turned back to Jennifer. 'When I tell you, throw that book onto the portal. Do *not* touch it, don't reach out over it, whatever you do, do *not*, for your own sake, step on it.' He looked her straight in the face to be certain she was taking him seriously, but all he could see was her open scepticism.

He shrugged. 'I don't have time for your doubts, Ms Sorenson, but if this is what you need to believe me, then fine.'

With that, Steven released the edge of the far portal. The moment the last corner of the tapestry struck the floor the energy level in the room rose, that same shimmer he and Mark had felt in Idaho Springs. Now Steven recognised the feeling: it was the same magic as the hickory staff. He felt it pulsing in the air, breathing him in and out, as if he were just a passerby interacting with an ancient force for a fraction of a second on its interminable journey though the ages.

He looked at Jennifer: she was standing in mute stupefaction: he had been telling the truth. 'Throw it!' he shouted, 'throw it, Ms Sorenson. Throw the book now.'

She threw the book awkwardly, but before it struck the tapestry, it disappeared. Steven used a small metal shovel he had taken from the array of fireplace tools beside Jennifer's hearth to create a shallow range of hilly wrinkles in the tapestry. In a moment, the shimmer in the air had faded away.

He crouched down and folded the portal in half, then moved to stand beside Jennifer, who was looking far older than her sixty years – decades older than the raving mother who had beaten seven shades of shit out of him earlier that afternoon. She stood looking down at her hands, thin and delicate, Hannah's hands, as if the book with its tasteful photographs, *études* of light and shadow, would somehow reappear in them. She was a practical woman, and believed her eyes.

For a few moments longer she struggled with the notion that greater things than anything she had ever imagined were at work right in her own living room, then she started to sob. 'She's alive? Hannah? Please— I'm sorry, Steven, but please tell me if she—'

Steven took the older woman in his arms and held her tightly as she shook with emotion. 'She *is* alive, Ms Sorenson, I promise you. She is in Praga, in Eldarn, and I have been trying with all my strength to get to her, but I've been trying to tell you all afternoon, I need your help.'

'Anything.' She took Steven's hands. 'My God, but look at you – what the hell is this place?'

'I've been through some difficult times, but I'm fine, and I *will* find her.' He felt about ready to collapse. Everything hurt, and he was exhausted – his nap on the bus that morning, as the sun rose above the prairie behind him, had been only a thimbleful of the rest he needed.

Thirty-eight minutes and he would be gone.

'This demon – what was his name?' Jennifer Sorenson's tears had slowed and her voice was steadier. She was back in control.

'He's not a demon, he's far worse. He is Eldarn's greatest sorcerer, the most gifted magician in thousands of Twinmoons – years, whatever – and he has been taken by an evil force. He's a matchstick compared with what's coming if we don't stop him.' He searched for an explanation that made sense. 'Nerak is the most powerful and destructive force any world has ever seen, and he's on his way to this spot right now.'

'Why?'

'Because we opened the portal.'

'Oh shit, Steven.'

The profanity was unexpected; he smiled. 'It's all right. Nerak doesn't want you, he wants me – he may not even show up at all, because he can go back on his own when the portal is opened. I doubt we gave him enough time just now, but I need you to close this portal as quickly as possible after I've gone through.'

'I can do that with this?' She picked up the shovel.

'Sure. That will do fine, just wrinkle the thing, and it shuts right down – but then you need to get away from here.'

'Where? How far away?'

'Not far necessarily, but someplace I don't know about, someplace Hannah would never have talked about, someplace I would never have mentioned to—' Steven hesitated, remembering the security guard's body on the floor of the bank. 'Someplace not even my bank colleagues would know.'

'I'm sorry, I'm being such a pest, Steven, but why? If he wants you, and you're gone, why would he come after me?'

'For the same reason I think he took one of my friends today. He wants what you know.' Jennifer blanched as he went on, 'He can take from your mind anything you know about me, about my intentions when I get back to Eldarn, or about the portal, anything.'

'But you haven't told me what you plan to do.' Her lower lip was trembling.

'He doesn't care.'

Jennifer straightened her spine. 'All right, I'll go to—'

'Please don't say it. I can't know. If I know, you'll be in danger. Just go someplace that I have never heard of, somewhere that wouldn't be swimming around in—' He stopped for a moment and swallowed hard. 'Well, someplace that Myrna Kessler wouldn't know about.'

'Myrna?'

'A friend of mine. I never told her this address, but she knew about your antiques store.'

'So if Nerak was already on his way to my father's store, then he might detect this rug—'

'Portal, yes,'

'Sorry, portal, and come over here now?'

'That's right.' Steven began organising his pack. His head ached fiercely and he sat down with a groan on Jennifer's couch. 'Do you have any aspirin?'

She laughed and looked fifteen years younger. 'I think we could both use some. I'll get the bottle.' She hurried to the kitchen while Steven pulled himself back into Howard's winter coat.

Four aspirin and a glass of water later, Steven handed the bottle back to Jennifer, who shook her head. 'Do they have aspirin there? You keep them.'

'You're right, thanks,' he tossed the container into his backpack. 'Now, I know this will be difficult, but I need you to open the portal again.'

'Fine. When?'

Steven did a quick mental calculation. 'Start in two months, that ought be enough time to find her. I want her back here with you as soon as possible, but it might take me that long to get there.' He paused a moment. 'What day is it?'

'The twelfth. Friday.'

'Okay. So, in two months, February twelfth, start opening the portal every day at five o'clock a.m. and five o'clock p.m. – for fifteen minutes only – you must be sure to close it at five fifteen without fail. Time is a bit different over there. I thought it was moving more quickly, but perhaps it isn't. Either way, I'll have this—' he held up Howard's watch. 'It'll keep the time here perfectly, even while I'm over there.'

'Five o'clock in the morning? Every morning?'

He laughed. 'Sorry, that is unreasonable, isn't it? How about seven o'clock – would that work? Seven in the evening and seven in the morning ... but just fifteen minutes, absolutely no more. I'll have to make sure the others know ...'

Jennifer still looked worried. 'What if the watch doesn't keep perfect time?'

'If it doesn't, then my already miserable day is about to deteriorate further. Mark and Garec are using my old watch to time my return right now, so I'll be testing my theory in seventeen minutes.'

He checked her wristwatch. 'Close enough. Now, promise me you will close the portal each time. You don't want Nerak coming through to find you, or if by naked, pastry-chef luck he gets stuck on this side, tracking you down. So you must swear you'll shut it down.' Steven didn't mean to scare her, but she had to understand how vital this was. 'One of those days, Hannah will appear. You cannot lose hope, Ms Sorenson, and you cannot miss a day, not ever.'

She looked determined. 'Absolutely. Seven o'clock, a.m. and p.m., every day, starting on February twelfth.'

'Thank you,' Steven smiled. 'She'll be back. I promise.'

Fifteen minutes later, as Steven checked Lessek's key was firmly secured in the front pocket of Howard's backpack, his hand closed around the second roast beef sandwich he'd stuffed in. He pulled it out and laughed. 'Mark will love this,' he said.

Jennifer gaped and, as if remembering her manners for the first time all day, burst forth, 'Oh my goodness, I'm a miserable hostess. I'm so embarrassed. Steven, what do they eat there? Do you want something before you go?'

'I only have two minutes, so no thanks, don't worry—'

'Wait. I have plenty of food. What can I—?' Her voice trailed off in embarrassment.

'Don't worry about it, we've managed just fine,' Steven said, patting her on the arm. 'More importantly, you remember what you have to do?'

'No problem. Seven o'clock, every twelve hours. I will be dead before I miss a turn – and I will not lose hope again, Steven.' She started to cry, reaching for him. 'Bring her back home, Steven.'

'I will,' he promised, and reached for the fire-shovel. His heart raced as he unfolded the far portal and the Larion magic swirled about the room. 'Don't forget: fold this up as soon as I'm gone, then take it and get out of here, as quickly as you possibly can.'

Her face still damp with tears, Hannah's mother repeated her promise. 'I will.'

Steven took hold of the backpack straps, checked Howard's watch, which read 5.04 p.m. and stepped onto the Larion far portal and out of Jennifer Sorenson's living room.

Jennifer crouched, watching tiny flecks of coloured light shimmer in the air above the tapestry like a cloud of Technicolor fireflies. Her tears had turned to stunned amazement; Steven Taylor had disappeared before her eyes. He had said he would, and the book had vanished, but until it actually happened, she had not realised how scary it would be. He had been telling the truth, the whole truth: Hannah was out there – Jennifer looked down at the ornate, if filthy, rug lying askew across her floor – *in there* somewhere. 'Bring her back, Steven,' she begged again, though she had no idea if he could still hear her. She was distracted by the sound of an accident outside – there were pile-ups on Lincoln or Broadway periodically, and Hannah invariably dashed the two blocks west so see if she could help until an ambulance arrived. But this was more than just the regular slam and shatter of a rush-hour crash: this was awesome, the musical tinkling of broken glass followed by the groan of tired steel and the *whump, whump, kablam!* of an exploding gas tank.

The sound slapped her back to reality; she heard Steven's voice again. *Nerak is the most powerful and destructive force any world has ever seen, and he is on his way to this spot right now – because we opened the portal.*

'Oh shit, Steven, oh shit, oh shit, oh shit, oh shit!' She stared at the portal, then whispered, 'Close the goddamned thing. Move!' She used the fire-shovel Steven had taken from the fireplace to fold one corner over and as she did so, the waves of energy in the room subsided. Jennifer guessed that with the disappearance of the mystical fireflies, it was safe for her to move the tapestry by hand, then escape to wherever it was she was going. She reached out her fingers, then stopped and retreated to the relative safety of the couch. She didn't consider herself a brave woman – her behaviour earlier in the day had truly shocked and appalled her – and she was glad no one was there now to watch as she scurried back and forth across her living room like a frightened rabbit.

'Enough,' she finally told herself, and steeled herself to touch the tapestry. Once she'd started it was easier than she'd expected, and she folded it into a surprisingly small lump, which she stuffed into a canvas bag. Then she rushed about her house, not really certain what essentials she would require. She grabbed her wallet and collected together a pile of clean underwear and socks and her favourite sweater. She unearthed the small fireproof strongbox she kept hidden in the space above the electric fuse panel. Now she could smell the pungent aroma of burning oil and melting plastic; people were crying for help and someone – or two, she couldn't tell – was screaming in agony.

He was here; he – *it* – whatever, Nerak was out there, less than two blocks away.

Jennifer rushed through the foyer, slipped one set of keys into her pocket, then without even a final look around her house stepped outside, locked the door behind her and hustled down the steps towards her car.

Nerak drove like a madman, with the window rolled down so he could drink in the bellow of the Mustang's racing engine. *These automobiles are fascinating*, he thought, picturing himself careening through the streets of Pellia – or, even better, Orindale or Estrad – maybe even in one of the colourful giants, *one of those trucks*, Myrna's memory supplied. Moving a plug of *Confederate Son* from one side of Myrna's mouth to the other, Nerak tried to spit brown juice out the window, but his current mouth was not yet trained and instead it dribbled down the inside of the door.

Traffic had been light, and the raging forest fire still flickering at the edges of the highway had discouraged all but the most intrepid of travellers from risking the journey east, but Nerak was becoming angry. The girl's memories told him that progress would be slower, but he had no idea how congested the road would be. There were hundreds – *thousands* – of clumsy, colourful roaring monsters lining the road, an endless caravan. *Where were all these people going?* He growled.

Home. Myrna's mind answered him. *They are going home.*

'Well, they are in the way,' Nerak said, and considered his options. He had used most of the bullets on his trip across the country – and a few more in Idaho Springs, just when people had tried to keep him from climbing the concrete ramp to the highway. But it hadn't taken many bullets to clear that path; Nerak had become quite a skilled marksman. He leaned out the window and spat another mouthful of tobacco juice onto the highway. This was too much; the gun was just a toy, anyway, nothing powerful enough to move all these people. He needed something more, another fire perhaps, or maybe a sand storm – just killing them all as he had in Port Denis wouldn't get their cars out of his way.

He searched Myrna's memories; all her thoughts, interactions, ideas and fears were neatly organised and it took only a moment for Nerak to find what he needed. 'Just to get through this traffic,' he said, Myrna's lips splitting to reveal teeth coated in brown fluid, bits of tobacco leaf stuck between her molars. He wiped the sticky open sore on the back of her wrist against one thigh, leaving a trail of blood and rotting flesh on her skirt. His eyes fluttered as he whispered a spell.

With Mantegna's new siren wailing and red lights flashing, Nerak drove with abandon, dodging parked cars and ignoring pedestrians scattering before him as he careened between cars and over sidewalks. Soon he spotted the row of antiques shops that ran along South Broadway Avenue. Meyers Antiques: Steven might be inside right now – perhaps that was where he planned to open the portal and take Lessek's key back to Fantus and the rest of the Ronan partisans.

'Not today, Steven,' Nerak growled, and pushed the accelerator to the floor. 'I might keep you alive just long enough for you to watch me eat your heart. That will make for a fitting end to an otherwise thrilling day.'

Perhaps he would crash through the front windows of the store: draw a crowd to witness Steven's pain. He was in a fine mood, for though he had temporarily lost Lessek's key, he was confident he would soon have it back – nearly a thousand Twinmoons later, he would reclaim what was rightly his. Lessek's key? Lessek had not suffered and struggled to earn that key – he may have chipped it from the granite slab that had eventually become the Larion spell table, but Nerak was the one who had earned its knowledge, its power. If it had not been for Pikan and that milksop, Kantu— He paused. He could barely control his rage: how close had he been that night?

Nerak felt a strange but familiar sensation; a tickle in his throat, along the left side of his face, but intent on Meyers Antiques, now only two blocks away, he ignored it – until, suddenly, its significance sank in.

'The portal!' he shouted, the power of his voice throwing a young man riding a bicycle into the wrought-iron gate of an upscale café. The portal was open, right now – *and it wasn't inside Meyers Antiques*. Steven Taylor was nearby; Nerak could smell him, could taste his foul foreign blood, but he wasn't inside the antiques store; Myrna had been wrong.

He searched her memories again: *Hannah Sorenson. Meyers Antiques. South Broadway Avenue, Denver, Colorado. Interstate 70 east to I-25 south to Broadway.*

'Where is he?' Nerak cried, shattering the car's windshield.

Hannah's home. Her parents. Her apartment.

Nerak cursed his own poor judgment, then shook his head. 'No matter. The portal will guide me now.' He honed in on the Larion magic, as loud now and resonant in this curious world as a thunderclap, gripped the wheel and turned left across the busy lanes of South Broadway Avenue.

He didn't make it. A large yellow moving van clipped the tail end of the Mustang, sending it into a spin. Nerak struggled for control, eventually giving up on the steering wheel and taking over with his mind, but it was too late and he slammed headlong through the wide plate-glass windows of a rare books store. The ensuing explosion as the gas tank erupted beneath him cast the Eldarni dictator out of Myrna Kessler's burning body.

Gilmour rolled over with a groan. The sun had not yet climbed high enough to bring any light to the fjord, but above he could see the earliest hues of dawn heralding another day. 'What time is it?' he asked in a hoarse whisper. Garec, sleeping soundly beside the remains of their campfire, didn't stir.

Pain flared in his chest and, wincing, Gilmour pulled his legs up tightly against his stomach. There were broken ribs, at least three, and maybe a bit of internal bleeding. With his fingertips, he felt the swelling beneath his armpits and grimaced. Was there any greater pain in life than broken ribs? And not just one, but three, great rutting lords. The damp mud of the shoreline provided a comfortable, if chilly bed, and Gilmour felt his head settle back into the concave dent where it had spent much of the previous night.

'What time is it?' he asked again, but Garec didn't move.

Lessek's spell book had lashed out at him; he hadn't been ready. Gilmour stared up at the sky. If Nerak had mastered the spells in that book, Gilmour would be destroyed. It was that simple. He had made a huge mistake by being too terrified to go back to the scroll library. 'The ash dream,' he whispered. The first folio was as far as he had got.

He forced himself to relax: one job at a time. He used magic to heal his fractured ribs, then sat up, groaning – this time in frustration – and shouted, 'Garec, what time is it?'

'What—?' Rudely awakened, Garec yawned widely, then sat up with a start, his eyes wide in sudden realisation. 'Did you sleep? Demonpiss, Gilmour, I hadn't expected you to sleep. Are we too late? Did we miss it?'

'Don't worry. I think there's still time.'

Garec studied Steven's watch with a furrowed brow. 'We have – ten moments before five clocks.'

'Minutes.'

'Yes, right, whatever. Ten. Tecan.' He walked stiffly to the boat and began rummaging in one of the canvas sacks.

'Yes, I'll have some tecan,' Gilmour said. 'Make a big pot this morning. I'll deal with the fire.' With a wave of his hand he moved several logs from a nearby stack into the fire-pit Garec had dug the previous night and set it alight with a gesture. The flames warmed and woodsmoke curled up and around his face in a gentle caress. For once, he really didn't know what to do – and he realised how much he missed Steven. 'How many minutes now?' he asked Garec.

'Four mimits, momets, whatever you called them.' Garec approached from across the campsite, a silent Mark Jenkins in tow. 'Ah, great fire, Gilmour. I wish you would teach me that one.'

He had no idea how much that stung. Gilmour turned towards the fjord, ostensibly to peer across the water, to keep the others from reading the insecurity in his face. 'Perhaps I will one day, Garec, but for now, I think I'll get the far portal ready,' he said.

Garec filled the tecan pot with water from a wineskin. 'I'll let you know when to open it.' He turned his attention to Mark. 'How are you this morning?'

'Can we do it today?' Mark didn't look up from the fire.

Garec shrugged despondently. 'I suppose today is as good a day as any.'

'Good.' Mark reached both palms towards the flames. 'What kind of wood do I need to find?'

'Several types will work just fine. I use rosewood. The grain is tight, very strong. But mahogany and walnut are excellent as well.' Garec stirred the tecan with a twig. 'The trick is not so much in selecting the right wood but rather in shaping the bow. You need a relatively thin length of wood from a thick green branch.'

'You shave away the outer layers?' Mark made eye contact with him for the first time in days.

'Lots of them. The best bows take a great deal of time to shape, because the most resilient, flexible wood is the core. The thicker and greener the branch, the more pliable and strong its core will be.' He gestured towards the twin hills in the east. 'When we get up in those woods later today, I'll show you what I mean.'

'I think I understand.' Mark reached over and took the twig from Garec. He stirred the tecan as Garec had done, then looked at Gilmour. 'You ought to check the time.'

Garec grinned. It warmed his heart to see Mark taking back control: the foreigner was a self-proclaimed expert on *frenchroastcoffee* and regularly criticised the others' tecan-making attempts. Although Garec had no idea what *frenchroastcoffee* was, he assumed being an expert had given Mark some deep insight into how to prepare the perfect pot of tecan. Either way, he was excited to see Mark moving back into one of his old roles. Taking over the morning tecan duties was a small step, but in the right direction.

He checked Steven's watch and called, 'Five clocks, Gilmour. Open it.'

Four minutes later, as the trio stood around the fire watching dawn over the fjord, Steven Taylor appeared beside the far portal. 'Hello, boys. Any tecan left?'

'Great rutters!' Gilmour shouted, spilling his drink down his tunic. He scurried over to clasp Steven in a bear-hug. Garec followed, while Mark knelt to close the far portal with the twig he was still holding.

'What happened to you?' Gilmour asked, holding Steven at arm's length and checking the lacerations on his head and the burn on his cheek. 'Are you badly hurt?'

'No. I'm fine – quite a journey, though.' He looked around, as if to check they were alone, then continued, 'But you were wrong, Gilmour. Nerak followed me; he pinpointed my cross-over spot even with the Colorado portal closed.'

Gilmour winced and nodded towards the leather book in the boat. 'I'm not surprised, Steven, but I'm sorry. And you're right; I think I underestimated a number of things about Nerak. The fact that he was able to follow you through the weaker portal may be just the beginning of a long list of surprises he has in store for us. But tell us – did you find it?' The three men were hanging on Steven's every word now. 'You managed to get back to the far portal, but Lessek's key?'

Steven reached into the backpack pocket. 'Rest easy: I did.'

There was an almost tangible exhalation of relief as he held it out, then Gilmour blanched and waved it away. 'No, no – uh, you hang onto it.' The book had just lashed out at him; the key was likely to kill him on the spot. *That was naught but the tiniest of tastes, Fantus, drawn from the very furthest reaches of my power.*

'All right,' Steven agreed, 'I'll keep it here.' He tucked the stone into the pocket of his coat, then, slapping Mark's shoulder, said, 'I brought you a few things, partner. Let me get a cup of that tecan, then I can show you what I picked up on my little vacation.' Steven didn't notice Mark's grim features as he walked to the fire, then looked around and asked, 'Hey – where's Brynne?'

Nerak took the first person he found, an elderly woman out walking her dog, an irritating Bijon with pink-rimmed eyes and an expensive coiffeur. The portal was closed, and the beacon he had followed was silent. The dark prince slammed into the old woman's body, killing her instantly as he demanded, 'Where does Sorenson live, Hannah Sorenson?'

The old woman had nothing in her memory to give Nerak any additional information. He dug deeper. 'Meyers Antiques? What do you know of Meyers Antiques?'

Dietrich Meyers. He came from Austria. Owned the store over on

Broadway. Died last year. It was closed up now. He seemed friendly enough. His wife used to make strudel before she died a long time ago – maybe fifteen years ago. I bought a tea set there once back in the 1970s, a nice floral, something British. Jeffrey broke two cups one morning, and I boxed it up. Ah, but that boy was a wrecking crew.

Nothing. Nerak cursed and left in a rush, ignoring the yammering of the wretched little animal as the woman's stout body fell in a rumpled heap, her thigh-length support hose exposed as the heavy folds of her wool skirt bunched above her puckered knees.

His next victim was a high school student, in the neighbourhood to catch an art film at a nearby theatre.

Nothing; a waste of time. Nerak left the boy's body slumped on a bus stop bench, an ad for a massage clinic showing behind the young man's varsity letter jacket.

A bartender on break, smoking a cigarette out behind a Broadway Avenue tavern, followed. 'Where does Hannah Sorenson live?' he asked the dead man's memories.

Hannah. Pretty girl. Great rack. Saw them once when she leaned over to tie her shoes. Drinks beer, sometimes has wine with her mother. They were working the sale at the old man's antiques store after he died. She lives over on Grant. Someplace near First.

He had it. First and Grant. The bartender filled in the blanks: two blocks over and one block down. Nerak enjoyed a final drag on the cigarette before allowing the bartender's body to collapse beside the tavern's loading dock, the wound on his wrist still wet.

At the corner of First and Grant, Nerak took a well-dressed woman, a financial analyst. She was home from work and taking out the rubbish, the only person outside in the street. Nerak had his answers almost before the woman died.

Jennifer and Hannah. They live right across the street. Three houses down. Tragic the way that girl disappeared. Her mother has never been the same. Used to be very cheerful, but losing her father and her daughter in the same year—

Nerak interrupted the dead woman's soliloquy: he had everything he needed for now: Jennifer Sorenson was Hannah's mother. So that's where Steven went. She'll have the portal.

He cast his thoughts ahead to examine the inside of the house. No one there. Not surprising; she would already be gone. Steven was reckless and overconfident, but he had not yet proven himself stupid.

'Where have you gone, Jennifer Sorenson?' Nerak asked out loud.

'Perhaps a bit of time in your house will help me track you down.'
He laughed, the sound of a soul in Hell. As he climbed the stairs
to Jennifer's front door he wondered if his latest victim was a fan
of *Confederate Son* chewing tobacco. 'We must introduce you,' he
promised the hapless body.

Jennifer flipped on the indicator and hoped that being lost in the
anonymity of the five o'clock rush hour would offer some protection
from the creature hunting her. As the radio DJs cracked jokes about
politics and religion, weight loss and divorce, she moved into the
centre lane, strangers' cars surrounding her on all sides and creating
a living barrier to protect her from Steven Taylor's demon.

She tried to decide where to go. Someplace no one would expect
her to be, that's what Steven had said, somewhere no one would
think of finding her, because apparently, Nerak had the ability to
read minds.

Jennifer had enough money to live comfortably for some time,
even if that meant staying in hotels. She had stashed a lot of cash
from the liquidation sale at Meyers Antiques in the metal strongbox
down in the basement, though she wasn't sure what she had planned
to do with the money. The cheques and credit card receipts were all
deposited at the bank, but she still had thousands of dollars tucked
inside her tote bag. Jennifer had been feeling a little guilty about
her taxes, but that was gone now: if the IRS knew the cash was to
save lives, her own life, her daughter's, and perhaps to help keep
the country safe from an evil force with the ability to tear the fabric
of the world apart, they might not mind if she kept a few dollars.
Or, if they did, maybe they would make arrangements for her to
have a corner cell, something with a view. Jennifer smiled. Being in
traffic *was* good; it was helping. As her thoughts cleared, she made
a decision.

With the Friday night ski traffic and a forest fire closing several
lanes in Idaho Springs, it would be hours before she reached
Silverthorn. She nestled herself back into the protective centre lane
and thought that another six or seven hours of traffic would be fine
with her.

'The forest of what?' Hannah spat a mouthful of tecan into the fire.
The brown liquid sizzled into steam. 'You can't be serious. There has
to be another way through.'

'Not one that isn't guarded by Malakasians,' Hoyt explained.

'They don't bother with this particular pass because no one would dare come that way.'

'Except us.'

'Well, yes, there is that, but it will get us into Malakasia without them knowing.' He tossed her an apple he had stolen from an orchard that morning. 'And we may get right through the forest without incident.'

'You don't sound convinced, Hoyt.' Hannah sounded sceptical. '*The forest of ghosts*, good Christ. All right. Um, what happens in the forest of ghosts? Do we meet Casper and the hitchhikers from the Haunted Mansion, or is there something else?'

Alen said, 'You misunderstand, Hannah. There are no *ghosts* in the forest of ghosts.'

'No ghosts in the forest of ghosts?'

'Only those we bring with us.'

'All right then, Churn, remind me not to bring any ghosts into the forest of ghosts. I want to go in alone and come out the other side entirely ghost-free. Can you help with a periodic reminder between now and then?' Hannah's sarcasm was not lost on the big mute, and Churn grunted a laugh. 'Thanks, Churn – or am I correct in assuming it's not that easy?'

'Uh, no,' Hoyt answered.

'The forest of ghosts is an enchanted place along a narrow stretch of foothills south of the Great Pragan Range, the mountains separating us from Malakasia,' Alen broke in. 'No one knows how or when the forest developed its curious power, but many travellers have been lost so now no one wanders through there on purpose.' His words carried a sense of finality that made Hannah shiver.

'What does it do?' she pressed.

'To some, nothing, but to others, it ensnares their minds, trapping them with memories of times in their lives – good times, bad times; no one knows really, because so few have experienced the visions and lived to reach the other side. Of those who have survived, the stories are always the same: they were trapped by the enchanter or the spirit of the place, and shown visions of their lives, pictures of essential moments that had led up to this journey. They always had some ambition or great goal ...'

'And if I'm just out for a morning jog, it will leave me alone?' Hannah considered the forest's curious nature. 'Why would it only target those pursuing lifelong goals?'

Alen went on, 'Because it feeds on the lies we tell ourselves to soften the blow of our memories. Maybe it grows stronger every time it keeps one of us from reaching our potential or fulfilling a dream. If it can show us the mistakes we have made, the lies – however small or infrequent – we have told ourselves or others to get to this moment, then it can trip us, perhaps convince us to give up – or worse.'

'Worse?'

'To stay,' Hoyt said. 'We can't be sure, but the forest may convince some travellers to wait there, reliving the same images from their past again and again until they succumb to hunger or thirst, completely oblivious to the fact that their lives are draining away while they re-enact some bygone moment.'

'How does it know if we are pursuing something so emotionally important?' Hannah was trying to find a flaw, a loophole through which she might slip without the forest's detection.

'I don't know,' Alen said simply. 'Somehow it reads our dreams. It knows if we are chasing down the last stages of something in which we have invested our passion.'

'So, of the four of us, who is in trouble?' Hannah asked.

'I certainly am,' Alen replied. 'Churn is also pursuing a lifelong desire for vengeance.'

Hannah gave the quiet giant a compassionate look; she could not imagine how he had suffered. The mute hadn't hesitated when Alen told them they would have to make their way inside Welstar Palace to send her back to Colorado. Hoyt was convinced that Churn had been tortured, forced to watch his family die, and then beaten nearly to death before managing to escape. The Pragan healer had found Churn still strapped to several pine planks, as if the big man had torn down a wall to free himself.

Alen added, 'And you, Hannah.'

My life's work? This? Nonsense. Hannah envisioned the faculty at the law school, cowled in black at last spring's graduation ceremony. 'This isn't my life's work. I'm not reaching any lifelong goals here. I just want out of this place. Granted, I would like to find Steven first, but if he is trying to get home as well, we may find him somewhere between here and there.'

'Not necessarily your life's work, Hannah,' Hoyt rejoined the conversation, 'but something in which you have invested your passion. This journey represents the most important thing you have done in – I don't know – how long?'

'Fine, okay, a long time, *years* even.' She used the English word to capture the depths of her anxiety. 'But don't you think the forest will – well, figure out that I'm just along because there is no other way for me to go?' She was embarrassed at being so selfish and so terrified out loud.

Thankfully, none of her companions appeared willing to judge her for her insecurity: all three had seen and experienced horrifying things in their past; each knew fear. The fact that Hannah was trying to find a way to avoid the forest of ghosts was a perfectly normal response.

Alen said, 'I'm afraid not, Hannah. If the forest behaves true to form, you will not pass freely.'

'Great. That's just frigging great.' Hannah stood and began walking back and forth between the fire and a gnarled oak from which she had hacked Churn a longer riding cane that morning. Searching her past, she tried to decide which images the forest of ghosts would use against her. *Might it be something wonderful?* she thought, *Meeting Steven? Feeling the power of those emotions?* She did not wish to remain trapped in the forest for the rest of her life, but if she had to relive something from the past, that would be her first choice. *Oh shit, though, what if it's something ugly?* Hannah considered the other side of the metaphysical coin. *I've got a lot of dirty laundry in there, too. Damn it!*

A thought suddenly occurred to her. 'Hey, what about Hoyt? How does he get off without having to wrestle one of these – whatever they are?'

'I may not,' Hoyt admitted. 'I may get in there and discover that I am as susceptible as you or Alen. But if we go by the legends, I ought to be able to move through unhindered.'

'Because you don't have anything invested in this little journey?' Hannah challenged.

'It is not my life's work, no.' Hoyt said, looking down at his boots to avoid eye contact with her.

'Well, Hoyt, it must be nice for once to be an outsider, huh? To be on the fringes of things that matter? Slash and burn, run and hide? Convenient, isn't it? Well, let's hope you're right about this place.' Hannah sounded furious, but without Hoyt she would still be pacing the hill overlooking Southport Harbour. Instead, pacing the camp, she wrung her hands in a frustrated gesture that said, *I am helpless, again. I have to give away control, again, and I am sick to death of it.* She kicked at a loose stone. 'All right, fine. Let's get going. If there is no other way in, we don't have a choice. Do we?'

Hoyt shrugged. 'No. If even one Malakasian soldier, some scout hiding in the brush above a mountain pass, sent word ahead that we were riding north, we would be stopped, interrogated, arrested – who knows what?'

'What about those towns you mentioned in the east?'

'Averil and Landry – we could try, but Churn and I have a reputation there. We've met some of the underground fighters, but it's been too long since our last visit to know whom we can still trust and who would sell us out to the nearest platoon lieutenant. It's too great a risk. Even if we utilised the network of thieves and spies at work between the border cities, we might get stopped on the street or the highway into town. That area is thick with Malakasians.'

'So, instead of sneaking in and maybe fighting a squad or two, we are going to butt heads with the supernatural?'

'We do have Alen,' Hoyt said. 'With his help, we should be able to link ourselves together using ropes, our horse bridles, anything, and walk right through.' Hoyt was irritated at how meek this response sounded, and he suddenly wanted to be gone, anywhere but there, trying to justify a potentially deadly risk the others had to take. Somehow he knew already that he would not have any difficulty crossing through the forest. They didn't want to go, especially Hannah, but here he was, the one taking essentially no risk, trying to convince her to dive in and trust a thief to see her through.

'So you'll lead us, and while leading us you'll listen in as we relive the most critical and emotionally impacting moments of our lives? The most devastating or wonderful times we have ever known? Do you really want to hear all that?'

Hoyt turned away, blushing. 'It might not be *those* memories, Hannah. It might be something horrible, and I promise you when we make it to the other side, I will drink myself into oblivion, until the whole ordeal is wiped from my memory.'

Suddenly serious once again, Hannah said, 'I wouldn't want to be you, Hoyt. I don't want to be me going through there, but having to haul us along while we fall apart? No thanks.'

'Come along, everyone,' Alen said, 'we'll never know if we don't get there.'

THE FJORD CAMP

Garec gnawed thoughtfully on one of the bars Steven had taken from Howard's kitchen. He turned it over in his fingers, looking at it sceptically. 'Why wouldn't they make them in the shape of something familiar?' He tried another bite. 'This doesn't look like anything that grows naturally – well, almost anything.'

'People are used to eating things that don't occur naturally where we come from, so the shape doesn't bother us.' Steven paused to consider the cylindrical brown morsel Garec twirled like a miniature baton. 'Although now that you mention it, it doesn't look very appetising, does it?'

Despite Garec's attempt at levity, the mood was grim. Mark told Steven of the *Prince Marek*'s destruction and of their subsequent failure to find Brynne among the floating wreckage. He had paused several times while telling the tale, but had refused to cry. When he finished, Steven had not known what to say, but looking into his old friend's eyes, he realised Mark had lost something vital; something had been extinguished inside him, leaving the dry vestiges of Mark Jenkins. No longer the fun-loving sceptic, Mark had shifted into the shadows. For the first time in his life, Steven feared his roommate. There would be no holding him back now; he would be an unchained force, running full-speed into Sandcliff, into Welstar Palace, wherever. Already he looked prepped for battle: his belt tightened snugly against his hips, a hunting knife, a short dagger and a new battle-axe strapped within easy reach of either hand. Mark, who had once joked about hacking off limbs, was ready to do just that. At that moment Steven profoundly regretted ever having found the key to William Higgins' safe-deposit box.

He passed out a few of the items he had managed to buy or steal on his journey across the country. Garec was especially excited at the idea of Colorado beer and had already placed the cans in the fjord to cool. Gilmour, thrilled to have Howard's American Civil War book, planned to check into an Orindale inn, bolt the door and steep himself in Gettysburg as soon as the Fold was closed for ever. As he paged through it absentmindedly, he pondered Steven's story; he was especially interested in how Steven had located the far portal and Lessek's key.

Pocketing the lighter, he asked Steven, 'So are you saying you could feel the staff's magic there in Idaho Springs?'

'I think it was the portal, or maybe the key,' Steven answered. 'I had been going so fast for so long – in such a hurry to get back. When I discovered that our house had burned down—' Steven glanced over at Mark, 'sorry about that, by the way—'

'It doesn't matter,' Mark said, emotionless. 'Go on, please.'

'Well, anyway – when I learned that our house had burned down, I figured Nerak had done it. He had beaten me there and had destroyed everything.' Steven looked across the fjord, allowing the images to take shape in his mind's eye. 'But he hadn't. The house had been gone for a while, long enough for them to come in and bulldoze the lot. There had been time for some real estate agent to put the land up for sale. So I figured the portal and the key must have been hauled up to the city landfill and dumped.'

'And that's where you felt the staff?' Garec pressed.

'It was more than just there. I guess it happened a few times along the way, but maybe it was my memory, you know, like muscle memory. Maybe I felt I needed the magic, and my body wanted to believe it was there.'

Gilmour nodded.

Steven rubbed his chin. He needed a shave again. 'Anyway, whatever it was, at the city dump, I felt the magic. It took me. I needed it, and it came in a blast. I think it came from the key. I can't be sure, but it did knock me down twice.'

'Why the key?' Gilmour leaned forward, his brow furrowed.

'Because the portal was still a good quarter of a mile away.' Steven saw Garec frown and added, 'About four hundred paces – and the key was right there, just a few paces away at the time.'

'How did it happen?' Mark joined the interrogation, suddenly interested.

Steven chuckled. 'I hit a speed bump, the same one, twice.'

Garec tried the words together, 'Speed bump?'

'Right. And who would have thought there would be speed bumps at the landfill? I mean, who goes in there but guys in pick-ups and big town dumper-trucks? Are there really enough pedestrians that they need speed bumps?'

'But it slowed you down just enough?'

'Knocked me down is more like it, and when I stood up, everything had changed. I knew right where to find the portal – and the key.'

Sensing something, Gilmour asked, 'But that wasn't all, was it?'

'No.' Steven kept his eyes on the fjord. 'I saw more than I expected. It was the Fold. It had to be.'

'And?'

'And there were rips in it, tears, like you would tear open a paper sack or the wrapping of a present – three tears.'

Gilmour ran a palm across his ribs, a gesture he had repeated several times that morning. He reached inside his tunic, withdrew his pipe and used Mikelson's lighter to ignite a leafy mound of Falkan tobacco.

'Great lords, but that's a handy device.' Garec was impressed.

Mark said, 'You should see some of the nonsensical toys we've invented, Garec. It would have your head spinning.'

'Speaking of which—' Steven tossed Mark the roast beef sandwich from his pocket.

Finally Mark perked up. 'Ah, thank you,' he said, heartfelt, and fumbled with the plastic wrapping. 'What kind is it?'

'Roast beef with mayo on wheat. It was all Howard had in his kitchen – well, all that looked safe enough to eat.'

'Thank you,' Mark repeated, and finally grinned. 'Try this, Garec.' He slashed the sandwich in two, offered half to Garec and gestured with the other half towards Gilmour.

'No thanks, Mark,' Gilmour indicated his pipe with a shrug. 'Anyway, Steven, these tears you saw – was anything moving through them?'

'No, and the funny thing about them is that I think I put them there – at least, at the time I was convinced I put them there.'

'You?' Garec took a bite of the sandwich and exclaimed, 'Great leaping whores! This is the best thing I've eaten in ten Twinmoons! Say again what it's called?'

'Roast beef with mayo. Mayonnaise.' Steven was amused.

'Roast beef with mayo. Gilmour, we have to learn to make mayo.' Garec wiped off a smear with his finger and licked it. He gave a moan of satisfaction. 'Great rutters—'

Smiling, Gilmour went back to the subject. 'How could you have created tears in the Fold?'

'That's just it, Gilmour. I don't know that I did, but I think I could have, or maybe – maybe it was perfectly all right with me that they were there, as if it didn't matter.'

'And you say there were three?'

'Three. Oblong, and standing on end, like narrow entrances to a tunnel or roughly hewn doorways, and when they disappeared – or rather, when I let them go – I knew right where to find the key and the portal.'

'And the magic came from inside you?'

'I don't know,' Steven said, matter-of-factly. 'I don't think so. Why would it? The staff was here, and I didn't have the key yet.' He looked across at the hickory staff leaning against the small sailboat. 'So I suppose the magic was the key. It had hit me hard in the knees, twice, so I wasn't feeling much of anything except pain – but when I reached out, I felt as though I could grab the air, as if it was there for me to take. That was when I saw the rips. They materialised in front of me, right where the big centre hill at the dump had been, but where the magic came from isn't actually as important as what began to take shape in my mind.'

'What's that?' Mark swallowed the last of the sandwich.

'That we can keep evil trapped inside the Fold.'

'How?' Gilmour looked bemused.

'By controlling the Fold itself.'

Garec laughed. 'Oh, of course. I thought you were going to suggest something difficult.'

'No, listen. The Fold is not the enemy, the Fold exists; if evil is trapped inside, and evil is our ultimate enemy, then our goal can only be to keep evil inside for ever. Gilmour, you said that the Fold is the absence of perception and therefore the absence of reality. So it's the place between what is real and what is unreal, the space separating expectations from actualisations. Right?'

'That's how I think of it in my mind, yes.' Gilmour wasn't sure yet about Steven trying to make his definition of the Fold into a tangible, controllable reality. 'But that doesn't make it any easier to grasp.'

'Yes it does.' Steven seemed convinced.

'Again, you have me on cloakpins, Steven. How?'

'Because if it exists and if we can conceptualise it accurately and if we can reach it via the spell table,' Steven withdrew Lessek's key and held it aloft between two fingers, 'then we can seal it, not by closing the door that the Larion Senate and Nerak and a handful of other travellers have used over the ages, but rather by building a wall around it, a box around it, a—' Steven laughed, '—a safe-deposit box for the whole frigging thing.'

'Steven, you're mixing two kinds of thinking,' Mark protested. 'You can't muddle the tangible and the intangible that way. You're creating a philosophical paradox. It won't work.'

'It *will* work. Everything can make sense if we take time to learn enough about it, about what it values, about what motivates it, about where it came from and why.' He searched their camp for an example. 'Look. Over there, that rock. Now, we all agree it's a rock, right?'

The others nodded, curious.

'We all agree it's a rock, but let's assume Garec is a masonry worker, and I am a geologist, and Mark is a miner, and Gilmour, you are a sculptor.'

'Wait – I see what you mean,' Garec interrupted, excitedly.

'We all might see it a bit differently, but no matter how hard we try, it will always be a rock. Whether it's a snapshot of Eldarni history, a valuable ore, a cornerstone for a public library, or even a beautiful three-dimensional realisation of a bird in flight, it's still just a rock. There is no way, even using all our will, that we can make that rock a fish, or a grizzly bear – or a roast beef sandwich.'

Gilmour, looking interested, said, 'So if I'm understanding your thinking: if we can understand the Fold, however intangible it may be, then we can – what?'

'Anything we want. We can paint the damned thing yellow if you want to,' Steven said. 'Don't you see? There is *no* paradox. We can do whatever we want to the Fold, if we are careful and thorough in developing our understanding of exactly what it is and how it works.'

Garec felt the rug come out from under them. 'How do we do that?'

'We need to know what Lessek knew. He found it, called it a pinprick in the universe. That's fine. Whatever. But he found it, and he knew how to get to it, how to arrive at that place where he could reach out and grab it – like the air at the city dump. It was no different than it had ever been, but I held it in my hands, pressed against it and moved it around.' He looked in turn at each of them. 'That's what we have to do.'

Gilmour slipped a hand back inside his tunic. Although his ribs no longer hurt, he could feel where he had mended them. *Only hurts when I breathe!* The three friends followed his gaze to where the leather-bound book of Lessek's spells lay waiting for him to come and try again.

'Once we know what Lessek knew, what will we use?' Garec broke the silence, making Gilmour jump visibly. 'The staff? That book?'

Steven replied, 'That remains to be determined, Garec, but at this point, I am fairly confident we will use compassion—'

Mark looked down, his head shaking.

'—magic—'

'And?'

'—and maths.' Steven gave him an amiable slap across the back. 'Mathematics, Garec.'

Garec went off in search of more wood, and Gilmour stood alone, ankle-deep in the fjord, enjoying a pipe and wrestling with his thoughts. They had made the decision to remain there another night, for they had talked until late in the day. Steven had put up a halfhearted fight when Mark told him where they were – he had assumed his friends were already in Praga, not well on their way to Sandcliff Palace. He had argued – for a few moments – then given in gracefully; much as he hated it, he knew that getting to Sandcliff as quickly as possible was more important than finding Hannah. He had known it when he told Jennifer Sorenson to wait two months before bothering to open the far portal again; it would most likely be even longer before he was reunited with Hannah.

Steven and Mark sat together near the fire, alone together for the first time that day.

'I'm sorry,' Steven said, leaning against a fallen log and staring into the flames of the campfire.

'For Brynne? Don't be. It wasn't your fault. She was over the stern rail and halfway to safety before she decided to climb back up.' Mark took a long swallow from one of the beer cans. 'She made her own decisions.'

'It's more than that.' Steven said. 'I'm sorry for the whole thing, for this whole mess. I never apologised to you. I ruined your life. Everyone thinks we're lying dead up there on Decatur Peak. I'm sure they've filled your job – hell, I might even have been responsible for the damned school burning down yesterday.'

'The students will hold a parade in your honour. You'll be the graduation speaker next spring.' Mark had been reading the newspaper articles Steven stole from Howard's refrigerator. Many had been ruined when Steven dived into Clear Creek, but enough had survived to give Mark a sense of the extent of the rescue and recovery efforts on the mountain trail west of town.

'I'm serious.' Steven tried to make eye contact; Mark avoided looking at him.

'It doesn't matter, Steven. I mean, I appreciate you saying it, but we are here. This is who we are and what we have to do with ourselves now. This is much bigger than being a high school teacher or a banker. These people need you and that staff. They need you here thinking the way you were thinking today, figuring things out, deciphering the magic to get the job done.' He finished the beer and tossed the can over his shoulder into the sailboat. 'You have nothing to be sorry for.'

'What about you?'

'I'm figuring out my role.'

'What does that mean?'

'It means until something better comes along, I am going to kill. I am going to learn to fight, to shoot and to defend myself, and I am going to kill them, one at a time until—'

'Until Brynne comes back?' Steven challenged.

'Maybe. Or maybe I'll just do it until one of them sends me along after her.' He reached for another beer. 'Either way, I don't care.'

'But there is something else bothering you, I see it now. I saw it before, long before Brynne— before she disappeared.' This was risky; Steven understood he was putting their friendship in jeopardy by pushing Mark along this emotional razor-high-wire. 'Isn't there?'

'Actually, you're right,' Mark said.

Steven was a little shocked – he had expected more resistance.

Mark refolded an article from the *Denver Post* and tucked it into the pocket of his new coat. 'I've been trying to work through something, and it's still bothering me. Do me a favour, give me Lessek's key.'

'What?' Steven was taken aback by the curious request, but didn't hesitate. 'Sure. Here it is.' He tossed the stone across to Mark who caught it in one hand. Neither noticed Gilmour turn to eavesdrop.

Mark closed his fist over the stone and went on, 'You know, I never touched this that night in our house, but when you opened that box, I experienced something strange.' He furrowed his brow, trying to remember exactly how the evening had unfolded. 'It's weird, and the only way I can explain it is like this: when I was a kid I had strange sleeping habits: I'd just pass out – the couch, the floor, wherever. So rather than try to lug me upstairs to my room, my mother would throw a blanket over me and leave me there. I never really woke up, but I could always sense when she'd covered me up. Do you know what I mean?'

Steven grunted in response; he didn't want to derail Mark's thoughts by interrupting at this point.

'Well, that night when you opened the box, that's what I felt: a warm sensation, like someone reached into our apartment and draped some old blanket over me.' He laughed, grimly. 'I know this isn't making sense, but bear with me. I'd been drinking, so at the time I dismissed it – I was just drunk, or stupid, or needing to pee, whatever.'

'But it came again?'

'When I came through onto that beach in Estrad, I was out of my mind. I thought I was going to lose it – and you know what happened?'

'Someone draped a blanket over you?' Steven felt gooseflesh rise up on his forearms.

'I remembered being a kid, out at the beach, Jones Beach, on the island. I was in Eldarn less than five goddamned minutes, losing it, going full-on screwball crazy, and all of a sudden, I got a reprieve.'

'What do you mean, a reprieve?'

'It wasn't permanent; before the end of the night, I did lose it, curled in a ball, crying like a child. I thought I was dead. But for about ten minutes, I was given a break – I'm sure of it. I certainly wasn't in any condition emotionally to look after myself, and someone came down to that beach and draped that old blanket over me.'

'Lessek.'

'And *Bingo!* You've won it all – the new car, the trip to Paris, and the showroom full of beautiful prizes,' Mark said with mock game-show enthusiasm.

'Holy shit.' Steven was stunned.

'You took the words right out of my mouth, cousin.' Mark drained his beer and leaned back against the log, shoulder to shoulder with his roommate.

'So what does it mean?' Steven pressed.

'I don't know, but I'm pretty sure I'm supposed to be remembering something about some afternoon out at Jones Beach with my family – something about my dad, I think – but our days at the beach were pretty much the same. The only thing I've managed to cling to is a

Red Sox-Yankees game, the night before, and the Sox won on some late-inning feat by Karl Yazstremski.'

'And your dad was pissed off about it?'

'Hell no, you know my father. He'd gladly go to his grave before supporting the "great scourge of the boroughs" – no, it's not that: he's a Sox fan, no matter that he took all kinds of shit for it at work all his life. The game isn't all of it, though: I think it's just a point of reference for me to get the day right.'

Steven pulled one of the saddlebags over and rummaged around for something to eat. Finding a block of cheese, he broke off a chunk and offered the rest to Mark. 'So what else do you remember?'

'Dad had a cooler full of beer and a couple of sandwiches. He wore a madras bathing suit, something he had bought back in the '60s, I'm sure, and he carried my mother's old yellow beach umbrella out there and stabbed it into the sand like Neil Armstrong claiming the moon for Earth.'

'How do you remember so many details? That was so long ago – how old were you? Six? Eight?' Mark's memory astounded Steven.

'I remember so much because I've relived it so often since we came across the Fold. It happened that night on the beach in Estrad. It came again in the cavern the night before we fought those bone-collector things—'

Steven shuddered. Mark had saved his life that day, swimming to the bottom of a subterranean lake to wrench his body from where it was trapped beneath the carcase of a dead monster.

'It came again today when you stepped through the far portal with the key in your pocket,' Mark continued. 'It was just like the other times – and it's happening right now as I sit here, touching Lessek's key: It's as though I'm there – as if part of my mind is there – reliving that day on the beach with my family.'

'So he's trying to tell you something. If you'd come up Seer's Peak, he would have visited you there.'

'Maybe, but if I'm right, he has already visited me, dropping a warm blanket on me that night in Estrad. He didn't need to see me at Seer's Peak: he needs me to figure out what the hell he meant by hauling me all the way back to Long Island twenty-five years ago.'

'Well?' Steven could barely contain his excitement.

'Well what?'

'So?'

'So what?'

'So, you've played it over and over again in your mind. You have the key right now. Talk it out. What looks strange? What are you not seeing that you're supposed to see?'

'If we ever get through this, Steven, please remind me to beat the shit out of you,' Mark said, amused.

'Why?'

'Don't you think I've done that? Don't you think I'm doing that now?'

'Well?'

'Christ. Don't start that again.' Now he *was* getting irritated.

'Tell me what you see.'

Mark closed his eyes and began to speak.

'Have you ever been to my parents' house?'

The question surprised Steven. He drew a blank for a moment, then said, 'Um – yeah – that night after the Mets game at Shea, remember? We decided not to fight the traffic back into the city.'

'You know that hallway that leads down to my sister's bedroom, across from my parents' room?'

Steven cast his thoughts back in time and visualised the house. 'Okay, right. What about it?'

'Things begin there—' Mark shook his head in frustration, 'no, that's not right. I guess I should say these visions, memories – they begin there.'

'In the hall?'

'Yep.' Mark reached out with one hand and gestured into the air above the fire. 'My dad comes down that hall. He has on that old madras bathing suit and a T-shirt from a deli in Amityville, something he got for playing softball one weekend, I think. Anyway, he doesn't come out of his room, and he's not coming out of Kim's room. He's just there, in the hallway until he turns and moves towards me.'

'What happens then?'

'Then we're outside. I'm helping him load everything into the back of the old station wagon.' Mark grinned and opened his eyes for a moment. 'I can't believe my mother ever drove around in that monster. I know time tends to exaggerate our recollection of things, but that old car must have been forty feet long; it was a beached whale. She couldn't have been getting more than three or four hundred feet to a gallon.'

Steven laughed. 'Well, gas was cheaper back then! But go on, what's significant about loading up the car?'

'Nothing. That's what's so damned frustrating. I can't think of anything. From the house, we'd go out onto route 27, take that west to the Meadowbrook Parkway, and from there, it was just a few miles out to Jones Beach.'

'Think about more of the details,' Steven urged. 'Slow things down. Take your time. What does it smell like, look like?'

Mark leaned back against the fallen log and closed his eyes. Just when Steven thought he would have to prod him awake, Mark said, 'The pavement was always hot, but I would leave my shoes in the car. My mom invariably yelled at me about it; she didn't want me cutting my feet on broken glass or getting splinters from the plank walkway.'

He looked at Steven. 'Jones Beach has this scrubby pine forest that runs along the north edge of the sand. I suppose, thinking about it now, it's a curious juxtaposition, pines and sand that way, but growing up out there, I never thought about it.' He closed his eyes again, took a sip from his beer and went on, 'I hated getting sand in my shoes and socks, so I'd leave them in the back of the whale, make the dash across the macadam – that was like running across molten rock – and leap for the relative safety of the plank walkway. By the time we went home, late afternoon, it never bothered me to walk back to the car.'

'This is better. Keep going like this,' Steven said encouragingly. 'What did your parents do? Were they fighting about anything? Disagreeing? How do you remember them?'

'Mom was always dealing with Kim and the food. Dad dealt with the umbrella and his chair. After that, I'm not sure they ever had much to say to each other at all – I remember them holding hands sometimes, even hugging out in the surf, but I don't remember them chatting on and on all day. Mom played with me and Kim – trying to keep us occupied underneath the umbrella, I guess. Dad always sat and watched the planes taking off and landing at Kennedy.' Mark hesitated. 'I guess that's something strange.'

'How do you mean?'

'He faced west.'

'Doesn't the beach run west to east?'

'Right, but the water is straight south. Who goes to the beach and doesn't face the ocean?'

'Maybe your dad wanted to get the most from the sun.' Steven tossed a log onto the fire, then looked for Garec; the Ronan was taking a long time to collect firewood. He noticed Gilmour and realised the old man had been listening. Catching Steven's eye, Gilmour twirled one hand, as if to say *keep him talking*. Steven nodded almost imperceptibly and turned back to Mark, who hadn't noticed the little byplay. 'Was your dad a sun guy? Did he like to lie around in the sun?'

'Dad?' Mark grimaced. 'Never. He hated the heat. It was all we could do to get him to the beach in the first place. Mom had to promise him he could bring a cooler full of cold beer just to get him there, and we always made at least one trip up the sand for ice cream. No, Dad wasn't much for the sun.'

Mark pursed his lips, picturing his father sitting in a folding beach-chair, his long legs stretched out before him, an incongruous image among the hundreds and thousands who turned their full attention to the sea. 'He'd sit all day like that, except for when he was in the water or playing with Kim and me.' Mark closed his eyes tighter in an effort to clarify the image, to bring his memory into sharper focus. 'He always sat that way. It crossed my mind once or twice when we were coming out of the Blackstones, after I dreamed about it in the underground cavern; I thought there had to be some connection between my arrival in Eldarn, half drunk on beer arriving at the beach, and those days out at Jones Beach when I was a kid, my dad drinking beer and—'

'And facing west towards Jersey,' Steven finished Mark's thought.

'Or further,' Mark whispered.

'Say that again.'

'Further.' Mark sat up.

Steven felt the connection begin to form in his mind and he raced to keep up with it before it dissipated in the nebulous fringes of his consciousness, the nether region where so many great dreams and ideas disappeared before he could get a firm handle on them. He stood up and started piecing the fragments together. 'The hallway. I remember that hallway.'

'Right. It runs from my parents' living room down to the bedrooms at the back of the house.'

'And there are pictures, right?'

'Yup. A whole family gallery. My father calls it the Jenkins Family British Museum, a complete photo-history of our lives.' Mark was standing now as well, and Gilmour moved through the shallows towards them.

Steven made several leaps in his mind, hoping to move two or three large pieces into place; he would form the outer edges of the puzzle later. It was time to connect the guts of the thing now. 'I remember those pictures. There are lots of pictures of that trip he's always talking about.'

'Sure: it was just about the defining moment of his adult life. He had planned for months, every place he wanted to see, all the parks, all the cities. He had never really been out of New York since he had started working full-time, or since Kim and I had been born.'

'There were all kinds of shots from out west,' Steven said, 'the hills, the Loop Railroad. Didn't you go to Pikes Peak, too?'

'We were supposed to be there for a few days and we ended up staying nearly two weeks. Dad absolutely loved the place. We hiked in the national forest, we went rafting. He hauled us down to Royal Gorge. It was as though he felt the need to see the whole state, to experience it all at once, as if he thought he would never get back.' Mark slowed.

'Or that he ought to have been there all along,' Steven said. 'When you think about it, it's odd that of all the photos in that hallway – and there have to be two hundred shots up there – why are so many of them ...' As Steven hesitated, Gilmour appeared suddenly at his side.

Mark said, 'He must have taken twenty-five rolls of film in those two weeks. Everything was worthy of a picture: streams, pine trees, rock formations, Kim and me, in all manner of poses – standing astride the Continental Divide, balancing on the USGS *mile high* marker – there were so many, and he took them all with that old Instamatic. When he blew them up—' Mark stopped, seeing confusion in Gilmour's face, and added tangentially, 'Most photographs are three-by-five or four-by-six inches – in other words, small.'

'Ah – and your father enlarged a number of these photo pictures?'

Mark nodded.

'Was he unhappy with them small?'

'No, they were his favourites, the most cherished photos he had ever taken; that's why he blew them up to display them.'

Gilmour nodded, understanding, and gestured at Mark to continue.

'They were in the living room at first, but then my mother wanted to redecorate. Dad didn't want them moved, but they finally agreed on a compromise: they would stay hanging on display, but he had to move them to the hallway.'

'He loved this place, your home, Colorado?'

'He did, Gilmour,' Mark said, 'more than I have ever known him to love any place else.'

'Why did he not live there?'

'Work. Family commitments. My mom is from the island, so he wanted her to be near her family – a whole barrel of reasons, I suppose.' Mark looked more like the young man who had arrived in Eldarn; Gilmour was glad he had found a moment's peace.

'Did he ever return?' Gilmour asked, carefully.

'I went to school there.'

Ah—' Gilmour nearly leaped across the fire-pit, 'why? Tell me why you chose that place.'

'I honestly don't know,' Mark said, surprised. 'I was eighteen; I wanted to get away from New York. I thought Colorado sounded rustic, provincial, wild – a long list of things Long Island is not. But maybe it was those photos.' Mark screwed up his face, trying to come up with a completely honest answer. 'Maybe looking at them day after day, year after year, influenced me.'

Steven said, 'So you might you have chosen Colorado State because he wanted you to?'

Mark, never one for arm-chair psychology, shrugged. 'Sure. I guess. Who knows why eighteen-year-olds decide anything? But I do know that I have felt more at home in Colorado than I ever did in New York.'

Gilmour asked, 'Did it take long for those feelings to emerge?'

'About twenty minutes, Gilmour. I think it was twenty minutes.'

Garec dropped an armload of wood at their feet, interrupting the conversation. 'Twenty minutes? I know that one; it's the four rune. The four, right? The four means twenty minutes on this absurd machine.' He held up Steven's watch. 'Why you don't just put a twenty on there, I have yet to understand.'

Mark, close to understanding at last, didn't speak, but wrapped an arm around Garec's shoulders and handed him a silver beer can. Garec pondered it briefly, then looked confused.

Tilting his own can for Garec's inspection, Steven said, 'Just pull the tab.'

Mark went on, 'So if my father faced west in moments of quiet – like the beach, when he wasn't working, when he had time to rest, to think and perhaps even to—'

'To be drawn,' Steven said, not certain he had chosen the right word.

'To be drawn,' Mark echoed, 'back to where he had been so—'

'Back home,' Gilmour said.

'But my father never lived in Colorado,' Mark cried. 'That trip, and all the memories he had over the years, all the pictures and all the stories – they were just his way of – I don't know.'

'They were his way of feeling that blanket,' Gilmour said. 'If Lessek has truly communicated these memories to you, now we must figure out why. What significance does Colorado have for your father? And for you, as your true home? And, most difficult to work out, what significance does your relationship with your father have to Nerak and our struggle here in Eldarn?'

Mark's reply was cut off by a rustling sound in the woods behind them: footsteps, stealthy at first and then closing at a run. Shadows painted the forest black, and it was impossible to see how many assailants there were, but in the instant before turning to flee, Mark saw at least two large figures armed with branches. Steven dived for the hickory staff, grabbing it as he rolled over and sprang to his feet. Garec stood frozen, unwilling to pick up his bow and quivers. His eyes flashed in the firelight as he peered back and forth at Steven and the men coming for them through the woods.

Gilmour shouted 'Seron!' and raised his hands, muttering; their small campfire exploded into a towering ball of flame, so hot that Garec fell backwards across the pile of firewood he had collected. He watched as three Seron, armoured in leather vests and chain-mail, charged, barking and grunting, between the trees. In the muted glow of Gilmour's explosion, the hardwood trunks looked like upright bones. The Seron moved as if through the half-buried ribcage of a decomposing god.

The last thing Mark saw before rushing into the night was Steven standing firm and twirling the hickory staff. His flight was a knee-jerk reaction to buy a few seconds to think how they would turn back what might be an entire platoon, hell, a whole frigging brigade of the soulless monsters. He hadn't expected the attack; he wasn't ready. That wouldn't happen again.

Mark risked a look over his shoulder. Gilmour had used magic to turn their sputtering campfire into a raging inferno and by its light it was clear that there were only a few Seron, possibly scouts for a larger force. He turned and began hustling back into the fray, certain Steven and Gilmour possessed enough power to dispatch the Seron even if they had been taken by surprise attack.

He watched as Gilmour held one Seron still; the old man's hand was pressed flat against the creature's chest, and though growling and spitting at the former Larion Senator, it was immobile, clutched in the grip of Gilmour's hastily woven spell.

Steven engaged the second of their attackers, nearly as large as Lahp, in a hand-to-hand fight that reminded Mark of an old Bruce Lee movie. Steven, trying to preserve life no matter how monstrous his assailant, used a fraction of the staff's power, just enough to sting the half-human nastily with each touch – first the soldier's knee, then a shoulder, thigh, collar bone, wrist, a series of neat blows that didn't appear solid enough to hurt a child ... but Mark could see pale greenish-yellow energy crossing from the staff to the Seron's body with each impact. The Seron barked, an inhuman yelp, each time Steven landed a blow and within moments the big Malakasian had collapsed to his knees, then toppled over.

Two down.

Their third attacker had somehow escaped the net of Gilmour's immobility spell, diving and rolling at precisely the right moment. Now, still gripping his makeshift cudgel, the Seron scrambled to regain his feet. Mark followed the Seron's line of sight to where Garec had fallen. With his companions bested, the creature would have only one opportunity to kill Garec. Mark would have to act quickly; this one would be his.

'Hey, you!' he shouted – he wasn't sure if he spoke in Ronan or English; he was too furious to care.

The Seron, so intent on reaching Garec, ignored him at first, but as Mark started shouting obscenities at him he finally turned.

'Come get me, you ugly motherhumper!' Mark cried, his feet ankle-deep in the fjord. 'I'm not armed – look!' He discarded Howard's Gore-tex coat and peeled his old red sweater over his head, leaving himself bare-chested, with a thin coat of perspiration despite the cold. 'C'mon, ugly rutter!' he shouted again, jumping up and down on the balls of his feet. 'I'm right here waiting, you frigging bastard!'

The Seron remained low the ground, crouched, his eyes fixed on the raving man only a few paces away.

'Yeah, yeah, you're so tough,' Mark growled. 'Come get me, you pussy. Stop stalking around like my sister's cat and get down here.' Mark flexed his arms, not entirely convinced he had made the right decision, but too far down this path to change his mind now. 'I'm going to kill you,' he shouted, an instant before the Seron pounced.

For a fraction of a second, Mark considered standing his ground. His rage was so overwhelming that he was certain he could beat the soulless half-human in a straight fight, but something echoed in his mind, that same voice he had imagined speaking to him in the Blackstones when he had nearly frozen to death, the voice that had awakened him when he had fallen asleep at the wheel on the Long Island Expressway. 'You can't win,' it said, and with just a hair's width separating them, Mark ducked beneath the Seron's grasp and dived into the black water.

He ignored the cold and kicked hard towards the bottom, thankful the water was deep right up to the shoreline, then, once he was thirty or forty feet out, he surfaced long enough to catch his breath. The Seron was paddling diligently after him.

'I'm over here,' he shouted, splashing a handful of dark water in the Seron's direction. 'You almost had me there. I was worried, I tell you.' He let the Seron get within an arm's length before slipping beneath the surface again. This time, on his way to the bottom, Mark reversed and gripped the warrior's ankles. He gave a firm tug, not enough to drown the creature, but sufficient to pull the Seron's head beneath the surface for a moment; it sent a powerful message. Mark knew he would have to surface and tempt the soldier again, or it might make the decision to turn and flee back towards shore.

Bobbing up through the darkness, Mark called again, 'I'm over here, dummy.' He had moved further away from their camp, from Gilmour's fire he judged the distance at about seventy-five feet, not yet enough to get the job done. He listened for sounds of the Seron's breathing: laboured and quick. 'Are you getting tired? That's a lot of armour you have on. I know I'm tired, and I'm just in boots and leggings. So, you must be wearing down.'

The Seron was starting to worry; he could tell. He swam closer to the struggling warrior. 'I tell you what – why don't you take off that leather vest and your chain-mail, and we can make a real contest out of this.'

The Seron, though obviously fatigued, lashed out with a fist like a hammer.

Mark took the glancing blow on the temple and saw stars for a moment. He let his rage numb the pain. 'Good punch, old man. I actually saw the lights of Denver that time.' He swam a few paces away. 'Now go ahead. Take your time. It's all right, I'm not going anywhere.'

The Seron ripped and tore at the heavy leather vest, then slipped out of his chain-mail, allowing it to sink to the bottom of the great inland cleft. The Malakasian killer seemed energised by his new buoyancy and growled a warning at Mark.

Watching him come, Mark gave his own warning, a quiet affirmation of what he was about to do. This was no parking-lot fight, throwing a few punches until someone broke it up or the police came: this was everything he had believed could never happen to him. He had never thought he would hate in this way – yet he was about to kill this thing in cold blood.

'So be it, rutter. Come get me,' he said as he slowly backstroked into even deeper water. Gilmour's bonfire looked like a lighthouse as Mark dived deep and waited. *Let the sonofabitch wonder.* Once he was confident the Seron had dived after him several times – he wanted him struggling for breath – Mark moved with the fluid grace of an underwater hunter, slowly coming up beneath the creature's legs. He grabbed one firmly with both hands and pulled hard for the bottom, releasing the creature at about twenty feet.

He surfaced, taking deep breaths, and checked his position against Gilmour's fire. He could hear the Seron, grunting and wheezing in dismay, begin paddling back towards shore – Mark thought how curious it was that the supposedly reckless killers would cling so ardently to life when they realised they had been beaten.

'Oh no you don't,' he whispered and slipped beneath the surface once more. Three times he pulled the coughing, spitting Seron warrior down, thinking of Brynne. *I love you*, she had said, mimicking Mark's own clumsy admission. Now he was about to get some revenge, a sliver, anyway. 'Three down, and I *am* keeping score, you bastard,' he shouted.

Rage at the thought of Brynne, freezing cold and sinking beneath the waves in Orindale Harbour, warmed him. Had she called out to him, treading water as long as she could in hopes he would come paddling over to rescue her? These questions tumbled through Mark's mind as he inhaled deeply and pounced on the Seron's back. Down and down they spiralled, the creature fighting furiously, but Mark wrapped his arms around the Seron's neck and took the blows until he felt the Malakasian stiffen, then go entirely limp.

Mark couldn't see in the black depths of the fjord, but he felt the body bob towards the surface for a moment, then, trapped by the cold and pressure of nearly fifty feet of water, spiral lazily towards the bottom.

He swam towards the shore and pulled himself onto land, his

body trembling with cold as reaction set in. Blood ran from his nose, and one eye was beginning to swell. He didn't speak as he strode across their camp, past the comforting warmth of Gilmour's fire to the little catboat he had stolen and rigged for their trip along the Ravenian Sea. He reached beneath his pack and withdrew the double-bladed battle-axe he had found in Orindale. He crossed back to where Garec was binding the Seron's wrists and ankles, ignoring Garec when he asked, 'Are you all right, Mark?'

Gilmour whispered, 'Don't.'

It was too late.

Mark hacked viciously into the first prisoner's neck. Blood splashed from the wound, dousing him. He took the second Seron while Gilmour was reaching out at him, but the spell on the old man's lips was a moment too late. Mark left the axe embedded in the Seron warrior's skull.

Mark barely heard his friends shouting. As he stumbled towards the fire, he was backlit by flames: a homicidal lunatic on a killing spree. Then Gilmour's spell wrapped around him and he collapsed into the dirt beside the fire.

'Do you like snow peas?'

'What? I'm sorry. What?' Jennifer jumped, startled. 'What did you say?' She turned to find the store manager standing beside her.

'I asked if you like snow peas.' He smiled. 'You seem to be interested in the frozen peas, but I have some nice snow peas, fresh in, over in the produce section.' He gestured towards the rear of the supermarket. 'It's eighty-nine cents for a half pound.'

'Uh, no, I mean, thank you, but no – I'm just looking for some—' Jennifer stammered to a halt. She had been replaying her conversation with Steven, and wondering where she could hide, someplace that no one would think of finding her, or even associate with her. A madman – no, a demon, worse than a demon – was looking for her, reading the thoughts and memories of people from her neighbourhood, her friends. They all knew where she went; Silverthorn certainly wasn't safe, not for long, anyway. Eventually, he would find someone who knew Bryan and Meg had a condominium up here, and then he – it – whatever it was would be on its way.

Steven had just disappeared. He had woven an absurd tale of magic and demons and monstrous creatures hunting him and probably Hannah in some fantastic world, a night-time story to frighten adolescent boys, and then Steven had disappeared. He had earned credibility the only way he could: he had proven it, vanishing from the room like the coffee table Frisbee book she had tossed onto the tapestry only a few minutes earlier.

And with that, Jennifer had been left alone with her charge: to get away, to protect the tapestry portal, and to open it on time, every time, without fail. No one cared that she was overwhelmed; he had not given her any time. She had lived through two months of anticipation, not for news that Hannah was still alive; Jennifer had been waiting for news that her daughter was dead. *You can think it now, because it's not true. It's not going to happen that way.* Steven hadn't given her enough time to get used to the fact that her daughter was alive, or that she might be pursued across the country by a homicidal creature bent on destruction. 'It wasn't enough time, Steven,' Jennifer muttered.

'David,' the store manager corrected. 'My name is David Johnson. I manage the store, and if you don't mind me suggesting, ma'am, if you don't think you've had enough time, would you please make your choice with the door closed?'

'What?'

'The door, ma'am, the freezer door. You've been holding it open for,' he glanced at his watch, 'for eight minutes now, ma'am.'

'What? Oh, God, I'm sorry. I'm so—' Embarrassed, Jennifer realised she was standing in the frozen foods aisle of the Silverthorn grocery store, the freezer held open in one chilly hand. Staring at the same rack of frozen peas for the past eight minutes, she blushed despite the billowing clouds of dry industrial cold wafting around her ankles. 'I'm sorry. I'm so embarrassed, Mr Johnson. I was thinking, and I got distracted, and I – can't believe I—'

'David,' he said, extending his hand.

'David?'

'Please call me David.' He smiled again, and Jennifer felt her already red face flush anew.

'Oh, and you're being nice to me,' she said, shaking his hand, 'and I'm sure I look like a madwoman standing here daydreaming.'

'Don't worry about it—' David paused.

'Jennifer.'

'Jennifer – really. It's no problem. I mean just last week I had a couple from Ohio out for a ski trip, and they stood and stared at the zucchini for almost twenty minutes. I think one of them lost a relative to a zucchini once, maybe back in Italy.'

Jennifer laughed, 'Must have been a mob hit.'

'Those overcooked side dishes can be lethal!'

They both laughed, and David asked, 'Can I show you those peas?'

'Really, Mr Johnson, we just met.' Jennifer feigned offence, then, holding a straight face for another moment, she burst out laughing, finding the humour. *It might be a long road*, she thought, *you ought to try and find some joy.*

Now it was David's turn to blush. 'Right back here,' he said, taking her gently by the arm. 'Are you in town long?'

'No, just a few days.' That was a lie; she had no idea how long she might be staying.

'Are you a skier?'

'No. I come up from Denver to spend time with my brother and his wife. They're the skiers.'

'So what do you do during the day?'

I worry. That's what I do most. I worry, and I miss my daughter, and I pray that she's all right, and I sometimes plan ways to kill or at least dismember whoever has her or anyone who might have hurt her. I have all sorts of sordid thoughts about torture and death. Just recently I learned that she's been transported somewhere, somewhere I can't go, and so I sometimes stand around with the freezer door open staring at the frozen foods for eight, ten, whatever, even twelve minutes at a time. 'Oh, I cook and read and write letters to friends. I love walking here. Some of the trails are gorgeous in the winter,' she said.

'The ones we plough anyway,' David was running out of things to interest her, and the produce section was coming up fast.

Jennifer stole a glance at the store manager. In her embarrassment, she had not realised that he was actually quite attractive. No wedding ring, fifty, maybe, with salt-and-pepper hair, brown eyes, a lean, honest face, and a small paunch engaged in a friendly wrestling competition with his belt, just the softening midsection of a middle-aged man who appeared to have been active for most of his life.

'I do, by the way,' she said.

'What's that?'

'I do like snow peas. I cook them all the time. My daughter loves them.' Jennifer picked through a handful, discarding several and dropping the rest in a clear plastic bag.

'Oh.' David was surprised. 'Is she here?'

'No.'

'Not a skier either?'

'Not this season, no.' Jennifer crammed two more handfuls of peas into the bag and tied a knot in it, suddenly in a hurry again.

David didn't notice her sudden haste. 'My kids either. They're in school now.'

Jennifer was silent. She wanted to get back to Bryan and Meg's condo, to consider her options and plan where she might go next. Tossing the bag of snow peas into the shopping cart, she said, 'Well, thank you, David. I appreciate the help, and I'm really sorry about—you know, with the freezer.'

'Please don't worry about it, and come back anytime. I'm here every day.'

'I will. Thanks,' Jennifer murmured the normal courtesies, then looked into David's eyes: he was gazing at her with calm, confident honesty. He was a nice man, and if he was attracted to her, he had picked just about the worst possible time in her life.

'Or if you need a walking partner,' he tried one last time.

'That sounds nice.' She wanted him to know that on any other occasion she would have been willing to stand here for the rest of the night, ice cream melting into a puddle of vanilla-soaked chocolate chips around her feet, to continue talking with him – but not tonight, and now perhaps not ever.

He smiled goodbye as she paid for her groceries, and watched as she pushed the trolley into the parking lot.

Outside, the afternoon had turned a muted ash-grey. Snow was falling above ten thousand feet; it would be in Silverthorn in a few minutes. Jennifer pushed the cart towards her car. She had bought enough groceries to last her at Bryan and Meg's for a few days, long enough to figure out where to flee next, but not so long that the thing she had passed on Broadway and Lincoln might guess where she had taken the portal tapestry. Wind from the river carried the distinct smell of woodsmoke, and Jennifer promised herself a fire when she arrived.

She had not slept well the night before; the events of the previous day had been too fresh in her mind, the thought of finding Hannah too prickly and hot to put down. With two months to wait before opening the portal, she had to find a way to get some sleep, to enjoy some semblance of normalcy, *to find some joy*. Jennifer glanced back at the grocery store and was surprised to see David Johnson watching her through the plate-glass windows. Standing between a red-and-white placard advertising *Paper Towels, $1.19 for 200* and a brightly coloured display hawking *Frozen Pizzas, 2 for $9*, she could see his smile across the parking lot. He waved, and turned back into the store.

Jennifer tilted her head slightly and furrowed her brow. 'A sense of normalcy?' she asked of the parking lot. 'That would be anything but normal.'

By the time she'd unpacked her groceries it was snowing; she got a warm, comforting blaze burning as quickly as she could, then poured a glass of wine – never too early, particularly not these days – and opened an atlas she had thrown into her car. She ran a fingertip over the state map of Colorado.

THE FOREST OF GHOSTS

Hannah Sorenson reined in to a dusty stop as Hoyt, Churn, and Alen rode ahead, unaware she had paused behind them. It had been six days since she had heard the legend of the forest of ghosts and Hannah was pretty sure that despite the others' silence on the subject, their small company was drawing near. Anxiety chilled her as images chased through her mind: running away, fleeing south – even just dismounting and refusing to go any further – until thoughts of Steven and home, her mother and the Rocky Mountains gave her a little strength.

The chill lifted a bit and Hannah urged her horse on again. If the forest of ghosts was the only way, then that was that; she would just have to fight to maintain her composure in front of the three men. She would go where they went, face what they faced and come through the forest ready for Welstar Palace. It was not a comforting thought: out of the frying pan and directly into Hell, but the displaced law student forced thoughts of Welstar Palace and all its nightmares from her mind: that was for another day.

The sun rising caressed her face and she squinted into the early rays to make out the lengthening foothills stretching towards the Ravenian Sea. The hard, flat farming land they had passed through had softened into green and brown folds, bending the landscape into ridges and smooth swells as it climbed towards the still invisible Pragan peaks. It was morning, and Hannah thought that ought to mean something significant; she had survived another night. On the run in a foreign world, she had made it to another dawn.

Hannah was embarrassed at how much she had taken for granted, like sleeping beneath a down comforter, an expensive one, in her own bed, the most comfortable place in the world to sleep – certainly better than the stacked logs and overturned rocks she had been using for the past several months. And she had pillows, glorious pillows, three of them. Imagine that; three pillows for one person, what luxury. Would she get back and be able to fall asleep in her own bed again? And would she wake with the opportunity to ignore the dawn or, better yet, to sleep right through it and welcome the day a few hours later?

As the sun exorcised the stubborn chill that had sneaked into her body, Hannah knew they would reach the forest of ghosts before the sun had passed overhead, and she would find the answers.

Alen suddenly tugged on his own reins, then dismounted with the agility of a man many Twinmoons his junior. If alcohol had ever impaired his physical, cognitive and mystical abilities, there had been no sign. He rode tall in the saddle and didn't appear to be suffering any back pain; he didn't complain of saddle soreness, of cramps, or any of the long list of ailments that had been irritating Hannah since she agreed to tackle this journey. He hadn't been drinking much, either – a few swallows around the fire each evening, a morning mouthful or two to wash out the overnight bitterness: that was it.

Hannah was proud of Alen and confident – more confident, anyway – that he might actually succeed in sending her back to Denver. His face had regained some colour, and she thought the former Larion Senator was feeling a renewed sense of mystical strength as long-untapped reserves of magic bubbled to life.

Alen had loosened his reins as Hoyt had dismounted, and indicated Churn and Hannah should do the same. He got some long leather straps from his saddlebag.

'What now?' she asked.

'Take one of these and thread it through your reins, then form a loop, like this.' Alen demonstrated by turning the leather strip back on itself and knotting it tightly several times. 'Then we'll clip yours to Churn's, his to Hoyt's, and Hoyt's to mine.'

Through the loop in his own reins, Alen drew a length of heavy twine which he knotted to the back of Hoyt's tunic belt, tugging on it sharply several times to ensure it would not come loose.

'There we are,' he said. 'Now, run your hand through the loop in your reins.'

Hannah did so, feeling the leather slide up her forearm and expose pale flesh beneath her tunic. 'What if it's not—' she began.

'Tight enough?' The old magician read her mind. 'Then unhook it, tighten the loop and try again, or use another strap to fix it to the wrist of your tunic. The horses shouldn't spook in the forest, and assuming Hoyt manages to lead them, they can drag the rest of us along until we clear the far edge.'

Hoyt asked, 'How will I know when we get there?'

'I imagine it will be when we stop raving,' Alen replied, cheerily.

Hannah used another length of leather to tie herself securely to the chain of reins linking the four horses. As brave as she was determined to be, she was not taking any chances. One glance at Churn assured her that the burly mute wasn't leaving his life to the fates either. She smiled at the sight of his massive forearm, as big around as one of her calves, looped several times in whatever loose string, rope, leather, even cloth Churn could find; wide-eyed, he stared back at her, looking as desperate for an alternative as she had been only a few minutes before.

At least I'm not the only one terrified, Hannah thought, wincing at what she could only imagine the silent Pragan might experience at the hands of the haunted forest.

'Sorry, Churn. But I think we just have to do this,' she whispered.

Signing slowly so Hannah could understand, he said, 'I don't want to go in,' in exaggerated gestures.

'Neither do I, my friend, but drinks are on me when we get to the other side,' Hannah said softly.

'Make it six, and I'll follow you anywhere.'

She laughed: she understood that! 'Done. Six it is.'

It would be impossible for them to ride like this, Hannah thought, wondering why Alen had insisted they link their mounts together so soon. As he double-checked the knots on the sacks, she asked, 'Why are we going on foot now? Shouldn't we ride until we get to the forest itself?'

Alen motioned towards a stand of white birch trees, their paper bark peeling in the autumn chill. The grove rained a cloudburst of tiny leaves with each gentle gust of wind that blew through the foothills. There, half-buried beneath a mound of yellow leaves was what remained of a traveller: man or woman, Hannah couldn't tell. Seated against a tree trunk, it looked like the figure had expired right there, legs crossed as if relaxing in the shade with a cold beer and a good book; there were no signs of struggle. The dusty grey cadaver was little more than a mummified husk; it looked like a statue. Hannah thought that if she wandered close enough, she might be able to read a bronze plaque, set with mortar into a carved piece of granite, *Sunday Afternoon by Michael Adams*.

'Good God, look at it,' she whispered. 'It died right there, sitting there.' Except for the few funerals of friends' grandparents, and the man Churn had killed while saving her life, Hannah had never seen a dead body up close, certainly not one who had died while wasting away an afternoon beneath a favourite backyard tree.

'What is this place, Alen?' she whispered as her eyes moved from the dead body to the old Larion Senator. 'What are we doing here?'

Alen smiled, summoning as much confidence as he could. 'We are taking the first of several difficult steps to send you home. So please, tie that loop tight and walk beside your horse. Let him lead you, and I will see you on the other side.' The old man brushed a strand of hair away from Hannah's forehead, then grabbed the wineskin Hoyt and Churn had been passing between them and took a gulp.

'All right Hoyt,' he said, wiping his mouth, 'straight north, all day, all night – however long it takes, do not stop.'

'Right.' Hoyt rubbed his palms on his leggings.

'Do you remember the words?' Alen had taught him a minor spell, something simple to dull his mind slightly and to keep his own memories from swirling about in his head like targets in an enchanted carnival shooting gallery.

'Yes.'

'Right then, lead on.' Alen looped his hand through the knot in his horse's reins and twisted it several times until it was tight about his wrist.

Hannah had expected the enchantment to overcome her the moment she stepped beneath the trees, so she was surprised that they were able to climb the slow-rising hill and descend into the shallow valley between it and the next before anything strange seemed to happen. Hoyt and Alen spent some of the time singing a Pragan song about friendship and courtship; Hannah had picked up most of the refrain before – in typical Hoyt fashion – the lyrics spiralled into a less appropriate libretto. Behind her, Churn grunted and giggled along, bursting out with an unnatural guttural sound every time his friend mentioned loose women, free beer or the incontinence of his eminence, Prince Malagon.

The melody and rhythm lulled Hannah into a false sense of security. *This isn't so bad – maybe nothing will happen. It can't be far – we've come a long way already.* She sang along until the song began to echo back at her from the forest, blurry, bent notes and odd angles that seemed to be creating lapses in time. *Weird jazz.* The boisterously loud refrain woke her from a daze – *a quick nap*, she told herself. Her eyes widened in her effort to stay awake.

*

The television was on – the boisterously loud refrain of a commercial awakened Hannah and her eyes widened in an effort to stay awake. *The couch again, rats.* She rubbed sleep from her eyes and waited for the commercial to end. It was something about soap and dress shirts; a bald fellow with a deadpan look was washing one white shirt at a time. *I'd hate to wait around while he does his laundry.* Hannah reached for the *TV Guide. What time is it?*

Before she could turn to check the hallway clock, the late news came on. Two men, one the anchor and the other a sports commentator – Hannah couldn't remember their names – were discussing football.

> *That's right, John Elway. He was the standout superstar at Stanford, and he does not want to play in Baltimore. He has told his agent. He has told the media. He won't go to Baltimore, and we are going to get him right here in Denver. I tell you, this kid has an arm like a god, and if we can get him here with the Broncos—*

Ten o'clock. No, later. They do sports later, almost at the end. So it has to be almost ten-thirty. Hannah sat up and was surprised to find her mother's old coverlet, the ratty one with the frayed edges, thrown over her. She had been sleeping longer than she thought. *Normally, I wake up when she covers me out here.* She curled back beneath the blanket, falling into the indentation she had left in the pillows, two pillows, and watched news clips of college football teams battling their way across a gridiron. She guessed that the focus of the report was a blond man, the quarterback from the team in red. *He's cute. He can play here. That's okay with me.*

The Sorensons' living room was located just off the kitchen, next to the area they used as a dining room for company. When it was just the three of them, they always ate their meals in the kitchenette, where a small table, easy to set and easy to clean, provided a pleasant place for family dinners and quick breakfasts before school. The dining room had a longer wooden table, conservative chairs, and a cabinet stacked nearly to overflowing with decorative china. A centrepiece of fake flowers adorned the table year round, their perpetually bright colours illuminated for dinner by candles in the candleholders Hannah's mother had bought one summer on a trip to Boston. When no one was visiting, the dining room remained dark, the door closed.

Tonight, light spilled through that doorway. Hannah craned her neck, not wanting to actually move to see who might be in there at this hour – she wished she could see around corners, a cool superhero power. Then she heard them, above the noise of the television news (more blather about John Elwood or whoever he was), her parents were sitting in the dining room talking – no, arguing. *This can't be good.* Hannah tried to go back to sleep. *They only sit in there when it's really bad.* She closed her eyes, certain if she kept them shut long enough she would drift off to sleep, but it was no good; closing her eyes just sharpened her hearing.

To get to her own room meant passing the open door – they would see her, and they would be angry; why was she listening, this was none of her business. Hannah pressed her head down into the pillows and ground her teeth, and focused on the news, listening to everything the sports commentator was saying about John Elwood. *That wasn't his name.* But they had already gone to another commercial. Sports were done for the night.

This time it was dog food. *What is a gravy train, anyway?* It was no use; Hannah could hear every word.

'But she loves you. Doesn't that make any difference to you?' Jennifer Sorenson was pleading with her husband. Hannah didn't know who *she* was.

'I don't give a fuck about her.'

Slurring. He's been drinking again.

'But she's left her husband; she's waiting for you. Are you going to tell her that you're planning to live here with us, or go to her? Either way, Gary, it's up to you, but you can't keep doing this to us – to Hannah or to me.'

'Just shut the fuck up about Hannah!' Gary Sorenson was yelling now. There was no drowning this out.

'I'm not going to cry, damn it. You are not going to make me cry again, Gary, you're not. But you have to decide. We love you – I love you, Gary, I still do, and Hannah idolises you, but you can't take advantage of us this way. Not me, and not your daughter – no more.' Jennifer, despite her promise, started crying.

Hannah rolled over on the couch, covering her ears with the pillows, trying not to hear her mother saying, 'I don't care about the women, Gary, because I believe you still love me, but you have to stop with the booze – it's going to kill you. You know that.'

Hannah heard the squeal of a chair being pushed back and her father shouting, 'I told you to shut the fuck up! Do you not

167

understand *shut the fuck up*? I will drink if I want to, and I will—'
The chair slammed against the dining room wall, rattling the porcelain. '—I will fucking go and fucking do what I want to!'

'Gary, I'll make it easy for you: just go. She loves you; she left her family for you – why, I don't— Well, anyway, I'll take Hannah, and we'll go to Bryan's. You can have three days, Gary, and then I want you gone, out of here.' Hannah heard her mother walk out of the dining room to the master bedroom. The door slammed.

What are you doing? Come and take it back, Mom, you don't want him to leave. I don't want him to leave. Where is he going? I don't want to go to Uncle Bryan's; I want to stay here. Mom! Take it back now! He'll leave if you don't come out here and tell him you're sorry.

She could sense her father's hesitation. He was probably standing beside the table, lighting another cigarette, or maybe pouring another glass of whatever was in the bottle he kept in the cabinet by the phone. Hannah was too terrified to move, so she pulled the blanket up beneath her neck and tucked in the sides until she was wrapped entirely in old knotted wool.

Hannah was seven years old and she had known for a while something was wrong. Her father was gone too much; when it was normal for dads to come home, her dad often didn't. Sometimes he came back two or three days later, arriving at seven o'clock in the morning, a funny time to get home. He would call into work and tell them he was sick, then sleep much of the day. By dinner time he was up and dressed. After a fight with her mom, he would be gone again.

But that doesn't mean I want him to leave for ever. Hannah used a corner of the blanket to wipe her face – then she felt a tug, gentle at first, like a friend gripping her hand and pulling her across the playground at school. But there was no one with her now.

What is that?

It came again, a tug on her wrist.

From the dining room, she heard her father lift the chair and slide it back into place beneath the table. He would sit there for the rest of the night, drinking and smoking until the sun came up. Then he would take a shower and leave for work. Some nights, he cooked eggs, adding whatever leftovers were in the refrigerator to his omelettes: green beans, chopped turkey, bits of hot dog, anything. The smell always lingered until Mom got up and sprayed the house. Some mornings Hannah would see him in the dining room asleep on his folded arms, an ashtray overflowing with cigarette butts and grey ash at one elbow.

There was a tug again. This time the little girl's wrist actually jumped up from the blanket, as if an invisible someone was lifting it. 'What is that? Who is doing that?' Hannah whispered, waving the offending wrist in front of her face, trying to see in the darkness if someone had sneaked in and tied a string around her arm.

She heard the dog pad in from the kitchen, his paws tapping out his approach on the linoleum. He was a big dog, like a wolf, and he climbed on the couch to curl up across Hannah's feet. As she felt the warmth of his fur, Hannah drifted back to sleep, wondering why she couldn't remember when they got a dog.

In the background the television was on. The boisterously loud refrain of a commercial woke Hannah from where she had fallen asleep. Her eyes widened in an effort to stay awake.

This time, the tugging came more frequently.

Churn woke to the snow tickling his nose and cheeks. The world, muted and out of focus, gradually exposed itself. Although he could feel it snowing, he wasn't cold; rather, it was uncomfortably warm. Churn couldn't recall the last time he had seen snow south of the Great Pragan Range. He was dimly aware that his body had been broken – he had so many injuries, there was no better way to describe it. A tugging sensation came from his left, as if he had been gripped by an invisible spectre, and Churn struggled to turn his head.

The soldiers had been brutal. The Malakasians had kicked, beaten and clubbed every inch of him. Churn assumed he was in shock, because except for his shoulders, nothing hurt any longer: his mind had closed off the part of itself that remembered the agony he had experienced that morning … *Or had it been the previous morning?* When he came fully awake, he drew a massive breath and screamed. He screamed for a long time, nearly half an aven, before passing out again.

Later, he woke in a panic, unable to breathe. His feet had slipped off the thin branch and now dangled high above the yard. The weight of his body pulling so hard on his shoulders made it impossible to breathe. He had been lucky to find that branch, though it was so narrow he was certain it would snap at any moment, but he mustn't slip again. He had to stay awake.

He had been terrified the whole time the soldiers spent getting him up here. He'd already been beaten near to death and he had no fight left in him. He hadn't fought back when the Malakasians tied him to a plank they'd found in the barn, not even when it snapped, the first time they tried to lift him. They hadn't been deterred, though; they'd just found a sturdier piece of wood.

While the soldiers lashed him to the new plank, one, a pretty woman, climbed the giant cottonwood next to the ditch. Once he was secure, the men tossed the other end of his rope to the girl in the tree.

In all his life, Churn had never seen anyone who could climb a tree like that girl – through the haze of his injuries he had wondered if she was some kind of magician, perhaps half-woman, half-cat, she climbed the old cottonwood with such graceful ease. She found a solid branch near the top and looped the rope over and back down to her companions, who were impatiently barking orders up at her. They were all obviously relishing stringing-up their trophy, the killer of three of their brethren, and looking forward to leaving him there to die, slowly and in great pain.

As soon as his feet left the ground, Churn had started gasping for breath; his head was bleeding and his body was in screaming agony, but he was more frightened of suffocation. His head and shoulders crashed through the lower branches, sometimes stopping with a jolt, but each time he thought they'd give up and tie him off there, the half-cat-girl with the grim, pretty face would swing over to dislodge him so he could continue his journey into the upper branches. When she finally secured him, fifty paces above his family farm, she hadn't noticed the thin branch jutting out of the trunk, but Churn counted it among the greatest strokes of good luck in his lifetime.

Though he faded in and out of consciousness, he remained lucid enough to keep his toes pressed firmly against the twig, taking enough of his weight that he could breathe a little. While he waited for it to snap, he thanked the snow for waking him.

He looked around, but there was no trace of the Malakasians below. He could see his sister and parents lying motionless in the grass below, and tried hoarsely to shout down to them. Perhaps they didn't know he was here …

There's that tugging again, from my left. Someone's pulling on my arm.

They were dead. There was no way they could have survived the beating they had taken. Churn didn't bother wondering why the squad had chosen this farm on this day (*was it yesterday? How long have I been up here?*) – trying to understand why the Malakasian Army acted with such brutality was like trying to understand their enigmatic leader.

The Pragan farmer who had grown as strong as a bull heaving bales up into the loft of his father's barn dangled like a macabre ornament from the snowy branches of the cottonwood tree. He could see his sister's cloak was soaked through where her neck had bled so badly. *There was so much blood* – it had stained the ground around her dark brown. *Blood is supposed to be red. This isn't right.*

His father's arm had been severed at the elbow. His old sword, little more than a rusty dagger, was still gripped in the missing hand. Churn would remember his father's wailing scream for the rest of his life: he screamed until one of the Malakasians had hit him hard across the temple with a cudgel. There had been a snapping sound, and his father's voice had been cut off in mid-cry.

His mother was dead too. She'd huddled on the ground, trying to revive Churn's father. She hadn't posed a threat; she hadn't fought back, and they might have overlooked her, if she hadn't run for the house when she saw the flames. There had been so much other brutality to distract them; they hadn't realised the soldiers' fire had kindled into a raging blaze, engulfing their house. Doren had been in there, Churn's younger brother, the baby of the family.

Churn's mother had ignored the inferno and burst through the front door, screaming to the gods of the Northern Forest – and then she had fallen silent. She hadn't come out, and Churn couldn't bear to think what his mother had seen before she had been swallowed by the flames.

Now his abused voice was a rasp at the back of his throat, but still Churn screamed as the smell of burning ash assaulted his nostrils. Flailing about in mental and physical agony, he finally managed to break the rope, and started crashing back down through the branches until the plank crossbeam caught in the juncture of two thick branches. Churn felt both shoulders come free from their sockets, the cartilage torn through, and he struck the ground with a thud that knocked the wind from his lungs – an unwelcome irony after he had struggled so hard to get any air in there at all. And then he screamed again, a dry wheeze that eventually faded to silence.

Kantu chanted the spell. It wasn't difficult to recall: he had used it thousands of times in the past five hundred Twinmoons. Just a few words, and the far portal would close and follow him – them – across the Fold. *But not all of us.* He closed his eyes and called it again just to be sure, steeling himself against the shrieking behind him. He couldn't stand to hear it for another moment. The Larion leader couldn't remember when he had started to cry; he was there now, crying, in the middle of the room. They had played with the baby here, reading her stories and watching her every move, as if nothing she might do or say in the entire span of her life was too insignificant to be missed by people who loved her that much. It was the room with the fireplace, but nothing burned in there now; it was too warm for a fire. Kantu wondered why there were still ashes in the fire grate. *Why had they not cleaned those out last spring? Why keep a fireplace full of ashes all summer?*

In front of him, the yellow and green flecks of Larion sorcery danced in the air above the portal. It was time. His stomach clenched into a knot at the thought of it, but it was time. Nerak would kill them – Reia too – if he knew Pikan had been pregnant, and they couldn't take that risk. But he would be back for her. That morning he had taken her out into the meadow beside the house, sat in the dewy grass, and wept. She had grabbed a lock of his hair in her tiny fist and cooed at him in her own esoteric language. It was there that Kantu's heart had finally broken, among the British wildflowers Pikan loved so much. *How could so many colours grow in one place together?*

He had promised Reia he would be back, soon, even if he had to kill Nerak himself.

Now, with Pikan wailing, Kantu called the spell a third time – unnecessary, but he needed something to do while Pikan said goodbye – and that would take time they didn't have. He was packed and ready, his notes rolled into scrolls. The portal was open and behind him – he couldn't look back – Pikan was crying, 'I can't leave her here! She's too small. She needs me. Please, please don't make me do this.'

There was nothing he could do to ease her pain. Kantu tossed their bag and his scrolls into the air above the portal. Both disappeared instantly. 'Come,' he said, firmly, trying not to sob himself, 'it's time.' He turned, still not looking at the baby; he knew if he looked at her, he would take her back, whatever the consequences. 'We'll be back for her.' He took Pikan by the shoulders, wrapped his arms around her and chanted the spell, avoiding her kicks.

He carried her to the far portal and she wept, 'I can't leave her! Don't make me leave her! Reia! I love you, Reia! I'll be back for you. Mama will be back!' Pikan was raving, reaching for the baby, who cried and screamed in the arms of the silent surrogate mother who would raise her until the Larion couple's return.

With a final glance at the cold, ash-filled fireplace, Kantu, carrying Pikan, stepped through the Fold and back into Eldarn.

Hoyt pulled at his horse's reins and the animal dutifully followed along. They had spent most of the day moving north through the forest of ghosts. Although he had been thankfully free of memories or visions from his own past, overhearing his friends as they relived anguish and pain had pushed him nearly to the screaming point himself. During a short midday-aven pause, Hoyt had tied a length of cloth over his ears in an effort to filter out Hannah's pleas, Churn's screams and Alen's curious chanting, but it hadn't helped.

Two avens later, as the sun faded in the west, Hoyt decided to skip the evening meal and continue walking their party north, even if it took all night to get clear of the enchanted woods. He had seen other people during the day: disheartened figures, some wandering around, talking to themselves or ghosts of themselves, their parents, lovers, whomever. Others were sitting, jabbering at nothing while some lay silent, emaciated, dehydrated and dying in the wilderness. There were corpses, rotting and foetid; a wayward step had cost him his breakfast as his foot plunged through the chest cavity of a woman who had died beside a brambly stand of evergreen brush. She had been so covered with leaves that he hadn't seen her there.

Several times Hoyt had tried to corral one of the other wanderers, but there had been no hope: none responded to his touch. They were all too far into madness to recognise or even care that someone might be attempting to lead them to safety. After a few aborted efforts, he had given up entirely.

It had been slow going, with each of his friends determined at one time or another to kneel or even lie down as they wrestled their demons. They had drunk greedily as Hoyt offered them water, and Churn had eaten a few bits of dried meat, though neither Alen nor Hannah would take any food. They had soiled their leggings at least once during the day.

Now they trudged behind him like walking dead, their wrists looped securely through the reins, responding when he tugged on their arms or clucked their horses along. None of them appeared to have emerged from their daze, even momentarily, all day. He stepped over a rotting log and as he turned to make certain each of his travelling companions could manage, Hoyt considered how many days they would be able to survive in the forest – only another day or two, he thought. Much longer than that, he would have to find some way to get them to eat. Keeping them hydrated was challenge enough, but feeding them while they screamed, begged or chanted verged on impossible.

The noise really was the worst part: Hoyt didn't mind that they had shat themselves or that they didn't eat; he could bear walking all day with no one to chat to, but the incessant repetition of whatever the forest of ghosts had found in their past was really driving him mad. Not even Alen's spell had done much good, though he was sure he has been saying it correctly. During the middlenight aven, he finally broke and shouted at them, 'Shut up! Shut up! Shut up, for the love of all the gods of the Northern Forest!'

The only response came from Hoyt's horse: startled at the sudden outburst, it nickered and pawed at the ground with one hoof.

'What? Oh, you think it's funny?' he asked the tired mount. 'Of course, you do. You don't mind six avens of mindless babble, and Churn – for rutting sake, Churn, who I have never heard speak – has not stopped screaming since morning.' Hoyt took a huge gulp from one of the wineskins and nibbled at a bit of stale bread. 'You'd think he would have lost his voice for good after screaming all day.'

Now even his horse ignored him. Hoyt spat a few curses at the Pragan night and pushed on through the trees. The Eldarni moons gave a little light, but Hoyt began to grow tired, and worried that one of them – or worse, one of the horses – might miss a step and turn an ankle or take a tumble. He shivered as an eerie moan drifted from somewhere off to his left: the sound of a lost soul wandering in the darkness.

'All right. One more hill, and then we'll rest for a while,' he said, giving a parting glance towards the voice, and tugged his horse's reins. 'Let's go.'

When they crested the next rise, the light from the twin moons and a hundred thousand Eldarni stars illuminated a massive clearing, dotted here and there with boulders and a few scrubby pines growing low to the ground. To the east, the rise and fall of the foothills hardened into a craggy cliff face jutting up in the first of what he guessed was row upon row of eastern peaks. To the west, he could see mountains rising in the distance.

Before them, the ground fell away; less than a hundred paces north, the world ended in a chasm that fractured the very foundations of the earth. Hoyt had no idea how deep it was, or how steeply it sloped, but he would take no chances. First he would lash his friends to a sturdy tree, then build a small fire and to take what rest he could before facing the next stage of their journey.

He dropped his reins and patted his horse on the neck. 'Good job today.'

'Hoyt?' someone called.

'Rutting whores!' he screeched, nearly tumbling down the slope.

'Hoyt?' The voice came again and for the first time since he stepped into the clearing, the Pragan realised his friends had fallen silent.

He scrambled to his feet and called, 'Yes. Who is that?'

'It's me, Alen – I'm pretty tired. Can we take a break here?' He was already spreading his cloak on the ground, apparently oblivious to the fact that he had walked all day without sitting, that he had eaten nothing since the pre-dawn aven and had relieved himself as he walked.

'Uh, yes, that's what I was checking,' Hoyt said. 'This is a good spot. You sleep. I'll make a fire.'

'Good. Thanks.' The old man was asleep beside Churn and Hannah almost before he'd stopped talking.

THE SALT MARSH

Brexan's foot came down in thick black mud that stank of salt and decay and she cursed as she pulled her boot out. It was cold this morning, made worse by the wind off the water. She was glad she had changed from her skirt, for the weather felt as though it had finally shifted from autumn into winter. The salt marsh stretched east and north, swallowing the Falkan coastline in a plain of wetlands. Rushes, most of them naked stalks this late in the season, dominated the coarse cordgrass and bog sedges which carpeted the ground in thick tufts of green, resiliently holding the vestiges of their summer colour despite the encroaching winter.

To her left, muddy flats sloped for several hundred paces to the lapping waters of the Ravenian Sea. The uniform expanse of low-tide mud was a monochromatic painting of the ocean floor and Brexan wondered if all the vast seas of the world were as boring beneath the surface. Far to the north she could just make out a stream meandering its way across the flats and into the sea.

As she scraped a clinging lump of mud from her boots, hundreds of tiny seeds exploded from the reeds and caught on her clothes and in her hair; Brexan imagined she looked frightful, splattered knee-deep in mud and decorated head and shoulders in marsh spores. She pressed on regardless, shouldering her way through the rushes using the patches of cordgrass as stepping stones to navigate a relatively dry path through the estuary.

It had been eight days since Sallax and Jacrys, locked in grim battle, had fallen into invisibility at the end of the alley behind the alehouse. She had spent every day since searching for Sallax, while checking in what she hoped were unpredictable intervals over her shoulder for the spy. Her daily explorations had been carefully planned; moving in concentric circles out from the alehouse, Brexan had searched, backtracked and searched again.

She had first seen Sallax in the woods south of the city, but when she found no sign of him there, she decided to search the salt marsh north of the city. The Ronan freedom fighter could find numerous places in which to hide in this beautiful – if inhospitable – territory. Brexan had seen no one out here all morning; it didn't look like the Orindale inhabitants made a habit of visiting the estuary during the winter.

'Or during the summer, for that matter,' she said. 'The rutting bugs and snakes would be thick on the ground – I suppose this is the best time to be slopping around in this muck.' She kicked at the discarded bones of a dead seabird, once a hearty meal for a marsh fox or perhaps a wildcat.

As a child, Brexan had been enthralled and terrified in equal part by the horror stories her father told her on cold winter evenings. There was nowhere in the Eastlands where the weather was quite as bitter as it was in Malakasia, and to pass the time, especially those interminable dark spells that blanketed most of her homeland in mid-winter, her father would make up stories of lunatic madmen on killing rampages, and demonic, one-eyed beasts hunting the Northern Forest for wayward children. From the adjacent room, her mother would invariably bark unheeded warnings to her father: 'She's not old enough for such tales,' and 'you can be the one to sit up with her all night, you great buffoon.' But Brexan hadn't cared; sleepless nights were never her concern. She would squeal with delight every time an unsuspecting villager wandered too far into the forest or when one of their wagons broke down, losing a wheel or ripping a leather bridle when they were too far into uncharted lands ever to make it home alive. And at the moment when the one-eyed ogre reached a muscular paw out from behind a stand of evergreens or a pack of rabid rodents gnawed through the leather slats holding the barn door closed to overwhelm the hero in a flurry of tiny teeth and poisoned claws, Brexan would dive beneath the blanket her father had been using to keep the chill off his legs and shiver and cry, frightened to within a hair's breadth of collapse – but still begging for just one more.

Later, when she had grown and enlisted in the Malakasian Army, Brexan had periodically run up against one of her father's old stories. Sleeping alone in a foreign inn, walking back from guard duty in the overnight avens or visiting the facilities after twilight, she would sometimes catch a chill scent or detect an imagined whisper caressing the nape of her neck. She would turn quickly on her heel, shouting, 'Who's there?' to the empty space. No one was ever behind her, no rabid rodents hunting her down; no ogres reaching out hungrily. Brexan couldn't escape those stories; scores of Twinmoons later, her father could scare her witless, even from the other side of Eldarn.

He had been with her this morning; on more than one occasion she had checked the cordgrass with a stick, half expecting to find a marsh adder coiled up and waiting for a taste of human blood or a pack of wild dogs crouching in the rushes, eager to hamstring her and rip mouthfuls of flesh from her defenceless body. As she tromped through the mud Brexan had tried to shut out her father's tales: it was a long walk back to the safety and anonymity of Orindale and she couldn't conduct a thorough search for Sallax with her father's ghosts leaping out from behind every clump of grass.

Periodically she stopped to stare out over the flats: if Sallax were on the marsh somewhere, she might catch a glimpse of him moving through the rushes or across the mud. Brexan figured he was still wearing the black cloak, but he should be easy to spot – even with the curious stooped position he'd adopted as part of his disguise as a beggar, he was still tall enough to stand out.

Sunlight gleamed off the stream; Brexan, certain she had spotted something out there, squinted into the blinding glare. *There it was*: a tiny indistinct hillock marring the perfection of the glass-flat stretch of mud. Brexan moved quickly, ignoring the marsh adders and rabid dogs, until she came to the edge of the cordgrass and started elbowing her way through the rushes once again. She groaned as she stepped back into the mud and began making her way towards the lump – *it's probably nothing, just a hunk of driftwood.*

The hump was a little over a hundred paces out and she was almost on top of it before she realised it was a body. She stopped dead in her tracks, sinking until the wet mud was almost at the top of her boots, as the odour of rotting flesh hit her. Trying not to breathe it in, she turned slowly in a full circle, feeling alone and vulnerable. Fear gripped her, and she thought again of home. *Curse you, father, did you have to visit me today?*

Breathing through her mouth, Brexan kicked the body over, almost retching as waves of putrefaction washed over her. In a clatter of armoured joints, a dozen or so crabs sidled a safe distance away; others stayed put, reaching up at her with their claws as if daring her to try and steal their prize. One small crab the size of a silver coin scurried over what had been the face – Brexan still couldn't tell if it had been a man or a woman – and into the open socket that had once held an eye. A translucent flap of seaweed covered the gaping mouth and with the sun directly overhead, Brexan could see straight through the empty skull. The face had been stripped of nearly all the exposed flesh, though a couple of lengths of striated muscle remained. That made things worse. Brexan looked away, unable to stand looking at it for another moment … this would be for ever waiting for her in the cordgrass, beside her father's marsh adders and rabid dogs.

She couldn't guess how long the body had been in the water; though the crabs and fish and who knew what other creatures had feasted on it, the torso and legs were pretty much intact, still wrapped in a tunic and homespun leggings. For the second time that morning, Brexan was glad winter was coming, because she couldn't imagine how disgusting this discovery would have been at the height of summer. She guessed this must have been someone killed during the last Twinmoon and dumped in the river or off the waterfront – there was a strong undertow round here and anything dropped in the water in Orindale would have been dragged along the bottom and deposited out here once the Eldarni moons broke off their relationship for another sixty days.

Confident the corpse had no link to Jacrys or Sallax , she turned to begin the long, sloppy trudge back to the relative comfort of the salt marsh. The sun had shifted just enough to ease the glare, but as she turned, something gleamed for a moment, just one flash – it blinded her for an instant and then was gone. She bent back over the body and this time spotted something shiny, a piece of jewellery, maybe, tucked just far enough up a sleeve for her to have overlooked it during her first cursory investigation.

'What do you have up there?' she asked, gripping the damp edge of the tunic sleeve with two fingers. Breathing quickly through her mouth, Brexan added a running commentary, hoping that would keep something dreadful from *actually* happening. 'And this is right about when my father would leap out of the chair and scream something horrible in a shrieking voice – you know, the voice of the young girl being pursued through the forest by the man-wolf or the lion-dog—' She tugged at the sleeve, but it was heavier than she'd expected and it slipped from her fingers. 'Or this is when the very dead body wakes up and uses its unfathomable strength to grip the unsuspecting soldier by the wrist and pull her down into the mud where she chokes to death while listening to its terrifying song … right, Father? Isn't that what happens about now, with the heroine exposed out here where no one can hear her scream—' The sleeve finally yielded up its secret: a curious piece of jewellery the like of which Brexan had never seen before.

'Now what in all the Eastlands is that?' she asked, picking at the buckle to untangle the mud-covered object from the rotting cloth. She turned it over in her hands several times, but it was too filthy to make out the detail, so she took it over to the stream, where she scrubbed the piece thoroughly. It was a bracelet, a round piece as bright as polished silver, held in place by a tiny leather belt. On the back of the roundel was an engraving: an odd, two-limbed tree surrounded by a series of runes.

'Hmm,' said Brexan out loud, 'I may have to take you to a jeweller. Maybe we can find out who you belonged to. I bet your family might want to know where to find the rest of … well, you know.'

The midday aven had passed, and Brexan didn't want to be alone on the estuary in the dark, so she turned and clumped her way back.

The four friends crossed the barren expanse of the Pragan foothills, moving towards the edge of the ravine splitting the Great Range north to south. The chasm was so wide and deep that Hoyt thought it might have been where the gods had gripped the land to pull Eldarn together, but finding there wasn't enough, they left the final seam gaping open. For as far as they could see the hills that rolled north into the granite slopes of the Great Range had been stripped bare; all the trees had been cut down or forcibly uprooted. Snow capped the highest peaks, and Hoyt shivered in anticipation of an overnight snowstorm.

Hannah, Churn and Alen had slept until midday, and once they'd cleaned up and eaten, the group set off for the western edge of the ravine, long stony bluffs that lined the chasm.

Despite his nearly incessant screaming the previous day, Churn had not made a sound since he woke; now he signed to Hoyt as they walked.

'I don't know who could have done this, Churn,' Hoyt answered. 'A farmer, perhaps?'

Churn's face scrunched into scepticism. He signed, 'It's the forest of ghosts. The farm hands wouldn't be able to go five paces before losing their senses.'

'True,' Hoyt admitted, 'but I'm not complaining. Hauling you through that forest yesterday was a rough business. I don't mind that someone shortened the trip.'

Alen interrupted, 'So it stopped when we emerged from the trees?'

'Right,' Hoyt said, 'as soon as you stepped out from beneath that big maple, the three of you collapsed. It was unnerving: there you all were, yammering away, not even pausing for breath, and then as soon as you broke through the tree line, that was it.'

Alen looked around at the rolling hills of barren earth. 'So, it's the trees.'

Hannah stopped beside him. 'And someone realised that, and came here to cut down the whole forest.'

'Right,' Alen said. 'But there's something missing.'

'What's that?' Hoyt asked.

'The trees. Where are they?'

Churn signed, 'Maybe they hauled them away.'

Alen nodded. 'I think you're right, Churn, but why?' He led them towards the edge of the ravine.

'To open a route south into Praga?' Hannah said.

'If they're Malakasian, there's no need to risk death just to cut a path into Praga. The Malakasians control every pass south. No. This is something else.'

As they stood on the edge of the chasm, Hoyt kicked a stone in front of him. They watched as it seemed to hang in the air for a moment before dropping from view.

As they peered over the edge, Hannah drew in a sharp breath. 'What on earth did that?' she whispered.

Below, lying in a huge tangled heap, were the skeletal remains of hundreds of thousands of trees, each stripped of leaves and bark. They spread across the valley floor and piled nearly halfway up the chasm.

Alen shook his head. 'I don't know, Hannah. I can't imagine who – or *what* – would have taken the time to do something like this.'

Hannah shuddered: it looked almost like a charnel house: millions of twisting branches woven into a gargantuan thicket. Here and there some of the majestic enchanted trees clung to the sides of the ravine, looking as if they were trying to claw their way back from the grave.

'Someone wanted the forest of ghosts cleared,' Hoyt said, 'but why shave them like that?'

'For a spell,' Alen answered. 'The bark and leaves of these trees must have some—'

He was cut off by a high-pitched creak, tired wood rubbing against tired wood, from behind them.

'What was that?' Hannah whispered.

'It came from over there.' Hoyt pointed north to where the swath of naked earth outlined a winding path towards Malakasia.

'Quiet,' Alen ordered, listening. The creaking came again, louder this time.

Churn signed to Hoyt, his hands a blur, 'A wagon or a cart.'

Alen whispered urgently, 'Take cover, quickly!'

'Where?' Hannah looked around in desperation; she could see no place to hide, and she wasn't about to run across the exposed crown of the hill to take cover in the forest of ghosts. She would face just about anything Eldarn could throw at her rather than set foot under those trees again. The memory of her father and mother warring incessantly was too alive in her mind, and cut too close to the bone. She felt hungover, exhausted, both physically and mentally, and she'd not even had the pleasure of drinking.

'There's no time,' Alen said. 'Just get down.'

Hannah did as he said, covering herself as well as she could with the folds of her cloak. She tried not to move as she heard the now-unmistakable sound of a wooden axle turning in a roughly hewn circular socket: a large cart of some kind. She shifted a few inches, holding her breath, and peeked out from beneath her hood, trying to see who had come over the hill.

She just could make out the large wagon as it rolled into view; it was full of people, but she couldn't see how many, or if they were men or women, young or old, soldiers or civilians. As it passed by, she realised it wasn't alone; a second loaded cart followed, then two more, side by side, with a fifth, empty, and a flatbed cart loaded with axes, saws, picks and metal implements for digging, stripping bark and hauling away lumber bringing up the rear.

The wagons rolled to a stop and Hannah watched two figures jump down. It was hard to be sure, but it looked like one was placing blocks around the wheels of the wagon; the other released the horses, which immediately started cropping what little grass remained on the nearly naked hillside. This one stood for a moment, watching as the horses moved off towards the ravine, as if to be certain none of his team were to wander downhill into the forest.

Once certain the horses were safe, the driver walked behind the wagon to join his companion and, working together, the duo hammered loose several planks to form a ramp.

Slowly, the passengers came down, in pairs: there were at least sixty people inside. They moved to a wide clearing south and west of where the Pragans lay hiding and were soon joined by those from the other carts – more than two hundred men and women – while the other drivers braced their conveyances and pastured their horses.

There was something curious about this group forming in the shadow of the haunted forest. Even from this distance, Hannah thought they didn't act like people who had been cramped together for ages: there was no general milling about, no stretching of muscles, bending of knees or rubbing of shoulders. Instead, they just stood and stared into the forest. There was no conversation that Hannah could detect either, and no one looked around, not even at the imposing peaks, forbidding cliffs and stark white glaciers of the Pragan Great Range.

Hannah wondered if they were slaves, and somehow protected against the forest's influence – they didn't appear afraid.

Then Hannah heard Alen murmuring something over and over again. She hoped it was a spell to make them invisible – there was no place to run, and little chance of getting over the cliff and down into the ravine unobtrusively. All their company could do was wait for darkness and try to slip north into the mountains. She squirmed quietly, trying to get more comfortable as Alen's voice continued the soft incantation. *Keep at it*, she thought. *A couple more hours and we'll be able to get out of here*.

She wondered about the passage north. It couldn't be that challenging, not if six horses could pull those wagons all the way from Malakasia. There might be guards, but those rickety carts would never have made it over rough terrain, certainly not loaded down with people – *zombies, whatever the hell they are* . . .

'Of course,' she muttered under her breath, 'the zombie things could have been ordered to get out and push the wagons over the highest passes.' If they steered clear of Malakasian soldiers, travellers on horseback should manage it with ease—

The horses!

Hannah nearly sat bolt upright, but caught herself just in time. *Where had they left the horses and the packs?* They had to be right there in plain view, beside the big maple where they had spent the night. *They'll see our stuff. They'll see the horses. There's nothing we can do about it. They'll know we're here.* She craned her neck, inching her way along the ground until she spotted the tree, at the edge of the forest – and there was no one between them and their possessions. The drivers and the zombie workers had moved some two hundred paces away, but not far enough: there was no way they could get to the horses, mount up and escape without someone seeing them. And once the zombies started chopping down the forest of ghosts, they might deploy all along this tree line – this very maple might be felled, stripped of its bark and thrown into the ravine.

Hannah looked into the shadows below the tree – the horses and packs *were* gone. Now she did move, lifting her head and staring. *It's the wrong one, stupid*, she thought. *Find the right maple.* But she kept coming back to the same tree, a positive flame-red poster tree for New England. There weren't any others that came close to it in size and colour. She couldn't be mistaking it.

Hannah searched the tree line for any sign of their belongings: something was strange. Her gaze locked on the base of the maple, right where she had left her pack that morning. Trying not to blink, she watched carefully as something flickered for a moment. A blurry patch caught her eye for a fraction of a second, then disappeared. It was there again, then it wavered and faded away.

Alen's muttering interrupted Hannah's thoughts again and finally she realised what was happening. It was magic. The former Larion Senator, the man who had claimed to have lost his confidence over the past one hundred and thirty-five years was casting a web of enchantment that was hiding four horses, several packs and a burning campfire.

Hannah watched transfixed, as rapt as when Alen's home had come into view properly for the first time. If he could do this, then perhaps he *could* get her back to Colorado – or at least get her back to Steven.

She grimaced. How the hell had she, a confident, self-sufficient woman, clear about who she was and what she wanted, managed to end up entirely at the mercy of a fallen-from-grace sorcerer with a hangover? Still, at least she had a little hope now, and silently she urged the old man to greatness: *You can do it, Alen. Make the whole place disappear. You can do it!*

Thunk!

A distant crash resonated from somewhere in the forest. Hannah didn't need to raise her head to know it was the first of what would doubtless be thousands as the zombies' axes chopped at the forest of ghosts. The intermittent sounds of isolated trees falling merged periodically into one drawn-out cry of shattering branches.

Finally, darkness fell and Hoyt slithered between Hannah and Alen. 'Churn and I will go for the horses. Hannah, can you ride?' He whispered, though Hannah didn't believe anyone could have heard him even if he had been shouting.

'I'm cramped, but I think I can.' She longed to stretch her legs, to twist her lower back until the bones cracked, and to straighten her knees.

'And you?' Hoyt asked Alen. 'You've been keeping that spell going all day.'

'I'm fine,' Alen said without hesitation. 'I'm drained, but it's a good feeling, tired out doing something useful.'

'Good,' Hoyt said, 'get ready. We'll walk the horses along the bluffs, mount up behind the hill here, and then make our way around to the north without being spotted.'

He had to thump the ground hard twice before Churn turned to look at him. He signed the plan, and with a nod and a quick gesture, Churn agreed. He gave Hannah a crooked smile and sidled carefully out from beneath his cloak. Staying low to the ground, he soon disappeared into the darkness. Hoyt rolled his shoulders back, shrugged off his own cloak and vanished after Churn. Hannah marvelled at how at home he was in the dark.

She stared out at nothing as the forest of ghosts fell beneath the Malakasian axes. She endeavoured to separate the sounds of axes falling, saws gnawing, and horses straining. There was little conversation; the din was only periodically interrupted by the call of one or other of the drivers as horses wrenched stumps from the ground or hauled heavy-limbed trees across the hillside. Once, she thought she had heard one of the workers shout in pain, an unnerving cry, gone almost as quickly as it had arisen. She didn't think these people – these zombies – would have much compassion for their injured colleagues. She didn't like to think what might have happened to the one who had been hurt.

She slipped closer to Alen. 'Who are those people?'

'I wouldn't want to say for certain, but from what I could see I would guess they are Seron.'

'Seron?'

'Seron warriors.' Alen's voice rose slightly. 'One of Nerak's little toys: he used to employ them for his most disagreeable tasks. They're tough, soulless killers he breeds in a sickening ceremony you don't even want to imagine. He hasn't used Seron in Twinmoons – rutters, I'd say maybe five or six hundred Twinmoons – but I'm pretty sure that's what they are.' He pulled back the hood of his cloak and searched the darkness for Hoyt and Churn.

'Warriors?' Hannah said. 'Why would warriors be here cutting down trees?'

'I don't think intimidating people would work for this – no matter how much under Nerak's control they might be, the ghosts would get them,' Alen explained. 'I'm not sure what, but my guess is that he's collecting the bark and leaves from these trees for something – doubtless something evil.'

'A potion?' Hannah couldn't believe she was discussing magical potions while lying face-down in the dirt hoping some zombie warrior wouldn't discover her while he was busy slaughtering innocent – okay, maybe not *innocent*, exactly – trees.

'Something like that, yes,' Alen said, 'but we don't call them potions.'

'They didn't seem to notice us – or anything. Are these Seron dangerous? They seemed like—' she stopped, not sure if the word meant anything here, then continued, 'well, they seemed like zombies to me.'

'Zombies,' Alen said. 'Interesting word.'

'It means— well, I guess it means the living dead, or the walking dead.'

'Well then, Seron are not zombies,' Alen said, 'they are very much alive; Nerak has never given them the chance to die – although I believe most of them would welcome death.'

'But are these Seron dangerous? They don't seem to be.'

Alen looked at her and Hannah could see fear mixed with amusement in his face. 'If they were to capture us tonight, Hannah, they would tear our bodies apart, most likely celebrate with a macabre ritual – using pieces of us – and then eat what was left over. Yes. They are extremely dangerous, and we will be exceedingly careful to avoid them.'

Hannah listened to the Seron working among the trees. 'Why doesn't the forest take over their minds like it did ours?'

'I am afraid that just being a Seron warrior is more terrifying than anything the forest of ghosts could show them: those men and women are constantly tortured by glimpses of who they once were, long ago. It must be tragic.'

'But you said Nerak breeds them.' Hannah was curious. 'What have they got to remember if they come from parents who have already lost their souls?'

'Seron produce human children, Hannah, because despite their appearance, they remain human. It is just that once a child is born to a Seron woman, it is—' He paused, searching for the right words.

'They are immediately expendable?'

'And once they have grown enough to perform basic survival needs, Nerak strips them of their sense of themselves, leaving a shell to fill with whatever values or ideas he likes. He has been known to experiment, filling Seron children with animal urges – dog and grettan senses … *hideous*.' Alen shuddered.

'How do you know so much about them when you said there haven't been any in over five hundred Twinmoons?' Hannah sounded sceptical.

The lines in Alen's face seemed to deepen. 'Because, Hannah, I was with him when he learned the process.' He stopped talking as Hoyt and Churn materialised out of the darkness. The horses' hooves were wrapped in torn cloth to deaden the sound.

Still moving close to the ground, Hoyt beckoned to the others and whispered, 'Let's go.'

Rising as silently as she could, Hannah felt the stiffness in her legs and promised herself a steaming hot bath, an icy-cold gin and tonic, and at least an hour with the *Denver Post* at the first decent hotel they passed. She struggled to get astride the saddle and felt Churn reach over and haul her onto it; he patted her on the back, slipped across to his own mount and waited for Hoyt to motion them forward.

Hannah reined in the horse to a slow but steady walk and tried not to think about the Seron children. It was the most appalling thing she had ever imagined, building an army over a generation of abuse, and focused cruelty. As the sounds of the Seron, chopping, sawing and stripping enchanted trees from the forest of ghosts, filled the night, Hannah swallowed hard: she had no idea that anything so terrible could exist – in any world.

As she followed Hoyt north along the path the wagons had taken earlier that day, she tried not to think what might be waiting for them as they moved closer to the Malakasian border and Welstar Palace.

THE FALKAN PLAIN

'That's it,' Garec said. 'Whittle it down, but don't cut it too deeply, or you'll leave weak spots – trust me, the last thing you want is to have an old bow shatter at full draw just because you chipped away too much at one area.'

'How do I know if it's too thin?' Mark stopped shaving the freshly cut branch and waited for clarification.

'You've got plenty of wood left right now,' Garec said. 'Keep going and when you've cleared some of the outer layers, use mine as a model. Gods know I don't want it any more.'

'But yours is wrapped. What is that? Leather? Hide?'

'Hide strips,' Garec nodded. 'I tan them from deerskin and use them to strengthen the bow. It's a tedious process, but if you dip them in salt water then wrap them across each other, they dry up and tighten into a tough but still pliable layer.'

'I want to do that too,' Mark said.

'Well,' Garec said, amused, 'first you've got to kill a deer.'

'That's fine. I'll shoot the next one I see.' Mark had never been a hunter. Apart from his attempt at fishing with Versen's bow and a few wild shots at flocks of ducks unfortunate enough to be flying over Port Jefferson one autumn many years earlier – none of the ducks were ever in any real danger – he had never fired a weapon of any kind.

'You'll have to find one,' Garec said. 'Then you'll have to hit it with an arrow – and forgive me for bringing it up, because I wasn't there, but didn't you struggle some with a bow the last time you tried this?'

Mark looked over at his Ronan friend; Garec could see the bruises where the Seron had punched him in the face. 'That was fishing, Garec. This is killing.'

Garec flashed back to the way Mark had used his superior swimming ability as a lethal weapon. He had no doubt Mark would use his new bow as often as he could. 'Trust me,' he said, 'you don't want to get so adept at killing that it begins to feel like fishing.'

'I think I know the difference.' Mark didn't look up from his work.

'For now, yes, but after a while, the lines begin to blur. It gets easier – too easy.'

Mark stopped whittling and looked at Garec. 'I don't need you to worry about my soul. If God exists – and I still believe He does – but He certainly hasn't been around this neighbourhood in a while. He and I can settle our accounts another day.'

Garec hesitated a moment, then, unnerved, asked, 'So your God doesn't permit killing?'

'Oh, He permits plenty of it, but He— He disapproves.'

'How does he feel about fishing then?' Garec forced a smile.

Mark laughed for the first time in days. 'I understand He was quite a fisherman himself, Garec! You just teach me to shoot this thing and I'll take care of the rest.' He held the branch aloft. 'How's this?'

Once, while exploring at Riverend Palace, Garec had come across a room that looked as if it had been an art room, maybe a classroom, filled with half-finished sculptures, figures struggling to emerge from otherwise nondescript sections of red oak or marble. The fire that destroyed the palace more than a thousand Twinmoons earlier had missed the chamber. Garec had been unsettled by his discovery – as though he had come upon something he shouldn't be seeing: two adulterers locked in a tryst, perhaps. The sculptures all evolved into something terrifying; not a flower emerging from a walnut log or a woman's face slipping free from marble bonds, but malformed, half-finished things – souls trapped between who they had been and who they might become. There were birds flying gracefully with one wing, trapped in the wood by the other, and an enormous red oak log in the centre of the room, taller than him, that halfway up changed into a man. Garec figured it was Prince Markon, but all his efforts to superimpose a kingly face and noble demeanour on the carving failed; the man had a desperate look in his eyes, and looked as if he was struggling to escape.

In all his time at Riverend Palace, Garec had never returned to the room. There was something wrong with those sculptures, a thousand Twinmoons old and still trapped. As he watched Mark whittle away at the length of green wood, Garec felt the same sense of unease; he was watching a killer being born with a few strokes of a hunting knife along a branch. He looked down at the foreigner's boots, nearly buried in a pile of shavings: would his feet disappear entirely before Mark was finished sculpting his bow?

'What's that?' Mark said.

'What?' Garec stammered, 'nothing— well, it's just that I wish you would reconsider this decision.'

'Sorry.'

'It doesn't make anything better. You realise that.' This last was a statement.

'I have to learn my own lessons, Garec – I always have. I don't want you to feel badly for me. We're friends, and I appreciate you helping, but this is something I have to do.'

Garec couldn't stand it any longer; he needed Mark to move, to see the shavings piled around Mark's ankles were not going to solidify and drink him bodily back into some wooden womb.

He blurted out the first thing that came to mind: 'Why don't you set that aside for now and we'll go and find a deer?'

'You're going to help me kill a deer?' Mark raised an eyebrow, his knife stilled in his lap.

'Sure.' Garec started to sweat, but he knew what had to be done. 'Someone has to teach you, or gods rest us, we'll all end up with arrows in our backsides.'

Mark stood up, his boots breaking free of the pile of wood off-cuts; Garec inwardly sighed in relief and gathered up his quivers.

Steven, sitting nearby mending a tear in his leggings, called after them, 'I like mine medium-well, with onions, tomatoes, mayo and pickles.'

'Pickles?' Mark called back. 'Yuk! Would you like fries with that, too?'

'And a beer!' Steven laughed and tossed a log on their fire as Mark and Garec disappeared into the trees. He looked around for Gilmour, who was making his way towards the camp; he'd been scouting ahead, trying to work out how far they'd travelled since leaving the fjord. Steven had a sense it was a good long way. Gilmour insisted that they ride at night. They had left the fjord the night Mark killed the Seron warriors – Steven thought of it as murder, but every time he tried to broach the topic, Mark shot him a withering glance that said, *you have no idea how I have suffered or how I still suffer, so back off.* And Steven had. While Mark slept, comforted by Gilmour's spell, the others packed hastily, needing to be away before any other Seron arrived. Then they'd awakened Mark and climbed out of the fjord, an easier journey than Steven had expected, even in the darkness.

They needed horses, and luck or fate had provided: a farmer who had a small homestead nestled in the hills had directed the travellers to a much larger farm less than a day's march away, where Garec bartered with a singularly disagreeable woman for four sturdy horses and saddlery. They paid too much, but with all of Central Falkan to cross, they were not in much of a position to complain.

At Gilmour's insistence, they were back in the saddle after nightfall. The old man galloped in front of the others, his cloak billowing out behind, and as he passed, Steven felt the hickory staff's magic, first as a faint prickle, then there in full force, wrapping him in a protective layer, as if it sensed something about to happen. But nothing attacked them, and Gilmour didn't lead them headlong over a cliff or into a lurking rank of homicidal wraiths. Steven, ready to shout out a warning at any moment, waited, wondering why the magic had suddenly sparked into life—

Then he noticed the plain ... There was nothing special about the ground beneath his horse's hoofs, nor did they *seem* to be moving unnaturally fast, but out beyond his field of view, the earth and sky had melted into one to form a blurry black backdrop: the world was moving past them faster than Steven had at first realised. He was glad Gilmour had ordered the night ride across Falkan, for it was very disconcerting, but at least the trip to the border between Falkan and Gorsk wouldn't take long.

He was disappointed they wouldn't see more of the vast and fertile Falkan Plain, for this huge area of rich arable soil provided fruit and vegetables for most of the Eastlands, as well as fine grazing for a wide variety of livestock. Farms abounded, and every town, no matter how small, had its daily market filled with local farmers selling or trading the autumn harvest. Winter was on its way and everyone was busy storing food for the leaner times ahead.

Steven didn't fool himself into thinking he had discovered a Utopian corner of Eldarn: it was plain the farmers here were not exactly revelling in lives of excess, any more than the dockers and townsfolk in Orindale. There was food as far as he could see, and the people of central Falkan ought to have looked much healthier, but most were thin, many to the point of gauntness, and clothes, though usually neat, were patched and mended. He didn't have to ask Garec to confirm that much of what had been harvested was earmarked for Malagon's occupation forces. This picturesque village, set amongst fertile fields and grassy meadows and heavy with the mouth-watering aromas of grilled meat, tecan and rich cheeses, was filled with sorrow and want.

These people needed someone to organise them: they needed to be educated about what could be possible if they only cut the head off the serpent – in this case, Nerak. Steven couldn't believe they hadn't already risen up together in defiance – everything here in Eldarn cried out for just that: revolution.

He started thinking about Garec's vision – Garec was certain he had witnessed a last-moment attempt to carry on the Ronan line, a grim coupling of a servant girl and a madman. Was that what they were supposed to do? Find that offspring and ensure he or she ascended to power and restored peace and prosperity to Eldarn? The breadth of what needed to be done overwhelmed him and he threw up his hands in frustration.

'First things first, Steven,' he told himself firmly, 'save the world now. *Fix it* later.' He tried not to be disheartened by what he was seeing: rich, dark soil tilled by starving people who no longer cared, for their crops were going to the enemy.

As Gilmour approached through the trees, Steven wondered how the old man was planning to bring prosperity to Eldarn – always assuming they survived the coming battle with Nerak, of course.

'You look deep in thought.' Gilmour sat down.

'There is *so* much to do.'

The old man chuckled. 'Just realising that now, are you?'

'You know what I mean,' Steven said.

'I do. I've been telling myself that for thousands of Twinmoons. I guess I know as well as anyone what has to happen for these lands to prosper.'

'But we have to save them first.' Steven fought an almost overwhelming feeling of despondency. He decided to change the subject. 'I'm worried about Mark.'

'Mark will be fine.'

'He's going to get himself killed.'

'Mark needs time – perhaps more time than we can give him – but there's nothing else that will ease his suffering right now. When you have lived as long and seen as much as I have, Steven, there are a few things you know, and one of them is that time can heal a wagonload of pain and suffering.'

Steven nodded. There was a long comfortable silence between them. Eventually, he gestured towards Gilmour's hands, lean and strong now, no longer the gnarled, arthritic hands of the old fisherman. 'You've made some improvements, I see.'

Gilmour turned his hands over and flexed his fingers. 'You noticed. I tightened a few cords, improved some muscle tone and—' he pointed two fingers at his eyes, '—sharpened my eyesight a notch or two.'

'It's amazing. I still can't get used to the fact that you can work such wonders.'

'You've done some wondrous things yourself, Steven,' Gilmour countered. 'You staved off an almor. No one has done that in thousands of Twinmoons. You fought a wraith army, saved Garec – twice – and saved the rest of us from the Seron that night in the foothills, and from what I understand you did quite a decent job of blowing up that bone-collector there in the cavern.'

'But nothing like you can do,' Steven said softly. 'The way you pounded away at Nerak: I was terrified. I couldn't have called up the staff's power that night; I just couldn't keep my thoughts straight. And now – how much ground are we covering? Are we really travelling four or five times faster than normal?'

Gilmour nodded. 'It's an old trick – a fairly simple one, actually. Nerak taught it to me when we were hurrying to get from Gorsk to a harvest festival outside Capehill in the south.' He broke off and sighed. 'We were still friends at the time – we were going for the wine, the music, the food and the women. Nerak created the spell for that trip. The last time he used this spell that I know of was when he went to Port Denis.'

Steven sat up straight. 'You mentioned Port Denis to him that night on the *Prince Marek.*'

'That's right. He rode there, ten or twelve days of hard riding, in a matter of avens.' Now Gilmour sounded despondent. 'His power is tremendous, and terrifying.'

'What happened when he got there?' Steven was still, almost frozen in place. He wasn't sure he wanted to know the answer to his question.

'Nerak wiped Port Denis clean of every living thing with a wave of one hand.'

'Sonofabitch,' Steven muttered, falling back into English. 'Where did he learn all this? How did he get to be so powerful – and so singularly destructive?'

'It probably helped that no one ever challenged him, especially early on. I certainly didn't, not after my embarrassing débâcle that night at Sandcliff Palace. It was never in me. Kantu was always much more adept at magic and sorcery than I, but he was wrestling demons of his own at the time and when he was finally ready to take on Nerak, the Nerak we had known all our lives, that man was already gone and the demon servant of the great evil lying dormant in the Fold had taken over.'

'How much did he get from that book? He was certain that was what we were after – have you read it? Will it teach you what you need to be ready for him?'

Gilmour swallowed hard and tucked his shaking hands beneath his thighs, hoping to still them.

Steven, misinterpreting Gilmour's silence, retrieved the spell book from the pack beside them and said, 'I've been paging through it a bit myself.'

Gilmour started. 'You have? When?'

'Sorry – I didn't think you'd mind.' A little abashed, Steven closed the book and tried to hand it over. 'You know, that night on the *Prince Marek*, it was different. When I touched the book, it was like I had fallen into a pit and couldn't get out – maybe didn't *want* to get out; there was light and colour, and things made sense, even things I had never imagined, things I never knew existed. Everything seemed logical, like there was an order to what was and what could or couldn't be.

'But since then, something's happened – maybe because the book isn't on the ship anymore – but I can touch it now, open it, read the text, whatever. But I didn't realise you wanted me to stay away from it, so I'll leave it to you. I'm really sorry.'

Gilmour ignored the spell book Steven was still holding out towards him. 'No, no, that's fine – of course you can read it if you wish.' He gestured for Steven to take it back, then said casually, 'Can you understand the text?'

'Nope, almost none of it – although I can make out a few words here and there. What language is this, anyway?' He turned a few pages idly.

'It is a very old, very dead form of Malakasian.' Gilmour was sweating now.

'So Nerak was from Malakasia?'

The old man struggled to hear over his pounding heart; it was getting harder to stay focused on their conversation.

'No, I guess Lessek had to be from Malakasia.' Steven answered his own question as he mouthed a word or two, and then snapped the book shut. 'Well, this is all yours, Gilmour – I'm afraid it won't do any good in my hands.' He held it out once again and this time, hesitantly, Gilmour took it.

In the moment before Steven closed the book, Gilmour had read the same words, *the ash dream*. He tried to hide the fact that he was in a state: he was panting as if a great weight had landed on his chest, and his ribs burned where they had cracked that night along the fjord.

For the first time since Gilmour had joined him, Steven noticed something was wrong. 'Are you okay? What do you think? Can you do it?'

'To answer your earlier question, yes, I have opened it. And can I use it? Honestly? No.' Gilmour retreated to the comforting idea that had kept him going. 'We have the key, and I know there is something in the third Windscroll that I am supposed to find, and that's a place to begin. We have to get to Sandcliff as quickly as possible, preferably before Nerak finds a way back from Colorado, because I shall need as much time as possible to find the scroll, open the spell table and work out how the two must work together if we're to banish him and seal the Fold for ever. I know something about your trip back home has made you confident we'll be able to do this, but I must admit, my own confidence has been waning somewhat since that night on the harbour.' He massaged his ribs again.

'But why? Because of the book? Maybe the book doesn't enter into the equation,' Steven cajoled him. 'Look, the key opened the Fold, Gilmour. I saw it. The whole world stopped and melted into a canvas with three rips in it. I saw right through one of them to where the far portal was buried beneath two tons of rotting meat and disposable diapers. That key is formidable. If it can give us the Fold's mystical dimensions – and it must have worked once, because Lessek was able to open the portal gates and keep them opened at will – then *we* can shut them, I know we can. *You* can do it, Gilmour, because we will have the same power Lessek had when he created the far portal in the first place.'

Gilmour sighed. 'I wish I had your confidence, my friend.'

'You *do* have my confidence,' Steven said, 'because closing the damned Fold for ever is only the first thing we need to do for Eldarn – and I *know* it can be done. I've seen it.'

'And then?'

'Then, we revolt.'

'All right.' Gilmour, looking tired, nodded more emphatically.

'All right. The third Windscroll. Gods grant it's still there.'

'It will be.'

'How do you know?'

'Because if Nerak knew his weaknesses were documented in that scroll, he would have destroyed it by now, or he would have—'

'Put it in your bank.'

'Put it in my bank, right.'

'The third Windscroll.' Gilmour held out his hand.

Steven clasped it and felt the sinewy strength of the old fisherman's grip. 'The third Windscroll. When can we get there?'

'It will only be a few more days.'

'Let's get on with it, as soon as Mark and Garec get back.'

Nerak slammed on the brakes, throwing the pick-up into a tailspin and causing several cars behind him to take to the shoulder in an effort to avoid a multi-car pile-up.

'Hey asshole!' someone shouted, 'play with it later in the bathroom, huh? Give us a break!'

The dark prince, cloaked now in Jennifer Sorenson's postman, a forty-six-year-old listed as missing with the Denver Police, glared at the passing motorist and noted the car, a white Ford driven by a woman with a comical hairstyle and three silver rings in her left earlobe. 'I will deal with you later,' he said, then, ignoring the horns and shouted abuse of the townsfolk and tourists making their way into Silverthorn, he rested his head against the rear window of the cab and closed his eyes.

It was the book; Fantus had opened the book again. How could the snivelling sap be that stupid? 'Did you not believe me, Fantus?' he muttered.

Almost as quickly as it had come, the sensation was gone; the book was closed, but Nerak wasn't concerned. 'I'll be waiting next time,' he promised, putting the car back into drive and pressing the accelerator. Though the tyres spun on the snow-packed highway, he picked up speed down the slope into Silverthorn. He had a sense of where he would find Jennifer and his far portal, but if Fantus and that irritating foreigner continued to experiment with Lessek's spell book, he wouldn't need her at all.

'Read all you like, Fantus,' Nerak said. 'It will be more than your ribs I break next time, my old friend.' As he pushed a wad of *Confederate Son* into his mouth, he came alongside the white Ford. He slowed to match the woman's speed, and waved until she turned to look at him, then offered her a broad, tobacco-stained grin. She tried to let him overtake, but Nerak kept pace with her, slowing as she slowed and speeding up as necessary, looking at her constantly through the window.

When she tried to turn onto the exit ramp for Silverthorn, Nerak took over, laughing as she struggled to turn the frozen steering wheel. He pressed his foot to the floor, revving the pick-up's engine, and this time the white Ford kept pace with him.

He drove faster and faster, until the pick-up's engine was screeching in protest, topping a hundred miles per hour, the dark prince gestured at the dashboard and the speedometer began climbing again: one hundred and five, one hundred and fifteen, one hundred and eighteen miles per hour – and still the woman in the white Ford kept pace. She was screaming now, and beating at her window, pleading with – God? – someone, anyway, in amusingly inaudible cries, for her shouts were drowned by the din of the two engines. He shattered both windows, his and hers, with a glance, all the better to hear her beg for her life.

'I'll think of you later as I play with it in the bathroom!' he shouted. 'And I thank you for the advice – I hadn't realised playing with it in the middle of the road was so inappropriate. I really do owe you my thanks.' He laughed, spraying tobacco-juice everywhere. Some dripped into the sore on the back of the postal worker's hand.

The woman screamed for him to stop, to slow down and to let her go.

Nerak turned his attention to the highway ahead. 'Ah,' he said, 'here's just the thing.' A logging truck, fully loaded with stripped pine trunks, was in the path of the speeding Ford as it inched up a short incline. Nerak turned to watch the woman again as her earrings caught the sunlight. At the last moment, her hands bloody and torn from ripping away the broken glass from the window, she tried to climb out of her car, but half out, she seemed to change her mind. Her blouse was ripped and she was bleeding from dozens of cuts. With the car bearing down on the trailer at over a hundred and twenty miles per hour, she made a final attempt to escape—

It was too late.

Nerak thought her the most beautifully wretched woman he had seen in several hundred Twinmoons.

'You ought to be more polite, my dear,' the dark prince shouted as he allowed his pick-up to break away and watched the Ford disappear beneath the back of the logging truck with a resounding crash of tearing metal and shattering glass.

The woman with the silly hairstyle and the silver earrings, trapped halfway out of the window, had been cut neatly in half. Now the upper part of her torso bounced along the highway until it came to rest in a snowbank. What was left of her car was dragged behind the truck for a while, then slid off the road into a snowy ditch as logs tumbled and rolled from the overturned trailer. Traffic screeched to a stop, and a few Samaritans hustled up the shoulder on foot.

Amusing himself with the irritating woman's murder had made Nerak miss the exits for Silverthorn and Breckenridge. He slowed down and, ignoring the cars in both directions blasting their horns as they stomped on their brakes to avoid hitting him, made a U-turn into the eastbound lane.

'Silverthorn,' he said firmly. 'She's in Silverthorn.'

It was dark when Garec and Mark returned from the meadow, lugging a deer's hind quarter and several bloody chunks of flesh, more than enough meat to sustain the four men for several nights. As sorry as Garec was to leave the bulk of the deer's body abandoned in the meadow, they would reach Traver's Notch before they would need to replenish their stores again. He doubted the deer's carcase would last the night; there was no shortage of local predators to make use of it.

Steven rose when he saw the others come into the firelight. 'All right, Garec! I'm glad to see you're back to normal – good for you!'

'Much as I appreciate the sentiment, Steven,' Garec said, 'tonight's credit goes to Mark.'

'No!' Steven looked as his friend in astonishment. 'You did this?'

Mark nodded.

'You? Mister-Greenpeace-Loving-Earth-First-Soya-Milk-Bleeding-Liberal-Anti-NRA-Gun-Control-Advocate-High-School-Teacher? You shot Bambi with a bow?'

'Bambi's mother, actually,' Mark smiled. 'Bambi was a buck.'

'A buck? You mean a little boy deer? You're from New York, Mark – since when do New Yorkers shoot Bambi's mother with a bow?'

'One shot,' Garec said, 'through the lung. It wasn't pretty and we had to track her for a stretch through those trees and then out into the plain, but she finally fell. It's sad that she suffered a bit.'

'Through the lung,' Mark repeated. 'I missed the heart. It was grim. I'll have to be more careful next time.'

'How about next time, we go into some town and buy a few grettan burgers?' Steven said. 'Really. On me. I've got several hundred thousand left in silver. I'll spring for pickles, onions, the works.'

Mark turned to Garec. 'Will the hide make it to the next town without rotting?'

Steven hadn't seen the length of rolled deerskin draped over Mark's shoulder. 'The hide? And what are we going to do with that, Uncas? Are you making a pair of trews? Planning to sing with the Doors this summer?'

'It's for my bow,' Mark said, waiting for Garec's answer.

'It should be fine,' Garec said. 'We've scraped it fairly clean and we'll salt and soak it tomorrow – even if it's not dry by the time we have to ride again, it will keep until we can stretch and tan it properly.'

'Great,' Steven said, 'well, keep me in mind for a nice football. Christmas is coming and I've got lovely woollen sweaters planned for you two. Of course, I'll just need to borrow your bow the next time we come across a herd of sheep, Garec.'

'Use the staff,' Garec joked. 'It'll be easier – and far less messy.'

'This will slow us down a bit tonight,' Gilmour said, interrupting the banter, 'but it's all right. Let's get it cooked and eaten, and let's get the rest wrapped up and ready to ride.' He moved off to continue packing.

'What's with him?' Mark asked.

Steven lowered his voice. 'He's not sure he's up to the task ahead. You've seen how fast we're travelling every night. He's moving towards a conflict that may kill us all – him too.'

'It's worse than that,' Garec whispered as well. 'If he can't use the key, or the scroll, it won't be much of a conflict at all.'

'You're right, Garec,' Mark said. 'We may get crushed before we have a chance to get in the game.'

'I wish he was more confident,' Steven said. 'I mean, what choice does he have now? Hell, we're going to be there in a couple of days.'

'One hundred and thirty-five years of preparation and hiding? I'd be nervous, too,' Mark said.

'Yes, but this is something more. He is questioning things *he* put in motion, that got us started along this path from the beginning. Remember when we came down from Seer's Peak? He was excited about the Windscrolls because Lessek told him Nerak's weakness lies elsewhere. He was relieved that we hadn't made the mistake of charging into Welstar Palace and getting ourselves killed.'

'Right,' Garec said, 'hearing from Lessek was lucky. So we turned to Sandcliff and the scroll library. What's your point?'

'I got the sense from him tonight that even this plan to get the key and the scroll might not be the right one.'

'But we've known that all along,' Mark said. 'Everyone knew we were essentially flying blind.'

'But it was *Gilmour's* confidence that got us here. He didn't want us doing anything until he read that scroll and had some time to experiment with the spell table.'

'And now he's questioning that?'

'Right – but I don't know why. Something happened to him while I was gone. Nerak must have said something, or done something – you should have seen him tonight; I couldn't even get him to touch that spell book, never mind read it. Did he look at it at all while I was gone?'

Garec looked thoughtful. 'Come to think of it, I've never even seen him open it.'

'Me neither,' Mark added. 'So what do we do?'

'I don't know,' Steven said. 'Ride hard, get to Sandcliff as quickly as we can, and do whatever we need to get him as much time with that table as possible before Old Shithead gets back. More than that, I'm at a loss.'

'What about the staff?' Garec asked. 'You seem to have some idea how to make it work for you these days.'

'Somewhat,' Steven answered, 'but most of the time, it feels like the magic comes and goes of its own will. I've called it up myself, but not as frequently as it has shown up unannounced.'

'Or not bothered to show up at all,' Mark said, recalling the staff's failure battling the river demon in Meyers' Vale.

'That's true, too, but I did something the day I was at the dump and I know if I could get back to that level of— I don't even know what, but that frame of mind I was in, maybe: if I can get back to that, I bet I *could* do it. I could close the Fold myself.' He tried to grip the air above their campfire – that was the clearest recollection he had, that he had been able to feel the very air around him. The Fold was everywhere, and that day Steven had been able to touch it.

Mark clapped his roommate on the shoulder, jolting him back to the present. 'You know I love you, buddy, but let's hope it doesn't all come down to your all-encompassing maths-and-compassion strategy.'

'It's right there, Mark. I can taste it ... but I can't quite get it in focus. It's like your struggle to make sense of Lessek and your dad. We are on the verge of having this entire dilemma worked out, but until we do ...' his voice trailed off.

'We're in some grand rutting trouble.' Garec finished the thought.

Steven nodded.

'Well, you heard Gilmour. We can continue pondering our collective quandaries while we skin and cook this meat. He's made it quite clear he wants to get moving, so let's get busy.'

ORINDALE'S SOUTHERN WHARF

'Great rutting whores,' Jacrys exclaimed, 'what's happened to you?'

Carpello Jax pulled the door closed and took a seat beside the spy. He did look different – thinner – and his beard had filled in nicely. The sore on the side of his nose was disgusting: raw and festering, obviously infected because he'd constantly picked at it. Now Carpello dabbed at it periodically with a handkerchief. He stretched his feet towards the fireplace. 'I am making some rudimentary changes to my appearance. It has come to my attention that this may be an appropriate time for me to fade into the background for a while.'

'You?' Jacrys laughed, 'when everyone knows who you are? Half the city works for you. Your captains cross the Ravenian Sea to Pellia on a timetable more predictable than the Twinmoon. Your cargo is hauled upriver on gigantic barges for everyone in Malakasia to see. You're supplying an army, Carpello … forgive me, but I don't believe shedding some excess blubber and carving a hole in the side of your face are going to make much of a difference. And good gods, why did you cut off half your nose, anyway?'

'It's no matter,' Carpello replied, waving the question away. 'It is something that needed to be attended to, and I have attended to it.' Versen's warning echoed in his memory: *you'll be dead and she will make it last for Twinmoons.* 'So tell me. Why are we meeting here and not at my home? And if you don't mind me saying, you are hardly one to talk about personal appearance: you look hideous yourself. When is the last time you slept in a real bed, Jacrys? And your clothes – you were always such a smart dresser!'

Jacrys resisted the urge to reach out and slap the bigger man across the face. 'We're meeting here, because I have Sallax Farro of Estrad here, and I look like this because I have been sleeping here, eating here and working here for I don't know how many days now, trying to get some information out of him.'

Carpello grimaced. 'I'm sure you've dealt with challenging prisoners before. What's the problem?'

'The problem is that he genuinely doesn't appear to recall that he is Sallax of Estrad,' Jacrys said. 'Last time I spoke to him was in the Blackstone Mountains, near Seer's Peak – he and the others had survived the grettans, a platoon of Seron, even an almor, and they were making good progress on their way here.'

'So what happened?'

'I don't know.' Jacrys rose and fetched a flagon of wine from a shelf behind the desk. He didn't offer any to Carpello. 'But while I was crossing, our prince told me to move west and then north, breaking off my pursuit of the partisans to meet with him here. He told me he was bringing something terrible, something to *address* the issue, and to retrieve the stone key.'

'And you think that whatever he sent to deal with the partisans left Sallax half mad?'

Jacrys nodded. 'I don't know how they survived the Blackstones. I killed Gilmour. The foreigner, Steven Taylor, had run off by himself and the other, the South Coaster, Mark Jenkins, was trailing him. An unholy storm blew through, snow almost to my waist – I thought for certain we were all going to die. The prince gave me a deer and even with that I barely made it here alive.

'Sallax's lot were broken, distraught at having lost Gilmour, and lost and separated in the worst storm I have ever seen – and yet they made it to Orindale *and* made their way through the pickets into the city, all without Gilmour's help.'

'How do you know they all arrived?'

Jacrys was not accustomed to explaining himself to the likes of Carpello, but for now, he needed the merchant's help. 'I know they made it here because I shot and possibly killed Garec Haile and because I have Sallax tied up in your warehouse, you horsecock!'

'All right, all right.' Carpello raised his hands in apology. 'Calm down, I've been away and I just need to catch up with what's been going on, that's all.'

'You've been away supervising a shipment – a likely story, Carpello; do you think the prince will believe you?'

The merchant mopped at the beads of sweat that trickled across his forehead. 'Look at you, Jacrys, you're a rutting mess yourself; it's glaringly obvious that you've fallen from the prince's good graces. All right, I admit it; I had a wretched trip. I lost both partisans. The whoresons jumped ship, even *bound*, they jumped and then – and you're going to love this – the rutting Seron he sent me jumped in too. No one could have survived, so yes, I did think it might be best to hide for a few days and maybe let the prince move on.'

'He's still here.'

Carpello stifled his gasp, swallowing hard.

'Actually,' Jacrys continued, 'no one has seen him in nearly a Moon, but he hasn't left the city. I'm assuming you know about the *Prince Marek*.'

Carpello nodded, then changed the subject back. 'So what exactly have you managed to get out of Sallax?'

'Not much.' Jacrys examined the wine goblet. 'He keeps talking about wraiths, a rock and a river.'

Carpello shrugged. 'It doesn't mean anything to me.'

'And he's a gods-rutting disaster. His shoulder looks like it was broken and left to heal in a horribly unnatural position. I brought a healer in a few days ago to re-break it and that was a nightmare – he's still as strong as a grettan. He was all bent over, twisted in pain all the time. He's tied up now in that cot you had back there.' The spy gestured towards the large storage area behind Carpello's office.

'You re-broke his shoulder?'

'Yes, I want him whole, healed, friendly with me again. He trusted me once and we helped each other get to Gilmour.'

'But that's done. Why keep Sallax alive now?'

Jacrys lowered his voice, leaning across the table and staring into Carpello's eyes. 'Because I want the stone and I want the—' He paused, deciding to leave out any mention of the curious staff Steven Taylor had wielded against the almor. 'I want the stone, and I want to deliver it to Prince Malagon in person: my last assignment before I retire. That'll be my grand gesture, handing the stone over to him. And then I want to get out of here.'

'So what role do I play?' Carpello lifted himself from his chair and rose to pour his own goblet of wine.

'I need information, and I want to know that every barge captain, every crewman, every carriage and wagon driver, every stevedore and every whore you have working for you is out looking for them. I need to know where they are and where they're going, and what they are doing when they get there – and I want to know it all yesterday.'

'So what's in it for me? Why should I help you with this?'

Jacrys' face reddened. 'Why should you help me? How about to keep me from cutting your bloated black heart out of your fat chest and feeding it to Sallax? And trust me, Carpello, the *thing* I have tied up back there would find it delicious.'

Carpello cringed; though a bully, he was a coward. Jacrys had no idea how the merchant had gained such power, but right now he didn't care – he would be very happy to kill Carpello as soon as he knew the whereabouts of Steven Taylor, the wooden staff and the keystone Prince Malagon wanted so badly.

Carpello marshalled his courage. 'Threatening me won't do you any good, Jacrys, not if you want me to help find your lost quarry. Again, what do *I* get out of this?'

Jacrys smiled. It wasn't reassuring. 'What do you want?'

Carpello leaned forward, his words almost tumbling over each other in his rush to speak – and before he was halfway through he was silently cursing himself for showing his naked desperation. 'I want to come with you, I know it's dangerous, but I want to be there when you hand the stone over. I want it to be from us. I want him to know that although I lost the bastards overboard, I didn't fail him.'

Jacrys sat back, contemplating his colleague. 'A wise decision, Carpello. You might just save your own life.'

'Is that yes?'

Jacrys said, 'You'll have everyone in your employment combing the country for them?'

'Done.' Carpello raised his glass in anticipation. 'There will be no place for them to hide.'

Jacrys reciprocated. 'Then we have an agreement.'

'Excellent,' Carpello said, draining his glass. 'Shall we visit your prisoner?'

The spy pursed his lips and nodded.

'Wake up, Sallax.' Jacrys tugged at the big Ronan's toes, exposed where they stuck out at the end of his blanket. 'Wake up, please.'

Jacrys had been thorough in his care: Sallax had been bathed, shaved and given a much-needed haircut. His leggings were clean, and his bare chest crisscrossed with bandages.

Carpello was impressed: Sallax was a powerful-looking man. The merchant wiped at his nose and said, 'I thought he was a mess. He looks just fine to me, apart from the shoulder and all. Healthy skin tone; and well-defined muscles: he looks good.'

'You should have seen him when I brought him here. Lucky for me he was so weak from malnutrition and dehydration because even so he nearly killed me. I had to cut him a couple of times across the chest – I stitched the slashes and wrapped them before the healer came in to re-set his shoulder.'

'It seems like a lot of trouble to go to for one man.'

'One man who knows more about the organised resistance in the southeast than anyone in Eldarn – the one person who knows how to get to Gilmour's home in Estrad, how to find Gilmour's writings, his personal effects – whatever I want. This man is too valuable to kill. I need him to trust me again.' He turned back to the cot. 'Sallax, wake up.'

With a groan, the man on the cot, clean and well nourished now, after who knew how long, tried to roll onto his side, but he was bound in place. He opened his eyes with a start, struggled for a moment to get free and then relaxed, obviously saving his strength. It was apparent he had been well trained, for as soon as he realised he was unable to break loose, he quieted. His gaze moved from Jacrys to Carpello. Even worn down and lashed to the cot as he was, Sallax still terrified the fat merchant.

'How are you tonight, Sallax?' Jacrys sat on the edge of the cot.

'Girl – the girl knew his name.' Sallax's voice came out more a groan that anything else; it sounded unused, grating.

'What girl, Sallax? You mentioned her before. Who is she?'

'She knew Sallax.'

'She knew Sallax? Well, that's interesting. Sallax, tell me where Steven and Garec are tonight. Do you know?'

At the mention of the partisans' names, Sallax bellowed, an anguished cry, devoid of hope. For a moment Carpello felt sorry for him as Sallax rocked his head back and forth across the pillow, screaming, 'Can't see him, can't see him. He's blurry, can't see him, too far away.'

Jacrys asked again, 'Who is, Sallax? Gilmour, Garec, or Steven Taylor?' His question elicited another despondent cry.

Carpello interjected, 'That certainly sets him off doesn't it? Can you stop asking him that?'

Jacrys frowned. 'He was there that night. He wanted Gilmour dead almost as much as I did. I don't know what this means, why he would be suffering about it now – this man is a killer; he has no problem with death. Why he's beating himself up about Gilmour is a mystery.'

'Pain or guilt, or sadness.' Carpello threw up his hands. 'Take your pick.'

Jacrys ignored him and continued to press the point. 'Sallax, tell me what happened in the Blackstones.'

Tears slipped from his eyes and tracked down his cheeks to soak into the pillow. 'Can't see him, he's too far away,' he wept. 'The girl knows. She knows Sallax.'

'The Blackstones, Sallax, what happened in the Blackstones?'

The big man's voice dropped to a coarse whisper. 'River ... wraith.'

Carpello leaned in a little closer. 'What did he say?'

'River ... wraith in the river,' Sallax repeated.

'A wraith?' Jacrys clarified. 'What kind of wraith?'

'In the river.'

'Did a wraith attack you in the river? Was it here in Orindale?' Jacrys rested one palm on the clean bandage strips wrapped across the partisan's broad chest, the touch of a caring friend – the Malakasian would have gutted him then and there if he had known about Sallax's nocturnal killing sprees in the alleys near the wharf.

'How did Sallax survive in the mountains? The wraith attack?' Jacrys' voice was soothing.

'River.'

'He was in the river? Was it cold?'

'Cold.' Sallax tilted his head towards his injured shoulder. 'Cold.'

'He must have fallen, broken his back, maybe,' Carpello said softly. 'He was in the river when Prince Malagon sent a wraith or a spirit or something up there after them. Maybe he was trying to treat himself with the cold water.'

'Or hiding in the most unlikely place,' Jacrys said.

'I wonder how they survived the wraith,' Carpello said, 'especially if they didn't have Sallax to fight for them – could they all have hidden in the water? That must have been deadly cold.' The fat man shivered sympathetically.

Jacrys shrugged. 'We'll not know anything for certain until we get him back on his feet.' He was confident that it would have been Steven and the staff that had ensured their safe passage, and wondered again if the stone somehow loaned its power to the deadly branch, for no one had defeated an almor in thousands of Twinmoons. Jacrys shook his head, and started again, calmly, quietly, insistently. 'Why was Sallax in the river?'

The big man gestured towards his bound shoulder. 'River – cold.'

Carpello joined the questioning. 'Does Sallax know if Steven has the stone key?'

Sallax opened his eyes and laughed, almost a bark, making both Jacrys and Carpello jump. The laugh was a punctuation mark that said, *absolutely not.*

'We don't understand.' Carpello tried to make his voice sound as gentle and as soothing as the spy's. 'Does Steven Taylor have the stone key?'

'No key – no key,' Sallax smiled an unlikely grin and said, 'no stone key.'

Carpello was frustrated; this was the wrong answer and he was bored of playing question and answer games with an addled enemy of Malakasia. Emboldened by his sudden anger, he stepped up close to the partisan leader and launched into a barrage of threats, culminating in the ultimatum, 'I want you to understand, Sallax of Estrad, that I don't care in the slightest that you feel oh-so-bad for your precious Gilmour.'

Sallax strained against his bonds and growled something unintelligible at the mention of the old man.

'I'll say it again: Gilmour, Gilmour, *Gilmour*. Does that make you feel sad or guilty? I don't care. I want to know about the key!' Carpello's jowls jounced in time with the finger he wagged in Sallax's face.

Jacrys, fully expecting Sallax to scream again, moved to shove Carpello bodily away from his patient – he needed the merchant, but he'd send him home that evening minus a finger or perhaps even an eye if Carpello insisted on badgering Sallax further.

'Ren.'

Jacrys turned back to the trussed-up figure and Carpello said, 'What's that? Have you come to your senses? Lucky for you.'

Carpello mopped again at his brow; this was working. He had already got further in one evening than Jacrys had managed in all the time he had been sequestered in this hole. 'Now, say it again.'

Sallax stared up at the merchant, his eyes ablaze. He drew a rattling breath and repeated, 'Ren.'

Jacrys suddenly realised that if the big Ronan had been free, he would have torn the fat man's throat out with his bare hands.

'Ren?' Carpello looked to Jacrys. 'What's Ren?'

Before Jacrys could reply, Sallax spoke again, his voice gravelly with disuse, but still recognisable. 'You cut off the mole.'

Carpello blanched. His throat closed and his limbs felt as though they were molten rock. 'I'll kill you,' he whispered down at the help-less man. 'Do you understand, Sallax? I'll kill you.'

'Ren,' said Sallax, his gaze fixed on the merchant. 'Sallax killed Ren and you cut off your mole.'

As Carpello's terror welled up, he screamed a string of curses that echoed through the great warehouse like the long-ago cries of the young women and girls he had beaten and raped. 'I'll kill you, you whoreson rutter!' Carpello screamed, towering over the Ronan with his fists clenched.

Sallax glared at him, daring him to strike, as if the surfacing memory was of a hatred so powerful that it had cleared his mind, even if just for a moment.

Finally Jacrys intervened, grasping Carpello by the collar and dragging him away from the cot. 'What's wrong with you, you stupid, stupid man?' he whispered furiously. 'Did you not hear a word I said?' He stood over Carpello, nearly incandescent with rage – but also interested in the merchant's response: Sallax had clearly touched a nerve. 'What's a ren?' he asked, more calmly.

Carpello was too agitated to answer. Shaking, he lifted himself off the floor of his own warehouse, a business he had built with his own superior intellect and crafty economic sense, and looked back at Sallax. The patient appeared to be grinning at him, daring him to come forward for another bedside visit.

Carpello ran a finger across the open sore where his mole had been.

She will make it last for Twinmoons.

There was no way to change his appearance; he would never be free. This broken man had recognised him even with the beard, much thinner and without the mole. He turned and, without a word to Jacrys, ran through the warehouse and out onto the pier. He shouted something as he left the building, but Jacrys couldn't understand what *Versen!* meant.

Brexan waited her turn at the bakery window, almost salivating as she eyed a plump loaf on the third shelf. A short woman with a kerchief on her head and a battered basket over one arm pushed in front of her – either she thought she was old enough to ignore social graces, or she had come to Orindale from some part of Falkan where queuing was not common practice. Brexan shoved her hands inside her tunic and bit down hard on her tongue; she had too much to do this morning to draw attention to herself thrashing some old bird.

When the rude woman indicated Brexan's loaf with a bony finger, though, Brexan lost it.

'That one is mine.' She leaned over the woman to illustrate that she was both younger and taller.

'Nonsense. You're behind me.' The woman didn't give Brexan more than a glance.

'Only because you ignored the queue,' Brexan said. 'I don't care that you broke in here. And you can take as much time as you like, buy whatever you need, but that loaf on the third shelf, that one is mine.' She cursed herself for skipping breakfast; she'd intended an early start locating Jacrys, Sallax or one of the Ronan partisans. So far all she had discovered was that it had grown significantly colder in the port city and the chance of finding a decent mug of tecan was remote.

'You are a rude young woman—' The old woman cut off each syllable, '—and you will learn to wait your turn.'

Brexan smiled, and as unobtrusively as possible, grasped the woman's wrist and bent it back enough to generate a mind-numbing pain. Unable to speak, the rude customer glared in horror at Brexan.

'Please listen,' Brexan whispered. 'If you buy that loaf of bread, I will ram it so far up that fat backside of yours that you will be shitting crust for the next Moon. You broke into the line, a line I have been standing in since before you awakened this morning. I am not in the mood for rudeness today. So choose another loaf, pay the gentleman and be on your way.' Brexan released the woman's wrist but continued to hold her hand, as if the two were friends.

The old woman shivered and without speaking, she pointed to another loaf, paid with a copper Marek and hurried away along the pier, careful not to look back.

'Enjoy your breakfast,' Brexan called after her; 'see you tomorrow!' She waved before turning back to the bakery window. 'Miserable old hen. Don't you hate it when someone does that?'

The baker, a gigantic man who appeared to have lived on nothing but unleavened dough for the past three hundred Twinmoons, had missed the whole by-play; he was far more interested in what his assistant, a much younger man, but already well on his way to baker's girth himself, was saying about an incident along the southern wharf the previous night.

'Ran all the way? Gods-rut-a-whore, but I would pay a Moon's wages to have seen that. I can just imagine it, all those cheeks and chins of his all jouncing along! And crying, too?'

'I heard he was crying,' the apprentice said, 'but I didn't see it. I guess he ran all the way across the bridge and out to his place near the barracks. He's probably still out of breath, hey.'

'Well,' the baker shrugged sympathetically, 'I know what that's like. And old Carpello, he's not quite as big as me – but I don't go running scared, hey. I stand and fight, you know.'

'Hey, I know, but running full-on and terrified of something, hey – maybe he saw old Prince Malagon? I mean, no one else has, hey.'

'Nah.' The bigger man laughed, a wet throaty chortle that left Brexan staring in wonder that he was not already dead. 'Old Carpello probably ran into one of his wives, huh, or maybe his wives ran into one another and he was running to get the coffers locked up, hey?'

'Yes and down on the southern wharf, too. If his wives are spending time down there, they're making their own money. You know what I'm saying?'

The baker laughed again and nodded towards Brexan. 'Which one, girly?'

Brexan gaped: she needed to find this man. She had been frightened in the alley, feeling Jacrys' breath on her skin as he pressed his dirk into her ribs, but had she not been attacked by the Malakasian spy she would never have known the man's name: Carpello, the Falkan merchant with the mole on his nose. 'Um, that one up there, please—' She indicated the loaf on the third shelf.

'This one?' The baker grabbed the wrong loaf, but Brexan was too busy trying to come up with a reasonable question which would keep the men talking.

'Something scared old Carpello last night?' she asked, controlling the quaver in her voice. 'Anyone know what it was?'

'His wives had a meeting.' The baker nearly howled at that as he sprayed the counter.

'Oh, really? Well, I think my mother was married to the fat old horsecock once or twice – I wonder if she was there.' Brexan was getting into the spirit now; all she had to do was pretend she was back in the regiment.

Both men roared and the younger of the two nearly lost his balance.

Brexan continued, 'The southern wharf, huh? Well, maybe I'll go down there and see if she's around. Actually, you'd better give me another loaf in case I find her.'

The baker's face reddened and broke out in a sweat. This was apparently the funniest thing he had heard in his lifetime. Unable to breathe, he coughed long and hard into a piece of soiled cloth, hacking up whatever was festering in his lungs. 'Oh girly, but that is the best I've heard in a Twinmoon. You come back any morning, any morning and visit us. If you find old Carpello down there, you tell him if all those wives are going to meet, he needs to build a bigger warehouse, huh.'

Brexan laughed herself, and repeated, 'Bigger warehouse, you bet!' She paid for her bread and waved cheerily before turning to hurry down the wharf.

Brexan had met Sallax Farro near the last pier on the southern wharf and she thought she knew the warehouses the bakers were talking about. She would be able to eliminate most of them just by asking around, although she might have to sneak inside two or three for a quick search. Gnawing thoughtfully on one of the loaves, she forgot her desire for a decent cup of tecan and instead bought a beer at a dockside tavern, one where she could sit and observe the pedestrian traffic outside.

The sun was bright this morning and except for the same black cloud that looked as if it had been hanging sentinel over the harbour since the day she arrived, the skies above the waterfront were clear. There was a pervasive chill, and the passersby all looked the same: bent over and clutching their cloaks tightly closed. They reminded her of Sallax; he had been stooped over as well.

Carpello would know. He would know where she could find Jacrys, too. She had originally planned to torture the bloated merchant simply because of what he had done to Versen. Now she could do both: Carpello's imminent interrogation would be closely followed by an agonisingly long session of creative revenge. Anyone who had ever told her that revenge felt hollow had obviously not been doing it properly – bleeding Haden to death had ranked among the most gratifying things she had ever done. She hadn't killed the scarred Seron to revive Versen; she had killed him out of a passionate lust for vengeance.

Now that lust flared again: as soon as he revealed Sallax's whereabouts, she would quench that fire with Carpello's blood. His mole, Brexan decided, she would hang from a string and present to Brynne if she ever managed to catch up with the rest of the Ronan freedom fighters.

By the evening, Brexan had worked out a rudimentary map of the southern wharf. There were numerous warehouses, owned by a mixture of individuals and companies, as far as she could make out, and roving teams of Malakasian guards patrolled the area. At least two of the buildings provided permanent offices for Malakasian customs officials, so those were discounted – though Carpello was working for Prince Malagon, Brexan didn't believe for a moment that all his business was legitimate.

Several storage facilities were obviously owned by the same person: they were marked with a red slash through a white triangle. She had chatted idly with a stevedore stacking empty crates – the only one who would to talk with her, for work was hard to find in Orindale and most of the dockers had learned to keep their mouths shut. He mentioned that he did not often see his employer, a Malakasian shipping magnate who lived most Twinmoons in Pellia, and Brexan struck five more warehouses from her mental map.

Finally she found someone who directed her to a series of storage units as far down the pier as she could go – he knew the ships loading and unloading along those piers were bound for Malakasia. 'You said he was from Falkan but that he had done well.' The brawny young man tossed a pallet up and through a roughly hewn window in the warehouse wall. Brexan heard it jounce over several others before coming to rest somewhere inside. 'No locals do well unless they run shipments back and forth for the prince. Try down there. You'll find him.'

NEAR THE GORSKAN BORDER

Gilmour took his time checking every hoof, each limb and all the saddlery while the rest of them bedded down for the night: it had been the hardest ride thus far. He knew their nights of using a Larion tailwind were over; in northern Falkan the land was too rough: rocks and granite boulders broke unevenly through the surface of the earth. Too often the previous night Gilmour had been forced to make last-moment changes in their path to avoid tripping one of the mounts; it was too dangerous to risk again.

Now he had determined that the horses were fine, and quite fit to ride later that day, but he dallied a few moments longer, watching the stream trickle by. Late autumn was moving quickly into winter and there wouldn't be much grass left anywhere this far north; they would need hay, and stables for the horses each night from this point forward.

He sighed. It had taken too long to get here, five, maybe six days. *Nerak could have made it in one.* Gilmour calculated that Traver's Notch was still a day or two north and east from the bare earth and the exposed rock of their current campsite.

Once he was certain his friends had fallen asleep he waved his hand slowly through the air and whispered a few words, ensuring none of them would awaken until well after the midday aven. 'They need the rest, anyway.' He reached into his saddlebag and withdrew the leatherbound spell book.

Nearly a thousand Twinmoons later and he still wasn't ready. He hadn't lied when he said he had spent all his time since the fall of the Larion Senate studying, preparing himself intellectually and mystically to face Nerak over the Larion spell table one day. And he had, scouring every destroyed university and blasted library, seeking books and scrolls on science, medicine, the arts and especially magic, any remnants that remained. Though there were pockets of renegade scholars, with secret laboratories or hidden libraries, dissemination of their findings was nearly impossible in the occupied nations, so Gilmour was left working with outdated information in a world filled with ageing academics.

He learned to create spells of his own, infusing his existing knowledge of magic with research, but every time he used magic, he had put himself at risk. Nerak knew when Gilmour practised one of the more complicated weaves and invariably sent along bounty hunters, Seron warriors, spies, assassins, even a demon or two, whenever he felt his former colleague experimenting.

So Gilmour had lived a life on the run, moving from place to place, from job to job, learning to move quickly, and knowing every time he worked one of the master spells, Nerak would be after him.

Over time, even with all the difficulties facing him, Gilmour had expanded his work. Was all hope completely lost because he hadn't studied Lessek's spell book? Certainly not. The old man stroked his horse's mane; brushing the long hair until it fell smoothly and he himself was calm again.

Then he bent to retrieve the spell book from the log where he'd placed it, flinching as his fingers closed about the binding in case the tome lashed out at him before he had even opened the cover.

The ash dream, folio one.

What secrets were hiding in these pages? He was certain the book represented a glimpse into Nerak's power – the dark prince must have cherished the book deeply to have carried it with him when he travelled ... or perhaps he had yet to master the magic inside, which was why he had it with him. Gilmour, fervently hoped for the latter.

The ash dream. He studied the first page and wondered if this was Lessek's handwriting, or if the Larion founder had employed a scribe. Lessek was a scholar. He studied the nature of everything he hoped to incorporate into a spell or an incantation and he used common threads to link one to another, to build ever more complex spells – and eventually to fashion the stone table. *I am the same*, Gilmour thought; *what Lessek had was time*.

Gilmour flipped through a few pages: each was lined top to bottom in the fine script, Lessek's thoughts, ideas and findings. Nothing had happened yet, and Gilmour's heart began to race. Perhaps this time he would be permitted inside, the moment he had been simultaneously hoping for and dreading. Heartened, he turned back to the opening folios, flattened his palm across the text and began to read.

Ash: of fire and wind. The first spell seemed to be—

Gilmour's thoughts eluded him. He swallowed, clearing his throat. It was a spell about – there it was again, a tightening feeling. He tried to unfasten the leather thongs holding his cloak together, but the bow had worked into a knot and he had to put the book down to sort it out. He shrugged the cloak off his shoulders and reached for the book, but this time, his throat closed entirely. An invisible fist came from the book and slammed into his neck, then encircled it with an iron band. He couldn't breathe, but that wasn't enough to stop the book's assault.

As it tightened, Gilmour tried to stay calm and think of a spell that would release him – whatever held him wasn't trying to suffocate him, for he would be unconscious already. As he felt muscles and tissues collapsing in on one another he realised it meant to rip his head off.

Get out of this body! Find another one, now – there has to be someone around you can take – just this once! Do it!

His eyes bulged and went blind as his cheeks caved in and blood spurted from his nostrils and mouth. Still the grip tightened. As the old fisherman's larynx caved in, Gilmour panicked; had he been thinking clearly, he would have slipped away, but he hesitated another moment, despite his own best counsel.

A great rush of warm air, redolent of organic decay and death, blew out from between the pages of the old spell book, then it was over. The invisible fist opened and he fell backwards over the log, clawing at his ruined throat, gasping for breath, almost blind in his panic. He knew no one would awake and help him; he had put them into an enchanted sleep himself.

Then a voice inside his head, called, 'Think, you fool – you're not going to die!'

Gilmour stopped struggling. *Right. That's right.* As he grew calmer, he searched his memory, the great filing system in which he kept most of the magic he knew: a key word there, a memorable phrase here – hundreds of spells at his fingertips. *Fix the damage,* he chided himself, and mouthed the words that would repair the injuries to his throat. *That's why it tried to pry your head off, stupid. It knew you didn't have a spell for that.*

Gilmour felt the old fisherman's lungs fill with cold air. He lay there for a long time, his bony knees still draped over the rotting pine trunk, enjoying the steady rhythm of his breathing. For a while he thought of nothing, content instead to bask in the joy of simply being alive: *two thousand Twinmoons and still alive.*

His thoughts drifted: there was no question now that they had to rely on the key, the spell table and the Windscrolls. The book would be no help. He hoped the faded pages had treated Nerak as inhospitably when the dark prince had endeavoured to read to them. He had no idea how Steven had managed to flip through the spell book so nonchalantly.

Tired now. He realised he hadn't slept since Steven's return to Colorado. He reached for his cloak and folded it over himself and drifted off for an aven's rest. He left the book where it had fallen closed beside the log.

Jennifer's foot broke through the new snow, leaving her standing knee-deep in the rest area parking lot. The bike path behind a row of evergreens had been ploughed – with nearly three hundred days of sunshine a year, bicyclists in the mountains enjoyed their winter riding and a bit of snow wasn't enough to interfere with that pastime. Jennifer wasn't here to go cycling, though: she was meeting David Johnson for a long walk, and maybe a quiet lunch in town.

She had run into him the previous night when she stopped at the grocery store; he had been happy to see her and had insisted that they get together before she left again. 'Nothing serious,' he said, 'but you mentioned you come up here for the walking and, well, I am an exceptional walker.'

'Oh are you?' She had been amused.

'Yes, just watch.' He turned and strode across the floor, much to the amusement of his employees and customers. 'See? A veritable world champion.'

She laughed. 'How are you over mixed terrain?'

David didn't miss a beat. 'You'll have to join me and find out for yourself.'

She gave in gracefully and agreed – she didn't plan to be in Silverthorn for more than two days, but while here, it wouldn't hurt to enjoy herself. She had been on the run for the past week, moving from one ski resort town to the next, taking rooms under assumed names and paying cash – trying to remain anonymous. She had twice been back to check Brian's place, but there was no sign of forced entry. She didn't want to stay there too long, but the constant moving was growing tiresome and expensive. She needed to find somewhere for a couple of months, but as family and friends were off limits, she was at a loss for where to go.

She hoped a day or two in Silverthorn would give her a chance to make contact with Brian and Meg, to impress upon them the need to be careful in the coming weeks and decide where to go next. She pondered on what to do about her brother and his wife; the truth was an unappetising option, and if she told them to avoid contact with strangers and remain in well-lighted, well-populated areas because she believed Hannah's disappearance was the result of foul play, Brian would insist that she call the police. As much as he loved her, he didn't trust her to make wise decisions about Hannah; he would promise not to interfere and as soon as she was gone, it would be the first thing he did.

Jennifer was still troubling over what to do when she heard David call from the parking lot.

She waved. 'Well, hello! Come on over, but be careful. It's deeper there than it looks. I nearly went in over my head.'

'I wish you had stayed in the shallow end until my arrival, young lady,' he chided. 'Did you at least wait forty-five minutes after eating?'

They walked together for over an hour as the village of Silverthorn gave way to the quiet solitude of the mountain forest. From time to time a bird or a squirrel would disturb the branches and snow would fall around them, but, lost in conversation, neither noticed as they walked, holding hands like school children, across the alpine wilderness, waving to the occasional cyclists who passed them. Jennifer was tempted to share her current predicament – David seemed open-minded enough – but each time she started to speak about Hannah and Steven, she caught herself. The last thing she wanted to do was to frighten this nice man off with fantastical talk of otherworldly monsters and demon hunters! As she gripped his hand she knew she wanted to come back here after Hannah was safely home; she just hoped he would forgive her when she disappeared in a day or two.

She caught sight of a young woman some distance ahead, wearing the same bright red apron David invariably donned while working at the supermarket. Gesturing down the path, she asked, 'Do you know that girl?'

David squinted into the late morning sun. 'It's Laura, I think – I wonder what she's doing out here today.'

'I hope nothing's wrong back at the store.' Jennifer felt a knot begin to twist in her stomach. *She should not have come back to Silverthorn.*

'Let's find out,' David said and hurried up the path with Jennifer close behind him. 'Laura,' he called as he reached her, 'what are you doing out here without a coat? Is something wrong at the store? Is everyone okay?' His breath came in great clouds; he was in good shape, but running at this altitude was hard for anyone.

'Hello Jennifer Sorenson,' the girl said, ignoring her boss. Her voice was almost a growl. 'I have been looking for you.'

Jennifer froze, waiting for billowy clouds of breath to form at Laura's lips, somehow knowing none would. The girl wasn't breathing.

'No, please no,' she whispered, 'oh, David. I'm so sorry—'

'What's going on?' David demanded. 'Laura? Please tell me what this is about—'

The girl broke in, 'Jennifer Sorenson, I need the portal, now. We can do this a friendly way, or—' Laura collapsed in a heap, a discarded pile of clothes and fleshed bones, but no spirit, no soul remained.

'—we can do this an unfriendly way.' David's voice had changed. He bent down and plucked something from the girl's hand, a packet of something, maybe.

Jennifer couldn't look at him. Overcoming her momentary paralysis, she turned and fled back along the path.

Too soon, she was exhausted – she wasn't in good sprinting-at-altitude shape – and she was forced to jog. She tried to ignore David's voice – no, not David, anymore, some demon prince – as he exhorted her to stop.

'You can't run, Jennifer Sorenson. You realise I have your daughter.'

That stopped her in her tracks. As she doubled over to catch her breath, the mother lioness within her roused itself. In spite of the icy cold, she was sweating. 'You motherless prick,' she snarled, 'if you hurt her, I swear to Christ I will tear out your black heart with my own hands.'

'Time is wasting and you have a choice to make,' David said, ignoring her toothless threat.

'What choice?' Jennifer didn't back away; she could see a wound on David's hand was dripping dark blood onto the snow. She shuddered.

'Turn the portal over to me and live, or die right now,' David said. 'I very rarely offer anyone a choice. You should consider yourself honoured.' He smiled, but like the voice, it was no longer David Johnson's smile, just a twisted caricature. 'So what will it be?'

'Why give me a choice?'

'Because either way, I get what I want, which is to return to Eldarn today.'

'That doesn't answer my question.'

'Insightful, too,' he said, 'how delightful.' He chuckled. 'I plan to kill Hannah, very slowly, and very painfully. If I let you live, then you will live knowing there is *nothing* you can do to save her and I can rejoice in the fact that I have driven you mad with helplessness and grief. For me, it's undoubtedly a win-win situation. For you, not so much.' The idiom sounded strange in that not-David voice; Jennifer lost control and charged the thing that had stolen David Johnson. She chose death.

As she ran blindly towards him, tears freezing on her cheeks, David's face changed. A quizzical look passed over his features, as if things were not working out the way he had planned; maybe Jennifer's actions had taken him by surprise. He tilted his head slightly, as though listening for something, ignoring the fact that a crazed, fifty-something woman was coming head-on at him.

Though distracted, he side-stepped her attack and sent her sprawling over Laura, the dead check-out girl. As she crashed down, Jennifer cried out in pain and tried to roll back to her feet for another lunge.

Not-David had gone back to contemplating the forest. He didn't look at her, but held up one hand in a wait-just-a-moment gesture, then said, 'Jennifer Sorenson. You are the luckiest woman in this unlovely world. I don't need you any more. Of course, I still plan to torture and kill Hannah, and I will be sure to bring a piece or two back here for you, but for now, I don't need you. A very good, very old friend of mine has allowed his curiosity to get the better of him again and he has just opened the door for me to go home. Goodbye, dear Jennifer Sorenson. We *will* meet again.'

With that, David Johnson seemed to shimmer – he looked like he was under attack by a cloud of yellow and green insects. He stepped from the bicycle path into the snow and faded away.

CARPELLO'S WAREHOUSE

Brexan was about to give up for the night. She'd spent two days searching and she was tired and cross, and only the thought of food was keeping her from screaming her frustration aloud – when she spotted Carpello Jax himself, slinking along the side of one of the warehouses she hadn't yet identified. He stayed in the shadows until he reached a window near the back. Huddling behind a pile of empty boxes, Brexan watched, but it was nearly half an aven before he moved back towards the pier. She ducked down low to the ground until he had turned the corner, then started to trail him, keeping her distance. This time she would be extra careful – no bumping into crates or scolding irritating children – the last thing she needed was a repeat of the Jacrys mission that had ended so ignominiously.

She followed the merchant through the sparse evening crowd, warm despite the cold night. She tried to work out what Carpello been doing back there – from what little she could see he had been eavesdropping at the window, but if that was his own warehouse, that didn't make any sense at all – unless ... the only thing Brexan could imagine frightening the fat man enough to make him run, weeping, in public, was someone trying to kill the rutter. Maybe that's why Carpello was sneaking about his own warehouse.

She watched him cross the great bridge before she did the same and descended onto the lively northern wharf. He walked away from the waterfront and into a street Brexan recognised as running to the barracks in the old imperial palace. The city was well-lit here, much more brightly than on the industrial southern wharf: if people came to Orindale to enjoy the food, the wine and the Ravenian Sea, they came to the northern pier, where the aromas of different cuisines perfumed the air, lively bellamir music lifted the spirits and young people flocked, looking for love but willing to settle for lust: here there was a nightly celebration of life in the occupied city. If they came to do business, maybe to seek their fortunes in the shipping industry, they came to the southern pier.

Walking carefully to avoid her boots clattering on the cobblestone street – this *was* an affluent part of the city – she marked the house Carpello let himself into: a tall, well-built and obviously expensive townhouse. The intricate stone masonry and stained-glass windows made it an easy place to find again in the daylight. She took in as much of the street as possible as she muttered, 'Now, I've got you, Carpello, you horsecock, and I am going to carve Versen's name in your chest.'

She grinned to herself and retraced her steps back to the southern wharf, where she spent the night huddled by the same window Carpello had visited earlier that evening. She dozed from time to time, but heard nothing; by the time the sun rose over the docks she had about decided it was abandoned. Just as she was about to leave to find some food and tecan, she heard the brace on the dock-side door slide back. Someone was coming out.

She dived behind the shelter of the building and hustled down the alley, ducking behind the same boxes she had used to hide from Carpello, but no one passed her, so she ventured out from behind her makeshift blind and moved cautiously onto the waterfront. Even from a distance, she could recognise the gait of the man walking away from her: Jacrys or Lafrent, Prince Malagon's spy and Lieutenant Bronfio's murderer always carried himself as though he knew something no one else knew. So Sallax hadn't killed him.

Brexan was cold and hungry herself, but she dared not move in that direction; Jacrys was sure to spot her; he had proven his skills in that arena. Instead, she decided to break into the warehouse: maybe she could discover what the spy was up to. As she stepped through the door, the black cloud that had been hovering in place over the harbour for the past Moon drifted back over the city, where it appeared to join forces with another, slightly smaller but the same threatening colour. The pair blew east, side-by-side, against the wind, as if they had been summoned.

Brexan moved quickly, scared that Jacrys would return soon. Peering through the window she could see the cavernous structure was empty, but at one end there were some rough doors; offices, maybe. Jacrys had left the main door unlocked. Brexan thought carelessness was not his style; now she was convinced he didn't intend being away for long. She hurried towards the rooms at the back.

Sallax was in the second room she visited, immediately behind what looked like Carpello's private office and, temporarily, at least, Jacrys' living quarters. The big Ronan was sleeping, and even in the dim light thrown by a bedside candle, she could see that he looked much healthier than the last time they met. He had obviously been well fed, his hair had been cut and he had been given a shave. Most importantly, he no longer stank like a midden. Brexan smiled in relief and moved closer.

His body was bound across the chest and one shoulder with clean strips of heavy fabric – Jacrys had obviously treated the partisan's injuries. She had thought him in disguise, bent over as if he were a wounded beggar, but seeing him bound up like this, she wondered if he had broken something coming over the Blackstones. Brexan marvelled at the strength of will that kept some people going. She wondered if she would have given up, but remembering her broken cheek and cracked ribs, decided to give herself more credit … perhaps she and Sallax were not so different after all. Suddenly she wanted very badly to take him away from Jacrys and this cold, damp warehouse. The tapestries on the walls and woven carpets on the floor did little to take the edge off the bitter cold; the Redstone would be far better for Sallax's convalescence – not to mention getting him out of Jacrys' grip. She had enough silver to stay on there at least another Twinmoon and in that time, she would nurse the big man back to health.

Her own transformation was complete: she had become a freedom fighter, just like Sallax, and Versen.

Sallax woke as she was severing the cords holding him down.

'The girl,' he started in a murmur, 'the girl knew Sallax.'

'Yes, Sallax,' she replied softly. His injuries were obviously more than just physical. 'I know you.'

'The girl,' he said again, watching her work.

Brexan sat on the edge of the bed, sheathed the knife and asked, 'Do you want to come with me, Sallax? I have a warm room, with good food and soft blankets. You'll be comfortable there.'

Sallax appeared anxious, uncertain how to respond.

Brexan glanced towards the chamber doorway. Nervous now, she tried not to show it in her voice. That might upset him. 'We need to decide pretty quickly, though. All right? Will you come with me?'

'The girl knew Sallax.' He grimaced, as if sitting up would be a great struggle and then smiled when he realised nothing was holding him down.

'I do know you, Sallax. I heard all about you from Versen. He spoke about you, all the time.' He was too thin, but she would see to that. The venison stew at the Redstone would fatten him up. She would help him regain a sense of who he was, and how he had come to be in Orindale. Brexan didn't know what could have turned Sallax's mind to such paste – maybe he had encountered one of the wraiths Gabriel O'Reilly had described and instead of killing him, they had addled his mind.

'Versen?' Sallax reached for her. Brexan started to back away, thought better of it and leaned forward to take his hands.

'Yes, Versen. I knew— I know Versen. He and I are close friends.' She swallowed the lump in her throat. This was no time to start crying; she had to get him up and out of this warehouse before Jacrys returned.

'You know where Versen is?'

Her shoulders heaved, and she smeared away tears. 'Yes, I know where Versen is.'

Sallax groaned as he lifted himself from the bed and swung his legs over the side. As he placed his bare feet on the carpet he began looking around the room for clothes. 'It's cold,' he muttered.

'You're right. It's too cold to take you all the way up there like that. You'll make it without boots, though – I can get you new boots when you are up and about. Wait here. I'll see what I can find in the other rooms.'

Brexan hustled into the spy's room; there was no point in going about on tiptoes; Jacrys was still out buying breakfast. She spotted a bag left open beside the fireplace. Inside, she found a tunic, a finely woven shirt of quality wool with a delicate pattern stitched around the collar and across each wrist. 'Fop,' she said, her lip curling, and put it back. She found a wool blanket on the cot Jacrys had moved in front of the fireplace. 'Sleeping in here with a blanket and fire blazing while Sallax freezes in the other room, motherless rutter,' she scolded. The more she discovered about the spy, the less she liked him.

'I wish you would leave my mother out of it,' a soft voice said. 'As for being a fop, what can I say? One has one's vices. Some, like our good friend in the other room, enjoy fighting for a cause. Our benefactor, the good Carpello, well, he gets his pleasure from a young girl from time to time. Me? I like fine clothing.' Jacrys stood in the doorway that separated Carpello's office from the vast emptiness of the warehouse. He held two loaves of warm bread, a block of strong cheese, two sausages and a flagon of what smelled like tecan.

She drew her knife as she turned; this time there was no point pretending she was anything but an enemy. 'I'm glad you brought in breakfast. I got hungry looking for you.'

'Under orders from General Oaklen again, I assume?' The spy placed his food on a broad walnut desk. 'Is he still determined for you to retrieve that stone?'

Brexan smirked. Jacrys still had no idea the stone was lost in another world an eternity away.

'What's funny?' Jacrys asked, drawing the dirk from his belt.

'Nothing, Jacrys, or Lafrent, or whoever you are today, nothing except that you are going to have to travel much further than you could even imagine if you want to get that stone.' She began circling, hoping she could be quick and ruthless as she had been fighting the Seron in the meadow on the Ronan border. There was no way out, except past Jacrys. She unfastened her cloak and let it drop to the floor.

'I'm sorry to say that when I am finished with you today, my dear, there will not be much left for old General Oaklen to—'

She cut him off. 'Oaklen didn't send me, you arrogant dryhump.'

'Oh, really?' Jacrys didn't appear to care. 'Working on your own – a Ronan girl with a passion for freedom? A freedom even your grandparents never knew?'

'I was one of Bronfio's platoon. I saw you murder him.'

'And I suppose you followed me all the way here to get revenge. Oh, but that is precious, my dear. You? A trained killer? Don't make me chuckle. You should have died with the rest of that wretched platoon in Riverend Palace.' He handled the dirk as if it were an extension of his own hand.

Brexan watched him, and tried to keep from looking frightened; he was obviously better than she with a short blade. The only chance she had was to defeat him mentally; beating him physically would need a stroke of exceptional luck.

'Do you hope I'll believe you are Prince Malagon's top field agent?' she asked, sneering. 'Look at you – you're a mess. I wonder if the prince knows you're holding one of the Resistance's top men as your private prisoner in a warehouse less than a quarter of an aven's amble from where he himself is in residence … and you, living in a warehouse yourself? You are on your own, Jacrys, just like me. So stop trying to sell me a new ploughhorse; I'm full to here with your blather.'

Jacrys lunged, as Brexan had expected, and she calmly parried his attack and moved back, content to let Carpello's desk stand between them for a moment.

'Not bad, my dear.' Jacrys circled again. He wasn't breathing heavily; Brexan tried to mask her own, heavier, breathing. 'Most of my opponents don't survive even this long. Sad, isn't it, that fighting with a short blade has become such a lost art. Too many have gone over to great heavy weapons, rapiers, and—'

Jacrys took the blow behind one ear and crumpled soundlessly to the floor beside the desk. Stepping over the spy's legs, Sallax delivered another hefty blow to his temple. The spy's body twitched several times before he lay still.

'Is he dead?' Brexan asked, retrieving the fancy tunic from the bag and helping Sallax into it.

Sallax shrugged and tossed his makeshift club – a table-leg, Brexan thought, towards the fireplace. She was pleased – and grateful – to see that he had not lost his skill.

She packed the breakfast Jacrys had so thoughtfully provided into another of the spy's shirts and picked up the flagon. As she stepped over the spy's body, she said, 'You know, Jacrys, you are so right: fighting with a short blade *is* a lost art – just as well cracking someone's skull with a piece of bedroom furniture just never seems to go out of style.'

She looked up at Sallax, who stared back at her, apparently oblivious to the fact that he had probably killed a Malakasian officer. 'You'll have to go without boots for now,' she said, 'his are too small for you, but I'll get you some as soon as we get to the Redstone. Here, wrap that blanket round you too; it's cold out there. Can you make it?'

'Versen?' Sallax asked.

'Yes, I have news of Versen.' Brexan uncorked the flagon with her teeth and took a drink. It was tecan, warm and tasty. She took another swallow, passed it to Sallax, who did likewise, and took him by the arm. 'Come,' she said calmly, 'let's get going.'

TRAVER'S NOTCH

'That coffee smells great,' Steven said, opening a saddlebag and rooting around for the last of the venison strips. 'When I was driving from Charleston to Denver, I must have drunk three gallons of the stuff.'

Mark looked up from where he had been carefully pouring hot water through one of the filters Steven had stolen from Howard's kitchen. 'I can't wait. I've grown so used to tecan, I'm worried I've lost my taste for it.' On the outskirts of Traver's Notch, a farm had provided milk, cheese, bread and vegetables to complement their venison. Mark had negotiated for a small metal pot for the brewing of coffee. Now he gripped the thin paper filter awkwardly between two fingers and trickled water slowly through the mound of ground coffee, trying to imitate the timing of their coffee maker at home. 'It's not the easiest thing in the world,' he admitted, 'but so far, it certainly smells like coffee.'

'I think it smells like burned dirt,' Garec said. 'And you prefer this muck to tecan? Look at the colour of it!'

'You need learn to have some faith, Garec,' Steven said. 'Just wait until you try some with a little milk and a few drops of that sugar extract Gilmour pretends he doesn't carry in his tunic next to his three hundred pipes.'

'Don't listen to him, Garec,' Mark said, 'you want it barefoot.'

'Barefoot?'

'Exactly,' Mark nodded, 'as it comes, direct from the pot, none of that creamy, sugary nonsense, just insert the needle and open the IV.'

Garec looked askance at the foreigner. 'I think Steven's way sounds better,' he said, 'but neither sounds good!'

Gilmour broke in, 'That aroma does bring back memories. My last cup must have been outside Gettysburg. Jed Harkness from Maine had a pot that brewed it right beside the fire, the water bubbled up in a little compartment, first clear, then brown and then almost black. It was wonderful ...' He sighed, and pulled his cloak close around his shoulders. It had grown noticeably colder in the days since they had resumed normal travelling, without the aid of what Garec had dubbed the *Larion push*. The ground was hard this morning and there was frost on the leaves and shrubs. The sky was slate-grey, and a glimmer in the southeast was all the sun they had seen that morning.

'Don't admit that, Gilmour,' Mark said, 'you're showing your age.'

'I am?' He looked at Steven. 'You've calculated the difference. How old would a two-thousand-Twinmoon grettan like me be in Colorado?'

Steven breathed a sigh through his nose. Mark recognised it: his maths sigh, a deep breath that said, *there are numbers and figures lining themselves up inside my head, so don't interrupt.*

'That's about two hundred and eighty years old, Gilmour.'

'Holy shit.' Mark stopped pouring and stared at the former Larion Senator. 'I have to apologise, Gilmour. The fact that you have any memories from your last visit at all is an impressive feat, never mind that they come from a time when my mother's mother's mother's mother was still in nappies. And I am embarrassed for my world that this little cup of trail coffee is the first you'll have to drink in a century and a half. I wish I could take you to the diner on I-84 just across the Newburgh–Beacon Bridge. That's the best coffee in America. I used to run up there when I was on break from school just to get a mug. It took all day.'

'If we ever get through this, I promise I'll go with you for a cup.' Gilmour forced a smile and rubbed his neck bruises absently.

'Speaking of which,' Steven changed the subject, 'we're about a Twinmoon early to meet Gita and the rest of the Eastern Resistance – when we made plans to meet in Traver's Notch, we thought you were dead. We figured we might need them to get us across the border.'

'Had I been dead, you would have needed them,' Gilmour said. 'But given our current situation, it's just as well that she is rallying the remainder of the Falkan forces here, for if we do succeed in vanquishing Nerak, we'll need a fighting force – however ramshackle they may be – to help with any pockets of occupation personnel who make the decision to stand fast.'

'I think they would relish that assignment,' Mark agreed. 'So how do we get across the border?'

'Magic, or if we don't want to be noisy, we creep in after dark, between the pickets,' Gilmour said. 'It'll be the only way – unless you fancy fighting your way through Malakasian soldiers whose sole purpose is to keep me – and Kantu, I suppose – from re-entering Gorsk.'

'No, that's fine,' Mark said quickly, 'I'm quite happy with door number two.'

Traver's Notch was a small village nestled between hills in a ridge running east to west along the Falkan-Gorsk border, south of the Twinmoon Mountains. The only road into town led between the hills through a miniature pass that ran up the draw and then down a series of gentle switchbacks until it reached the main town on the valley floor. It wasn't hidden – several homes and what looked like shops were clearly visible on the slopes above the city – but flanked to the north as it was by deeper valleys and steep foothills, Traver's Notch was well protected and easily defensible from any force, either approaching over the mountains or along the Falkan plain. It looked like it was engaged in a daily battle to keep from being swallowed entirely by the mixed hardwood and evergreen forests that spilled over from Gorsk.

As they crested the final hill, Traver's Notch spread out before them. Steven guessed the valley was over a mile wild and perhaps half a mile across, with most of the buildings tucked neatly into the great natural bowl. A narrow river ran through the middle of the valley, and the centre of town, spanned here and there by bridges. Along the river were a handful of large stone buildings, colourful standards waving in the midday breeze.

Steven had no idea what they represented, but he gestured in their direction. 'That looks like as good a place as any to start looking for the inn.'

'What good will that do us?' Garec asked. 'I can't imagine Gita managed to get the passwords up here already.'

'You're probably right,' Steven agreed, 'but let's see if we can find the place, figure out which innkeeper she meant – and make certain we all know the code.'

'Some maths thing, right?'

'Why am I not surprised?' Mark rolled his eyes.

'Hey,' Steven said, 'be grateful! If it hadn't been for my maths obsession, we never would have made it this far.'

'Oh yes, I forgot,' Mark said. 'Malagon's safe-deposit box, right? Your telephones and calculators problem?'

'Yup,' Steven answered proudly. 'Jeff Simmons will never believe it.'

'I have to admit, I was impressed,' Gilmour said. 'It was one of the more harrowing moments of my life – and we've already determined that I'm older than most civilisations.'

'It's not that bad, Gilmour,' Mark said, 'there are plenty of civilisations far older than you.'

The others laughed. They found a barn where they paid to stable their horses for a few nights, then crossed a sturdy wooden bridge into the main part of town. At the far end of the span, a merchant was selling pelts, flagons of warm tecan and blocks of cheese from a cart. He was a short, thin man, and grimy. His gloves, cloak and leggings were in tatters; on his head, he wore a scarf of some sort, badly made from the hide of an unrecognisable animal. Steven glanced at it furtively, afraid it might raise its head and snarl at him, but he nodded affably to the fellow as they moved past the impromptu store. His cart was not much more than a slatted wagon with a pair of boards nailed to each corner creating space for hanging pelts. The tecan smelled good, but with the lingering aroma of freshly brewed coffee on his mind, Steven ignored the temptation.

'Wine, sire?' the merchant asked. His voice was gravel underfoot. 'Or maybe some cheese, sire?'

'No, thank you,' Steven said.

'A splash of tecan then, sire?' As the filthy man stepped out from behind his cart, Steven was able to see just how pitiable he was. One leg dragged, and he shuffled along in an ungainly creep that made Steven think of every war B-movie he had ever seen, and every character actor who had ever dragged his broken form up the Normandy beaches for entertainment's sake.

'No. Thank you again,' Steven insisted, moving away more quickly.

'Right, then, sire,' the crippled salesman persisted, 'maybe I'll carry your bag then, sire? Maybe carry it for you? What do you think, sire? Maybe for a copper Marek or two?'

'All right, look,' Steven turned with a frustrated shrug, his hands raised in surrender. 'I will give you a copper coin if you will go back to your cart and leave us in peace. Agreed?'

'Sorry, sire. I can't take it if I don't do something, sire … something, sire. You need something carried, sire? Your bags? Maybe I'll see to the horses, sire? They tethered across the bridge, sire?'

'Yes,' Steven gave up. 'Our horses are tethered across the bridge, but I have already paid for them to be well cared for. You wish to carry my bags, but you've left your stand. Aren't you worried someone will come along and steal your goods?'

'No, sire, oh no,' the man answered. 'I'm well known here. This is my bridge, sire. Everyone knows me here.'

'I see.' Steven looked to the others, his eyes begging for help. 'Anyone have any ideas?'

'Go ahead, Steven,' Mark encouraged. 'Let him carry the saddle-bag. You're going to give him a couple of those kopeks, anyway. Let him haul the stuff.'

'He's dragging his leg,' Steven said as if only he had noticed.

'He has made that fairly obvious,' Mark answered, 'but he doesn't seem bothered by it. Go ahead. And if he runs, I'm sure we can catch him. He's not going to be competing for any international records in the hundred metre sprint, let's face it.'

Steven hesitated a moment longer, then handed over the saddle-bag. 'Here you go, but if you run off, I'm going to break your neck. Do you understand me?'

'Of course, sire. I'll not run off, sire. Where are you going, sire? Maybe I know the way.'

Steven was irritated by the way the little man ended each phrase with *sire* – it got under his skin. Steven regretted giving up his bag.

'And the stick, sire?' The intrepid salesman gestured towards the hickory staff.

'No. I'll carry the stick, my friend.'

'Very well, sire. Very well.' He scratched at his chin for a moment, turned to the others and asked, 'Any bags, you sires?'

'No,' Garec answered for the rest of the company, 'we're doing just fine on our own.'

'Very well, sires. Very well. Where are you going?'

Steven answered, 'We're looking for an inn.'

'Which one, sire? There are many here in the Notch, sire, many.'

'I'm not sure of the name, but it's got a yellow and red standard, a sign depicting a bowman at the hunt. Do you know it?' Steven flexed the fingers of his right hand into a fist several times, as if working out a cramp; something was bothering him.

'I do, sire. This way, sire. It's not far. Good food in there too, sire. Comfortable beds, cool beer, warm stew, sire. A wise choice you make going there, sire.' The little man pushed passed Steven to lead them through town and as he did, Steven caught a hint of something familiar, a faint aroma, maybe lingering around the man's clothing. It wasn't overt, almost a memory of something. Coffee? Was he remembering the coffee, or was this something else?

'This way, sire, this way.'

'Right.' Steven shook his head and flexed his fingers again. They were stiff. He needed to get out of the cold, to eat something other than old venison strips. But the coffee had been delicious.

Was it coffee?

Steven sidled up behind the man as he turned a corner into the wind. Though he inhaled deeply, he couldn't pick up the scent; he decided that he must be really tired, or at least thirsty for another pot of Howard's French roast. Once they were settled, they'd find a bigger pot and brew up a cauldron of the stuff ... 'Inside,' he whispered to himself, 'inside someplace warm.'

'Yes, sire. Yes. Inside. Someplace warm, the Bowman, a clean place, sire. Good food, cool beer, sire. Follow me.' The little man had heard him. Making surprisingly good time on one ruined leg, he half-hopped and half-scurried. Except for the bridges, the streets were either dirt or cobblestone, and the tree-lined boulevards, tidy dwellings and clean shops gave the place a sense of having been well cared for. In fact, there was nothing about Traver's Notch that Steven found disagreeable – he thought it might be a pleasant place to spend a few days when he located Hannah again.

Calling back to Gilmour, he asked, 'What kind of industry keeps this place going?'

'Mining,' the old man answered. 'Look up there.' Gilmour gestured towards an area of the valley wall that had been hidden during their descent and Steven saw the telltale sign of lode shafts dug deep into the mountains, great triangular swaths of brown dirt and rubble, tailings spilled in teardrops marking the hillsides from top to bottom.

'Mining, sire. Yes, mining,' the merchant turned and spoke only to Steven, as though he were passing on a secret. Lowering his voice, he added, 'Mining, sire. It ruined my leg, sire. Can't do it any more, sire. See?' He dropped the saddlebag and drew up his hose to expose what remained of his lower leg.

Steven gasped at the carnage: the vivid scars looked as if they had been drawn by a child with a crayon, a roadmap of recent pain. The skin bulged in unlikely places too; Steven guessed bones had been fractured in multiple places and left to knit themselves together in whatever arrangement they saw fit. 'Good Christ,' he whispered.

'Yes, sire, he is,' the little man mumbled, dropping his leggings back into place.

'What's that?' Steven asked. 'What did you say?'

'Nothing, sire,' he said, 'I didn't say anything, sire.'

Steven caught the aroma again, something tangy and pleasant, but not coffee. He stopped and sniffed at the air again.

Mark looked at him quizzically. 'What's up?' He clapped a hand across Steven's shoulder.

'Do you smell that?'

'Nope. What is it?'

'I can't put my finger on it, maybe it's just me, but I keep getting a hint of something—' He paused, sniffing again. 'You sure you don't smell anything ... anything from home?'

Mark tested the air again. 'Nope. Sorry.'

'All right, it's me going mad.' Steven moved along after the crippled ex-miner. 'I just need a couple of nights in a bed, that's all.'

'Yes, sire. A bed. The Bowman, they have comfortable beds, sire. Warm stew, cool beer, sire.'

'Would you stop that?' Steven asked as politely as he could.

'Stop what, sire?'

'Stop calling me *sire*. I'm not— well, I don't need to— yes, just stop. Can you do that?'

'Yes, sire,' the man grinned and pointed towards a two-level building at the top of a short rise. 'The Bowman, sire. There it is, sire. Come this way. It's a shortcut, sire.' He moved off through a small wooded area, a city park maybe, that ran along the edge of the brook and cut off the corner between the street and the inn at the top of the rise. 'Just through the trees here, sire.'

Steven followed him in, glancing back to see Garec shrug and gesture him forward. Mark came after and Gilmour trailed behind, gazing along the street, an inquisitive look on his face, as if he had dropped something and didn't know where to begin searching for it.

'You all right, Gilmour?' Steven asked.

'Oh, yes, for a moment I thought I felt something back there, but then it was gone.'

'This way, sire. This way,' their guide insisted, 'here, through the trees, sire, a shortcut.'

233

'Right, right, we're coming,' Steven said irritably. Looking back again, he saw Gilmour hesitate. The grove of trees was small but relatively thick, and the old man appeared strangely well-lighted outside the overhanging branches.

Steven's foot splashed through a puddle, invisible in the darkness beneath the trees. 'Ah, shit,' he said. 'Look at that; now my feet are wet. I'll be so glad to be under a roof again. Do you think they have hot and cold running water?'

'I wouldn't get my hopes up,' Mark answered as he moved ahead of Garec. 'From the look of this ground, it must have rained or snowed here recently. That doesn't bode well for us heading into those hills. We'll be slogging through drifts in no time.'

The crippled merchant muttered something and Steven froze. 'What did you say?' Shadows of dying leaves, faded dusty brown, were caught in scattered puddles marking the trail through the grove. Steven watched his own shadow pass over a puddle. Ahead, the little man had stopped, turning to wait for them. Steven moved forward and inhaled deeply again, still seeking the curiously elusive aroma he had detected earlier. He flexed his fingers.

Mark's voice came to him, as if from far away. 'I agree, I am so owed a hot bath. A shower would be even better, but I know that won't happen.' Steven heard Mark's boots slosh through the same puddle, and waiting, holding his breath, he heard the Falkan miner's reply.

'Yes, sire. Yes. Hot water. They have hot water at the Bowman, my prince.'

Mark looked ahead. 'What was that?' He gave a startled cry when Steven whirled on their guide, swinging the hickory staff in a deadly arc. The staff, glowing with rage and ancient power, sliced through the cool air, leaving its own contrail. It didn't appear to slow as it passed through the man's body and tore through clothing, sinew, flesh and brittle, undernourished bone to emerge on the other side.

Mark watched in horror as the small man simply fell apart. Save for the terrible look in Steven's eye and the heartrending scream that accompanied the attack, it was an almost comical caricature of death as the broken man split at the waist. There was no blood, though, no wet entrails. Nothing splashed up to hit Mark except for the backsplash from the puddles he danced through to get clear of the hickory staff, still aglow with rage.

'Holy shit, Steven!' Mark fell backwards into Garec, who stumbled, but managed to keep both of them upright. 'What did you do?'

Steven was standing over the remains of their guide and staring at Gilmour. 'You didn't feel it?' he asked calmly, 'how could you not feel it?' Neither Garec nor Mark spoke.

Gilmour stammered, 'I thought I did – out there on the street, I thought – I don't know.' His neck throbbed and his ribs burned as if they had been rebroken. 'I don't know what's wrong with me.' He lowered his eyes to the ground.

'No time for that now!' Steven was agitated. 'He'll be back. I don't know where he is, but he'll be back. Can you cloak us?'

'I—'

'Gilmour!' Steven barked. 'Can you do it? Can you cloak us?' The old man's form stood out stark against the trees. 'Well? Can you cloak us?' he asked again.

'Are you sure?' Gilmour took a few tentative steps forward.

Without replying, Steven knelt beside the body and dug through the threadbare clothes until he found what he was looking for.

'Yes,' he said firmly, 'I'm sure.'

Gilmour's features hardened and a glimmer of angry confidence flashed in his eyes. 'Then we must run, as quickly as possible. Come, right now, back the way we came. It's the shortest path out of the valley.'

'Can you cloak us?'

'I don't – I'm not certain … I'll try, but we must run anyway. A cloaking spell won't protect us for long.'

Mark regained his composure and yelled, 'Steven what the hell is going on? You just hacked that guy in two. Jesus Christ, you killed him in cold blood. What's this about?'

Steven tossed his roommate the thing he had removed from the dead man's clothes: a crumpled red, white and blue pouch of *Confederate Son* chewing tobacco. 'I knew I smelled something. I smelled it that day when he came after me in the mountains. Believe it or not, I could smell it on that old ram's breath as it was pressing its face through the windshield of Howard's T-Bird. This bastard had been chewing it sometime today.'

'But how can that be?' Mark didn't know whether to look to Gilmour or to Steven for his answer. 'I thought he had to—'

'I don't know,' Steven said abruptly, 'but Nerak's back and he's here, right here somewhere.' He kicked the dead body aside, retrieved his saddlebag and began running back towards the street. 'Come on. There's no telling what he'll do when he gets over the hit he just took.'

Nerak roared and the middlenight darkness that had swallowed him shuddered. Huge monolithic towers, ornate with carvings and stained-glass, rose up before him and collapsed beneath their own weight, the thunderous echo of destruction in their wake. Cities grew, withered and died before his scream faded and the light came, brightened, blinded him momentarily and then passed away. Smoke from gigantic forest fires rose in billowy clouds, lending colour to the night and choking off the cries of souls trapped for ever in his cavernous prison. Part of him was back inside the Fold. How had that happened? He could feel the earth, the frosty grass and the chill of the little river that passed through Traver's Notch, but he couldn't see them.

He screamed again, and his rage rattled the nothingness. Great stone keeps, palaces of granite and mortar, welled grandly up from the abyss, only to shatter in a hailstorm of grey and black stones. Reaching out with his mind, he found himself, dazed and wandering in the foothills outside Traver's Notch. With careful concentration, Nerak elbowed his way back through the Fold and into northern Falkan.

He would kill Steven Taylor; nothing in the past thousand Twinmoons would come close to the pleasure he would enjoy torturing that boy for all time, an immortal prisoner for ever in pain, in an endless, empty cave.

It had been that rutting stick again. What *had* Fantus done to that thing? It had to be the most complicated and intricate spell the old milksop had ever done. He would get that stick. And that saddlebag had contained the key. It was inside a jacket, a colourful jacket of some foreign material, hidden inside the bag so as not to draw attention to the foreigners. But it was there. He would take the brown leather saddlebag and the wooden staff.

Steven Taylor had swiped at him in the Blackstone Mountains as well, but that had been when he had come as a grettan. Nerak had underestimated its strength that night and he had underestimated it again in Traver's Notch. He had Jacrys to blame for that; the spy had never mentioned the power of that stick. He himself had not been able to detect it, even with his most sensitive and delicate webs. No matter. Jacrys' day of reckoning was coming as well.

Reunited with his Eldarni form, Nerak tried to move back towards Traver's Notch. He would wipe out the entire valley, eradicate every last person, in one swift and decisive blow. He would teach them to harbour his enemy, whether they knew what they were doing or not.

But something was amiss and he couldn't make the connection complete. It wasn't physical, whatever kept him from rejoining the frayed ends of his spirit, but something intangible, a gap in who he was and who he had been moments before Steven slashed at him.

Whatever had happened, Nerak was forced to take time to mend the rift Steven had torn in his being. That boy was dangerous; he would be Nerak's next target, no matter that it was earlier than he had planned. He had figured to use Hannah Sorenson – she was easier to reach – but the hickory staff changed things. It would be Steven Taylor, and he would provide the final pieces to a puzzle he had been trying to complete for over a thousand Twinmoons. And it would be soon.

Struggling – and failing – to reconcile the twin halves of himself in the forested hillside above Traver's Notch, Nerak's anger overwhelmed him. 'Steven Taylor!' he screamed and entered a broad walnut tree, exploding it outwards into thousands of jagged splinters. The blast was deafening, and knocked a frightened forester to the ground. As he swirled about between the trees, Nerak felt better. He chose another, an old maple that still boasted a few bright red leaves, and blew it apart from within, shattering the relative silence and knocking the forester down for a second time. The devastation felt good, but Nerak wanted to be back in Traver's Notch, watching Steven Taylor's face as he first killed the bowman and then took the ignorant South Coaster. 'My prince,' he whispered contemptuously as he flitted through the trees.

When Nerak came across the terrified woodsman, he took him effortlessly, as he had done to so many others, so many times over the Twinmoons. They were all there to serve him: children, horses, women, it didn't make any difference. The last one's leg had dragged, broken worthless cripple that he was, but he had worked the cart, enjoying a mouthful of good South Carolina tobacco while he waited for Fantus to lead his pathetic little company across the bridge. That one hadn't screamed either; too shocked or too rutting sorry for himself – many of his victims forgot to scream. Too surprised that it could possibly be happening to them – proud trash, that's what they were. The woodsman had been no exception: he had stiffened for a moment as the life drained from his body, his hopes and dreams and memories pooling in a puddle at his feet. Nerak picked up the man's axe, wiped his bloody wrist on his leggings and started back towards town.

Nerak looked down on Traver's Notch and contemplated the valley. He couldn't detect Fantus or the others anywhere below. He considered wiping the Traver's Notch slate clean, as he had in Port Denis – it wouldn't take much: a simple gesture and a few key words to call up the web of mystical power he had woven over the Twinmoons and Traver's Notch would be gone.

But the dark prince hesitated. 'If you do, they'll know you're back,' he rationalised. He needed Fantus to believe him gone, perhaps for ever, but certainly struggling to recover from Steven Taylor's attack – but this time he had surprise on his side, and he wouldn't hesitate. He knew where the key was hidden. Steven Taylor and Fantus – *Fantus!* – were his biggest problems, so he would take one of them first, quickly and without warning. His desire to see if Steven Taylor screamed in the moment before death was overwhelming. He strode down into the town, intent on finding the party and discovering the answer for himself.

Then he stopped. 'They're making for Sandcliff,' he said out loud. 'They have the key and they're heading for Sandcliff Palace.' He started laughing. 'What a perfect tomb for you, Fantus.' He cast a fast-moving spell out and over the ridge to the east. He would find them; it wouldn't take long. 'Enjoy your journey, Fantus,' he shouted. 'Be sure I'll be back to perform your rites.'

'You have to do it,' Gilmour shouted as they forced their way through the forest along the base of the ridge.

Steven shook his head. 'No, I can't. I don't know how.'

'But you do. You have to trust that you do.'

'*You* know the spell. All right, you were a bit flustered back there and I don't know what's wrong, but you need to get your wits back, Gilmour. You didn't feel him, but we'll worry about that another time. Right now, you have to figure out a way to keep him from finding us.' Steven was adamant.

'That's my point,' Gilmour said. 'Any spell I use right now, he's going to find me. We're too close. He'll sniff me out in no time.'

'I don't know how,' Steven stammered, looking to Garec and Mark for help. 'Yes, you do,' Garec said. 'Think of the night you saved me. If you hadn't been there, I would be dead.' He still wore his bow over one shoulder, but except for Mark's lessons, he hadn't nocked an arrow since leaving Orindale.

'I can't just call it up,' Steven argued. 'It wells up when it wants to – I'm lucky to be able to manipulate it at all.'

'That's not true,' Mark stopped. The others turned to wait. 'Steven, that's not true and I think you know it.'

'What do you mean?'

'Remember when you used the staff in the foothills? You broke it against that Seron's back and it was obvious that it was more than broken, because it didn't just break like a stick breaks, it damned near shattered in your hands. You decided that it shattered because you had used it in anger to wound that Seron maliciously and that there was something about the staff that refused to be used like that. Isn't that right?'

Steven nodded. 'It always feels most right when I use it in a – well, in a *compassionate* way. I know that sounds stupid, because I'm fighting, but when I use it to help our cause and I show mercy, it's stronger – it's at its most powerful when I am controlling a situation so that no one gets hurt or killed.'

'But that's when the staff responds to your needs, to *our* needs, and I believe it does, Steven, I agree with you. Sometimes the magic does come of its own volition, but I don't think you realise what you are capable of doing. I've seen you call up the magic – Hell, Steven, I've seen you do it without the staff. That day when Lessek's key kept knocking you down at the dump? I'd bet dollars to doughnuts you were calling the magic up there, too, all the way back at home.'

There was an explosion behind them that echoed along the ridge. Steven turned to continue riding, but the others stood fast. 'That was him,' Steven said. 'He's back.'

Mark ignored him. 'Steven, tell me why the staff didn't shatter that day in the hills when you got so angry with Garec, you two almost killed each other?'

Steven recalled the morning with embarrassment – it hadn't been his finest hour in Eldarn. By the end of that day, his leg was bitten through and he was bleeding to death in the snow. If Lahp hadn't been shadowing him, he would have died alone that night. 'I don't know why. You're right, I did it in a rage and the staff should have broken against that tree.' He shrugged. 'Can we discuss this someplace else?'

'No,' Mark said, 'Something else happened that morning and it happened again our first night in the cavern.'

Steven was sweating despite the chill.

'I could see home, Steven. It took a while to figure out what it was, but when you slashed through that big pine, I could see the corner of Miner and Tenth. There was neon. At first, I couldn't believe you had missed it. It was a clear view across the Fold. And then in the cavern, the little campfire went out the moment you fell asleep. It was as if the thing needed you to be awake to keep it burning. Garec and I woke you up and asked you to start another fire, a real fire, with one of the logs from the *Capina Fair*.' Mark smirked recalling their awkward raft. 'And you did it.'

'So?' Steven was nervous, as he continued to glance back along the ridge he was only half-listening to his roommate. 'So what's your point? I've made fifty fires. They're not that hard to do. The staff is always ready to get one going – they're something this company needs.'

'You're not paying attention!' Mark almost shouted.

'Steven, that night you started a fire without the staff,' Garec said. 'You sat up, glanced at the fire-pit, called up a nice little blaze and went right back to sleep. The staff wasn't anywhere near you.'

'And that night, I saw home again,' Mark said, 'the 10-minute lube joint on the corner, that awful orange sign we can see from the driveway.'

Steven knew the sign – he had seen it as he ran towards Miner Street after realising Lessek's key had been hauled away to the city dump. He looked at his friends. 'So what? What do you want me to do? I'm telling you I can't just turn it on like a faucet.'

'And we're telling you that you turn it on like a faucet all the time,' Mark said. 'I'm not trying to manipulate you. I'm telling you the truth. Why didn't the staff shatter against that tree in the Blackstones?'

'I don't know.'

'Yes, you do, Steven and so do I. It wasn't the staff's magic that knocked the tree down.' Mark stared at him, unblinking. 'It was yours.'

'Oh, good Christ, Mark,' Steven was flustered. 'Do you not get it? Nerak is coming here to kill us, right now. I don't have any magic. I'm a bank teller, for shit's sake, and a pretty poor bank teller at that. I don't know where this magic is coming from. Maybe I *have* done from time to time without the staff, but I'm quite sure it's the staff's magic. Maybe it's around me like a cloud. Maybe it works if the staff is nearby. Maybe—'

He was interrupted by another explosion, as devastating as the first, from somewhere on the ridge above them.

'How did you know?' Mark pressed, 'just now, how did you know it was Nerak?'

'I smelled tobacco juice on his breath.'

'But there was more, wasn't there? And it didn't come from the staff.'

'I ... I don't know. Maybe, yes.'

'Yes,' Mark said, 'yes, because Gilmour didn't feel him there and the staff didn't feel him there. He was well hidden, Steven, but *you* felt him, didn't you?'

Steven nodded, almost imperceptibly. It was true. He had felt Nerak, smelled him, even disguised as that broken little man. His hands had stiffened and he had balled up his fists in an effort to stretch them. He had thought he was tired, or cold, but he had felt something. The tobacco juice had simply confirmed his suspicions.

'And you tagged the dog-piss out of him,' Garec interjected. 'Was that the staff, or was that you?'

Steven looked at Garec and then at Gilmour. The old man had said nothing. 'It was both, I think,' Steven answered. 'I lashed out, and I know the staff's magic was there, it just blew up in my hands, but there was some of the other in there as well.'

'So *you* do it,' Mark insisted. 'You cloak us now, because anything Gilmour does to hide us will be like lighting a signal flare.'

'Okay. I'll try.'

'No. Don't try, Steven, just do it. When you came back through the Fold, you were certain you could take it over. We needed maths, magic and compassion. How in all Hell you're going to do it, I have no idea, but you were confident. That's what we need you to do right now, recapture whatever it was that had you believing so strongly.'

'You said, "We can paint the damned thing yellow if we want to!",' Garec quoted.

'That's right,' Mark slapped a hand hard against Garec's back. 'That's what he said. Well, Steven, get painting.'

Steven took a deep breath. It was hard to concentrate, knowing Nerak was so close by; he didn't know how to keep his mind focused. Turning to Gilmour, he asked, 'Is there a spell I should try?'

Mark interrupted, 'No. You don't need one. In all the time we've been here, you haven't uttered one spell. I want you to do just like you did in the cavern with that wall of fire or those flying rocks. You needed them. You imagined them and *ka-blam!*, they were there. I saw what was left of the grettan that attacked you. It looked like someone rammed a Tomahawk missile up its ass. And you did that *after* you lost consciousness – *and* while the ugly bastard was having your leg for a snack. Steven, you just gave Nerak the first beating he has taken in five generations. He had *no* idea what hit him.'

Steven nodded seriously, listening carefully now to what Mark was saying.

'I'm almost sure of it now,' Mark went on, 'he has no clue what's inside that stick of yours, and even less notion that you have found some hidden power inside yourself, or inside this world or between you and the staff or— well, shit, who knows? But as long as he can't feel you, he has to fly blind. That gives you the upper hand.'

Steven looked again to Gilmour, 'What do you think?'

'I think for the time being, I can be of little help.' His neck and his ribs had ached since the moment Steven slashed through Nerak's disguise and he had a terrible suspicion that it was he who had allowed Nerak back into Eldarn, when he had opened the book of Lessek's spells. In trying to learn what he needed to defeat his old nemesis, he had opened the gate for Nerak to come back: that rush of warm, humid air, that had been Nerak. Gilmour had failed again.

'That doesn't instil me with a lot of confidence,' Steven replied.

'Mark is right, though,' the old man said, 'remember the way you saved Garec that night on the beach.'

Steven tried to corral his thoughts and recall the energy he felt battling the wraith army, the power at his fingertips when he called up the wall of fire, the way his knowledge of physiology had transferred itself to the staff when he healed Garec's injuries. He let all the images wash over him, bringing whatever insight they might have. He remembered the dump, the thin air that took his breath away when he climbed the fence, and then the thick air, dense with potential and power, that he had reached out and felt swallowing his hand. It had pressed back against him as he watched three tears open in the Fold. He concentrated: Nerak was close by and searching for them right now.

How could he create a cloaking spell without knowing what a cloaking spell ought to do? Did they need to be invisible? He was certain that was beyond his reach – but invisible to Nerak's power? That might work…. but how to think it? What to feel? Gilmour was supposed to be the sorcerer, not him.

Well, Steven, get painting. He heard Mark and Garec urging him on, could feel their eyes on him. He felt embarrassed ... 'This isn't working,' he sighed.

'Why? What's the matter?'

He looked around. 'Let me try it over there. Maybe that'll help.' He dismounted and moved off a little way into the woods, away from where the others could watch him so closely. He heard something large and fast rush by overhead – at home, it would have been a low-flying jet, but here – here, he knew it was the dark prince, casting about for them. *Hurry up*, he told himself, *Steven, you'd better hurry up.*

He sat down on a moss-covered boulder and focused his attention inward: the wall of fire, Garec's lung, the great pine in the Blackstone forest – but again he was derailed by his inability to think of how a cloaking device should work. 'This isn't going well,' he called back to the others.

'Take your time,' Mark encouraged. 'We're fine. We'll watch and listen. You don't think about anything but keeping us hidden, protected from his sight.'

Protected from his sight. They needed camouflage. Camouflage, like the absurd head-to-toe drapings Howard used to wear for his annual trip to Nebraska during goose season. He remembered Myrna saying, 'I can still see you, Howard. You're still here? I can— oh wait, I almost lost you there for a minute, but there you are. I can still see you.'

Focus, Steven. You're not focusing. Hidden from sight – how do we get hidden from sight? We need to be camouflaged but not invisible. Howard might have been invisible to the geese, but he was never invisible to Myrna. Myrna. Think, Steven.

Another seeking spell rushed by overhead. Steven recoiled reflexively and opened his eyes. 'He's getting closer.'

'Keep at it! I know you'll get there.' Mark's confidence was infectious, but it didn't help. It was cold. He wished he had put on the ski jacket from his saddlebag before moving into the brush. He would start wearing it beneath the cloak; that would be warm, as warm as a heavy blanket, a wool—

'That's it,' he cried, looking back at the others.

'What's it?' Garec asked, but Steven didn't answer. His friends had already begun to come more sharply into view, framed in front of the acrylic canvas of the forest as trees, shrubs, fallen leaves and scattered rocks all began slowly to melt together, to soften into a malleable whole. Reaching out, he could feel the air, that familiar sense that it had grown more dense, as heavy as the most humid day he could remember: Mexico, or New Orleans in the summertime. He wore the air like a glove, a perfect fit, and Steven turned his hand over and over, gaining a sense of how he could push and pull, manipulate and build from this perspective.

Well, Steven, get painting – yes, painting a woollen blanket, one with holes in the weave, holes he could see through, but that was fine, they needed to see where they were going. It was the perfect camouflage – was someone under there? Of course. No one could become invisible … but you couldn't tell who was hiding beneath that old blanket. Mark had said something about a blanket, the comforting feeling of falling asleep on the floor or the couch and waking up later covered by his mother's wool blanket. Why had Mark mentioned that? It had something to do with Karl Yasztremski and the Red Sox, with his father and Jones Beach out on Long Island.

Without realising what he was doing, Steven walked back to where his friends watched, thrilled that he had succeeded in calling up the magic, yet still dumbstruck at the breadth of his power. He held aloft the hickory staff and gestured with it from horizon to horizon, east to west, and then north to south. It glowed a faint red where his palms touched it, much as it had the night Gilmour rebuilt it from splinters he found scattered across the ground.

Mark traced the line of the staff in the air; he was looking for something in particular. When he found it, he nodded grimly to himself. Steven was camouflaging them, protecting them from Nerak's sight.

When he was finished, Steven leaned the staff up against his horse's flank, turned to the others and said, 'That should do it. I'm not sure how long it will last, but I think I can do it again if I have to.'

'What did you do?' Gilmour asked. 'I felt nothing, no ripple, no tension, no spark, and if I felt nothing, I'm sure Nerak has no sense at all of what just happened.'

'I put a blanket over us.'

'A blanket?'

'Yeah, an old blanket my mother used to keep draped across the back of the couch.' He smiled at Mark. 'It was your idea.'

'My dad, and those pictures in the hall,' Mark said. 'I knew it was working.'

'How?'

'Abe is running a sale on Bud and Bud Light. I saw the poster.'

Steven nodded and climbed back into the saddle. 'Let's get out of here. Which way, Gilmour?'

'East, my friends.' He did not look well, but he patted his horse and led the others through the Falkan forest.

THE GORGE

Hannah was worried about her mother, and worried about Steven and Mark. She wished there was some way to get a message to them, to let them to know she was doing well – still lost, but no longer alone in this curious land. She was certain the two roommates were in Eldarn too, somewhere, and she was still hoping she might encounter them by pure chance – things like that happened all the time; people met longtime friends and lost relatives on beaches and at used car lots, on station platforms and in supermarkets. Well, maybe not *all* the time, because for all the lost friends one met in the queue at a department store, there were ten thousand who never showed up ...

Still Hannah looked closely at every stranger they met on the road, and gazed about as they passed through villages. She sighed to herself, imagining the scenario: Steven and Mark would shout to her through the window of a pub and she would join them for a few drinks. She knew they would pick up where they had left off, as if nothing as improbable as this had ever happened.

She still hadn't discovered any way of getting a message across the Fold to her mother, either. She didn't want much, just a momentary tear in the fabric of the cosmos. She had never done well in physics; that was Steven's *forte*, and she guessed that even her world's greatest physicists would be confounded by her current situation, so she hoped for a chance discovery that might allow her to shout, as if from across an airport parking lot, that she was scared but fine, and working on a way to get home.

Hannah and her new friends were still picking their way through the Great Pragan Range, moving slowly north towards the Malakasian border. The forest of ghosts was ample deterrent for most travellers and none of her friends had been this way before; Hannah had realised that no one knew *exactly* where the border was. Blocking the sun with one hand and peering into the fading daylight, she tried to determine if there was a navigable pass between two hills off to their left. The hills would be considered mountains by most standards, but in comparison with the rest of the sawtoothed Pragan range, these were little more than speed bumps.

This guess-and-check orienteering without a map was really slowing their progress. Twice now they had been forced to backtrack to find a workable pass. Most of the time, though, they had been what Hannah called 'holy fucking lucky' – Churn found the notion hilarious, but Hoyt and Alen understood the grave implication of the foreign woman's joke: winter was upon them and finding a low-elevation passage was critical. Not even a fool would climb the Great Pragans until the high altitude snow melted the following spring. And here they were, moving steadily north

Still squinting into the west, she asked, 'What do you think?'

'A pass there? It's hard to guess,' Hoyt said. 'This sloping meadow cuts off too much of our view to be sure.'

Hannah sighed. 'You're right, I know, but just look at the rest of them. See anything more promising? If we can't get through there, I foresee a long snowy winter right here in the centre of this frozen field.'

Hoyt shivered. 'Let's go.'

The periodic snow on the ground had made it easy for them to follow the route taken by the wagonloads of Seron tree cutters – the noise the carts made gave plenty of notice and they hid in the underbrush until the Malakasians had disappeared – but the previous night the group had taken a wrong turn and a thorough search of the meadow yielded no evidence that the Malakasian transports had come this way.

'But there couldn't have been any other way to get those wagons through here,' Hannah said. 'I'm sure we'll pick up their trail between those two hills. It's the only low-elevation pass along this ridge.' She gestured west to east, as if Alen couldn't see for himself that the way was blocked. 'And I don't know how the hell anyone in Malakasia thinks they'll continue to make this journey, either going or coming back, for much longer.'

'Prince Malagon will have his Seron pick up the wagons and carry them over these passes, and he won't think twice about it if every last one of them freezes to death – he wants the bark, and it looks like he wants *all* of it, as much as they can harvest. Lives lost in the process will mean nothing to him.'

Hannah nodded, her lips pressed together against the cold. 'Cheery thought, Alen. Thanks. Are you ready?'

'Lead on.'

They moved across the open meadow and into a crowded stand of pine trees, the wind that had been brushing at their hair and tickling the backs of their necks becoming tangled in the branches. Hannah's heart sank when they emerged and started climbing the slope, for the pines had given away to leafless deciduous tress that offered little shelter from the wind. Without speaking, they hastened on, hoping for better shelter over the rise.

When they reached the rounded hilltop they realised why Prince Malagon's wagons had taken a different path: below, a river rushed its winding course towards the Ravenian Sea. The pass they had seen from the meadow looked to be a viable alternative to freezing to death, but reaching the base of those hills from their current position would be challenging. The little river cut a canyon two hundred paces beneath their feet, running in a southwesterly direction. At the base of the hill, it curved back on itself, carving a deep gorge into the hillside, and disappeared into the trees. They could clearly see the pass, and given an early start the following morning, they could be well on their way down the opposite side by the midday aven.

Now they had to decide whether to cross the river, at the risk of soaking everything they wore or carried, or backtrack to pick up the Malakasian trail. Crossing the river ran a real danger of hypothermia, and building a large enough fire to dry themselves was another risky proposal – with Seron moving so freely through the country, they would likely be dead by morning. But Hannah didn't like the idea of going back either; losing another day of travel meant one day closer to real winter setting in.

There was a third option: they could move northwest beneath the hollow edge of the gorge's lip, hanging on to anything they could to ensure no one slipped down the incline and into the eddy swirling below. It would be difficult for their horses, and Hannah feared that if they lost even one, the remaining animals wouldn't be strong enough to get them through the mountains and over the border.

With daylight fading, the scene before her took on a grey aspect, presaging a long fall and an icy swim through the turbulent water.

'We can't do this,' she said finally.

'Actually, I think we can,' Hoyt said, who had been silently staring across the gorge. 'Look up there at that slope: it's gradual all the way around. We shouldn't organise any dances up there, but if we hold fast to that lip, it's a good two or three paces wide, and it's actually fairly level.'

'What about over there?' Alen pointed to a place along the curved hollow of the gorge where a lone pine with broad branches effectively blocked their way.

'We'll have to go above it,' Hoyt smiled, the reckless smile of a young man who still believed himself invincible.

'You're going to get us all killed,' Hannah said.

'No,' Hoyt answered, 'and look, if it gets too bad, less than halfway around, we can climb up the slope and over the lip.'

'To find *what* on the other side, exactly?' Hannah asked, 'a good Pragan restaurant? Hoyt, what if we get out there and decide we have to climb over and the other side is worse than this?'

Hoyt smiled again. 'Hannah, what could be worse than this? I know you don't want to go all the way back trying to find a wagon track in the dark.'

That much was true, but falling over exposed rocks to land in a freezing mountain river as the sun punched its time card was not the most appetising suggestion either. She turned to look at Alen, her eyes pleading for help.

The old man threw up his hands. 'It would save time.'

'Churn?' For the first time since the argument had begun, Hannah looked at the big mute. He looked as though he might pass out right there and Hannah felt a moment's guilt: they hadn't even considered Churn's fear of heights.

He was still uncomfortable sitting in the saddle all day; right now he was pretty certain he'd be safer walking back and single-handedly grappling with an entire wagonload of Seron, rather than walk around beneath the lip of this gorge. He tried to swallow, and failed; his throat was too dry.

He looked at Hannah and tried to grin. He had survived the forest of ghosts; he had survived being beaten and hanged from the highest branches of his family's cottonwood tree. He hated high places, but he had survived ... and this gorge had a slope and a thin path so there wasn't a straight fall. There would be places to grab on to, should he slip, and he'd have to slide far through the mud, and then over the rocks, before getting to the edge and falling into the river. This would be a grim few moments – but it wouldn't be as bad as the forest of ghosts. *Nothing* could be that bad.

Churn straightened his shoulders and grinned again, a proper smile this time. He took out a length of rope from his saddlebag, tied one end about his waist and handed the other to Hannah, motioning for her to do the same.

'Yeah, Churn, great idea,' Hannah said, 'unless, of course, you fall – then I'm going down like the stern colours on the *Andrea Doria*.'

Churn grunted. He didn't understand.

'Just don't fall, all right?' she said, and checked the rope was tied tightly. 'Okay, guys, Churn has spoken – let's get going. It's already getting dark.' Alen and Hoyt led their horses out onto the narrow sloping ledge encircling the half-moon gorge while Hannah, distracted thinking of the number of ways disaster could find them in the next twenty minutes, didn't notice Churn facing her, one hand on his hip and one behind his back. She suddenly realised the others were nearly out of sight while she and Churn had yet to leave and, a little irritated, asked, 'What is it, Churn? We need to move.'

Churn motioned towards his hidden fist.

'What? Oh, not now – you want to play now? To see who goes first? Are we really going to do this, Churn?'

He didn't budge.

'All right, all right,' Hannah acquiesced. 'On my count … one, two, three!' Simultaneously, they both extended their hands, Hannah's in a fist and Churn's with two fingers extended. 'Rock breaks scissors. I won!' she crowed, exultant, 'hey, I won, I really won! So what's the total score at this point – 673 to one?' She thought on it a moment longer, then asked, 'But does that mean I have to go first or that I get to choose?'

Churn gestured slowly enough for her to understand. 'You choose.'

'Then you go first, my friend, and I will follow along and watch your footing.'

'Very good,' Churn signed.

She knew that one. 'And remember, don't fall.'

'I won't.'

'And try to keep solid footing in case I fall.'

'I will.'

'All right, go ahead. Get going.'

'I'm trying. You just keep—' Churn checked his own knot a final time, then sighed and led his horse out onto the slope.

Leading her own horse by the bridle, she followed. 'Thanks Churn,' Hannah whispered.

Halfway through the gorge, Hannah was seriously regretting letting Hoyt talk her into coming this way and angry at Alen for not backing her. The footing was difficult, and the mud that lined the gorge wall was like hardening paste, making decent handholds rare. She and Churn stopped to watch as Hoyt and Alen led their horses past the lone pine blocking the path. Her heart was in her throat as one of the horses slipped, but it was momentarily and they were soon out of danger. As they headed for the top of the gorge, the two men looked like children racing to be crowned King of the Mountain. Finally Hoyt stood on firm ground and waved back at them. 'It's easier going up here,' he shouted down. 'Still narrow, but better than along the slope. Come around as far as the tree and then climb out.'

Churn, moving ahead of her, hummed an off-key melody in time to his careful footsteps. He kept a tight grip on his horse's reins with one hand and used the other to hang on to whatever purchase he could find on the gorge wall. He concentrated on keeping his weight into the wall and pressed his feet firmly into the dirt, ready in an instant to support his weight, and Hannah's, if necessary – he was quite strong enough to lift her entire body with one arm, should she slide down the slope, but he didn't want to risk a weak foothold and end up following her into the river.

As he got closer to the tree in the path he began to feel better. He was still afraid of heights – the memory of the cottonwood tree and the carnage below was still too vivid – but helping Hannah had stopped him being paralysed by terror; concentrating on her had distracted him enough to make it through.

He didn't even notice the ice that crusted the mud as his foot slid – Hannah had a moment to wonder if he might regain his footing – then he and his horse spilled over the edge, an inarticulate scream echoing back.

In her own mind, Hannah was screaming for Churn to find a foothold while she struggled to unfasten the knot holding the two of them together, but there wasn't enough time. She watched as the burly Pragan tumbled down the slope and the line stretched taut, caught for a moment on a jagged outcrop, then came free and dragged her down behind him.

Hannah felt her hand close around a root, and for an instant she thought they were saved – but no sooner did she feel a wave of relief wash over her than she was torn bodily away from the gorge wall, a broken end of muddy root in one hand, to continue freefalling through the air towards the river. Just below her, Churn hit the water like a boulder, followed closely by his horse, which crashed through the surface with a resounding splash and was swallowed whole by the grey water.

Disoriented by the frigid cold, Churn flailed wildly in the current, then came to his senses: he needed to swim for the opposite shore and kindle a fire as quickly as possible if he were to survive this bone-numbing chill.

When his horse struck the water, it landed on the rope – which in turn yanked Hannah from her trajectory towards the centre of the river and sent her crashing into the muddy slope, where she slid gracelessly to a flat rock protruding into the eddy. Hannah slipped in and out of consciousness, fleetingly aware of the sound of the river hurrying by.

Then Churn, ghostly-white and shivering, was with her, holding fast to her rock while his legs trailed in the current. In the distance, a horse whinnied loudly, and Churn managed a wry grin as the animal climbed from the shallows on the opposite bank and turned to shake its head at them impatiently.

Churn tried to lift his head when Hannah groaned. Blood matted her hair and painted her face red; the heavy homespun tunic was soaked in mud and blood.

'Shit, Churn, I'm hurt,' she whispered, trying to roll onto her side. A sharp pain flared in her shoulder and her left arm tingled with pins and needles, then went numb. She tried to move her arm, but it lay useless at her side. 'I broke my arm, Churn,' Hannah said plaintively, reaching for him, 'and my head is bleeding.' Her vision blurred. 'I hit it hard, Churn. I think I'm going to pass out. We need to get away from here before I do ...' She inched her way across the rock, trying to ignore the pain as she dragged herself on one hip. She focused on Churn, whose head rested on his folded arms while the bulk of his body was still submerged in the water.

'Come on, Churn,' she encouraged, her voice breaking, 'let's get you up here too.' She grasped one of his hands as firmly as she could with her own good hand, gritting her teeth to ignore the jags of pain that radiated from her shoulder to her fingers. Even healthy, she didn't have the strength to heave Churn onto the rock, but she hoped the power of her touch would motivate him.

'Come on, buddy,' she said, her vision tunnelling now. She knew she wouldn't be conscious for much longer. 'A little help, my friend,' Hannah groaned.

He finally lifted his head, and as she succumbed to the encroaching darkness, she thought, *he will be all right*. Churn took a deep breath and pulled himself painfully out of the water. The cold bit hard; his arms and legs had begun to tingle numbly and he struggled to remain lucid as he looked Hannah over more closely. As well as the head wound, which was still bleeding, one collarbone was almost protruding through her skin and the arm looked pretty nasty as well. Hoyt would have to set and bind that one. Her knees and elbows were bleeding, but none of her other limbs appeared to have snapped. He ran his fingers over her ribs, but his own hands were so cramped with cold, he was unable to feel if any of them had broken.

Rutting mess, Churn thought, *this will slow us down. We should have gone back and circled around.* He made a solemn promise to himself: if he were able to carry Hannah back up the slope, he would never again return to another high place – not a ledge, nor a building, and certainly not another icy mud slope above a swirling, freezing mountain river – no matter who might be chasing him.

Churn shook his head to keep his thoughts clear: he had to move Hannah, before she lapsed into a coma. He searched the hillside, waiting for Hoyt and Alen to pass down a rope: he could climb the embankment with Hannah over one shoulder, if they pulled from the top. His main concern was to give the injured woman as gentle a ride as possible.

First things first: he needed to immobilise Hannah's shoulder. Keeping it from moving would be critical if they were to make a safe ascent, and Churn thought it best that she remain unconscious until he had her safely out of the gorge. Jouncing the broken collarbone might wake the girl (*she had looked like a sea nymph that day in Southport*) and then she might jerk away and cause them both to tumble back down. Ignoring the fact that he was freezing himself, Churn started to unhook his cloak; he needed it for bandages – but as he did so, something glinted in the sun.

He crawled painfully over to the shining object – a cloak pin, holding closed a thick woollen wrap being worn by what was undoubtedly a dead man. It looked as if he had fallen, like they had, but he hadn't been as lucky: a pace or two further and the mud would have cushioned his fall, as it had Hannah's.

Churn peered closely at the body; he reckoned the man, a forester, maybe, judging by his clothes, had been dead for several days, though the chill air had stopped the corpse from rotting. The body rested half on and half off the rocky ledge. It looked like the man had cracked his skull, killing him on impact. Churn warmed somewhat at the notion of another dead Malakasian, then got to work pillaging the corpse for anything he might use to make safer his and

Hannah's potentially dangerous journey up the muddy embankment. The man had a knife and a small wood axe, nothing appropriate for battle, tucked in his belt. He tore the man's cloak into strips which he used to bind up Hannah's injured shoulder, being especially thorough, then he attended to her head, using another makeshift bandage to tie around her forehead, stopping the flow of blood from her wound. He dipped a bit of cloth into the river and used it to clean her face.

From somewhere above, Churn heard Hoyt and Alen calling, but he couldn't call back; he could just hope they found him soon. He returned to the corpse and reached for a leather pouch, small but bulging with what he hoped was silver. It was tied tightly at the top with a wet leather thong. Churn fumbled with the tie for a moment, the cold making his fingers cramp, and then gave up and drew his own knife to slice through the leather and open the pouch.

Almost immediately, he was gone. It wasn't cold and he wasn't wet. The snow was falling again, warm weather snow, tickling his face and catching in his hair. His shoulders ached, but he was happy to be free from the frigid waters. He tried and failed to free one of his hands to brush the snow from his face.

He was back in the cottonwood tree, but this time he didn't look down. Instead, he forced himself to keep his gaze focused on the perfect azure sky, Gods of the forest, but it was a beautiful sky. Churn wouldn't pull his gaze away from the cloudless expanse of Pragan blue perfection, despite the heavy aroma of smoke and ash. He was back, but it wasn't real. It was a dream. The smells made him want to look down, but he wouldn't; he would look up at that sky for the rest of his life if necessary.

Then he heard them: there were at least two, above him someplace, hiding in the Pragan sky, but they called him and he didn't answer – he *couldn't* answer. There was no shouting left in him, certainly not from the top of this rutting tree where he had shouted and cried for so long. Instead, he shook his head, a gesture he had perfected in those few moments after climbing from the river, and he would use it again now. It helped him ward off the cold. It was cold now, even there in the cottonwood tree. Perhaps it *was* winter snow. Churn knew, without looking down from the branches, that Hannah Sorenson was not down there on the ground outside his family farmhouse; she was somewhere else – he tried to remember where she had fallen, but the vast Pragan sky called him back and he forgot the woman for a moment, just long enough to smell the ashes burning below ...

Churn dropped the leather pouch. *Demonpiss! It's more of that cursed bark*, he screamed in his mind. He dipped his hands in the river and wiped them repeatedly across his leggings, hoping to wipe any vestiges away. Adrenalin surged through his body, warming him for what he needed to do. He picked up the pouch and secured it with the leather thongs, then tied it safely onto his belt. Then he stood for the first time since crawling from the river and looked up the embankment. The curve of the hillside blocked his view, but he could hear Hoyt and Alen right above him, shouting his name

Cry out to them, he thought, *yell up to them now*. Churn threw his head back, rounded his shoulders and drew a deep breath – but nothing emerged, not a squeak. He couldn't make himself shout, and as he couldn't see them, he guessed that they couldn't see him or Hannah either – and still he couldn't make himself shout up to his companions. *Why would you not call out to them? What is the matter with you?* he asked himself, shuffling from foot to foot. *Do it now – they need to know where you are! Call up to them, you great stupid rutter!*

A length of rope, tied in clumsy knots to three sets of leather reins, landed in the river some distance off to his right and swirled there for a moment before it began moving downriver towards him: Hoyt and Alen had thrown down a lifeline and were dragging it the length of the gorge, hoping he or Hannah would grab hold and offer them a reassuring tug.

Hoyt.

Gods keep Hoyt for a thousand Twinmoons. His old friend had come up with this strategy; Churn swore he would crush the little thief in a bear-hug if he made it back to the top. He watched as the rope came ever closer, then bent to lift Hannah gently over his shoulder. As soon as he moved her, she awakened briefly, screamed what he guessed was a string of obscenities in her own language, and then passed out again. When the line reached the flat stone, he grabbed it, wrapped it several times around his free wrist, tugged twice to let Hoyt and Alen know he was ready and then worked his way up the slope, digging in with the toes of his boots and allowing the two men to haul him and Hannah back to the upper edge of the gorge.

Churn was careful not to look down until well after they had reached the safety of the forested hilltop.

THE BORDER CROSSING

'We would have known, right?' Steven asked.

'I suppose so,' Gilmour answered, 'although I can't be certain anymore – I've lost track of myself recently ...'

'I think you're underestimating yourself, Gilmour. Maybe you're tired – we've been going at breakneck speed since Mark and I arrived, and that's just been the past Twinmoon or so. You've been pushing yourself for much longer: you've been running on fumes since Orindale.' Steven held back a branch to let the old man past. The forest they were walking through was thick with young growth, periodically interspersed with the charred remains of an older tree, still standing, but truncated by fire and crusted in black ash. Steven released the pliable branch with a snap. 'Anyway, I'm sure we would have felt it.'

'I agree,' Gilmour nodded, 'if he had levelled the city, we would have known. I felt the Port Denis spell from all the way across Eldarn, so even in my current state I think I would have sensed it if Nerak reduced Traver's Notch to rubble three days' ride from here.' He tried to sound encouraged, but he wasn't happy at the idea of resting at Sandcliff; the site of the massacre that had killed nearly all of his closest friends was not the most relaxing prospect. 'You may be right, Steven,' he continued. 'I'm not young any more – I haven't been young in nearly two thousand Twinmoons.' He laughed. 'But *on fumes*? That I don't understand.'

'Fumes, yes,' Steven said, 'gas fumes – it's a car reference, Gilmour. Automobiles: you're going to love them.'

'Automobiles.' He considered the word. 'Very well; we shall see in due course.'

Comforted by the idea that Traver's Notch still stood, Steven changed the subject and asked, 'Where are we, anyway?'

'You see that hill over there?' Gilmour pointed across a shallow valley to the north. 'That's Gorsk. Sandcliff is probably four or five days' ride north of there, longer if Nerak has the hills patrolled and we have to work our way up the coast.'

'What's keeping us from just riding through the valley and heading north right here?' Steven indicated the gentle downward slope from their current position on top of a long ridge running west to east along the border. He was anxious to cross over into Gorsk; he needed to feel as though the final leg of their journey had begun. Lessek's key had been feeling especially heavy in his pocket.

Gilmour stared for a moment across the valley, then said, 'I'm no expert on foreign affairs, but I suspect they might have some questions for us.' He pointed down into the draw where smoke swirled among the treetops that encircled a clearing. There were several rows of large canvas tents.

'Holy shit,' Steven exclaimed, 'where did they come from?'

'They are encamped all along this ridge,' the Larion sorcerer said. 'Take a look back there.' He pointed west, the way they had come.

Squinting, Steven could see more tendrils of smoke snaking their way skywards from within the trees. 'Jeez, they're everywhere,' he said, then, as if noticing their position for the first time, 'Shouldn't we take cover?'

'Why?'

'For one, the only cover we have right now is a few charred stumps. And two, well ... there is no two, but *one* seems a healthy enough reason to duck down for me, wouldn't you agree?

'I wouldn't worry, Steven,' the old man said calmly.

Steven looked incredulous. 'And why not?'

'Your mother's blanket, remember?'

Steven stopped and rubbed his horse's nose. 'It works on them too?'

'From what I can gather, your spell was very thorough.' Gilmour didn't elaborate.

Steven looked around, suddenly uncomfortable, and gripped a fistful of mane. 'All right then. If they don't know we're here, let's go, before they find us some other way. What are we waiting for?'

'Did I mention that I'm a little uncertain of my own skills right now?'

Steven nodded. 'And?'

'I don't doubt your magic at all, but I would hate to attempt a crossing and have someone hear our horses whinny, or see too many tree branches moving against the wind – they'd be bound to investigate.'

'Oh.' Steven sounded dejected.

'Don't get downhearted.' Gilmour tried to sound reassuring. 'You did a very thorough job and I am quite sure Nerak has no idea where we are – at least for now.'

'I think I've felt him looking for us,' Steven said.

'Me, too,' Gilmour said. 'But until I am convinced we won't be riding into an enemy prison, I want to continue east until the patrols thin out enough that we could cross in one of your fuming automobiles and no one would be any wiser.'

'All right then.' Steven turned back to the trail.

Gilmour said, 'I was impressed, by the way.'

Steven looked surprised at the unexpected compliment. 'You were?'

'No spells, no fancy incantations, just focus and concentration: you are far, far ahead of any Larion sorcerer I ever knew, Steven, even some who had been studying for twenty Twinmoons or more – except Kantu, Pikan and Nerak, of course, but they were exceptional.' He sighed and climbed into the saddle. 'I was impressed. Come on, I think we can ride from here.'

Steven looked back to where Garec and Mark were engrossed in a conversation about arrows and homemade fletching. 'Mount up, boys,' he called softly. 'We're going to ride from here.'

'Oh, hurrah,' Mark groaned. He was still clumsy in the saddle and would have been far happier jogging all the way to Sandcliff Palace. 'How much further today?'

'We need to get past that encampment, and Gilmour says we might have to go another day or two east towards the coast.'

Garec agreed with Gilmour. 'They won't patrol as much out there, especially east of the Merchants' Highway. There's nothing out there.'

As they set off, Mark tried to pull the wrinkles out of his leggings where the unruly fabric had bunched up to expose his lower legs; he cursed and nearly fell into the dirt beside the trail. 'Goddamn these creatures,' he muttered, pulling himself straight again.

Gilmour, confident Steven's cloaking spell would effectively distract any one who thought they detected something out of the ordinary, allowed a small fire behind a house-sized boulder left on the ridge by a god building a mountain somewhere further north. It wasn't strictly necessary – they had plenty of dried meat and cheese still – but Gilmour had been craving a cup of coffee himself, and as the milk wouldn't last much longer, he decided a break would do them all good. Everyone was anxious to cross the border into Gorsk and he couldn't blame them; he was a little excited as well. He hoped they had come east far enough to slip north safely.

As Mark busied himself with the coffee pans, Gilmour moved around the boulder and gazed at the hills rolling towards Sandcliff Palace. In the twilight they were brown fading to purple, flanked by the grey-black northern mountains. He pitied those who died late on a winter's day: the journey to the Northern Forest – a journey Gilmour wasn't even sure he believed in any more – would be long and tiresome, especially for someone his age. To pass this way after the leaves had fallen, the naked trees and hills cold in the late day sun, would be an anticlimax to a life filled with love, passion and engaging pursuits. He reached out with his mind, hoping to detect a soul making its way across the burned-over ridge, to offer a greeting and ease the loneliness of that final trek, but he could sense nothing.

He had just started back towards the fire when he heard Mark shouting.

'Stand still – right there! Show me your hands!' The foreigner's voice drowned out whatever anyone else was trying to say.

Another, unfamiliar, voice answered, 'I didn't see you. I can't believe I didn't see you.' He didn't sound that concerned that he might be run through in the next breath, but rather, someone genuinely surprised. 'Four horses and three men— four men—' Gilmour had come around the corner, '—and I didn't see you. Gods rut a dog; you've got a fire burning and I didn't see you!'

'Hands, asshole!' Mark, an arrow drawn full, didn't notice his slip back into English.

'My hands? What? What should I do with them?' The stranger spoke calmly, apparently unafraid of the angry bowman.

'Turn them over. I want to see your wrists,' Mark said.

'What an odd thing to—'

'Now, asshole, or I will drill you through the neck.'

'I don't know why—'

'Shut up,' Mark interrupted, 'and pay attention! I want to see the backs of your wrists, so turn your hands over. Do it now, or die. No discussion; your decision. I will not care, not for one moment, if your body rots on this hill for an eternity.'

The man stretched out his arms, causing his tunic sleeves to ride up his wrists, and did his best to show his hands from every angle. 'I must say, I have been detained from time to time in my life, but this is the most curious demand I've ever heard,' he said conversationally. 'Where did you all come from? Is it magic?'

Mark ignored him. 'Do you see anything?' he asked.

'No,' Garec answered.

'Nothing from over here either,' Steven said, 'and I'm getting nothing from—well, you know.'

Mark still held the arrow nocked. 'What are you doing here?'

The man, who looked somewhat younger than Garec, was dressed in the ubiquitous leggings, a wool tunic with a leather bandolier and a heavy brown cloak. His hood was up, but he had made some effort to cast it back from his face, hoping that eye contact with his assailants might convince them of his peaceful intentions. Still waggling his wrists, he said, 'My name is Rodler Varn. I'm from Capehill. I make, uh, well, deliveries into Gorsk from time to time.' He indicated the bandolier with his chin. 'A bit of root, that's all, and not much. I'm not greedy. I take what I can carry and go in on foot.'

'Fennaroot,' Garec said, surprised, 'you sell fennaroot in Gorsk?'

'What's fennaroot?' Mark kept the arrow trained on Rodler's chest but looked to the Ronans for clarification.

Gilmour said, 'You remember your first day out of Estrad, Mark? The root I sliced for you?'

'Oh, yes, right: it gave a real kick. We tried to get some in Orindale, but it was out of season or something.'

'Malagon made it illegal,' Garec added. 'That's why we had trouble finding it.' He moved over to the man and opened one of the leather pockets in the bandolier. He held up a piece of nondescript dirt-covered root. 'He's telling the truth.'

'It's dope?' Mark asked. 'So you're a drug dealer? Oh, that's just terrific, the one person we meet out here is a drug smuggler.' He chuckled and lowered the bow.

'Fennaroot has many uses, Mark,' Gilmour said, keeping an eye on Rodler Varn. 'It's not very powerful in its raw form—'

'But let me guess,' Steven interjected, 'dried and crushed into powder, it packs a significantly more powerful punch.'

'Yup,' Mark said, 'just sprinkle a little on your pancakes and you'll be swimming the English Channel.'

Rodler, still exposing his wrists for their inspection, called, 'Hey, Southie, can I come up now?'

Wheeling back, Mark drew the bow again and trained it on the stranger. Rage twisted his face and for a moment Gilmour feared he would kill the fennaroot smuggler. Mark's voice was grim. 'My family has put up with racism for generations, and where I come from, the appropriate thing for me to do right now would be to express my sincere outrage and disgust at your narrowmindedness. But guess what, asshole, we aren't there, are we?' Gita Kamrec of Orindale had called him a South Coaster in the caverns below Meyers' Vale, but Mark had let it pass; there had been nothing pejorative in her usage, and she had obviously earned the respect of the numerous black members of her small fighting force. But that had been some while ago, before something fundamentally good had snapped inside Mark's mind.

'I don't believe Eldarn will miss you,' he continued. 'They might pin a medal on my lapel. Ridding the world – even this rotting nightmare you call a world – of a racist drug smuggler might be the best thing I've done since I got here.' Mark laughed, an unfunny sound that rattled around in the back of his throat and died.

'Wait, wait, one moment, wait, please,' Rodler begged. 'I'm sorry. I'm sorry. I didn't think there was anything—'

'And that makes it even worse—'

'But wait, wait, if you're heading for Gorsk, I can get you in,' Rodler was pleading. 'I can get you past the patrols.'

'We'll be fine,' Mark said, his tone still uncompromising.

The man fell to his knees. 'I can get you silver, lots of silver. Is that what you're doing out here? Or is it Sandcliff? I can get you into Sandcliff.' His voice cracked in desperation; Mark grinned, wondering if he had pissed his leggings.

'What do you know of Sandcliff?' Gilmour interrupted, raising one hand to Mark as if to stay the execution – even if only for a moment.

'The Larion palace, I can get in there.' Rodler's eyes were pleading; maybe the old man was the leader of this odd company. 'That's where you're going, right? Sandcliff?'

'How do you know?'

'Well, you're an old man, really old – what else would you be doing out here during this Twinmoon, running along the edge of the border and heading east?'

'Adding ageism to your list of transgressions is not impressing me, shithead.' Mark refused to look at Steven.

Rodler tried to explain, his voice still shaking. 'You built a small fire in the lee of this rock, hoping the smoke will disappear in the twilight. You obviously have some magic, because I nearly stepped on you and I don't generally miss four men, four horses and a burning campfire, especially when they're directly in my path. So I'm guessing you have some cloaking spell keeping you hidden, or at least keeping people around you distracted by other things.

'And him.' Rodler pointed at Steven. 'He looks fit enough to run from here to Capehill, so why carry a staff? He doesn't need it for walking – his legs aren't injured and he has a horse—' Rodler's half-guesses were coming more quickly now, 'and I have never seen anyone this close to the border who hadn't planned somehow to get into Gorsk. Of course, no one I have ever met along this ridge was going into Gorsk for benevolent reasons. Resistance fighters, root peddlers like me, even a few merchants, but no one comes this way to see the sights.' Rodler paused in his rant to check on Mark, who still had a shaft nocked and drawn full. 'But I know things about Gorsk – I'm well connected there. And I will never again use that term, I promise, and I am deeply sorry I offended you. No offence was intended, I swear. I'm telling the truth: If you want to get into Sandcliff, I can get you in.'

Gilmour gestured for Mark to lower his bow and, reluctantly, he complied, saying as he returned the arrow to its quiver, 'If I get even the faintest hint that you are thinking of me or of my race as anything other than your equal – your *better* – you drug-dealing piece of mooseshit, I will drop you in your tracks. You will have no idea death is coming, but it will be final. Do you understand?'

Rodler nodded, still sweating.

Gilmour indicated he should join them around the fire. Mark bent to his coffee and tried to ignore the conversation.

'How much do you carry?' Garec asked.

'Just this,' Rodler indicated several pouches along the bandolier; it looked like they ran round his back as well, but he pulled his cloak close again.

'We're not here for your drugs,' Steven said. 'None of us are interested.'

Rodler calmed noticeably. He looked again at the hickory staff and asked, 'That magic, then?'

'I can get hockey games on it when the wind is right, but sometimes the audio is fuzzy,' Steven said. Mark, in spite of himself, barked a laugh as Garec looked quizzical.

'Not willing to tell me, huh? Well, what's that language you and your— your friend speak? *Asshole*? *Hockey*?'

'It's the language we speak where we live.' Mark had used too many slang terms for him to believe they were anything but foreigners now.

'A different place? A different world?'

Steven nodded. 'You don't seem surprised.'

'My great-grandmother told my mother all about the Larion Senate – although I think they were all dead before even she was born. But she never forgot the stories about when magic and mystical things happened all over Eldarn. It wasn't just the dark prince's nonsense, but real magic, and fascinating inventions and ideas and innovations the senators had brought back here from— well, from somewhere else.'

'Your great-grandmother was right,' Gilmour said. 'It was a magical time.'

Rodler smiled for the first time since joining them. 'You sound as though you were there.'

Gilmour raised his eyebrows.

Rodler gave up. 'So did you plan to cross tonight?'

'We had thought about moving further east, at least across the Merchants' Highway, and crossing there,' Garec said, and then regretted divulging that much information, but neither Gilmour and Steven seemed upset with him for it.

'You could do that, but there's no need,' Rodler said. 'Right here is fine. There's a big encampment back about a half day's ride—'

'We saw it yesterday,' Steven agreed.

'But that's it until you reach the highway and the border stations.'

'How do you know?' Garec asked. 'I thought you said you only make these deliveries from time to time.'

'Sometimes more frequently than others.' Rodler sniffed the air. 'What is that? Burned tecan?'

Garec answered, 'It's called coffee and I recommend you try it barefoot.'

'All right.' Rodler shrugged and began pulling off his boots.

Steven didn't attempt to explain. 'What can you tell us of Sandcliff Palace?'

'So I was right. That's where you're going.' No one responded, so Rodler continued, 'I think there must be some old Larion magic still working in that place, because you would never know it had been abandoned for so long. The grounds are a tangle and the forest has just about swallowed the place, but it doesn't look at all run down. It's as if its heart is still beating, and with a few folks to clear the brush, it would be back to the glory we all heard about as kids. It's not falling down, or even dusty. The windows aren't broken – well, one big one above the main hall, but that's the only one I remember seeing – and the inside is as clean as my mother's bedroom.'

Gilmour grimaced at the mention of the broken window, but quickly hid his embarrassment. 'How did you get inside?'

'I was in a hurry one morning after a business undertaking un-ravelled—'

'Tried to sell to the wrong people?' Garec interrupted.

'No. It wasn't a fennaroot deal. I was at the university.'

Steven frowned and Gilmour explained, 'There is a small university near Sandcliff – the Larion Senators did much of their work there.' He chose his words carefully: Rodler appeared to have been honest with them and it was clear he was not Nerak disguised, but he had yet to prove himself trustworthy.

'So you were there trying to enrol in a class?' Garec asked pointedly. 'The universities have been closed since Prince Marek took the Eastlands.'

Rodler cast his eyes down towards the fire. 'I make a number of trips up here. Some trips are more lucrative than others. Often I'll stop by the university—'

'Books,' Steven interrupted. 'You're stealing old books.'

'I do a bit of book business in Capehill, yes.'

Garec shook his head.

'What?' Rodler defended himself, 'I have to make a living. How do you feed *your* family?'

'I'm a farmer in Rona,' Garec said.

'You've come a long way from home since harvest, then.' The quick-witted smuggler didn't miss much. 'When did you get all the crops in? A few days ago? You're quite a speedy traveller.'

Garec didn't back down. 'I cover some ground, yes.'

'You were saying—' Gilmour interrupted.

'What? Oh, right, Sandcliff, well, I was at the university and I ran into some Malakasian officials whose business ethics did not entirely align with my own and I had to run like a raving madman to get free. I figured they would assume I made my way back into town; so instead, I headed up towards the old palace. When I reached the lower gardens, I thought I was clear, but there they were, waiting.'

'I understand they're thorough about such things,' Garec said.

'So I moved through the lower garden – well, the brush – trying to find some cover. They'd fanned out and were hard on my heels when I found a grate, like a drainage grate for rain runoff, or melted snow, maybe, running through the gardens – I've never seen anything like it, it was a simple idea really, just an underground trench to allow for excess water to run down from the garden—' He broke off, as if to rhapsodise further about the Larion drain, but a look from Mark brought him back on track.

'There was nothing covering the opening now – I guess it might have been wood once, or maybe metal that rusted away, but either way, it was gone, so I crawled inside and made my way up the trench.' The way he told the story, it sounded as if eluding Malakasian patrols was something he did every day. 'The trench ran through a narrow breach in the wall into the scullery, just about wide enough for people to empty water pots or old beer barrels in, I guess, but I managed to squeeze through.'

Gilmour shook his head wryly. 'I'm quite sure the Larion leadership never thought of that opening as a potential breach in the palace's defences,' he murmured.

'It wasn't much of one, I tell you,' Rodler said, 'it would take a rutting Twinmoon to get a decent-sized fighting force through there. The palace wouldn't ever have been under any real threat from that trench, but we were always told it was hard to get into Sandcliff via the main entrance, what with all the spells and such, so I was surprised that I could just crawl into the place.'

'So what did you find inside?' Gilmour wiped a few beads of nervous sweat from his forehead.

'Nothing,' Rodler said, 'I wasn't raiding the place. Well, I did try to find the library – but really I just went in to hide while the prince's squad tore the gardens up looking for me outside. I waited until they were gone and then thought about going back out.'

'But not before you went looking for books,' Garec reminded him.

'Of course – I'm a businessman, just like anybody else.'

'But you couldn't get to the library,' Gilmour stated more than asked.

'Rutting mothers, no. I couldn't get out of the stinking scullery. The doors, windows, nothing would open.' Rodler pursed his lips. 'That's when I knew the place still had some leftover magic in it.'

Again, no one replied.

'So that's why you want to go up there, you want to tap into that force somehow – with that stick? Or is it you?' He pointed at Gilmour. 'You seem to know a lot about the Larion Senate.'

Gilmour shook his head. 'I had a grandmother much like yours.' He changed the subject swiftly. 'How would you recommend we get into Gorsk?'

The sun had set by the time they reached the river, but the water reflected moonlight in hundreds of tiny sparkles, illuminating a surprisingly bright path into Gorsk. 'It will be cold,' Rodler said, not bothering to whisper – unless a patrol was right on top of them, the perpetual background roar of the water would muffle their voices. 'But we don't have to be in it for long, a few hundred paces, that's all. The patrols from the highway station come up to this river on that shore. Patrols from the encampment in the west come up as far as this shore. Neither patrols the centre ... I'd prefer it a bit darker, but we ought to be able to pass by tonight without incident.'

'What makes you so confident?' Garec asked quietly.

'I almost stepped in your campfire – if one of you isn't wielding powerful magic to mask your whereabouts, someone is watching over you. I think we could be screaming songs and playing a bellamir and no one would know we had passed. But it'll be very cold, so we have to move quickly.' He gestured and moved into the water.

Steven shrugged and followed, leading his horse. The mountain water was icy-cold and for a moment he feared the horses would refuse to move, or worse, might bolt and give away their location, but apart from a few irritated shakes of her head, the mare allowed herself to be drawn towards the centre of the river. Their packs were tied onto the saddle, but he retained the hickory staff, warm in his hand despite the frigid, numbing cold in his legs, and Lessek's key, an indistinct lump in his pocket. Rodler hadn't commented on the curious cut and colour of the Gore-tex coats; he appeared to have learned when to keep his mouth shut.

They picked their way carefully upriver, but after what felt like an hour, Steven began to worry that he might never regain feeling in his legs. He was seriously considering an attempt to warm the water as it rushed by when Rodler turned and pointed.

'Just up here, up past that big willow,' he said, indicating a willow tree standing sentinel on the bank, its leafless branches hanging like the thinning hair of an ageing woman. Steven waited until Rodler was distracted and then quickly moved between his friends, drying their leggings and warming their feet with the hickory staff.

'Thanks, Steven,' Mark said. 'Do me a favour and leave him wet, okay?'

'He got us here,' Steven said firmly.

'Where's here?' Mark asked. 'How do we know Eldarn's answer to the Gulag Archipelago doesn't lie just over the next hill? We can warm up beside the fire with Al Solzhenitsyn.'

'Nah, he got out,' Steven said.

'Do you know where we are?' Mark asked Gilmour.

The old man nodded. 'I used to fish in this river – if we follow it north, we'll begin to see landmarks I'll recognise; then we can turn east to Sandcliff.'

'Should we risk a fire?' Garec asked. 'I'm freezing.'

'Not here,' Rodler answered, 'let's ride further north. There's a copse upstream where I keep a fire-pit ready to dry me out after coming through. I've yet to hear a patrol come by while I'm in there.'

'Come here first,' Steven said. 'I owe you at least this much.' He used the staff to dry Rodler's leggings and boots.

'Well, that's a neat trick,' he said, grinning. 'I knew that stick was special.' He reached out to touch it, but recoiled, wondering if it might strike him dead on the spot. Coming across the four travellers had put an unfortunate kink in his plans; agreeing to guide them into Gorsk was a desperate offer to save his life, but he was curious about Steven and the wooden staff, and he wanted very badly to pillage the library at Sandcliff Palace. Rodler decided to remain with the four strangers for a while – at least until he had a better understanding of their intentions.

Steven and Mark turned into the car park next to the Air Force Academy Aquatics Centre just north of Colorado Springs. They had made the trip to the Colorado State Championships to support one of Mark's swimmers, Bridget Kenyon, who was a favourite in several events. Bridget was behind them in a titanic SUV with her parents, her two younger brothers and her grandmother.

Steven asked, 'Why do they hold this all the way down here and not in Denver?'

'The facility is state-of-the-art: an Olympic-size pool cuts down on the number of turns the kids have to make so in the end, the times are faster.' As Mark opened the truck door, the winter air rushed inside, chilling them both.

'It's a long ride to watch one girl swim.'

'Ah, but wait until you see this girl swim.' Mark zipped up his jacket, pulled on his gloves and stepped outside. 'You'll agree it was worth the trip.'

'All right, but you're buying the hot dogs.' Steven realised he had forgotten his gloves and pushed his hands deep into his pockets. 'Let's hurry. I'm cold.'

'You're such a wimp, Steven,' Mark teased.

'But I'm good at it – nearly world class!'

Inside the centre they split up; Steven headed upstairs to find their seats while Mark escorted Bridget down to the pool, distracting her with inane jokes to keep her mind off the early heats. As they emerged into the pool area, a wave of voices washed over them and Mark heard someone say, 'There's that Kenyon girl. She's picked to win the 200 free.'

'Bridget. I think that's her name,' someone else replied. 'I saw her swim at Regions. She put on a freakin' clinic that day, I tell you.'

'We may be able to take second or third, but she's the one, over there, that's her, she'll take the 100 butterfly.'

'That's right. That's right. She's the one with the nigger coach from Idaho Springs. Oh, yeah, I hear great things about him, too. He was tough in his day.'

Mark wheeled on the crowd, drawing an arrow. 'Who said that?' he shouted. The bow felt good in his hands. He had made it himself, whittling down the green branch, even killing the deer whose hide provided the crossed leather strips that made the weapon so resilient.

'Hey Southie, can I come up now?'

'Right, the one with the nigger coach from Idaho Springs. Oh, yeah, I hear great things about him.'

'The nigger coach from Idaho Springs. I hear great things about him.'

'Hey Southie, can I come up now?'

Mark homed in on the voice. It was Rodler Varn, the Falkan drug smuggler. He was here in the stands somewhere. There, beside that guy, whatshisname, the bigot in the green Fort Collins sweatshirt. Smiling, the racist waved and offered Mark an ironic thumbs-up.

'That's just great,' Mark said, 'smile and wave. No one heard you, asshole, but this ought to get your attention.' He exhaled slowly and released the bowstring.

The man in the green sweatshirt took the arrow in the chest, just above the second *L* in Collins. Two more followed with muted thuds. One dotted the *I*; the other found its way inside the tiny hillock of the *N*. Garec's coaching was paying off.

'I warned you,' Mark snapped, nocking another arrow. 'My family has been putting up with that bullshit for generations and the appropriate thing for me to do right now is to express my outrage at your narrow-mindedness. Well, I'm expressing it this way, asshole.' A fourth arrow pierced the man's throat. 'That'll shut him up,' Mark said with satisfaction.

'Hey Southie,' Rodler called from his seat beside the body. He reached over to finger the fletching on one of Mark's arrows. The other parents and coaches chatted, sharing swimming gossip. No one seemed to notice that Mark Jenkins, the talented young coach from Idaho Springs, had just fired arrows into a spectator's chest.

'Southie, can I come up now?'

'I'm going to kill you, asshole.' Now Mark started loosing arrows aimlessly into the humid air of the aquatics centre; most found their way into the man in the green sweatshirt until the body tumbled off the bleachers and rolled to a stop behind the girls' bench.

Frustrated, Mark turned to Bridget. 'Did you hear what they were saying about me?'

The girl smiled up at him, her dirty-blonde tresses tied back in a utilitarian ponytail, soon to be coiled up, snakelike, and tucked inside her swimming cap. Holding two ends of the rolled towel she had draped over her shoulder, Bridget said, 'Maybe I'll carry your bag then, sire? Maybe carry it for you? What do you think, sire? Maybe for a copper Marek or two?'

'What?' It was noisy in the arena and he shouted over the din, 'Bridget, I didn't hear you.'

Grinning to expose her teeth, two perfect rows of white, ortho-dontically sculpted masterpieces, Bridget said, 'The water's cold in here today, but they have warm water at the Bowman, my prince.'

'I'm not a prince, Bridget,' Mark said. 'Go swim, will you? You need to get warmed up if the water's cold.'

'They have warm water at the Bowman, my prince,' she repeated and moved towards the starting blocks at the end of the pool.

Mark watched her walk away, then called after, 'I'm not a prince.'

Bridget turned and mouthed a few words Mark couldn't hear. Tossing her towel onto the blue-and-white bench running the length of the pool, she climbed onto the third starting block. A large number 3 had been painted on the front of the block; Mark wondered if it were important for the swimmers to know which lane they were in during the race. He glanced down at the water and whispered, 'I'm not a prince.'

He saw it move, a flash of something opaque and indistinct. Was it a trick of the light? Then he saw it again, this time rushing towards the other end of the pool, and he knew what it was. He started towards Bridget Kenyon at a run, screaming, though the noise had grown so loud, he couldn't hear his own voice.

Bridget didn't hear him either. She had tucked her ponytail under the rubber swimming cap and was ready to dive in for a few warm-up laps. 'Bridget!' Mark shouted again, 'No! Don't go in the water!'

His heart stopped as the young girl dived lazily into the pool. Bridget Kenyon never hit the water.

The almor burst through the surface and took the girl in mid-air. She was dead in an instant; as the demon carried her to the bottom of the deepest part of the pool, Mark could already see her muscular back and powerful thighs thinning to leather and bone in the creature's unholy grasp. A moment later the almor released her body and a wet sack of bones drifted to rest against the far wall beneath the three-metre diving board.

Mark stood at the side of the pool, waiting for the almor to surface, certain that it would: it had come for him and he was ready to die if necessary, whatever it took to rid the world of this monster.

He expected the demon to explode from the pool like a tidal wave, but instead, the almor bobbed above the surface, a nearly translucent, shapeless creature. He fired arrows into it as quickly as he could draw and release, but they passed through the demon and ended up on the bottom of the pool where they lay together: an underwater game of pick-up sticks.

The water is cold today, but they have warm water at the Bowman, my prince. The almor's laughter came from inside his own head. Mark thought he might pass out from the pounding reverberation.

Panting, he managed, 'I'm not the prince.' He couldn't bear to look down at what was left of Bridget's body. 'I'm not the prince.'

As the almor disappeared through the filtering system and out into the Colorado Springs water supply, Mark heard its words: *Not yet.* That was what Bridget Kenyon had mouthed to him, he now realised.

Not yet.

Mark awakened and was on his feet before he realised it had been a dream. His cheeks were damp: he had been crying in his sleep. Gilmour, stirring the coals in their small campfire, leaned over and whispered, 'Are you all right?'

Mark rubbed his hands over his face and across the back of his neck. He felt like he was having a breakdown; his heart was racing, and he was panting and sweating now, as if he had just finished a strenuous workout. He couldn't even see clearly. He crossed to where Steven was lying, wrapped up tightly in his coat and a blanket, and kicked his roommate firmly on the soles of his boots. 'Wake up,' he muttered.

'What?' Steven groaned, rolling onto his back, then his eyes adjusted to the firelight and he could see Mark standing over him. He sat bolt upright and reached for the hickory staff. 'What is it?' he asked urgently. 'What's happened?'

Gilmour crouched beside Steven. 'You look terrible, Mark. Are you sick?'

'It was Lessek. I'm sure of it,' he gasped, still trying to slow his breathing.

'What did you see?' Steven's grip tightened on the wooden staff. He looked over at Rodler and Garec, but both appeared to be sleeping still.

'Steven, that moment before you hacked that tramp in half, what did he say?'

Steven's brow furrowed. 'I wasn't really listening – he was so irritating, calling me *sire* all the time, prattling on and on about five hundred different things. I kind of tuned him out as soon as I suspected it was Nerak. I was concentrating on sniffing for any hint of tobacco on his breath.' Steven smoothed his blanket over his legs while he thought. 'Sorry, I can't remember.'

'Was it something about the water?'

Steven's eyes widened. 'That's it!' he started to shout, then, lowering his voice again, he said, 'He was talking about getting cleaned up, or getting clean clothes— no, it was a bath. He'd said something when he disappeared into the trees and I hadn't really heard him because you and I were talking about the Bowman and whether or not they would have hot and cold running water. It was obviously a joke, but then—' Steven paused. 'You know what? He was talking to *you*. Right before I decided to use the staff, that little bastard was talking to you. He said, *they have warm water at the Bowman, sire.*'

'Was it sire? Did he say *sire*? Or was it something else?' Mark glanced over at Gilmour, who was shaking his head.

'He said, *my prince*,' Gilmour muttered, 'I'm sure of it. I remember thinking exactly what you were thinking: what did he mean by that? Mark, you stopped to look up at him – that was just a breath before Steven sent him to the Northern Forest.'

'I just needed to be sure I wasn't losing my mind,' Mark said.

'Did you dream? Was it Traver's Notch?'

'Yes and no – not here, but the state swimming championships last year. You remember, Steven? Down at the Air Force Academy?'

'With that girl Kenyon?'

'Bridget, right,' Mark answered. 'I have no idea why – if it *was* Lessek talking to me – he chose that day. Or it may be just a bad memory sparked by our new friend over there.' He gestured towards Rodler, who was curled in his cloak.

'How was that a bad memory? I thought she swam brilliantly that day.' Steven uncorked a wineskin and offered it round.

'It wasn't her. It was this guy from Fort Collins – I don't remember his name, but his daughter was swimming against Bridget. When we walked in, I heard him say something rude about me. I don't know that he meant it to be cruel, and at the time I dismissed it because I just figured he didn't think anything of calling me a nigger.'

'So what did you do?'

'Nothing.' Mark shook his head. 'Oh, well, I did the usual thing all intellectuals do when met with that kind of situation: I frowned, acted displeased, expressed my outrage at his narrow-mindedness and *blah, blah, blah, bullshit, bullshit, bullshit*, but I didn't kick him in the teeth or call him a white trash asshole or anything like that.'

'But you wanted to,' Gilmour said.

'Of course I wanted to,' Mark said. 'I always want to.'

'And today, when Rodler called you a Southie and you almost filled his chest with arrows—'

'I guess it woke up the fury I felt that day at the pool.' Mark looked over at the Falkan drug smuggler again. 'But, Gilmour, there was more to it. The girl I was coaching, she called me *my prince*, just like Nerak did. And there was an almor, a big mother, right in the pool, and it called me prince as well. It said, "There is warm water at the Bowman, my prince".'

'That's it – the last thing Nerak said before I clubbed him,' Steven added.

Mark sighed. Everything that had been on his mind the past weeks came back in a rush – now he needed a few moments to sit by himself and sort them out. The process would go more smoothly if he could take a break from the conversation to determine if he was actually prepared to pursue this particular uncomfortable notion further, but from the look on Steven and Gilmour's faces, he knew there was no chance of putting them on hold while he wandered about the copse arranging puzzle pieces.

'What are you thinking, Mark?' Gilmour asked.

'Is it that obvious?'

'I can smell the smoke,' Steven joked, and the three men laughed softly together.

'This may be nothing, but I need Garec to confirm a nasty suspicion I'm having.' There was no going back.

Steven nodded and poked at Garec with the hickory staff. 'Hey, Garec, wake up,' he whispered.

The young Ronan rolled over, quickly lucid, and demanded, 'Why? What's happening?'

'Lessek may be visiting again tonight,' Mark said.

'Grand,' Garec groaned. 'The last time he showed up we got attacked by a demon.' He sat up and sniffed noisily. 'What are we doing?'

Mark said, 'I need you to think back to your dream at Seer's Peak.'

'My dream? How can I forget? First I have to stand and watch as the most beautiful woman in Eldarn has sex with a frothing freak while a bunch of guards and soldiers wait around in case she needs assistance. Then as if that wasn't bad enough, I get to see Rona devastated by some kind of plague and my favourite woods haunted by an army of wraiths. And afterward, for everyone's enjoyment, I am forced to repeat my dream over and over and over again until the details become so firmly lodged in my memory that I will probably be able to recall every moment on my deathbed three hundred Twinmoons from now. That, of course, was thanks to Gilmour – so anything you need from my particular vision is well preserved right up here.' He tapped a knuckle on the side of his head.

Mark grinned. 'All I need to know is if the woman that Doctor—' He paused, trying to remember the name.

'Tenner,' Gilmour supplied.

'Yes, that's it, Doctor Tenner. The woman he chose to carry on Eldarn's line, the woman having sex with the crazy, crippled prince, was she black?'

'What do you mean, black?'

'Did she have black skin? I don't mean black, like shadow-black, but did she have dark skin, like mine?'

Garec nodded. 'She did. When she came in she looked like a servant – there's no difference once we all get out of our clothes, but from what she was wearing when I first saw her, I would guess she had been a servant at Riverend Palace.'

'A South Coaster?' Mark was on eggshells.

'Yes, definitely,' Garec said. 'What are you trying to work out? That was a long time ago, and even if they did succeed in getting that woman pregnant – well, you read Doctor Tenner's letter: she went off to live in Randel with someone named Weslox Thervan. If Tenner died in the fire, there was no one to produce that baby as Prince or Princess of Rona.'

'But that baby would have been Eldarn's true monarch, Rona's prince.'

Gilmour nodded.

'Mark,' Steven said, 'where are you going with this? Nerak might have been jerking your chain – he called you *prince*, but he called *me* sire about sixty-three times.'

'But not in my dream,' Mark said. 'If my dreams are coming from Lessek, then it's Lessek trying to draw my attention back to those words from Nerak, "There is warm water at the Bowman, my prince." Did you notice that was the only thing Nerak said to me then? He asked the rest of us – once – if he could carry anything else, but apart from that, he mostly talked with you, Steven.'

'So Lessek wants you to remember that comment. Why?' Garec asked, 'is it because you come from the South Coast?'

'I don't, Garec. My family comes from New York. Before that, we were lost in the confusion surrounding the American Civil War. No one has been able to trace back far enough to know what my origins were. Educated guesswork invariably leads to a slave ship that arrived somewhere in the American south after 1619.'

'So South Coasters in your world are slaves?'

'*Were*, Garec,' Steven said. 'It was long ago, a grim time for our world.' Turning back to Mark, he asked, 'Are you thinking that the servant girl—'

'Regona Carvic,' Garec said, 'remember, from Tenner's letter?'

'Are you thinking that Regona somehow came through the portal to your world? That she's related to you?'

Mark shrugged. 'Why else would Nerak and then Lessek draw my attention to that comment, *my prince*?'

'Holy shit, buddy, but that's assuming a lot,' Steven said. 'I don't see how it would be possible – the far portals have been in Nerak's control ever since Sandcliff Palace fell, and Regona was taken to

Prince Danmark's chambers at least a Twinmoon after that. If Nerak had the portals, how could she have got through?'

Mark turned to Gilmour. 'When Nerak was in Estrad, busying himself with Doctor Tenner and the fire at Riverend, where was the portal?'

'I don't know. All I can work out is that Nerak had it hidden somewhere in the city where no one would find it; he most likely did the same thing the day he took Prince Marek in Pellia. He probably hid the portal at Welstar Palace, made the trip downriver to the capital and took the prince right there at his father's side.'

'But the portal wouldn't have been in his control when he was out causing havoc or taking souls?' Mark felt another piece slip into place.

'No. Theoretically, the portal would have been available, if not open, for someone else to use.'

Mark wished he had some time to himself, to draw a diagram or a crude timeline. He drank from the wineskin, then wiped his mouth and asked, 'Steven, why do we live in Idaho Springs?'

'What do you mean?'

'What are we doing there? I love it there, but I freely admit I don't fit in as well as I might someplace else. And you, you're worse than me. How many decent jobs did you pass up after finishing your MBA? Three? Four?'

'What's your point?'

'Maybe we don't have a choice. Maybe we were *supposed* to find Lessek's key and we couldn't leave. Look at you: you do magic with no spells or potions. You just think of things you want to happen; you *will* them to happen and they happen. Is that the staff, Steven, or is that you? Are you a real sorcerer, or are you a guy who found a magic stick that somehow got into his bones? I'm asking because I don't know. But then I couple that with the fact that I left Fort Collins to come to the foothills and take a teaching job that pays less than just about any job I could have found down in Denver or in one of the suburbs. So I wonder what we're doing there, and if we are there by choice.'

'No one is forcing me to live in Idaho Springs, Mark,' Steven said with a degree of uncertainty. 'My parents live there.'

'But why? Do you think they had a choice?' Steven was about to respond when Mark pressed on, 'Think about the communication I have allegedly had from Lessek. He quiets my fears moments after I arrive in Eldarn. It's a memory from a day at the beach with

275

my family. My dad is drinking beer. I had been drinking beer; I'm comforted by the memory and it takes me weeks to realise I'm supposed to be thinking about my dad. Lessek didn't give a pinch of shit whether I was comfortable or not. He hit me with a memory of home, because he needed me thinking about why my dad was such an anomaly: he's the only guy on the beach facing west; he has three hundred pictures of a family vacation that spanned thirty-seven states and almost all of them were taken within one hundred miles of Idaho Springs. He was drawn there, Steven, just like us.'

Steven was shaking his head. 'You aren't the prince of Eldarn, Mark.'

'You're right,' he answered, hearing the almor's cavernous voice echo in his head, 'I'm not – not yet – because I believe my dad is Rona's prince, Eldarn's king. I won't be until he dies, and that's fine with me, I hope he lives to be a hundred and six.'

Steven stood up. 'Do we have any wine left? I need a drink. Mark, this is crazy. You can't be the prince of Rona, and I am not a sorcerer. We weren't *drawn* to Idaho Springs, because there was nothing in Idaho Springs to draw us there.'

'Yes there was,' Mark interrupted. 'You have it in your coat pocket.'

'Lessek's key?'

'That night in our house, we chucked it away – we thought it was nothing, maybe a hunk of some crazy miner's rock – and yet I felt it that night, Steven, and I felt it again when you came back here, that day by the fjord. It's something I can't explain, but it reminds me of when I get a flight back to Long Island to see my family: it's about feeling safe, like I belong – feeling like I'm at home. That hunk of ore makes me feel like that – when I stand next to you and you have it in your pocket, and when I stand next to your bloody saddlebag when you have it packed away. At any given moment, I can pinpoint the location of that stone, even blindfolded.'

'This is too much, Mark,' Steven said. 'You had a bad dream. I'm sorry Rodler called you a Southie, but you can't take that insult and decide it means you're sovereign of Eldarn.' He was growing exasperated. 'It's too great a leap. You can't explain the portals. I know for a fact that the safe-deposit box was never opened at the bank because the key was missing until I found it at Hannah's shop. There are no records of any deposits or withdrawals from the day William Higgins opened the accounts in 1870. That portal was secure.'

'But the other was not,' Mark argued. 'Imagine if Doctor Tenner, before he died in the fire, made arrangements to send Regona through the portal. Think about where she would be safest from Nerak – it's certainly not in Randel with Weslox. She would be safest delivering that baby in a medically advanced society – even in 1870 – and then raising it there. He probably figured he would go and find her later, after the trouble had passed – he might even have drafted the letter I found behind the fireplace as a decoy, after all, everyone talks about this guy as if he was a genius.'

'That couldn't be the case,' Gilmour said.

Mark turned on the old man, his argument ready, but Gilmour went on, 'It would have been Lessek.'

There was an almost tangible silence, broken only by Rodler's breathing and the ever-present babble of the nearby river. It was Steven who finally spoke. 'Not you, too, Gilmour. This is madness.'

'Actually, it makes sense, except Tenner – he was a brilliant physician and an excellent advisor to Prince Marek, but he knew nothing of the Larion portals. After the Larion Senate fell, only Kantu and I knew they existed, and how to use them to cross the Fold. Kantu was in Middle Fork; I was wandering broken and lost. The only person who could have done it was Lessek – he could have detected the portal and sent Regona across the Fold. He might have known that Eldarn's monarch would be drawn to the keystone, one of our world's most powerful talismans, even across great expanses of open land or water. Mark's deductions, however fantastic, are quite reasonable. I'm not saying this is true, but it certainly could be. Lessek could have intercepted Regona on her way to Randel and sent her across the Fold to your world.'

'But how?' Steven was still far from convinced. 'If Nerak was in Riverend, kindling Estrad's biggest bonfire and killing off the rest of the Ronan royal family, how much time would Regona and Lessek have had? Nerak couldn't have been there for very long.'

'Lessek would have been able to detect the portal, even when closed—'

'I believe *that*,' Mark interrupted 'When we opened it that night in our house, we could feel its energy as soon as Steven cracked the seal on the cylinder.'

'Why isn't it doing that now?' Steven asked suddenly. 'It's there in my pack. Why can't we feel it?'

'You've grown accustomed to it,' Gilmour said. 'If we took that portal to somewhere never touched by Larion magic, the people there would feel a tingling in the air like you did. Regardless, if

Lessek was on hand, he could have escorted Regona to the far portal and allowed her to open it.'

'She had to do it?' Mark asked.

'Lessek would have been a wraith,' Gilmour said. 'He may have looked like a normal man, but he would not have been able to open the portal by himself.'

Steven considered their argument aloud. 'So Lessek knows Nerak has the portal hidden in Estrad. He meets Regona *outside* the palace while Nerak is *inside*, burning the place to the ground. Lessek encourages Regona to open the portal and proceed, alone and pregnant, to a foreign world, where she is drawn by the force of his key to Idaho Springs, Colorado – oh, and somewhere along the line gives birth to Mark's great-great-great-grandmother?'

'Or grandfather,' Mark said. 'Otherwise, yep, that about sums it up.'

'I see.' Scepticism was thick in Steven's voice. 'But you're overlooking the fact that your family isn't from Colorado.'

'True, but my great-grandmother moved west when she was married and my grandfather worked for the railroad, crisscrossing the west from their home in Cheyenne. My father was actually born in St Louis and lived in the Midwest before moving to New York. I'm telling you, Steven, he and Mom had planned for that trip to San Francisco for years. They literally saved every penny they could for it – they had a big jar on the kitchen counter. It was their dream to go to the Pacific and we had to pry Dad out of those mountains with a crowbar. He just didn't want to leave. And in what community in 1870 would a dark-skinned, single mother have been accepted? If she was in the United States, it had to be the black community: no whites would have had anything to do with her.'

Steven said, 'Your great-great-great-grandmother was from Rona.'

'I don't know,' Mark sighed. 'I know it's crazy – but Lessek is trying to tell me *something*; he's been trying since my first night here, on the beach near Estrad. I just haven't been able to figure out what it is, and this is the only thing that makes sense.'

'If you're right, how would Nerak know?'

'I have no idea,' Mark answered. 'Unless he knew the key would have pulled me to Idaho Springs, and your bank.'

'What about me? He doesn't seem to know anything about me, and I worked in the damned bank for three years – and we share the house. If what you say is true, I've been a victim of Lessek's key as well. Why doesn't Nerak know who I am?'

'I can't begin to say, but if the opportunity ever arises, we should definitely ask him.' Mark walked over to where Rodler slept and, kicking the smuggler a good deal harder than he had his roommate, said sharply, 'Wake up, asshole.'

Rodler was up like a cornered animal, a thin dirk held tightly in one fist, no trace of sleep in his sharply focused eyes. 'What's happening? Is it a patrol?'

For a moment, Mark was impressed with the man's response, though sleeping with one eye open was most likely a necessity for him. Still, he didn't like Rodler and didn't approve of his business. He had decided he would kill Malakasians without guilt, his way of dealing with the helplessness he felt in the wake of Brynne's death. Mark might not like war, but he recognised there were times when it was inevitable. Diplomacy in Eldarn had died the night Nerak killed Prince Markon at Riverend Palace and he had taken up arms for the oppressed. He might kill, but he would never deal in drugs, no matter how lucrative it might be.

Now grinning at Rodler, Mark asked, 'You wouldn't happen to have been in Colorado Springs last winter for the Colorado State Swimming Championships, would you? Maybe sitting next to a man from Fort Collins? He had on a green sweatshirt.'

The man blinked several times in confusion, then sheathed his dirk. 'Mark Jenkins, I don't even know what most of those words mean. But no, I was not in Color-ado last winter. I have never heard of that territory. Is it in Rona?'

'I'm relieved to hear that – but I woke you up to make certain you understand that if you ever disparage me, my skin colour or my race again, I will kill you. All right?'

'Gods rut a mule, Mark, but I thought we were already beyond this.' He shook his head in disappointment. 'I was doing my own thing, when you appeared and started shouting. I would have been very happy to have missed the four of you by a thousand paces, believe me.'

'Just so you understand – and Rodler, I truly am glad that you weren't in Colorado Springs last winter.'

'And why is that?' The younger man sighed.

'Because you would be dead already.' Mark turned back to his blankets. 'Good night.'

THE RAID

'Wake up,' Brexan whispered, 'Sallax, wake up. It's another raid.' She rolled to her feet. Her back ached from eight nights of sleeping on a hard wooden floor, but she ignored it and squirmed into her tunic.

From the bed, Sallax groaned and opened his eyes.

'No peeking, you rutter!' She turned towards the wall, then said, 'No, never mind, just get up – hurry! I can hear them, maybe two doors down. We have to get you down the back stairs.' Her hair a tangle and her tunic unbelted, Brexan rushed to his side and began unwrapping his injured shoulder. It was healing; Jacrys had done an admirable job of rebreaking and setting the bones, but it should have remained bound, without interruption, for the next Moon.

Sallax winced.

'I know. I know,' she whispered. 'We have to, just until they're gone.' The Malakasian soldiers and their Seron escort (Prince Malagon's Seron warriors were brutal and efficient, but not adept at espionage) were searching for a woman travelling with an injured man who was addled, and nearly incoherent in his speech. The raids had started two days after she and Sallax fled Carpello's warehouse. She thought she had left Jacrys dead, but when the searches began she realised that somehow the resilient bastard spy had survived Sallax clobbering him with the wooden table leg. Now Jacrys was obviously directing the periodic raids – maybe even from his hospital bed – as the soldiers and Seron crawled into every cabinet, beneath every building and inside every cargo hold.

They had her description; of that Brexan was certain, so she sheared off her hair – and nearly burst into tears when an emaciated, cropped-haired ghost stared back at her from the mirror. But what Jacrys had planned for her would be far worse than a tragic hair-cut.

'Come on,' she said, 'they're close this time.' From outside the window, Brexan heard the screams of those Orindale citizens unfortunate enough to be the search subjects this pre-dawn aven. The shouting was more a warning that a raid was coming than the city folk being badly injured by the searchers.

Sallax was up and dressed when she heard the front room door burst open, kicked off its hinges as the first of the Seron made their way into the inn. 'Pissing demons,' she said, 'they're here already. Come on. Down the back stairs, right away.' She hurried Sallax out the door and along the darkened hallway, careful not to touch his shoulder, waiting to hear a barked command to halt at any moment. In her haste, she had forgotten her belt; now she scurried downstairs without any weapons.

'Trenchers again?' Sallax drawled.

'Is that all right? Can you do trenchers this morning? I will get you all the trenchers in the kitchen if you promise not to say anything to anyone but me.'

'Trenchers, yes,' Sallax said, 'and he won't say anything.'

'Good job. Outstanding, and you just wash the trenchers until I come back for you. It will be just a few moments, all right?'

'Trenchers, yes.'

They reached the service entrance and Brexan hurriedly lit several paraffin tapers from coals still burning in the fireplace. Illuminating the small room, she positioned the big Ronan at a tub of water, pushed a cloth into his hand – and then discovered that every trencher in the scullery had been scrubbed clean and stacked neatly beside the hearth. From the front room, she heard the sound of heavily booted feet stomping up the stairs to the guest chambers. 'Bleeding whores,' she said, sweating, 'every rutting dish is already clean.' She sidled across to a large pot of leftover stew, ladled some into as many trenchers as she dared and piled the soiled dishes beside the tub. 'Can you clean these?'

'Trenchers,' Sallax said, hefting one to eye level and watching as bits of stew dribbled down his wrist to the wooden tabletop.

'Excellent,' she said, kissing him quickly on the cheek. 'You clean up. I'll be back.'

She had paid the tavern owner an extra silver piece to be permitted to secrete Sallax into the kitchen whenever the Redstone was searched. This was the third time in eight days. She worried that some smart officer might wonder why a scullery worker would be cleaning trenchers during the overnight and predawn avens, but thus far, her luck had prevailed: the raiding parties stormed through the inn, searching every room, including the kitchen, and left without a second glance at the big simpleton.

Hiding herself the first night had been challenging: at a loss for any other option, Brexan had slipped into the squalid chamber where the tavern staff bedded down and, stripping off her tunic and leggings, she had dived into bed with that same waiter who had been her antidote to loneliness: too much wine and sex with a stranger. She shocked the young man near to death as she helped him out of his bed clothes and began fondling him beneath the blankets, but when the soldiers burst into the room and she had feigned shock and terror along with the others, they were in no doubt about what the kitchen maid and the waiter were up to.

As soon as the door closed behind them, Brexan had kissed the confused boy affectionately and slipped back into her clothes, then headed off to retrieve Sallax.

That evening, the young man had looked at her questioningly. Not knowing whether she would be forced to take refuge beneath his covers of his bed again, she smiled at him. 'Shame we were so rudely interrupted,' she whispered, 'but I guess that's what we have to put up with these days.' She didn't want him to know she was the target of the raid.

This morning all the tavern staff were already awake when she arrived, stirred by the sounds of raiders stomping upstairs and through the guest chambers. Several had lit bedside tapers, and no one appeared surprised when Brexan entered the room.

'Oh, lords, you aren't going to make me do this with the candles lit, are you?' She didn't wait for a response from the bleary-eyed staff but steeled herself, pulled her tunic over her head and slipped into bed with the young waiter. As she settled beneath the covers, Brexan found him already stripped and waiting for her.

'I thought you might be back,' he said as seductively as the clumsy encounter permitted.

'I would be so grateful if you help me make this look as convincing as possible,' she said, smiling down at him.

When the door crashed open a moment later, two Seron tried to press inside, but stuck in the doorway until the larger of the two pushed the other violently out of the way, clearing a path for himself. Behind them, a Malakasian officer dragged the elderly tavern owner by one arm. The innkeeper made eye contact with Brexan briefly, and then looked away.

'See? I told you,' he said to the soldier, 'just these five.'

'But only four beds?' The Malakasian moved through the room, tugging down blankets, moving piles of clothing, and peering behind the crates the employees used for storage. 'Does someone always share a bed in here? What kind of place is this, eh?'

'These two ...' The old man stammered as he pointed at Brexan and her young waiter with a quivering finger. He was too nervous; Brexan held her breath. At least her bare shoulder was exposed outside the blanket – more convincing than finding her there in a tunic and boots. 'These two came together from Strandson,' the tavern owner said.

The officer nodded, and Brexan exhaled slowly. He didn't care about who she was or what she was doing in this filthy, malodorous chamber: he was upset at having been deployed on a pointless search by a spy who outranked him in the field and strutted around in a rich man's wardrobe. The man and woman had obviously slipped through the barricade around the city – anyone could these days, with Prince Malagon gone and his generals bickering about it like elderly women.

He glanced down at Brexan, hoping to see more than just her shoulder, then turned back to the tavern owner. 'The one in the kitchen?'

'My overnight worker,' the old man said. 'He comes in late and cleans until dawn. He's addled, kicked in the head by his father's horse. I let him clean the trenchers and keep the fire going. That's about all he's good for.'

The officer whistled softly, then said, 'Fine,' and to the Seron, 'You two, let's go. Find the others and move on.' A moment later, they were gone.

Back in their room, Brexan rewrapped Sallax's shoulder. She was tired, and desperately wanted to sleep another half-aven, but the dishevelled hillock of abandoned blankets thrown across the floor did not look very appealing. 'You did well this morning,' she said. 'I don't think they'll be back now – they've been here three times. It's Jacrys sending them.'

Sallax growled threateningly under his breath. 'He tried to fool. He tried to be nice. Sallax knew him from Rona.'

'I know.'

'Praga, too.'

'Praga?'

'Sallax is from Praga, not Rona. Brynne too.'

'I didn't know that,' she said. 'I thought you were from Rona.'

He grimaced as she pulled the bandages close around his shoulder.

'Does it still hurt?'

'Not like before.'

'What happened?' Brexan felt that she was making progress with Sallax, building his trust and helping him face whatever nightmares had changed him from the proud, tough freedom fighter to the crippled, filthy dock scavenger she had met south of the city. This was more than he'd said in eight days.

'The wraiths found Sallax.' He stared at a point in the woodwork.

'A wraith?'

'Many wraiths. They were hunting for the old man.' Since the night she helped him escape from Carpello's warehouse, Brexan had not heard Sallax use Gilmour's name. 'There were many, and they came across the hills and up the river valley. Sallax was in the river.'

'In the river? Why?'

'This needed cold.' He indicated his shoulder with a tilt of his head, but his eyes never left the opposite wall. 'It was broken that day. Lahp, a Seron, broke it. Sallax tried to fix it on the rock, but it didn't work, and he needed to make it cold.'

'The wraiths found you in the river? In the cold water?'

'Very cold. He was in there a long time. Everything was blue and white, even the old man. There was nothing but the blue and the white, and the cold did it. The river. This only felt better there.' A tilt of his head again.

'Why did the wraiths want to find Gilmour?'

'They thought he had the stone. He didn't. They wanted to find him and the others. Sallax doesn't know if they did or not. They found Sallax and hurt him.'

'Your shoulder? They hurt your shoulder again?'

'No, here.' He tapped at his forehead. 'They wanted to kill the others, but when they found Sallax, they didn't kill him. It was more—' He stopped.

'Entertaining.' Brexan completed his thought, 'more entertaining to make you think—'

'About the old man,' he reciprocated.

'Gilmour.'

'He's dead.'

'Dead?'

'Sallax helped to kill him. The wraiths thought that Sallax's pain was funny. They wanted to kill the others, but they let Sallax live.'

'They were ghosts?'

'Lost souls. People once. They were trapped, and it made them angry. They wanted to get free but couldn't. They wanted to find their friends and children, their families. When they realised what Sallax had done, they went wild. It was mad, a raving spirit dance there at the river. They had been trapped a long time. Sallax was not as good as they were, but he was free. They didn't like that.'

'So they trapped you in here.' She tapped two fingers on his forehead as well. 'We have to find you in there, Sallax. You have too much strength, you're too valuable to be wandering lost and alone like this. People need you.'

'People needed the old man.'

That tack backfired, so Brexan decided to change the subject. 'Tell me about Brynne.'

A hint of a smile graced the big man's face. 'She was just a baby when her parents died. She needed lots of nappies.'

'Babies do.'

'She had a lunatic's hair. It was curly and all over. Nothing could tame it.' He twirled one finger above his head, sketching a crop of unruly locks badly in need of a trim.

'Did she follow you that day along the river?'

'She was older then, but yes. She came with Mark, the one from the portal who left the stone. Sallax hid. They didn't find him.'

'Did the wraiths find Brynne?'

'I don't know.'

'She was coming here to Orindale. Do you remember that?'

'You knew?'

'Versen told me.'

Sallax smiled again. 'He could eat more shellfish than Sallax could carry.'

Now Brexan laughed. 'I'm not at all surprised to hear it.'

'He's dead, too?'

'Yes.'

'The almor killed him at Seer's Peak.' Sallax seemed certain he knew what had happened.

Brexan was about to correct him and then decided against it: there was nothing to be gained by confusing his memories. She felt a chill thinking of Versen, though, and was embarrassed that she had been diving into bed with a stranger for the past several days. She knew he would have laughed, but she was still embarrassed that he might be watching her, checking in from the Northern Forest.

'He talked about you all the time,' Brexan said.

'He and Sallax are good friends.'

'He said you emptied out his house when he turned two hundred Twinmoons.'

'We set everything up outside, exactly as it had been inside, everything but one boot. That we left in the middle of the floor. Then we hid in the woods to watch. Versen was very angry.'

'You said *we*.' She didn't want to push him, but this was the slip she had been hoping to hear. 'Sallax?'

'Yes. Garec, Brynne, Mika, Jerond, Sallax, and the old man,' he said. 'We emptied out his house.'

'You?'

'Yes.'

'Sallax.'

'Yes, I did.'

'Yes, you did,' Brexan sighed. It wasn't much, but it felt like progress. She didn't know how to treat him. His physical health was returning, and when his shoulder healed, he would be nearly as fit and as strong as before the initial fracture, but his mental health was not much better than when she first saw him, when he had dragged her into the sunlit ferns.

'He's dead now, like the others?'

'Versen is dead, yes.'

'The almor killed him at Seer's Peak.'

'Sallax,' Brexan decided to take another risk, 'do you remember the fat man from the warehouse?'

At that, the big Ronan's countenance changed. His body tensed and his mouth split into a wicked grin. 'Yes, he almost killed Brynne, a long time ago. She was sick for many Twinmoons. Ren was the boy who led her to him.'

'Ren?'

'I killed him.'

There it was again. '*You* did?'

'Sallax did, yes. I used a dirk, slipped it right in. He died in the street in Estrad, but I never found the fat man. He will be alive when Brynne gets here. Brynne will kill him slowly.'

It sounded like the fat man had raped Brynne when she was just a child. Brexan shuddered. 'I have my own account with the fat man as well. His name is Carpello Jax, and I know where he lives. I know which ships are his and which warehouses he uses to store his cargoes. He runs ships up and down the Ravenian Sea, from Strandson across to Pellia. I'm not sure what he's shipping or why, but he serves Prince Malagon. He often moors here in Orindale – maybe he has some arrangement with the customs officers down on that southern wharf. I've watched him while you've been asleep. He has cut his hair, grown a beard, lost some weight, and sliced the mole off his nose, but it's still him, the bloated whoreson.'

'Did you kill him?' Sallax was obviously agitated at the possibility that Brynne wouldn't be the one to torture and kill the man.

'No, just watching. It's easy to move through this city unseen; you learned that.'

Sallax nodded, recalling a huge overturned wine cask outside a rowdy tavern.

'I wasn't very good in the beginning,' Brexan told him. 'I would be dead if you hadn't been watching that first night, but I've learned a lot. Unless Carpello ships out again – which I doubt, he's not much of a seaman – he'll be here when we find Brynne. But Sallax, I need you to think about Gilmour and Brynne, and Garec and the two foreigners. Where were they going after they lost Versen? Welstar Palace?'

'Brynne will kill Carpello.'

'Yes, we can all do it together, but we have to find them first.' Brexan had found no sign of them in Orindale, but she knew Jacrys hadn't either; maybe they'd moved further north – or if they survived the wraith attack in the Blackstones, perhaps they went back down south, to Strandson or one of the port villages in western Rona. The longer she spent in Orindale, the more she thought the odds of finding them were slimming to nothing. 'Sallax, can you remember *anything* about where they were going?'

'Orindale,' he said simply. If he did know anything else, it was lost in his damaged mind.

'You rest now,' Brexan said. 'We'll get some food after the midday aven. I'm going to check on Carpello now – I want to know what he's doing today.'

'Don't kill him.'

'I won't. We'll wait for Brynne.'

That night, while Sallax slept Brexan sat staring into the glass, watching her reflection through tired eyes. By the flicker of the bedside candle she strained to make out her shorn hair and drawn features. Perhaps it was better that there was little light.

It had been a productive day: Brexan was encouraged that Sallax had spoken of himself in the first person for the first time: saying *I* was a huge step forward. She knew nothing about mental health, but she was all he had. She wouldn't press him to remember anything painful – rushing his recovery wouldn't help.

She had made friends with some of the stevedores working the southern docks; though none of them had seen anyone resembling the partisans, a few copper Mareks had elicited a lot of information about Carpello's business dealings, routines and schedules.

Once she'd followed the fat merchant to a brothel in a nice part of the city – at first she thought he had been calling on friends, or business associates, but the parade of well-dressed men going in and out at regular intervals gave the game away. As she stood watching the windows, she thought of Brynne, a child taken against her will, and nausea hit her hard. She was very much looking forward to killing Carpello. It was taking all her willpower to keep from breaking into the whorehouse, kicking down the fat man's door and chopping him up right there on top of whatever trollop had been coerced into servicing him.

When he left, his frilly tunic askew, she followed him back to his apartments. She could have finished him quickly and quietly, right there in the stairwell of his own home, but instead, she let him live another day.

As the unbearable need for revenge washed over Brexan again, she turned from the glass and began undressing. She nearly leaped out of her skin when she saw Sallax materialise out of the darkness behind her.

'Good rutting Pragans!' she shrieked, grabbing her tunic to cover herself, somewhat inadequately. 'You aren't supposed to see me like this!'

Sallax loomed over her, a look of pensive concentration on his face.

Brexan backed away. 'Get back to bed, Sallax – just because I'm out of my clothes you can't—'

He reached out to grip her wrist.

'Ow!' She tried to twist out of his grasp. 'Sallax, please, don't do this.' All of a sudden she was a little scared, but Sallax didn't do anything more, he simply stared at her muscular, outstretched arm.

Finally he said, 'Where did you get this?'

'What? Get what?' Brexan's heart was still pounding nineteen to the dozen. 'This.' He turned her wrist back, exposing the strange bit of jewellery she had taken from the corpse on the salt flats. It had cleaned up nicely and she'd worn it buckled about her wrist ever since. Sallax must have seen it hundreds of times over the past few days; she didn't understand why it caught his attention now.

'I found it.' She hesitated, not really wanting to admit that she had purloined it from a dead body.

'Where?'

'On the marsh, north of the harbour. I was out there looking for you one day last Twinmoon when I found it – it was so beautiful, and so unusual. I thought I'd find a jeweller in the city to tell me what it was, but I never had the chance to show it to anyone.' Brexan was embarrassed: she had been caught, a thief flaunting her stolen goods. She had not imagined for a moment that Sallax would recognise the small circular bracelet.

He let her go and sat dejectedly on the side of the bed, his face buried in his hands while she pulled on her tunic properly. 'It's called a watch,' he said at last.

'A watch? Am I supposed to watch it?'

'It tells the time of day and night.'

'Really?' Fascinated now, she picked up the candle to study the trinket more closely. 'I don't understand. How does it work?'

'It doesn't tell the time here.'

'Well, what good—?' She stopped. 'Oh gods, oh gods, oh gods, Sallax, how do you know of this watch?'

The big man started to cry, the sobs shaking his body. Brexan sat beside him, rubbing his shoulders and crooning comfortingly to the distraught man for an aven or more, until he drifted off into uneasy slumber. She washed the tears from her own face, and unclasped the watch from her wrist and left it beside the candle. She lay awake and listened for sounds of raiding parties outside.

Later, still awake, Brexan watched the sun come up over the city.

Captain Thadrake eyed the pastries; one had been bitten nearly in half, but the other two were untouched. Beside the plate was a flagon of wine, Falkan red, he guessed, the best wine in Eldarn, and a half-empty goblet. He didn't understand how anyone could get so blasé as to ignore such delicacies, but he forced his attention from the bedside table.

The captain was standing in a lavishly appointed apartment in the one-time imperial palace in Orindale, formerly occupied by one of Prince Malagon's generals. The general and several members of his staff had been killed in an unexplained explosion during the last Twinmoon and several days ago the apartment had become an impromptu hospital, with one bed in the centre of the room for the patient. The bedding was the finest Orindale could offer: down-filled pillows, thick, soft blankets and a firm mattress softened with several layers of goose-down. A fire crackled day and night in the fireplace.

He noticed a leather-bound book, tucked beneath the pillow as if in a hasty effort to hide it from visitors. He shuffled his feet nervously.

'Who is he?' Not much of the patient was visible – his head was bandaged and only one eye, part of his nose and a corner of his mouth showed outside the gauze wrap – but it was obvious he was irritated.

'My assistant, sir, Hendrick.'

'Well, get him out of here, you rutting fool! Why don't you just parade me in front of the entire army? Let's make certain everyone can see me: oh, yes, there goes the prince's spymaster; everyone knows him. Great whoring monks …'

'What is your name, Captain?'

'Thadrake, sir.' He tried not to cringe.

'Captain Thadrake, do you want to be responsible for everyone knowing what I look like?'

It was obvious a crunching blow to the back of the head had left the spy near death, but Thadrake had no idea why Jacrys Marseth had come here, to a public Malakasian facility, to recuperate. Most spies found ways to deal with their injuries without jeopardising their cover. Maybe it was because no one had seen Prince Malagon in the past Moon, or perhaps the spy was to be assigned to another Eldarni territory under a new identity. Whatever the reason, Jacrys was obviously in no mood to discuss his decision to come in from the field, and Thadrake wasn't about to ask why. He loathed Jacrys, and everything the man represented. They were an occupation army, the most powerful military force in Eldarn; they didn't need spies scurrying about, eating pastries and drinking good Falkan wines.

Thadrake would have been quite happy to face the combined Resistance forces in the Eastlands in a final, conclusive battle – that would be far preferable to the cowardly terror strikes along the Merchants' Highway and all the throat-slitting that went on in the streets of Orindale after dark. His corps had lost several officers to a terrorist, a merciless cowled man who stalked the back alleys. Thadrake himself had been part of the response team, rounding up any suspected Resistance members – and a good few who had never before been under suspicion – each time an officer had been murdered.

The Malakasian response had been swift, brutal and public and whilst the people of Orindale were not happy about hangings in the imperial gardens, Captain Thadrake didn't care. If they wanted the capricious justice to stop, they had to hand over this homicidal rutter themselves. He was quite sure they all knew who he was; they probably toasted his very good health every night in those filthy waterfront taverns.

'What progress have you made in your search?' The spy's voice was muffled by bandages.

'Which search, sir?' Thadrake wanted to hear the spy say out loud that he was more interested in their search for his assailants than for the caped lunatic killing Malakasian soldiers – *his* men. Given the number of people lost to terrorists in the past Twinmoon, all their attention needed to be on nightly sweeps of the waterfront area; if the Ronan partisans turned up, good, but if not, at least they were making a concerted effort to avenge those Malakasians who had given their lives. The increased patrols did appear to be having an effect, for the murders had stopped – at least for the time being – but the extra raids were taking their toll on the army.

How he hated working with Seron … Thadrake couldn't stand the sight or the smell of them, and racing through Orindale during the middlenight aven, pursuing some so-called Resistance leader and a traitor soldier who were obviously well into Rona by now seemed a pointless, self-indulgent directive.

When Jacrys didn't answer right away, Thadrake asked again, 'I'm sorry, but which search do you mean? Sir?'

'The search for my attackers, you whore-spawned rutter!' It looked as if he was about to choke on his bandages.

Thadrake fought back a smile. 'Sorry, sir, but we have not yet found anyone fitting those descriptions.'

'Have you been thorough?'

'I have a map of the city, sir. Each night we have searched random, unpredictable quadrants, but thus far, we have turned up nothing.'

'Then you are an idiot, Captain Thadrake.'

'Yes, sir,' the officer said, thinking, *I am an idiot for not leaving with Hendrick.*

'I understand that the woman might be able to secrete herself somewhere, but Sallax? He is as big as a blazing mountain. He has long black hair, pale skin, and he is a gods-rutting dolt who can barely speak. He doesn't make eye contact, and he looks as though he has been kicked squarely in the head by a horse, Captain. So I don't know what you have been doing each night, but you had better find a way to tighten the noose about this city and to find those two for me, or I will have your—'

'Sorry, sir,' Thadrake interrupted, 'but would you repeat that?'

Jacrys grunted. 'What?'

'What you just said, sir.'

'Sallax Farro is a piece of limp-brained grettan shit.'

'Who looks as though he has been kicked in the head by a horse, sir?'

'Exactly, yes. Captain, let me remind you that when I am speaking—'

'Sorry, sir.'

'You did it again, you son of a bleeding whore!'

'I know where he is, sir.' Thadrake snapped a salute, turned on his heel and started out. Several steps away, he froze, realised his mistake and turned back smartly. 'Sorry, sir, but am I excused? I expect I can have Sallax here by the midday aven, sir.'

Jacrys was almost speechless. 'Yes, by all means, go. Get him now, and bring him here with the girl. But Captain, if she should resist, feel free to kill her.'

'She's a traitor, sir?'

'Yes'

'She should be hanged, sir.'

'Captain, if she resists, cut her down, but I want Sallax Farro alive. Understand?'

When Jacrys paused, the captain snapped to attention once again, saluted, and said, 'I'm sorry for the breach of protocol, sir.'

'Just bring Sallax Farro to me, Captain.'

'Should I clear these plates, sir?'

'Yes, and the bottle, too. That rutting vintage makes my head hurt.'

Captain Thadrake was already on his way out of the door with the pastries in one hand and the wine in the other.

*

292

As Hannah sat bolt upright pain ripped through her shoulder, and with a shriek she fell into her blankets, dizzy with the agony. A moment later, Hoyt was by her side. 'I see you're up. It's about time,' he said cheerily.

'You wait until I'm back in one piece, Hoyt. I am kicking the shit out of you,' Hannah said through shallow breaths.

'Out of *me*?' Hoyt feigned incredulity. 'I put you back together, Hannah, and trust me, it was not an easy task.'

Mimicking his accent, Hannah repeated, 'We shouldn't organise any dances up there, but if we hold fast to that lip, it's a good two or three paces wide, and it's actually fairly level.'

Hoyt laughed. 'I'm not the one who tied myself to the millstone.' He motioned to where Churn lay sleeping, a nondescript lump under two heavy blankets.

'How is he?'

'Fine,' Hoyt said, 'it would take more than falling off a mountain to hurt him. He was a bit cold when we finally got you back up on the porch, but Alen worked an interesting spell, warmed the two of you right there in the mud, dried your clothes, too. I was impressed.'

With Hoyt supporting her, Hannah sat up a bit straighter. 'Where are we?' she asked.

'We're back in that grove of pines we crossed through before climbing up onto the cavern ledge. That big meadow is just through there. We've kept a fire going with anything we've been able to find that won't smoke up too much. The branches in here are such a rutting tangle, no one would know we were here unless they actually walked into us, but none of the Malakasians have passed anywhere near us. You were right. They must have another path somewhere south of here.'

'So we're safe enough – but how long has it been?'

Hoyt hesitated. 'Two days.'

Hannah almost choked. 'Two days?'

'Well, three, this morning.'

'Oh, Hoyt, I'm sorry. If I hadn't slipped, we could have hauled Churn up, dried him off and been on our way.' She looked around. 'Did it snow?'

'Some, a couple days ago, but it's been quiet since then.' He reached over to open one of their packs. 'Are you hungry?'

'Yes, please,' she said, gratefully accepting two handfuls of crumbly bread, a small block of cheese and some cold sausage. Between mouthfuls, she continued asking questions. 'Why did I sleep so long? What did I do to myself?'

'Not much,' Hoyt assured her. 'You broke your collarbone and split the skin across your forehead. The head wound was messy – head wounds bleed like a rutting sieve – but setting the bone was the nastier of the two. Apart from those, it was nothing, really: assorted bumps and bruises, not a lot to brag about at a chainball tournament.'

'A broken bone shouldn't have knocked me senseless for so long.' She shifted in her seat, trying to move her shoulder beneath its heavy wrapping.

'Normally it wouldn't, but it was a bad break and I had to treat it with querlis.' Hannah looked at him questioningly, and he went on, 'that's a plant we use to treat all manner of injuries. It speeds up the natural healing process at a remarkable rate, but it takes its toll. Most people sleep for some time after a querlis application. You ought to be feeling better soon.'

'Well enough to ride?'

'Gods, yes. You don't plan to walk over these hills, do you? You can ride with me. We lost Churn's horse. The wretch is probably on some Pragan farm right now, eating winter hay and sleeping in a stable full of mares.'

'Churn saved me.'

Hoyt nodded, 'Yes he did, but he also hauled you down there to begin with, and for that, I think we ought to tease him for the next two hundred Twinmoons.'

She was serious. 'And you put me back together.'

'I did.' This time, Hoyt didn't make a joke.

'How did you do it? I don't remember any of it. You would think setting a bone would have been a horrible thing, especially one that had nearly broken through my skin.' She ran two fingers over the bulging swath of bandages and torn tunics the Pragan healer had used to immobilise the injury.

'Well,' Hoyt began tentatively, 'when you were down there on the rock, Churn found a body, one of the Malakasian engineers.'

'So at least one of them did come this way.'

'He did, and our guess is that he was trying to get away on his own.'

'Why?'

'Because he was carrying a pouch filled with ghost tree bark.' Hoyt reached into a pack and withdrew a small leather sack bulging at the seams with bark from the enchanted forest.

Hannah nodded. 'And he wanted some for himself, so he came through there thinking he would work his way north with a bag full of great magic.'

'Or medicine, or drugs, whatever,' Hoyt said. 'Either way, he fell and died, right about where Churn found you.'

'So what does this have to do with me?'

'I didn't have any way of knocking you out, or getting you to sleep long enough to set the bone; so I—' He paused.

'So you used the bark,' Hannah finished his thought. 'You sent me back to my childhood, to my parent's house, that night I fell asleep on the couch.'

'I don't know what you were reliving, but it wasn't as bad as the day we came through the forest. You kept going on and on about never having a dog.'

Hannah's brow furrowed. 'There was a dog, a big black one, or dark brown, maybe. It looked like rather like a wolf. He was there the night my mother decided ... well, the night I relived in the forest of ghosts.'

'All right, why is that an issue?'

'I never had a dog, Hoyt.'

He tossed the pouch back inside the pack. 'Who knows what this stuff does? Maybe it's just a hallucinogen that sends you flying over the hills and valleys of your past. You get a whiff of this, whether it's magic or not, and you go back in time, peek in a few windows, see your parents cooking eggs, beating each other up, whatever, and then you come back. Maybe people get caught by the forest because they can't get out before they wither away.'

Hannah shook her head. 'It's more than that, Hoyt. I was there. I was actually there in the room, and the dog was part of it, as real as I was.' She tried to stand, swooned again, and sat back down.

'Keep resting. Those two are still sleeping, and my watch ends with breakfast, so close your eyes for a while. If you're feeling rested enough later, you can ride with me and we'll make our way back to find that trail.'

'Three days lost,' Hannah murmured.

'Not a total loss,' Hoyt said. 'If Alen can work out what a sorcerer might be able to do with a handful of bark from the forest of ghosts, we may have stumbled ... literally ... onto something important. I doubt it was the engineer's lust for adventure in high places that made him try to cross alone.'

Hannah lay back, closing her eyes and hoping for a couple hours' sleep. Three days lost, and she had not been heartened by anything she heard after waking. She was glad that Churn was safe. As for their pocketful of enchanted forest, if it helped Alen figure out a way to send her home, then she would be happy they had found it, but for now, she was wary of it: it was mystical and dangerous, and it had trapped her in her past with her parents and that big dog until Hoyt had dragged her out. Hannah didn't trust it. She remembered the dead body on the southern edge of the Great Range – *Sunday Morning by Michael Adams* – some poor soul who had wandered into the forest of ghosts, become enslaved by a memory and sat down beside a stand of white birch to while away the days for ever.

She accidentally rolled onto her shoulder, and was painfully reminded that she had fallen two hundred feet onto a rock. Eventually, she slept again.

This time when she awakened, the sun was fully out and brightening the snow at the edge of the meadow. Hoyt was still awake, cooking sausages in the small pan he carried. The food smelled good; despite the fact that she had eaten only a short while earlier, she was famished. On the opposite side of the campfire, Alen was sleeping. She guessed that anyone who had lived as long as Alen would need a great deal of sleep – and the former Larion Senator was world class at it: there were few places Alen did not manage to sleep like a cadaver from dark to dawn. Hannah frequently worried that the older man had died in his sleep, and she often forced Churn or Hoyt to go back to their rooms and make certain Alen was still breathing.

She would have been surprised to know that, unlike Gilmour, Alen chose to sleep. He revelled in it, enjoying the feeling of being completely fatigued, especially in the moments right before drifting off. Gilmour slept only when he felt the need to rejuvenate his physical self.

With one arm, Hannah pushed herself into a sitting position, a definite improvement. 'What's for breakfast?' she called.

'You ate already,' Hoyt tried to sound indignant. 'What kind of place do you think I'm operating here?'

'A place where I get to eat when I'm hungry, and right now, I'm good and hungry. So keep your comments to yourself, my intrepid thief – but you had better share the bounty from that frying pan.'

'Or else?'

'Or else, I will beat your sorry ass one-handed – and think about it, every time your so-called friends have one too many beers, there it will be all over again: the hilarious account of the time Hoyt got thoroughly whipped by a one-armed woman.'

'Fine, fine, just keep your one-armed whipping to yourself, all right?' Hoyt tore another lump from the loaf he had shared with her earlier that morning.

'Where's Churn?'

'Scouting the meadow,' Hoyt said. 'If you're feeling better, I think it's time to try to find a trail.'

Hannah nodded vigorously as she had chewed. 'Yes, by all means, let's get going. I've held us up here too long.'

As if overhearing them, the Pragan giant returned to camp, ducking brambly needles as he shouldered his way through the grove.

'What news?' Hoyt signed.

Churn shrugged, 'Nothing new, a few tracks.'

'Wagon tracks?' Hoyt passed his friend a chunk of bread with hot sausages and melted cheese tucked inside.

'No.' Churn took a bite, fanned at his open mouth with a palm, then put down the bread and finished, 'Dog tracks. One dog, a big one.'

SANDCLIFF PALACE

'There it is.' Gilmour was as excited as a schoolboy starting the harvest holiday. He pointed through the scraggly branches of a roadside oak. 'Can you see it?'

'Which one?' Garec asked, shielding his eyes from the morning sunlight. On the opposite hilltop, he could see a group of buildings organised around a blocky stone structure in the centre, and a taller, more majestic building on a rise to the north. Grouped in clusters, the shorter buildings appeared to have been constructed around common areas, but he was too far away to determine any reason for the peculiar layout.

'The one at the top, with three towers, the highest in the north.' Gilmour had not yet taken his eyes off his former home.

'All that, Gilmour?' Mark asked. 'I thought you said it was smaller than Riverend. That place is gigantic.'

'No, no, no,' the older man corrected, 'it's just the one at the top. All those others below are the university buildings. The residences are there in the south, and the classrooms and laboratories are those short stone buildings. That ugly rectangular beast in the centre is the university library. Gods rut a demon, but that was a fight. I think it ruins the look of the whole place. Modern architecture, gods of the Northern Forest, look what it did to the arena. Now the fields are just little stretches of green tucked in between the residences and that great, grey-boned monster. It's a shame it never fell in on itself.'

Rodler Varn raised an eyebrow at the older man. 'Careful, Gilmour: your age is showing.'

'What?' Gilmour stammered. 'Oh yes, well, I've done quite a bit of research into the Larion Senate, and as far as I can understand it, the library caused a commotion among those who appreciated more traditional architectural styles.'

'What? Stone on stone over stone?' the smuggler joked. 'Or stone over mortar between stone? I can't tell the difference, myself.'

'I think it must be the same everywhere, when intellectuals get together to do something permanent and creative. I'd just as soon lead a brigade into war,' Steven said.

Gilmour said, 'It's no matter now, anyway. That was a long time ago. It's silly for us to spend time worrying over arguments Larion Senators had two thousand Twinmoons ago. But let's get up there, shall we?' He started back along the road.

Rodler interrupted, 'We shouldn't go up that way.'

'Why not?'

'The only place this road leads is up to the campus and the old palace. Both are off-limits and patrolled regularly. When we climbed out of that last village on this road, we started taking a risk – there's no reason to be up here, so the further we travel the more suspicious we look.'

Mark realised that the road was in disrepair – it didn't appear to have seen more than cursory traffic in years. Turning in the saddle, he asked, 'Which way then?'

'Down this slope and then up the opposite hillside. The villagers hunt and trap along a trail that runs just about all the way up to the palace. We can ride the horses most of the way, and then walk them the last few hundred paces to the university. Once there, we ought to tether them in the forest and go ahead on foot. I didn't hear a patrol in the village this morning, certainly not one of any significant size, but that doesn't mean there won't be one up there already.'

'Why would they be up there for any stretch of time?' Steven asked.

'They're patrolling a campus that has been closed for almost a thousand Twinmoons. Not too many people stop by to raid it these days. The campus is a nice place to stay for a while, to have a smoke, maybe a few beers they carry up there. Sometimes they stay a couple of days.'

'You know from experience?' Mark asked.

'I am here to help, my friends, and happy to do so, but once I get you in the palace, I am going my own way.' Rodler sneaked a glance at Mark, but the foreign bowman was looking down the valley.

'Rodler, you and Steven lead the way.' Gilmour turned his horse. 'I think I know of the path you mentioned: it's the one my research highlighted as a popular way for intrepid students to sneak out after dark.'

'Whatever you say, Gilmour.' Rodler ushered Steven towards a break in the trees and a slope falling away from the road to cross a shallow gulley. 'It should be easy going, but be careful of these slopes. Some of this loose rock can trip the horses. That would be a blazing mess.'

They rode through the morning, climbing inexorably towards the summit and the abandoned university. Steven finally got his first clear view of Sandcliff Palace, a proud edifice overseeing the sprawling school from its place just north of the campus. As they drew closer, he saw that Rodler's description had been accurate. The old place appeared to have withstood time well – *too* well.

'Do you know if there is any magic still working up there?' he asked Gilmour quietly.

Gilmour had apparently been thinking the same thing. 'There must be – I know there were spells to repair minor breaks, leaks, cracks and so on, and Rodler was unable to get out of the kitchen so the spells securing the doors and windows must still be in place.'

Rodler asked, 'So what are we doing up here, old man? You're going to crawl into the scullery to discover for yourself that the palace is impregnable? Call me a madman, but that's an awfully long, hard trip just to get yourself locked in some dead sorcerer's kitchen.'

Gilmour peered up at the old keep, awash in sunlight and bearded in unruly tangles of autumn-brown ivy over halfway up to its slate shingle roof. They had done great work in that building, bringing enlightened ideas, innovation and useful technologies to Eldarn. He had been at his best while living here, and Gilmour felt his heart race at the idea of stepping foot back inside once again. He wasn't young; he would never be young again, but in Sandcliff he would remember what it had been like.

'You didn't answer my question,' Rodler said. 'What exactly are you going to do, locked inside the kitchen?'

Gilmour pulled out his pipe and filled the bowl, then, deliberately lighting it without benefit of a flint and steel, he blew a cloud of billowy smoke towards the Falkan smuggler. 'I think we'll manage, Rodler,' he said, matter-of-factly.

'I knew it! Rutting dogs, but I knew it!' Rodler twisted so far that he nearly fell off Steven's horse. 'You are some kind of magician, a real sorcerer! So with your spells and Steven's stick, you think you can get inside that old barn and raid the place for all it's worth? Well, my payment for bringing you up here – all I ask – is a few books. Nothing much, just a couple of satchels full.'

Puffing contentedly, Gilmour didn't answer.

Rodler thanked the gods of the Northern Forest he'd stayed with them and turned back to look up at Sandcliff Palace. 'Excellent luck meeting you, just excellent luck,' he murmured.

'That will remain to be seen, my friend,' Steven said caustically, 'but I wouldn't count on it.'

They approached cautiously, tethering their horses in the forest as Rodler had suggested. Garec and Steven checked for signs of patrols, until, finding nothing, they motioned the others forward. Gilmour hustled to the front. The stone staircase from the university to the main gate was lined on both sides by a diverse assortment of trees, now leafless, but still imposing. Steven imagined the arboreal corridor had made quite an impression, especially during the peak of autumn's splendour, but many had grown too large; now inquisitive roots cracked the polished steps.

Halfway up, Steven paused to look at a curious pairing: an old cottonwood had grown so huge that its trunk pressed outward against its neighbour, a birch, hung about with epiphytic clumps of mistletoe. The birch, not to be denied access to the sun, had grown around the cottonwood, like the coiling embrace of a jungle serpent. In their hundred-and-forty-year battle for survival, the trees had grown so intertwined that Steven couldn't disentangle the upper branches.

Garec and Mark joined him and looked on silently.

'The battle of two titans,' Steven said poetically, 'fighting for the highest point on the hill.'

'That's where all the best sunshine falls,' Garec said. 'You can't blame them.'

'It certainly looks to be worth the fight,' Mark agreed – but Steven had already left, sprinting up the remaining stairs.

'What's wrong?' Garec asked.

'The fight for the top of the hill,' Mark mused, shaking his head – then suddenly his eyes grew wide; he ran after Steven as fast as he could in his effort to reach the gates in time.

Garec heard Steven shouting, 'Wait! No, Gilmour, stop!' By the time he reached the top of the great staircase, Garec realised Mark and Steven had been too late.

Steven had taken the stairs two at a time, struggling for breath in the altitude, then leaped from the top step to a stone walkway to the ponderous oak and steel portcullis, shouting, 'Wait! No, Gilmour, stop!' Behind him, the slope led down to the relatively flat area where the Larion brotherhood had built their university, and below that, the wintry hills rolled away towards the horizon where the sea met the coast of Gorsk in a sunlit backdrop of blue, green and brown. Had Steven turned to admire the view, he would have found it one of the most beautiful he had ever seen.

'It's just up here,' Gilmour said, leading Rodler along the walkway towards the main gate. 'Not far now.' He was almost giddy with excitement, distracted by rich memories and feeling better than he could remember. The old man ran the last few paces, his cloak fluttering out behind him.

'The gardens are just through here,' Rodler said, pointing. 'I don't think it will take me long to find that drainage ditch. If you don't mind a tight squeeze, I can get you inside without much trouble.'

'Nonsense, boy,' Gilmour said. 'We're going in the front gate.'

'But it's enchanted – it won't open for anyone but a Larion Senator, and they're all dead, so we are out of rutting luck on that point. And all the Larion spells were lost when Prince Marek closed the schools.' Rodler wasn't hopeful. 'I know you have a bit of magic, but you're talking about getting inside the most protected edifice in the Eastlands – almost as secure as Welstar Palace.'

'Come, watch this.' Gilmour raised his hands above his head, faced the portcullis with a broad smile and chanted a simple spell, a quiet curling phrase he repeated three times before lowering his hands. 'Not much to it really.'

Rodler pursed his lips; still sceptical, he watched the gate, wondering if he had made the mistake of following an insane old codger all the way up this hill just to watch him play pretend sorcerer. When the portcullis slid upwards, as smoothly as if on recently oiled hinges, Rodler gasped.

'Rut a monk!' he whispered. 'Did you see that? Gilmour, how did you—?'

His question was cut off by Steven's scream. The thin, wild-eyed foreigner was running towards them, the hickory staff raised as if to strike, shouting, 'Wait! No, Gilmour. Stop!'

As the portcullis disappeared up into the recesses above the granite archway, Gilmour turned. 'What's wrong?' he asked, his eyebrows raised in consternation, 'what's happened?'

His chest heaving with the effort, Steven leaned on the staff to catch his breath. Finally he pointed towards the open gate. 'You just alerted Nerak.'

Gilmour felt the blood rush from his face. His hopeful, nostalgic mood fled, leaving him hollow. 'Oh dearest gods of the Northern— I can't believe I did that …' Dejected, the former master of this palace shuffled his way beneath the archway and into the stone foyer. Without lifting his head even to look around, he climbed the few steps to the great room and crossed to an old wooden bench beside an equally battered table and sat down, burying his face in his hands. This was not the homecoming he had imagined. His failures rushed in to haunt him: here was a third misstep, when missteps were too costly to commit at all.

He was responsible for them; if Nerak arrived in the next aven, Gilmour would face his former friend alone.

Alen awakened and looked about the small tavern. They had come upon the village early that morning, two mud streets crossing in a valley tucked behind the range of hills they had spent the past several days crossing. There were a handful of stone dwellings arranged around the public house, and Alen guessed the village was Malakasia's southernmost outpost, a mountain hideaway for miners, woodsmen and seasonal trappers.

The tavern didn't have any rooms upstairs; the barman said so few travellers ever passed through that there was no need for guestrooms, but, looking at Hannah's bandages, he said he could make arrangements for them to sleep in a woodshed behind a local cutter's house. It wouldn't cost them much, a few copper Mareks, and the shed had a stove; they would be warm for the night.

Hoyt thanked the barman, paid for their midday meal, and cordially declined the offer. Encouraged by the realisation that they were descending into civilisation once again, however slowly, they planned on travelling as far as possible while daylight lasted.

Alen had been dozing in a high-backed chair near the fireplace, too tired even to assist with meal preparations at their table, when his eyes juddered open and he leapt to his feet. He walked quickly to the window and gazed along the narrow street outside.

Hannah came up behind him. 'What is it? Did you see something?'

'Someone just opened the gates at Sandcliff Palace.' He did not turn to look at her.

'What does that mean for us?'

'It depends on who it was. If it was Fantus, my old friend Gilmour, I have great hope for the future. But if it was Nerak, my other *old friend*, then we may have reached the end of a long road, Hannah. I'm sorry you'll be here to witness it.'

'So what do we do?' Her voice broke, and she cleared her throat.

'There is not much we can do – we're too far away. Our only option is to press on. We need to get to Welstar Palace and to try and have you home before things begin to come apart over here.'

'That's it?'

'I can try to contact Fantus, but it's very difficult – unless he's in a place where he is prepared, and willing to hear me, he won't. I hesitate to try it until I know who is at Sandcliff – if it's Nerak, he would be able to locate us.'

'Why, if he's way over there?'

'He has some pretty reprehensible characters working for him over here, Hannah.'

She shrugged. He was right; she should have thought of that. They had no choice but to push ahead and wait for Nerak to unleash a horror that would either destroy them, or enslave them for all time. 'How will you know if Nerak is the one there?' She wasn't sure she wanted to hear his answer.

'If we live out the Twinmoon, I will be fairly confident that Fantus opened the gates. Otherwise, I don't believe it will take long for Nerak to eradicate all of us here in Eldarn.'

'You should come with me. You all should. It's safe over there, absurdly safe, compared to this place. The most I do for safety each day is wear a bike helmet, and most of the time that's just because my mother insists.'

Alen shook his head. 'Hoyt may go with you. He has always been a seeker of wild adventures. Churn and I have business here.'

Hannah grabbed his arm, determined to be heard. 'It doesn't have to be that way, Alen. You don't all have to die.'

Placating her, he nodded. 'Perhaps not.' Then leading her back to their table, he added, 'Let's eat. We may all be dead tomorrow, anyway, so we might as well enjoy some decent food while we can.'

The man was shaking with what Brexan guessed were equal parts rage and terror. 'I want you out of here.' He wasn't certain if the un-predictable woman was about to draw a knife and open his throat.

'I paid you well.' She kept her voice low, not wanting Sallax to overhear their discussion. His sister's death had plunged him back inside himself, closing Brexan out and refusing to speak about it. She worried whatever progress they had made together had been completely lost; she was horribly afraid the mumbling, violent creature she had encountered in the streets would return without warning; she didn't need the tavern keeper's intransigence as well.

Worrying about Sallax had worn her down; waiting each night for the raiding parties had not helped either. Her back ached; her neck hurt, and she fought off a huge yawn as she deliberated with the old man.

'I'll give you that silver back,' he stammered, 'or what's left of it, but you two can't stay another night.' He looked as though throwing them out was the hardest thing he had ever done – he must have kicked out hundreds of drunk, poor or violent customers in the past two hundred Twinmoons, so why he was so scared of her was a mystery.

Brexan glanced past him to where the staff were eavesdropping near the scullery door. Although many had grown angry when they realised she and Sallax were the reason the Redstone had been searched again and again, they stared at the floor, embarrassed at their own cowardice – even the young waiter who had helped keep up Brexan's cover. She frowned at them. She was pretty sure it was they who had pressed the owner to evict the fugitives.

'Are you having trouble hearing me? I said I want you out now,' he repeated, as he cowered beneath the bar, his hands raised to ward her off.

Brexan knew she couldn't blame them for being wary: no one wanted to draw the attention of the Malakasian forces, and neither she nor Sallax were one of them, after all. Having Seron warriors kicking doors down every night would invariably mean some of them would be hanging from the rafters, tags marking them out as traitors looped around their necks.

'Fine,' she said finally. 'I want the silver back, at least what you have left of it. We'll be gone before midday.'

'You need to understand that—'

'I don't need to understand anything,' she snapped and he shut up, backing away from her. 'I will get our things together and we'll go. You just find your purse – and keep your rutting mouth shut.' She flushed. Before the last Twinmoon, she would never have even imagined herself speaking this way to an elderly person, regardless of how reprehensible or irritating he might be. She didn't recognise herself any more, not emotionally, not physically: she was too thin and her hair was crooked. Her body ached all over – and worst of all, she was a fugitive, a traitor playing nursemaid to an enemy of Malakasia. Suddenly she wanted to apologise, to say she understood he was just protecting his business and his people – but he was already gone.

Keep the coins. I stole the silver, anyway, she thought to herself sadly.

In the front room, she leaned over Sallax and whispered, 'Stay here. Try to eat something. I'll be right back.' She took some bread and a chunk of cheese from his plate and went up to their room.

It didn't take long for her to pack; she had stolen what they could carry from Carpello's office, but that didn't amount to much more than a few items of clean clothing for Sallax. Brexan stuffed everything into the bag she had lifted on her first morning in the city, donned her cloak and threw Sallax's over her arm. She had seen a quiet place on the outskirts of the city, the day she discovered Brynne's body on the salt marsh. They would go there.

Sallax needed time, and Brexan had to provide it; without him, her only option would be to start making enquiries about the Resistance, and she didn't fancy her chances there. So Brexan would steal all the silver they needed to stay on in Orindale until Sallax recovered and they found Garec and the partisans from Estrad, and until both Carpello and Jacrys lay dead.

She slipped through the doorway into the upstairs hall. She had become talented at moving through the city undetected; if she could discover what Carpello and Jacrys were shipping to Pellia, that information might earn her a position with the Eastern Resistance. She would torture Carpello until he told her everything – but Jacrys would never break under interrogation; Brexan had read that in his eyes. She wouldn't bother trying to question him; she would just kill him.

She was nearing the top of the stairs leading down to the front room when she heard the tavern door crash in. *Sallax!* Without thinking, she hurried down a few steps and bent to get a clear view of the front room.

Two Malakasian officers, one the captain who had led the last raid, appeared in the door, trailed by five Seron warriors, who immediately fanned out and began moving patrons to the back of the room. One customer, a middle-aged man sitting alone, hesitated, apparently too frightened to move. One Seron punched the man across the temple and he toppled backwards over his chair and fell to the floor, where he lay quivering in a gathering puddle of blood. This was more than a raid; someone had made the connection between the inn and the two fugitives. Brexan couldn't see Sallax, so turning as quietly as she could, she moved back up the steps to the landing.

A guttural shout from below told her that she was too late; an instant later, she heard the heavy clumping of Seron boots as one of the monsters charged up the stairs after her. As Brexan ran for the back stairwell he was close behind; she could almost feel his foul breath on her neck. She glanced back for an instant: the half-human animal had wild eyes, flaring nostrils and huge, crooked yellow teeth. It – maybe a *he* – was gaining ground fast. Brexan threw the bag at its feet, hoping it might trip and give her an instant more to escape, but the ploy didn't work.

The Seron was reaching for her with large hairy hands that looked so human it was unnerving, though the nails were gnawed down to the cuticle, and they were filthy, as if the warrior had spent all morning digging in pig-shit. Brexan froze, remembering the horrible moment when Lahp, the big Seron at Seer's Peak, had punched her hard enough to crack her cheek and leave her senseless. This Seron was not interested in punching her, though, so clutching Sallax's cloak like a lifeline, she leaped out over the stairs, throwing herself down to the lower landing behind the kitchen.

Brexan landed with a bone-jarring thud and tumbled into a stack of wooden crates. She felt something go in her ankle, but whatever she had injured, it held together long enough for her to crash through the back door and out into the alley behind the Redstone.

She had gone just three or four paces when she heard the Seron burst through the door and start down the alley after her. She was not going to get away; it would catch her and probably kill her before realising it … she hoped the Malakasian captain punished the creature for bringing back a corpse; even through her fear she grinned at the thought that the Seron's penchant for brutality might mean its own execution.

As she rounded the corner, rough hands reached out and seized her, pulling her violently into a dead-end corner.

'No!' she cried, flinging back her arms in a futile effort to break free. Whoever it was let go, and tossed her back into the alcove between two buildings.

It was Sallax.

'Demonpiss, Sallax! He's right behind—'

The Seron, still running at full speed, turned the corner, saw them and skidded to an awkward stop, blocking their only escape route.

As Brexan bent to catch her breath, her mind flashed to the morning she and Versen had charged Haden, the scarred creature who had beaten her and torn out Versen's throat. Drawing her knife, she sliced the leather strap holding her cloak closed and it fell to the dirt.

Sallax had slipped out of his bandages and she guessed his shoulder must have been blazing with pain. He backed towards her until she was pressed up against the wall then, never taking his eyes off the Seron, he felt around for Brexan's arm. He followed it down to her hand and took the knife. He brandished it and walked back towards their assailant.

'Come on, motherhumper,' Sallax rasped. 'I'm just one man. Take me.'

The Seron growled a warning and sprang.

Sallax stood his ground, his hair falling in greasy strands about his face, his shoulders drooping. With his eyes focused on the Seron's waist, he looked as though he was waiting for a pretty woman to turn him down at a harvest festival dance.

Brexan was certain he had taken the knife from her to ensure the Seron attacked and killed him first – suicide at the hands of an enemy. She screamed when the creature leaped out at him.

A few moments later, Brexan was thanking the forest gods she hadn't been with her platoon the day Lieutenant Bronfio led the attack on Riverend Palace to flush out the Ronan partisans. Had she remained inside with her fellow soldiers, she might have come face to face with Sallax Farro, one of the most dangerous men in Eldarn, and Sallax would have killed her in an instant.

The big Ronan kept her knife extended towards the Seron, the most rudimentary mistake all fencing students made: extending themselves too far and opening themselves up to an opponent's counterthrust. Sallax looked like an instructor's demonstration on how to get killed in the first moments of any battle.

But when the Seron flew at him, it leaped for the knife. In a blur, Sallax turned and removed his own blade from the back of his belt. As the creature lunged towards him, grabbing at Brexan's knife, Sallax brought his own up and into the creature's ribs with a slash that opened a ragged gash across the Seron's ribcage before burying itself to the hilt in the monster's back. The Seron screamed as it rolled away, releasing Sallax's arm and tumbling to the dirt.

As it rolled back to its feet, barking insults, the Seron grabbed for the knife, but it couldn't reach it. Brexan watched the soldier struggle, turning in circles like a dog chasing its tail, while its gurgling complaints became ever more choked.

Sallax watched without expression; he could see frothy red bubbles between the warrior's lips, then he lunged, using Brexan's knife to stab the monster in the throat. He opened the carotid artery and they watched the Seron bleed to death in a matter of moments.

Brexan stared in mute horror, the pounding of her heart almost deafening her.

Sallax wiped both blades on the Seron's tunic, sheathed one and handed the other back to Brexan. 'Come on,' he said, and led her out of the alley into the street.

Brexan followed in stupefied silence, following Sallax's lead as he ducked behind wagons and into shop doors to avoid Malakasian soldiers. She lost all sense of direction, but she couldn't summon the strength to argue.

Left then right, another right and then left again, they moved stealthily, quickly, across wide boulevards, through alleys and down side-streets. They crossed a bridge and followed the shoreline of a river until the path climbed up an embankment and ended beside a run-down waterfront business; Brexan guessed it might be an alehouse – but before she had a moment to take in her surroundings, Sallax shoved her roughly inside a huge cask, one of a number of enormous barrels someone had rolled out onto the quay above the river and obviously forgotten. The only light came through a tiny crack in one of the slats.

Brexan realised she had been crying and dried her tears on a corner of Sallax's tunic; she had forgotten her cloak where it had fallen in the dirt. Sallax reached over to place a hand gently on her shoulder. She reached up with her own to take his. It felt good, strong and warm in the darkness.

'Carpello,' Sallax said.

Brexan nodded, though he couldn't see it. 'You're right. Next is Carpello.'

'Soldiers will be looking.'

'After your little demo of short-blade combat, I bet they will, lots of them.'

'But we will find Carpello?'

'Yes, after we find someplace to stay for a few days, maybe a Moon, while that shoulder of yours heals. Fighting can't have been very good for it. That'll give things a chance to quieten down – and after that, we'll find Carpello.'

'For Brynne.' He reached into his tunic and removed the watch Mark Jenkins had given his sister and buckled it back around Brexan's wrist.

'For Brynne,' she said, 'and for Versen.'

THE SPELL CHAMBER

'Gilmour,' Steven shook the old man's shoulder, 'Gilmour, you need to get up. We may not have much time here and we *must* find that Windscroll. If you want to go back down to the village and hide somewhere, that's fine, but let's get that scroll.'

'I let him back in, Steven,' Gilmour said.

'Nerak? What do you mean?'

'I tried to read the spell book. He reached across the Fold and knocked the shit out of me. I had not a clue how to free myself. The second time, he did the same, then came through as a rush of wind and power. I let him back in, and now I've lit a rutting signal fire.'

'I don't care if Nerak's back, Gilmour – in fact, I prefer having him here, where we have the resources to destroy him, rather than over there where he might kill my parents or my friends. He already killed Myrna Kessler. I watched him burn down the entire south face of the canyon above Idaho Springs. For all I know, he left Denver in ruins before he came back looking for us. So to tell the truth, I'm glad he's here. As for him knowing where we are, why do you suppose he met us in Traver's Notch? He knows we have the key. He's been trying to get it since the day we arrived in Estrad. He damned near shat himself when he discovered it was on my desk that entire Twinmoon, and he raced me across the United States to get to it. So he's always known we were coming here; opening the gate only confirmed that we had arrived.'

Gilmour lifted his head from his hands and looked around the great room. It would have been dwarfed by the main dining hall at Riverend Palace, but it had been the scene of so many debates and drunken discussions. A wry grin crossed Gilmour's face despite his mood. Even with the sun directly overhead, little light broke through the arched windows lining each wall. Above, a narrow balcony ran around the entire hall; tapestries decorated with the crests of each territory and the various branches of the Larion Senate hung from the walkway, their tail ends limp above the main floor.

Gilmour rolled his shoulders back. 'Let's get some light in here,' he said.

'Garec,' Steven ordered, 'grab that torch over there; I'll use the staff.'

'Don't bother, Garec,' Gilmour interrupted, reaching a hand towards the ceiling. As he chanted a brief spell, turning on his heel to point at the torches and fireplaces, they all burst into flame and the mood in the hall changed at once. Steven could see that this had been a welcome meeting place, not the cold, inhospitable hall it had first appeared.

Mark hugged Gilmour comfortingly. 'Don't worry about it. This way we know where the bastard is.'

'I don't know if that makes me feel any better, Mark, but thanks anyway.'

'I like the trick with the torches, too. Steven did it down in the cavern below Meyers' Vale and scared the wits out of Gita and her Falkan roughnecks. Do you know any others? Like maybe how to open the kitchen?'

'I can open the kitchen, Mark, but I'm afraid there weren't any spells working to preserve the food. All we'll find in those cupboards is dust.'

'How about the wine cellar – or at least some water?'

'Ah,' Gilmour perked up again. 'I can get the water going.' He chanted again, and cast a half-moon arc over his head.

For a moment nothing happened; then Mark heard a low groaning noise, like tired metal shifting. 'What's that? A dragon in the basement?'

'An aqueduct,' Gilmour said.

'I just wanted a drink, and maybe a nice shower – you didn't need to open the hose quite so far!'

Just as all the torches had come to light at once, so all the fountains in Sandcliff Palace began simultaneously to spout, pour, dump or seep water, depending on their particular design. In this chamber alone there were four fountains and soon the lively crackle of the fires was punctuated with the tinkle of clear mountain water as basins beneath sculpted fountains began to fill.

'It should be clean,' Gilmour said. 'Drink all you like. We can fill the skins before leaving. As for a wine cellar, Mark, I don't know if we have time, but we had nearly four hundred casks – most of it has probably turned by now, but there were a few vintages that should have aged quite well. There's nothing like a thousand Twinmoons to bring out the flavour in a Falkan grape.'

'Great,' Mark said, 'well, if old Demon Prince Ugly doesn't join us right away, maybe we can run down there and grab a few flagons for the road.'

'I wouldn't count on it.' He gestured for the others. 'Let's go. It's not far to the north tower.' Gilmour led the way up a spiral staircase tucked into a back corner to the balcony. Gilmour paused to look back across the open expanse above the dining room.

'What is it?' Steven asked.

'There will be some bodies between here and the tower – probably quite a few. I'm sure they'll be nothing but bones now, but ...' He swallowed hard. 'The carnage that night was unprecedented. I don't know what Nerak might have done with the bodies after I left. So be warned.'

'Why do you suppose he did something with their remains?' Steven asked.

'Because this is where I stood, with that old broadsword still dangling from my hand, and I faced Nerak, in Pikan's body, right over there. From here I could see Callena and Janel, the two young senators Nerak killed first, across the balcony over there.' He pointed towards the other side of the room. 'Nerak threw their bodies down into the main hall, right in front of that fireplace, but they're gone now. I'm not sure why, or to where. I had planned to cover their remains with one of the tapestries, but that's when I saw her – *him* – here. And the sword is missing too.'

'The broadsword you carried?' Garec asked.

Gilmour stared towards the far end, his voice a murmur. 'I dropped it right here before sprinting all the way across the balcony and jumping through that window to the stone walkway outside.' He nodded towards the still-shattered panes of a broad circular window.

'It'll be all right,' Steven said. 'We've seen a lot on this journey; we're too close to let a few piles of bones frighten us into turning back.'

Gilmour turned and smiled. 'I know. Maybe I'm the one who needs convincing.'

They made their way up two more levels towards a chamber at the end of a corridor lined with wooden doors. Some of the doors had been left slightly ajar, others were wide open. The only closed room was a corner chamber at the end. As he had on the *Prince Marek*, Steven stood by while Gilmour placed a palm flat against the wooden doorframe.

'Anything?' he asked.

The old man shook his head. He pulled at the latch and the door swung open without a creak.

Steven's view was blocked momentarily, but when he heard Gilmour gasp, he pushed past, afraid that Nerak might be waiting for them. He needed only a glance to understand: this had been Gilmour's room. Much of the chamber was undisturbed: books, brittle and disintegrating over the Twinmoons, rested on a small table near the window. A paraffin taper lay in a shallow dish. A crammed bookshelf stood against the wall, next to a narrow closet still full of clothes.

Gilmour's bed was pushed against the wall, little more than a wood and leather-strap cot. The straw mattress that had once provided some measure of comfort had rotted away and a threadbare blanket was all that remained of Gilmour's bedding, but far more disturbing was the skeleton, clothed in the rotting remains of a pair of under-breeches, lying on the bed. The stark grey-white bones were held together by bits of putrefied ligament. The skeleton's arms were draped over its chest and its fingers gripped the pommel of a rusty old broadsword, a crude weapon.

Steven knew at once that this was Pikan Tettarak, Nerak's assistant and the one Senator powerful enough to mount any kind of counterassault against Nerak. She had failed; Gilmour had been busy in the scroll library when the fallen Larion sorcerer attacked, but had he been at Pikan's side, he would not have survived the devastation either. Watching the old Larion leader gaze down at the remains of the brave woman, Steven understood that his friend was wishing he had been beside her, hands with hers deep inside the spell table, when the end had come.

Rodler, surprising them all, acted first. Stepping into the closet, he removed an old cloak, tattered and moth-eaten but whole enough to cover the body. 'Whoever he is, he shouldn't be laying there with nothing covering him,' he said firmly. 'I understand we don't have time to give him his rites, but leaving him like that is unholy.'

'She,' Gilmour managed, 'her name was Pikan.'

'*She* then.' Rodler draped the cloak over the skeleton. 'Do you want the sword?'

There was a long silence in which no one moved. Finally, the wear-worn sorcerer, looking old, and thoroughly defeated, in the torchlight, said, 'No. Leave it.' He pushed his way past Garec and Mark and back into the corridor.

As he followed the others, Rodler was surprised to find Mark waiting for him. 'That was a nice thing you did back there,' Mark said, offering his hand.

'Thank you, Mark.' Rodler looked down, uncertain what to do. 'What is this?'

'This is one way we say *I'm sorry* where I come from.'

Rodler extended his own hand, and the two men settled their differences without another word.

They climbed staircases and crossed hallways, Gilmour mouthing incantations at every new junction to get through the restricted access, until they reached a short spiral of five or six stairs that ended at a heavy wooden door. Whispering a command, he pressed it open.

Steven felt a cold rush of wintry air swirl across the darkened landing: the door led to an exposed causeway of sorts, only a few paces wide, that ran from the top floor of the keep to the middle of the north tower.

'It's not far now, my friends,' Gilmour said as he stepped out into the late-day sun. 'The spell chamber is up there.' He pointed towards the upper room. 'That was where Nerak did the greatest damage.'

'Let's just get up there and grab that scroll,' Mark said. 'We'll haul the table out and hide it in one of those university buildings, or maybe at the bottom of the gorge, down in the village.'

They crossed the bridge and stepped inside the tower, taking a moment to allow their vision to readjust to torchlight, then pressed on towards the scroll library, quickly and silently.

No one appeared to have noticed the storm blowing in from the west.

On the uppermost landing, Gilmour knelt beside a body he identified as Harren Bonn. He had ordered him to guard the spell chamber door, knowing it was a death sentence; Harren had realised it also. While Pikan's remains had been recognisable as human, Harren was a jumble of cracked and shattered bits of bone in an untidy pile on the floor. Gilmour didn't care to let himself imagine what the dark prince had done to the novice Senator.

Joining him on the landing, Rodler asked, 'Is this someone else you knew?' He had casually accepted Gilmour as – *somehow* – a Larion Senator, one who had survived the past five generations and was returning to Sandcliff Palace for the first time.

Two thousand Twinmoons of accumulated wisdom and experience couldn't compete with feelings of guilt, sadness and regret. 'This should have been me as well.'

'Like the woman in your room?'

'Yes, like her.' Gilmour drew a sleeve across his face. They had all come too far for him to collapse, blubbering, beside what was left of a farmer's son he had sent to his death. He couldn't allow his guilt to debilitate him now, not this close to the end. If he died in the spell chamber, battling Nerak for control of the Fold, then so be it. Harren, Pikan and scores of his friends and colleagues had died doing their duty to Eldarn; he would do the same.

Gilmour rested one hand gently on the largest identifiable piece of Harren's skull. 'We're done, my boy. It's been a long time, but we're done.' He stood, ushered Rodler gently out of the way, and kicked what was left of the spell chamber door, which fell from its final hinge with a dusty, resounding crash.

As he stepped across the threshold, Gilmour felt a renewed sense of purpose, and confident determination – despite his recent failings – that he would see this through to its end. He stood for a moment in the spell chamber, taking in the small room, before his knees gave way and he collapsed unconscious to the floor.

The Larion spell table was gone.

'Holy shit!' Steven cried, 'Gilmour!' He knelt by the old man's side.

'What happened?' Garec asked, joining them on the floor.

'Look,' Steven said, gesturing into the empty room.

'I don't understand,' Garec said.

'This is it. This is the spell chamber, and *there's no spell table*.' Steven slapped Gilmour gently, trying to startle him awake, but he remained unconscious.

'Oh rutters, no, this is one of your hideous jokes. Isn't it—?' Garec stood in the centre of the small room and turned a full circle, somehow expecting to see the stone table tucked away in a corner, or maybe artfully camouflaged with some clever cloaking spell. 'Gods, please tell me we did not come all this way for nothing.'

'I'm afraid we did,' Steven said, glancing up at Mark, who simply shook his head.

The laughter began as a hollow rhythmic vibration, barely audible above their voices. It was joined by a clattering sound, like marbles dropped down a stairwell.

'Hahahaha!' The amused chuckle was insidious, terrible. 'What a creative spell that was, Steven. I *am* impressed. I assume it was you; I would have known if Fantus had been cloaking your little party all this time.' It was Nerak, though Steven couldn't see him. His voice felt as though it was coming from everywhere at once. Then the clatter came again, louder this time, and Steven turned towards the door.

The hundreds of shattered bits of Harren's broken body, en-shrouded in a tattered robe, began to pull themselves back together. Scraping and clattering against the cold stone of the north tower stairwell, the long-dead Larion Senator rose awkwardly to his feet, his ribs misplaced, one shoulder dislocated, and his skull askew above his spine.

Shuffling into the spell chamber, the pieced-together skeleton focused its vacant gaze on Steven. 'Did you really think I would just have left it here? You are fools for following him. Look at him, Steven. He's finished, beaten, and he knows it. Give me the key now, and I'll let you go home. Give me the key now, and I'll let Hannah go home as well.'

Steven stood, the hickory staff alive in his hands. 'How did you enjoy Traver's Notch, Nerak?' he said quietly. 'Not expecting that one, were you? Did it hurt?'

The dark prince ignored him. 'Right now, she and her friends are moving north towards Welstar Palace, *my palace*. Can you believe that? She hopes to find you and go home. Would you like that? Give me the key, and you can go.' Harren extended a bony hand.

Steven's stomach turned at the thought of giving in. 'Not today, Nerak,' he said as he nudged Gilmour with the toe of his boot. 'Gilmour, wake up. Wake up now.' When the old man still didn't stir, Steven tapped him in the ribs with the hickory staff, sending a bolt of lighting juddering through his body and shocking him back to consciousness.

'Rutting whores!' the old man shouted. 'What was that?'

'Get up, Gilmour,' Steven hissed, 'on your feet, now!'

Harren's empty eye sockets glowed amber for a moment, then faded to black. 'Hello Fantus, so good to see you again,' Nerak said through his skeletal mouthpiece. 'I am so very glad you came all this way for nothing. Was it a hard journey?' Harren's jawbone hung open as the dark prince laughed. 'It's been gone for a long, long time, Fantus, and you'll never find it. Eldarn itself wards the spell table for me, Eldarn and Eldarn's most ruthless gatekeepers. Forget the spell table, Fantus. It's mine. It has *always* been mine.'

Gilmour's gaze fell to the floor; he couldn't summon the courage to look at Harren's ruined body, now Nerak's prisoner.

Nerak was enjoying the moment immensely. He turned on Mark Jenkins. 'And you, my prince, you have everything figured out yet? If you believe you do, you're wrong. Keep at it, though, because our day is coming.'

Grimacing, Mark stepped towards the skeleton, his battle-axe drawn and raised to strike. 'Stop calling me that.'

'My prince? Oh, that? Enjoy it while you can. I have a special place for you in the Fold. It's dark in there, Mark. I hope you're not afraid of the dark.'

With a cry, Mark attacked the skeleton, hacking away one arm. Nerak grabbed him by the throat with Harren's remaining hand; its grip was impossibly strong, and Mark tugged hard at one bony finger until it snapped.

His friends were still frozen in shock, but finally Rodler moved, swinging his fist like a cudgel to break through the bones of Harren' forearm. As they snapped, Nerak's vice-like grip was released and the remaining fingers fell away. They disintegrated to dust when Mark, in disgust, cast them against the chamber wall.

Armless, Harren turned back to Steven. 'Give me the key, and you can go home, you and Hannah. I regret that I can't let Mark Jenkins go with you, for he and I have other plans, don't we, Mark?'

Mark rubbed feeling back into his throat and growled, 'Any day, sister. I'm right here.' He threw the axe and it crashed through Harren's ribcage and clattered on the floor behind him. Nerak was unfazed.

'The key, Steven. It is up to you.' With that, what was left of Harren's skeleton collapsed in a dusty pile.

'Cover your wrists!' Mark yelled. 'Jesus Christ, cover your wrists!' He folded his hands under his armpits, not really believing that would keep the dark prince from taking him.

'Don't worry,' Steven said, 'he can't attack us.'

'How do you know?' Garec asked, staring at the backs of his wrists, waiting for the skin to discolour.

'Because he's not really here,' Steven said. 'Did you see the eyes glow yellow? He's not here. He may not even be in Gorsk, never mind the palace. That was a phone call.'

'A what?' Rodler asked, his hands shaking and sweat streaming from his face.

'We're safe.' Steven wrapped an arm around Gilmour's shoulders, trying to comfort the weary old man.

'Safe? I can't say I feel safe.' He looked at Mark, who nodded silent thanks. Rodler punched him softly in the upper arm, and both men smiled, grateful to be alive.

The first drops to strike the floor went unnoticed, then Garec said, 'What is that? Rain?'

Mark shook his head. 'Nah. It's too cold for rain.'

'Maybe it's snow, melting on the roof. Those torches are throwing off a little heat now.'

Rodler reached out and caught a droplet with a celebratory cry. 'Hah, got one!'

Mark wheeled on him. 'Wipe it off! Wipe it off now!'

'What? What is it?'

'It's acid,' he said, 'it's eating through the roof. We have to get out of here, now.'

Rodler yelped as the acid bubbled its way through the skin on his palm. Rubbing his hand against his cloak, he looked to the others for some explanation, his eyes wide with terror.

'The Windscroll,' Steven said, 'Gilmour, where is the third Windscroll? We have to get it, fast.'

'I— I don't ... I'm not sure I know which—'

'Gilmour!' Steven swatted the old man again with the hickory staff and another bolt of fire lanced through his body.

'Gods rut!' Gilmour bellowed, 'I wish you wouldn't do that!'

'Then pay attention. We need the third Windscroll, now, before this rain kills us all. Go!'

Finally fully conscious again, Gilmour hustled across the spell chamber and disappeared down a short flight of stairs into an adjacent room: Lessek's scroll library. He watched as more droplets smoked their way through the ancient wood and slate of the tower ceiling.

'It's those clouds,' Mark said redundantly.

'The clouds from Orindale,' Garec agreed. 'Gita and her men described them: acid in a living cloud. What kind of twisted animal comes up with something like that?'

A low hissing sound filled the chamber as wood and stone disintegrated above them: the entire structure was gradually being eaten away. Soon they would not need to dodge periodic drips; before long the deadly fluid would rain down on them in torrents.

A shingle gave way and a thin stream of deadly acid began running into the spell chamber, a harbinger of what was coming. 'Hurry up, Gilmour,' Steven shouted, 'things are getting bad out here.'

'I think I have it – *ah*!'

'Are you all right?'

'Yes, I'm fine. A drop fell on the back of my neck – it burns, but I'm all right for now.' Gilmour appeared in the doorway, his feet skidding on the stone as he tried to avoid charging headlong through the acid stream pouring through the ceiling. He had several scrolls tucked under one arm. 'Let's go.'

As they started down the spiral staircase, the ceiling of the Larion spell chamber gave way with a crash and what was left of poor Harren's bones dissolved in the flooded room. The trickle of almost living liquid grew moment-by-moment into a steady stream, running down the stairs behind the fleeing party.

Rodler, disconcerted at the size of the burning wound caused by just one droplet of the noxious fluid, shouted, 'We have to hurry, boys. It's coming down behind us!'

Steven looked back as well. 'Holy shit, look at that! Everybody, keep to your feet – we can't fall. If we fall, we're dead. Don't think about anything but quick feet and keeping your balance. Run, now, move it!' As they pounded down the worn staircase, the river of acid gained ground on them with every step.

'Keep your feet! Keep your feet! Move it! Move it! Move it!' Steven chanted in rhythm to encourage them.

Rodler hesitated long enough to check back again, and cursed himself for doing so: the acid was right on his heels, just five steps back, then four. It was coming too fast, and he was last in line. How in the name of the gods of the Northern Forest did he end up last in line?

'You have to run, boys. Jump down the gods-rutting stairs if you have to – we're losing this race,' he screamed.

They picked up the pace, trying to avoid slipping, loudly cursing the Larion Senators for building such a tall tower with such smoothly polished stone steps. One tumble, one mistake, and they would all be bathed in deadly acid.

Three steps back, then two. Rodler, realising the poisonous stream was hugging the insides of the steps, was running on the outside of the spiral staircase. *That makes it faster*, he thought. He could hear the hissing, like ten thousand angry snakes, coming up behind him, eating away at the very foundations of the tower. When he looked down again, the acid was keeping pace with him, running on the inside of the same steps he traversed on the outside. It was too late; he would be the first to step in it. He wondered how much protection his boots would actually provide and was horribly afraid of the answer: *not much*.

Finally he heard Garec burst through the doorway, and a moment later he too was outside and the acid river was flowing past them, down the remaining stairs to the tower's basement. Gasping, he collapsed on the stone walkway. 'That was too close, my friends. I was just on my way to work when I ran into you. Never saw you – that was a rutting good spell you cast, Steven. I never saw you ... and I wish with all my heart I had never stumbled into you ...'

Beside him, sprawled out on the stone bridge, Mark began to laugh. 'That certainly wasn't your day, was it?'

The others joined in. Garec said in an effeminate voice, 'So dearheart, how was work today?' Even Gilmour roared at this, his thin frame doubled over. They had lost. He had given up; the stress was too much for him to bear. He laughed inanely until he couldn't catch his breath, then lay down beside Mark, the cold of the nearly frozen stone chilling the acid burn on the back of his neck.

'Wait,' Steven said, 'wait!'

'Catch your breath first, Steven,' Mark said. 'We're still trying to get over the last one.'

'No, wait. It's no joke. Look up there.' He pointed towards the top of the north tower where grey-black clouds were dissolving much of the tower's uppermost level in their unholy acid bath. Even the outer layers of stone had grown discoloured and it was only a matter of time before the peak collapsed.

What alarmed Steven was not that the Larion spell chamber and scroll library had been destroyed, but that one of the clouds had broken away from its partner and was dropping down on them. He rolled to his feet and screamed, 'Move!'

He raced to the doorway and tugged on the latch. Nothing happened – he couldn't budge it. It must be locked from the inside. The cloud fell towards them, an acrid bath of death descending from heaven like an Old Testament nightmare. He grasped the latch and tugged, hoping to break the ancient clasp with muscles and the sheer strength of his will, but it was as solid as a mountain.

He peered over the side of the causeway and wondered if they would survive the jump, if perhaps there would be water, a deep river or maybe a lake far below. But his hopes were dashed: all he could see were rocks, trees and forbidding cold ground. It was too far to jump;

it would kill them. He reached for the staff; he had five seconds to think of something to save them – but nothing came to mind. He was too terrified. He held the staff over his head, praying it might act of its own volition, generating some miracle to keep them safe.

Then Gilmour was beside him, throwing his hands up to the door and chanting. It opened. Garec and Rodler dived past him and down the few stairs to the corridor below, then Mark grabbed his roommate by the collar and heaved him through the archway to tumble down the unforgiving steps. Steven was glad there were only five or six of them as the two friends landed painfully on the hallway floor. Gilmour dived for the protection of the corridor and shouted; his spell caused the door to slam shut and the hollow thud resonated out into the palace.

In the instant before the door closed, Steven saw the acid cloud strike the causeway with a vengeance, raining noxious fluid and for ever cutting off access to the north tower. The stone bridge dissolved like a paraffin taper.

Rodler looked around at the collected members of their company. 'I need to find a fountain. My hand is burning,' he said, matter-of-factly.

'I do as well.' Gilmour regained his feet with a groan. 'I took a thick drop on the back of my neck. I think I'll feel it boring in there for the next Twinmoon. Come on, Rodler, there's one down the hall. The aqueduct is a long way from those clouds, so the water should still be clean.'

'I'll come with you,' Mark said. 'I need something to drink.'

'I'm afraid it's just water, Mark.'

'Yes, but with Nerak out and about somewhere and those clouds slowly eating this place as a snack, I figure we've plenty of time to raid your wine cellar.' He started down the hall. 'Don't forget your scrolls.'

Gilmour gathered up the parchment rolls and turned to follow Rodler and Mark down the corridor to a small fountain, a delicate trickle splashing into a carved stone basin.

Rodler reached the fountain first, but he gestured for Mark to go ahead of him and drink his fill.

'Don't be silly. You just saved my life, and for your efforts you were burned – you've got the honours. ' Mark gave a bow, and ushered the young man forward to wash his injured hand.

'All right,' Rodler said as the water washed over his wound, 'thanks Mark. I appreciate it.'

'My pleasure—'

The almor struck with such ferocity that Mark was knocked off his feet and into the opposite wall. The demon took Rodler Varn of Capehill and he was dead in an instant, *as dead as Bridget Kenyon there in the deep end of the Air Force Academy pool*—

Mark heard Gilmour shout from somewhere behind him, and felt the Larion sorcerer's magic blast by him like a mortar round to slam into the creature and rip the fountain out of the wall. Flailing in the almor's grip, one of Rodler's hands came forward; Mark seized it and began to pull – but instead of tugging the smuggler free, Mark felt his own life siphoning away. Rodler's fingers collapsed and shrank to bony twigs, as unnervingly brittle as Harren's when clasped about his neck.

Repulsed, Mark finally gave up, released Rodler and watched as the milky creature retreated back into the palace wall. It all happened in an instant; there had been nothing anyone could do. Falling to his knees in a puddle beside the ruined fountain, Mark Jenkins began to cry.

Steven stared in shocked disbelief for several moments before he rose to his feet, peeled off his jacket and ran down the hall towards his friend. By the time he reached Mark, he was in a rage, his eyes dancing with anger and the hickory staff glowing red.

'No!' he roared, raising the staff. 'No! No! No! You did not just do that! You did not just kill him!' Steven struck the wall above the broken fountain and the foundations of Sandcliff Palace seemed to quiver.

An explosion knocked the others off their feet and tumbled Mark from his knees into a foetal position, looking so vulnerable that Steven reared back and struck the wall once again. When the smoke and dust finally cleared, a hole big enough to accommodate the small party comfortably had been opened in the blocks between the corridor and an apparently abandoned chamber beyond. Running down through the masonry was a makeshift tube – broken now beyond repair – that Steven guessed was connected somehow to the palace's central aqueduct. The fountains weren't magic; it was a simple system of pressure and abundant supply that kept the water flowing at Sandcliff. Jabbing the hickory staff into the cracked ends of the ceramic pipe, he released a devastating blast of destructive energy that tore through the palace.

Hoping he had done enough to frighten the almor away, or at

least stun it, Steven kneeled down beside Mark. 'Are you all right?'

Mark choked. 'I hate it here, Steven; I really do. Clouds of living acid, water demons – how are we supposed to fight?'

Steven had no answer. He stared at the shattered fountain lying on the stone floor beside the leathery sack that had been Rodler Varn of Capehill.

'That was supposed to be me,' Mark went on through his tears. 'He wanted me to drink first. That was supposed to be me. I insisted he go first. Can you fucking stand that?'

Steven was already on his feet. Stepping over the body, he reached out with two fingers and wiped them gently around the spout that had carried water through the tiny sculpture and into the marble bowl. Rubbing his fingers together, he said, 'Sonofabitch. Look at that.'

Gilmour was by his side, still shaking, and thrilled and frightened at the crushing blast he had called up to tear the fountain from the wall; he suspected it was his magic that caused the almor to scurry back into the dark recesses of the Sandcliff cistern. 'What is it, Steven?' he asked.

'You said there was an aqueduct. Where?' He was so intense now, and Gilmour could feel the power of the hickory staff surrounding him, charging the stale air of the old hallway.

'It comes in through the east wall, below the main hall, turns a wheel downstairs and dumps into various lines that feed the fountains throughout the keep.' He stepped away a little, nervous that the staff might touch him and inadvertently stop his heart, or blow a hole in his chest – he was still smarting from the firebolts Steven had used to shock him back to consciousness.

'Garec, take Mark downstairs. Get to the lowest level you can reach without getting wet, or being near any water supply – I mean it. I don't want you in sight of *any* water at all.'

Garec helped Mark to his feet and as they made their way down the corridor, Steven called after them, 'Keep your heads down, and wait for us to come get you.'

'Right,' Garec said, 'I understand. It's going to be bad.'

Gilmour asked, 'What are you going to do?'

'The clouds are eating this place stone by stone, and they won't stop until they have consumed us, right down to socks and boots. There is a demon in the water supply. I'm not going to have any of it, Gilmour. I think I know how to deal with both of them at once, but I need to know if we can get to a place on the aqueduct

– without those clouds detecting us – where I might climb up and access the water supply.'

'Water won't do anything to those clouds, Steven,' Gilmour warned.

'Don't worry about that: can we get there without those clouds noticing?'

Gilmour's face was layered in wrinkles as he concentrated. Finally he said, 'Yes, I think we can.' Then almost boyishly, he added, 'Gods rut it, but Steven, I can get you there. Let's go.' He led the way towards the centre of the keep.

Steven ran through the forest and up the sharp incline beside Sandcliff Palace. He kept his head low, hoping the clouds gnawing the north wing of the Larion keep down to its bones would ignore Gilmour and him as they moved towards the top of the aqueduct. The woods were thick enough to mask their movements, but they did little to diffuse the hissing as the acid melted the ancient stone.

Arriving at the aqueduct, Steven and Gilmour huddled amongst the trees that grew along the base of the stone waterway. The Larion aqueduct was enormous, a marvel of engineering and architecture, the gigantic mortared stone archways supporting a veritable river; they climbed the hillside to the top of the mountain. Steven had no doubt that Larion Senators had spent time in Italy during the Renaissance.

He whistled quietly as he looked up the bone-grey wall to where a stream of water ran into the cisterns beneath Sandcliff's east wing. 'Sheez, Gilmour,' Steven shook his head. 'You didn't mention it was quite this big.'

'What can I say? We had a lot of fountains. We had hundreds of students studying at the university,' Gilmour replied. 'Now will you tell me what you plan to do?'

'Well, I will tell you that I don't plan to get killed,' Steven said, 'just in case you were wondering.'

'It had crossed my mind …'

Peeking beneath one of the stone arches, Steven could see that the clouds continued to work their insidious magic, dissolving what was left of the tower to rubble. Soon they would break through the walls of the main building, and from there it was just a short step to Mark and Garec's hiding place.

Tucking the hickory staff into his belt, Steven climbed the aque-duct and carefully ran along the narrow edge – keeping his feet dry for as long as possible was critical; he didn't want to alert the almor until the last possible moment.

He moved quickly back down the slope to where the aqueduct spilled through a tiny breach in the palace wall and into the great cistern. Once he found a suitable spot he stepped into the ankle-deep stream of rushing water and bent low to examine the joints between two of the sections of funnel-shaped ceramic tubing the water ran in. He found an old carpentry nail holding them together and scraped a fingernail across the metallic head, then rubbed his fingertip against the fleshy part of his thumb. 'Good enough,' he said to himself, then turned towards the acid clouds and began to shout.

'Hey! Hey you, over there, you— whatever you are, *cloud things*! I'm over here! Come on over and get me!' Steven shouted, trying to taunt the clouds into attacking him; he had never realised how difficult it was to insult a cloud. Still screaming into the sky, he felt the hickory staff warm into a rage once again. *This had to work.* He just needed one more thing to fall into place.

Steven stood in the water, taking a gamble that the magic had driven the almor far enough out of the palace that the creature wouldn't come up behind him from somewhere in the cistern. It had been a powerful blast – and he knew the staff had enough strength to kill an almor; he had done it before. It had most likely been driven up into the mountains, where it would wait for another opportunity to ambush them, but Steven wasn't willing to sit around and be hunted by a demon every time he took a drink of water. He stomped his feet in the aqueduct stream, egging the almor on, while he continued to berate the far-off acid clouds.

Then the twin clouds broke away from the north tower and, independent of the prevailing winds, moved over to where Steven waited, the staff a red glow of vengeance in his fists. 'Come on, come on you bastards,' Steven said, uncertain if the clouds could hear him. They had detected him there, and that was enough. Now he needed the almor. He looked for Gilmour below in the trees, but the old man was nowhere to be found, probably hiding in the shadows.

He stomped his feet again, splashing as much as possible without tumbling over the side and plummeting to a broken neck on the frozen ground below. 'Come on, where are you?' he shouted. 'Come and get me, you bastard, I'm right here – I'm standing in the water, for Christ's sake. What more do you need, a goddamned invitation?'

Looking back to the clouds, he realised it was too late: they would be on him before he had a chance to draw the almor in for the kill. 'Motherless dry-humping bastards,' he cursed; this was bad luck: the almor could hit him at any time, probably while he was busy battling the clouds.

'Shit and double red shit,' he said, 'burned to death with acid while being sucked dry by a waterlogged demon. This was a great idea, Steven. No, really, one of your absolute best!'

He waited, furious; the acid clouds were coming, with or without the almor, and he was about to fight. He took a deep breath, murmured insults at the acid monsters, and braced for their assault – until Gilmour's shouting and splashing distracted him from his immediate doom. The old man was dancing and jumping about barefoot in the water near the top of the aqueduct and even from this distance, he could hear the song Gilmour was singing, an off-key, off-colour ode to a sexually active young man with a wooden leg, surely one of the most hilarious pieces of folk poetry he had ever heard. But now was most definitely not the time; he was quite sure that Gilmour had gone stark raving mad.

'What the hell are you doing?' Steven shouted, looking back and forth between the dancing sorcerer and the clouds. 'You're going to get yourself killed. Take cover. Get out of here now!'

But Gilmour danced and sang; jumping about, he was a dripping mess of wet wool and matted hair – until the Larion Senator turned suddenly and gestured over his shoulder.

The almor was coming.

'Get down, Gilmour, jump for it,' Steven cried, but the last few words were lost. The clouds were just overhead.

Gilmour screamed again and Steven risked watching as the old man took a few tottering steps towards him, then dived headlong into the smooth ceramic channel. Steven was surprised by Gilmour's over-the-edge antics, until he realised that Gilmour's cry had been one of excitement, not fear or panic, as he came onwards, head-first and bellowing the third verse defiantly. Out of nowhere, Steven recalled a water-park near Denver where periodically a drunk forty-year-old would leap headfirst down the tallest slide and end up airlifted to the nearest hospital. He wondered what might happen when a three-hundred-year-old man tried his hand at such a game.

As he came closer, Gilmour's song changed from the rhythmic thump of a drinking tune; now he was shouting, 'Behind me, Steven, look behind me!'

Finally he realised what the crazy sorcerer had been doing as an ivory blur pursued him down the aqueduct, rapidly closing the distance between them. Timing would be everything if this were to work. Steven stepped out of the stream and stood astride the chute on tiptoes, hoping he'd left enough space for Gilmour to pass between his legs. His eyes moved from the almor to the acid clouds: the demon was coming fast, almost too fast now, down the chute, nothing more than a hillock of fast-moving current. Above, the clouds were massing, one spinning tumult of acid death.

Steven found himself remembering a science class on weather: were these stratocumulus, cumulonimbus, stratonymphopolyphonic – whatever? They were weaving themselves together to rain their deadly fluid down on this young fool – and, in a stroke of great luck, poison the water in the palace at the same time.

The almor was close now and Steven watched as one shapeless arm broke the surface and stretched towards Gilmour's feet. In another few seconds it would have him. 'Hurry, Gilmour, come on,' Steven urged under his breath, and called forth the magic of the hickory staff, right at his fingertips—

The acid cloud dropped, a terrifying storm of pestilence and burning death. It was little more than twenty feet above his head when Steven glimpsed the old man passing beneath him and with a primitive cry, he slammed the hickory staff down into the water between Gilmour and the almor. His magic responded instantaneously, blowing the stream up and out into the acid storm above, carrying the almor aloft as well. Its cry was deafening, reverberating waves of punishing sound.

Steven intensified the magic, calling forth all the water from the aqueduct, throwing great waves of icy snowmelt overhead.

He caught every drop of water and cast it skywards, and when the half-moon channel was empty, the hickory staff pulled forth reserves of water from the mountains, deep caverns of inky-black water, summoned into the skies above Sandcliff Palace. Wave after wave drenched the acid cloud, and when the deadly nimbus realised what was happening, it tried to flee.

Steven screamed, nothing intelligible, just a release of pent-up anger, frustration and fear. He understood Gilmour's lunatic behaviour now as he continued to pour thousands and thousands of gallons of water into the cloud. His senses sharpened by the magic, he caught sight of the almor, acid-scarred and full of hatred, below him, sliding towards a rapidly diminishing puddle.

'Not so fast,' Steven cried from his place atop the makeshift river, 'back you go to the hell that spawned you!' He used the magic to toss the opaque demon back into the acid cloud. Again the almor screamed, but Steven kept his feet and continued his barrage.

All of a sudden it was over. The cloud, saturated, fell across the hillside in a rainy death, killing some of the trees and shrubs, but mostly absorbed by the cold dirt above the palace. The north tower looked as though it had melted away. Steven hoped the Windscroll would give them the answers they needed, because anything left in those tower rooms, Harren's remains included, had dissolved to nothingness.

Steven searched the hillside, through the wispy clouds of foul-smelling mist, for the almor. He was certain it had survived – an acid bath wasn't enough to kill it, but it would have annoyed the demon, and hopefully made clear that Steven and the hickory staff were a formidable enemy. It was just a matter of time before the two of them battled again.

His rage sated and his need to avenge Rodler met, Steven felt the magic recede. Maybe Mark had been right: there were no hickory trees in the foothills where he had found the staff; that was anomalous enough, but it responded to Steven's needs so perhaps there was something to Mark's claims that he was a sorcerer, compelled to remain in Idaho Springs all those years by Lessek's key. Steven inspected the familiar length of hickory for any damage and wished he had the answers.

If Mark really was a king and he really was a sorcerer, they were doing a right hideous job of saving the world.

'Steven?' Gilmour's voice came from the forest below. 'Are you all right, Steven?'

'Am I all right?' Steven shouted back. 'I'm not the one who did a full-on Charlie Hustle all the way down this aqueduct. Where's your head, Gilmour? That thing could have caught you and sucked you dry before I had any chance of warding it off. How did you know it wouldn't catch you?'

Gilmour's face was bloody and one arm hung at his side, unmistakably broken, but he sounded fine, even enthusiastic. 'I was right rutting surprised at how fast it came after me. I *do* love it when we take the fight to them, though, don't you?' Gilmour was enjoying himself, as if he had momentarily forgotten that the spell table was missing.

'Oh, yeah, sure,' Steven said. 'It's invariably the highlight of my day. I find few things as invigorating as going toe-to-toe with homicidal clouds and ancient demons. It's like a double shot of espresso. How do I get down there?'

'I came the easy way.' He pointed towards the palace wall, 'Bounced right off and fell into that bush over there. It was quick, but I don't recommend it. I'm going to have to do some work on this old fisherman's body, I'm afraid. I suggest you hike back up the chute and jump down.'

'I think I'll take option two,' Steven said. Water began flowing down the chute from the hidden caverns and subterranean aquifers, chilling his feet even through his boots.

Ignoring his injuries, Gilmour kept pace. 'How did you know the water would drive off those clouds?' he asked.

'It wasn't just water. That fountain was caked with limestone, deposited over the Twinmoons by that trickle. The water flowing into the palace is heavy with lime – you can scrape it off the nails holding these joints together.'

'Limestone?'

'Calcium carbonate, Gilmour, simple high school chemistry: in solution, limestone raises the ph of water.' The old man still looked bemused. Steven clarified, 'It makes water less acidic: the solution can be used to neutralise acids. I didn't know what the concentration was, or whether it was enough to stave off those clouds, so I used a lot.'

'I'll say!' Gilmour grabbed a low-hanging tree branch with his good arm and pulled himself up the slope next to where Steven could jump down from the elevated waterway. 'I wasn't sure there would be any water left in the mountain after that little display.'

Steven landed beside him and started mopping the blood from Gilmour's face. 'You're a damned mess.'

'Oh, I'll fix it,' he said. 'It seems I've rediscovered a few vagrant skills here at the old homestead.'

'I'm glad to hear that,' Steven said. 'We're going to need them to find that table.'

Gilmour's enthusiasm faded.

'Sorry,' Steven said, 'I didn't mean to remind you.'

'Oh, it's all right.' Gilmour forced a smile. 'But I *do* love it when we take the fight to them!'

From somewhere on the hillside, the almor screamed, a raging cry of anger and frustration. Its hunger wouldn't wane until it had taken them all. Steven winced as the inhuman shriek resonated along his

MALAKASIA

'Thank you, Alen.' Hoyt's eyes brimmed with tears. 'Where did you get these?'

Alen gestured as if all of Eldarn were within his reach – yet Hoyt had never known the old man to be anywhere but Middle Fork. 'Oh, here and there.'

'But these are vintage – nothing like this has been printed in over nine hundred Twinmoons.' Hoyt brushed the cover of the top volume in the stack of thirty or more: the most comprehensive collection of medical texts he had ever seen.

'There are more,' Alen said.

'Where?' Hoyt immediately hated the fact that he sounded so greedy and tried to curb his enthusiasm slightly. 'Sorry, I mean— thank you so very much for these, Alen. It would have taken me ten Twinmoons or more to steal this collection – I'd love to know where you managed to find them. And if there are others, well, you know I just want to be as thorough as possible in my training—'

'Please stop apologising,' Alen said with a smile. 'There are more, and I want you to have them. They're doing no one any good where they are. Once you get this bunch stashed away somewhere, I'll show you a significant private library here in Praga, and another over in Rona.' He considered his pipe and rapped the bowl against the fireplace to empty it, then stored it in a rack on the mantel. The old man's dog wandered in from the hallway, nuzzled against Hoyt's hip until he patted the big animal behind the ears. Satisfied for the moment, it padded over to a rug near the fire to sleep away the morning aven.

Hoyt had dreamed of such books. He had wanted for so long to be a healer – more than that, he wanted to be a *doctor*. Stitching a wound, setting a bone, even delivering a baby: these skills he had learned during his travels, and he was respected in Southport as a talented healer, but it wasn't enough to satisfy him. A thousand

Twinmoons of Malakasian rule had seen the deterioration of so much in Eldarn – education, public health, welfare, scientific research, and especially medicine. Given the opportunity, Hoyt Navarra of Southport was happy to burden himself with the resurrection of medicine in Eldarn. These books were a good start.

Being found with even one of these publications would mean death; being detained with thirty ancient medical treatises would almost certainly ensure a slow, tortured death: a tag hanging. He would be forced to wear a placard naming him as an illegal smuggler of outlaw writing, and then hanged for an entire Twinmoon until his body rotted. Hoyt had seen tag hangings before; by the end of the Twinmoon, the foul stench of decay was overwhelming. Once he had seen a woman caught with fennaroot; she'd refused to put on the placard so the Malakasian officials had acted swiftly. A soldier nailed the placard to her chest.

Getting Alen's generous gift home would be challenging, but … 'I can get these back,' he said confidently. 'Thank you, Alen, thank you!'

'It is my pleasure,' he smiled. 'Use them well. Teach others. Make it your goal in life to see this information applied throughout Eldarn, and then update them, Hoyt – it's been nearly a thousand Twinmoons since anyone has published anything new. Even more important than becoming a doctor: your charge will be to find the right people to add knowledge.'

Hoyt ordered the tenderloin, a first for him in a public house. It was expensive, and a rarity – few people had spare silver to be ordering such elaborate meals from a tavern – but this was a celebration, after all. If anyone tried to roll him, they'd get a bit of a surprise: Hoyt invariably carried a homemade scalpel in easy reach; any would-be assailant would get more than he had bargained for. Still, neither the two elderly gentlemen throwing multi-sided dice, nor the young couple talking over a flagon of wine, nor the small group of men engrossed in some business discussion looked at all interested. He turned his attention to his meal.

He had waited for this day half his life; now Alen had made it a reality. All he had to do was work out how to get this treasure trove back to Southport. That would need some planning.

While he was contemplating options, a young woman approached and, without asking, took a seat across from him.

'Good evening,' she said.

Hoyt, both his thoughts and his meal interrupted, was irritated. 'Not tonight,' he said shortly as he reached for the wine, and gestured towards the door. 'Go find someone else.'

The woman, several Twinmoons older than Hoyt, was wearing a simple wool skirt and a light tunic with loose-fitting sleeves. She had a thin leather strap of some sort around her neck. She ignored him and motioned for service.

'I'll have the same,' she told the barman, 'and another flagon of that too, please.'

Hoyt reached for his goblet again, and said, 'I'm sorry, maybe you didn't hear me. I'm not interested. And I am not buying you dinner.'

She tossed a leather pouch onto the table which jangled with the unmistakable sound of Mareks – a bold move, showing off that much money. Despite the fact that no one appeared to have noticed, Hoyt was uncomfortable with such a public demonstration of wealth.

'I'm not a prostitute; so relax,' she said softly. 'I can pay my own way. I was just looking for someone interesting with whom to have dinner.'

Hoyt raised an eyebrow. She was straightforward; he appreciated that quality, and as he sneaked a longer look he realised that she was not unattractive. Her curly hair was closely cropped, her eyes were large and wide-set over a narrow nose. Her face was scarred – beneath one eye, across her chin, and through the gentle incline of her upper lip; Hoyt found that curiously endearing: the perfect women who cavorted with Malagon's generals or lived in his palaces could learn something from a woman like this. Maybe this woman's scars came from a rough-and-tumble childhood; maybe from her more recent past – either way, she had captured his attention.

He pushed his chair back and turned to order more wine for himself, and as he did so he caught sight of her tanned deerhide boots rising halfway up her calves, the soft double-wrapped type popular with those who spent much of their time on their feet. In one was stashed a bone-handled knife, sheathed in an inside flap for quick access, not the type of blade one used to slice bread or cut meat from a spit.

Hoyt smiled. His attractive dinner companion smiled back. Her teeth were straight and clean; she had obviously grown up in a privileged community, probably somewhere in Malakasia. 'So no chance I can get you to leave?' he said, this time bantering.

'Oh no, not now I've just ordered dinner. That looks delicious. How is it?'

'One of the best tenderloins I've eaten in Middle Fork.' This was the first time Hoyt had ever tasted it, anywhere in Eldarn – but it was undeniably delicious.

'Are you celebrating something?'

He shook his head. 'No. I just enjoy good food. It's my one vice.'

She laughed, and to his surprise, Hoyt found he desperately wanted to hear it again.

'Do you want to know what my vices are?' she asked.

His hand started to shake. 'No—'

'Why not?' Her seductive manner was difficult to resist; Hoyt moved his hand to keep it from rattling the plates. He enjoyed the charade of being a wealthy man, and he hoped she was enjoying her role as the temptress, but it hadn't taken him long to know who she really was.

'Because I am too busy tonight to spend time on silly pursuits.'

'Since when is love silly?'

'Since the very first time it was mistaken as love by someone – probably a man – in the throes of lust.' His hand had stopped trembling now and he deliberately picked up his fork and speared a piece of meat, then popped it into his mouth and savoured the taste.

'What a negative outlook on human emotion.' She reached across the table and took his hand, and in spite of himself he felt his heart race. Perhaps there *was* something to be said for a full-blown case of raging lust. She toyed with his fingers, almost absentmindedly. 'You need a strong woman to take you to heights of pleasure you will remember for the rest of your life.'

'Ah, now I understand.' He withdrew his hand. 'A half-aven of pleasure followed by two hundred Twinmoons of wishing I could recapture it, even once. Forgive me, but that doesn't sound like a terribly appetising offer.'

Her food arrived, and as she sorted out coins from her purse, the barman tried to steal a clear look down her tunic.

A withering glare from Hoyt sent him on his way. 'You ought to close that up. People kill for that much silver.'

'I'll be all right.' She slipped it back inside her tunic. 'You realise my offer doesn't have to be just one night.' As much as Hoyt wanted to feel the woman's fingers entwined with his again, he kept his hands busy with his cutlery.

'Ah, but it would be, wouldn't it?'

'What makes you say that?' Her voice had dropped again and Hoyt felt it resonate in his bones, stirring him from within. He wanted to clear the table and take her right there, in the tavern – but that was what she wanted him to feel; she had been manipulating him from the start. His body responded to his desire, playing into her hands.

Hoyt smiled, it had been a thoroughly enjoyable game – and now he had to end it.

He leaned in close to her, enjoying the triumphant smile that crossed her lips. 'Because, my dear, you are a thief,' he whispered, enjoying even more the sudden change of expression. 'Your entire persona screams *I am a thief*, louder than if you were standing on top of this building, screaming it out to all of Middle Fork. You have a knife tucked into a hidden sheath in your boots, which in turn are tough but more importantly, *silent*. You're wearing a tight-fitting skirt, but I would guess your loose-fitting tunic has sleeves filled with all sorts of nasty sticking and stabbing devices. Your hair is short – quite attractive, I would add – but short enough to stay out of your way when you've tucked it beneath a hood or a mask. You have exceedingly strong hands and fingers, a quick wit, and three scars on your face that I very much doubt came from playing chainball with your older brothers. You are obviously not a prostitute, and obviously not a businesswoman, but you're carrying enough silver to buy much of Middle Fork.

'So unless you're a Malakasian general's wife holidaying in the southern territories, amusing yourself with a bit of local colour, you're a thief. Probably quite a good one.'

A brief look of horror passed over her face, replaced almost immediately by a look of fear. 'Who are you?' she whispered, unobtrusively sliding one hand beneath the table.

Hoyt liked her other voice much better. 'I am the one who is going to break that hand if you don't keep it up here where I can see it.'

She complied, and he added, 'Good. Thanks. You should have listened when I asked you to go away, but I guess I was about the only target here – and I did enjoy the seduction routine; you're very good at it.'

'Pissing demons,' she said, staring at him. Without looking down, she stabbed a piece of meat and bit it off the blade, then chewed slowly. 'You're a thief,' she said finally.

'Nice to meet you. I'm Hoyt. I'm from Southport.'

Knowing she had been bested, at least on this occasion, she smiled. 'I'm Ramella. I'm from Landry.'

'A pleasure, Ramella of Landry.' Hoyt offered to pour her a goblet of wine, but she took the flagon from him and helped herself.

'You must have done well today.' She gestured towards the meal.

'Ramella,' Hoyt decided to take the risk, 'I have had one of the most glorious days of my life, and I will be completely honest with you, I don't have a heavy purse, but I do have enough for this meal, and a bit left for my room upstairs. If you actually meant what you said, I would be *very* happy to take you up on your offer – we have, after all, moved beyond that awkward "getting to know you" phase, so why not?'

Ramella leaned back in the chair, sipping her wine and fiddled with the leather thong tied loosely about her neck. Nothing dangled from it, no charms, jewellery or icons; it was just a leather tie, but Hoyt couldn't take his eyes off the way the leather strip caressed the soft skin above her tunic.

Smiling her seductive grin, Ramella leaned forward, and gestured for him to do likewise. As he did so, Hoyt could feel her breath on his cheeks, could smell the heady aroma of wine and venison. He held his breath, not wanting to cloud the air with anything but her scent. He waited, expecting her to kiss him and praying she wasn't about to knife him beneath the table.

When she spoke, he was confused – her words were nowhere in the long list of possible replies to his invitation.

Ramella of Landry leaned across the table, breathing pungent fumes into Hoyt's face, and said, 'I think he's coming out of it.'

'I think he's coming out of it,' Hannah repeated, working some of the stiffness from her shoulder. The querlis had helped – Hoyt rewrapped it each morning with a new poultice – but her arm remained immobile. She felt stronger, though, and was desperate to try going without her shoulder wrapped or her arm in a sling.

'Yes, you're right,' Alen said, 'and it worked blazingly fast. Great rutting lords, but this is a remarkable substance.'

Hoyt blinked to clear his eyes. Instead of a beautiful thief, Alen and Hannah were staring back at him. Hannah's shoulder was wrapped, and he recognised his handiwork. Cold, confused, and utterly surprised to find them here, outside, he asked, 'Where's Ramella?'

Alen laughed. 'I'd like to know that, too, Hoyt. You never mentioned her before. She sounded quite intoxicating.'

Hoyt thought his head might crack open. 'Is she here? Where are we?'

Hannah sat beside him. 'We're in Malakasia, north of the Great Pragan Range and moving towards Welstar Palace. Do you remember any of that?' There was a concerned look in her eyes.

In a rush, everything came back to him: their journey, the forest of ghosts, the pouch of bark Churn had found on the Malakasian corpse – and his crazy decision to test it out. As his memories washed over him in a wave, he started to tremble. Hannah put her good arm around him, and he revelled in the warmth of her touch.

'Unholy whores, but that was real!' he cried. 'I was *there*, Alen, there in your house. It was like yesterday – there were details I would never be able to remember now, not even on my best day with my clearest recollections. I saw it all: your house, the fireplace off that little room you called your study, the one with the green and brown rug on the floor – I haven't seen that rug in a hundred Twinmoons, but I could weave it for you, today, without missing a detail. I don't remember you smoking, though, or having a dog, but the rest of it was so real.' He paused, shaking his head as if to clear it.

'It was the day you gave me the first books in my collection. I never told you what happened afterwards, but I left your place that night and I met a woman. She was a thief, and gods, but I was in love with her.'

'Sounded more like lust from where we were sitting,' Hannah said.

'Call it what you like,' Hoyt chuckled, 'but she was the sexiest woman I've ever seen. I asked her to stay with me that night. I couldn't help it; my whole head was caving in just looking at her. I couldn't—' He paused, considered his rambling storyline and ended with, 'I don't suppose you need all those details, do you?'

'We need a few,' Alen said. 'I don't recall smoking, and I have never had a dog.'

Several tumblers clicked into place in Hoyt's mind. 'The dog. Hannah, *you* remembered a dog, too, both when you came through the forest of ghosts, and again when I set the bone in your shoulder. Isn't that right?'

She nodded. 'It was more than remembering him. When I was in the forest, it was as if reality had changed. I was there with my parents, and the dog was there too – that dog was there at my parent's house in Denver, *but we never had a dog*. I spent a long time wondering which were my real memories.'

'How very odd.' Hoyt shook the last of the fog from his mind. 'What do you think, Alen? Is it just some strange effect of the narcotics in this bark?'

'It must be,' Alen said. 'I wouldn't worry about it. It's clear that we all experienced the most memorable times in our lives, and whether they were a highest high – collecting that medical library in Middle Fork – or a lowest low, like Churn's family massacre or my leaving Reia in England, the memories are as vivid as any dream we've ever experienced. And they're repetitive and very real – and captivating, in that none of us have been able to escape them without some outside intervention.'

'What happened to me?'

'You were out all day, so we cut the strip holding the piece of bark around your neck. It wasn't long after we took it off that you started to come back to us.' Hannah held up the thong on which Alen had carefully affixed a piece of the bark.

'A leather strip,' Hoyt said under his breath. 'That's another detail.'

'What?' Hannah asked.

'It's nothing, but Alen is right, some of the details are things we seem to be adding. The dog is one. I don't know why you added it to your memories, and I can only guess that I added it because you mentioned it after your last episode, so you must have put the idea in my head. The dog appeared in my memory as an added bonus, just like this leather strip: I knew you had attached the bark to my neck with it, and as a result it appeared in my memory as an exceedingly seductive piece of jewellery Ramella was wearing the night we met. But I can't remember if she really was wearing a leather thong around her neck the night we met.'

'She probably wasn't,' Hannah said. 'I am convinced we had a dog at the house in Denver, but I *know* we never did.'

Hoyt turned to Alen. 'Well, let's document that as a side-effect.'

'Added details and embellished memories?'

'Ramella's breasts didn't get bigger, if that's what you mean, but yes, the dog and the leather thong both seem very real to me now – yet I know you never had a dog when I used to visit in those days.'

'Right, and I didn't smoke, either.'

'There's that, too. The dog sort of makes sense, in an odd, shared way between me and Hannah, but the smoking? I can't figure it.'

'I don't know either, but we have learned a few things. We've

342

discovered that the bark appears to work on everyone – you went under in moments, even though you were unaffected by the forest.' Alen was trying to tally a mental list before any elusive details escaped him. 'That's why you volunteered, because we already knew it would work on the rest of us. You looked as though you'd go on reliving that one day over and over again for the rest of your life if we didn't cut the strip from around your throat. And like Hannah, you added details to your memories. Neither Churn nor I can recall adding anything to ours.' Alen looked to the big man, who nodded in agreement.

Alen went on, 'You were under its spell all day, like we were, but you were able to communicate with us – at least to hear us.'

'How do you know that?'

'Look,' Alen said, and stepped aside to reveal a stack of firewood, enough logs to keep a significant blaze going for several days.

Hoyt didn't understand; he signed to Churn, 'Pissing demons, did you think we were going to stay here all Twinmoon?'

Churn smirked and signed, 'You did it.'

'I did this?' Hoyt walked over to the pile and took a log from the top. He looked at it uncomprehendingly, then dropped it into the fire, as if to confirm that the stack was real. 'How did I do this if I was back there all day?' Hoyt gestured into the past as if it existed somewhere on the other side of their camp.

Churn went on, 'Alen asked you to get some firewood. You did.'

'But— This can't be. Alen, I was there with you. It was a conversation we had for maybe half an aven. We ate, then I left to steal a wheelbarrow. It took an aven, start to finish, if that.'

Alen crossed to his friend. 'You collected firewood for nearly four avens today, Hoyt. One of us was always with you, but you worked nonstop until we made you sit down and cut away the bark.'

'But I don't feel tired,' he protested. 'Look at how much wood there is: I'd be flat on my back if I worked that hard! And look at the size of those logs – I could barely lift one of those on my own, never mind pile them up like that!'

'That's another interesting detail we need to consider as we analyse this bark and examine the forest of ghosts more closely – I think I've an idea of why Nerak wants so much. Imagine what he could make the people of Malakasia do … Hoyt, we hung this around your neck and the bark took you – it was quick and painless, and you were gone. I protected my fingers as I fixed this piece to your throat, Hoyt, and it barely touched your flesh all day, but you didn't break from your memories for four avens *and* you worked steadily the whole time. Imagine what might happen if Nerak uses this on his army, or his servants – and what if he gives it to them internally, what might happen then?'

'But I'm not tired,' Hoyt repeated, still unwilling to believe the evidence.

'Still,' Hannah said, 'we should take rooms in the next town. We don't know what might happen once he starts travelling again. He might pass out or fall asleep. We should be someplace warm and safe tonight.'

'I agree,' Alen said and began packing up.

'Alen, are you suggesting that Nerak would be able to make these effects permanent?'

'I shudder to think that, but yes, he might. Imagine the workforce he would have—'

'But would Hoyt have been able to make us do things when we went through the forest of ghosts? Gather firewood or build mortar outhouses or sack Sparta?'

'I had trouble getting you to walk most of the time,' Hoyt agreed.

Alen looked up from the saddle bags. 'That is precisely why I believe Nerak wants the bark. He can refine it, or do *something* to control it, I'd bet my bones on that.'

'But he already has the occupation army, the taxes and tariffs – what more could he squeeze out of Eldarn that he would need a village full of hysterical, screaming, babbling slaves?' Hoyt still wasn't convinced.

Alen frowned. Was it obvious only to him? 'Nerak wants what Nerak has always wanted, my friends: supreme power, power and control over everything. He wants life and death in his hands. He wants to reign like a god over all he can see and all he can imagine. There is an awesome evil waiting out there for Nerak to open the door and when it arrives, it will bring down death and devastation, and Nerak will finally have what he wants. He will have brought about the end of all things.' *And he wants Pikan. But he cannot have her, not any more.*

'Nerak can use this bark to control the minds of the living, and he can revel in our suffering while he works to bring about the end of us all. So to answer your question: Nerak would want this because no one else in Eldarn would be hideous enough to ensnare who knows how many in the worst nightmare of their lives while they toil away at whatever reprehensible task he has dreamed up, either just for his own enjoyment, or, worse, for the eventual destruction of all we know.'

Alen kicked out their campfire. 'We will see things between here and Welstar Palace, even *inside* Welstar Palace, that will stay with us for the rest of our lives, and whatever it is he is using this bark for will be one of those horrors. You can bet on it, my friends.'

Hoyt swallowed hard. 'Now I'm feeling a bit tired.'

'You and me both,' Hannah said.

Alen smiled and tucked the pouch back inside his cloak. 'Then let's get ourselves to a nice warm inn. We'll go wild and get comfortable beds with down pillows and soft wool blankets.'

'And venison, with gravy – tenderloin,' Hoyt added in a burst of enthusiasm.

'Expensive choice, Hoyt, but you've had a hard day gathering firewood.' Alen considered the immense pile of sticks and branches. 'Venison all round then.'

That night, Hoyt fell asleep earlier than usual, though he really hadn't suffered from any overwhelming feeling of fatigue. Churn followed his friend a short time later, carrying a flagon of wine as an aid to sleep; Hannah heard the wooden steps groan and creak in protest as the big man passed.

Alen reached for the remaining wine and started to refill Hannah's goblet when she stopped him, protesting, 'No thanks, Alen, I'm already getting dizzy. I'll have some of the water, please.'

'As you like.' He complied, pouring from the stoneware pitcher beside Hoyt's empty trencher. 'But I don't recommend the water – it's a boring vintage, horribly similar to last year's.'

Hannah chuckled at the reference to her world. 'How many trips did you make across the Fold?'

'Too many to count,' he answered. 'I learned so many languages on my journeys back and forth that they started to become confused in my head, all those tenses and cases jumbling together. Do you know how many ways there are to make reference to pasta in Italian?'

'No.' She grinned at the thought.

'No one does, but there have to be hundreds, maybe thousands. All that *oni, illi, elli*, I just want it in a bowl, gods, is that too much to ask?' He slapped the table with one hand, a little drunk himself, the first time Hannah had seen Alen like this since they had left Praga. He drank, and held the goblet against his chest as he sat back in his chair. 'Yes, there were many wonderful journeys.'

'Yet I see so little of our world here. Why is that?'

Alen sat forward, the long-ago lost teacher in him coming into hazy focus for a moment. 'Oh, there used to be much more, but we have let it all fade, or we've forgotten how to do things properly. It's remarkable how quickly an advanced society on the edge of greatness can disintegrate when people don't have what they need to survive. The whole world's focus changes, turns inwards, and progress grinds to a halt. Back then, it was industrial-age technology, that's what we were after at the time: printing, education, public health, medicine … We had made such progress here, and our own scientists and researchers were finding ways to enrich our efforts with the magic inherent in this land. But those days, the exciting news was the industrial boom. Gods, but I would have given anything to figure out how to bring back a blast furnace.'

'Why not just build one here?'

'We would have, if Nerak hadn't ruined everything. Do you know that there were metal ships in your world at the time? Imagine a navy with metal ships …'

'I don't have to imagine it, Alen,' Hannah said, reaching for the water pitcher again, 'I've seen it all, and you're right: a fleet of wooden ships would be sunk in less than half an aven. The fight would be over before our modern ships had appeared over the horizon.'

Alen was hanging on her every word. 'So it remains a wondrous place then?'

'We have some way to go still, but all things considered, it is a remarkable place, yes. Mind you, there are drawbacks, and we've got our oddities too: we have to print warnings on coffee cups saying the drink's hot! Can you imagine anything that absurd?'

Alen, a little taken aback, asked, 'Is your coffee not served hot any more? I remember it being quite delicious that way. Tea also.'

'Like I said,' Hannah dismissed it with a wave of her hand, 'some oddities and a few drawbacks.'

'Regardless, I would love to see it again. One more trip.' He stacked his plate neatly on top of Hoyt's, then added Churn's.

'You can,' Hannah said. 'You should all come back with me. You've said yourself, time and again, that there's nothing left for you here. Your family is gone. Why stay just to die? Is it because of Lessek? Is it really his intention that you live this long, in solitude, then just march into Welstar Palace and die?'

'No, I'm sure there's more, and I'm sure it has something to do with you. But after that's done, I will rest.'

Hannah changed the subject. 'Tell me about Nerak.'

'Why? I was having a nice time.' Alen glanced towards the door as three soldiers entered the tavern. They looked as if they were off duty for the evening. The former Larion Senator scowled at them. 'Grand. And now we add these scum to the evening. This place is falling apart around us, Hannah. We should flee into the night, or at least until we find a different tavern.'

'Right here will be fine, Alen, and as for that crew, just ignore them. All we're doing is having a late dinner and a few drinks.' She filled a goblet with water and pushed it across to the old man; having him falling-down drunk wouldn't do now, not with Malakasians in the room. She would have been happy to ignore one night of revelry, but if he began making disparaging comments now, it could mean the imprisonment and torture of them both. 'Here,' she said, 'have some of this.'

Alen shrugged. He was too tired to argue with her. Gripping both goblets, he asked, 'Now, what were we talking about?'

Hannah raised a finger as if to say, *wait one moment*. The soldiers were heading for the bar and she wanted to listen to their conversation as they passed. She couldn't glean much, just a few snippets. She still wasn't familiar with the curious lilt of the Malakasian dialect; she'd never be able to fool anyone into believing she was a native.

Was in Orindale Harbour, but I hear it sank, she heard.

Not seen him in a Moon at least.

Rutter may have gone down with the ship.

Already breaking up. Whole brigades moving out of Orindale, rutting Seron, too.

Generals don't know whether to shit or scratch.

Glad we're not them, eh?

Right. What's drinking?

Across the table, Alen waited, folding and refolding a cloth napkin repeatedly as the soldiers passed, determined not to make eye contact with them. Hannah immediately felt better; perhaps he wasn't as drunk as he'd appeared.

'Well, that was interesting,' she said quietly, once they were out of earshot.

'Not now,' Alen cautioned, even more quietly. 'We'll talk about it later.'

She went back to her previous question. 'Why don't you want to talk about Nerak?'

'Because he is a mean, reprehensible, smelly old fart, and he always has been.' Alen grinned. Hannah imagined he must have been quite attractive an eternity ago, when he was young.

'Come on,' she urged, 'you two worked together, lived together, built the Larion Senate together ... at least tell me about those days, before everything began to unravel.'

Alen shifted in his curious way, adjusting himself and then coming to rest exactly where he had been before. 'I suppose there were good Twinmoons, but things began to come apart over a very long period of time. There were grim shadows of our future quite early in our time together at Sandcliff; there was a darkness to Nerak from the beginning. Sometimes the pall over him was so thick you felt as though you could peel it off and paste it on a wall if you could get close enough to him.'

'He was frightening?'

'No, not at first. In the beginning, he was contagiously enthusiastic, driven unlike any of us. But his lust for power and knowledge coupled with his desire for Pikan drove him mad.'

'All over a woman?' Hannah looked askance at him. 'I find it hard to believe Nerak would allow everything to come apart over the love of one woman.'

'He didn't allow everything to come apart. Instead, he pushed too far too quickly. He was well on his way to becoming the greatest sorcerer since Lessek, Lessek's heir apparent, but he was prone to bouts of anger – well, rage really. He pressed himself too hard, delved too deeply into the spell table. In the end, it consumed him. Would he have done it if Pikan had loved him instead of me? Eventually, yes, I think so – but I also believe he was taken by something hideous because he was in there too frequently and too early in his development as a sorcerer. If Pikan had loved him, he might have made different decisions.'

'She must have been quite a woman.'

'She was. Since her death, I've lived almost a thousand Twinmoons sequestered in the same house in the same town, never venturing further than it took to buy greenroot, potatoes and pepper weed. I'd say she was quite something.'

Hannah checked the soldiers at the bar were still engrossed in their beers and said, 'But she didn't choose him, Alen, she chose you, and that was entirely her choice to make. And no matter how many ways you pick it apart, or how long you hide in the basement blaming yourself, Nerak's fall from grace was his own doing.'

'Oh, I don't disagree with you; it's just that he had so much to offer. It's really quite—'

'Tragic.'

'Tragic, yes.'

'Did you never have times when you collaborated and succeeded in reaching the Senate's common goals?'

'Absolutely,' Alen said, 'many times, especially in the beginning. That may be why we all stayed so long, despite the darkness hidden in Nerak. We were teachers and leaders, but we were magicians, and even though magic was much more common in Eldarn than in Denver, it was not always easy for us to find a niche in Eldarni society. Before the Larion Senate, if you were a magician, you became a healer, an entertainer, sometimes an artist, but never a teacher. It took a long time for people to feel comfortable knowing their children were working with sorcerers.'

'But your early successes changed some of that?'

'That's what made it so special. All over Eldarn people wanted their children to come to Sandcliff to study at the university; we even had waiting lists. Pikan, Nerak and I often travelled together to find those who showed more potential.'

Hannah, caught up in the old man's tale, poured herself more wine. 'So students had varying degrees of skill?'

'Oh yes, we'd get urgent messages from parents convinced their little one was Eldarn's next Lessek – mostly when some child managed to wilt the flowers on the mantel, or perhaps rolled a few beans around a trencher. We made trips to find the strong ones, the children who blew their grandfather's barn down with a breath, who lit the dog on fire with a thought, or who lured all the region's fireflies into the house for reading light.'

Hannah mimicked the mothers she knew: 'My kid's gifted. No, *my* kid's gifted. *Your* kid? Stop it. My kid's gifted.' She laughed. 'Is that where you were going when you had the fight?'

The old man's mood darkened; Hannah was sorry she had asked the question. 'No. That trip, we were heading for Larion Isle, where we went to work new spells and to document those that were successful. And to protect the rest of Eldarn from those that ... well, weren't successful. No sense holding back now, eh? That trip was the beginning of the end. I know I said that there had been something dark about Nerak, but that was when we should have realised that the Larion Senate was doomed as long as Nerak had access to Lessek's key.'

'I thought the fight was over Pikan,' Hannah said.

'It was. The initial confrontation was two lovesick fools fighting over a woman. Can you believe it? And he could have killed me. I know he wanted to, but his love for her stopped him, I'm sure of it. Nerak knew she would have been crushed if he had killed me, so I came out of it with a nasty ankle injury and a sorely bruised sense of my own abilities as a sorcerer. It ruined the trip to Larion Isle. I'd always enjoyed those journeys, because Pikan and Nerak led the magicians and I went just as a researcher – and because it was a great boat trip.' He finished the wine and started in on the water. 'This tastes dreadful. Do you want some tecan?'

'I'd love some, sure. Do we have enough money? I know it's a bad time to ask now that we've eaten the most expensive meal in the place, but how are we holding up?'

'I haven't been out in nearly a thousand Twinmoons, Hannah.' He gestured for the barman. 'We have plenty.'

'Good. Then, yes, please. It will help clear my head.'

'So where was I? Oh, yes, the fight: I hurt my ankle and lied to everyone that I did it getting off the ship. He wasn't telling anyone the truth, so I let it go as well, but he began to pick at me. First, he insisted on climbing the highest mountains on the island just to run the tests. Pikan always went along, because someone had to keep the records. That would have been my role, but I couldn't get there. Then there were the walking sticks I cut. I must have cut myself five or six, and most of them were burned when it was his turn to set the campfire. He knew they were my crutches, but he cut them up and tossed them in the flames just to be irritating. Some mornings I would wake to find my sticks on the other side of my room, or out in the common room.'

'That sounds awfully childish, Alen, especially for someone who took himself so seriously.'

'Love makes fools of us all, Hannah. If you haven't discovered that, yet, be patient; you will.'

Hannah thought back to her drive up the canyon from Denver to Idaho Springs to look for Steven. Part of her had gone to confront him; if he wanted their relationship to end, he needed to say so. She supposed a part of her had gone because she was genuinely worried something might have happened to him or to Mark, but Hannah knew in her heart that she had driven up the canyon, broken into the house and fallen victim to the ugly rug because she had been falling in love with Steven Taylor. And she had not wanted to be the only one – if her heart was going to break, Hannah wanted it to be on her terms, not at 4.30 a.m. along some freezing cold trail beneath Decatur Peak. 'Perhaps I have already,' she murmured.

She turned the conversation back to Larion Isle. 'Was the trip a bust because you two were fighting, or did you get what you needed while you were out there?'

Alen's brow furrowed. 'I have been asking myself that question on and off for the past thousand Twinmoons, and I have to say honestly that I don't know. We wrote the Windscrolls on that trip. Pikan called them that because it had been so rutting windy the entire time we were out there. How anything ever grew on that island was a mystery to me. Anyway, the Windscrolls: there were at least three, spells for protection, deception, destruction, culling minerals from the land, cleansing contaminated water, numbing the body during medical procedures – even killing viral and bacterial infections in people and livestock. The big spells were the first few on the First Windscroll: common-phrase spells for deception, destruction, mining, farming, mass production of goods from raw materials, grand spells we hoped would have a sweeping impact on Eldarn.'

'Destruction? Deception? And you wanted these to have a world-wide impact?' Hannah was incredulous. Alen could read it in her face.

'Clear cutting land for lumber or blasting through bedrock to get at rich veins of ore, that sort of destruction. I suppose you might say they were spells that helped us control the devastation inherent in powerful magic.'

'And deception?'

'Similar in a sense to destruction; magic has an enormous capacity to change the way we perceive things. Think about the dog in your parents' home. You're convinced that dog was real, but you *know* the dog was not there. You were deceived by magic. We wrote spells to control that deceptive ability; it helped us continue to work spells in the table without waking the next day believing we were all dancers or professional bellamir players.' That was the best explanation he could give for the moment.

The tecan arrived and they paused to pour out and sip from the steaming mugs. Hannah inhaled deeply, then asked, 'So what happened then?'

'You know the rest. We brought the Windscrolls back to Sandcliff and left for England. There was a common-phrase spell for cleansing contaminated water that Pikan was particularly interested in, so she and I made the research trip to Durham, to study how they handled waste and waste-water. She carried Reia to term, and I did all the work. When we returned, everything was crumbling in Gorsk, and we swore we would get back to England, even if it meant confronting Nerak and perhaps losing one of us in the process.'

'But you never had the chance?'

'I had to go to Middle Fork. It was a short assignment. I ended up staying there for most of my life.' He stared across the table at her, still suffering the anguish of a decision made almost a century and a half earlier.

'Would you like some more?' Hannah said, offering the tecan jug, hoping to stop the old man breaking apart. She changed the subject. 'Do you suppose my friends are alive?'

'Steven and—'

'Mark. Mark Jenkins and Steven Taylor. I'm certain they came across the Fold together sometime during the day before I landed in Southport.'

Alen shook his head. 'I cannot begin to say, Hannah. I'm sorry.'

Her efforts to distract him were failing. He was lost in England, reliving the worst decision of his life, without the help of any enchanted bark or the forest of ghosts.

She tried again. 'Have you given any more thought to why Nerak might want so much of that bark?' She tried to be as upbeat as she could.

'You don't need to do this, Hannah.' Alen cut her short. 'I have lived with this for a long time, long before you were born, and I will live with it for the time I have left. Ignoring or forgetting it would mitigate everything that my life has become. I want those memories clear when this all spins itself out.'

Hannah nodded.

'When we get near Welstar Palace, I will try to contact Fantus. I hope it was he who opened the doors at Sandcliff.'

'Yes, I remember,' she said. 'If it was him, we live. If it was Nerak, we die.'

'You don't cloud the air with a lot of unnecessary details; that's an admirable trait. And yes, if Fantus is at Sandcliff, and if we are exceedingly lucky, he may know something of your friends.'

'I appreciate you asking him, but why contact him in the first place?' Hannah asked.

'He has been out and about these past Twinmoons; I felt him working spells, before I lost much of my ability to feel anything at all. Perhaps he knows something of Welstar Palace.' Alen rose to pay their bill. 'Good night, Hannah.'

'Good night,' she said, worrying that he might succumb to his grief, his alcohol poisoning or his guilt and die before dawn. The wooden stairs were silent as he passed.

Hannah suddenly felt as lost and alone as she had felt since her arrival. The three Malakasian soldiers drinking at the bar were a stark reminder of the dangers that had found her so soon after her arrival in Southport. Turning quickly, she took the rest of the tecan and a mug and followed Alen upstairs.

THE TOPGALLANT BOARDING HOUSE

The sky had just begun to whiten in the east when Brexan woke. The Ravenian Sea and the salt marsh remained dark, insubstantial in the pre-dawn aven. Slipping into her tunic, she crept into the front room, stoked the overnight embers and put on a kettle of water; Nedra Daubert, the woman who owned the Topgallant Boarding House, was happy to wake to a ready-made fire and a pot of tecan already brewing. She had asked no questions when Sallax and Brexan arrived, dirty, shivering and without any bags, but taken the last silver coin Brexan had and invited the couple to stay on with her until their luck changed.

'There's enough silver here to last the next Moon, and that's with meals,' she told them, clucking around them in a motherly fashion. 'If you don't have any more, or you haven't earned any by then, well, I suppose you'll be able to stay on for a while after that. What difference does it make? That dog-rutting Malagon taxes most of what I take anyway.'

Sallax had grinned and they had accepted her offer to join her for a flagon of wine and a few slices of just-baked bread.

For the next twenty days, the Topgallant had seen only two other boarders, travelling merchants who stayed a night or two before moving on, but Nedra's front room was invariably filled to bursting every night. Her seafood stew was justly renowned. Brexan and Sallax helped out in the kitchen, then, worn out from the countless trips back and forth between the front room, the bar and the kitchen, the three tired workers would eat their fill while Nedra counted the evening's copper Mareks. Each time they helped, the innkeeper would separate out a few coins, slide them across to Brexan, and say, 'There's a bit of spending money, and you've earned another five nights' room and meals.'

Brexan tried to argue that she was being too generous, but Nedra would not listen to the younger woman's objections. After a while, she realised Nedra loved having company around the Topgallant, and any loss of revenue was a small price to pay. There was no danger of the Topgallant going out of business; the boarding part was just an excuse to have new faces around the house.

Brexan wondered if she might one day live like this: with Versen dead, the former Malakasian soldier worried she might find herself keeping a tidy house, caring for her pets, cooking seven-course meals for one, and suffering in silent loneliness until the end of her days. She would have liked to have stayed on at the Topgallant, keeping her new friend company, but that wasn't possible. Sallax's shoulder was growing stronger every day, and it would soon be time to exact their revenge on the fat merchant and the spy. Killing Carpello and Jacrys would result in another wave of citywide raids, public hangings and general unrest and neither she nor Sallax would feel comfortable placing Nedra in harm's way after all she'd done for them.

Instead, they would move west into Praga in hopes of finding Garec and the staff-wielding foreigner.

When Brexan returned to their room, Sallax was awake and standing at the window watching dawn colour the marsh where Brynne's body had washed ashore. They had gone looking for her together their first morning at the Topgallant, but Brynne was gone, long ago washed out to sea on a Twinmoon tide. Sallax was recovering well; he stood at the window lifting a heavy log he had pilfered from Nedra's woodpile, to exercise his damaged arm.

'Good morning,' Brexan said cheerily.

'I did it, you know.'

'What's that?' She folded their blankets and draped them over the foot of the bed.

'I killed Gilmour, me, Sallax Farro of Estrad. Just me. I did it.'

'I know,' she said, straightening the sheets. 'But Versen told me about Nerak, the one controlling Prince Malagon, and you didn't have much of a choice. He wasn't playing fair with you.'

'I know, but I should be stronger than that.'

'Aren't you strong enough? Who else could have survived the way you did, on the streets, eating what you ate?' She shuddered. 'And yet here you are, having just bested a Seron with a knife.' She moved to his side, but he avoided looking at her. 'You may be the strongest of us all, Sallax, and you're getting more so every day.'

'No, I'm not.' His words fell like stones. 'There's something wrong with me, Brexan. Those wraiths did something, and I don't know if time will be enough to set me free – I don't even know if I want to be free from it.'

She turned to look out the window with him.

Sallax went on, 'It's as if a curtain has been drawn across my mind. For a long time I couldn't see anything through it, just shadows.'

'But now?'

'Now I can see, and think, and remember – some things anyway – but I still can't find the centre of things. It's a place in my mind, my heart, my soul ... I don't rutting know, but it's the place where *I* used to be, the centre point from which I used to look out at the world.' He paused.

'And?' Brexan prompted gently.

'Now I'm not allowed back there. For some reason I'm off to one side,' he gestured, 'where I can see and think and do, but it's as if the focal point of me is over there somewhere in the corner and I can't get back there.'

'Is that the wraiths' curse, or is it guilt?'

Sallax grunted in amusement. 'Which is worse?'

Again, Brexan had no reply.

'I think the only person who could lift this last veil – and it's not black any more, it's just irritatingly dark, as though someone has drawn a cloud over the sun and everything has faded slightly – well, the only way I could open it again would be to see Gilmour, to explain it to him, and to have him tell me that he understands what happened. So maybe it *is* just guilt. Gilmour never wanted anything except to serve the people of Eldarn – and *I* arranged his execution. I used to sneak out of camp after everyone had gone to sleep; Steven caught me twice. I would meet him in the forest, or in an inn, wherever he ordered. All I had to do was wander back the way we'd come and he would call to me, reach out for me, pull me in.'

'Jacrys?'

'Jacrys. Yes. I told him everything – except that we didn't have Lessek's key; somehow that seemed too important, it was bigger than Gilmour and me. I couldn't bring myself to tell him that. I hated Rona and everything about Rona, because raiders had killed my family. I truly believed they had been led by Gilmour. I wanted to go to Praga, but whenever I thought about it, something kept me in Estrad. Now I know it was Prince Malagon. The wraith, O'Reilly, showed me that.'

'But think of the work you'll do from here on. Isn't that enough?'

'I don't know.' Finally he looked at her. 'I wish he were here. I would tell him everything, and then I would beg him to forgive me.'

'He would.'

'That's exactly what Steven tried to tell me the morning Lahp broke my shoulder, but I didn't want to hear it. I guess a part of me still doesn't; I need to hear it from him. I suppose when I get to the Northern Forest I will ask him.'

'Maybe that's why the wraiths didn't kill you that night in the river – maybe they realised you needed time to figure things out, and to recognise that Gilmour's death wasn't really your fault. Maybe they set you up: gave you a sort of vantage point from where you could see and think and *be* Sallax of Estrad, but from where you could also observe yourself healing. Maybe they did it on purpose.'

'They were a marauding band of homicidal monsters, Brexan. They did this to me to amuse themselves. They soaked up my pain and spun it so it would torture me for ever; much more entertaining than simply killing me. You told me that.'

Brexan nodded. 'You're right. But perhaps it was a gift anyway.'

'To live like this?'

'To live at all. Do something with it, Sallax: make them regret not killing you.'

The sun finally crested the horizon and the salt marsh burst into glistening gold as the sun's early rays refracted off the thin ice that covered everything.

Shielding her eyes, Brexan said, 'I think we ought to distract you.'

'Carpello?'

'That's a good place to start.'

Turning back to the window, Sallax squinted. 'It's the perfect day for it.'

Carpello leaned back in his chair, watching the girl, Rishta, Rexa, whatever her name was. She had disposed of her skirt as she entered the room and the gossamer-thin, loose-fitting tunic that had already fallen off her shoulders barely covered her tightly encased bottom – those breeches looked painted-on, he thought to himself, barely restraining the drool as he watched for the curve of her breasts through the almost see-through material. Craning in his chair, he felt like a schoolboy. RishtaRexawhatever's brown hair hung in drooping ringlets, jouncing about and getting in the way: just when he felt certain he was going to get a warm-up glimpse of that delicious young package, her cursed hair swept down like a dressing-room curtain.

What kind of a prostitute was she? You don't take your skirt off as soon as you come into the room; that's not how it's supposed to happen. Carpello felt a flush of anger redden his face; with it came a stirring in his groin. *Yes, give her a good beating: teach her some good whoring technique.* He felt his body respond to the thought of violence as he watched her pour drinks and slice off slivers of fennaroot – that was mostly for herself, but he would have a slice himself tonight, perhaps two. *Have all you want, my dear,* he thought lasciviously, *for tonight you are going to learn how to be seductive – and what happens when you get it wrong . . .*

RishtaRexawhatever stood up, the loose neckline of her tunic falling closed, and stared vacantly at Carpello: too much fennaroot. Now she was adrift in a narcotic dream of colourful nymphs, floating castles and great winged horses, and that made Carpello angry, that the girl was so wrecked before she'd completed her night's work. His anger fuelled his erection; he didn't care; his pleasure was yet to come and she would do just fine – in fact, once she realised what was about to happen, that might even sober her up; it did so many of them.

Although he didn't much like using whores, especially fennaroot addicts like this one, they all retreated back into that state of youthful shyness he desired. It was true that they couldn't cry like the virgins when they finally understood where he was about to take them; those nights were like grand holidays, glorious events – but even the most street-hardened prostitute managed a satisfactory squeal or two when she realised what was happening to her.

There was no fighting back, of course: Carpello was not a strong man, but he knew how to use his considerable weight to his best advantage. This street whore with the droopy hair and the floppy breasts would be shrieking in terror and pain before the night was over, and no fennaroot haze was deep enough to protect her from that.

As she eyed him in what he was certain she considered a seductive manner, Carpello thought she looked like she had just smelled something disagreeable. He longed to beat that absurd pout off her face. Standing fully erect now, rock-hard in his excitement, he moved to take her. RishtaRexawhatever pulled the thin tunic over her head, exposing a soft roll of flab hanging over her skin-tight breeches. Carpello, distracted by it, ignored the breasts he had been trying so diligently to glimpse earlier; having them bared in front of him wasn't nearly as enticing.

'You're fat,' he said, amused.

She giggled, sucking on one fingertip and beckoning him closer.

Carpello smiled, but made no move to unfasten his belt; there would be time for that later.

When he punched her in the face, she screeched, a short, high-pitched, wavering cry, and as RishtaRexawhatever tumbled over the table, spilling the wine and fennaroot onto the floor, Carpello felt himself about to burst. She rolled onto her side, still too lost in her drugged haze to cry, and pushed herself up on one arm, shaking her head as if to clear it. Then Carpello kicked her in the ribs and she fell back to the floor again, wheezing, fighting to catch her breath.

RishtaRexawhatever reached up feebly to ward off the huge man descending through the hazy fog of her nightmare, but it was too late.

He was on her.

Normally he preferred to start slowly, squeezing a breast a bit too firmly, or biting a little too deeply, and sometimes he would be gently corrected, told he was playing too rough, and then, then he would deliver his first few punches, still nothing brutal, not that early, for he liked to feel his excitement build, the great waves of pleasure in his loins intensifying and he raised the levels of brutality: beating, biting, scratching, choking— until he felt himself explode in pleasure.

But tonight he was too angry, angry that he had allowed her so much fennaroot; that he had allowed her tunic and hair to infuriate him; that he had not made her put her skirt back at the start ... Although he was aroused, the little slut had already cheated him out of a night of true ecstasy by forcing him to hit her so hard and so early. She was a sneaky whore, a trickster slut prostitute with a roll of flab, two floppy breasts and a filthy, sneaky demeanour, and he hated that about her, and now he would make her regret tricking him into punching her.

Carpello's heart was hammering; he was soaked in sweat and panting. He *had* to get himself under control or he would fall over, dead ... He raised his fist, his fat fingers closed together tightly in a vicious human cudgel. On the floor, RishtaRexawhatever squirmed, moaning and slapping at his great bulging gut with her hands, tiny little things in comparison with his; Carpello barely felt them.

'You ruined what could have been a pleasant evening,' he gasped. 'You tricked me, and I don't appreciate that. I wanted this to be a nice night for both of us, but now you've ruined it, and I have to punish you.'

'No, plea—' RishtaRexawhatever's voice failed as Carpello's fist slammed into her face, shattering her nose and sending frothy, mucus-filled blood splattering across her cheeks and onto his expensive rug.

'There we go,' Carpello shouted, almost singing, rubbing his erection furiously against her stomach as she writhed, desperate to escape. He reared back again. 'One more just like the last, what do you say?'

The prostitute screamed, the fennaroot fog well and truly dissipated now, and a great white light burst in her mind as unbridled terror took over. She wailed like a child, terrified of the dark, still hitting fruitlessly at his immeasurable bulk, but he didn't budge. RishtaRexawhatever tumbled away into the dark recesses of her mind as she waited for the great hammer of his fist to fall back into her face.

There was a thud, an audible grunt.

Then Carpello fell off her. He slumped to the floor and she heard the wine goblets clink together. Something broke – maybe the ceramic plate she'd sliced the fennaroot on.

Then there was silence, broken only by her ragged, uncontrollable sobs.

'Up here, dear,' a soothing voice said after a while. RishtaRexawhatever felt someone take her by the forearms and she lashed out again, shrieking, 'No! No! Get off!'

'It's all right,' the same voice said calmly, kindly, 'It's all right. He's gone. She felt the hands take hers; they were small, a woman's hands. Slowly she forced open one eye – the other was already swollen shut – and she could dimly make out a pleasant-faced woman kneeling beside her holding a blanket. 'Here, wrap yourself up in this and let me help you up,' she said. 'What's your name?'

Name? The question rattled around in her head; after a while she whispered, 'Rishta.'

'Here we go, Rishta, drink some water, and then let me look at your face. Is anything broken?'

'I— I don't know,' she croaked. 'I hurt all over, but I don't think so.' With the strange woman's help she managed to limp to the armchair the merchant had been using, but the stench of his musty

360

sweat rose up from it and she started shaking again. 'Not here,' she said. 'I can't sit here.'

'All right,' the woman said, helping her up again, 'let's try here.'

As Rishta sat down on the ornately carved sofa, adrenalin flushing the last of the drugs from her system, she tried to regain some composure. For the first time she realised there was a second man in the room with them. Carpello lay still on the floor. 'Is he dead?' she asked in a soft voice, as if he might hear.

'Gods-rut-a-whore, but I hope so,' the woman replied, then added, 'Sorry.'

She didn't sound in the least bit sorry and despite herself, Rishta laughed. Pain flared from her broken nose. 'Don't worry about it. I've heard worse. Who are you?'

'I'm Brexan Carderic. This is Sallax. Please don't worry – we came to get him.' She gestured towards the hummock of flab splayed awkwardly across the floor. 'He's a killer, a traitor.' Brexan pulled a chair up and sat down. 'Rishta, I need to set your nose. It'll hurt like a rutting mule kick, but it'll have to be done. I see you've had a bit of fennaroot—'

'A bit too much,' Rishta admitted. 'I might throw up.'

'I don't care. I hate these rugs anyway. You can chuck up all you like. If you've got a little fennaroot in your system, this won't hurt as much as it would if we waited an aven or two.'

The prostitute trembled. 'Do we have to? Is it bad?'

'It's fine if you want to smell what's cooking off to starboard for the rest of your life.'

Again Rishta laughed. 'All right, go ahead, but try to be quick.'

'Okay, let's have you lying down. I think it'll be easier that way.'

Rishta pulled the blanket tighter and allowed herself to be stretched out on the soft cushions of Carpello's sofa. 'Maybe this way I can bleed *and* throw up on his furniture too,' she mumbled, trying not to show her fear.

'We'll make an evening of it,' Brexan agreed. She reached for the girl's shattered nose, clasped it firmly and, without warning, shifted it back into place. As the cartilage crunched beneath her fingers she felt her stomach flop and a gust of nausea blew through her.

Rishta's screech faded to a moan.

'You rest there for a while,' Brexan said. She looked around and picked up the napkin that had been covering the fennaroot platter. 'Here, for the blood,' she said, passing it to Rishta.

'Thank you – I think. Is it straight?' She mopped up the fresh blood and squinted with her one good eye, but she couldn't see a thing.

'Nearly perfect.' Brexan said as she considered her handiwork. 'It looks a good deal better than mine, even all swollen and bloody. Imagine that.'

Rishta giggled, wiped away tears and blood, and rested her head back against the cushions while Brexan turned to Sallax.

'Is he dead?' she asked quietly.

'No.' Sallax grimaced.

'Good. Let's wake him up.' She picked up a jug of water standing on a sideboard and walked back to Carpello. 'I'm surprised that didn't kill him, Sallax,' she said, looking down at the swollen, bloody lump bulging from the back of his head, then poured the water over him and stepped back.

He groaned, and tried to roll over, then caught sight of Brexan and Sallax. He began to sob. 'What are you doing here?' he whimpered.

'We've come to kill you,' Brexan answered matter-of-factly.

'But I posted guards!' Carpello whined. 'I've had an escort ever since you escaped.'

'Guards?' Brexan was amused. 'My sister could have run them through with a knitting needle. Sallax eats guards like that to stay in shape.'

'I like them with red wine,' Sallax interjected.

Brexan grinned; Sallax's first real joke.

'You can't just come in here and kill me,' Carpello moaned, 'I did nothing to you, it was all Jacrys, he killed Gilmour, not me. Why would you come here?' He turned to Brexan. 'And who are—?' He froze, a dawning recognition in his face. 'You? But you can't—That swim; it was too—' His voice tailed off and he went even whiter. 'You can't have lived,' he whispered.

'Oh, but I did,' Brexan said. 'We both did.'

'Versen.'

Brexan flushed with anger and kicked Carpello hard. 'Don't you *ever* say his name again, you—! Don't you ever say it! Do you understand?'

Carpello wailed, 'It wasn't me, I didn't want anything to happen to you, I would have brought you back to Orindale, but you had to—'

'Shut up, just shut up!' She kicked him again.

Behind her, Rishta slipped out of the blanket and began hurriedly pulling on her clothes.

Brexan shouted, 'You tied him up, you dragged him behind your ship: you don't tell me what you *would* have done because you *didn't*. I was there!'

Rishta looked around for her shoes.

'Your Seron?' Brexan lowered her voice a little, but to Rishta she sounded even scarier. 'Old scar-face? It took almost all day for him to die. I watched him. With you it will take longer.'

Carpello lifted his face to Sallax and cried, 'Please, don't let her do this to me! Please don't.' He was as reprehensible a human being as Sallax had ever seen, his whole fat, filthy, sweat-soaked, blood-streaked body quivering. It made Sallax feel sick just to look at him.

He kneeled beside Carpello and leaned in close. 'Ren,' he whispered, 'do you remember Ren?'

Versen's voice reverberated in the merchant's head. *You'll be dead, and she will make it last for Twinmoons* ... He wiped his arm across his face. 'What was she to you, Sallax? That was a long time ago.'

'You cut off your mole,' Sallax said.

'He *did*,' Brexan said, 'and I wanted to do that myself, to put it on a string for Brynne to wear on holidays.'

'Brynne? That was her name?'

'Brynne was – *is* – my sister, and you should thank the gods of the Northern Forest she's not here with us today.' Sallax lashed out with his knife, so fast it was almost blurred, and sliced the end off Carpello's nose.

Not realising what had happened, he reached up, feeling for his face like a blind man. His fingers came away soaked in blood, and Carpello began to scream.

Rishta screamed along with him and ran for the chamber door. Before Brexan and Sallax could stop her, she was out of Carpello's apartments and into the hallway.

'Rutters,' Brexan cursed. 'That'll bring the neighbours. We have to get him out of here.'

'Right,' Sallax said, and clubbed Carpello with the hilt of his knife. 'How are we going to carry him?'

'I don't know.' Brexan looked nervous. 'We've got to take him to find out what he's shipping to Pellia. Garec and the others need to know and this bloated piece of rancid meat is the only one who can tell us.'

'Not the only one.'

'No.' She shook her head firmly. 'We're not talking with *him*.'

'What do we do?'

'Bind him. Bandage his nose – wrap his whole rutting head if you want. Wait a quarter-aven, then haul him down the stairs. I'll find a cart or a wagon and we'll wheel him up to the Topgallant. We can interrogate him there.'

Sallax nodded agreement.

'Oh, and take whatever silver you can find – when the investigators come, I want them to think it was a robbery. Plus, we owe Nedra.' She pulled up her hood, slipped into the hallway and ran swiftly down the wooden stairs to the street.

THE LARION SENATORS

The almor screamed from somewhere inside the palace. The shrill echo ran into every corner, violating every space and silence, the terrible cry of a soul sentenced to an eternity in Hell. Mark imagined the flames in the cavernous Larion fireplace cowering, shrinking back from the sound.

Garec jumped at the demon's shriek. 'Demonpiss, but I will never get used to that thing,' he growled.

Mark nodded. 'Maybe it thinks if we can't get any sleep, we might make a mistake and drink from a fountain or something.' He shuddered; he'd seen some hideous things since his arrival in Rona, but Rodler's death would haunt him for ever.

'It may not have to wait for us to misstep,' Garec said. 'It might just starve us out.'

'Or keep us here while the army surrounds the palace. That'd be a fun day, huh? Weak from lack of food, we burst through the main gate to deal with a tireless demon-hunter and the legions of soldiers Nerak has sent to make certain we all die.' Mark slid closer to the fire.

Winter had arrived, imprisoning them at Sandcliff, for the regular snowfall meant the almor could reach them anywhere outside the palace. It was too dangerous to leave the dry stone of the upper levels. Gilmour had shut down the waterwheel feeding the shattered pipes in the north wing, but the halls and chambers had frozen over and the almor was probably lurking up there, waiting for them to make the fatal mistake of trying to pass through.

No one blamed Steven; he had saved them all when he neutralised the acid clouds, and he had beaten the almor, singeing it with acid and leaving it crippled and furious in the damp soil outside – but he hadn't killed the demon. All he had done was annoy it, and now it reared up periodically to scream a reminder that it was there, waiting, and it would remain until it had sucked each of their emaciated frames to a husk.

Now Garec and Mark sat together in the great hall, feeding what wood they had left into one of the huge fireplaces. They had burned the long-untouched stores of firewood, the empty wine casks Mark discovered in the cellar, and much of the furniture in the hall itself. Soon they would be forced to go foraging for more tables and chairs – there were plenty scattered throughout the old keep, but no one relished the idea of wandering around; it would be too easy to step into a room that had developed a leak and become the almor's next victim.

'I wonder why he hasn't come himself?' Garec mused.

'Who, Nerak?'

'Why haven't we seen him again?'

'Maybe because he knows we're trapped and running out of food. The wine is wonderful, but one cannot live on wine alone. And we can only refill our water when we hear the bastard almor screaming outside. So maybe Nerak hasn't shown up because he knows this situation is handled.'

'Or perhaps he's busy taking care of other business while Steven and Gilmour are locked in here.'

'Could be,' Mark agreed. 'What was his daughter's name? Malagon's daughter?'

'Belle— No, Bella something,' Garec said. 'I don't remember. Do you think he's gone back to Welstar Palace to take her?'

'Judging from Eldarn's history, that'll certainly be high on his to-do list. People have got to be wondering what's happened to their dictator, regardless of how nasty the old bastard was. If he's dead, they'll want a fresh start; it doesn't matter how long they've toiled under the thumb of a grade-A prick, they'll all be praying for a new beginning under Whatshername's rule. If Nerak has any doubts about sorting us out, or working the spell table – wherever that is – he wouldn't leave Eldarn to flop around like a fish on dry land, will he? He'll get back there and start running things as Bellawhatshername.'

'That makes sense,' Garec said, 'especially if Malagon's body came floating up on shore in Orindale. Those generals won't know what to do, but I'm sure most of them would rather cut off a hand than take orders from a *girl*.'

Mark laughed. Some things didn't change, no matter what world you were in. 'He'll take her – the poor kid never had a chance – and do something ugly right from the start. They'll all get the message that Daddy's little girl is just as cruel as the old man.'

Garec laughed. 'Imagine being a doll in her dollhouse!' He looked around. 'Where are the others now?'

'Steven is upstairs staring at the wall again, and I don't know what happened to Gilmour this morning. He's been in quite a funk,' Mark said. 'The fight was good for him; he was almost back to normal, but now he's reverted to being all wet and beaten up. I suppose he's spending these days working spells to make up for lost opportunity; I guess he figures Nerak knows where he is so he can make as much mystical noise as he wants.'

'I'm worried about him,' Garec agreed. 'He just about came apart when he saw that empty spell chamber.'

'Who can blame him?' Mark sighed. 'If I were him, I'd be downstairs locked in the wine cellar. It's probably good that he's back there blasting away. Gives him a chance to bone up on his skills while we wait.'

'That is what we're doing, isn't it?' Garec asked, 'waiting?'

'I don't know what else you'd call it. Waiting for someone to figure out where we're going or what we're doing, waiting for the snow to melt so we can get past the almor, waiting for Gita and the Falkan Resistance to get to Traver's Notch, waiting for Gilmour to discover something in that Windscroll he brought down with him? I don't know, Garec. I wish someone would tell me.'

'Steven's not had any luck either?'

Mark shook his head. 'If he had, he wouldn't be in there staring at it.'

'I'm not sure he's going to get anything out of it.'

'He hasn't had a glimmer.'

'What does it say? I can't remember it exactly.'

Mark laughed, hollowly. 'I have it memorised. It says: *It's been gone for a long, long time, Fantus, and you'll never find it. Eldarn itself wards the spell table for me, Eldarn and Eldarn's most ruthless gatekeepers. Forget the spell table, Fantus. It's mine. It always has been mine.* Steven wrote it using ashes from the fireplace. That was a bit odd, actually, with all the sealed canisters of ink in the library, but the ashes worked.'

'He's still convinced there's a hidden meaning, even though he's stared at those words every single day ...' Garec's voice trailed off as he gazed into the flames.

'Not so much a hidden meaning. I'm with him on this: Nerak's a brash sonofabitch, too confident and too certain of victory, and it's quite possible he said something that will lead us to the spell table.

But it's been what – twenty days? – since Nerak was here and none of us have come up with a damned thing.' He dipped a ladle into one of the buckets they had drawn from the cistern the evening before, filled a goblet and handed it to Garec, then filled another for himself.

'Thanks,' Garec said, then asked, 'sunonabitch?'

Mark shrugged. 'Close enough. I add it for colour; it's one of my favourites.'

'What does it mean?'

He thought about it, then said, 'In a literal sense it's an insult to one's mother.'

'Those are always effective.' Garec drank.

'But the way I use it is more to say that Nerak is a great pile of cat-shit.'

'All right, thanks.' Garec grimaced. 'You know, there really is nothing worse than cat-shit.'

Mark laughed. 'How did we get here?'

'We're here to save Eldarn and send you back to Colorado. Have you forgotten?'

'Oh, yes, right, save Eldarn. Of course, I had better write that down. I'll see if Steven has any ash left. I'll scrawl it here on my water goblet so I don't forget.' He refilled his cup.

Garec reached back for a piece of chair, tossed it on the flames and said, 'But first we have to figure out how Eldarn itself might ward the Larion spell table.'

'And then we have to get through Eldarn's greatest gatekeepers.'

'Most ruthless gatekeepers,' Garec corrected.

'Sorry, most ruthless gatekeepers,' Mark said.

'I wonder what aven it is.'

Mark looked surprised. 'Does it matter?'

'We're sitting here drinking water. Whose idea was that?'

'You think it's late enough for wine?'

'We'd have to go back down into the cellar. I don't like it, but I'll risk it.'

'Yeah, I'd hate to get caught down there. Too dark, too many damp places. That miserable almor could be down there anywhere waiting for us. Maybe we'll stick with water for a while and send Steven down there when he takes a break. At least he'll have the staff with him.'

'Right,' Garec said. 'We wouldn't want to get trapped down there.'

Mark had leaned over the water bucket when he heard Garec's goblet clatter to the floor. The Ronan was already running towards the stairwell at the far end of the great hall. 'Hey,' Mark shouted, his echo coming back at him from fifteen stone hallways at once, 'where are you going?'

'Sunonabitch!' Garec called without looking back.

Garec burst into Steven's chamber without knocking and was surprised to find Gilmour there, considering the crooked ash letters Steven had scrawled on the grey stone wall. 'I know where this is,' he panted, heaving in great swallows of air. Gilmour and Steven offered him twin blank stares as he waved a hand at the writing and gasped out again, 'I know where this is. The spell table, I know where we can find it.'

'Sit down, boy, relax.' Gilmour was obviously unconvinced. 'Get your breath back and tell us how – or rather, *where*.' He looked at Mark questioningly as he too ran into the room, but Mark just shrugged and raised his eyebrows.

'I just figured it out downstairs with Mark. We were—' He stopped and laughed nervously; he didn't want to be wrong after bursting into the room like a bad actor in a second-rate melodrama. 'Well, we were downstairs, drinking water we collected yesterday from the cistern – it isn't bad, but it tastes like lake water, all full of minerals and fishy things. And we were talking about going downstairs to get some wine, which is a good deal more pleasant, anyway, we decided to wait and send Steven down there, because to tell the truth the almor scares the dog piss out of both of us, and neither of us wanted to go down to fill the flagons.'

'Gosh, thanks Garec,' Steven said dryly.

'Well, at least you'd have the staff with you,' Garec explained.

'Oh sure. Talk about hoping someone else will pick up the bar tab.' Steven grinned. 'Here at Sandcliff Wine and Ale, drinking really *is* hazardous to your health.'

Gilmour, clearly not amused, interrupted again. 'I hate to be such a killjoy, but get to the point, please, Garec. Where is the spell table?'

'It's buried beneath a pile of rocks on the bottom of a river flowing out of the Blackstones into southern Falkan.' Garec found himself squirming under the scrutiny of a Larion Senate leader, not the kindly gaze of his mentor and longtime friend. 'I wondered if that might be the place where Eldarn itself would ward the table, but when I heard Mark clarify the part about the gatekeepers, Eldarn's most *ruthless* gatekeepers, I knew that had to be it.'

Steven turned back to the text he had scrawled on the wall; he had been staring at it for days, vainly hoping some cartoon light bulb would pop on above his head, or the hickory staff would reveal the truth. Now he nodded. 'That day on the river, yes. Gilmour, you were— well, dead at the time. We were coming downriver on our raft.'

'The *Capina Fair*,' Mark said, as if the name were an important piece of the puzzle.

'I went swimming, and managed to get myself trapped at the bottom of the river – something grabbed me and wouldn't let go. Garec came down to help, and soon he was stuck along with me. We used the staff to breathe, sort of, but that's all it did – we barely got away with our lives.'

Gilmour looked at them. 'How did you finally break free?'

Steven was quick to answer. 'I remember this, because it was so odd. I'd been using the staff, blasting away at the river bottom, drilling it with everything I could muster, but it didn't budge.'

'Instead, it began to drag us towards this underwater rock formation, Steven by the ankle and me by my wrists,' Garec said. 'I thought we were dead. And then it just let go.'

'Actually,' Steven interjected, 'it didn't – and I'm not certain I'm right on this, but I'll say it anyway: I believe it had something to do with what I was thinking.'

Gilmour cocked an eyebrow. 'Go on.'

'At first I was pounding away, all my frustration and fear blasting into the riverbed, and it was pointless, then I forced myself to relax. We were breathing all right, and I knew that even in the cold, we had a few seconds before we started to lose our senses.' He looked at Garec, checking he wasn't leaving out any details. Garec gestured for him to continue.

'It was then that I thought about our goal, to reach the spell table and to defeat Nerak. I focused on it, concentrating all my will on our quest—'

'And the staff responded,' Gilmour said.

'No,' Steven shook his head. 'I never landed another blow with the staff. The riverbed just let us go. Maybe it was a coincidence, but if it wasn't, then something down there essentially read my thoughts and changed its mind about killing us.'

'Or it was your own power,' Mark said. 'Maybe your own magic was stronger than the staff's that day.'

Steven didn't answer; he was still uncomfortable when Mark insisted that he was more than just a conduit for the hickory staff, even though Mark had a legitimate argument.

Gilmour asked, 'What else do you remember?'

He closed his eyes, trying to recall as much as he could. 'It was so cold. I do remember those rocks.'

'It was like a cave,' Garec agreed, 'an underground cave, and the sand was pulling us towards the opening. Rutting terrifying is what it was, and I was going in head-first.'

'It was more than that,' Steven said, pointing a finger at Garec. 'He's right, but it was more than that: it was like a sculpture, a perfectly random, natural, flawed, beautiful sculpture – nothing you'd see in a Florence gallery, but perfectly awkward and clumsily done, as if a passionate idiot had built it out of rocks and sticks—' He paused, certain he was going to sound foolish. 'It was like an altar. I even kneeled down in front of it, twice. The second time was when it decided to grab me.'

Garec echoed the text scribbled on the wall. 'Eldarn itself wards the spell table.'

'Nerak took it from here and buried it there.' Steven had not yet said as much, but he agreed with Garec.

'Why not take it to Welstar Palace?' Mark asked, 'wouldn't it be safer there?'

'It's too obvious a hiding place,' Garec answered. 'If anyone were ever to figure out how to get into Welstar Palace – a challenge, I admit – the spell table would be there. Burying it beneath an Era's worth of rock, sand and mountain runoff – who would know where to start looking, never mind how to get it out of there? It's the perfect hiding place: nowhere.'

Mark nodded reluctantly. It made sense, but there were still holes in the argument. 'So why did it let you go?' he asked. 'If it wasn't your magic, and if Eldarn itself wards the spell table, why did the riverbed let you go when it read your quest?'

'No idea,' Steven said, 'maybe Nerak has cast some kind of spell that keeps the table under close watch – and maybe the river freed us because Eldarn itself wards the spell table, against its will. I want to believe that Eldarn itself wants us to be successful.'

'That's awfully presumptuous of us,' Mark said. 'And what of the ruthless gatekeepers? Is that the rocks and the dirt as well?'

Garec said, 'No, the ruthless gatekeepers are those sunonabitch bone-collectors we met in that cavern.'

'But that was days later – we were much further down the river. That can't be what he means.'

'But think about that cavern,' Garec said. 'There were hundreds of thousands of bones stacked up against that wall; where do you suppose they came from? There's no way that many people just wandered into that cavern: those creatures come out and hunt.'

Remembering the huge eyes he hacked out with his battle-axe, Mark said, 'They must be nocturnal – but some of those bones were ancient. They disintegrated when we touched them. Those things have been gathering bones down there for ages and ages. The spell table has only been gone for a few generations.'

'So what?' Steven said. 'So they gathered bones for ten thousand generations; that doesn't stop Nerak enslaving them as his gate-keepers nine hundred and eighty Twinmoons ago.'

Mark conceded the point and threw up his hands. 'Hey, it beats sitting around here waiting for whomever or whatever is next on Nerak's list to show up and kill us. What do you say, Gilmour?'

'Can we find it again?'

'I know right where it is,' Steven assured. 'There's a mountain above the river with a stand of pines growing right out of the rock, sticking out all over, almost marking every point on the compass. I've never seen anything like it before. We can't miss it.'

'You're sure?'

'Absolutely. I stared at it for what felt like hours while I was lying there thinking the staff's magic had run out.'

Gilmour was silent, pacing back and forth across the chamber. He looked too thin, too tired and too old for the challenges that lay ahead. He ran a hand over forehead.

Everyone knew he was wishing he had been with them on the river. How much easier this would be if he had not been such a fool as to go to sleep. How many times in the past five hundred Twinmoons had he done that: fifteen? Twenty, maybe? But thinking he should build up some energy for their trip over the pass the following day, he had rolled himself up in his blankets for an aven or two – and why not? Kantu slept all the time – drunk too, mostly – and no one chided him for it. But the first time Gilmour slept in uncounted Twinmoons, an assassin had come into their camp and driven a knife into his chest, a quick, clean killing. He hadn't seen the man, though he had known someone was following them. He, one of the most powerful sorcerers in Eldarn, had been tricked by a carnival magician's cloaking spell, and it had cost him dearly.

Now Gilmour wrestled with the uncertainty of leaving again: would his magic wane when he stepped outside his home? Mark was right: there was no point in remaining at Sandcliff, and there was nothing in the third Windscroll other than a protection spell that he thought Pikan had planned to use to protect herself and her team from Nerak when he came through the doorway. Even then, Gilmour had failed, for he hadn't found the scroll in time and Pikan had not been given an opportunity to use it.

'All right,' he said finally. 'Let's go.'

'What? When? *Now?*' Steven hadn't expected to leave so suddenly. 'Don't you have more work to do with the Windscroll? You've been poring over it, and working so many spells in the back hall; are you ready? Do you need more time? Gilmour, as long as we have the key, we control the pace of this horrible cat-and-mouse game.'

'No, Steven, I'm ready,' Gilmour said, straightening his shoulders. 'The Windscroll is an engaging riddle, and I think I'm onto something, but I can keep that research going as we travel south.' The lie tripped easily off his tongue. He looked at each of them in turn. 'You've all convinced me. Let's go.'

Nerak's weakness lies elsewhere – he heard Lessek's voice echo in his memory and worried for a moment that the others heard it too; it was followed by Pikan saying, *I need the third Windscroll. It's in the library near the top shelf behind Lessek's desk.* Why had she wanted that scroll? Did she know – wherever she was – how hard he had worked and how far he had come to get it?

Nerak's weakness lies elsewhere.

'Where, gods rut it?' Gilmour barked aloud.

'Where what?' Steven asked.

'Nothing, sorry!' Gilmour found he had begun to sweat and dragged a sleeve over his brow in an effort to hide his discomfort. The pieces had fallen into place. Nerak's weakness. Pikan had known what to do; Gilmour had lived with that assumption since those terrifying few moments cowering in the corner of the spell chamber, gripping the pommel of that absurd broadsword.

If Nerak's weakness lies elsewhere, and it doesn't lie in the third Windscroll, then where in all the wide world does it lie?

Fantus, are you there?

Nerak, you bastard. Where are you? Why don't you just come and settle this together, face to face, here at home, where we belong?

Fantus, it's Kantu. Is it you, Fantus?

Gilmour felt dizzy: the voices inside his head had taken on a mind of their own. First Nerak, then Pikan, and now *Kantu* – what was happening to him? Sweat poured off his forehead and stung his eyes. He mopped repeatedly at his brow and shut his eyes hard, trying to keep the salty sweat from blinding him.

Fantus! It's me, Kantu. Can you hear me?

He answered, *What could you possibly want? To ride along with the others as I lose my mind? And what brings you out at this time of day? I figured you'd be—*

Fantus. Shut up and listen!

He was really there. It wasn't his imagination ...

Gilmour tried to relax and to open his mind – as scrambled as it had become in the past half-aven – and allow his old friend to speak with him. *Sorry. I'm sorry, Kantu. Give me a moment. I must attend to one thing and then I'll lie down.*

Please hurry. I am in a safe place, but this will tire us both immensely.

Gilmour opened his eyes to find his young companions standing frozen in place, each staring at him with wild-eyed incomprehension. He realised he was gasping for breath, sweating and talking with the demons in his head.

He sent them away, reassuring them he was all right, but pushing them firmly out of the room. 'I need to be by myself,' he said, forcing a smile. 'I'll be fine. I'll come and find you tomorrow.'

Steven was the first to protest. 'Gilmour, we don't think—'

'Nonsense,' he cut them off. 'I'm fine. I have a few things to work out in my mind before we go, and I am going to need quiet for that. I beg you not to worry. I'll join you all for the midday meal: whatever perishables we have left. Pack for travel, because we need to investigate this river of yours before we do anything else.'

The others eyed him suspiciously, but no one offered another argument. Steven, following Garec and Mark out, asked once more, 'You sure you're all right?'

'Just fine, really,' he replied. 'I'll see you tomorrow, midday.'

'Good night, Gilmour.'

'Sorry to be so abrupt, but I've just figured out a few things that need to happen before we go. I want to take care of them tonight.'

Steven nodded and pulled the door closed as he left.

In the hall, Mark said, 'What's with him?'

'He's losing his mind,' Garec said. 'Did you see him? I thought he was going to fall down.'

374

'If he's not right tomorrow, we'll insist on staying here for a few more days,' Steven said.

'We don't have food for a few more days – we're pretty much out of everything, and even drinking the water is dangerous.' Mark had run out of ideas, so he clung to the notion that they needed to get to the river right away. Of course, there was the problem of the almor waiting for them outside, not to mention an entire army ...

Steven read his mind. 'If he's in there getting things sorted, then we have to do our part out here.'

'What do you mean?'

'I mean, if he's working out the details of the Windscroll, whatever he needs to crush Nerak with the spell table, then we need to make certain we're ready to travel.'

Garec was confused. 'What? Pack?'

'Yes,' Steven said. 'You two get us packed.'

'What are you going to do?' Mark looked sceptically at his roommate.

'I'm going outside,' Steven said.

'Oh, that's just—'

'Don't try to stop me. You know as well as I do that it has to happen. If it doesn't, then we're just stuck here staring at the walls and drinking vinegar until Nerak sends something in here to kill us.' He shouldered the staff. 'I have to do it.'

Kantu! Gilmour called into the darkness gathering in his mind's eye.

Fantus! Are you losing your mind, my old friend? Kantu's voice came to him across the void. Communicating this way was horribly difficult; it required a masterful use of energy to completely empty one's mind of thoughts or images that might distract one of them and in turn break the connection between them.

For the moment, yes, I think I am. But how are you? Are you in Middle Fork?

I am well, but I am not in Middle Fork. I hoped I would find you at Sandcliff. I felt the gate open during the last Twinmoon and knew it was either you or him. I have not had an opportunity to try and reach you since then. We have been travelling a great deal. In a secluded corner room on the second floor of a surprisingly comfortable inn, Alen Jasper of Middle Fork lay on a straw mattress, apparently fast asleep. Downstairs, his friends were enjoying a fine dinner, with an extra flagon of wine with his compliments.

It was me.

I'm glad.

Where are you?

I'm in central Malakasia, heading for Welstar Palace.

Gilmour's surprise nearly severed their contact. *Great gods, why?*

I have business there, Fantus. That's why I contacted you. I need to know if you have learned anything at all that might get me safely inside.

He pondered this question before responding. *I don't know why you would want to go in there. Nerak is here, not right here, but near here, and he isn't—*

Please, Fantus, anything at all?

I'm sorry. No.

That's all right. It was a hope; that's all.

Why are you going there?

Someone has found the key, Fantus. Someone might have brought it back to Eldarn. I have met a young woman who has come across the Fold through our far portal. She found one in Colorado.

I know, I know. Her friends are with me. We have Lessek's key and the second portal with us.

There was a long silence; Gilmour's mind was an empty cave. Then Kantu spoke again. *The one called Steven Taylor?*

You would love him, Kantu. He reminds me of you. And speaking of which, do you have any recollection of a staff? A hardwood staff, hickory, nondescript really, that might have been imbued with something experimental, something powerful? Anyone working with hickory that you remember?

Working with hickory? There was another pause. *No. Not that I can remember.*

Ah well, it was a hope; that's all.

Why are you back home, Fantus?

I came for the third Windscroll. I thought it might have some secret to help me defeat Nerak.

The Windscrolls? That's funny. I was just thinking about those. But why the third? There's just one spell, isn't there? A common-phrase weave for protection, right?

Gilmour was growing weary; he felt his body sink comfortably into the blankets. He tried to ignore the fatigue. *It's a protection spell, but I never knew that. And it's written in Pikan's hand. Were you not there for that trip?*

I was, but I injured my leg and was not able to make the climb with them for the final tests. Pikan kept the records for us that time out.

She did? That's curious.

Why?

Well, the night that things came to an end here at Sandcliff, she was working the spell table, trying anything to cast Nerak's demon back into the Fold. When I arrived, she sent me for the third Windscroll. I've studied it now for the past twenty days or so and I can't imagine why she wanted it, except as a last-breath shield for her team.

Kantu was silent again. Gilmour felt rather than heard a heavy sigh resonate sonorously from somewhere far to the west. *She would have wanted it for herself, Fantus.*

Gilmour didn't see anything to be gained by passing judgment on a dead magician. *We were all scared that night, Kantu. I don't blame her.*

She wanted to live.

So did I.

She wanted it for other reasons.

I don't understand.

She was a mother. She would have asked for the third Windscroll to preserve her own life. It was her only goal, to get back to the baby.

Taken aback, Gilmour asked, *How do you know this?*

I was the father.

Gilmour tiptoed towards the edge of the great empty space in his mind, knowing he was about to fall in. *So the third Windscroll—*

Will offer you nothing against Nerak. I'm sure if she called for it, she was trying to stay alive for the baby, our baby, Reia. This time Kantu did sigh, and it echoed for a moment inside Gilmour's head.

Don't go in there, Kantu.

I was going to send Hannah home, but if you have the portal . . .

Turn back.

Perhaps I'll go in alone.

You should bring her here. We can send all of them home together.

Do you know that he has had magicians, slaves, I'm sure, searching for me night and day for the past nine hundred Twinmoons? Did you know that, Fantus?

He has done the same with me – except those pursuing me have periodically come wandering in for a visit.

I want to kill him myself.

He's already dead, Kantu. You can't kill him.

I'll find a way.

You'll get killed, and you know it.

There was a pause, then Kantu spoke again. *Where are you going?*

Traver's Notch, to meet with what's left of the Resistance over here, and then to a valley in the Blackstones. I'm not exactly sure where it is.

Kantu didn't reply.

Will you bring Hannah here? Will you join us? It would be good to have you here, Kantu, good for me. I have not been very effective recently, but being home has helped me hone some of my skills. It would be nice to work together again.

Kantu ignored Gilmour's plea. *Where is he?*

He thinks he has us fooled, that he has hidden the spell table where we won't find it, but we believe we know where it is. We have the key, so he won't be far from us, of that I am convinced. He has tried on numerous occasions to get it, but so far, we've been lucky.

Lucky?

Absolutely. Gilmour would not take credit for any of the successes his company had experienced in the past two Twinmoons, but he added, *Luck, and the hickory staff I mentioned, which has proven both powerful and effective.*

First I've heard of something like that.

No matter. Gilmour pressed again. *Will you contact me from Orindale?*

Malagon's daughter is there.

Who cares?

I care; I had a daughter, Fantus. Reia was my daughter, and I will never forgive him, not ever. I have lived a long time, and I can still feel her there, Fantus. She is as real in my heart as the day she was born, and I will not go on like this one more day. I will never go back to Middle Fork. I am through hiding. For the first time since they began speaking, Kantu's voice rose. Gilmour was surprised that his friend was able to shout. He did not recall anyone ever being able to yell in this manner before.

Killing Bellan will do nothing to ease your suffering, my friend.

But it won't hurt.

Don't risk Hannah for your personal vendetta. That's not who you are.

You don't know me any more, Fantus.

Contact me from Orindale, please.

Afterwards, perhaps.

Please.

I may, if I . . . well, you know.

Thank you.

Keep well, Fantus, and sorry about the Windscroll.

378

It's all right. Gilmour lied. It was not all right. He felt the world opening up to swallow him. *Fine; let it take me. I need the rest, anyway.*

Goodbye, Fantus.

Orindale, Kantu. Contact me from Orindale. Gilmour tumbled backwards, knees over head, into the sorrow and confusion that had welled up to take him. He would remain there for the night and much of the following day, sleeping fitfully. The third Windscroll, held open on his chamber table with two stones and an old inkwell, went unread that evening. Pikan's thin script noted the common-phrase spell she had hoped to employ in the moments before Nerak broke into the tower that night long ago. As he tumbled away, Gilmour was reminded – from some disembodied spirit of himself lingering in the hollow well of his insecurity – that if Nerak's weakness really did lie elsewhere, there was no one who had any notion where that might be.

'I want to go outside with you.' Garec came up behind him, making Steven jump.

'Jesus, Garec, didn't anyone ever tell you not to do that to some-one about to challenge a demon to a fistfight?'

'I want to come.' He wore his quivers and carried the rosewood bow.

'I thought you were finished with that thing.'

'I don't know when I'll kill another animal, and I hope to live out my days without ever shooting another person, but this is different. You're going outside into the snow, Steven, *snow*. Here in Eldarn, we make our snow out of water.'

Steven chuckled. 'Yes, us too – but what can you do? Forgive me for being blunt, but you can't fight it, Garec, and with you out there, I'll be worried about you and if I'm not paying attention, it may come on us without warning.'

The young man Sallax had once dubbed the *Bringer of Death* held out his longbow. 'Remember the cabin? Let's try again. Maybe it'll work a second time.'

Steven withheld the magic but reached out with the staff and touched the bow, anyway.

'Come on,' Garec chided, 'do it properly.'

'I don't want you out there,' Steven confessed. 'This thing is an unholy killer. We already lost Versen to an almor and I'm not about to risk your life, just to have a back up in a one-on-one fight.'

'Try again,' Garec insisted, 'for real this time.'

Steven exhaled and let the magic come; it wasn't difficult. The staff understood they were about to go into battle and was prepared for his summons. The air around the wooden shaft lit up with mystical energy.

Steven tapped it lightly against Garec's bow and then against each of the quivers. 'Anything?' he asked.

Garec shook his head. 'Not like before.'

'Sorry.'

'No, I'm sorry. I don't like the idea of you going out there by yourself.'

'I can only think of about fifteen hundred things I'd rather be doing, but we don't have a choice. If we leave here tomorrow, it will hit one of us before we reach the top of the staircase. We haven't been to the stables since this last snowfall. If the horses are still alive, I'd like to know they'll survive the night as well.' Steven smiled and said, 'I won't be long.'

'Call out if you need help.' Garec was serious.

Steven stifled a laugh. 'Maybe I'll just toss a few snowballs in that window Gilmour broke when he dived out of here.'

'Whatever gets our attention.'

'Good luck.' Mark came in with Steven's jacket. He didn't try to talk Steven out of his decision to face the almor alone. 'Just remember, *you* have the magic. I've seen it.'

'Thanks,' Steven said. 'Help me with the gate, will you?'

Mark and Garec gripped the wooden handles on either side of the gate that closed the foyer off from the wintry weather, lifted their latches free and pushed, opening a crack just wide enough for Steven to slip out

As the gate slammed shut behind him, Steven took stock. He was protected under a stone archway, his feet safe on dry granite steps. It was too dark to see, never mind to do battle with an otherworldly demon, so Steven gestured with the staff, igniting a bright ball of flame above his head to illuminate the archway and much of the stone walk leading away from the portcullis. A short distance across the lawn he could see a swirling wind pick up wisps of snow, a flurry of tiny tornadoes dancing in the fireball's light.

All at once he was uncomfortable with what he was about to do – what had seemed like a good idea a few minutes earlier was beginning to unravel in his mind. His clothes were uncomfortable; Howard's woollen sweater scratched at his neck; it was far too big for him. Even his coat felt like it had grown too large. He thought he might take it off before calling the demon out – one didn't get in a bar fight in baggy clothes; too much material for some drunk to grip hold of. The almor might somehow grasp the jacket in one of its opaque appendages and use it to hold him fast as it sucked life from his eyes, or maybe out his navel: that was where life first went in, wasn't it?

He slipped the jacket off carefully, always holding onto the hickory staff, and allowed it to fall to the ground behind him, then repeated the process with the sweater until he stood there in the cotton T-shirt he had bought while racing Nerak across the Midwest. He was confident stripping off the layers had been a wise first move; now he nodded towards the staff, summoning forth the magic.

Nothing happened.

'Ah, shit, not now,' he said. 'Talk about the worst possible time to get stage fright.'

And remember, you have the magic, Steven, I've seen it. Mark's words came back to him, confusing him and leaving him feeling vulnerable.

'Thanks, buddy,' Steven said, 'but that wasn't at all what I needed to hear.' He gripped the staff more tightly. 'Come on, baby, light up for me. Let's go. You and me. Let's beat this creepy bastard and get in out of the cold.'

Still nothing came from the staff. Steven shivered, wondering if he ought to knock on the gate and wait for his friends to let him back inside. There would be no shame; he wouldn't go back with his tail between his legs – it took courage even to step foot outside the palace. He had seen how fast the almor could move, and the snowfall meant it could be anywhere, right at the bottom of the steps perhaps.

Steven stood fast and thought about the landfill above Idaho Springs. It would be burned over now, after the forest fire Nerak had brought down the canyon. He had felt so confident that day, certain he understood the Fold and knew how to manipulate it – *paint the damned thing yellow if we want to.* Why? What about that day had made such sense? He gritted his teeth: perhaps Mark was right and he *was* as powerful as the staff, more powerful, even.

It would be down to maths, because mathematics could explain anything in any world. Prince Malagon's lock-box, his Malakasian safe-deposit box, had proved that, and once he knew enough about the Fold to understand it, he could calculate parameters to define it. There would be compassion, because anything less would mean failure; Nerak – in all his forms – would fail in the face of true compassion and mercy. And there would be magic. But which magic? Him or the hickory staff? Maybe the spell table? That question remained to be answered. It was sufficient now that he knew magic would play a role, had to play a role against the combined strength of the Larion sorcerer and his evil captor.

Maths, magic, and compassion were the variables that came to him that afternoon, and at the time it all made sense. He longed now to feel a similar level of confidence as he stood there freezing, trying to find the courage to step into the snow. The key had knocked him over twice that day, dropping him to the icy pavement until he worked out what he was being told. He wished that something would show him the way here; he needed something to reach over and take his knees out from under him. Then he knew he would be able to connect with the hickory staff and defeat the almor.

Steven watched the snow blowing back and forth across the Larion courtyard and realised his fireball was still burning brightly.

'Wait a minute,' he said, 'who turned on the light? Me?' Did it matter? He had turned the staff in his hands, imagined the size, shape and intensity of the ball, and it had appeared. He had stepped onto the speed bump, and the key had tripped him.

'Step into the darkness, Steven,' he smiled. 'Is it that easy?'

He ignored the cold, took the staff and gestured out of the archway and into the air above the stone walk. The fireball complied, floating effortlessly out until it illuminated the grounds. He knew his ability to see in the dark would have nothing to do with destroying the demon, but old habits died hard; he felt more comfortable risking his life with the lights on.

'Step into the darkness, Steven,' he said again. 'Get the right context, dummy, and don't trip.'

With that, he breathed out, long and slow, lifted one foot from the safety of the dry stone and stepped into ankle-deep snow. Almost immediately, the staff flared to life and his fireball grew in intensity until he could clearly see the winding staircase, the snowy hillside to the east and the intricate stained-glass window in the huge stone wall that Gilmour had ruined nearly a thousand Twinmoons earlier.

Standing now with both feet in the snow, the glass began to blur, melting before his eyes into a gold and black backdrop, flecked here and there with snowy white. Was this his magic, or the staff's? Did it matter?

The almor screamed a shrill greeting from somewhere out beyond the fireball's reach, but this time the demon's cry didn't frighten him; instead, he heard the sound of a crying baby, the child that had died in the explosion at Charleston Airport. The young mother had been taken by Nerak before she and the child boarded the plane and the baby had cried from the time they passed down the aisle to the moment the plane exploded around them. Steven seethed with rage, remembering that sound.

'Come down here!' he shouted up the snowy slope. In his hands, the staff glowed and the hillside melted away, matching the window's waxy texture and blurred colour: it would be easy to see the almor. Steven felt it coming now, but he was ready.

THE INTERROGATION

'Is he waking up?' Brexan's voice came from far away. 'I think so too. There he is.'

Carpello opened his eyes.

'Welcome back. Did you miss us?'

Pain lanced through his lower back, his side and especially his head and face. He had been clubbed into a stupor twice in one evening and his thoughts were coming together more slowly than usual. He had difficulty clearing his mind, and he couldn't focus properly; he was certain irreparable damage had been done to his head. Panic overtook him and he tried to scream for help, but to no avail, for his mouth had been bound with the same bandaging Sallax used to stem the flow of blood from his nose. Carpello guessed his entire head was wrapped in it, with just enough room for him to draw shallow breaths through his disfigured nose. He trembled, and he felt his bowels let loose, filling his leggings and adding to the already disagreeable smell.

'There we go,' Brexan said lightly. 'I was wondering when that would happen. You are a predictable little milksop, aren't you? Great gods, but what have you been eating?'

He tried to beg for his life, to promise anything he could to change these madmen's minds about killing him, but all he could do was grunt. It was dark outside, and he assumed he had not been unconscious for six full avens, so it must be the same night.

Not that long ago he'd sought out and then escorted home the floppy-breasted prostitute with the endearing little roll of flab ... it must be quite late now; dawn would soon brighten the sky outside. It was difficult to dispose of a body after sunrise; so if he could stay alive long enough to see the sun crest the horizon, there was a chance he might live through the day.

Carpello checked out the room; he had no idea where he was. A bedside table matched a chest against the wall. No carpets on the floor, no tapestries on the walls: this was a guest room. An inn, maybe? He hoped there were plenty of guests that night: he would wait for dawn and then, when he heard someone moving outside, he would cry for help. It wasn't the best strategy, but it was the best he could do right now. His head ached and he longed for sleep.

'I want you to pay attention,' Brexan said.

His eyes shifted to Sallax, and Brexan slashed him across one thigh.

Both his cry of pain and sobs were muffled. His pulse quickened and his breathing was laboured as he heaved back and forth in the chair he was bound to with leather straps. He stared wide-eyed back at Brexan.

'That's better. I want you to pay attention. When you don't, I am going to cut you. Does that make sense? I'm keeping it simple.'

He nodded as quickly as he could, never taking his eyes off her, trying to ignore the feeling of warm blood trickling across his lap.

'Very good.' Brexan leaned forward until her face was close to his. Carpello thought that if he had any flesh left on the end of his nose, it would be pressing against hers. 'I will ask you a question, and then I will loosen your bonds enough for you to reply. If you say anything that is not a direct response to my question, I will tighten them back up, and I will cut you. Make sense?'

Again Carpello nodded vigorously.

'See? You're doing fine.' Still face to face with him, Brexan asked, 'What are you shipping to Pellia?' She reached up and loosened the bandage around his mouth, which hung limp beneath his lower lip, damp with saliva and blood.

Carpello breathed deeply for the first time since waking and took a moment to regain his composure before answering, 'I'm not sure what it does, but it comes from Rona. There's a forest outside Estrad Village, and another along the South Coast, forbidden forests, closed off – they have been for almost a thousand Twinmoons.'

Brexan raised the knife. 'You haven't answered my question.'

Carpello whimpered, 'I am, but I don't really know what it is. It's wood, processed wood, but not lumber – bark and shavings, leaves, and roots and stuff. I don't know what he wants with it, but he wants as much as I can ship. He pays anything I ask.'

Sallax stood. 'I know that forest, near the old palace. We hunt in those woods; there isn't anyone in there harvesting any trees.'

'I'm trying to save my life,' Carpello said, 'what chance do I have if I lie? I'm telling you the truth.'

Brexan pressed her lips together; she believed him. 'My platoon used to patrol the edge of those woods. Every now and then we would hang a poacher, but most of the time, we looked the other way.'

'Did you hear of people cutting down trees?' Sallax's scepticism was evident.

'No, and it isn't possible that wagons of timber could come out of there without us knowing. You need to do better than this, Carpello.'

The fat man spoke rapidly, filling the air with as much information as he could. 'It doesn't come out in wagons; then everyone in Rona would know. Prince Malagon is aware that patrols along that forest are token; it's the end of the world out there, and anyway, no one really cares what happens in Estrad. The cargo comes via launch to my ships – my captains moor off the peninsula. The loads are ferried out. There hasn't been a Ronan boat around that peninsula since Prince Marek closed the forest five generations ago; not even the bravest fishermen go out there, for fear they'll be sunk immediately by the Malakasian Navy.'

Sallax shook his head. 'Versen and Garec have hunted that forest since we were kids. It's a competition with them, who can get the most deer. They would know if there was cutting going on.'

'How far out do they go?' Carpello asked, glad for the excuse to keep the two partisans talking. 'Is it all the way to the coast? Do they go out onto the peninsula?'

'I would guess …' Sallax hesitated, looking at Brexan. 'I don't know.'

'Can we loosen these a bit more?' Carpello ventured, warily.

Brexan's hand moved so swiftly he barely saw it. Blood seeped through the new gash, parallel to the first. 'Don't stray from the topic, or I will gut you right now.'

Carpello whimpered; he was almost paralysed with fear. His eyes were red with fatigue.

Brexan worried that he might pass out on her. 'Stay awake,' she ordered. 'I need you focused on the conversation.'

'Whatever you say, just please don't cut me,' he pleaded. 'Please don't cut me again.' His body shook, great rolls of fat quivering as he sobbed.

'How much have you shipped?'

'Twelve vessels in the last eighteen Twinmoons – as fast as they can harvest it.'

'What are you paid?'

'Five hundred silver pieces per ship.'

Brexan did a quick calculation. 'Six thousand pieces of silver! You have done well, haven't you? You could live like a prince on that much – for eight or nine lifetimes.'

'I have costs,' he said, a little sulkily. 'Ships are lost, sailors die, cargoes sink. There are always risks.'

Another slash, this one deeper, in line with the first two. 'Did I ask about your overheads?'

The merchant emitted a high-pitched whine. He kept it going, without a break, for a surprisingly long time, until Brexan slapped him hard, drawing blood from his lip.

'Stop that squealing – you sound like the pig you are. I'm losing patience. What happens in Strandson?'

Carpello stopped shrieking and after a moment replied, 'It's where we pick up shipments from the South Coast. I transport the cargoes via wagon to the village.'

'Why not moor and ferry them out from down south?'

'No good anchorage off the coast where Prince Marek closed the forest. It's easier – cheaper – to run the wagons into Strandson and pick them up there.'

'What happens in Pellia?'

'I've never done that leg of the journey. I don't do well at sea.'

'I recall.'

'Right, um, I'm told that there is a deep-water dock. The cargo is unloaded onto barges and towed upriver to someplace near Welstar Palace. That's all I know. I swear it.'

'Who pays you?'

'A general, here in Orindale, who deals with the prince's financial affairs in the Eastlands, but he was killed in an explosion. He was living in the old imperial palace – where they took the spy after his encounter with you two. I don't know if he's still there. I don't know who will pay me now, for these shipments, or the next.'

Brexan frowned. 'There will be no more shipments.'

Carpello, afraid of being cut again, bit down on his tongue in an effort to control his sobbing. In his peripheral vision he could see the sun coming up, but he dared not look out the window. Instead, he kept his gaze focused on the bridge of Brexan's nose. He was too frightened to look into her eyes; nothing he saw there gave him any hope that he would live another aven. Warm blood continued to ooze out and trickle down his leg, puddling on the floor beneath his chair. He thought for a moment that he could smell it, but in truth all he could smell was his own excrement.

Brexan left his side and moved to the window. 'Have you ever been lost at sea, Carpello?' she asked him, conversationally.

'No.'

'Have you ever been submerged in water so cold that you can't feel your toes or fingers? That you forget your extremities – ever been there?'

'No.'

'Have you ever feared what might be waiting for you at the bottom of the ocean?'

'When I was young, I was afraid of the—'

'Shut up!' Brexan turned back and glared at him. The lines across her brow and at the corners of her eyes were deep slashes in the dim light. 'I don't want to hear it, do you understand? The sound of your voice only makes me want to kill you even more.' Tears welled in her eyes and her voice cracked as she shouted, 'You don't have any idea what it was like! I held him up, I carried him, and he was bigger and stronger than I am, but I did it anyway, because he was so tired and so cold. And do you know why he was that cold? Because you dragged him behind your ship; do you remember that, Carpello?'

He said nothing.

Brexan turned back to the window and watched dawn colour the salt marsh. 'But then we were saved,' she whispered. 'We were saved and I thought I would live for ever. We didn't have anything but a big, smelly fish, but I didn't need anything. We were alive, and we were free, and we were together.'

She wiped the tears away and returned to the shaking merchant's side. She bent down and asked quietly, 'Do you know what happened then?'

Still Carpello kept silent. He could read his death in Brexan's voice, in her stance, in the air. Begging would do nothing but hasten that eventuality.

'Your scarred Seron happened. He came after us. It was just after dawn, about this time of day. The light was just like this; that meadow was so pretty, and I could smell the sea. It was a beautiful day.' She took a selfish moment to allow the memories to wash over her, then she punched Carpello solidly beneath his chin.

The prisoner tumbled backwards, crushing the wooden chair beneath his weight and coming free from the leather straps, but neither Brexan nor Sallax feared that he would be able to escape.

Instead, he rolled into a foetal position and lay there keening to himself.

'Gods, look at what a pathetic creature you are,' Brexan said in disgust, and then turned to Sallax. 'Go ahead,' she said.

Sallax got up from the end of the bed and stood over Carpello. 'My sister's name was Brynne,' he said. 'Say it.'

Carpello rolled onto his back, looking like a bloody stranded whale. 'What?' he muttered.

Sallax kicked him in the ribs. At least one snapped.

Carpello screamed, a hoarse rattling cry, until his voice gave up and faded to a whisper.

'I said my sister's name was Brynne. Say it.'

'Brynne.' The word was barely audible.

'My sister's name was Brynne. Say it!'

'Brynne,' Carpello repeated, a little louder. 'Brynne.'

'That's right, Brynne.' Sallax almost choked. 'Brynne: an innocent little girl, you foul beast.' Sallax ignored the tears coursing noiselessly down his cheeks. 'She was a child when you ruined her. You tore her apart. It took Twinmoons for her to heal physically, but she never got past what you did to her.'

'I'm sorry. I'm so sorry.' Carpello's voice was a whisper. He reached out with both hands to Sallax, as if the big man might kneel down and embrace him, his apology accepted.

But instead, Sallax placed the heel of his boot on the fat man's jowly throat and started pressing down. 'My sister's name was Brynne. She was a loving, caring, wonderful person who would have done anything for anyone. And she died an angry, knife-wielding killer, because of you. Do you understand that? My sister's name was Byrnne,' Sallax shouted down at him, 'say it. Say it!'

All that emerged was a rasp, a coarse rattle, as Carpello gasped for air. Sallax removed his boot and, crying openly now, crossed the room to Brexan, who hugged him, hard.

Seeing them momentarily preoccupied with one another, Carpello summoned the last measure of his strength and, rolling to all fours, half-crawled and half-dived for the door. He crashed into it, feeling his rib flare, and the door flew out on its hinges, slamming against the wall with a satisfactory crash.

That ought to wake someone, he thought, but he tried to shout for help as well. 'Please, help, someone,' he rasped. He could barely hear himself.

Behind him, he heard Sallax and Brexan, and pulled himself

painfully, clumsily to his feet. Neither had yet grabbed him, and he revelled in a wave of adrenalin: he had a chance, freedom looked to be just a few steps away. If he could reach the front room, there might be someone who could help him ... One step, then two; he was nearly there. He drew what felt like the biggest, cleanest breath of fresh air he had ever tasted, and prepared a great bellowing cry for help. *How can they not help me?* he thought. *Look at me: I'm cut to pieces, my face is a mess, my clothes are soiled – someone will help me.* He shouted, his voice still hoarse but significantly louder than it had been only moments before, 'Please, some—'

Carpello was silenced by a crushing blow to the back of his head. He lost consciousness immediately, but his onwards momentum propelled him headlong into the stone fireplace in Nedra's front room. A sickening crack echoed as his head hit the carved mantelpiece and Carpello's body fell to the floor. It twitched and jerked for several moments before stilling.

Sallax and Brexan had reached the door in time to see Carpello take his last flying leap into the mantelpiece. Turning towards the scullery, they saw Nedra standing in mute horror. A splintered log dangled from one hand.

Sallax reached over to take it.

'Is he a thief?' she asked. 'I didn't mean for him to—'

'He was an evil man,' Brexan said, wrapping an arm around Nedra's shoulders. 'He was a hideous monster.'

Nedra nodded, her eyes still wide, taking in the gruesome scene in her dining room.

'We'll take care of this,' Sallax said, tossing the log onto the overnight embers. They watched while it caught fire and began crackling brightly.

'The tide will be high soon,' Nedra said, almost in a daze. 'I get rid of pallen and lobster shells, gansel bones, whatever. I just leave it a few paces below the high water mark. Half an aven later, it's gone.'

Brexan looked over at Sallax, who nodded. 'That should do just fine.'

As the tide turned, the three of them stood together among the skeletal stalks of winter cordgrass. Almost everything on the marsh had died, but the remains were still there, frozen and delicate, like finely blown glass. The water had come up, taken Carpello in its frigid embrace and carried his corpulent form out to sea. They could still see him, floating in the distance. Brexan watched closely, hoping to see the inky waters pull him down into the darkness.

Sallax put an arm around her shoulders. 'We got what we needed.'

She nodded. 'He's at the old imperial palace.'

'It will be difficult to get in, even more challenging to get back out,' Sallax lied. He knew it would be suicide to try to assassinate Jacrys in the Barstag family residence.

'But he won't be expecting us.'

Alen belted his tunic tightly and pulled his cloak loosely about his neck. Communicating with Fantus, even for those few moments, had drained him noticeably and he had slept like a dead man for the rest of the night. He could have done with another aven or two in bed, but with Churn, Hoyt and Hannah already out and about in Treven, investigating safe passage down the Welstar River, he felt compelled to rouse himself.

In the bar he armed himself with a flagon of tecan, a hunk of bread and some cheese, then dropped some copper Mareks next to the bread basket. He waved to the innkeeper, gesturing that he would return the flagon later; the innkeeper, absorbed with repairs to a torn leather satchel, nodded in understanding.

Alen stepped into the street and felt the cold work its way inside the folds of his cloak. Winter was upon Malakasia; this far north it had been for much of the past Moon, but it was colder along the river than it had been descending the foothills and crossing the arable plains south of Treven.

Treven was more of a large town than a city, but it had a very healthy economy, thanks to its position as the first major settlement upriver from Welstar Palace. Treven's shipping and merchant fraternity were kept busy running goods in and out of the military encampment next to Prince Malagon's hilltop residence.

Hoyt was out searching for a barge captain willing to sign them on – as crew, they'd have legitimate papers to get past the customs officials who checked everyone on the river around the military base. Alen wanted an opportunity to reconnoitre, and floating by the encampment was the only way they could come up with to gain even a cursory look at the defences through which they would have to pass to reach the palace.

As he walked down a steep hill towards the docks, Alen was troubled. The news from Fantus had been disappointing: Nerak was not in Malakasia, so there would be no final battle between the two of them, at least not yet, and there was no password to Welstar. He was still determined to get into the palace, and to kill the magicians who had forced him to remain in hiding since Sandcliff fell.

You did that to yourself, his conscience chided him.

He wanted to kill them, and he wanted to kill Bellan. He tried to convince himself it was because she was Nerak's only opportunity to continue ruling Eldarn from Welstar Palace, but the truth was, Alen wanted Bellan dead because she was Malagon's daughter. Alen wanted to be the one to look into the girl's eyes and watch as her life faded. It wouldn't bring Pikan or Reia back, but that didn't matter: what mattered was vengeance.

Fantus had had other troubling news, though: if there was no far portal in the palace, there was no reason to take Hannah, Hoyt and Churn with him – there was certainly no sense risking their lives to achieve his own selfish goal of vengeance for his wife and daughter. He would have to find some way to trick them, to break away and sneak inside the palace alone – perhaps masked by the same spell he had used to hide their horses and satchels outside the forest of ghosts. He smiled at the thought of Hannah's reaction: she would be furious, she would rave like a madwoman for avens. He hoped news of Steven Taylor and his Larion far portal would persuade her to leave Malakasia and to go with Hoyt – Churn would probably remain behind – to the Eastlands to find Fantus and the other foreigners.

As he picked his way towards the river, he spotted Hoyt and Churn emerging from a dockside tavern, each carrying a flagon of something. The Pragan giant saw him and raised his in greeting.

'Well met, boys,' Alen called. 'I take it you slept well.'

'Not like you,' Hoyt said, 'Alen, you sleep like a champion! How you do it escapes me.'

'I have a talent for it; that I admit. However, last night was something special.'

'Difficult spell?'

'The worst I know.'

'What did you do? We didn't notice anything, no phantom dragons, no hugely breasted women, not even a talking dog.'

'I contacted an old friend, Fantus. He is in Gorsk.'

Churn signed, 'That's tiring?'

Alen nodded 'We didn't speak for long, but it left me shattered.'

'Fantus – that's Gilmour, isn't it? The famous partisan from the Eastlands? Did you reach him?'

'Yes, yes and yes.'

'So what's the news?'

Alen shrugged. 'Not much. He's moving towards Traver's Notch, hoping to make contact with members of the Falkan Resistance.'

'They mounting an attack?'

'He didn't say.'

'It would make sense, given what we've learned in the past few avens. First off, we found a barge captain. He's a pretty disagreeable fellow, but for a bit of silver he—'

'Where's Hannah?' Alen interrupted.

'Oh, she's inside. The kitchen workers had some gansel eggs, and Hannah's paid them just about all the copper she had on her to cook them herself. Can you believe it? And what a mess: eggs with cheese and bits of ham, pepper weed, even sausage, all mixed in together. Good rutting whores, but it looks like it's already been eaten at least once.' Hoyt grimaced. 'She'll be done in a bit. We came out here to get away from the smell. It was grim.'

Alen smiled. Looked like the omelette wouldn't take off in Eldarn just yet. 'Go on about the captain, please.'

'He'll give four members of his own crew a few days' leave – once he got a look at Churn, he offered five or six! We pay him for the cruise, work the barge for him, and he gets his normal take from the stops we'll make along the way. There's no downside for him.'

'So if we get boarded, we're legitimate?'

'We are legitimate, perfectly legal and beyond reproach.'

'Is he willing to make more than one pass?'

'Only if we work the return trip,' Hoyt said. 'He nearly shut down negotiations when I mentioned lingering a few avens near the palace. He doesn't strike me as the kind of person who's afraid of much, but he went white and nearly passed out right there on his deck when I asked if we could play in Malagon's back yard for a few days.'

'So down and back?' Alen confirmed.

'Right, but we have stops at the military docks on both journeys, so we'll have two decent opportunities to survey the place and plenty of time in between to scribble out a map or to note areas we want to examine more closely on our second pass.'

Alen pursed his lips. 'Good,' he said finally. 'That's fine. Thank you both.'

Hoyt shrugged his cloak up higher across his shoulders. 'It's not ideal, but I can't think of any other way to get near the palace.

Wagon shipments are all taken over by the army and carried in by military transports. Even on the river we'll most likely have a naval escort most of the way.'

'When do we leave?'

'Two days from now – but it will take two days to get down there.'

'And when do we report for duty?'

'Funny you should ask.' Hoyt glanced at Churn. 'We're hired from dawn tomorrow – I gather we'll have quite a few crates of vegetables to load.'

'Grand,' Alen said wryly. 'At least it'll keep us warm. Let's go and find Hannah; we've plans to make.'

THE BORDER GUARDS

'You think it's safe?' Garec stuffed the last of his belongings into a saddlebag.

'Of course,' Mark said. 'Steven said it was, and I don't have any reason not to believe him – anyway, didn't you hear it screeching all night? It didn't sound especially healthy to me.'

Garec shivered. 'The sounds of it dying – those coarse coughs, like barks, were so unnerving I could hardly sleep. Just when I thought it was dead and was finally going to lie still, it started up again.'

'Steven said he did something so that the almor couldn't escape, then it was just a matter of following it up into the hills,' Mark said. 'Even with the staff to keep him warm, it can't have been much fun hiking back with no coat or sweater.'

Garec looked at Steven, asleep beside the fire in the great hall. When he came in earlier that morning, wet, cold and worn out, he'd just assured them they would be safe going down to the stables to check on the horses, then he curled up in the tapestry they'd been using as a rug in front of the fire and promptly passed out. Now, with both sorcerers sleeping off the rigours of the night's work, Mark and Garec were left to make preparations for the journey south.

They probably wouldn't travel far before stopping first, most likely in the village at the bottom of the valley, where there was at least one decent inn. Garec, folding blankets as tightly as he could, started to imagine a wooden table piled high with winter delicacies – gansel stew, thick sauces, fresh bread – followed by a long night's sleep in a comfortable bed – until Mark interrupted, shattering his fantasy.

'Do you want to take the rest of this down there, or will you wait for me?'

'I'll wait,' Garec replied. 'Together we can make it in one trip.' He stood and stretched, reaching for the buttressed stone ceiling until he felt his muscles loosen. He had lost weight since leaving

Estrad; he shuddered to think what his mother would say when she saw him. He hadn't been especially large before setting out from the orchard that grey morning; but he imagined he now looked like one of Malagon's wraiths. Garec promised his absent parent he would spend an entire Moon eating if he ever saw the end of this business and returned home.

Both Garec and Mark were looking forward to leaving the Larion stronghold; they had spent much of the past twenty days or more idling the time away while Steven and Gilmour worked. Garec noticed Gilmour never opened Lessek's spell book, and though Steven flipped through the pages from time to time, it wasn't that often, so it appeared that whatever magic the two men hoped to employ in their ultimate battle with Nerak, it would only come from the hickory staff, the Windscroll and Lessek's key.

With little else to do, Garec and Mark had explored the Larion library, investigated all the decent vintages in the wine cellar – careful not to step in or near anything that might be damp – and had spent many avens perfecting a game Mark called *Larion Golf*, something he developed to take his mind off Rodler's death. He couldn't help feeling guilty, thinking the almor had been waiting for *him* specifically, but eventually he realised the demon wasn't actually choosy: it wanted them *all* dead.

After a sleepless night agonising over his treatment of the smuggler, Mark took himself in hand. He called Garec over and spread a large piece of parchment out on the floor beside the fireplace. The parchment was covered with crosses, arrows and circles, and near the top were the words *Larion Golf, The Front Nine, Par 27*. He read it out for Garec, who couldn't decipher the loops and whorls of the foreign script.

'This, my friend, is how you and I are going to practise archery without boring ourselves to death,' Mark said proudly.

'What do those words mean?' He ran a finger across the top of the folio.

'Shoot straight and win drinks.'

'My kind of game, then,' Garec laughed. He studied the parchment, recognising it now as a crudely drawn map of the palace, from cellar to towers. 'How do we play?'

Mark set up a course of nine holes of archery golf. Each had a tee, a series of wooden targets to hit from a particular spot at a particular angle, and a difficult, near-impossible final shot, through masonry cracks, lattice windows or stone crevices.

He'd worked out a tally system too: they teed off together, took three shots per hole, and counted once for every time a bowstring snapped. If their arrow reached each of the interim targets, and then embedded into the final target without bouncing off, deflecting, or missing entirely, it was scored par for that hole. Every time one of the competitors had to draw and fire again – either at an interim target or at the final mark – he had to add one shot to his final tally.

At the end of nine holes, the winner got to wait by the fire while the loser went, alone, into the wine cellar to fetch whatever vintage the winner requested. It was up to the winner to decide whether or not to share the wine, but every time Garec won – and of course he won every time – he graciously split the wine. In Garec's opinion, Mark had earned the drinks simply for creating Larion Golf. Garec had never known how much fun shooting an old palace full of arrows could be.

Now he picked up Mark's quiver and checked the contents. There were few arrows left with decent tips and many had damaged fletching. 'We have to get you some new shafts and tips,' he said. 'And I need to teach you how to repair these.'

'No laughing, Wonder Boy,' Mark smiled. 'Just because you've spent your whole life practising doesn't mean you get to laugh at the beginner when he narrowly loses in heated competition.'

'You never finished the course within six shots – and just look at these arrows! It looks like you clipped every stone in the place.'

'I said, no laughing.' Mark took one of the arrows and examined it; he grimaced when he saw how badly the tip had eroded.

'I am joking,' Garec said. 'Most great archers need fifty Twinmoons to learn what you've learned in one; you're an outstanding shot.'

'But I'm not you.'

'No one is me, Mark.' Garec's voice dropped. 'I have—'

'A special gift.'

'If that's what you want to call it, fine.'

'I still don't know how you do it.' Mark said, 'and the more I learn, the more in awe I am. Like those shots through the lattice window: they're impossible. I didn't make one. You never missed.'

'I'm not just an archer,' Garec said. 'I've moved beyond that. My bow is more like a part of me – and you'll be that good some day.' He was confident Mark would become one of Eldarn's great archers. 'You have a natural affinity for it.'

'For killing? I would never have thought that about myself.'

'I meant for archery,' Garec corrected. 'Killing is something altogether different.'

'I don't think so.'

'You will.'

Mark diverted to a safer topic. 'So what do I need to fix these up?'

Garec laughed. 'How about a whole new quiver full of decent shafts? These are all a mess. You won't get one straight shot out of the bunch. It was a great game, though.'

'That it was,' Mark said. 'Can we get fletching and tips in the village down here?'

'Probably not,' Garec said, 'but I'm sure we can find someone with polished stones.'

'Stone tips?' Mark was unconvinced. 'I don't know about that.'

'Oh, you'll get used to them. I have a whole quiver full of stone tips, most of them polished myself – they can be deadly effective.' He swallowed hard at his choice of words.

Mark didn't comment, but as he tied down the last of Steven's belongings with a half hitch and hefted both sacks over his shoulder, asked, 'Ready?'

'Yes. Should we see if Gilmour is awake?'

'No,' Mark shook his head; 'let them sleep. Who knows what kind of night Gilmour had? They deserve an extra aven; we can get the horses ready and be on our way just after midday.'

'After you,' Garec said.

Outside a strong wind blew the dry snow into flurries. The day was slate-grey, the sun a white ball shrouded in layers of clouds, dimly visible, and the cold was intensified somehow by the lack of colour. Garec hesitated beneath the stone archway, where his feet were still dry. Several steps down, the ankle-deep snow – disturbed here and there by Steven's boot prints – waited for them. He looked over at Mark, chuckled nervously, and stepped onto the stone walk.

'Well, that was harder than I thought it would be.'

'For me too,' Mark said. 'I'm glad we took the plunge together. Still alive?'

'Still alive.'

The duo covered the distance to the top of the staircase quickly, as if hustling would keep the memory of the almor from detecting them outside the palace, then hurried down the steps, past the anomalous cottonwood-birch trees, to the narrow defile where the Larion Senators had kept their horses. A wooden stable, one box wide, but several hundred paces long, ran against the south wall of the gorge. The Larion Senators had been famous for their frugal lifestyle, but from the look of their stables, they had invested plenty of time, energy and resources in their horses.

The thin, craggy passage ran back into the hills away from the university campus until it opened onto a hidden meadow in a shallow box-canyon. The two men secured saddlebags and packs, tied down blanket rolls and bridled their horses in preparation for what they assumed would be a brief, late-day trip down the draw and into the village.

Baggage stashed, they wandered along the enormous stables, hoping to find a bale of hay, maybe left by Rodler or other border runners, for the animals were also suffering from too little food and looked barely capable of carrying the packs, let alone riders too. In the picturesque meadow at the far end of the stables, Garec and Mark found the remains of a dilapidated fence and an old corral.

'Would you look at that?' Mark said. 'They stabled the horses in that crevice and brought them out here for exercise and training.'

'Ingenious,' Garec agreed, 'look at this place. It's perfect for it.' He peered back through the narrow gorge. 'I wouldn't want to have been a stable hand, though.'

'No way,' Mark agreed. 'You'd walk ten miles a day just feeding and watering them.'

'If that means a long distance, then I agree,' Garec said. 'You—'

The first arrow missed Garec, passing over his shoulder with an audible *pffft!* to bury itself in the flesh above Mark's right knee.

Mark cursed in shock and fell, his hands wrapped around the colourful fletching; blood bloomed across his leg and seeped between his fingers. It was a deep wound.

Garec reacted in an instant, diving on his friend and shouting, 'Don't pull it out! You'll make it worse!' He dragged Mark towards a clump of aspen trees growing between a stand of rocks that had fallen from the gorge. He didn't bother to look back; he knew where their assailants were, on the forested hillside to the east. The hunters had a clear shot at them until they reached the rocks. Blood oozed from Mark's leg, leaving a dark crimson trail.

'Come on,' Garec said, his voice charged with fear, 'we're dead if we don't get out of here.'

An arrow zinged past his head; another stabbed into the ground beside his hand. A third struck him in the calf, and he heard a fourth hit Mark with a dull thud. *They had to keep moving.* Ignoring the pain, Garec clawed and scraped his way through the snow to dive behind the rocks.

Mark continued screaming.

'Let me see it,' Garec shouted over him, 'let me see where you're hit.'

'Just here,' Mark groaned, 'just in my knee.'

'There was a second,' he gasped, needing to catch his breath. It wouldn't be long before whoever was firing at them came down to finish the job. 'I heard it. The second one, where did it hit you?'

Mark pointed with a bloody finger, indicating Garec's side. As if seeing another person's body, he stared down at the second shaft, buried halfway into his hip. Garec had heard the thud, but he hadn't felt anything.

'Rutting whores,' he cursed.

Mark pulled himself up behind the rock, his knee ignored for the moment. 'How many are there?'

'I don't know. I didn't have time to look – if we'd stayed out there, it wouldn't matter how many, we'd be dead.'

'Good point,' Mark said, drawing an arrow from his quiver. 'Get ready,' he directed, his hands trembling as he tried to fix it on the string.

Garec's stomach turned; he made no move towards his bow.

Mark took aim along a Larion Golf-battered arrow and fired into the trees on the opposite side of the corral. The arrow flew up and away from his target. 'Missed him,' Mark growled, and fired again, this time at a shadow that passed beneath the outstretched limb of a clumsy oak tree. Again, the imperfect shaft flew high and wide. 'Mother—!' He turned on Garec, ignoring the blood-stained snow beneath his knee. 'Give me some of your arrows; these are rubbish – I can't even hit the bloody hillside.' He checked his friend's hip again. 'Are you all right? Can you shoot?'

Garec groaned, stammered something, then fell silent.

'Garec!' Mark shouted, worried he might pass out. 'Garec, I need you. We're in a bad spot here, buddy. You've got to keep it together.' Angrily he continued to draw and release, aiming at anything that moved. After a minute or two of wild shooting, he realised there was no return fire.

Crouched beside Garec, Mark put the bow down and waited.

A squad of Malakasian archers, border guards from the look of their uniforms, stepped from the trees on the opposite side of the meadow and began marching down, obviously a well-disciplined group. Garec peered over the rocks to count them: nine. He shook his head. He could have dropped all nine of them before they reached the near side of the corral. The errant shots had lulled them into thinking they were in little danger. Mark was skilled, but he had no experience in battle and his injuries and his excitement had caused the shafts to fly all over the place. The squad obviously assumed Mark was the only one capable of mounting any kind of defence.

Little did they realise that in two breaths they could all be dead – *if* Garec decided to stand and fight. Dropping his forehead to the cold stone, he closed his eyes. He wouldn't do it.

'We're dead now,' Mark whispered.

'Throw out your bow,' Garec said, 'throw them both out. At least let them see we won't be fighting back. They know they've hit us. Maybe they'll take us prisoner.'

'Terrific.'

'It's better than any alternative we have,' he said. 'Throw out the bows.'

Mark did, and Garec watched as the squad slowed. Several of the men nocked arrows, aiming at the rocks, taking no chances.

Garec shouted loudly, 'We are injured and unarmed!'

A husky voice answered, 'Stand up. Now.'

'We have to,' Garec said to Mark. 'They'll kill us if we don't.'

'Look at the way they move together,' Mark said. 'They're well trained.' He winced with the effort to get up. 'We have to hope they're well-trained soldiers and not well-trained killers.'

'They're soldiers,' Garec said, 'look at their uniforms. This far from Malakasia, and they're that disciplined: these are proper soldiers, border guards, probably.'

'Let's hope you're right.' Mark leaned on the rock for support. He could feel his knee was badly injured. Garec put a supporting arm around his waist, in case one of the soldiers might mistake falling down as reaching for weapons.

'And the other weapons,' the voice came again. Garec couldn't see who it was, but he was somewhere to their left.

Garec drew his hunting knife and tossed it out in front of the rocks. Mark did likewise.

'Anything else?'

'No,' Garec shouted back.

'Come out slowly and lie down, face-down, away from your weapons.' The disciplined line advanced as one.

'Let's go,' Garec said. 'I don't think they're going to kill us.'

'Because they would have already?'

'Something like that. But look at that fellow on their left, the short one with the stomach. He's the one in charge.'

'So what? Fat people don't kill indiscriminately?'

'Look at his uniform. He's not an officer. He's a sergeant.'

Mark grimaced with pain. 'I hate to belabour a point, Garec, but so what?'

Garec was sweating, despite the chill; he was losing too much blood. He looked forward to lying down in the snow, at least there he could rest for a moment and cool off. His heart was racing, he was breathing heavily and on the verge of losing consciousness.

He pulled himself around the rocks, motioning for Mark to do the same. 'Look at his gloves,' he said softly. 'They aren't standard issue. He's in knitted mittens, and he's not carrying a bow. Old, unarmed sergeants in knitted mittens don't kill indiscriminately.'

'How do you know that?'

'Because he's out here by himself, that's how. He's been around for a while, long enough to substitute standard-issue gloves with something one of his daughters made for him back home, probably because he was complaining about working in Gorsk. His squad is disciplined, and no one has fired a shot since we threw out the bows. Finally, where's his lieutenant? Back in the barracks, nice and warm beside the fire, because he trusts this guy.' Garec felt his head loll momentarily to one side; he shook it several times to clear his thoughts. 'We're not going to die, Mark, not here.'

'That's great news, thanks.' His voice faded as he fell forward in the snow.

Dropping down beside him, Garec winced as he jerked the arrow-head in his side. The squad moved into position, surrounding them.

'Lay down, son,' the sergeant said, coming forward. He pulled off one of the knit mittens and tucked it beneath his arm for safe keeping, then reached up to remove a wool hat emblazoned with the crest of Prince Malagon's Border Guard. 'Where are the others, son? Still up at the palace?'

Garec tried to remember what Rodler had said when Mark first threatened to kill him. 'We're from Capehill,' he said. 'We do a bit of book business down there. That's all. This old palace has a library, most of it rotten or torn up, but there are a few volumes here that bring a decent price at home.'

The sergeant nodded. He had arranged his thinning hair to cover as much of his pate as possible, but there wasn't much left to cover the pale skin, dotted with liver spots. From the look of his paunch, he was a beer drinker. His yellowing teeth suggested a tobacco habit. Garec thought this man might be any of their grandfathers; what he was doing serving along the Gorskan border at his age was a mystery.

'A book business, eh? Well, that's illegal, but you know that. And what about the root?'

Garec shrugged, affecting a sheepish child caught with one hand in the pastry drawer. 'We do a bit of a fennaroot business as well, yes sir.'

'And you, Southie? You're pretty far north, eh, Southie? Books and fennaroot pay your way, did they?'

'Don't call me that,' Mark was lying in the snow, his eyes closed, fading in and out of consciousness, 'fat Irish flatfoot.'

'What's that then?' The sergeant stepped over to him. 'I didn't hear you, but from your tone, Southie, I'd guess you just disparaged my parents, eh?' He kicked Mark solidly in the ribs. 'Eh, Southie?'

Mark groaned, and gurgled something unintelligible.

'Raskin!'

'Sergeant?'

'This one needs surgery.'

A young soldier, lean and wiry, shouldered her bow and stepped forward. 'Field surgery, Sergeant or tavern surgery?'

He pinched the bridge of his nose with two fingers and closed his eyes. 'Rutting headaches, um, make it tavern surgery. We don't have all day to play at party games out here.'

'Right,' The soldier, Raskin, motioned for two others to join her. 'Mox, Denny, hold him down.' One broad-shouldered young man lay across Mark's upper body, pinning his arms to the ground; another gripped his lower legs in a powerful hug, bending his knee to expose the arrow for Raskin. She removed a scarf from her neck and tied it around Mark's thigh, tightening it with a piece of whittled wood she took from her belt, then she gripped the arrow with one hand.

'One surgical procedure, tavern method, ready to go, sir,' she announced. 'Hang on boys,' she said, looking at the two soldiers holding Mark fast, and drew the arrow with a tremendous wrenching pull. Mark, who was not strong enough to resist, screamed long and shrilly, and then fell silent.

The sergeant gave the trio an approving grin. 'Well done, Raskin. Now, bind that up, quickly, mind.'

'Right away, Sergeant,' the woman said, removing the makeshift tourniquet and exposing the wound. Someone handed her a wad of cloth dampened with water from a canteen and she cleaned it, pressing too far into the flesh for Garec's comfort, then bound it snugly with a length of gauze someone else had ready.

'Does he need querlis?' Garec asked.

The woman glanced up at her sergeant, who nodded. 'He might need it later,' she said. 'It's bleeding now, but I'll check it after the blood has clotted. If it looks like it could become infected, I'll give him some then.'

'Thanks,' Garec's vision blurred again and he flushed. His stomach knotted, but he managed to quell the rush of nausea by pressing his face into the snow to cool the rush of blood and quiet his raging system. He croaked, 'If you don't mind, I think I prefer field surgery to tavern surgery.' The last thing he heard as he passed out was the sergeant bellowing a hearty laugh, a grandfather's laugh; nothing dangerous in it. Garec felt confident as he drifted away that he and Mark would live.

He didn't wake, nor did he feel any pain when Raskin extracted the arrows from his hip and leg.

'So it's just a minor change in plans, that's all.' Hannah dried her tears and laughed. 'Look at me, will you? I'm a mess.'

Alen's heart wrenched. He hadn't mentioned the far portal, but he had told Hannah that Steven and Mark were on their way to Traver's Notch and that it was just a matter of time – and a significant dose of good luck – before they were reunited and returned safely to Colorado. She had flung her arms around his neck and squeezed him harder than anyone had in nearly a thousand Twinmoons. When she finally released him, her face was already tearstained.

'We can steal the far portal, right? It's not too large? If it's like the one in Steven and Mark's house, it's a rug. We can roll it up and carry it between us, that shouldn't be a problem. We can take a ship to Orindale, and you can contact Gilmour again – if it isn't too hard to do. Is it? I mean, it doesn't hurt, does it?'

'No, I just get a bit—'

'Oh, good then, because if it was painful, we could find some other way to locate them, but if you contact Gilmour from Orindale, or maybe from the ship on the way over – ships are a nice place to sleep, what with all that rocking – and then we can find them, and we can go home. Oh, Alen, thank you, thank you, thank you. I can't tell you what this means.' Hannah was almost incoherent, and the others left her to carry on until she was finished. She had come a long way, through many stressful and unfamiliar challenges, desperately praying someone would tell her that Steven Taylor was alive and that they could go home together. No one interrupted her as she veered wildly between laughter and tears until she stopped to catch her breath.

Calming finally, she said, 'But we still have to go inside the palace to steal the portal. That's still dangerous, and I don't want to get my hopes too high, because that could still kill one or more, or *damn* – sorry – all of us. But I don't want to think that way; I want to believe we can do it. We can get in the palace, can't we? We can get inside and find the portal – I suppose we have to leave that to you, Alen – and then we can take it with us. If we get in, we can get out. And we can take the portal to Falkan with us, and Steven and Mark and I can go home.'

Then her eyes widened; she smiled as an idea took shape in her mind. 'And you all can come with us. You should think about it, really, it's wonderful there, especially in Colorado, there are so many places to visit, things to see and enjoy – and it's so much safer than it is here. You could find happiness there. I know you could.'

Hoyt reached across the table and took her hand. He laughed and said, 'Hannah, gods keep you this happy for ever, I mean it, but you are *not* going into that castle.'

'Why not?' Hannah asked. 'We've come so far.'

'That's right,' Hoyt made Alen's argument for him, 'and if we don't need to send you home from the palace, there is no need for you to go inside.'

'Well, how are we going to—?'

'I'll go get it.'

'Not by yourself,' she protested.

'It's what I do, Hannah. I am one of the best: I can get in there, grab the portal and be out before anyone knows I'm gone.'

'I'll need to be there too,' Alen said.

'Not without me,' Churn signed.

'No and no,' Hoyt said to each of them. 'There's no need to risk everyone's lives to retrieve this rug. Alone, I can be invisible. If we find a way inside, I can get in, get the portal, and get back out quickly. No one will even see me there. I'll find Malagon's chambers, wait for him to step out, even for a moment, and be inside without a sound.'

Alen shook his head. 'The prince's chambers will be sealed with a spell. You need me with you.'

Churn signed again, 'Not without me.'

Finally, Hoyt stood, jouncing the table and nearly upsetting several tankards. 'Fine, fine. You two can come along, but *not* Hannah. There's no reason to endanger her.'

'I agree,' Alen said.

Churn nodded.

'But you know what this means, both of you.' Hoyt was visibly upset. 'This changes the entire operation. What should have been one person going in quietly now becomes three, and that means we triple the possibility that we will end up fighting our way out – or worse.'

'We don't have a choice,' Alen said. He had no intention of Hoyt or Churn going anywhere near the palace. 'At the very least I *have* to go in; whether I can unlock all the doors Prince Malagon will have sealed, I don't know, but I can, to some extent, mask my own movements. Hoyt, I don't see any reason for you to come along – except that, like your burly companion, you seem determined to be there.'

'I am going in,' Churn signed.

Hoyt looked dejectedly down at his beer. 'Fine. I hate this idea, but fine.' He sulked another moment, then turned on Churn. 'And you. What are you thinking? You want to die in there, is that it? *He* does. Did you know that?' He gestured over at Alen. 'He wants to face Prince Malagon and kill the prince and himself at the same time. Is that what you want?'

'I am going in.' He swallowed half his beer in one massive gulp.

'I hate to interrupt, but what can I be doing while you three are in there stealing the portal?' Hannah had no desire to enter Welstar Palace. Hoyt and Churn were thieves by profession; she had never stolen more than an extra carton of milk at school. She wasn't skilled with a bow, a rapier or a short blade, and if she did go along, her safety would be an added burden on her friends.

'I know it makes no sense for me to go inside with you,' she went on, 'so I won't ask to come along, but there must be something I can do to make sure we get away safely.'

'You can build three pyres,' Hoyt said sarcastically. *That's right. We're going in there to get this portal so you can go home. The rest of us have nothing to gain in there, and these two don't plan on coming back out again.*

'You've known all along,' Alen interrupted, glaring at the younger man, 'that you do not have to accompany us on this journey. Hannah and Churn have business here in Malakasia. I have issues to address. You came for the trip, Hoyt. We are all glad you did, but you should feel no obligation to enter Welstar Palace, and certainly not on your own.'

Hoyt softened. 'You're right. Sorry, Hannah.'

'I'll go in,' she said. 'You've already done so much for me, and I'll not ask you to risk your life again, especially for nothing but the chance to cheat death against tremendous odds. I'm not afraid to admit that I don't want to go in, but I don't think you want to, either.'

'Don't worry about it – what kind of freedom fighter would I be if I turned down a chance to deny Prince Malagon one of his favourite toys?'

'And to answer your question, Hannah,' Alen broke the momentary silence, 'when we escape the palace, we will either make our way west into the mountains on horseback, or we will move downriver under cover of darkness; whichever we decide, our packs, supplies and horses, or our barge, raft, canoe, whatever it is we use, will need looking after, so you are the only person left to ensure our speedy departure.'

Hannah was pleased to have something to do; she was still a little embarrassed at Hoyt's comment. She reminded herself Steven was alive and waiting for her in the east.

Hoyt rose. 'I'm going to get a few things we need for the river trip.'

'Nothing to eat?' Churn asked.

'I'm not hungry,' he signed back.

'I'll come with you.'

'No, you eat, you big bear. We need you strong tomorrow morning. We have vegetables to load, and we both know how grumpy you'll be tonight if you don't eat.'

'You all right?' Hannah asked.

'I'm fine.' He turned to leave.

'Let him go,' Alen whispered. 'He has to make a decision; we need to give him some time.'

'But he's going into the palace for me,' Hannah insisted. 'I don't want that on my shoulders for the rest of my life.'

'Hannah, take it from an exceedingly old man; if it saves your life and allows you to return home with Steven Taylor and Mark Jenkins, then yes, of course you want it on your shoulders for the rest of your life. Don't try to tell me otherwise, because I am too old for bravery, pride and sacrifice for one's values, that's all grettan shit, and I'm not interested in wallowing in it. Hoyt is not going into Welstar Palace for you, he's going in for everyone: for Churn's family, for my family, for all the miserable, oppressed people of Eldarn who never had a chance to enjoy freedom or prosperity in their lives, and especially for one very talented thief who would have been a wonderful, caring doctor had he been given a chance. This is all much bigger than you, Hannah. Hoyt knows it; he just needs a little time to realise it.'

And I will have done one final good deed for my friend. Then I will be able to go in. Alone.

When Garec woke it was nearly dark and he was sweating. It had been cold that morning, when he and Mark set out to load the horses; he remembered the wind swirling clouds of snow about the grounds and the wintry bite of the air. It wasn't much warmer here. From the slate-grey colour of his surroundings, he guessed he and Mark were under cover of a Malakasian Army tent.

The woman had treated him with querlis; that's why he was sweating, and why he had slept the day away. He lifted his head from the damp blankets, enough to see that he and Mark were on cots in an eight-person tent, similar to those Gilmour had pointed out from the ridge south of the border. It was a big square, easily as large as the front room in Garec's parents' house, but he and Mark were its only occupants. Near the back was a table piled with bags and bits and pieces, and a tripod brazier, which was currently unused.

Garec tried to assess the damage to his hip and lower leg. He felt relatively little pain, other than a dull throb pulsing in his side. Mostly, he felt numb. *That's the querlis*, he thought. *When it wears off you're going to feel like someone has been shooting arrows into your backside.* He was glad to have been unconscious when the soldiers removed the arrows. Although he had requested field surgery, Garec did not fool himself into thinking that he had been treated more gently than Mark. *Tavern surgery*, he thought. *Remind me never to go to that tavern.*

A strong breeze caused the tent flaps to flutter noisily. Outside, the snow looked less deep; maybe they'd been carried downhill from Sandcliff. Garec heard Mark stir from the other side of the shelter and whispered urgently, 'Mark, wake up.'

Mark moaned and rolled onto his side, still asleep.

Garec listened for sounds of the soldiers outside. He thought he could make out two or three voices, but they were muffled by distance and wind; even straining, he was unable to eavesdrop on the conversation. 'Mark,' he said sharply, 'Mark, wake up.'

Mark shifted again and opened his eyes. 'Garec?' He tried to lift his head, but was overcome by dizziness and fell back into the blankets.

'I'm over here.'

'Where are we?'

'In a Malakasian tent; they were a border patrol. How's your leg?' Garec pushed himself up on his elbow.

'I feel like I've been shot.'

Garec laughed and a blast of pain ran through his hip. 'Me too.'

Without opening his eyes, Mark said, 'Lovely place, this Gorsk. Remind me to look into the local timeshares; maybe we can go in on one together.'

Garec asked, 'Can you walk?'

'Walk?' Mark was incredulous, 'Garec, I don't even know if I can sit up.'

'That's the querlis – it's powerful, but you'll heal very quickly. It does make you drowsy.'

'Drowsy?' Mark laughed again, a happy drunk. 'I feel like I've been hit over the left-field wall. Sorry, it's a baseball reference. You wouldn't know.'

'We'd say you've played the ball in a chainball tournament, about the same thing, I guess,' Garec said. 'Versen used to say that every time he drank Ronan wine.'

Mark forced himself to sit up. 'So how do we get out of here?'

'I don't know,' Garec answered. 'There's less snow here, so I guess we have to assume they brought us down the valley. It looks like it's getting dark outside, but I don't know how long we slept.'

'So we don't know how far we've travelled, and we won't be moving very quickly with these injuries. If we can get to high ground, I'm sure we'll be able to see enough to find Sandcliff, or at least the village below it.'

'Can you climb?'

'No,' Mark was honest, 'probably not, but together, we have two good legs. We might be able to drag ourselves up high enough to get our bearings.'

'That's not much of a plan.'

'No. Where are our weapons?'

Garec looked around. 'Not in here, as far as I can see.'

'How about our cloaks?'

'Mine's here.' Garec peered through the gathering darkness. 'That might be your coat, bunched up beneath the foot of your cot.'

'All right, so assuming, they don't come in here and beat us to death, or torture us to give information we don't have, we might be able to get past a guard late tonight.'

'I doubt it,' Garec said. 'If they don't beat us or tie us up, they'll have that woman—'

'Raskin, he called her; did you see the way she pulled that arrow out of my knee? I'm going to need surgery.'

'Field surgery?'

'Real goddamned Rose-Medical-Center-in-Denver surgery!'

'She'll treat us again.'

'What, with that queer stuff?'

'Querlis, yes.'

'Great,' Mark sighed, 'another beating with the pharmaceutical cudgel. We'll never get out of here if she keeps us doped up on that.'

'But it's good for our injuries, the best thing we have in Eldarn,' Garec insisted.

'Can we get some in a village somewhere?'

'It's difficult to find, but any significant town will have querlis. Traver's Notch has healers.'

'Then I'm skipping my next dose,' Mark said, shifting enough to get his feet onto the ground. He rested his face in his hands.

'You're not ready to travel, Mark.'

'You're right,' he said, 'but I will be if we can get clear of this camp. Have you been able to see outside?'

'Just that it's not as snowy.'

'Let's do that first.' He braced himself on the cot and pushed up with his arms, trying to stand, but as he did so, the tent flaps opened and the woman came in. Mark allowed himself to fall back into the blankets. 'Ah, Dr Mengele, lovely to see you,' he said.

'What are you doing up? You shouldn't be putting weight on that leg.' She moved to his bedside. 'Here, let me see it.'

'No way!' Mark spat and swung for her, tumbling her into the wooden table at the back of the tent. The table collapsed over her, spilling packs, supplies, food and what looked like medical implements. Rolling to her feet, Raskin advanced with her own fists clenched. She stopped when she saw the tent flaps open.

'Now that wasn't very polite,' said the sergeant, who had followed her in. He crossed quickly to Mark's cot.

'I don't want her touching me again,' Mark said angrily.

'No, son, you don't want *me* touching you.' He slammed a fist down on Mark's injured knee and Mark screamed, curled into a ball and rolled from his cot.

The sergeant stooped to help Mark back into bed. 'I hated to do that, son, but I can't have you striking my soldiers. Raskin is the best healer we have in the northern corps, and you're lucky to have her looking after you.' He covered Mark with a wool blanket, careful to tuck the edges beneath the young man's writhing frame. 'Now, get control of yourself, because we have to talk.'

'Leave him alone,' Garec threatened from his cot.

'Or you'll do what? Shoot me with that fancy bow of yours?' The sergeant turned to Garec. 'I noticed you didn't fire one shot this morning, not one. And that after we stuck two arrows in you. Then you throw out one of the nicest rosewood bows I have ever seen. So I figure you're either a coward or a rich coward. Either way, you shut yourself up until I tell you to speak. I'm not interested in getting involved in a lot of bureaucratic nonsense. If you're border runners, you'll go to the lock-up and await your hanging. I don't read, myself, but books are books; I don't begrudge a man the chance to make a bit of silver. I don't like fennaroot runners, and you two claim to be root runners as well as rare book dealers. But you've got no root on you, you've got no books on you, so what am I to do with you?

'I tend to hang fennaroot runners, and though you didn't have anything on you today, if I hang you, no one is going to care. Unless you had it stashed there at the university, you're lying to me, because I know there is no place to sell fennaroot on that hillside – it's not a popular spot, that hillside, doesn't draw a lot of visitors, especially not in the winter.' He looked over at Mark again.

'I don't believe you know a way into the palace, because *I* don't know a way into the palace, and I've been up here since before both of you were even born. If you had any root on you, you'd be dead. If you had any books on you, we might negotiate for a small fee, and you'd be on your way. But you didn't have any books, and you don't have hardly any silver at all. So what do I do with you?'

'I think—' Garec interrupted.

'Shut yourself up firm and quick, boy. I am not making a joke with you,' the sergeant said firmly. 'I will ruin your life right this moment if you don't shut your lip right now.'

Garec complied without another word and the sergeant continued, 'So, boys. There've been reports of some strange goings-on up at the palace: clouds that move against the winds, explosions, demon screams late at night. The villagers complain and our captain sends us up here to check on the place. Mind you, our lieutenant didn't come along with the rest of us, because that would have meant getting up off his delicate little backside, and he doesn't like to do that during this season. So we make the trip up and find you two, *book dealers* with no books, *root runners* with no root. I am a very reasonable man, me, and I didn't kill you. I actually had my girl *treat* you *with querlis*, because I do not, not for one moment, believe anything you have told me.' He spat onto the frozen ground by Mark's head.

'I am not famous for having border runners rush to tell me the truth, and normally I would just hang you boys and be done with this situation. But there are too many coincidences here. First, you aren't who you say you are; I can see that. Second, you appear at the same time we get reports of odd – some might say *magical* – goings on up at the palace. And third, we find you two just at the moment our orders from Capehill fade to a trickle. You see, we here on the border receive our orders from a general in Capehill. He doesn't come up this way too often, because it's cold and grey and the wine doesn't travel well out here in the territory. We have received no orders in the past Twinmoon except to come out here and check up on things. Now, rumour has it that Prince Malagon is dead – gone, killed, hiding out in a basement in Orindale, whatever – and I can assure you boys, I don't care one rutting pinch if he's on a dairy farm enjoying sexual relations with a heifer. But when I put all these pieces together at the same time, something tells me I need to keep you two alive long enough to satisfy my curiosity that these things are not somehow all related. What do you think?'

Raskin had begun changing the dressing on Garec's injuries, peeling away the querlis leaves and replacing them with a fresh poultice. So much for escaping during the night. He nodded his thanks when she finished and watched as she moved warily to Mark's cot.

'If he so much as twitches, you leave his wound untended, you hear, girl? He can tie it up himself if he's that tough.' The sergeant stared down at Mark as he spoke.

'So, boys, what do you think of my summary? Am I about right?'

Garec had been trying to work out their story. 'You're right about much of it, sir, although we truly don't know anything about any

412

screaming demon or magic clouds. We *do* know a way into the palace, and we *do* have a stash, root, a few books and a purse of silver we left inside. We were going to go back for it, after we made a run down into the village for some supplies.'

The sergeant grinned at him. 'I'll give you ten points for coming close to the truth, boy, but you missed it, didn't you? Just by a bit, but you missed the truth.' With that, he pressed the flat of his palm against Garec's injured hip and began to lean forward. Pain flared up despite the fresh querlis and Garec groaned, fighting the urge to scream.

'You want to try again, boy? You two weren't going into that village for supplies. That village is a day-trip. You two were carrying everything you own, and if you were going in for supplies, you'd have taken more than the few copper Mareks you had on you. You were on your way out of those hills, right?'

'Yes, yes, all right, all right,' Garec spoke as quickly as he could between shallow breaths. His leg throbbed with every heartbeat, and his foot began to twitch involuntarily as his body fought the need to pass out. 'You're right. We were leaving.'

The sergeant withdrew his hand. Garec rolled onto his back, sweating.

'We were leaving for a few days. We'd done the first part of our job. The books were there in the library and the root was hidden inside the palace scullery.' Garec decided to try lying one more time, assuming that if the sergeant pressed against his hip again, he would be unconscious until morning, anyway. 'Our job was to get the root across the border and to hide it at Sandcliff. Our partner is the one with the connection here in Gorsk. He sells the root, brings the silver back and we return three days later to carry both the coins and the books across the border into Capehill.'

'Ah, a partner now? This is getting thick, isn't it?' The sergeant approached again. 'And I am quite sure you will be happy to share your partner's name, will you not?'

Garec prayed the sergeant really had been a border guard as long as he claimed. 'Rodler Varn of Capehill,' he said. 'I'm Garec Haile; I come from Randel, down in Rona, but I live in Capehill now. That's Mark Jenkins. He's from the South Coast, obviously, but he lives in Capehill too, at least for the autumn harvest and our winter runs across the border. We get into the palace through a drainage track that runs from the scullery to the gardens. It was a fluke; our partner found it one morning running from a squad of your guards.'

'Rodler Varn?' The sergeant glanced at Raskin, who tried to hide her excitement. 'That name might be familiar ... Rodler Varn. Hmmm.' Garec could see the Malakasian was prevaricating; it was quite clear that young Rodler had been eluding them for some time; he was probably quite a thorn in their sides. 'And you say he'll be stopping by the palace in the next three days?'

'Did I say that?'

'Don't play games with me, boy. What you say in the next two breaths may save your life – your Southie friend's life, too.'

Garec felt a rush of adrenalin; the wind had changed in their favour. Now was his chance to misdirect the greedy border guards. 'We can take you back. We can get you inside – though not many can fit through the opening. *You* won't be able to, and the others we saw this morning, they won't fit either.'

'Mox and Denny,' Mark said quietly.

'Good memory, boy,' the sergeant said with a laugh. 'You *were* paying attention this morning.'

'One tends to remember the names of people who have been so helpful.' He shot Raskin a grim look.

'Right. Denny and Mox. They won't be able to fit, but *she* will.' Garec indicated Raskin. 'We could get her inside.'

'And she could open the doors for the rest of us?'

'I don't know,' Garec answered. 'We've never tried to open them. We figured if anyone – you in particular – was monitoring the palace, you'd know if the main gate had been breached.'

'Wise of you, young man, very wise.' He turned to Raskin. 'You'll go inside with them.' It wasn't a question.

'Rutters, yes, Sergeant,' Raskin said

'Good, good. We'll ride up that way in the morning. Trust me, boy, if you have someone waiting in that scullery for my soldiers, they'll be dead. You, too.'

He turned back to Raskin and said, 'Send Mox and Denny back with two of the others to watch the place. I don't want young Rodler Varn of Capehill coming and going before we can snare him. Have them go up the draw south of here. It's faster.'

Raskin looked concerned. 'Are you sure? The regular path up there is—'

'It's cold enough. No one has seen or heard one of them creatures in the last Moon. With this snow, they'll all be down on the plain hunting livestock. It'll be all right.'

The sergeant pulled his hat down over his ears and tugged the

414

knitted mittens back on his hands. 'If we do capture your partner, boys, you'll have the fun of a tag hanging down in the village.'

Neither Mark nor Garec replied; they hadn't been invited to speak. Garec was feeling drowsy as the querlis began to take effect, but before allowing himself to fall asleep, he made eye contact with Mark. They had learned something useful: none of the ranking officers were alarmed about the strange happenings at the old Larion keep; they hadn't even bothered to send out a full platoon. That was good news for the partisans: they had infiltrated Gorsk and engaged in a noisy battle with Prince Malagon's minions without alerting the entire army.

The challenge now was not just to escape, but to make sure no one managed to spread the word that a company of partisans had breached the walls at Sandcliff.

Garec's vision began to blur and he slipped smoothly into the darkness. His last thought was that Mark had been right: Nerak hadn't sent anyone to Sandcliff, because he thought the almor and the acid clouds would kill them off; he hadn't even alerted his own border patrols. Garec hoped to make it a mistake the fallen Larion sorcerer would regret.

At midmorning the following day they came upon what remained of Mox and Denny and the two soldiers dispatched to assist them at Sandcliff. Mark and Garec were riding one behind the other on a large roan which was quite comfortable carrying both men as long as it didn't involve galloping. They were still groggy with the lingering effects of querlis, and in pain, even though the poultices had reduced the swelling and speeded the healing process. Raskin had visited several times during the night to make sure they were drinking enough water and, in the aven just before dawn, to change their dressings for the ride back to the palace. Garec didn't believe they would have received such attention had Rodler's name not been mentioned; he suspected transporting a few bandoliers of fennaroot was the least of the young man's crimes north of the Gorskan border.

They had been riding for nearly an aven, the roan's reins securely attached to Raskin's pommel, when they heard the sergeant cry out. A flurry of activity as soldiers dismounted and ran forward preceded screams of horror. One of the guards leant over and vomited repeatedly in the snow.

Raskin remained in the saddle, her sword drawn. Neither Mark nor Garec made any move, both watching their guard carefully: it was obvious something nasty had happened to her colleagues.

Garec wanted to sympathise, for Raskin had been good to them. He had lost Mika and Jerond, Versen and Sallax – he *knew* what was going through Raskin's mind as she listened to her fellow soldiers crying out to the gods of the Northern Forest. He set his jaw, determined not to feel sorry for the border guard: she, like the rest of them, was Nerak's servant, and thus his enemy.

He gave her credit for being a steadfast soldier; maybe if she'd grown up in Estrad she might now be fighting for the Resistance.

'It was grettans,' Garec said.

'Shut yourself up,' Raskin scowled. She sat straighter, trying in vain to see what was happening ahead. After a bit, she said, 'What makes you think it was grettans?'

'Look at where we are,' Garec said. 'This is a game trail, running from the pond we passed near your encampment. Every animal in this forest probably comes down here for water and I imagine grettans hunt back and forth across the trail, waiting for the opportunity to attack downhill. They would be deadly fast downhill.'

The soldier, despite her discipline, began to shake. 'Oh, gods, Denny—' she whispered to herself. 'Poor Mox—'

'Go and see for yourself, Raskin,' Mark said in a kindly tone. 'We aren't going anywhere – neither of us could even get off this horse without help, and it would be suicide for us to try and outrun you with two of us in the saddle. We'll be here when you get back.'

Raskin pulled herself together and put her shoulders back. 'I'm fine. Sergeant Greson will get everything in order.'

'Raskin,' Garec hoped using her name would soften her, 'those were your friends. Mark and I would be crushed if we knew four of our friends were lying mutil— well, you know, just up the path. Go ahead. We will be here when you get back.'

'He's right,' Mark said. 'You know we can't ride far.'

'Or take us with you if you must,' Garec went on, ignoring Mark's hard poke in the ribs. 'You can't get up there with both horses; so dismount and lead ours along.'

Her eyes grew distant for a moment. 'Maybe that will be all right – it's not like I'm leaving you alone.'

'We've both lost friends, Raskin,' Garec said soothingly. 'We know how difficult it is.'

'All right,' she said, 'but any move and I swear I'll run you both through.' She untied their reins from her pommel and slid from the saddle, never taking her eyes off the two prisoners. Walking backwards through the snow, she led the big roan by the bridle. After a few paces, and nothing untoward from Garec or Mark, she relented and turned her attention to the trail ahead.

As soon as she did, Mark whispered, 'Are you insane? She was going to leave us.'

'I wanted to get up the ridge,' Garec said. 'Being down there does us no good – we could run headlong into another patrol without seeing a thing.'

'Can you ride?'

'It's going to hurt. You?'

'Same, I'm afraid.'

'Our bows and quivers are tied to the back of the sergeant's saddle. If they stayed in line, his horse will be second from the front, the dapple-grey mare with the braid in her mane.'

'You get us close enough and I'll get the bows.'

'Can you turn and fire?'

'Like a Parthian.'

'Does that mean yes?'

'It's going to hurt.'

'We'll deal with that later. If they're scattered all over this clearing, we'll have one chance to break away. The ever-charming Sergeant Greson won't lose control of this group for very long. If they're on their knees or huddled together, that'll be our only chance.'

'I'll bet dollars to doughnuts their discipline returns as soon as they see us.'

'Right. So you'll have to be quick.'

As they neared the clearing, Garec numbered off the remaining soldiers: two were bent over a fallen tree. The sergeant was pushing his way through deeper snow off to one side of the trail, pushing back branches and peering into scrubby patches of brush. At first, Garec couldn't work out what he was doing, then he realised he was collecting the pieces of his men left by the grettan pack. The sergeant was muttering inaudibly to himself: the worst thing that could ever happen had come to pass that morning: he had lost half his squad, young people he had taught, disciplined, and most certainly loved.

Finally Mark spotted the fourth, a middle-aged man of perhaps three hundred Twinmoons who knelt in the snow clutching an unidentifiable limb resting across his lap.

A squad this tight-knit was closer than family, and with four men lost, and so gruesomely, the Malakasians had forgotten – just for the moment – that they were soldiers, with prisoners. If they were to escape, Mark and Garec had one brief window of opportunity.

Raskin's boots crunched through the snow as she approached the scene. Shaking noticeably, she brought her hands to her face, still holding the roan's bridle, and covered her eyes. Mark hadn't known the dead men; he'd used a whole quiver of arrows trying to kill them … but he winced when he saw the carnage left by the grettan pack.

The trail was awash with blood, staining the trampled snow, pooling in beastly footprints, coating trees and bushes – drops had even frozen into jewel-like icicles. And strewn about were sundry pieces of men and horse and bits of accoutrements: a hunk of shoulder, arm partly attached, still sporting epaulettes and the insignia of the Malakasian border guard; half a hand adorned by a flattened ring with huge tooth marks in the metal; a horse's head, intact save for a torn ear, rearing up out of the ground, the bridle bit gripped between bloody teeth: a war horse even in death.

They understood now why supposedly hardened soldiers were shaking and throwing up like novices.

'Dear Mother of Christ,' Mark whispered in English.

Garec didn't need a translation. 'Rutting dogs, what these people must have gone through—'

'Either way,' Mark caught hold of himself, 'we need to mourn them later. Right now you have to get me close to that grey mare.'

'Don't worry,' Garec said confidently, 'we'll be long gone before any of them, least of all our dear Sergeant Greson, has any idea we've run.' The guards would certainly give chase, but he was gambling on their current confusion, coupled with their state of mind, to provide a significant head-start. He hoped Mark would give good enough account of himself with the bow – at the risk of incurring yet more deaths – to turn their pursuers back.

He surreptitiously checked the trail ahead: the path itself was clear of major obstacles, and they wouldn't have far to go before they were under cover of the forest. As long as he could guide the roan by the mane initially, they'd be all right; he didn't want to reach for the reins until they were out of sight. He peered down at the tracks and froze.

'Oh, Versen,' Garec whispered.

'What?'

'I wish Versen were here.'

'Me too,' Mark said. 'He's a much better shot than I am.'

'No,' Garec gestured into the clearing, 'that's not what I meant. Look at those tracks.'

'Well, of course there are tracks,' Mark said dismissively. 'There was an ungodly fight – by my count it was grettans four, Malakasians zero.'

'The grettans would have been hunting this valley; they would have gone downhill for water overnight.'

'Good. I'm glad they're behind us. What's your point?'

'They're not.' Garec peered into the trees. 'That's my point. They didn't move downhill.'

'What?' Mark's voice rose. 'Are you saying they're still hunting?'

'Ssssh, don't attract attention. They're still up here, somewhere.'

'Oh, shit,' Mark whispered. 'All right. All right. Breathe. We still have to get the bows.'

'Yes,' Garec said, 'get ready.'

Behind them, one of the horses whinnied; their roan nickered in response, shaking its mane irritably in Garec's face. 'Easy, easy,' Garec said in a normal tone, smiling down at Raskin when she looked back at them.

'They're nervous,' she said.

'They're spooked by the smell of blood, and the lingering scent of the grettans,' Garec whispered, in mock deference to the soldiers' suffering. 'But they're war horses. They'll be all right.'

The roan's ears pricked back and Garec closed his eyes, listening as closely as he could to the sounds of the forest: the background rustle of the light wind through the leafless branches. Somewhere off to his left he could hear a small animal moving, a squirrel or a rabbit, maybe.

There it was: a rumble, like that of a wooden cart over a log bridge. Garec tensed.

'What is it?' Mark whispered, afraid for his friend's answer.

'They're here.' Garec nodded off to his left. 'West of us, maybe a hundred paces.'

Behind them, one of the horses cried out, a terrified whinny, and bolted. Another followed.

'This is it,' Garec said, and then cried loudly, 'Grettans!' He manoeuvred their horse next to the dapple-grey and pulled the reins from Raskin's loose grip. The young woman wheeled on them, terror in her eyes. Her sword was hanging limply at her side.

Mark needed a moment to wrestle with the knots securing their weapons; he nudged Garec to keep her attention focused away from his hands.

'They're over there,' Garec said, pointing into the forest. 'Raskin, *move!* Get your horse before it bolts – take it by the reins, don't try to get in the saddle. They're too skittish now.'

Raskin stared dumbly at him, shaking visibly.

'Get your horse, now!' Garec's cry slapped her back to reality and she hurried back along the path, not even looking at them.

'Sergeant,' she screamed, 'they're coming! We're got to get out of here!'

To Mark, Garec said, 'You have about half a breath to get those untied, my friend, because things are about to get very bad around here.'

'Got 'em,' Mark shouted, 'go!'

Garec jabbed his heels hard into the roan's side, kicking it into a gallop, ignoring Sergeant Greson, who was reaching out a mittened hand to grab their reins. Mark reached over and slugged the man, tumbling him into the horse's severed head. 'Grettans are coming,' he shouted at the soldiers, 'and if you don't move, you'll be as dead as them!'

'Come on,' Garec urged their horse, 'come on. You can do it – let's go, Roan, let's go!' Awkwardly at first, and then gradually faster as the big horse eased into its stride, they climbed the slope at a run.

'You'll kill him if you keep up this pace,' Mark said.

'Just a bit further,' Garec replied, 'we have to make the ridge before we can ease off. Anyone behind?'

'Nothing yet,' Mark said.

As if in response, a horse screamed and the unmistakable sounds of a grettan attack reached them through the trees. Both men shuddered as they visualised the beasts falling on the small party. Human cries came now, a shrill call for help that was cut off so suddenly their minds were filled with images of throats being torn out mid-plea.

'Maybe Raskin will escape,' Mark said quietly, knowing it was a forlorn hope.

The horse missed its footing for a moment, jouncing its riders badly, reminding them both that they had been shot the previous day.

'Sonofabitch,' Mark shouted, 'watch the road, will you?'

'Sorry,' Garec said, 'I have to get the reins. We won't make it far steering with a handful of hair.'

'Well, slow down and grab them,' Mark said. 'We can spare a

moment.' He grimaced and muttered to himself, 'I do hate riding these things.'

Garec eased the roan to a trot while he leaned forward and slipped the reins effortlessly over the horse's head. Garec grinned. 'Easy,' he announced.

'Yeah, yeah,' Mark groaned, 'just watch the potholes.'

Garec heard a rumble, an echo of the growl he had caught back in the clearing. This was not the scream of a grettan attacking, this was a grettan stalking. It was coming for them.

'Gods of the Northern Forest,' Garec said. 'Did you hear that?'

'Shit, Garec. Is there another?'

'At least one.'

'Get us out of here, quick!'

'We can't outrun them, believe me. I've tried – and on my Renna, who's twice as fast as this old carthorse.'

'What do you propose we do?'

'Get ready to shoot. Draw several arrows, tuck them in my belt. Put four or five in there, no more. If you can't stop them with those, we'll be dead anyway.' The growl came again, closer this time but still off to the west. 'Hurry!'

They had covered another hundred paces before Mark caught sight of the creature, coming at them through the trees, its great hindquarters propelling it forward at high speed.

Mark's stomach felt as though it had been filled with concrete; his arms went numb with fear. Coming towards them was something out of a nightmare, a beast unlike anything he had ever seen. He had only glimpsed the grettan Nerak had sent against them in the Blackstone forest, but that animal had been fleeing into the trees, one leg severed, shrieking in pain. This grettan was in rude good health, and coming for them full pelt, crashing through the undergrowth as if there was nothing there. It had small black eyes, set wide apart over a short snout and a snarling mouth of spiked canines. Its fur was dense and black, covering the corded muscles propelling the beast towards them.

It was coming too fast; he wouldn't get a shot off, there was no way – and even if he did, it would be a token gesture, nothing good enough to stop or even slow the grettan. Garec's voice woke him from his stupor.

'Shoot the rutter!' he screamed, 'can't you see it?' Garec was fighting to keep the horse under control as the scent and sounds of charging grettan drove it wild.

Mark's hand shook as he tried to nock an arrow but it finally gripped and he drew, took aim and felt the shaft slip off the bowstring. 'Hell,' he barked, lowering the bow and starting again, 'I can't ride a horse! I can't shoot a bow! Sonofabitch!'

Garec shouted back at him, 'Breathe. Take your time. Aim, breathe and release. You've practised, Mark, now make the shot.' Garec soothed the horse, urging the animal on. 'Make it count, Mark. You won't have many chances.'

The grettan broke from the trees some hundred paces behind them, turned up the hillside and began closing the gap. Mark turned as far as he could in the saddle, ignoring the pain as the hole in his knee broke open and began bleeding again. Watching the monster come up behind them was like watching a train coming down the track: he needed a rifle, a hand grenade, an RPG to stop this thing, not an *arrow*.

'This isn't going to work, Garec,' he said despairingly.

'Just breathe, aim and fire. You can do it.'

Mark wished he was back in Idaho Springs teaching history, telling his students about the Parthian shot: the great bowmen were famous for the feat of turning in their saddles while retreating and shooting surprisingly accurate parting shots at their enemies. Instead, here he was in a fantasy land, about to try the same trick himself. He drew a deep breath and, timing his shot to the creature's rhythmic stride, released the arrow.

The shaft took the snarling monster in the right shoulder, sinking deep into the muscle and slowing the grettan for a moment as it reared back and howled into the treetops. But the injury stopped it for only a moment, long enough for the roan to make up fifteen or twenty paces, then it was after them again.

Emboldened by his success, Mark drew and fired a second time, screaming obscenities at the beast. This arrow tore through the thin flesh between the grettan's eyes and flopped up and down in time to its leaps, a grisly metronome. Mark shouted a victory cry, but it choked in his throat when he realised the direct hit had done nothing to slow the creature down.

His hands trembling again, he struggled to prepare his third shaft, aiming and releasing a scant moment before the grettan, its face stained with blood, leaped onto the roan's hindquarters, spilling him and Garec into the snow.

Mark rolled head over heels, crashing through the rotten wood of a fallen tree trunk. His injured knee was bleeding badly now as he slipped and slid down the hillside, bouncing off trees and through brambles before coming to rest against a rock protruding out of the frozen ground. From above, he heard the roan wail several times like a frightened child and then fall silent. The horse was dead.

Trying to regain his composure, Mark cleared the snow from his face. His knee was a mess; the bandages Raskin had applied that morning had disappeared during his precipitous descent. He had a sharp pain in his shoulder, the damaged knee was throbbing badly and there was a steady, dull pain in his lower back, but he felt as if he could manage to walk. He could hear the grettan, snarling and tearing at the carcase of the horse, and he looked around for a tree he might climb to elude the creature long enough for it to lose interest or wander away. The nearest looked to be fifteen yards or so up the hillside, one he had slammed into moments earlier.

He searched around for Garec, but there was no sign of him. He shook himself and began trudging back up the slope, calling out, 'Garec!' – and immediately realising how stupid he'd been. Instead of Garec's voice, Mark heard the snarling and growling come to an abrupt halt; a palpable stillness fell over the forested hillside.

Mark took another few steps, just far enough to see that instead of feeding on the horse's carcase, the grettan had lifted its head and was staring down at him.

'Ah, hell,' Mark groaned, unsure whether to run, freeze or pray for a massive heart attack. He measured the distance to the nearest branches. 'There's no way.' He glanced around, hoping someone had passed through the forest earlier that morning and accidentally forgotten their machine-gun. Apart from a stocky length of rotten oak, there was nothing. He bent down to pick up the stick, hoping that, like Steven, he might choose the one branch in the entire forest imbued with enough mystical energy to blast this grettan into pixie dust, but the branch just crumbled in his hand.

The grettan moved down the hill, like a jungle cat stalking its prey. Mark thought for a second about running, but he didn't much fancy the idea of being hamstrung, so instead, he froze.

His legs buried calf-deep in the snow, Mark Jenkins stood his ground, trembling, and waiting for the monster – that's what the grettan was, a monster from a child's nightmare – to pounce on him and tear out his throat. He waited for his life to flash before his eyes, but nothing happened; all he could think about was when the creature would leap, and how quickly it would tear him apart. He started to cry. This was *not* how he had ever imagined he would die.

'Come on, then,' he sobbed. 'Come and get me.'

The grettan moved down the hill, low to the ground, sliding like mercury between the rocks and trees, the consummate hunter.

'I'm right here!' Mark looked for a stick, a rock, anything he might use to land one decent blow. Maybe he could blind the creature, or crack its skull ... but there was nothing nearby but snow and the rotten branch lying in a crumble beside his feet.

Mark decided to go out in a flurry of noise and anger, to leave Eldarn a raving wild man. He started bellowing, whatever came into his mind, his last testament a loose collection of words and phrases, the stream-of-consciousness farewell of a condemned man.

Pffft! The arrow took the grettan in the throat. *Pffft!* Another sank deep, inches from the first, until only the fletching protruded. The grettan shrieked, rose up on its hind legs and growled. *Pffft!* Thud! Another hit. *Pffft!* Thud! Yet another, and this one was a miracle shot, into the soft flesh behind the animal's ear and below the curve of its skull; there weren't a handful of people in the world, *any* world, Eldarn included, who could have made that shot.

Garec kept the arrows coming, but they were unnecessary, for the miracle shot had finished the grettan. Only adrenalin kept it coming at Mark, dragging its injured legs, screaming at each new arrow that pierced its hide, determined to kill, even in its final moments. Finally, just a few paces away, the creature slumped to the ground and lay still, growling a warning as its life drained away.

Mark wisely gave the dying grettan a wide berth as he climbed back up the hill to join Garec, who was standing by the ravaged carcase of the roan horse, his rosewood longbow still drawn.

'Here,' Garec handed him the bow. 'You finish it.'

Mark shook his head. 'No. It'll be dead in a moment anyway.'

'You don't want a shot?'

'No.'

Garec understood; shouldering his bow, he offered a hand to Mark and laughed. 'What did you say earlier? We have two good legs between us?'

'Something like that.' Mark took his arm. Together they pulled themselves up the hillside.

THE BARSTAG RESIDENCE

When Orindale fell to Prince Marek, the imperial gardens surrounding the Barstag family residence became a tent-camp for the occupation forces maintaining order in the city. Tidy rows of delphiniums, larkspur and hollyhocks were trampled to the ground; lilac and buddleia bushes, full to bursting with sweet-smelling blossom, were chopped down for the watch-fires, and thousands upon thousands of rosemary and lavender plants were used to soften the ground beneath many a soldier's blankets. The fragrance of the bruised stalks perfumed the air for weeks.

The civil unrest that marked the early Twinmoons of Marek's dictatorship gave way to a more prosperous era. The busy seaport saw a decrease in Malakasia's military presence, especially as commerce and trade recovered. For hundreds of Twinmoons following Marek's takeover the imperial palace served as a barracks for the soldiers charged with patrolling the city and overseeing customs and shipping along the wharf.

Orindale was the natural choice for those supervising the steady export of goods and taxes to Malakasia, and most of these officials chose the upper floors of the opulent Barstag family palace for their private quarters. On the few occasions when a significant threat to the Malakasian hegemony rose in the east, the old structure became a command centre for the officers deploying troops to put down whatever grass roots uprising was taking shape in the Eastlands. When civil war broke out, the imperial gardens – a city park in more peaceful Twinmoons – reverted to its former guise as an encampment for foot soldiers securing the city and once again whatever flowers and shrubs had reclaimed the greensward were trodden into the mud, burned in campfires and used to soften the ground where soldiers slept.

Sallax, approaching the imperial grounds from the south, noticed that the broad, tree-lined park was full of square eight-person tents, wooden carts, fire-pits and buried latrine trenches. A half-rotten, half-eaten mound of hay lay abandoned beside a ramshackle corral, though none of the soldiers still quartered on the palace grounds appeared to have been assigned horses, and the army's work-horses were stabled in a far larger enclosure out near what remained of the eastern pickets.

'A Moon ago, this whole park was tents,' Brexan said.

'They don't know what they're doing,' Sallax replied. 'Malagon's carriage hasn't moved all Twinmoon. Most of the generals probably think he died in the explosion.'

'Wouldn't that be nice?'

'They must be bickering about what to do by now.'

'But surely it must be obvious to them that no major attack is coming?' Brexan wondered. 'Why stay dug in now that it's so cold?'

Sallax knelt to slip through a breach in a hedge that looked like some enterprising squaddies had enlarged a natural break to gain easier access to the street. 'There was an assault on the lines not too long ago,' he said. 'At the docks Sallax heard them saying several thousand partisans threw themselves on the Malakasian lines, after word spread that the prince was en route from Pellia.'

Brexan stopped. 'Are you all right?'

'Yes – why?'

'You said Sallax.'

'Never mind that.' He thumped the side of his head. 'I think I'm going to be just left of centre for a long time. I need to learn to live with it.'

'What happened to the partisans?' Brexan slipped through the hedge behind him.

'Torn to ribbons, by Seron mostly, but there were rumours of worse: killer winds or rains, or something weird. It sounded bad.'

'They were routed?'

'I don't know even if it went that well. I wasn't terribly healthy at the time. I think I remember hearing that calling it "driven back" was too generous.'

Brexan looked pale in the moonlight. 'There were many more soldiers here then, though.'

'True. Actually, I'm surprised. I expected we'd have to work our way past more than this crew to reach the palace tonight. I'm glad many of these divisions have moved on.'

Brexan ducked behind a stack of hay bales near the first of the tent-camps they had to pass on their way to the palace's southern gate. 'More than this?' she whispered. 'I think there are soldiers here enough to capture, torture and hang us if we're caught.'

'We won't be,' Sallax said. 'Jacrys can't be planning on staying here much longer. Sallax hit him – there, I did it again – *I* hit him hard, but he'll be recovered by now, and if we let him get back in the field, we'll never find him again. He's a ghost; you know that.'

'I suppose you're right.' She craned her neck to see over the bales. No one moved inside the encampment. 'Come on. Let's go.'

Skirting the silent tents, avoiding the token guard posted near the watch-fires, they ran along the tall hedge that enclosed the park and closed out the noise and crowds of the city beyond.

'At least we're already inside,' Brexan said when they slipped behind an enormous old oak tree that looked as though it had been there long before King Remond started construction on his Orindale home.

'I didn't think they'd have much of a guard posted, especially at this aven.' Sallax pointed towards the south entrance. 'They'll have guards at the gates, and again at the doors, but from here we may only have to pass one sentry.'

'Because no one would be stupid enough to plan an assault on the palace that meant getting through the entire Malakasian Army first?' Brexan's voice rose with her anxiety.

'Crafty and brave enough, you meant to say.'

'That too.'

'When we get up there, we have to take the guard out silently. If there are two, we'd better do it together. Remember to be quick and quiet.'

'What if there are three?'

'Then we're dead.' Sallax crouched low to the ground and disappeared, soundless and deadly, into the shadows.

He was wrong. There were several guards posted along the stone walk running between the south gate and the tent-camp. Young, tough-looking, the three men and two women paced back and forth, talking amiably. Some smoked pipes, while others ate from a canvas bag open on the ground between them, fruits or nuts, maybe. The south entrance to the palace was well secured: they were obviously on watch duty for the night; despite whatever disagreements Prince Malagon's generals might be having, this group were taking their night watch seriously. None of them even looked tired.

As Brexan watched them from behind a holly bush, she scowled. 'We can't go in here,' she whispered.

'That window near the back,' Sallax answered, 'that may be our only chance. We can worry about getting out once we're inside.'

'This is insane,' Brexan said. 'There has to be another way.'

'We'll be fine. This is the hard part. No one will expect us to be inside, because no one can get in. Once we're in, we'll be able to move about easily.' He reached over and squeezed her shoulder. 'Trust me.'

Brexan stifled a giggle. 'We're going to die.'

'Someday, and far from here.'

'Promise?'

'As absurd a request as that is, I will grant it.' He placed a hand over his heart, 'I promise.'

'How do we get in the window—? Stay put,' Brexan said suddenly. 'I have an idea.' Without waiting for him to answer, she slipped away.

Sallax waited, straining to see back the way they had come. Save for the watch-fires, spaced unevenly where islands of tents remained after the mass military exodus, the park was in darkness. He could see no movement, and he couldn't find Brexan in any of the shadows. 'She has learned to vanish when she needs to,' he said to himself. 'A very talented spy.'

Soon Sallax began to grow uneasy. He had just about decided to go back and look for his wayward partner when he thought he saw a glow brighten the near side of the park, behind the first row of tents. He thought perhaps his eyes were fooling him, too much straining to see things that weren't really there, and he shook his head and turned back to trying to work out a path between the sleeping soldiers – then Brexan was beside him.

'Great whores, but you scared me,' he whispered, certain the hammering of his heart was loud enough to wake the entire camp.

Brexan grabbed his wrist. 'Back to the holly bush, quickly,' she ordered.

Sallax didn't argue, but followed her silently back to their vantage point. He looked at Brexan expectantly.

'Just another moment now,' she whispered.

'What did you do?'

'Hopefully, I managed to get us inside. The last sentry we passed, I think that's him over there; he left his post back near that first row of tents to come up here and eat whatever that stuff is they're gobbling down. He left that near patch of tents unguarded.' Brexan looked back over her shoulder.

Sallax saw it now, an orange glow, only a few paces from where they lay nearly face down in the snow and mud. 'You started a fire?'

'I had a taper in my pack. I was worried that it might be dark when we got inside the palace. I went for one of the big tents,' Brexan whispered, keeping as low to the ground as she could. 'I tried to make it look like an accident—'

She was cut off by the first of many shouts from inside the tent; pandemonium followed. Soon the entire encampment was alive with soldiers rushing here and there, some carrying water and others simply moving about, uncertain what was happening and whether they should put out the fire or prepare for battle.

Is it an attack?

Where are they?

Partisans?

The fire, fools, the fire!

Over here, we need water over here!

The cries overlapped, creating a nearly incoherent wall of noise. Sallax watched, enjoying the fiery carnage, especially when the big tent finally toppled and ignited its neighbour. 'You got two.' He elbowed Brexan in the ribs, but the young woman ignored him; her attention was focused on the guards posted beside the south gate. Three had already dashed back into the camp to assist their comrades.

'Two more to go,' she said to herself. 'Just another moment—' She rose up on her elbows. 'Now,' her voice was harsh, 'let's go.'

Sallax was surprised when Brexan stood up and began running towards the palace gate. An iron fence, rusted nearly through, separated them from the stone archway and the shadowed doors beyond. If they could get inside the gate, the darkness beneath the arch would hide them until they determined if the door was unlocked, or if they had to try the window near the back of the building. Without slowing, Brexan pushed on the gate with all her strength, praying it wouldn't creak and give them away – but it did grate, a long, whining squeal that made Sallax hold his breath. 'Pissing demons, Brexan, stop!' he whispered. 'We don't have to fit a grettan pack through here, you know.'

She stopped pushing, let him step through and then closed the gate, clenching her teeth at the piercing creak that rent the night and cried out for them to be captured and hanged right then and there. 'Sorry,' she muttered.

'No matter,' he said, 'none of them heard it. Look at them, scurrying about like mice!' Some fought the burgeoning fire, while others brandished weapons and crept warily from shrub to shrub. 'We'll have to stay inside until all this quietens down again,' he said.

'We have about an aven before dawn,' Brexan said. 'That should be enough time.'

'Let's hope no one is posted inside the door.' Sallax moved past her.

'Why would there be with five standing sentry out here?'

'To ruin my night.'

'Try the latch,' Brexan forced herself to whisper.

Silence. Then—

'It's unlocked, thank all the gods of the Northern Forest.' Sallax pulled the door open a crack and slipped through. Brexan followed. No one guarded the foyer.

They could see five smoothly worn stone steps leading to a landing and a second door, but there were no windows and when Sallax pulled the door closed behind them, they were left in total darkness. He felt his way up the steps and across the landing. 'This is unlocked as well.'

A leather strap threaded through the door released the latch with a *click!* that echoed through the chamber. Brexan held her breath, waiting to hear the sound of boots clacking on the floor as guards came to investigate the noise.

Nothing.

Sallax opened the door just far enough for them to slip through into a long chamber with high buttressed ceilings and wooden support beams. The smooth floor was carpeted in places with the remnants of old rugs and tapestries the Barstag family had imported from Praga, though not nearly enough of them to mask the sound of two intruders moving through the hall. A lone torch burned in a sconce at the base of a stairwell.

'That must lead up to the south wing,' he breathed into Brexan's ear.

'Where Jacrys is staying,' she answered.

'It's a good place to start looking.'

'How are we going to get out of here afterwards?'

'I'm working on it.' He was already creeping on tiptoe towards the pool of light and the stairs to the upper floors of the south wing.

The wide stone stairs, like the main floor, were polished smooth from use, carpeted down the middle with a thin layer of woven wool.

Brexan kept to the carpeted pathway, imagining generations of King Remond's descendants walking up and down this same ribbon of fabric.

At the first landing a torch illuminated a few paces in either direction along a corridor lined with wooden doors. Sallax mimed *soldiers sleeping* in awkward gestures and Brexan nodded. Anything they did to call attention to themselves meant they would have to make their way down through a full platoon of groggy, upset soldiers. As if reading their minds, one of the far doors opened, and a half-dressed young man emerged carrying a chamber-pot.

They fell back into the shadows, watching as the soldier walked to a window at the end of the hall, opened it with a shoulder and emptied the pot into the shrubbery below. As soon as he disappeared back into his room, Sallax turned the corner and started up the next flight of stairs, which narrowed into darkness.

Uneasy at the sight of the narrow passageway, Brexan slipped back to the landing and lit her taper from the torch; it wasn't much light, but it was better than nothing. Sallax nodded thanks and gestured that she lead the way upstairs.

As Brexan sidled past, she heard him slip his knife from its sheath. Sallax wore a rapier, compliments of Carpello, but that remained in its scabbard for the moment. Neither of them were keen on a sword-fight with Jacrys, who was obviously well trained with blade. They would be quite content just to knife the spy in his sleep, if only they could find him without waking the entire residence.

Brexan felt her pulse begin to throb in her temples. She had been nervous coming through the Malakasian encampment, nervous enough to make a potentially costly mistake with the wrought-iron gate, and although they'd been lucky, her failure to think of the rusty hinges haunted her. How had she been so stupid? Were her nerves clogging up her brain? She was desperately worried that she might be overlooking something lethal, right now.

She couldn't hear anything above her heartbeat; she hoped Sallax wasn't whispering anything to her. Even though he was just a pace behind, she was certain this was the loneliest she had ever felt. Despite the chill, Brexan started to sweat.

She turned the corner at the next landing and started up what she hoped was the final set of stairs. Ahead, she could see light from another torch illuminating a tiny landing, just wide enough for two or three people to stand together, with a wooden door at the back. Brexan hoped it led into Jacrys' quarters.

She couldn't see the torch, but assumed it was suspended above the stairwell – until she heard the sound of a wooden chair sliding across the floor above. *Oh gods, a sentry!* She held her breath; every muscle in her body was poised to take her back, but instead of bolting for the lower level, she stood frozen, paralysed by fear.

'Who's there? Who is that?' The man had obviously been drowsing at his post and was fighting to sound official. The yawn ruined the effect.

Think of something. Think of something. Think of something. She opened her mouth, but nothing emerged, she couldn't even gasp with any authority.

Then she felt Sallax reach for her, his hand firmly on her back. His touch calmed her enough that she was able to draw a stabilising breath.

'Who is that?'

The torchlight flickered and the ancient sconce creaked as the sentry withdrew the burning bundle and brandished it down the stairwell.

'Riders,' she croaked and cleared her throat, feigning a coughing fit. 'Who?' the soldier interrupted.

'Riders,' she said again, 'from General Oaklen.' The old general's name had stayed her execution once before; she prayed it would work again.

'General Oaklen?' the sentry asked, 'he was just here a few days ago. What does he want?'

'That's none of your concern, you dumb rutter.' Brexan would have welcomed a swift death at that moment. 'We have a message for the spymaster Jacrys. We've been riding for two days.' She was glad that they were both thoroughly covered in mud.

'Why are you out of uniform?'

'Good rutters, but they do station the dumbest soldiers here, don't they?'

Sallax nodded in agreement.

'We can't ride through Falkan alone in uniform, you mule-kicked idiot!' Brexan barked. 'Now, are you going to stand aside and grant us entry, or shall we just wait here while you fetch your superior and explain to him why I have been delayed from carrying out the general's command by some jumped-up little squaddie's inability to UNDERSTAND ORDERS?'

The guard shuffled his feet; this would not look good on his record. The spymaster would be angry that someone had been allowed to reach this floor in the first place, and Captain Thadrake would slice him from groin to gullet if he knew that he'd fallen asleep at his post. The spy was already furious with the captain for allowing the partisans to escape; the captain had, in turn, taken his anger out on the entire third platoon, which was now reassigned to guard duty here. Any one of them would rather have been ordered to scrape the hull of every ship that passed through the harbour than take guard duty – and he'd had fallen asleep! Bleeding whores.

'Well?' The woman's impatient voice came from the stairwell again.

'What's the pass?' he asked, trying to match the woman's irritated tone.

Brexan felt the wind go out of her lungs. *A password? Three floors up in the most secure building in the Eastlands and you have a whoring password?* She would have to distract the sentry and give Sallax an opportunity to knife the soldier and end this absurd exchange.

She took a wary step forward; the guard drew his sword and Brexan stopped.

'What's the pass?' he called down at them again, louder this time; Brexan worried he might start shouting and alert the entire building to their presence.

She'd take an educated guess; she'd been a soldier long enough. If it failed, she'd make a run for him and try to get a blade in his throat before he could scream.

'Lafrent,' Brexan said, the spy's other identity, the name he was using when first she met him. It was the only one of millions of possibilities racing through her mind that had any chance of being correct. She grasped it in desperation.

Miraculously, the soldier lowered his sword. 'Come on up.'

They climbed the rest of the stairs.

'What's happening outside?' the guard asked. 'If he's awake and I went off for a look, he'd have my guts for breakfast …'

'Oh, the commotion? Someone's tent caught fire. Half the rutting camp was sleeping, and someone thought it was an attack; people kept tripping over each other trying to find water. It was a mess.' Brexan remained in front of Sallax, effectively blocking the guard's view of the big Ronan. 'What room is he in?'

'It's just through here, the second door on the left. I have to walk you down there. He's a bit tiresome about procedures. You know the type. I just wish—'

His final wish drowned in a gruesome rattle as Sallax's blade took him in the throat. He fell to his knees, blood staining his hands as he clutched at the wound, and tried to swear at them, instead choking and coughing up blood that splattered their cloaks and stained the darkened stairwell. When he finally collapsed, drowning in his own blood, neither Brexan nor Sallax gave him a second glance.

'Through here,' Sallax said, opening the hallway door. 'There's no one, just an empty hallway.'

They hurried to the door the guard had pointed out. After checking to see if it was locked, Sallax leaned against it as gently as he could, sliding it inwards a crack, careful not to allow the leather hinges to creak as the door swung open. Brexan followed him through.

Jacrys' bed was positioned in the centre of what was still, even after Twinmoons of neglect, an opulent apartment. Sallax left the torch hanging in a doorway sconce and they moved stealthily across the floor.

For a moment, Brexan feared they would find the chamber empty and Jacrys, somehow warned of their approach, vanished down a hidden stairway, but as they reached his bedside, she saw that he was there, snoring away, sleeping the deep sleep of one who felt safe. Jacrys didn't stir, even as Sallax gestured that Brexan should kill him without further delay. In the torchlight, she could see the sentry's blood drying on the big man's fingers.

She drew her knife and checked her position. She thought briefly of Versen, and Lieutenant Bronfio, whose murder had started this whole adventure for her, and drew a breath to strike. It had to be deep, into the heart, and enough to shock him awake for long enough to see his killer – but not give him time to cry out. *Use two hands,* she thought, and squeezed the wrapped leather grip with all her strength. *Do it now, Brexan, she thought, just do it* – but then she hesitated, backing away a step and staring down at the sleeping man's face. *What's the matter with you?* she asked herself. *Just kill him and go home. This man is a monster, the reason Malagon knew where to send the Seron who took you prisoner and broke your cheek. He killed Bronfio and made sure Versen was delivered into enemy hands. Just kill him!*

Sallax struck while Brexan was still caught in her crisis of conscience, slamming his own knife into Jacrys' chest. He held it for a moment as the spy woke with a gasp and stared, eyes wide in horror, into the faces of his killers. Sallax lowered his face and growled, 'This is for Gilmour.'

Jacrys' mouth moved, but he couldn't manage to make a sound. His eyes fluttered and his nostrils flared with his efforts to breathe, and then he tensed as his body went into spasm. As consciousness fled, so the rigid tension dissipated.

Sallax released the bloody hilt, leaving it standing erect in the spy's chest. 'Done,' he said. 'Let's get out of here.'

Brexan nodded, staring down, waiting for Jacrys' eyes to close. She was remotely aware of Sallax crossing the room to retrieve the torch and then coming back.

He bent to examine a stack of papers spread across a wooden table. 'Come look at these,' he called in a whisper.

'What?' She watched Jacrys' eyes catch the firelight, his mouth still stuck somewhere half-open and half-closed. A trickle of bloody saliva drooled down his chin as he fought to stay alive. She wondered if he could see her, if he recognised her, or if he was just staring at the faded tapestries that hung around the walls.

'Over here,' Sallax interrupted. 'Do you recognise these?'

She pulled herself away from the dying man and, gathering her wits, moved to stand beside Sallax. 'They're maps.' She bent over the table to look at them more closely. 'This is Pellia.'

'And these?' Sallax shuffled two or three others to the top of the stack.

'That's the river, and these are the heights above Welstar Palace. That mark right there must be the keep.' She ran her finger over a semi-circular area around the castle. 'All this is a Malakasian encampment. It's the biggest army I've ever seen.'

'Good rutters,' Sallax said under his breath. 'We have to take these. Look at the marks on there. These are maps of the river. Look at these boxes and circles. They must be places along the waterway for barges to load and unload whatever it is that Carpello is shipping – *was* shipping – from Strandson and Orindale.'

'And look here,' Brexan pointed to another map. 'This is the Great Pragan Range, the mountains on the southern border. I wonder what's happening down there.'

'I don't know, but let's take them all; we can study them as closely as we like later. But for now, let's—'

A clamour rose from a lower floor, a wildly ringing bell, as if someone was trying to rouse the entire city against a pending invasion.

Sallax and Brexan stopped, their eyes meeting across the wooden table. 'What's that?' she asked nervously.

Sallax turned back towards the spy and over his shoulder, Brexan could see what Jacrys had been staring at. A trail of blood, viscous, black in the half light, led from the spy's empty bed to the wall, where, in front of one of the ancient tapestries, hung a bell rope, dangling from an old system of pulleys and cables that obviously ran to the servants' quarters and the scullery below.

Jacrys tugged the rope with all his remaining strength, sitting with his back propped awkwardly against the wall. A grim smile split his cadaverous face: the triumphant grin of one who has emerged victorious despite overwhelming odds. He twitched as waves of pain assailed him, but it didn't change the smug assurance that, try as they might to escape, there would be no leaving the palace alive.

'Come quickly!' Sallax barked, no longer trying for stealth. 'We have to get below the first level before anyone gets to those stairs.' He scooped up as many of the maps as he could, folded them under his arm and charged through the door into the hallway.

Brexan considered crossing the room to cut the spy's throat, but shrugged and hurried out behind Sallax. She ran back to the small landing and headlong into Sallax, who had stopped. Brexan stepped back. 'What is it? Let's get going. Are they already on the stairs?'

Sallax didn't answer as the maps slipped from beneath his arm and spilled down the stone stairway.

'What is it?' She pushed past him onto the landing.

The lone sentry was lying with his legs hanging off the first step, his torso propped up between the door and the wall. Sallax staggered and fell to his knees and Brexan managed to slip past him, over the dying guard, to grab the torch Sallax had dropped. Brexan picked it up, fanned it back to life and propped it between the fallen man's legs.

The flickering glow illuminated the rapier protruding from Sallax's chest, the last attack of the dying guard. A long, wheezing rattle came from the sentry's chest. Brexan gasped and reached for Sallax.

'I'm dying,' he murmured. 'I'm dying.'

'No, you're not,' she said firmly, ignoring her tears. 'Come with me. We have to hurry.'

Below, the incessant ringing merged with the groaning and shuffling of soldiers rousing themselves from sleep. From the annoyed sounds that filtered upstairs, the groggy guards thought some gods-forsaken officer had spent too long with his head dipped in a wine cask and was now mustering them all for a late-night inspection.

Thankfully, none of them appeared to be coming up the stairs, not yet.

Sallax fell forward, and Brexan caught him beneath his arms. As she hugged him close, she flashed back to Versen, and how heavy he had been that day she'd tried to keep him afloat in the Ravenian Sea. 'Please, Sallax, please,' she cried softly, 'you can do this. You're so strong and it isn't far, just a few stairs. Come on; we can make it.'

'Leave me here, Brexan,' Sallax whispered. 'You can get out.' He struggled to lift himself off her and fell back against the door, slamming it shut with an echo that rolled down the stairs. 'Hurry now; you can make it.' He reached for her with a bloody hand, and she held it in both of hers.

He wriggled his hand free and reached for her again, stretching. She tried to take his hand, but he shook her off. 'What is it?'

'You can make it out,' he said, 'but you need—' Gripping her tunic belt, he pulled on it, his strength failing, until the tongue was drawn back through the buckle.

'What do you want me to do?'

'I want you to get out, but you have to make it look like—' Again he tugged at her belt. Suddenly Brexan understood.

'No, Sallax, I'll stay here and fight beside you.'

He ignored her. 'You can do this.'

Brexan angrily fought back tears as she unfastened her belt and untied the strap holding her cloak closed. Dropping the belt and her weapons, she pulled the tunic over her head.

Sallax looked away, with a hoarse laugh. 'I'm not supposed to peek,' he murmured.

Now she did cry. She gave him a long kiss on the temple, hugged him to her naked torso until enough blood smeared her body, then picked up her cloak and screwed it up into a ball. 'Goodbye,' she said, a sob in her voice.

Sallax looked at her, his eyes glassy in the torchlight. 'Tell Garec the truth about what happened. Make sure he knows.'

Brexan sobbed, 'I will. I promise. I will find him.'

The bell rang on into the night and Brexan cursed Jacrys, wishing with all her heart he would die before Sallax, so her friend would hear the bell fall silent, but it didn't happen. Sallax's eyes fluttered open several times, then his head slumped on his chest, and Brexan watched as his final breath sighed from his body.

'Oh gods,' Brexan started quietly, then, fulfilling her promise, allowed her cries to grow in volume until they were enormous, great heaving sobs that echoed through the upper floors of the old residence. 'Oh gods, oh gods!' Holding her cloak and tunic, Brexan ran, half naked and splattered with blood, down the stairs and into the midst of the confused platoon milling about below. 'Oh gods!' She grabbed the first soldier she encountered, ensured he took a long look at her body, and then shouted, 'They're killing him! Please help, upstairs, please help! They're killing him!'

He turned and ran, followed by others, taking the stairs three at a time; then Brexan heard shouts echo down from the landing.

Come quick!

Bring weapons!

We need a healer up here!

One soldier walked her to the top step of the lower stairway. 'You wait here,' he said gently, helping her pull her cloak about her shoulders. 'I'll be right back; you can tell the lieutenant what happened.'

'I didn't do anything,' she wailed, 'please. I was just – you know, working.'

'I understand, and I don't want you to worry. You'll be fine.'

In a moment he was gone and Brexan, still crying, slipped down the stairs and across the main hall.

At the front entrance to the palace she was able to lose herself in the noise and bustle, slipping behind the tall hedge that encircled the grounds, where she pulled on her tunic and cloak and disappeared into the city. As she rounded a corner into an alley off the main thoroughfare, weeping and furious with herself for leaving Sallax alone, she could still hear that wretched little bell jangling. Jacrys was still alive.

THE WELSTAR RIVER

Captain Reddig Millard stood at the helm of the *River Prince*, his eyes fixed downriver. A Malakasian naval vessel had been flanking the barge for nearly half an aven and he was waiting for them to come alongside, give the order to heave to and deploy a boarding party to examine his papers, his cargo and his crew – but he would not turn and look at them.

He had been working the Welstar passage to Pellia for too many Twinmoons to allow any puny cutter make him sweat; his cargo was legal, his crew was legal and his documents had been approved by the customs officer in Treven. No baby-faced so-called officer all got up in that absurd black-and-gold fancy dress was going to get under his skin, not on this trip. Millard was not going to worry about the four who'd bought passage, nor did he care that they'd asked to linger a while on the great bend below Prince Malagon's castle. He had agreed to ship them with no questions asked and that's what he was doing.

Of course, he stood to make a handful of extra silver: free money, and nothing the customs officers in Pellia would notice, because his overhead costs were always the same, and his take for a load of crates and military passengers was always within a few Mareks of the same bottom line, give or take a beer or two. It was worth the risk. He'd pocket the silver, and the customs officer in Pellia would check his papers, ask about the weather and accept a donation of a few bottles of decent wine. He might be slipped a tin or two of tobacco in thanks for the wine, but then he would be allowed to unload whatever was left of his shipment after the military had purchased what they needed for the palace encampment. The drill was always the same.

Something was making Millard nervous, though; being shadowed this long by a navy cutter, and his crew, the old man especially – *why would anyone want to linger on that stretch of the river?*

Doggedly determined not to look back at the wet-nosed cutter captain, Millard kept his eyes trained on the river ahead, charting the speed and heading of other vessels. A notion began to irritate him, lingering at the back of his mind like an itch he couldn't reach: this was not going to be another routine passage. He unfastened the leather ties holding his tunic closed; his skin was warm with sweat despite the chill along the water.

His new crew bothered him: at first he thought they were fennaroot runners, or maybe deserters, but he was beginning to fear that they represented something much more dangerous to him and his ship.

In the broad but shallow cargo area below the raised helm, the crewmen lounged in the midday sun, smoking, drinking tecan and picking at what remained of their midday meal, all but the four strangers, who huddled together in the forward corner, talking among themselves and taking turns marking the cutter's progress.

It's a faster ship. Millard wished they could hear his thoughts. *There is no point staring back at them; they'll catch up with this hulk whenever they please, so stop giving them reason to believe we're up to no good!*

Millard nearly succumbed to his anxiety and turned for a quick glance, but he gripped the wheel with both hands until his knuckles whitened. 'No,' he said aloud. 'The moment I turn round, they'll know they have me, the bleeding whores.'

The *River Prince* was like all the barges that worked the passage between central Malakasia and Pellia; she could haul three times the number of crates they could pile inside a schooner, and Captain Millard needed only one-third the draft: even at the height of the dry season, he could run the river from south of Treven all the way into Pellia with two thousand crates of summer vegetables or fifty pallets of freshly cut lumber.

The barge captains had all developed a healthy, if wary, relationship with the region's customs and naval officers: Prince Malagon's army needed daily shipments to stay well-fed, well-supplied and ready for immediate deployment. The barge captains didn't skim too much off the top or forge their papers and in turn the officials looked the other way if a few extra crates of wine, beer or tobacco were unloaded at an unscheduled stop somewhere along the river. Those who ran weapons or who cheated the military simply disappeared; their ships still made the river run, but with a new captain at the helm.

Millard had dabbled a little in extra trade, but as he looked down at his new crew members nervously marking the naval cutter, he worried that he had allowed his desire for a quick score to cloud his judgment.

'Round that next bend,' Millard said to himself, 'and he'll see where I'm bound. He'll tack off towards the centre of the river. Good rutting monks, but there's Sal and the *Black Water*. You rutters know he's got at least two crates of root in there. Go follow him for an aven or two.' But Captain Millard didn't need to watch to know the cutter was staying right behind him as the *River Prince* sailed north to the Welstar docks.

As he navigated the last turn before coming into view of the Welstar military encampment, the captain nodded to a young woman, who hustled up the creaky wooden steps and rooted around in a box beneath the binnacle. She pulled out three small banners, one yellow and green, one blue and white and one bright orange. The captain nodded.

'Run those up, Bree,' he ordered. The flags that flapped noisily in the brisk wind would tell the cutter that he meant to dock at Welstar and offload crates of vegetables.

'Up in the bow with you, Bree, and keep an eye peeled for our mooring colours.'

'Yes, sir.' The girl scurried through the hold and up onto the bow platform. Shielding her eyes against the sun, she watched until one of the dock stewards ran up the same set of coloured pennants. 'Three, sir,' she shouted, pointing at the third wooden dock from the end.

The twenty-one wooden piers jutting from the wharf at Welstar were a hive of activity during any season, but on most winter runs, Millard and his crew never saw Pellia, for the army normally bought everything he carried; he expected them to take all his vegetables this time as well.

He had promised the strangers two opportunities to take in as much as they could of the Welstar Palace encampment; if the supply officer striding officiously out the dock to greet them cleaned him out today, he would see if the military needed anything hauled downriver to Pellia. If they didn't require his services, Millard would allow the barge to drift with the current past the old palace while his crew made a few minor repairs – to what, he had no idea yet, but the *River Prince* was an old tub and there was always something that needed fixing. Then, once the strange foursome had enjoyed their second look at the castle and its grounds, he'd begin the arduous task of tacking back upriver to the narrows north of the Welstar docks. There, Millard would hand over the Mareks to lash on to the next available oxen team, and try to ignore the inane drivel of their driver as the *River Dancer* was towed upstream to the swirling, deep-water eddies above Treven.

And if his new crew members were unhappy with that arrangement, he would have them thrown overboard; that was quite sufficient risk for one journey. Millard looked forward to pocketing his silver and being done with this business for good.

As he headed the barge towards the long row of evenly spaced wooden piers Captain Millard discovered that the cutter was shadowing the *River Prince* into port.

'Now why would he be coming in here after me?' he asked the empty bridge. 'I've run up my colours, is all, even a blind man can see I'm shipping winter vegetables. What's wrong with winter vegetables?'

He barked orders and the small team of sailors scampered over mountains of wooden crates and boxes, untying tarps and loosening cargo lines. The girl, Bree, remained in the bow, a length of rope in one hand, until they were close enough for her to toss the line to the dock steward waiting near a stanchion.

The captain felt his hull bump against the wooden dock with a muted thud as the cutter closed in at flank speed. His hands trembled a little as he reached inside his tunic and withdrew his shipping papers. Something was about to happen, but he didn't have a clue what, or why; instead, he'd behave as normal. If he went along as if everything was normal, producing his manifests, greeting the supply officer, chatting with the customs officials, the pending trouble might somehow pass them by.

When the cutter furled sheets and dropped anchor off the slip between docks three and four, Captain Millard knew his hopes were for naught: the *River Prince* was boxed in. He swallowed an order to cut the dock lines and break free, even though his barge could easily smash the cutter to splinters.

As a squad of soldiers approached at a quick march, the crew began to mill about nervously, looking at the captain for answers; Millard gestured for them to stand down, trying to convey reassurance: *it'll be all right. We'll be back on the river soon.*

'Captain?' A supply officer he recognised approached along the pier.

Millard searched for the man's name, and replied cheerily, 'Lieutenant Warren,' waving his manifest again. 'What's happening, sir?'

The officer gave him a look that said he had no idea why the military had taken a sudden interest in the *River Prince*. 'Captain, join me on the pier.'

'What's happening, Lieutenant?' Millard repeated, moving warily towards the rail. 'I'm hauling vegetables, and I'm happy to sell them right here.'

'Join me up here, Captain, I need you to comply right away,' the official said. 'On orders, I am impounding the *River Prince* and its cargo until further notice. You and your crew will be placed under arrest.'

The soldiers lined up along the port rail, weapons drawn. Captain Millard looked back towards the river and saw two ranks of bowmen, arrows nocked, lining the cutter's rail. There was no escape; he leaned forward and whispered, 'You are not taking my boat, Warren.'

The lieutenant did the same, checking to be certain none of the soldiers along the pier heard him. 'I'm sure it's all right, sir. Please come with me. The major has been grumpy all this Moon. His foot has been bothering him again.'

Millard nodded imperceptibly, then shouted to his crew, 'All hands, up here now. Follow me.' He jumped ashore and started down the dock.

'They need to relinquish their weapons, sir,' Lieutenant Warren said, as firmly as he dared.

'They don't carry weapons, Lieutenant. They're sailors.'

'The knives, sir.'

Millard shrugged, irritated, but shouted down regardless, 'Leave your knives, and anything else you might have on you.'

Everyone complied; no one said a word. Once everyone was ashore, Captain Millard gripped his manifests in one hand and followed the lieutenant towards the wharf and the major's office. Halfway down the pier, he had to sidestep the mangiest dog he had ever seen. Its paws were caked with dried blood and it had lost an eye and part of an ear. One of its hind legs appeared to have been broken and mended crookedly. The animal watched him pass, peering at him until he crossed the wharf and entered the customs office.

When the *River Prince* made her final turn into the Welstar Palace encampment, Hoyt cursed. 'I can't believe he's going to dock,' he muttered. 'Can't he see them? What's he thinking?'

'He's thinking that there is no way to run for a great hulking barge laden full of winter vegetables with little breeze and barely a current. We'd be run down, strafed with arrows, holed and boarded in time to save the cargo before we went down.' Alen watched past Churn's shoulder as they were followed towards the docks that reached out into the river like so many skeletal fingers.

'We should run,' Hoyt insisted.

'Captain Millard makes this stop every time he comes down the river. If he deviates from normal practice, he might as well shout out loud that we're up to something. His only choice is to tie up and go about his business.' Alen stood and stretched; it was clumsy and awkward, but it did enable him to get a long look at the cutter in the distance. 'We'll follow Millard's orders, but we will keep our wits about us; we did not come all the way down here to get arrested because some halfwit bargee has fennaroot stashed somewhere between the potatoes and the greenroot. Keep your heads down. Speak only when one of them asks you a direct question. We don't need any additional attention drawn to us.'

Hannah said, 'So you think they're after Captain Millard?'

'Who knows?' Alen said. 'Maybe this is standard procedure.'

'Look at Millard,' she said. 'He's too stiff; he hasn't looked at them, not once. This isn't standard; he's sweating like a guilty pig.'

'Either way, we can't fight our way out of this, so until we know what's happening, we play along. Agreed?'

The others nodded, Hoyt somewhat hesitantly.

As the barge got blocked in, Hoyt whispered to Hannah, 'This is bad.'

When the squad formed along the port rail and drew their swords, Hannah replied, 'I think it just got worse.'

'You're not joking.' Hoyt forced a half smile.

'Look,' she said under her breath. 'It looks like the captain knows that one.'

'He's a supply officer. I'm sure they know each other.'

'Maybe he'll tell Millard what's going on.'

'And maybe he'll have us all hanged for treason.'

Hannah shivered as a sharp wind blew off the river. She stepped closer to Churn; maybe being near the Pragan giant would help her feel more at ease. She welcomed the feel of his massive hand on her shoulder as she whispered, 'What do you think?'

'Not good,' Churn signed with one hand. 'Stay near me.'

Hoyt dropped his knife when ordered, but retained the silver scalpel; he'd been able to hide the small blade before. He hoped the search was cursory. They followed the *River Prince*'s crew along the pier, all careful to avoid eye contact with any of the soldiers escorting them towards a rank of stone buildings. The wharf marked the riverside entrance to the village that supported the palace and the military encampment. They were all silent, until Hannah passed by the filthy dog padding back and forth along the pier excitedly, its hind leg oddly out of rhythm with the other three.

'My dog,' she blurted suddenly, but quickly fell silent again.

They were herded to the customs office, then left outside under guard while Captain Millard went in to find out what was going on. None of the crew spoke; Hoyt and Churn wandered off a few paces and then turned to face the others.

Hannah, following Churn's directive to stay close, moved to join him, until he signed, 'wait there'.

She looked at them: to an observer, they were just crewmembers, nervous, shuffling their feet and waiting to see what was about to happen, but with a few paces separating them, they could each check the area for possible routes to freedom, should the discussion going on inside the major's office go badly.

Hoyt nodded pleasantly to one of their guards and signed, '*What dog?*'

It took a moment for Hannah to understand, but after Hoyt repeated the gesture several times, she finally got it. '*Sorry. My dog. Back there, the dog from my . . .*' She didn't know the sign for dream, or vision, but they appeared to understand what she meant.

'*That was Alen's dog. The dog from my . . .*' Hoyt gestured as if he was waving flies away from his face; Hannah guessed that was Churn's sign for *dream*.

'*It's real?*' Churn asked.

'*It is a real dog, but it isn't mine, and it wasn't Hannah's.*' Alen joined the conversation.

'Branag's!' Hoyt exclaimed out loud, then hid his outburst behind a feigned coughing spasm.

'*What?*' Hannah asked.

Hoyt's hands moved quickly, but he punctuated his comments with coughing fits, hoping to cover the curious way he was standing alone waving his hands about. '*It's Branag's dog, the old dog that follows him everywhere. That's his dog.*'

445

Churn turned to look along the dock; the dog was coming towards them. *'You're right!'* Churn agreed. *'That's Branag's wolfhound. Remember?'*

Now Hannah remembered: Southport, and the dog that padded back and forth down the short hallway between the saddlery shop and the workroom in the back. She, Hoyt and Churn had hidden in there for days after Churn killed the soldier along the road above the village. The dog had made for pleasant company. She signed, *'Why is it here?'*

'It must be following us. That's why we were stopped. They knew we were coming.'

'How can that be?'

'You came through the portal. Nerak knew.'

'So he sent a dog to follow me?'

'Not him, no.'

'Who?' Hannah was confused now.

'I think I know who.' Alen turned towards the palace which rose above the army encampment and the village.

'It came this far? How can that be?' Hannah asked.

'Look at it. The thing is a mess,' Hoyt signed. The wolfhound limped over to Alen and nuzzled the old man's palm; Alen patted it on the head, leaned over and whispered into the animal's remaining ear, 'You tell him I'm here. It's Kantu. You tell him, wherever you are. Tell him to come out here and meet me. I'm waiting.'

The dog growled and Alen stood back up, turning away from it.

'What did you say?' Hannah asked.

'I told it goodbye.' Alen's face was angry; he mouthed a few words, nothing anyone around him could hear. Then feigning an itch on his opposite shoulder, he gestured towards the animal as it backed away across the wharf. Almost immediately, the dog began to cough, raspy and laboured. It started panting for breath and it turned to yelp in their direction, then, dragging its crooked hind leg, Branag's old wolfhound, emaciated and scarred, slunk behind a stack of pallets.

The door to the customs house flew open and an angry Captain Millard stepped into the street growling. 'Gouty whoreson, no wonder his foot's bad.' He waved his copy of the *River Prince*'s manifest at the upstairs window, an act of defiance. Lieutenant Warren followed closely behind.

'Tell them, Captain, and make sure they come peacefully. I would hate to have your crew—Well, you know.' It was obvious that the major had just berated Lieutenant Warren for allowing the furious captain anywhere near his private office.

'Oh, shut up Warren,' Millard said, ignoring the fact that he was insulting a Malakasian officer with a squad of armed soldiers standing by.

'What do we do?' Hannah signed, her hands shaking.

'Wait,' Alen replied. *'Just wait.'*

Lieutenant Warren's response shocked all of them, Captain Millard most of all, as he drew a short sword and levelled its point at Millard's throat. 'Soldier!' Warren barked, and the squad immediately stood to attention.

'Sir!' shouted the man nearest.

'Bind this man. If he speaks again, bind his mouth. If he resists at all, kill him. Understood?'

'Sir!' He pulled a length of rope from his pocket and gestured at the captain, who was still gripping his winter vegetable manifest.

For the first time Millard looked scared as his hands were bound behind his back.

'They aren't going to kill us,' Hoyt signed.

'How do you know?' Hannah asked.

'Because they're tying him up, not hanging him.'

Lieutenant Warren gestured to five soldiers from the squad. 'Take the crew and get the barge unloaded.' As the soldiers started moving, the lieutenant interrupted, 'Not those four. They're coming with me. Bind them hand and mouth. If they resist or speak out of turn, kill them. We need only one of them alive. Confine Captain Millard to his cabin, bound, until he learns to control his tongue or until I order his release. Understood?'

'Sir,' the squad responded in unison.

Hannah heard a rush of sound, like a great blast of wind that drowned out the noise of the docks and she began to shake. 'Not inside the palace,' she said. 'They can't take us in there. Please, no.'

'Quiet,' Alen signed. *'It will be all right, but you have to be quiet.'* Then they tied his hands.

Churn looked to Hoyt, his hands still free. *'Now?'*

'No.'

'When?'

'Not now. Inside.'

The big man relaxed, dropped his arms to his side and allowed the soldiers to bind his wrists. One of them prodded him in the back of the knees with the flat of a sword. 'Kneel down,' he ordered, and

Churn complied quietly; the soldier was not tall enough to reach his mouth.

Before they could gag him, Alen called out, 'Lieutenant, please.'

Warren cocked an eyebrow at the old man.

'Can I speak?'

'Make it quick.'

'Prince Malagon's daughter, Bellan, can you tell me if she has changed yet?'

'What?'

'Changed. Begun wearing gloves all the time? Maybe taken to her chambers and not been seen for days?'

Lieutenant Warren looked at him in curiosity. 'Because the chances are slim that you will live through the day, old man, I'll tell you that I have never been above the lower level of the palace, and I have only been in there once. I don't like going up that hill, and since you are the reason I have to go up there today, I don't like you. I have never seen Princess Bellan, nor do I care what she wears. But I will tell you that if you speak to me of her again, I will run you through myself. Do you understand?'

'One last question?' Alen dared.

Lieutenant Warren shook his head in mock-despair and put his band on his sword-hilt. 'I told you, old man, I would—'

'Get word to the palace; let them know that Kantu is here. They'll know who I am. Just let them know. Kantu.'

'Gag this rutter!' Warren snapped. 'Make it tight.'

Still shaking, Hannah allowed herself to be guided towards the sloping road that led through the village. Behind her, the waterway was abuzz as naval vessels patrolled back and forth and barges, too many to count, moved up and down the channel, some stacked high with crates, others starting their return journey unladen. Hannah saw, in the shadows, Branag's dog, the wolfhound she had seen padding into the living room from her mother's kitchen as clearly, lying dead, its broken form motionless.

Ahead, Welstar Palace rose above the village, a dark structure with windows that appeared to absorb rather than reflect light: depthless pools of midnight black staring out at passersby. There were three towers, and wings stretching out and back from the elaborate main gate, and a series of enclosed courtyards, but there were no pennants flying from the ramparts, no flags hoisted above the towers and no smoke rising from chimneys; no sign of life inside at all.

Hannah thought it was the most forbidding place she had ever seen. The grim façade seemed to hum, *stay away*, resonating out through the dirt beneath her feet.

THE BOWMAN INN

'Beer.'

'Beer.'

'Beer.'

'All right, three beers and two half-goblets of wine coming right up.' Steven draped his cloak over the back of his chair. The Goretex coats were hidden in Garec's saddlebag.

'And aspirin,' Mark said. 'My leg is cramping again.'

'I have aspirin. I took it from Howard's place.'

'I need three.'

'They're in the bottle in my pack. You can get them while I get the drinks.'

'Good, I like them better with beer, anyway.' Mark dug into Steven's bag and opened the plastic container discreetly. Cupping the pills in his hand, he said, 'I like Traver's Notch.'

Garec nodded. 'It's a nice little town, clean and quiet. I'll bet there's good fishing too.'

'Too bad we can't stay,' Mark said.

'Time is running out on us.' Gilmour traced the grain on their tabletop with a fingertip. 'We have to get south. If you know where the spell table is, we must get there as soon as possible, before Nerak beats us there.'

'Won't he be looking for us?' Garec asked, 'knowing we have the key, won't he be waiting for us out here somewhere?'

'Perhaps not. If Nerak travelled back to Malakasia to take over Bellan and resume command of the occupation forces, then we may have some time before he comes back to the East.'

'But why would he waste time doing that?' The young Ronan checked the front room for eavesdroppers.

'Because he can, and because the occupation forces are valuable to him. They are a formidable army – and don't forget, as far as Nerak is concerned, we don't know where the spell table is, and we are effectively trapped in Sandcliff Palace.' At that, Gilmour smiled.

'Unless he felt Steven killing the almor and wiping out those clouds,' Mark said.

'He can't detect Steven's magic. If he could, we'd have known by now. So if he returned to Welstar Palace to collect Bellan, to proclaim Prince Malagon dead and to restore order among the occupation forces, we may have a little time in which to travel unaccosted. He may be thinking he can take Bellan, return to Sandcliff in person, and finish us off, but with Steven's cloaking spell—'

'Yup, Mom's old blanket,' Mark said, appreciatively.

'Well, with that we may be able to move south without him knowing we've escaped.' Gilmour gestured south as if Meyers' Vale were just across the street.

'Could he somehow have had the almor reporting back to him?' Garec asked.

'Perhaps,' Gilmour shrugged, 'but that's a risk we can't avoid these days. Our best option is to get there as quickly as we can. He has no idea we're closing in on the spell table; that's to our advantage. We have Steven's cloaking spell. And finally—'

'We have the key.'

'Yes.'

'So someplace between here and the spell table, he'll confront us in person, not long-distance threats or talking Larion skeletons,' Mark said.

'Unless we manage to get all the way down there without him detecting us, or without his spies getting word to him of our whereabouts. Although at this juncture I suppose I should say *her* spies.'

'So Nerak is now Princess Bellan?' Garec sat up straighter, half expecting the woman herself to step into the room.

'I'm pretty sure – of course, she won't be Princess Bellan in the eyes of his occupation leaders until someone produces Malagon's body.'

'Which is floating somewhere off Charleston, South Carolina,' Mark said. Gilmour chuckled. 'That's right, and as long as that's the case, Bellan will have a hard time convincing the generals they need to follow her.'

'Won't she just kill anyone who resists her?' Garec wondered why a being as powerful as Nerak would spend time trying to convince mortal generals that they should follow him.

'A few, yes, and after a while that will get the others' attention. We want her distracted by that as long as possible.'

'How long will it take us to cross Falkan?' Mark asked.

'Maybe fifteen days from here, riding flat-out.'

'We should travel like we did before,' Garec suggested. 'That was incredible. We crossed the plains in just a few days.'

'Nerak was still in Colorado then. If we do that now, he'll track us all the way.' Gilmour closed his eyes for a moment; he was not looking forward to the journey.

'You're right, sorry. So we travel the old-fashioned way. That's fine; it gives us a chance to see the scenery.'

'A mostly flat, arable plain lying fallow during winter,' Mark quipped. 'That will make for some picturesque vistas.'

'No matter,' Gilmour said. 'We'll travel as far and as fast as the horses can stand.'

'When we get to that bend in the river, assuming we can find it again, how will we get the spell table out?' Garec checked the bar to see what was keeping Steven so long.

'I don't know,' Gilmour said matter-of-factly. 'I haven't seen this place.'

'Imagine ice and snow over a rushing river and an underwater moraine as big as your mother's house. There's nothing south of there but the Blackstones and nothing north except days and days of river, and then that cavern with those bone-collecting things.' Mark popped one of the aspirins into his mouth and swallowed it dry.

Gilmour filled a pipe and lit it from a taper on the table. 'I trust you, and that's why we're going all the way down there. Nerak thinks he has the best of us – of me, I suppose, because I was too stupid to realise he wouldn't have left the spell table at Sandcliff. Any half-wit would guess if it isn't at Sandcliff, then Nerak must keep it at Welstar Palace, but I think you may have stumbled onto it completely out of naked— what was it, Mark?'

'Pastry-chef luck.'

'Naked, pastry-chef luck.' He puffed contentedly at the pipe. 'Anyway, if it is Eldarn warding the spell table, and it was Eldarn that trapped you down there, then I will need some time to find the root of the spell he's used to control the ground, the water and the rocks. It will be a slow process.'

'Can you unweave it?' Garec wasn't sure how to ask what he wanted to know.

'Probably not,' Gilmour said, surprising them, 'but I'll wager he can.' He nodded towards Steven, standing patiently at the bar.

Steven was waiting for the innkeeper. Gita had told him to look for a tall man, heavy around the middle, with flowing grey hair and ruddy, wrinkled skin. His name was Ranvid; he had been a member of the Falkan Resistance for almost two hundred Twinmoons. Malakasian forces regularly moved through Traver's Notch, so Ranvid was always assimilating bits of news about the occupation which he passed through various channels to Gita and the other Resistance cell leaders. His methods were simple, and effective: the Bowman was known to welcome Malakasian soldiers: they got good service, cheap booze and plentiful meals, and officers *always* drank for free.

Over time, the local occupation forces had come to think of the Bowman as an establishment sympathetic to Prince Malagon and word spread as the army moved throughout the country. Ranvid gleaned a wealth of valuable information, ranging from which general loathed which down to specific troop movements. He even knew when an enormous force started mustering outside Welstar Palace.

The innkeeper had never participated in a raid, taken up arms against a local patrol or killed a Malakasian soldier, but he was invaluable to the Falkan Resistance, a hero who risked his life daily.

When he finally stepped out from the kitchen, Steven recognised him immediately from Gita's description.

'Yes, sir, what do you need?' He collected an armful of dirty trenchers that had been left along the raised counter.

'Three beers, and two half-goblets of wine, one red and one white.'

Ranvid froze, then turned to look Steven in the face. 'You plan to mix them to make a whole pink?'

'No,' Steven said, 'I don't like to drink that much.'

He placed the trenchers in a bucket half filled with greasy water that made Steven lose his appetite and drew three beers from a wooden cask behind the bar. 'I knew a woman once who drank pink wine,' he said conversationally.

'I hear she died,' Steven continued the exchange he'd memorised.

'No, she's still around.'

'I'd like to meet her.'

The innkeeper placed the beers in front of him, then poured out two half-goblets of wine from ceramic pitchers. Steven paid with a few copper Mareks and reached for the drinks, but almost imperceptibly, Ranvid shook his head. 'You want food?'

'No, thanks,' Steven said, his stomach still recoiling from the sight of the oily bucket. 'We have to be moving on.'

'You want food.' It was not a request this time.

Steven sipped the surprisingly good white wine and agreed, understanding belatedly that the man wanted him to wait beside the bar. 'Actually, why not? What's good?' *Anything but stew*, he thought to himself.

'The stew is tasty.'

He swallowed hard. 'Good then. Four stews, and bread, please.'

'A fine choice.' Ranvid turned to the kitchen and shouted, 'Four up!'

Someone called back, 'Come get them yourself.'

Ranvid motioned for Steven to wait and disappeared into the kitchen. A moment later, Steven winced at a loud slap, a shriek and the sound of a large pan full of something wet and sloppy tumbling to the floor.

The innkeeper returned and grinned. 'Your food'll be right out.' He waved away Steven's thanks and busied himself at the bar, clearing goblets, scraping trenchers and tossing half-eaten loaves into a woven straw basket at his feet.

Steven stayed where he was, content to watch and wait.

Without making eye contact, Ranvid said softly, 'You wield the staff, yes?'

Steven examined an etched pattern on the side of his wine goblet. 'That's right.'

'The woman is here. Many of her men are in the Notch; there's a camp on the north side of the wall.'

'The wall?'

'The northernmost hill behind Traver's Notch. There's a pass; we keep it open through the winter. Any horse can cross with no trouble.' He waved to three locals sitting near a window, raised his eyebrows, and nodded. 'Three more, right away,' he called.

Steven finished the white wine and started in on the red. 'How do I find her?' he asked as Ranvid finished drawing the men's drinks.

'Across the western bridge and up the hill road. Near the top there's a dirt path leading back into the trees. Follow that to the cottage at the end behind the birch trees.'

He disappeared back in to the kitchen and reappeared with four trenchers. 'Enjoy, sir,' he said heartily.

'Thank you.' Steven left a silver coin on the bar and loaded up the trenchers.

'She's a great leader, and a great fighter.' Ranvid's voice was barely there. 'She has great hopes for you.'

'I won't let her down,' he replied.

'Steven Taylor!' Gita Kamrec met them outside the cottage, running to him and throwing her arms around him. 'Gods, but I am glad to see you're still alive.'

'Me too,' Steven replied, returning her embrace one-handed, the hickory staff in the other.

Gita released him and stepped back. 'Gods! Be careful where you point that thing. It makes me nervous.' She hugged Garec and Mark in turn. 'Garec the bowman, and Jenkins, the horseman from the South Coast, welcome to Traver's Notch.'

Mark smiled. 'Nice to see you again, Gita.'

'What happened to your leg?'

'We met a border patrol in Gorsk.'

'Gorsk? How long have you been up here? I thought you were going to Praga to find Kantu. What were you doing in Gorsk?'

Mark said, 'We've a lot to tell you.'

'And where's Brynne? My earlobes have healed, and I think the scars just about match; I don't think I'm lopsided.' When no one answered, Gita's countenance fell. She looked back and forth between them. 'Brynne, too?'

'We lost her in Orindale,' Garec said. 'We're hoping she's alive, but we don't know.'

The Falkan leader pressed her lips into a thin line. 'And Sallax?'

'In Orindale, we hope,' Garec said. 'We heard nothing from him, nor could we find him while we were there.'

'Gilmour, Sallax, Brynne, Timmon – not to mention my soldiers: this is a costly a business, boys. I hope we'll all be around when it ends.'

'I'll buy the drinks.' Garec said, anxious to move on to something more pleasant.

'The rutting blazes you will,' Gita quipped, smiling again. 'I'm an old lady, and it's an old lady's prerogative to decide who picks up the tavern bill. I'll have no arguing about it. The drinks will be on me.'

'Done,' Gilmour said, approaching warily.

'And who's this? Are you Kantu? I've heard of you.'

'It's me, Gita.'

'Which *me*?' She looked askance at him. 'Do I know you?'

'You have known me for a long time,' Gilmour said, looking into her eyes. 'When days in Rona grow balmy—'

'Drink Falkan wine after Twinmoon,' she said in a whisper. She turned to Garec. 'Did you teach him that?'

Garec shook his head. 'It really is him, Gita. It's a long story.'

She leaned in, squinted as if, blurry, he might somehow become familiar to her. Then, inhaling sharply, she said, 'They told me you were dead.'

Gilmour said, 'I suppose part of me has been for some Twinmoons now, but as you can see, the parts that count are still doing quite well.'

'I always knew there was something about you, you old ... is it really you?'

He nodded.

Now she *was* awestruck. 'What kind of magic is this?'

'Larion.'

She laughed. 'That's funny, but no, I mean, what kind—' Gita waited for Gilmour's expression to change, and when it didn't, her eyes grew wide. 'Then you would have to be—'

'Yes.'

'And that would make you like – gods! I can't even figure it without a piece of paper.'

'Two thousand, probably more.'

'I need to sit down. I need a drink, a lot of drinks.' She reached for Garec and he slipped an arm around her waist. 'Let's go inside.'

Three men, bodyguards, Steven guessed, materialised from the woods beside the cottage when Gita reached up and signed *all clear*. He remembered the covert communication the Falkan Resistance forces had used in the underground cavern. Two remained outside watching for any indication that their hideaway had been discovered. The third, a young man wearing an eye-patch, joined them inside.

Steven tried not to look at the soldier's face, but couldn't help wondering if the man was one of those he had injured when he had used magic to hurl a cloud of stones into the Falkan ranks; he toyed with the idea of asking and apologising, but every time he geared himself up to do so, someone interrupted, derailing his good intentions.

Another of Gita's commanders joined them for the discussion. As Brand Krug walked in, Steven noticed that he still wore a brace of throwing knives at his belt. As he had in the underground cavern, Brand immediately asked for news of Sallax; he looked angry and disappointed when Garec told him they had not located their friend.

Gita paced back and forth before the fireplace, thinking through their story, and their intention to move south towards the Blackstones. Steven watched her, hoping she wouldn't try to accompany them into Meyers' Vale; he didn't want a military escort. If their group got any larger, it would slow them down and make them an obvious target for the army.

Gita said finally, 'We've received information that the forces around Orindale have broken up and battalions are moving to take up their regular patrols. The prince's generals argued for almost a Moon after Malagon disappeared and they have finally decided there is nothing to protect; that the prince must have left the city incognito.'

Garec said, 'They'll be scattered all over the countryside. It'll be difficult to avoid them.'

'You won't avoid them,' Gita said. 'You need to take some of us along. Brand's company can escort you.'

'How many men do you have?' Garec asked.

'Ninety-seven here now with more on the way.'

Steven shook his head. 'That's foolish, Gita. We'll succeed in nothing but getting them hacked to pieces. Gilmour and I can see us into the Vale.'

'A stray arrow, Steven, one single arrow will silence you or Gilmour. We can't afford it. You have to be escorted. Brand's soldiers are tough, solid fighters. They've lived a long time, and through hundreds of raids. They know what they're doing, and they can travel fast. If you're attacked, the orders will be clear. Brand and a squad will ride with you, while the lieutenants engage and retreat, engage and retreat, pulling them off your back. Afterward, if they can get past the Malakasian forces, they'll meet with you along the road further south.' She stared down at a map of the flatlands in central Falkan. 'They will see you through the first skirmish, anyway.'

Steven didn't like the idea, but he waited to hear what the others thought.

Mark spoke up first. 'I think it's a good idea.' He looked to Brand. 'Chances are you'll lose some of your soldiers, but this trip is critical to Falkan's freedom and Prince Malagon's defeat. If we can't avoid encountering soldiers, then we need help.'

'Gilmour, what do you think?' Gita asked.

'I understand Steven's point. Alone, we are powerful and very fast. But you're right as well: one lucky shot, and we lose Steven—'

Steven interrupted, 'But that could happen anyway. It's a risk we have to take.'

'That is a risk we have to mitigate as much as possible and then take,' Gilmour corrected. 'I agree. We should accept Gita's offer and move south with Brand's escort.'

'A hundred people? We'll be ringing the clarion all the way down there. Every Malakasian soldier and informer in the midlands will be on our tail.' Steven tried not to get too emotional, but Hannah was alive and possibly on her way to Orindale right now, and he was not about to take unnecessary risks. The odds of a stray arrow taking him would go up severalfold if he were travelling with an armed Falkan escort. If the Malakasian forces were dispersing, the only way to reach Meyers' Vale would be to move in the shadows, off the main roads, hiding at every sight of black and gold uniforms, otherwise it would be suicide. 'Think about what comes next.'

'What do you mean?' Brand asked.

'If we get to Meyers' Vale and find the table, Falkan and the Eastlands will need a solid fighting force to move across the plain, dividing the occupation army in half, and trying to turn either north or south, to establish a foothold over here. That's going to be a back-breaking task as it is and there's no way you could attempt it without Brand's company.'

'You are right, Steven,' Gita said, 'you're really not bad as a military tactician. However, I have others gathering every able-bodied soldier up here to join us. At first, I thought we would come together here, see you into Gorsk, and then turn back towards Orindale for our final stand. But knowing how disorganised the Eastern Army has become in the wake of Prince Malagon's disappearance, we might be able to take a corner of the Eastlands, a stretch of Falkan with a port, perhaps Capehill, if we can capitalise on a momentary lapse in their command hierarchy.'

Mark finished her thought, 'And taking leadership from Welstar Palace out of the equation, we create exactly that opportunity.'

'Does that mean we won't have to face Seron, those ground demons, or any more of the cloud creatures?'

'If my speculations about Prince Malagon are even close to correct, Gita, that's exactly right – although I'm not sure about the Seron. They may be here for good,' Mark said.

'But the almor, and the cloud creatures?'

'And the wraiths,' Mark added, 'all of them, they'll still be in Eldarn, but I'm betting they won't be following orders any longer. I have a strong belief that Prince Malagon has a weakness, maybe something to do with Steven and his stick. All the creatures he has sent against us have a few things in common and if we deal with Prince Malagon in Meyers' Vale, I believe it will take care of those creatures as well.'

'Steven has already proven himself against the clouds and the almor,' Garec added.

Gita laughed. 'When you put it that way, I think we have the easier task taking over the Eastlands.'

'When will the rest of the Resistance arrive?' Gilmour asked.

'It's hard to say. We weren't expecting you fellows for a while, so I would guess another Twinmoon.' Gita looked again at the maps spread across the table. 'I'd like to give them that long, anyway.'

'That should give us time to get there, but we don't know how long it'll take to excavate the table – *if* we find the table.' Garec joined Gita near the fire.

'It will be enough time,' Gilmour said. 'Do you have anyone under your command who can work magic, even simple festival tricks? Anyone at all?'

Gita glanced at Brand; something passed between them.

'I don't know where he is,' Brand finally said.

'Can we get him here in the next Twinmoon?'

'I can send a rider, but Gita, he's a mess. He can't—'

Gilmour interrupted. 'He won't need to work any spells. He'll simply need to receive a message from me.'

'You'll talk to him?' Brand asked sceptically, 'from the Blackstones?' Gilmour laughed, 'No; it'll seem like he's been belted by an invisible fist – unless he's very talented, he won't know what hit him, but it will at least confirm that we've been successful.'

'So we bring him here and watch him until you clobber him senseless from somewhere south of Orindale?'

'Exactly.'

'And all he has to do is ...'

'Have a thimbleful of magic in his bones and take a solid, unexpected punch to the head.'

Now Brand laughed. 'That, I would like to see.'

'Send the rider,' Gita directed.

'Very well.'

'Who is this man?' Gilmour asked.

'His name is Stalwick,' Gita said. 'He rode with us for a time but then he ...' She searched for the right description.

'He's a blazing idiot,' Brand finished for her. 'But if all you need him to do is be around here until you kick his head in, he can handle that.'

'Where is he?'

'Capehill.'

'Good,' Gita clapped her hands together. 'It's decided then. Brand's company will ride south with you. We'll bring Stalwick here and continue to build up our forces. We have many friends and supporters in the Notch, and the local mining industry provides us with an excellent cover. When Stalwick collapses, I will assume that you have done whatever it is you plan to do with this table you seek and that we should begin our march to Capehill.'

'And we'll meet you there,' Gilmour finished.

'After we go to Orindale,' Steven interjected.

'Orindale?'

'Hannah and Kantu,' he reminded.

Gilmour nodded, 'That's right – unless, of course, they join us along the way.'

They stayed in the cottage that night. Mark woke in the pre-dawn aven and slipped out to pile logs onto the fire. He was not surprised to find Gilmour awake and pouring over Gita's maps.

'Looking for an overland route to the West Indies?' Mark asked.

'How'd you know?' Gilmour said.

'I'll give you a hint. They're islands; you need a boat.'

'How's your leg?'

'Getting better.'

'You need more querlis?'

'No. That stuff just makes me sleep.'

'Come and sit down.'

Mark did. 'What are you looking for?'

'Nothing particularly; I just don't sleep all that often.'

'You'd do well in corporate America.'

'Not me,' Gilmour said. 'I never had a head for business.'

'I find that hard to believe.'

'I heard what you said before.' The Larion sorcerer changed the subject.

'About what?'

'About Nerak and his minions.'

'Oh, that.' Mark examined a map of Estrad and southern Rona. 'I've been thinking about him, and all the creatures he's sent to find us. They all fall along the same continuum, from real to unreal, or whole to less-than-whole, so they might have common weaknesses as well.'

'I don't understand,' Gilmour admitted.

'If Nerak only creates or summons creatures that fit a certain profile, it may tell us something about his weaknesses. He has sent ravenous beasts, wild animals, half-humans and wraiths, and all of them are similar in certain respects: they hunt, use some mystical energy either to search or to exist and they all fall beneath the power of the staff. It makes me think that might be the place to look for weak spots in his armour.'

'That's quite an array of nasty creatures, Mark; I'm afraid I don't understand,' Gilmour said.

'Why didn't he create a plague? Why didn't he open the earth and swallow Sandcliff Palace with us in it? Why didn't he have the water in Orindale Harbour swell up and drown us that night? I'm betting it's because he can't. There are tremendously powerful things he can do, and all of Eldarn has been living in fear of him for almost a thousand Twinmoons, but let's think about the things he can't do.'

Gilmour nodded, beginning to understand. 'He can't sense the hickory staff.'

'Nope, and he can't open the Fold and allow his evil master to just step outside – if he could have opened the Fold without the spell table, he would have done it by now and all of us would have been obliterated, or enslaved for an eternity.'

'But he crossed the Fold when I opened the spell book.'

'Sure, crossed it, but he can't open the Fold with that book. There is nothing in there to allow his master to emerge into Eldarn.'

'Fine, I agree – but what's the point of what Nerak might or might not be able to do with his power?' Gilmour rolled up the map and placed it to one side.

'We have seen real evidence of things that can be done that *Nerak* has not been able to do.' Mark was speaking quickly in his excitement.

'Such as—'

'Such as keeping you and Kantu alive for two thousand Twinmoons, such as sending visions of things we need to understand, such as intercepting Regona and sending her through the portal to raise Eldarn's heir in my world.'

'Lessek?'

'Lessek.'

'And you truly believe you are somehow related to Regona? I know Nerak called you *prince*, but I don't know how he would have known Regona at all.'

'Doctor Tenner.' Mark reached for a flagon of wine and uncorked it. He poured two goblets.

Gilmour stood and walked towards the fireplace. Crouching before it, he reached out to warm his hands. 'Tenner's letter.'

'Or Tenner himself. Suppose Nerak took Tenner the night he burned Riverend Palace. He would have known all that Tenner knew at the time.'

'But all Nerak would have known was that Regona went to Randel to live with Weslox.'

'Sure, so Nerak goes to Randel – he had all the time in the world – and learns—'

'That Regona never arrived,' Gilmour finished.

'Lessek took her through the far portal, or at least he showed her the way through.'

The Larion Senator rubbed his palms together. 'She wouldn't have been able to touch him, but he would have looked real enough.'

Mark sipped the wine. 'It's evidence of yet another skill Lessek perfected that Nerak did not. If the evil minion that took Nerak only inherited Nerak's power, then it doesn't know the extent of what's possible; what a *great* sorcerer can accomplish. Eldarn has been measuring sorcery by Nerak's benchmark for a thousand Twinmoons when you should have been measuring Nerak against Lessek, the true master.'

'But how could Nerak have hidden his weaknesses from the evil minion? Nerak knew his own weaknesses; we all do – he wouldn't have been able to mask them inside his own mind. What came through the Fold hit him like a rogue wave; he had no time to cry out for his own mother, let alone hide any thoughts in his head.'

'And thus we come to the place where all my best deductions fall apart: I just can't get past that. But I *am* confident there are plenty of magical possibilities to defeat Nerak, and I bet you a case of beer the place to start is with Steven's staff. There's something he just doesn't understand, and it will be his weakness; I know it.'

'"Nerak's weakness lies elsewhere",' Gilmour quoted.

THE PRISON WING

Hannah woke to the sound of the underground pistons, popping and churning, popping and churning. She didn't know if that's what they actually were; she imagined furnaces boiling water to build steam that spun cranks, pushed pistons and blew warm air up through the palace vents, or perhaps heated air that expanded inside great balloons then exhaled through ducts servicing the keep above. All her imagined machines were gangly-limbed monsters that sputtered and farted great belches of humid air up through the palace. Were an attack ever to come on the ancient castle, all Prince Malagon had to do was loose his heating system on the enemy lines.

As she lay there on the floor, she felt the heat begin seeping into her cell until she was sweating freely; later, when the massive creature was chained back in its place, the heat would wane and she would wrap herself in the cloak and await the onset of another frigid night.

She had seen no light – except for guards passing who carried torches – since the soldiers wrestled her, kicking and scratching, into her cell. She had no real idea whether it was day or night; she charted time by the heat, or lack of it; soon after the furnace started up, the door would open just enough for one of the guards to slip a bowl of brown mush inside. She counted that as morning.

At first, she had refused to eat it, her stomach in knots as anger and fear warred for control, until Hannah's indignant stand – *I'm an American, damnit* – gave way to terror and she curled up in the corner and cried herself to sleep.

After a few days, the hunger pangs grew too painful to ignore and Hannah forced herself to eat the tasteless gloop; now its arrival represented the highlight of her day. She always thanked the soldier, but so far no one had said a word to her.

She tried to mark the days, but was it fifteen now, or twenty? She couldn't find anything sharp enough to mark the walls of her cell, giving up after tearing two fingernails to the quick. Besides, there was only ever light for the few moments it took to shove her gloop through the door, so scratching lines in the rock seemed pointless.

Instead, she named the days: her father was fanatical about baseball, and obsessed with the 1975-76 Cincinnati Reds; he claimed it was the greatest baseball team ever assembled on one field. Now Hannah tallied her stay in the Malakasian prison: 'Gullett, because you have to start with Gullett, Bench, Perez, Morgan, Rose, Concepcion, Foster, Geronimo, Griffey, Senior not Junior, although the kid can get it done when he needs to; then, Plummer, Armbrister, a lucky call there in game three, Eddie; and Rawlins Jackson Eastwick, the Third. That's just a name you have to say out loud. Okay, so what's that, twelve days, plus a few before I started the count, so that's – fifteen days? Right, fifteen. Tomorrow, we'll go back to the utility infielders.'

When she ran out of Cincinnati Reds, she moved on to the New York Yankee squad from the '76 World Series, but it was hard to remember all the players. Then she tried making up song lyrics, which amused her for a day or two. It seemed important for her to occupy her mind, because otherwise she'd start thinking of her arrival in Welstar Palace ...

They had been bound and gagged, and dragged from the Welstar docks, through the encampment to the palace, and Hannah had her first up-close encounter with Seron, the creatures she had seen in the distance outside the forest of ghosts. Nothing her friends had said had prepared her for these huge monsters, staring vacuously, apparently oblivious to the open sores, boils and pox marks that covered their bodies. Even now the memory of the stench made Hannah retch: the stink of death and decaying, foetid flesh ... part of her hoped that she would die there, rather than having to cross that field of pestilence again. What kind of soldier stood staring without a care while his flesh rotted from his body? These people – if they were people – would be the grimmest fighting force ever assembled – what good would it do to shoot one of them with an arrow? Or even with a rifle?

Hannah blinked away the tears and started again. 'Gullett, Bench, Perez, Morgan, what a strange swing you had, Joe; Rose, Concepcion...'

One morning Hannah missed a meal. She had waited all night for her brown gloop; when it arrived, she forgot it. The following morning a soldier picked up the untouched trencher and swapped it for a fresh serving of mush. Hannah started to shake: things were getting worse. She filled her mind with batting averages, prices of antiques stacked in her grandfather's store, the names of all the peaks she had climbed in Colorado, the keys and key signatures of all twelve tones in the chromatic scale. She decided she must be on the threshold of madness because one night, battling the particularly insidious chill, she managed to recall a quadratic formula she had no memory of ever learning, let alone what it was supposed to do.

For water, Hannah had a trickle running down the back wall. She awakened each day apparently free of dysentery, so she drank as much as she could, reminding herself, especially during the blazingly hot days, to stay hydrated. At night, the trickle sang as it ran down the wall and dripped down between the flagstones. When she couldn't sleep, she made up songs to the rhythm of the rill.

The key of C, C, C.
It has no sharps.
The key of C, C, C.
It's the hairy smelly key of C.
The key of G, G, G.
It has F sharp.
The key of G, G, G.
It's the filthy rotten key of G.
The key of D, D, D.
It has F and C sharp.
The key of D, D, D.
It's the tired wrinkled key of—.

A loud click emanated from somewhere along the hallway outside her cell; Hannah quieted, listening intently, and heard a second click and footsteps approaching along the hall. She peered through the cracks between the wooden door, expecting to see the flicker of torchlight, but the hall remained dark. She whispered more nonsense under her breath.

The key of F sharp, F sharp, F sharp.
It has F, C, G, D, A and E sharp.
The key of F sharp, F sharp, F sharp.
It's the crippled beggar key of F#.
The key of C sharp—

The footsteps paused, then came towards her cell.

'Hannah?'

'Steven?' She was embarrassed at the hoarse rattle in her throat. 'Steven, is that you?'

'Where are you?'

Adrenalin flooded through her and she stood and stumbled across the chamber, shouting, 'I'm in here, Steven. I'm in this one, right down here.' She banged her fist against the door, hearing the echo resonate along the cavernous hallway. He had to hear her; she was making enough noise to wake the dead.

'Hannah?' the voice called back, 'where are you?'

Something slimy slithered across her foot. She screamed, twisting away so violently she felt something in her back snap, a tendon or a ligament stretched too far. She ignored the throbbing pain as she huddled in her corner and screamed, 'Steven! Can you hear me, Steven? I'm in here, Steven! Please let me out! Steven, please!'

The voice didn't answer and Hannah strained her ears, keeping her eyes tightly closed. Her breath was too loud; she was panting in fear of whatever had slipped over her feet— She felt around for her boots and pulled them on: she needed to get a hold of herself, control her breathing if she was going to hear him. She forced herself to take several long, deep breaths.

'Steven?' Hannah whispered, and tiptoed back towards the door. There was no answer. She pressed hard against the wooden frame, until her skin came away marked with the grain pattern. 'Steven?'

For a time – Hannah lost track – she stood and called into the darkness; after a while some part of her mind took charge and told her she had been hearing things; there was no way Steven Taylor could have been in the hallway outside her cell.

When the less-than-entirely sane part of her mind finally accepted that, Hannah fell apart. She trundled back to her corner, wrapped herself in her cloak and cried until she fell asleep. She didn't wake when the guard brought her morning gloop, nor did she wake when he arrived the following day to replace that trencher with a fresh one.

Eventually, Hannah's cell door opened and torchlight flooded in, blinding her. She buried her face in her cloak as a young soldier stepped inside. She squinted up at him: he wore the Malakasian crest emblazoned in gold across a leather vest, and his muscular arm was marked with sergeant's stripes. His sandy-brown hair was tousled; his skin was pale, and he wore heavy boots and leather gloves, which Hannah found a curious choice given the heat.

He wasn't carrying the disgusting mush.

'So?' she said, her voice hoarse, her lips cracking and bleeding as they moved. She pushed her matted hair from her eyes with bruised fingers, revealing the sores that had opened on her skin.

'Hannah, oh gods ... I've been looking for days.'

Confused, she tried to make a joke. 'Oh, that's nice. Is there a dance or something?'

'Hannah, it's me. Alen.'

Hannah tried to stand, but as she struggled to her feet, her vision tunnelled and she slumped back onto her knees. The soldier, whoever he was, moved to assist her.

'Sit down,' he said, 'you're weak.'

Hannah barely heard him as nausea gripped her and the tiny cell spun around her; she couldn't make sense of what the soldier was saying.

'—lost so much weight; look at you!'

Finally she struggled to a sitting position and swallowed hard, trying to keep her stomach calm. 'Say what you said before,' she croaked.

'It's me, Alen.'

'No—' She toppled over and allowed her head to rest against the stone floor.

The man squatted down beside her and took her hand. 'Hannah, you grew up in Colorado,' he said in English. 'You're American. I'm Alen; I've found you—'

'How—?' She was almost convinced. She pulled herself upright again.

'This?' Alen looked down at the young man's body. 'I broke a hundred and thirty-nine Larion Senate rules, but we're in a bit of a spot and I needed to do something to free us.'

'But your body, your old body, where is it?' Her head was still spinning, but she began to hope.

'In the cell, burned by now. I assume they think I'm dead.'

'But where have you been all this time?'

'I was looking for you, and this morning, I finally tracked you all down – this place is enormous. You're the only one on this floor – well, the only one still with a mind, I should say—'

He broke off as Hannah groaned in anguish.

'Hannah, listen, I'm getting you out now, so just hang on in. The day after I took the guard – well, I got posted to the docks; it took me eight days to get back and assigned to the prison wing yesterday.'

'How many days?' Hannah asked.

'Too many, my dear; I had to make a good show of it until I located you all; like this I'm able to move freely about the palace – well, at least until they discover I'm gone. You need proper food, and querlis.' He looked about the tiny cell. 'Let's get you some air first. I've found a place where you'll be safe.' He stood up and pulled her to her feet, then put one of her arms over his shoulder, his arm around her waist.

Hannah concentrated on walking, trying not to look at the thick oak doors that lined the hallway. She shuddered at the idea that such a prison had been constructed before Nerak destroyed the Larion Senate – what could they have needed with such a facility?

'Where are we going?' she whispered.

'To the servants' quarters, there's an empty hall, maybe housing for seasonal workers, but it's all locked up and ignored; it's the perfect place for you to recover. I'll settle you in, then go find Hoyt and Churn.'

'You've been out all this time?'

'I've been doing some research while searching for you all; I've learned a great deal.'

'Is Nerak here?' She shuddered at the thought.

Alen shook his head. 'No. People believe he was lost in an explosion in Orindale, or that he went down with his ship, the *Prince Marek*. I felt the magicians – well, most of them – give up their search for me; I suppose that was the night he disappeared.'

'Most of them?'

'At least one has continued looking for me, probably at Nerak's insistence.'

'How do you know that?'

'Branag's dog,' Alen held the torch out in front of them, illuminating a section of uneven flagstones. 'Careful here. Nerak must have detected you coming through the portal, but Steven and Mark were already here and I think he knew they had Lessek's key, so he concentrated on finding them. But he wasn't going to just leave you to wander about, so he had one of his slaves watching you. When Nerak disappeared, this one hunter must have kept working, tracking you with Branag's wolfhound. He must have soiled himself when you arrived in Middle Fork and found me.'

'A two-for-one special,' she murmured.

'Just that. They've been trying to find me for a thousand Twinmoons, the bastards,' Alen said. 'Whoever this is, he ran that poor dog into the ground – that was a mercy killing on my part.'

'But you spoke with the magician before killing the dog.'

'I know.' Alen frowned. 'Rutting stupid of me – but as long as he thinks I'm dead down here, I'll have surprise on my side when I finally locate him.'

'You haven't yet?' Hannah asked.

'Not yet. I've scoured those levels of the palace I can get into without raising suspicion, but Malagon and Bellan's apartments are on the top three floors, and no one but Malagon's personal guard can get up there. I'm not – this man – wasn't cleared for it.'

'Maybe the magician is up there too.'

'That's my guess.' They reached the end of the corridor; Alen said, 'No talking now. If we run into anyone out there, start coughing; I'll convince them the prince wants you alive and that I'm taking you to a palace healer.'

Hannah nodded. 'That shouldn't be difficult to fake.'

She fell onto the mattress, little more than a canvas covering over a thick pad of hay, but to Hannah, it was bliss. Her breath was rasping in her chest and she hoped it was just a cold, not anything more worrying, like pneumonia. Dust motes danced in the sunlight that flooded the room and Hannah watched them as they settled back to the floor; before the last one fell she was asleep.

She woke to the sound of the door creaking open and watched as the young man claiming to be Alen entered, followed by Hoyt and Churn. Hoyt staggered over to her; his clothes, like hers, were torn and dirty, and he had open sores on his face and blood drying on his lips. His hands were stained with blood, and most of the nails on his fingers had been torn away. He stank, but Hannah didn't mind – she probably looked and smelled much the same.

'Move over,' Hoyt whispered, obviously barely able to stand by himself.

'What, no hello?' She tried to make a joke.

'Later,' he said and collapsed onto the bed beside her.

Hannah tried to make as much room as possible; even in her dazed state she was amused at the thought that sharing a bed with someone for the first time was never easy, even when both were suffering from malnutrition and crippling fatigue. She tried to think of something witty to say, but Hoyt was already asleep.

Hannah looked at Churn, about to offer him her place on the mattress as she had slept a while, although she didn't know for how long. It was still daylight, but the angle of the sun had changed; night would be upon them soon. 'Churn,' she whispered, 'do you want—?'

But it was too late: the big man had walked to the nearest patch of sun and collapsed. Now, lying on the floor with the light on his face, he slept, a fallen Goliath. Hannah watched him for a moment, making certain his chest was rising and falling in a steady rhythm, then she drifted off again herself.

WELLHAM RIDGE

The road was an endless ribbon of mottled brown and white, hoof prints and wagon tracks frozen in the snow-covered mud. The Central Plain was a wasteland, sleeping away the winter, with only a few forgotten corn stalks or the occasional patch of winter wheat breaking through the monotony.

Garec had lost count of time since they had ridden out from Traver's Notch; they'd been more than fifteen days on the road, but how many more, he had no idea. He couldn't even recall what they'd eaten for dinner; the meals had begun to blur together. They had had no trouble finding accommodation so far; they made sure to enter any village or town from various points, not together, and the scattered occupation patrols had given them no more than a passing glance.

Townsfolk, merchants and farmers had welcomed the partisans into their barns, haylofts, cellars, offices, even the occasional guest room, as they made their way south as quickly and inconspicuously as possible. The previous night had been the first time they hadn't reached shelter in time, and sleeping outside had been painfully cold.

Now as they cantered down the roadway, Garec felt the prickly sting of winter needles across his cheeks and forehead; he smiled, thinking of his mother, hearing her voice in his mind warning him to watch out for skin freeze – she always called it *icebeard*.

If that was the least of his worries, he'd be lucky. So far their trip had been pretty uneventful, all things considered. It was four days before they met their first soldiers, when, cresting a short rise, the company had overtaken a five-man patrol. Without slowing, Brand led his men straight at them: the black-and-gold-clad horsemen had no chance as the Resistance soldiers ran them down, slashed them to bloody tatters and left their broken bodies lying in a gulley.

There had been a few other small skirmishes; by Garec's tally,

Brand had lost seven of his men, but had accounted for very many more – none of the Malakasians they encountered escaped, so the occupation army had no idea that an enemy company was on the move. He worried for those people in the towns and villages where Malakasians were killed; the dark prince had never been one for leniency, especially not where guerrillas were concerned. Malakasian retaliation would be bloody, and cruel: many innocents would die for each Malakasian body they left on the roadside or behind a village tavern.

Later that morning, when Brand called a rest halt, Garec slipped from the saddle to stretch his stiff, sore back and legs; a night on the freezing ground had left most of them with painful limbs, though Garec noticed Gilmour, the oldest of the company, wasn't even limping as he walked over.

'Stiff?' Gilmour asked, sympathetically.

'Ha! Not all of us have the benefit of Larion magic to limber up our muscles each day,' he grumbled.

'Of course you do.'

'I do? How?' Garec winced as his leg cramped again.

'Like this.' Gilmour rubbed his hands together slowly until they glowed a dull red, then pressed his palm against Garec's lower back; in a moment, the young man felt his joints loosen as a rush of warmth spread into his extremities. His pain subsided and then faded entirely.

'Now that is a spell worth knowing,' he said gratefully, 'and you have my deepest thanks, Gilmour. It's too bad you're not ambitious: you could have made a fortune as a healer.'

'Nah, too many sick people,' he laughed.

'So you'd rather be a soldier?'

'Look at where we are, how lovely and refreshing it is, out in all this healthy fresh air.'

'It's freezing air,' Garec corrected, 'and speaking of where we are – where are we?'

'You remember that fjord we navigated last Twinmoon? I think the eastern end is about three day's ride from here, putting us two days east of Orindale.' He filled his pipe, lit it with a spell and began smoking.

'Morning boys,' said Mark, riding over to join them.

'Get out of the saddle, Mark. The air down here is fine.' Garec offered a hand.

'No, I'm too stiff – the only way I'm getting off is if the wind blows me down.' He grimaced. 'I don't like riding these miserable animals at the best of times, and all stiff and twisted with cold makes it ten times worse, so I'm doubly cranky this morning.' He searched along their ranks. 'Where's Steven?'

Garec pointed forward. 'I saw him near the front with Brand a while ago.'

'I'll catch up with you later then,' he said. 'Gee up, Dobbin.'

Gilmour and Garec watched him ride off, feeling the animal's hoofbeats through the frozen mud. 'We ought to make Wellham Ridge late tonight,' Gilmour said, 'and if we're up and out early tomorrow, I suspect we'll end the day in sight of the foothills. We're making good time.'

'Until we reach a city,' Garec corrected.

'But that's not to be helped. All the time we spend making our way into any town undetected is time well spent. Think of the alternatives.'

'Sleeping outside?'

'For one.'

'No thanks. I suppose I can live—' The vibrations began again, resonating up through his boots. 'Do you feel that?'

Gilmour had gone white. 'Mount up,' he whispered, and then, shouting, 'Mount up! In the saddle, now! Mount up!'

Garec dived for his horse as with each moment the vibrations beneath his feet grew stronger. Behind him, Gilmour ran back to where he had left his own horse, still shouting, but many of Brand's men were slow to realise what he was saying.

Garec, now mounted, started urging them into action. 'Let's go. It's riders, coming fast. Get up! Let's go!' Instinctively checking for his friends, he saw Mark near the front, one of the only riders still in the saddle. He watched as Mark reached into his quiver and nocked an arrow.

Hundreds of riders were coming hard at them across the plain; they were close.

Garec rode forward to join Steven and Mark; Gilmour would not be far from Steven and Lessek's key. As he closed the distance, he saw Mark draw his bow full, aim and release an arrow into the wintry sky. Garec tried to keep his eye on it, but Mark's angle was too high for any accuracy; Garec hoped that meant the approaching forces were still some distance off, but as he came alongside Mark's horse, he saw what they were facing for the first time.

A battalion of Malakasian soldiers, some five hundred men, were closing on them at a gallop, thundering across the plain with stand-ards flapping.

'This is very bad,' Mark groaned. 'There are too many; we can't fight that many.'

'Maybe Steven will—'

'He won't, that would be mass murder. He'd never do that.'

'Maybe he can slow them down.'

'How? They're a tidal wave.'

'Where is he?'

'Over there with Brand and that squad of scared-looking icicles we're calling the Resistance Army.' Mark drew another shaft, aimed to the heavens and released with a twang. They couldn't see if it hit anyone in the blurry cloud of black, brown and gold.

'Steven!' Garec cried, pressing forward. 'Steven, we have to get you and the key out of here.'

'I agree.' Gilmour appeared beside him. 'We have to ride south as fast as we can; the Malakasians have big Falkan stallions and they'll run us to ground. Let's go.'

'He's right,' Brand agreed. 'We'll cover you, and hope they don't see you.'

Steven shook his head resolutely. 'We can't leave you here alone.'

'Yes, you can,' Brand said firmly, 'and you must – don't think we'll dig in here and fight to the death; no one can stand against a cavalry charge, not even you and that staff. Prince Malagon isn't with them and this is no suicide mission: we'll draw them away and try to keep them distracted long enough for you to disappear.'

Uncertainty was clear in Steven's face. There was another thrum as Mark loosed another arrow; Garec thought he might have seen a rider go down.

'All right, fine,' Steven said, 'let's go.' He rode off a few paces then reined in. 'Brand, you're not digging in?'

Brand shook his head. 'I will see you again, Steven Taylor, and if I can find you in the next several days, I will. But go now, because the longer you wait, the longer we have to wait.'

'Thanks,' Steven said, and without another word, he thundered off, with Garec, Mark, and Gilmour hot on his heels.

Brand watched until the four riders had crossed into the next field, then nodded to one of his lieutenants. 'Take the company north. Make a lot of noise doing it. I want that whole battalion following you. Don't stop. Pass the word for everyone to retreat by squads. Find villages, towns, farms, caves, I don't care where, to hide out, but break up and make your way back to Traver's Notch. Send our fastest rider – Greves or Mallac – ahead to inform Gita. Understand?'

The man nodded agreement and Brand continued, 'I'm taking one squad with me. I'm following them.' Brand gestured the way the four had ridden. 'Stay here long enough for us to get clear, then ride like all the gods of the Northern Forest were after you. Understand?'

'Yes sir – and good luck.'

'Squad!' Brand shouted, 'We can't take the risk that Gilmour and the others were seen, so we'll cover their flanks, give them as much time and room to run as possible.'

The rag-tag band of hardened partisan riders nodded, grim understanding on their faces. They would be the sorcerers' last line of defence.

Brand clapped his lieutenant on the shoulder and pulled his horse round, then took off, but he and his squad had barely crossed into the next field when a group of cavalrymen broke off from the main charge, angled across the plain, and took up the pursuit.

The lieutenant shook his head; there was nothing he could do for them. The brunt of the day's unpleasant responsibilities now rested on his shoulders. He rode back along the lines, shouting, 'Retreat to the north! Retreat by squads! Retreat to the north!'

Gilmour rode hard down the dry streambed that was providing some cover. They had been galloping for a quarter of an aven now and he was worried that the horses would not be able to keep up this breakneck pace for much longer. They had no spare mounts, and losing an animal this far outside Wellham Ridge would be a disaster. They would have to stop soon.

He used a rudimentary spell – nothing that would resonate enough for Nerak to locate them – to confirm that they were being followed, but he had some vague sense that their pursuers were friendly. He guessed Brand had sent a handful of riders after them, and that bothered him; he hated that Gita had demanded they use Brand and his company as a live shield. He supposed he ought to harden his heart to such sacrifices, but it hadn't been easy to look them in the eye; they all knew why they had been sent on this mission.

While Gilmour felt responsible for having led Brand's company into the Malakasians' path, he didn't wish to make a stand against a cavalry charge, certainly not with his magic alone. He wondered for a moment if Steven would be able to help without losing the camouflage spell he had cast when they left Sandcliff Palace, but the old Larion Senator decided that risk was too great: any spell powerful enough to divert a cavalry charge would tell Nerak exactly where they were.

The gulley rounded a lazy bend and turned southeast; if this stream had once spilled into the Medera River and run through Orindale to the Ravenian Sea, then their current path would take them too far east. They had to leave the streambed. Gilmour looked around: if they were forced to expose themselves, they might as well seek whatever high ground they could find and use it to their advantage.

A thousand paces further on, he saw what he had been looking for: a tight bend in the riverbed had left an era's worth of dirt and rocks accumulated above the turn, a little hillock. Given the paucity of heights in the Falkan landscape, this would have to do. At the bend, Gilmour slowed and urged his horse up the rise.

'Where are you going?' Steven shouted. 'We have cover down here.'

'This stream will run into Orindale. It's the wrong way. Besides, we're being followed and I don't think it's the Malakasians.' He crested the hill; reluctantly, the others followed.

'Who is it?' Steven asked.

Gilmour peered back along their trail, and was surprised to see no one approaching across the plain. 'They must be in the streambed,' he said, scanning the area until he detected a faint cloud of dust and dirt billowing up from the twisting crevasse they had been using to mask their movements. 'There,' he pointed, 'past that stone wall on this side of the far field.'

Steven, Mark and Garec all strained to see where Gilmour was pointing, but none of them had improved their vision with Larion magic; they saw only the barren expanse of fallow fields.

Garec rode back down into the gulley and dismounted, then patted his frothing horse gently on the neck. 'Not much further,' he said encouragingly, then sprawled on the ground and pressed his cheek against the frozen dirt. The sound was unmistakable. Rising to his knees, he called, 'They're not far, but nowhere near as many as earlier.'

'Well, that's good news,' Mark said. 'I think.'

'It's Brand,' Gilmour said.

'How do you know?' Steven asked.

'I checked – nothing that will alert Nerak – and I can feel that it isn't Malakasians.'

'That may be,' Garec said, 'but we should keep riding, nevertheless.'

'My horse can't keep it up much longer.' Mark ran a hand through the animal's mane.

'Mine either,' Steven added.

Garec said, 'We'll slow the pace. Mark and I will hang back and just trot for a while. They'll see our trail run up the side of this gulley. When they get to the top, we'll know who's back there. If it's Brand, we have nothing to worry about. If it isn't, we'll ride up behind you. You'll hear us coming like rutting thunder.'

Garec looked at Mark, who pressed his lips together and nodded. 'Give your horses a rest, but canter just the same. Get as much distance out from us as you can. If we get separated, we'll find you in Wellham Ridge tonight.'

'You understand that we can't—' Gilmour started, 'that Nerak would—'

'Don't worry about it,' Mark said. 'I don't want that motherless bastard knowing where we are either. I just hope Steven's blanket still covers us when you two are gone.'

'I don't know,' Steven said, apologetically.

'It doesn't matter,' Garec said. 'It's not us he wants, anyway. We could stand naked out here singing bawdy songs and he wouldn't look twice at us.'

Steven laughed. 'Well, can you blame him?'

'Go.'

Garec and Mark watched them lope off southwest. Garec asked, 'How many arrows do you have?'

'Maybe twenty. You?'

'About the same.'

'We can't stop them with a couple of bows and a handful of arrows.'

'I know,' Garec said, thankful that Mark hadn't suggested they make a stand there on the riverbank.

'This is not good.'

'We can't run the horses any longer. We have to hope theirs are in a similar condition.'

'We've been riding hard for more than fifteen days now. If they're coming from Orindale, they've been in the saddle for two, maybe three. They'll catch us, Garec.'

The bowman didn't reply, but turned back towards the knoll above the stream and watched as it gradually shrank to a lump. Still, no one emerged from the winding riverbed. 'I suppose all we can hope to do is delay them long enough for Gilmour and Steven to get free.'

'Or pray it's just Brand coming up to cover our backs.'

'That too.'

When Brand and what remained of his squad burst from the streambed, it was like watching cavalry emerging from an underworld kingdom. His horse was swathed in froth, its nostrils flaring and bloody, as he led five men and women Garec recognised from their journey south.

As he closed on Garec and Mark, he started shouting, but his incomprehensible cries became obvious as a rank of Malakasian riders rose up from the streambed and began pursuing the Falkans across the plain. They fanned out like unfurling wings on a low-flying demon, narrowing the gap as the nearly spent freedom fighters struggled to get away.

'Stupid bastard,' Mark spat, 'he's led them right here. What in hell is he thinking?'

'He must have decided to cover our flank, and then was seen riding off.'

'With five soldiers?'

'I don't know,' Garec said, 'maybe there were others; maybe they led some of them away.'

'Shit and shit and *shit*, this is bad,' Mark spat. He nocked an arrow and waited. 'How long until they're in range?'

Garec's hands began to tremble. 'Let's ride, Mark. We can't stop them. There are – what? Fifteen or twenty of them? We can't ... let's run for it. Come on.' He was scared.

Mark shot him a withering look. 'How long until they're in range, Garec?' He was ready to die; this was his moment. Brynne was watching; his final stand would make her proud.

Garec gripped his pommel with both hands until they stopped shaking. He focused on the advancing line and shook his head. 'Not yet. Not yet.'

Mark held the bow ready as Brand's voice came to them across the field, shouting 'Pick them off! As many as you can!'

'Now?' Mark's voice was urgent. 'Garec?'

'What?' He shivered. *Please don't make me do this.*

'Now?'

'Yes, now, *now*!' He felt the air go out of his lungs. He couldn't fire. He hung his head.

Brand's voice came again. 'Garec! Garec, kill them, Garec!'

Mark loosed his first shot and shouted victoriously when one of the Malakasians fell. He nocked another arrow, aimed over Brand's head and fired into the Malakasian line. This one took a horse in the chest, and the animal tumbled headlong across the frozen plain. As he fired over and over again, nocking, drawing and loosing like an automaton, he paused only once to look at Garec with a mixture of pity and disgust. There was no time to talk, so he carried on trying to wound or kill as many of the soldiers as possible before they closed for the hand-to-hand fight.

Garec wouldn't fight; it was up to him, Brand and five exhausted soldiers, to defeat an entire squad of Malakasian cavalry.

Three dead. Four dead. Five injured. Six dead. Mark kept a mental tally. *Seven injured, maybe dead. Eight injured. Nine dead.*

And then Brand was with him.

'What the holy hell is the matter with you, bastard?' Mark screamed in English, too fired up with adrenalin to remember to speak Common.

'What?' Brand shouted despite the fact that they were side by side. Two of his soldiers had drawn their bows and had joined Mark, firing into the charging line.

'You led them here,' Mark screamed, 'what were you thinking?' He fired again. *Ten injured. Eleven dead.*

'I lost men leading them away from here,' Brand said, drawing his short sword and charging into what was left of the Malakasians.

Mark tossed his bow aside, shrugged out of his quiver and drew his battle-axe. Throwing his head back, he screamed, then dug his heels into his horse's sides and galloped into the fray.

Garec never moved, and those few moments were the longest, hardest of his life. He didn't have the strength to watch, but focused on his horse's trailing mane, gripping the pommel of his saddle tightly. His stomach clenched at the screaming, and he winced when his face was splashed with someone's blood. The noise of battle was gruesome, terrifying, unbearable: the sounds of suffering, pain and death.

Someone threw a sword and it slashed across his horse's rump, opening a deep gash. With a furious whinny the animal reared and Garec fell to the ground, where he lay, immobile, waiting to be trampled to death.

Then it was over.

Only Mark, Brand, and a woman named Kellin remained in the saddle; everyone else lay dead or wounded. Brand dismounted to see to his injured soldiers, trying to keep his face immobile as he realised none would survive to see the midday aven; Garec rolled onto his side, his back to the carnage, and rested his head on the icy field.

Later, when the pyres were lit and the dead had been given their rites, the four remaining partisans mounted and rode slowly towards Wellham Ridge. Garec, without a horse, rode in silence behind Kellin. He was too ashamed to look at anyone; he couldn't stand the thought of what he might see in Mark's face: disappointment, regret, anger, hatred. Instead he watched Kellin's light brown hair moving against the heavy weave of her cloak.

It was dark when they arrived in the village, but Steven and Gilmour were not difficult to find; they were sitting together in the front room of a tavern called the Twinmoon. The ever-shrinking group was reunited, but Garec, dejected and embarrassed, excused himself. He would go in search of a new horse in the morning; he told the others to leave without him and neither Mark nor Brand argued.

Steven looked closely at Garec, and agreed.

'Please,' he murmured. 'I'll catch up with you tomorrow or the following night at the latest.' As long as they rode south and followed the river into Meyers' Vale, he wouldn't have any trouble finding their trail. He needed the space to think; if being alone meant he was captured, interrogated and killed by Malakasians, well, that would be fine too.

THE SLAVE QUARTERS

As the door closed behind him, Alen let out a long sigh. 'Too close, old man,' he murmured to himself.

He had spent the past several days ignoring his new body's responsibilities while he searched Welstar Palace for the slave magicians. A thousand Twinmoons ago these men and women would have been trained as Larion Senators, but since the collapse of the Larion brotherhood, Nerak had brought Eldarn's most promising young sorcerers here to serve his own mystical needs.

Alen guessed that six or seven enslaved magical hunters were permanently searching for him; over the Twinmoons there had never been a break in the energy sweeping the land for some sign of him. His home in Middle Fork had been his only refuge – every time he had ventured out, even just into the village for bread, he had been at risk of discovery. Over the past fifteen Twinmoons he had stopped bothering; his house remained camouflaged, but he used little more than a rudimentary cloaking spell when he left the protection of his home for the nearest tavern, where he invariably drank himself into a stupor.

Alen was determined to find and kill these magicians, and Bellan, Prince Malagon's only daughter. He had intended to find and challenge Nerak himself to a battle that would – hopefully – end both their lives, but Nerak had fouled his plans by travelling east. Alen flushed with anger at the thought that he and his friends had made the trip to Malakasia for nothing – even the Larion far portal, the only way to send Hannah back to Colorado, was in the east, under Fantus' protection. There had been no need for Hannah, Hoyt and Churn to accompany him into the palace, but he hadn't had the heart to tell them they had come this far for nothing.

When they were taken prisoner, Alen had decided he had to live long enough to see his friends safely back to Treven, or onto a barge headed north to Pellia; only then would he return to the palace to await Nerak's return.

Now, while they recovered from the rigours of their imprisonment, he spent every spare moment searching for the slave magicians, and for Bellan. He also made sure the Malakasians didn't discover three empty cells, which wasn't always easy: this morning he'd got a little lost in the endless corridors and nearly blown it, running into an officer as he hustled down to intercept the morning mush delivery. It was rare for an officer to actually make an appearance in the dank prison levels, and this time it nearly cost the old Larion sorcerer his cover.

'Late this morning, Sergeant?' the lieutenant asked pointedly.

'Sorry, sir,' Alen said, saluting smartly. 'I had word that new prisoners were coming in, and I wanted to be sure we had cells available on that wing, sir.'

'I know nothing of new prisoners, Sergeant.'

'No sir. Confused information, sir.' Alen took the trenchers from the soldier, who had probably been standing rigidly at attention from the moment the officer had entered the hall. 'Thank you, Tandrek.'

'In the future, Sergeant, I would appreciate it if you would not go haring off without checking with me first,' the young lieutenant said, still irritated. 'You are responsible for the security of these halls and the feeding of prisoners, not a one-man welcoming committee. Deployment of cells and sentences is my job. Is that understood?'

'Yes, sir.' Alen tried to salute smartly, but a dollop of gloop splashed on his boots, ruining the effect.

'And get those polished before you come upstairs, Sergeant.'

'Yes sir. Sorry, sir.'

The officer strode down the hall and left without looking back.

Alen breathed again and looked at Tandrek. 'Thanks,' he said quietly.

'No problem, Sergeant – bit of a shock to see him down here this morning. I don't suppose we'll see him again for another ten or twelve Twinmoons.'

Alen laughed. 'Take a break, Tandrek. I'll deal with this.'

'Thank you, Sergeant. Sir, Abbott is out for a few days. Boils.' He winced in sympathy. 'Should I take care of the deliveries to the lower chambers?'

'Yes, do. Good thinking,' Alen said, his close escape leaving him a little distracted.

'Thank you, Sergeant. All right if I borrow a cart from the scullery? They get real food down there and it's too much to carry in one journey.' At Alen's nod the man saluted and left the hallway.

Alen sighed in relief again and moved off down the dark hallway. He had memorised the path from the scullery hall to Hannah's cell, down the moss-covered stone ramp and through the old archway to Hoyt's cell, then across the hall and up two flights of spiral steps to the cruelly small enclosure selected for Churn. At each door he emptied the day's mush into a pile that was smelling worse each day, left that trencher on the floor and retrieved the previous day's bowl.

No one had yet questioned why he was making the food run. Tandrek didn't care why his superior insisted on lugging the trenchers through the dank, humid prison; he was pleased to be relieved of that unpleasant duty and often bragged to his fellow squaddies that he had the easiest post in the platoon.

As he stepped inside Churn's former cell and dumped the trencher's contents into the pile in the corner, Alen slipped and nearly fell to his knees.

'Gods, but this is disgusting. I can't believe they find anyone to make it, never mind feed it to other ...' His voice trailed off as he looked at the foetid pile and the flies that danced around it.

They get real food down there.

'Down there,' he murmured, 'down *where*, Tandrek? *What* lower chambers?' Alen picked up the old trencher and ran back to the scullery.

'Tandrek!' Alen cried. 'Thanks the gods of the Northern Forest; I was beginning to think I'd rot down here!'

The soldier, a little shocked to find his superior hunting for him in the catacombs, assumed he had committed some grave military offence and snapped immediately to attention. 'Sir!'

'Where are we?' Alen was out of breath, and completely lost in the maze of passageways beneath the old keep. 'We must be three hundred paces beneath the mountain. This rutting sergeant must—' He caught himself. 'I've never been down here.'

'Of course not, Sergeant,' Tandrek said, surprise on his face. 'This is Abbott's job – your predecessor assigned him and you never re-scinded or changed the order, sir: if it ain't broke, don't fix it, you said, sir—' He broke off, not sure if repeating his sergeant's words back to him was the right thing to do.

'Of course, Tandrek, you're right.' Alen hit his head lightly and laughed. 'My rutting memory: can't remember anything from one day to the next. And Abbott's sick and you take on his duties when he's down ...' He held his torch up to illuminate the young soldier's face. 'So where are we?'

Tandrek laughed, then immediately stifled it, 'Sorry, Sergeant.'

'No offence, soldier '

'If you don't mind me asking, Sergeant, what *are* you doing down here?'

Alen had to cover himself for one more day; that's all he needed to finish his business here and see his friends safely down the river. 'I'm trying to familiarise myself with the whole prison,' he said. 'I don't send my men to do jobs I'm not prepared to do myself. I need a better idea of our overall responsibilities if I'm to be an effective leader.' He knew from the sergeant's memories he'd not long been assigned to Welstar, but he couldn't make out how much the man was supposed to know about the various levels. He didn't want to over-egg the pudding, but he needed Tandrek on his side, even unwittingly.

'I'm ambitious, Tandrek, and I'm still young: I intend to be an officer, and when I get promoted, I will need effective men under me. Knowledge is the key to that,' he said.

Tandrek grinned. 'Well, Sergeant, since it's just me and you here, I'll stick my neck out and tell you we all would love to have you as our lieutenant – Willis is a horsecock! Sir!'

Alen chuckled, playing along. 'And as it's just between me and you, I didn't hear that, soldier! Going deaf in my old age!' He clapped Tandrek on the back and looked around. 'So where is this chamber?'

'Right down here, Sergeant.' Tandrek pointed, and started down the hall. Their torches cast surprisingly bright light in the narrow passage, which looked as if it had been tunnelled through the bedrock on which Welstar Palace was built. It felt like a mineshaft to Alen, the roughly hewn walls making him feel a little claustrophobic. He imagined a cool breeze blowing across his face and shook his head in an effort to clear his thoughts, but it came a second time and he realised it wasn't his mind playing tricks on him.

'Tandrek, is that a draught?'

'Yes, Sergeant. There are fissures in the rock down here, a system of caves in the hillside behind the palace. There's plenty of air blowing in.' He stopped, and Alen saw someone had carved a crooked M on the wall. 'From here, I have to remember it in couplets, sir. Right-left, left-left, right-left,' he chanted, turning into a new passageway with each instruction until the tunnel widened and ended in a pair of large double doors, not unlike the oak doors lining the halls in the prison wing.

Alen tried the handle and wasn't surprised to find it locked.

'I've no idea who's in here,' Tandrek confided, wiping beads of sweat off his face. 'I don't think Abbott knows either; we just bring the food down and take back the empty dishes.' He indicated the pushcart he'd been dragging, which was stacked with covered plates and bowls, some corked flagons and loaves of fresh bread.

'I'll take it from here, Tandrek. Good work, soldier. I won't forget it.'

'Thank you, Sergeant, but I don't think you're supposed to—'

'Not to worry. I'll be fine.'

'Do you remember the way back out?' Tandrek asked, wondering what the sergeant was up to.

'In couplets backwards: left-right, left-left, left-right.'

Tandrek nodded. 'Most people get it wrong, just going back with the same couplets that brought them down – stupid rutters. Abbott has to come down here every Moon or so to find some other blazing idiot who's got himself lost, but you've got it, Sergeant.'

'Thanks, Tandrek. You're a good soldier, and I'll remember that. Back to the prison wing with you, and keep things together until I get back. I won't be long.'

Tandrek saluted and started back along the passageway, his torch-light fading as he rounded the first corner.

When he was certain he was alone, Alen sat down beside the cart and uncorked one of the flagons. He sniffed appreciatively at the aroma of hops and barley and helped himself to the beer as he counted to one hundred. Then he called out, 'Tandrek? Are you there, soldier?'

His voice echoed back, but nothing else; he was alone. The beer reminded him how much he liked that first drink of the morning; he wanted more before going inside.

Alen put the empty flagon back and placed his palm against the centre of the doors; he whispered a spell and, with his eyes closed, imagined the locking device lifting, releasing an inside latch. It opened with a click, and he cursed under his breath. 'Too loud, fool.'

He stepped back as the heavy doors swung open without a sound, bathing the passageway in light. Alen knew in a moment that he had found what he was looking for: the light was artificial, sorcerer's light, and although the bundles resting in the sconces were similar to traditional torches, Alen didn't have to examine them closely to see that these particular torches would never burn down, or extinguish in water.

A hallway stretched before him, the walls covered with tapestries and thick carpeting under foot. Alen ran through the lexicon of spells he had learned over a thousand Twinmoons, hoping his memory, addled by Twinmoons of alcoholism, did not fail him today. He regretted every slice of fennaroot, every beer, every flagon of wine ... even in this young soldier's body he felt every bit of his two thousand Twinmoons. To Hannah Sorenson, that was around two hundred and eighty years; somehow that sounded better. He scolded himself for procrastinating: Twinmoons or years, it was all the same; he was an old man.

Further down the hall was a room too wide to see across, but there was enough light for Alen to realise that Sandcliff Palace no longer housed Eldarn's largest library. The floor-to-ceiling racks of books disappeared into the darkness at the far edges of the chamber, the spoils of war as Prince Marek and his army rolled through Praga and across the Eastlands, burning presses, closing universities and confiscating essentially every book in the land.

Alen reached for a book of music tablature: *Liber Primus* by Valentin Barkfark-Greff. 'This one came from Sandcliff,' he murmured, furious. 'This might even have been mine.' He pushed it back into place and looked around. 'Hoyt would give his life to see this place.' He fought the urge to immerse himself in this horde of stolen treasures and continued down the hall.

He passed several rooms, including an unused kitchen and a nicely decorated sitting room, possibly a reading room for the library; the furniture reminded him of a Larion visit to the land of Portugal.

In another, he found all manner of maps, on parchment, hide, wooden boards, even paper, maps of Praga, Rona and the Eastlands, of the Louisiana Territory, the Mason and Dixon survey, of Lima and St Petersburg; he even found the village they had called home during visits to Larion Isle. Alen was entranced: here was Durham, the city with the old stone castle and the curiously winding river, and Paris, Constantinople and Estrad, with the Forbidden Forest inked out in black crosses. There were charts of the Tigris and Euphrates Rivers printed in Vienna, pictorial representations of the ancient cities of Madras and Delhi, from Cairo, and of the great mountains of Tibet. On the walls were maps of islands in the Pacific Ocean, Pellia, Port Denis, and Petrópolis in Brasil. On a table in the corner was a piece of buffalo hide with a berry-juice sketch of the Beaver River in Dakota; he stared at this one for a time, entranced.

He promised himself just a few moments more and started picking through scrolls he found organised in cylindrical stacks. Here was his home, Middle Fork in Praga; leaning over the table, he tried to locate his street and nearly toppled the entire collection when he heard a small voice ask, 'Are you Prince Nerak?'

A blazing attack spell ready at his fingertips, Alen wheeled on the unexpected visitor, preparing to strike a death blow. His curiosity had cost him the element of surprise, but he couldn't help it now. As he mouthed the words, he readied himself – and then stopped, holding the crippling blast of Larion fire back as he surveyed the little girl in the doorway. She was clad in a filthy dress that might once have been pink, and clutched what appeared to be a stuffed toy dog to her chest.

She looked quizzically up at the man visiting her underground home and asked again, 'Are you Prince Nerak?' Her voice was light, sweet; Alen's eyes widened, for he could feel there was powerful magic in this child.

'No, my dear.'

'Are you one of his soldiers? Because soldiers aren't supposed to come in here.' She wiped her nose on the back of her hand, shaking her mass of tangled red-blonde curls.

'Yes, I am one of his soldiers, and I have special permission to be here today. Prince Nerak said it would be all right if I came for a visit.' Alen moved slowly around the table and approached the little girl with caution.

'Is he back?' She walked into the room and climbed into a great armchair by the fireplace, settling the dog in her lap.

The question might be a test. Alen knelt down beside her and answered truthfully. 'Not yet, my dear, but he'll be back soon. Why do you ask?

She shrugged. Alen was enchanted. 'The others are sick,' she said. 'Maybe when he gets back he can help them get better.'

'How long have they been sick?'

'Don't know,' she said. 'A Twinmoon? I don't tell time as good as them, but it's a lot of days.'

Alen smiled. 'How old are you?'

Her face lit up. 'I am thirty-one Twinmoons. Mama taught me how to count them myself. I'm big.'

'Yes you are,' Alen said. 'Thirty-one whole Twinmoons!'

'How old are you?' she asked seriously.

'I am as old as my nose and a little older than my teeth,' he answered, remembering his father's favourite response.

She giggled uncontrollably, wrinkling her nose at him. 'You're not that old.'

'Ah, but I am,' Alen said. He glanced towards the door. 'What's your name, Pepperweed?'

'You can't call me Pepperweed,' she giggled. 'That's not my name. My name is—'

Please, please, please don't let her say Reia. Please—

'Milla.'

Alen sighed in relief. 'Milla,' he repeated, 'that is quite the prettiest name I have heard in a long time. Did Mama give you that name?'

'Uh huh.'

'Milla, where are the others?'

'Down the hall in the back. They're sick.'

'And where is Mama?'

Milla's face fell and Alen felt his heart wrench. 'She's home.'

'And where is home, Pepperweed?'

Grinning again, Milla said, 'Falkan. Mama lives in Falkan still, but she said she would come and visit me when she can get across the Rasivian Sea.'

'Ravenian Sea.'

'Rasvenial Sea. That's it.'

'What does Mama call you?' Alen glanced again at the hallway door, listening for the sound of anyone moving into position to strike at him.

'Mama calls me Milly ... 'cept if I've been bad. Then she calls me Milla in a cross voice. So I don't be bad because I don't like her cross voice.'

Alen reached a hand out to her. 'Can you take me to where the others are, Milly?'

'Uh huh. C'mon.' She led him from the room, dragging the dog by its hind leg. As they crossed what looked like a common room, a chill wind blew through; Alen looked up and noticed the fissures Tandrek had mentioned in the rocky roof. Milla looked at the smokeless fires burning throughout the room, and the flames

492

leapt higher. 'It gets cold in here sometimes,' she said. 'That wind is always coming in.'

'But I see you know how to make it warmer.'

'Uh huh, and nobody taught me that one,' she said, proudly. 'I just could do it when I got here.'

The old Larion sorcerer felt the warm air and wished that time would stop, so he wouldn't be forced to do what he was about to do. He had visions of making love with Pikan beneath a heavy blanket at Sandcliff Palace, the heady aroma of her body mixing with the dank odour of the coverlet. They had conceived Reia on one of those cold autumn nights, and the following spring they had left her in Durham, the village with the old castle and the curiously winding river. He had walked with her that morning, in the meadow with the wildflowers; the scent had been intoxicating and Alen was certain he would never again see anything so beautiful.

He tried not to look down at the little girl by his side: she was a hunter, in service to the dark prince, and he had come to kill them all, sick or not. Sweating, he dropped Milla's hand.

'Is it too hot?' she asked, turning down the fires with a glance.

He was impressed; this wild-haired little girl would have made a powerful Larion Senator. 'No, Pepperweed, I'm fine. Tell me, how long have you been here?'

'Four Twinmoons, I think. Rabeth tells me when another Twinmoon comes, but I keep count myself too.'

'Four,' Alen said, almost to himself, 'that's not very long.'

'It is a long time!' she said, shaking her head.

'Where are the others?'

'Through there,' she said, and pointed to a door at the other end of the common room. 'That's Rabeth's room. He's got the most rooms. They're in there together.'

Alen squatted down on the edge of what looked like a Persian carpet. 'Milly, I need you to wait for me out here,' he said quietly. 'I'll be right back.'

'You're mad at them, huh?'

'No, no, I'm just going in to see if I can help them, because they're sick.' He didn't think she would believe him.

'No,' she said matter-of-factly, 'you're mad at them; I can tell.'

'Really?'

'Uh huh. I can tell things sometimes. Rabeth can't, but I can.'

'Will you wait here, Pepperweed?'

'Uh huh.'

493

'Good girl.' He walked across the room and used the same spell that had let him into the underground residence to unlatch door.

The smell of disease washed over him in a rank embrace and the beer he had swallowed a little while earlier churned about in his stomach. It took a moment of fierce concentration to keep from vomiting across the threshold. Then Alen stepped inside and brightened the mystical torches.

He could see a large sitting room with two doors on the back wall. Though the room was cluttered with furniture – over-stuffed sofas, soft armchairs, and beds that looked out of place, as if they had been dragged in from other rooms – it was luxurious. Book shelves lined three walls, and a fire burned in the fireplace on the fourth. On the mantelpiece were crystal sculptures and a ship's clock. More Persian rugs covered the floor. Alen guessed the people lying about the room were what remained of six slave-magicians. He tried to keep his temper as he looked around: they had lived in complete luxury, enjoying the treasures generations of Larion Senators had brought back through the far portals, while they served the dark prince, visiting uncounted atrocities on Eldarn's people. They had probably worked their evil magic from these very rooms, standing barefoot on a priceless carpet from ancient Persia, drinking wine from Falkan and eating cheese from Switzerland.

The Larion Senators had brought these things through, hoping the Eldarni people would learn from them, but Nerak had stolen them and used them to create a wonderful environment for his slaves.

Warm mixing with cold; dank mixing with fresh. Sex and love mixing with passion and murder.

They were slaves, though: for all the displayed wealth, they were trapped here, and now they were dying. In another time, they would have come to Sandcliff, learned to travel across the Fold in service to Eldarn, but Nerak's lust for power had forced them into a different world. They may have lived in a world filled with riches and beauty, but they had lived there as slaves – and killers.

Now he wondered what had happened; did their power fade when Nerak disappeared? As he looked closer, he saw four of them were unconscious. One woman was awake, but she sat facing a corner, rocking back and forth and running a finger up and down a crack in the wall. She had worn her fingertip away – literally. Alen could see the bone, and blood ran down the crack.

One man was sitting up in bed, watching Alen cross the room; as he neared the sallow, cadaverous man, Alen nodded and said, 'Rabeth, I gather?'

'Sergeant,' Rabeth's voice was a hoarse whisper. Alen thought he saw dust billowing like tobacco smoke from the dying man's lips. 'What can I do for you?'

'Nothing,' Alen said, coming closer.

Rabeth wheezed and squinted, as if to improve his vision, and then grunted with what might have been laughter. 'You?'

'Yes.'

Another grunt, definitely laughter this time. 'Where were you?'

'Middle Fork.'

'Ah,' Rabeth rasped, 'ah, I *knew* it. I knew it. Tallis there owes me a silver piece.' He pointed to an emaciated shell of a man, barely breathing, scarcely more than a moment or two away from death. 'I don't think he'll be paying, though.'

'Why did you do it?'

'We had no choice. He brought us here, gave us everything. He said it was better than the Larion Senate ever would have been, and in the beginning it was.'

Alen waited patiently as the old man struggled for each breath. 'How long have you been here?' he asked. It was strange, but his anger had dissipated.

Rabeth shrugged, like an animated skeleton with an itch. 'Six hundred, seven hundred Twinmoons, I don't know. We made the Seron for him, and processed the bark and the leaves for the others. We summoned the demons when he wanted to strike out at you or Fantus.'

'You did all that?'

Rabeth nodded. 'That, and so much more. My whole life I looked for you.'

'And then I came to you.'

'You did. Ironic.'

'And Hannah Sorenson? The wolfhound?'

Rabeth shook his head. Alen didn't have any reason to think the man would lie to him now.

'Why did you stay here so long?'

'We can't leave.' He held up his wrist. 'These bracelets; I tried for two hundred Twinmoons, and I can't get the spell.'

Alen saw each of the slave-magicians wore a similar bracelet: three bands of silver woven together. 'Suicide?' he asked.

Again, Rabeth held up the bracelet. 'I tried, six times. Just made him angry.'

Alen was speechless at the tragedy he had discovered. This was worse than anything he had ever imagined. He took Rabeth's wrist in his hand, whispered a few words and felt the silver bracelet break apart, falling to the mattress in tiny shimmering pieces. Crossing to the fingerless woman, he repeated the incantation, but even when her bracelet fell to the ground, she continued rocking back and forth.

'He lied to you,' Alen said. 'I was never the greatest sorcerer, but I learned that spell a few Twinmoons after I arrived at Sandcliff. You should have been Larion Senators, all of you. We lived a simple life, but it was a paradise compared with this.' He started back towards the common room.

'Wait,' Rabeth called.

'What?'

'Kill us, please. Grant us mercy.'

Alen pressed his lips together to keep them from quivering. He went back to Rabeth's side, reached out with both hands and touched the dying man on his forehead. He wove a spell, then slipped quickly through the room, touching and incanting the same few words for each of the slave-magicians.

When he finished, he addressed all of them. 'I have given you what strength I can. I assume that you are in here together because Nerak abandoned you, and a lifetime of constant spell-weaving has taken its toll. I imagine Nerak used his own power to keep you all strong, but that power came from a dark and evil place. When Lessek's key returned to Eldarn, Nerak withdrew from you to bring the sum of his own magic together inside himself. After all these Twinmoons, you are addicted to his support, his power; without it, you haven't the strength in yourselves. But I'll wager you all you feel cleaner, even in your misery, without his cold, despicable magic inside you.

'I won't kill you. You have enough of your own strength now to take your own lives if that is what you want. Or do something good for once; you have that power too.

'That's my mercy: I give you your choice. Goodbye.'

Alen closed the door behind him, shutting the foul stench inside the room, and walked quickly to where Milla was sitting on a high-backed mahogany chair, her feet dangling above the ground. Though his heart hammered in his chest, he felt strong, renewed of purpose, and as clear-headed as the night the slave-magicians had stopped their search, when he had recovered his dulled senses and his magical ability.

'Did you hurt them?' she asked softly.

'No,' he said with mock offence, 'I told you I wasn't mad at them.'

'Yes, you were, I told you.' She played with the fabric dog, not looking at him.

'Pepperweed?'

'Uh?'

'Did you send the dog to follow the girl?'

Milla turned away; she had been caught. 'I get so tired, and I need to sleep sometimes, so I asked the dog to follow the girl. Prince Nerak told me I had to do it, but I get so tired. The dog didn't mind. He is the nicest dog.'

Alen felt choked. This is why Lessek hadn't allowed him to die; it wasn't Hannah Sorenson at all. 'Pepperweed?' He coughed to clear his throat. 'Milly, you need to be a Larion Senator.'

'What are those?'

'You'll see,' he said, stroking her tangled hair.

'Are you sad?' she asked.

'A little bit, Reia,' he said, wiping his nose.

'How many names do you have for me?' She flapped her arms at him in frustration.

'Sorry, Pepperweed, my mistake.' He stood and reached out for her. 'Come on, then. Time to go.'

'Where are we going?' Milla took his hand.

'Back to Falkan, to find your mother.'

Milla's eyes widened, and she leaped from the chair. 'Really truly?'

'Really truly.'

As quickly as it had brightened, though, her mood disintegrated. 'Prince Nerak won't let me go.'

Alen bit back rage. 'You leave Prince Nerak to me, Pepperweed.'

She held up her wrist; a silver bracelet hung there, but it was loose. *Room to grow.* He knew it wouldn't fall off, though it was bigger than her hand. He held the links between two fingers, incanted the spell and watched in satisfaction as the bracelet shattered and rained silver pieces across the Persian carpet.

'Wow!' Milla exclaimed. 'I've been trying to do that for such a long time.'

BRINGER OF DEATH

Garec pointed his horse, a pinto mare of no more than five summers, towards the wall of pines. She was strong and quick, but she was no Renna. He missed his mare desperately, and promised himself that he would return to Rona and search for her as soon as he could.

The day was bright and cold, and the morning sun bouncing off the snow hurt his eyes, so he had to squint to pick out the trail. He was less than a day behind now, and would catch up with Steven, Mark and Gilmour by the day's end. If he loosened the reins and let the horse run, he might overtake them by the midday aven, but right now he was in no hurry. He was enjoying the solitude. He had found a replacement horse quickly enough, and he could have been with them the previous evening, but he was not yet prepared to face Mark, or Brand.

Visions of the bloody skirmish on the Falkan plain haunted him; when he closed his eyes, Garec could see Mark, staring back at him in disgust. Perhaps by nightfall he would be ready to stand among them, and beg their forgiveness for his behaviour two days earlier.

Garec knew his future with the Resistance was in question. He had refused to fight beside them, and his failure to fire even a single arrow had cost lives. It would be quite some time before Brand would forget. But they didn't understand how easy it had always been for him: he had been the *Bringer of Death*; it had never taken more than his willingness to fire.

He was also plagued by the memories of being shot himself, feeling the stone arrowhead break his skin, shatter his ribs and come to rest inside his lung, a constant reminder his days as a killer were behind him.

To the east, the river babbled and gurgled on its roundabout path to the Ravenian Sea; from time to time Garec caught sight of it between the ranks of pin-straight pine trunks that covered this part of what Steven called Meyers' Vale. It was virgin forest, but he wasn't surprised: this was the bone-collectors' hunting ground.

'Not a great place for a summer cottage,' he warned the disinterested horse. He laughed and turned up a short rise. A deer leaped across the path, and Garec held the reins firmly to keep the mare from spooking. 'Could've had him,' he said, 'a going-away shot into his left shoulder. It would have dropped him on his face before he reached the river. What do you think?'

The mare ignored him.

The sun's rays burst through a break in the trees and Garec idled in the light for a few moments, looking at a wide clearing, in summer probably painted bright with wildflowers. He figured he could ride across the meadow, enjoying the sunshine, then rejoin the snowy path beneath the pines at the far end of the clearing.

He led the horse off into deeper snow. 'Come on, Paint,' he said cheerily. 'Let's go and get sunburned.' The mare broke a trail out towards the meadow while the sun marked their passage between the twin ranks of shadowy pines. A crust of ice broke easily beneath them, making their approach noisy, and Garec hummed a song Brynne had been fond of, until the sound of a rising commotion interrupted him. He reached for his bow, praying to the gods of the Northern Forest he wouldn't be forced to use it again. Three deer bounded through a thicket next to the clearing, leaping over fallen logs and snowy drifts; the animals barely slowed when they reached the deeper snow along the path

'I wonder what scared them,' Garec said. 'Our big feet crunching all this ice, maybe? What do you think, Paint?' A few moments of silence passed, and he added, 'You aren't much of a conversationalist, are you? All right, we'll hurry. Maybe Steven or Mark's horse will have something more interesting to say.'

They were only a few steps into the frozen meadow when Garec realised what had spooked the deer: a squad of soldiers, looking like ghosts of those Mark killed outside Wellham Ridge, galloped across the meadow towards the pine forest and the river. They were well ahead of him and would pick up his friends' trail as soon as they reached the trees.

'Grettan shit,' Garec swore, looking around and hoping some solution might present itself. 'They'll beat us to the path. There's no way to get ahead of them.'

Instinctively, he reached for an arrow. 'Steven will stop them,' he told the mare. 'Steven and Gilmour together, they could handle anything, right?' The riders crossed his field of view; he watched them go, oblivious to the fact that if they turned around, they would see him sitting there, gaping, in the corner of the meadow. 'Not again, please, not again,' he begged silently.

No one can stand against a cavalry charge, not even you and that staff.

He was their only protection; Steven and Gilmour, Mark, Brand and Kellin – they were exposed because they knew Garec was following them. They would be caught unawares, by cavalry riding hard and armed for close combat.

'Steven and Gilmour—' Garec looked down at the painted mare, closed his eyes and gripped the bridge of his nose between two fingers. 'Please, don't make me do this. Please.'

The Malakasians were nearly across the meadow now, their black-and-gold uniforms blurring together in the morning sunlight. Garec cursed his luck. 'They must be part of the battalion we evaded the other day,' he said, watching as flying hooves tore through the brilliantly white snow, leaving it churned up in their wake. 'Please,' he begged again to no one, 'please, I don't want to do this.'

His hands shook as he drew the first shaft from his quiver, but they were as still as stone as he nocked the arrow and peered across the meadow. Perhaps if he waited too long, it would be too late, they would be out of range, or into the trees. 'No,' he muttered finally, 'not today. You're not attacking my friends today.'

No one can stand against a cavalry charge, not even you and that staff.

Ignoring the churning sensation in his stomach and the beads of cold sweat on his forehead, Garec drew the rosewood longbow and held his breath.

There was no need for him to watch the shot; he had released two more shafts before the first struck the lead horseman. The rider collapsed to the ground and rolled from his saddle; others ran over their fallen leader and one of the horses lost its footing, audibly snapping a leg as it tumbled into the snow. Garec tasted something unpleasant at the back of his throat; grimacing, he swallowed it down and reached for another arrow.

He could hear them now as shouts of surprise and rage filled the air. Two more arrows, two more men down, and the entire squad, disrupted for a moment, regained its collective composure and turned towards him, as he had hoped. He fired again and a man slipped from the saddle, the colourful fletching jutting from his chest.

How many are there?
Get under cover, under cover, now.
Only one!
There's only one?
He's there. In the clearing!

Their shouts washed over him as he sat tall in the saddle. Six had fallen; nine faced him, watching to see if the bowman was truly alone – he would have to be mad to stand alone against a heavy cavalry unit geared for battle. They waited, watching the trees that encircled the meadow, hoping to detect a branch moving out of turn or a clump of thicket rustling too nosily for the morning wind. But nothing stirred: there was no one in the forest except for the archer who sat deathly still in the saddle, almost as if inviting them to cut him down. He didn't fire on them, didn't rant or shout, but he didn't try to escape, either. It had to be a bold suicide attempt; there was no other explanation.

Then Garec convinced the Malakasians he *was* insane, and alone: this fool, skilled, but a madman, nevertheless, dismounted and slapped the painted horse hard on the flank, sending it trotting into the forest. Armed with only his bow, he faced the Malakasian cavalry squad and shouted, 'I'm truly sorry. Please believe me.'

As one, they drew their swords and spurred their mounts into a gallop, to ride him down and grind his bones into the snow until he was little more than a muddy red patch in the once-pristine winter meadow.

Garec stood still, his arms at his sides, unfazed.

Corporal Wellin, from southern Malakasia, pushed himself up painfully, his whole body jarred. His horse had broken its foreleg tripping over the sergeant's body. Wellin had a bloody cut on his forehead, a mass of bruises on his legs and back and a broken finger; he was lucky. He shouted to Gransen and Tory that he was all right, but that they should get under cover; there were bowmen in the trees, and five of their comrades lay dead or dying in the snow. Neither of his friends seemed to hear so Wellin craned higher, trying to see what was going on.

One man sat astride a mottled horse at the far end of the meadow. He looked quite young, and the corporal guessed he was either a partisan assigned to lure the entire squad into an ambush, or he was a woodsman, maybe a hunter, but whatever he was, he'd obviously gone dribbling mad, attacking a cavalry squad alone. Either way,

Wellin wanted to see him dead. His horse was screaming, sending rolling waves of pain through the corporal's already aching head.

'Shut up,' he cried, 'I'm coming.' As he stood up, wobbling a little, he saw the lone man had dismounted and sent his own animal into the trees. 'Ah now, don't do that, you fool,' he shouted, 'I need a horse.' He sat down next to his own horse and stroked the big head sadly, then sliced the horse's throat, leaning back to avoid the fierce spurt of blood. 'Look at what you did to mine, you rutter.' The animal shuddered for a moment and then went still. 'Sorry, old man,' Corporal Wellin said, a note of genuine regret in his voice, and turned back to his comrades.

Someone gave the order and the remaining men spurred their big chargers into a mad gallop, thundering across the meadow, snow flying up from their hooves in a white spray.

'Go, boys! Go get him,' Wellin shouted, falling to the ground again as the pain in his legs and back hit. He watched the charge from beside his dead horse, and found himself witness to one of the most incredible displays of archery he had ever seen. The archer was Death; the corporal was certain his squad had been visited by an angry god as one man fell after another. It should not have been possible, but not one of the nine men reached the other side of the meadow alive.

'No one man can stand against a cavalry charge,' Wellin whispered, aghast at the devastation. He dragged a sleeve over his face to wipe the blood from his forehead, and then pulled his broken finger back into place. He shuddered at the faintly audible crunch.

'Motherless whores,' he cried, and fell to his knees.

The bowman was still there, standing stock-still. Perhaps his feet were numb as well.

'What do you want?' Wellin murmured. 'There's none of us left.' He knew the man couldn't hear him from this distance, but he gave an exaggerated shrug.

The bowman stared back at him; it wasn't over yet.

Wellin didn't see the final arrow as it came for him through the air. One moment he was shrugging in the bowman's direction; the next, he was on his back, his hands clasped around the smooth wooden shaft he found buried in his chest. As he died, he whispered, 'What god are you that would do this?'

No one heard him. The far corner of the meadow was already empty.

*

Hoyt checked over the short sword: good steel, but it had been clumsily honed, probably by a smith's apprentice, leaving an uneven edge. Still, better than nothing; he sheathed it and tossed it to Churn. 'This one's good.'

Churn discarded the rapier he had been examining. 'This one isn't.'

'That's all right,' Hoyt signed, 'we've plenty here. I'm sure we'll find enough decent blades.' He looked at Hannah who had just rolled from bed. 'You want one?'

'So that I can stab myself during our little suicide mission?' Hannah stretched until her back cracked. 'No thanks.'

'I like to think of it as a prison break rather than a suicide mission.'

'Whatever,' Hannah said. 'I still think there has to be a better way than this. Alen says there are guards all over the keep.'

'Exactly the reason we'll walk right out – who would be so stupid to try such a thing?'

'No one?'

'No one. Exactly.' He tossed another short sword to Churn. 'No one would try it; so no one will expect it. And as long as Alen can find us three uniforms, we'll be out before anyone notices we're even missing.' The thief in Hoyt was enjoying the challenge of seeing the four of them safely through the palace and back to the river. While he hoped they could find a barge to take them to Pellia, he was quite prepared to steal something and make a run for shallow water, where they couldn't be run down by the navy.

Hannah stuffed some cheese into a chunk of bread and poured herself a mug of cold tecan. 'The being outside here is the part that worries me almost as much as parading through the palace. Do you remember what was out there?'

Hoyt nodded. 'It was bad. And we never saw what was on the northeast side of the palace either; if there are more of them – well, I don't like to think about what will happen to the Resistance—'

'You don't have a Resistance Army big enough to stand against them?'

'Hannah, I don't believe Eldarn has *ever* had an army that could stand against them, not even when King Remond was in charge. It was as if those Seron monsters were— I don't know, as if their brains had been scrambled by something nightmarish, but their bodies were still programmed to fight.'

Hannah shuddered, unsure which challenge she feared most:

getting out of the palace or crossing the monsters' encampment.

'So no sword?' Hoyt asked.

'No, I'll stay behind Churn.'

'Good idea,' Churn agreed.

'You should wear this' Hoyt said. He belted a dagger around her waist. 'It's light and well balanced, almost a throwing knife.'

'Good, because I won't do anything but throw it away at the first sign of trouble, anyway.'

'I don't care; it will help with your disguise, and it might just save your life if we get into a fight.' He stepped back and looked at her. 'Try to relax; you're too stiff. It's not going to stab you in the leg.'

'It just might.' She held the leather scabbard as if it were a live snake. 'I'll be some NRA statistic, another hunter shot by a shit-faced brother-in-law with a rifle.'

Hoyt looked to Churn.

'No idea,' the big man signed.

'Let's say we reach the river.' Hannah gave up arguing; she wasn't getting anywhere. 'What then?'

'Either we hop a barge, or we steal a boat. We ought to get out of here before dawn, because we'll need at least an aven to get down-river and find some shallow water.'

'Assuming Alen has the far portal.'

'That's where he said he was going.'

'You think he'll get it?'

'I think he wants to kill Bellan. If the portal is in her chamber or a nearby chamber, I think he'll get it. If not, then our suicide mission will have to wait until tomorrow night.'

'I like the sound of prison break better,' Hannah said.

The door opened and Alen stepped inside, talking to someone. 'In here, Pepperweed. Don't be afraid. They're nice, too.'

Just before it faded for the night the sun invariably brightened, a final swell of light before slipping off to bed, Hannah thought. *I'll be back*, it might have shouted, *don't forget me*, even as Eldarn's twin moons shouldered it out of the sky for another lap around the heavens.

'We have to get it,' she heard Hoyt say.

'No, we don't. We have to get Milla and all of you out of here.' Alen was adamant.

He hadn't found the far portal. Although Hannah was as en-chanted with the little girl as any of them, she worried that the old man had forgotten why they were in Malakasia at all. She watched the last rays of sunlight and tried not to cry as she asked, 'How will I get home, Alen?'

'We have to get away,' Alen said, his hands resting on Milla's shoulders.

'We will,' Hoyt said, 'but what's wrong with you? We came here for the portal.'

'I know,' he said, 'and a few other things, but—'

'But what? What has changed so dramatically that we're going to leave here without the far portal?'

Alen tried to sidestep the question. 'A soldier named Tandrek is taking over the delivery of food – if you can call it that – to the cells. I have been doing that job for the past five days. He believes he is doing me a favour, and keeping both of us in the officers' good graces, but he will discover that you aren't in your cells, and haven't been in your cells for some days, and the alarm will sound. So please understand, we have to leave right now.'

'We can't go without the portal, Alen!' Hoyt shouted. 'Think of Hannah.'

'I am thinking of Hannah.' The old man tried not to raise his voice.

'No, you're not, you are thinking of yourself and your personal vendettas – what happened, Alen? Did you kill Bellan? Is that it? Did you kill these slave-magicians who have been hunting you for so long? Did you get all your slaughtering done and then realise that we didn't have the far portal?'

'Enough!' Alen shouted. Milla jumped and scurried away from him. Ignoring the others, he kneeled and whispered to her, 'I'm sorry, Pepperweed. I'm sorry. I shouldn't shout like that. I'm sorry.'

Her lip quivering, Milla clutched the straw-stuffed dog in a death grip.

'I'm sorry,' he said again. She gave him a watery smile.

'Alen,' Hoyt interrupted impatiently, 'we have to get it. Let's go; Hannah can stay with Milla.'

Alen got up and shrugged helplessly. 'It's not here, Hoyt, it's in a town called Traver's Notch, with my old colleague Fantus, Gilmour Stow. He and Steven Taylor managed to get it away from Nerak; I don't know how.'

They stared at him in shock, and he said quickly, 'I never had any intention of bringing you into the palace – who knew the bastard was watching us all the way? I am truly sorry, Hoyt; I wasn't going to put you at risk, but I needed to come here.' The words, so long pent up, bubbled out of him as he begged for their understanding.

'I needed to kill Malagon's daughter, because he took Reia from me, and I needed to kill those who have made me a prisoner in my own home for the past nine hundred Twinmoons, but none of that matters now, because the portal is in Falkan, and Fantus – Gilmour – has it. We *will* send Steven, Mark and Hannah safely back home.'

Hannah's heart lifted; she almost sobbed in relief. He hadn't forgotten her. Churn put a comforting arm on her shoulder.

'Right now, the most important thing is to get this little girl out of this place safely,' Alen continued. 'She's important, that I know, and that's the reason I've lived this long, Hoyt, I'm sure of it: this is the path to the Northern Forest. That's what Lessek wanted me to know; that's why he let them watch me all those Twinmoons. He needed me enraged enough to come up here and rescue this little girl.'

Hoyt bit his lower lip, considering the old magician in the young sergeant's body. Drawing a deep breath, he said, 'You know, Alen, I'd wager that you could probably meet some really attractive women in that body.'

'Oh, Jesus Christ,' Hannah breathed.

The former Larion leader smiled in relief. 'It's been so long, Hoyt, I wouldn't know how,' he said with a laugh. 'Now, are we ready to go?'

'Not at all.'

'Good. It will be more fun figuring it out along the way.' Hoyt checked his weapons. 'Churn, you stay with Hannah, no matter what.'

'Right.'

Alen said, 'Hoyt, you and I will take the lead; you carry Milla. If we run into anyone, she is Colonel Strellek's daughter, and we are ordered to deliver her to him out near the river where he is inspecting a shipment from Treven. Got it?'

'Colonel Strellek?' asked Hoyt.

'There is no Strellek, so it will confuse the issue long enough for us to get away, or to silence whoever is questioning us. We stop for nothing, but we don't run. Walk purposefully, as if you are going somewhere. Don't linger, drag your feet or stop for any reason. People don't interrupt those who appear to be on their way to do something important. It's just our nature.'

Hoyt handed Hannah a leather strip. 'Tie your hair up. It's like a rutting flag hanging down like that.'

'Got it,' she said, tying her hair into a ponytail, then tucking the end underneath and securing the whole lot. It didn't feel terribly secure, but it was the best she could do.

'Here's the route,' Alen continued. 'Out the door to the right and down the stairs, two levels. At the bottom go left past the doors to the main dining hall. The kitchen is across the hall. Take the first stairs we reach on our right; it's about a third of the way down the hall. Down two short flights to the grand foyer, cross the foyer and go out the main gate. From the moment we pass the first level hallway, one flight down, we will be among Malakasians. There is never a time when that hall is empty, so we might as well go when it is full to bursting – there is a guard change after the evening meal, so that's right about now.

'Don't make eye contact with anyone, but don't be too obvious in looking away, either.'

Hannah felt her stomach flopping over and she was already damp with nervous sweat. 'Where do we go if they come after us?'

Alen shook his head. 'If we're caught, there will be no place to go, certainly not down to the foyer. If that does happen, I'll try to create enough disturbance for the rest of you to melt into the crowd. Let's hope we're lucky enough that there are no guards at the main gate.'

'Who would be insane enough to attack this palace?' Hoyt asked rhetorically.

'Right. Are we ready?'

'Let's go,' Churn signed for all of them.

Alen leaned over and reached out for Milla. 'Are you ready to go find your Mama? You'll have to let Hoyt carry you; is that all right?'

The little girl squealed. 'Will we be there soon?'

'It will take a few days; we have to cross the Ravenian Sea, remember?'

'How do we do that?'

'In a boat.'

'A big boat?'

'Yes, a big boat,' Alen said, and nodded to the others. 'It will have a kitchen and a place to sleep and maybe even a puppy that lives on the boat all the time.'

'I bet his name is Resta.'

'I bet it is, too, Pepperweed, but for now, we have to be quiet. Can you do that for me?'

'A being quiet game?'

'Yes, a being quiet game.'

'All right, but later I want to play grambles.'

They had just started down the first stairs when their plan began to unravel. Churn, in front, gave a hurried salute to a sergeant who was rushing up the stairs so quickly that he barely acknowledged the gesture, but as he passed Alen, he stumbled. 'Sergeant Willis!' Alen exclaimed, 'Where are you going?'

The other man frowned. 'Where the rutters have you been? We've got squad members looking all over for you – Tandrek's down there by himself. You've had a break, three prisoners – can you rutting believe it?' He stopped and looked over the curious group. 'Who is this child?'

'Colonel Strellek's daughter; that's where I've been. He got called out to the docks, something he was expecting from Treven. He asked me to bring her after she'd eaten.'

'Strellek? Who's that?' Sergeant Willis sounded bemused.

Hoyt interrupted, 'Sorry, Sergeant, we are assigned to Colonel Strellek, but he didn't want us bringing the girl out through the gates and then the encampment without at least a sergeant with us. He wanted to find the lieutenant, but none of us knew where he was at the time.' Hoyt could lie like a professional; given half a chance he would have stood on the stairs the rest of the aven, spinning a wrinkle-free tale that would have had all of them believing they had been ordered to bring Milla out to her father on the wharf.

'The lieutenant?' Willis was confused. 'He's down in the prison wing cursing your name all the way to the Northern Forest. If I were you, I'd let these three take the girl out while you get yourself—' His gaze fell to Hoyt's hands, which were still a grim testament to his efforts to break out of his cell. 'Soldier,' he interrupted himself. 'How did you get—?'

Hoyt nonchalantly clasped his hands behind his back. 'Sorry, Sergeant?'

'They're here!' Sergeant Willis screamed, 'I have them up—'

Churn's punch took Sergeant Willis beneath the chin, lifting him clear off the stairs. He rolled into a heap, eight or nine steps below, and Hannah wondered if he was dead – until a commotion erupted from the main floor two levels down. 'They're coming,' she said, the words feeling strange in her dry mouth. 'What do we do?'

'Up this way,' Alen ordered, 'quickly.'

Hannah felt the world crash into the sun. 'Not up, no, we can't go up. There's no way out up there.'

'You have to trust me.' Alen was trying to remain as calm as possible.

'Where are we going?' Hoyt asked.

'There's an atrium at the end of the hall. Across the way is a courtyard.'

'Alen, we're three levels up,' Hoyt said.

'No, no, no,' Churn was signing furiously, 'I won't go out there, I won't.'

'We've no choice,' Alen said. 'The courtyard is off a banquet hall or a meeting hall on the second level of the other wing. It's a short fall. I'm sure we can jump it. It's that or them.' Alen pointed down the stairs.

Hoyt tweaked Milla's nose. 'Can you fly?'

Milla nodded, grinning. 'A little bit. Can you?'

'I'd better be able to.'

Alen had already started up the stairs and down the upper hall. Hoyt followed. Churn waited with Hannah.

'I can't do it,' he signed.

'Jump down to a courtyard? I can't imagine why not.'

'Maybe they'll think of something before we get there.'

'Whatever – we can't stay here.' She reached for his hand and the two of them hurried after the others.

MEYERS' VALE

'What do you suppose happened to them?'

'He might have thrown them away.'

'Garec?' Steven was incredulous. 'You've seen the pride he takes in them – he made them himself; if he truly planned never to fire another shot, he would have given them to you.'

'He hasn't said anything.' Mark checked to be sure Garec was still out of earshot. They were riding south along the river through Meyers' Vale into the Blackstone foothills. 'Ever since he got back, he's been staring into space. Something happened to him, Steven.'

'Of course it did,' Steven retorted. 'He failed to raise a finger to help you and Brand; he knows you're disappointed with him. We're within inches of wrapping this whole wretched business up, and he feels like he's fumbled the ball inside the five – *of course* he's embarrassed. But you and Brand aren't making it any easier for him. Let's face it: this has been the worst nightmare any of us could ever imagine, and you're holding an outbreak of honest-to-goodness compassionate conscientious objectorness – or whatever you call it – against Garec. He chose to die rather than to kill; I don't know if I could have been that brave given the circumstances.'

Mark grimaced. 'Okay, you're right. I've been a bastard – but I don't think that's it. Something happened between there and here.'

'Ask him,' Steven said. For a few seconds they were back in Idaho Springs, in a place where things made sense. 'He's your friend,' Steven went on, 'whether you're disappointed in him or not. If you think something happened on the way down here that caused him to fire—'

'Twenty. He had about twenty in his quiver.'

'Okay, so about twenty arrows ... I bet he'll tell you. Give up the grudge; ask him what's wrong.' Steven guided his horse around a tree partially blocking the trail. Mark ducked and rode under it, wondering if there was some Eldarni superstition – seven hundred Twinmoons of bad luck, boils, locusts and flatulence, maybe – that was all he needed to cap a terrifically abysmal few days. He smiled at Steven, then slowed to allow Garec to catch up with him.

'Hey,' he said as Garec came alongside.

'Is that a greeting in Colorado, Mark?'

'Yep.'

'A good greeting or a bad greeting?' Garec looked grim; he slouched in the saddle as if he were carrying the world on his shoulders.

'One of the best,' Mark said.

'Well, *hey* then.'

In the ensuing uncomfortable silence, Mark thought about dropping it, but finally he said, 'I'm sorry about the other day. It was wrong of me to expect you to kill if you choose not to.'

'You had the best interests of the Resistance at heart, Mark. I was the one at fault.' Garec's voice was flatly matter-of-fact.

'No, I didn't,' Mark said, 'I've never given a pinch of raccoon shit about the Resistance.' Garec looked at him, and Mark shrugged. 'What can I say? I wanted to learn to shoot because I was in love with Brynne and she was taken from me – from all of us – because I wasn't a killer, I wasn't in control of those nightmarish circumstances. Well, now I am a killer, and I'm happy to go on killing.'

'Then I'm sorry for you,' Garec said. 'Some day it will catch up with you.'

'As it did you?'

Garec nodded.

'It might,' Mark said, 'and you've been doing it for a lot longer than me, so you've probably got some insights into these things that I don't. I may have found enough rage inside me to kill, but I'm not stupid, so what do I learn from you? I learn that many of the things I had to abandon in myself are still there somewhere, sublimated under five hundred layers of anger, hatred, disgust, whatever. But putting pressure on you to kill those soldiers the other day, that's about the worst thing I have ever done. It's far worse than killing people who are attacking me. So I'm sorry, Garec. I won't let it happen again.'

He looked grim as he continued, 'I have these hazy memories of living in a place and a time where killing another person would never be a possibility, not in a month – a Twinmoon – of Sundays, and yet here I am, a bloodthirsty monster out hunting for Malakasian soldiers to mount on the wall of my living room.'

'We all have untapped potential,' Garec said. Mark felt a chill run up his spine.

'I'm sorry.'

'Thank you.'

'So what happened?'

'It's not important.'

'Not important? By my count, you're down about twenty arrows – and no matter how badly you want to snap that bow in two, you still carry it with you. You didn't throw those arrows away, Garec; Steven's right. So what happened?'

Garec reached over and took Mark's forearm. 'When the time comes, I'll be ready. You needn't worry.' His eyes blazed, and for the first time that day he sat tall in the saddle, looking deadly dangerous. Mark recoiled slightly; he might think himself a killer, but he would fold were he ever to face Garec one-on-one.

'You took out a soldier?'

'Fifteen soldiers, maybe seventeen. They were coming up behind you; there was nothing else I could do.'

'Good Christ,' Mark said, '*why*? You could have let them come – we're on horseback, they wouldn't have caught up with us.'

'They were cavalry.'

The enormity of Garec's accomplishment was not lost on Mark, especially now he had been attacked by a cavalry charge himself. Just the thought of facing them alone made him shudder ... Sallax had been right: this young man truly was the *Bringer of Death*. Mark reached out to take Garec's hand. 'I'm truly sorry,' he said. 'This is a hideous time.'

'Yes, it is, but I will be ready,' Garec repeated.

Mark took out half his arrows, which Garec accepted without saying a word.

'My father always used to say that the lowest of low points in his life were always the start of the next good thing,' Mark said.

'Did your father enjoy plenty of good things in his life?'

'I think he did, yes.'

'Then he must have had plenty of low points as well,' Garec said.

'I think he did that too,' Mark agreed.

'If we see the other side of this business, I'll pay for my actions. I'm not sure how, but that day is coming. Perhaps it will be the start of the next good thing.' Garec was staring straight ahead; Mark wondered if he were talking to himself.

He slapped the bowman on the back. 'If we see the other side of this business, and you find a way to atone, I'll go with you and atone as well.'

Finally Garec smiled. 'That will be fine with me. And I think Brynne would like that too.'

Steven was watching Mark and Garec out of the corner of one eye; he felt the tension ease somewhat when Mark slapped Garec on the back and Garec smiled, however briefly; they would be all right now, both of them.

As he rode in silence beside Gilmour, he took in the wintry beauty of Meyers' Vale, and thanked God they weren't attempting to cross the Blackstones during this season. He wondered if any of them would have survived had they begun their journey from Estrad even a Twinmoon later. The terrain had changed now they were off the Central Plain and he was careful to guide his horse around the plentiful rocks and stumps as they followed the river upstream. Gently rolling hills were interrupted periodically by upland meadows; now and then the river widened into bogland and slowed to a more majestic pace.

'How far was it from the canyon to the place where you think Nerak buried the spell table?' Gilmour finally broke the silence.

'It was at least ten days on the *Capina Fair*, but some of those days were less productive than others. If we keep along this path, I know I'll recognise that hilltop.'

The old man filled his pipe and began puffing. 'I ask, because from what Brand says about the underground cavern and the partisans' caves, we are two or three days' ride from the canyon you found.'

'That makes sense,' Steven said, 'it'll be just a day or two before we are well into the foothills, and then maybe another two or three days to the place on the river – although that's the bit I can't really predict, because we were on the raft and most days we were happy to be there because the terrain on either bank didn't look like the most hospitable place to travel – and that was during autumn.'

'Perhaps we'll get lucky and find a smooth way through.'

'Here's hoping,' Steven agreed.

'How are you doing with that spell?'

'Which one? Our camouflage blanket? I hardly think about it now; it feels almost as though it will just keep itself going until I tell it to stop.'

'Or until you grow old and die. Many spells are like that. That's

514

why it was so easy for me to open the doors at Sandcliff, to turn on the fountains and ignite all the torches. Magic is funny that way: once you get it started, it has a wonderful – if sometimes terrifying – propensity to spin itself out over and over again.'

'As if you change what is real, and then step away,' Steven mused.

'That's exactly right.' Gilmour patted his horse contemplatively. 'Sometimes what's real does change; other times, well, it's just an illusion. That's what separates us from carnival magicians.'

'It's an emotional undertaking,' Steven said, wondering if the Larion sorcerer would agree. 'I mean, I know the staff is more powerful when I'm motivated by the right emotions. Does that make sense to you?'

'Yes, I think you're right: the power *we* wield is so malleable, it can be almost—'

'Wait,' Steven cut him off.

'What is it?' Gilmour turned in the saddle, checked the forest around them and looked back at the others to see if any of them had detected anything.

'The trees up there.' Steven gestured to the edge of a hillside that fell away to an area along the river they couldn't see.

'What about them?' Gilmour raised a hand to stop the others.

'They're blurry.'

'Blurry?'

'Blurry, melting, you know, like things have been getting ever since Lessek's key knocked me down at the landfill. They're softening up, as if, when I get closer, they are going to begin to run together, and—'

'Critical elements will become clear.' Gilmour tentatively finished his thought.

'The magic has been doing that for me ever since Idaho Springs,' Steven explained. 'It's happened a few times; it seems to get rid of everything I can overlook, allowing me to focus on what's most important.' His voice faded to a whisper. 'When you are running, run.'

'What's that?'

'*When you are running, run,*' he said. 'My old cross-country coach was a man of few words.'

The line of trees continued to soften as they approached. Steven dismounted, pushed his way into the undergrowth and dropped to his knees, where he started digging frantically in the snow.

'What are you doing?' Mark called.

'He's here, just over that hill,' Steven answered, reaching into his pocket and removing Lessek's key. He could feel his heart pounding, thrumming in his temples, rushing blood to his cold fingers and causing him to fumble awkwardly with the crooked little stone. He looked up at Gilmour and waited. When the old man nodded, he dropped the key into the hole, covered it with snow and burned a black cross in a nearby tree with one end of the hickory staff.

Steven stood. 'I don't know how he could have known we were here.'

Gilmour deliberately tapped the ashes from his pipe and replaced it inside his tunic.

'Please,' Steven implored the others, 'stay here. Don't come up. Even better, go back to Wellham Ridge and wait there. We were fools to bring you down here.'

No one moved; Steven climbed back into the saddle and rode forward. Gilmour moved to ride beside him. When they reached the top of the short rise, Gilmour said, 'Yes, you're right. I can feel him now.'

The hickory staff began to glow, warming Steven's hands.

The hill sloped down gradually to an irregularly shaped clearing interrupted in several places by isolated clumps of trees. The snow was pristine, with not even animal tracks marring its surface. To the east, the clearing narrowed, and a thin line of snow ran down into the glen and up to the water's edge. The river there was dark, shadowed, even in the bright midday sun. Several large boulders, some as big as houses, were scattered in the water, creating deep, swirling eddies.

Darkness, deep water, cold shadows, and a wintry clearing that narrowed to a point where rushing water met sedentary earth, and in the middle of it all, a titanic boulder reared out of the water. A young girl sat on top of the boulder, dangling her feet over the edge and gnawing on an apple. She was pretty, with shoulder-length hair, a narrow face and oval eyes set perfectly over the thin bridge of her nose.

'Who the hell is this?' Steven whispered.

'That's Bellan Whitward,' Gilmour said, 'Princess Bellan. Malagon's daughter. Look at her hands.'

The girl sitting there – she couldn't have been more than seventeen years old – was wearing black leather gloves. She was already dead, her soul imprisoned alongside her father's, somewhere in the profound emptiness of the Fold.

'Welcome Fantus, Steven Taylor,' she called, her light voice making them all shiver. 'I must commend you on your powers of deduction, Fantus. I admit, I don't know how you did it. But given your presence here, I must assume that you have somehow worked out where to find the spell table – maybe you've even worked out how to extract it.'

Bellan tossed the apple core into the river, reached inside her tunic and withdrew a red, white and blue pouch of *Confederate Son* chewing tobacco. She delicately teased out a lump and popped it into her mouth and sat there chewing quietly for a while, savouring the flavour, then she spat bubbly brown juice into the swirling eddy below.

'I suppose I must blame myself,' she said. 'I obviously said too much at Sandcliff, and now here we are.'

Steven rode into the clearing as the trees around him faded from view, melting into one another and leaving just the wintry carpet, the boulder and the girl for him to consider.

Bellan continued, 'Remind me, Fantus, did I mention the guards?'

Gilmour reined in beside Steven. 'You said the table was warded by Eldarn itself, and Eldarn's most ruthless gatekeepers.'

Bellan's face split in a smile that managed to be both gruesome and coquettish. 'I did say that, didn't I? Well, grand. Would you like to meet them, Fantus? Steven? Would you like to meet Eldarn's most ruthless gatekeepers? Because I have been literally *dying* to introduce you.' She giggled and waved a hand; the river started to bubble as small ripples spread across the water, churning white when a number of the horribly familiar bone-collecting monsters tumbled out and skidded across the clearing.

Steven was ready for them. The staff flared to life, glowing red-hot with impatient rage and untapped power. He slid from the saddle, trying not to worry about his horse as the animal reared, whinnied in terror and bolted.

'I'll handle these things,' he said to Gilmour; 'you keep your eye on Bellan, or Nerak, or whoever it is up there.'

'Careful, Steven, careful,' Gilmour warned. 'There is much more to face here than just these monsters.'

Steven moved purposefully, intent on engaging the bone-collectors before they could reach the slope and his friends, but he was just a few paces away when something inside him – the staff, Lessek's key, or even some primitive survival instinct – shouted a warning, *On your left!*

Steven ducked, and whirled to his left, swiping the hickory staff through the air between him and the blurry trees. There was a tear, a rip in the world like those he had seen in the hills above Idaho Springs, and flying out at him was a wraith, one of Nerak's immortal slaves. He barely brought the staff around in time to slice through the gossamer body and send the ghostly shards reeling through the clearing like so much tobacco smoke; killing it was easy, but there had been something oddly familiar about this wraith and Steven froze as the creature's wild-eyed, homicidal visage flashed into his mind's eye.

'No!' he screamed, and killed the first bone-collector with a massive bolt from the staff; the subterranean monster exploded in front of him, hundreds of armour-plated legs like so much chitin shrapnel firing through the clearing, into the river and out among the trees.

Steven's mind raced. It couldn't be. *Please don't let it be true; not her . . . please tell me I didn't just send her soul back into the Fold—*

'When you are running, Steven, run.' Gilmour's voice reached through his anguish. 'When you are running, run, and when you are fighting, *fight*.'

'When you are fighting, fight,' Steven repeated. 'When you are fighting, fight.'

We might not make it.

'When you are fighting, fight,' he said again, the rhythm of the words helping him regain his composure.

'It was her,' Bellan called sweetly from her perch on top of the boulder, 'and you just sent her soul back into the Fold for ever. Some friend you are, Steven Taylor. Poor old Myrna Kessler.'

Steven fought to contain his rage. *Compassion, Steven. Fight with compassion. It is the strongest emotion in the world: stronger than rage, stronger than fear and stronger than hatred.*

'She will be in there for ever now – and let me tell you, it is an unpleasant place; I've been in there once or twice myself,' Bellan laughed, a cackling chortle that made Steven's blood rush to his head.

'When you are fighting, fight, Steven,' Gilmour called again. 'Don't think about anything else.'

Steven tried to clear Myrna Kessler's face from his mind, but it burned there, leaving an indelible impression: Nerak had killed her and then sent her against him, and he had damned her soul to the Fold for ever.

THE ATRIUM

The third level of Welstar Palace was as far up as anyone outside Prince Malagon's personal staff was able to go without permission: a long, wide carpeted hallway hung with tapestries. Torches burned in wall sconces, and the whole floor felt homey, comfortable. Hannah wondered who lived here.

From the main hall lots of smaller hallways ran east or west, some emptying into large rooms and others spilling out through etched-glass doorways onto balconies overlooking the encampment and the river beyond. Halfway down the hall, Hannah nearly ran into a Malakasian soldier, a woman. She had obviously been off duty, for she was struggling to buckle on her tunic belt when Hannah rushed by.

'What's happening?' she asked.

Hannah allowed her terror to diffuse into her lies. 'Back there. It's some kind of attack. We're going to get Colonel Strellek. He's supposed to be here in the atrium. But you go, they need help – second level.'

The woman nodded obediently and turned towards the commotion, but she had gone barely two steps when Churn grabbed her by the throat.

'Churn,' Hannah cried, 'what are you doing?'

'Go,' he signed, then drew the woman's sword from its scabbard and tossed it across the hall.

'Churn!'

'Go.' He tightened his grip and lifted the soldier from the ground; she kicked furiously and pried at his fingers, trying to break free.

'What—?' she croaked, her face turning red and her eyes bulging.

Churn lowered his face to hers, and a horrifying moment of recognition passed over the woman's face. She remembered him.

'You— you were dead,' she croaked, 'the— the tree.'

Churn nodded, lowered her to the floor and relaxed his grip long enough for her to take a breath; a moment later, he closed his fingers again.

'Please don't,' she rasped, 'so sorry.' Her face was red, and her eyes had begun to bulge from their sockets again. Churn wondered idly if he squeezed hard enough, would they would pop out and bounce across the floor? What kind of noise might that make? She had such a pretty face; he remembered it so well, her pretty face, and the way she had climbed the tree so nimbly. She had been the most beautiful woman he had ever seen; he would have told her that if he could have summoned the strength to speak that day. But he couldn't speak, and his parents, his sister and the baby had all died that day. This pretty, nimble woman had left him there, a crucified joke, hanging in the cottonwood tree.

And now here she was, a gift from the gods. Churn thought about letting her take another breath, but the noise from the other end of the hall was too loud now. They were too close. He didn't have time to torture her, though he had dreamed of this moment for so long. From the atrium, he heard glass shatter: Hoyt and Alen had broken through the window.

I'm not going out there, he thought. *I don't care if it's dark, and I can't see down. I'm not going out there.*

Looking back, Churn saw the first soldier reach the third-level hall. There would be a few moments of confusion before they realised who he was ... he still couldn't jump. *I guess this won't help my case,* he thought as he slammed the woman's head into the stone wall. It was quick, crushing her skull, and gruesome, but what made it worse was that he didn't feel anything; there was no great wellspring of satisfaction. He dropped the woman's body and ran down the hall behind Hannah. He had nearly reached the atrium when the first arrow struck him in the shoulder.

'You go first,' Alen said. 'Get a good grip, and I'll hand Milla out to you. Then I'll come out and take her while you jump across.'

'And then?'

Alen didn't want to say it out loud; instead, he gestured, *I'll throw her to you.*

'All right. There's no time to think about it, anyway.' Hoyt smashed out the window over the sloping stone buttress with the hilt of his dagger, then bashed out the remaining shards from the lead frame. He nearly slipped off the stone precipice, not realising how steeply it sloped, but he clamped his thighs together and gripped either side of the buttress, then reached up to take Milla. The little girl came willingly, giggling as she was folded into Hoyt's arms.

'This is high up,' she said. 'Do we have to stay here long?'

'No,' Hoyt said, 'not long at all. Ready?'

'Ready.'

'Here we go.' He loosened his grip and began slipping backwards, towards the raised end of the buttress; it wasn't much, just a few stones and some mortar, but it would be enough to stop him from tumbling into the darkness. He could already see Alen sliding towards them.

'This was a great idea,' Hoyt called. 'I tell you, a view like this would cost a fortune anywhere else.'

Alen glanced quickly across the encampment towards the river. The watch-fires lining the path between the palace's main gate and the wharf were great blazes, and there were literally thousands of campfires, looking as though Nerak had scattered handfuls of fiery gemstones to flicker on the frozen hills around Welstar Palace.

'Funny,' said Alen, 'but I'm afraid if we don't hurry, we'll be getting a much closer view.'

'Take her,' Hoyt shouted. 'I'm going over. You're right; it isn't far to the courtyard.'

Alen let go with his hands and felt his stomach clench into an iron knot as he lost his centre of balance, but that was enough to get what remained of the dead sergeant's adrenalin flowing and he felt his legs strengthen to an almost inhuman degree. 'Come here, Pepperweed. I've got you,' he said encouragingly.

'Where is he going?' she asked, apparently nowhere near as afraid of heights as either of her self-appointed protectors.

'Just over to that snowy patch of grass right there.'

'That's not far.'

'Do you want to jump it together with me, or by yourself?'

'I'll go by myself. Will he catch me?'

'Yes he will,' Alen assured her. 'Just don't look down.'

Hoyt made the leap easily, rolling to his feet when he landed. The 'courtyard' was in fact a second-level balcony laid out as a miniature botanical garden, now winter-bare, with just a few patches of grass poking through the snow.

'I think I'm scared,' Milla said. 'Can we go back inside?'

'Just another moment, Pepperweed,' Alen said comfortingly,

allowing himself to slip down to the raised stones at the end of the buttress.

'It's cold.'

'I know, Pepperweed, but it's just another moment.' He checked to be sure Hoyt was standing, arms raised and waiting for her. 'All right, turn around.'

'I really don't want to.'

'Pepperweed, you have to.' He held her fast, gripping the buttress with all the strength in his fit young thighs, then lifted her up until she was standing on the end the sloped beam. 'Close your eyes now.'

'I don't want to,' she whined, 'I don't want to.'

Ignoring her, he said soothingly, 'Close your eyes and—' he tossed her with all his strength, '*go!*'

Hoyt couldn't hear over the sound of the wind rushing between the wings of the old castle. As he stood waiting, he squinted into the darkness, to make sure he saw Milla when Alen threw her over the short but deadly-deep abyss separating them.

There she was! Hoyt pressed himself into the wall, feeling like his timing was off; something about the darkness had first made the girl appear much closer, but now she seemed to be falling from a great height, or maybe taking an inordinately long time to come down.

Then she was there, light as a feather pillow, landing softly in his arms. Hoyt realised this child was special. 'You *can* fly!' he exclaimed, hugging her to his chest and twirling her round.

'People can't fly, silly,' Milla said. 'I just know how not to fall bad. I used to fall a lot when I was little, well, littler than now, and I made that up so all the bonks wouldn't hurt.'

'You made it up?'

Alen leaped over the gap to join them.

Hoyt repeated his question. 'You made it up?'

'So falling and bonking hard won't hurt any more, but it's not flying.'

He looked to the former Larion Senator; Alen raised his eyebrows and nodded.

'Good job, Milly. You were the best of all.'

Then Hannah screamed and slipped off the buttress.

THE GLEN

The concussion from Steven's explosion knocked Gilmour to the snowy ground, the blast still ringing in his ears. Bits of bone-collecting monster fell like armour-plated rain and he rolled quickly to avoid a large piece of the creature as it crashed down beside him.

He felt his own magic respond and hoped it would be enough – the insecurities and crippling failures of the past Twinmoons almost made him wish it would disappear entirely; at least things would be simpler then. He thought of the spell book he had stolen from the *Prince Marek*; he wished he had never taken it, for all it had done was to show him vast tracts of magic about which he knew nothing. He had been convinced the Windscrolls held some clue, because Pikan had screamed for them that night so long ago, but no: she had just been desperate to save her life. Larion magic had been a cruel bedfellow this past Twinmoon; feeling it come alive inside him did not instil Gilmour with the confidence it might have long ago.

For nine hundred and eighty Twinmoons, Gilmour had learned to weave common-phrase spells, working wonders with Larion magic – but it had never been enough. Every time he had tested a large weave, he had been forced to go underground again. Working a Larion spell was like ringing a bell and screaming, *Come and get me, Nerak, I'm right here in Estrad Village.* Running had cost him valuable Twinmoons of his life, perhaps too many; were it not for Steven Taylor and the hickory staff, Gilmour wasn't sure he would be alive today.

But here he was, armed with some notoriously mercurial magic, standing beside the staff-wielding foreigner who had returned Lessek's key to Eldarn. Gilmour had done his best to help Steven learn as much as possible, although it had never felt like enough. He wondered why Lessek, the old Larion founder, had permitted him to live so long – for hundreds of Twinmoons, he thought it was because it would be up to him eventually to face Nerak and restore freedom and prosperity to Eldarn, but now, sitting in the snow, cold and damp, his ears still ringing from the hickory staff's explosive attack, he thought perhaps it was because of Steven Taylor: he had to see this young man to this place and time.

Gilmour felt emboldened by the notion that perhaps his role was to teach, not to work spells. 'Lessek?' he murmured, wrestling the old fisherman's body back to its feet. 'Is that what you did? Is that why I'm here?'

He looked over at Steven and saw the younger man was still struggling with the fact that he had just condemned his friend's soul to an eternity inside the Fold. Gilmour's heart broke for him. *Say something, you doddering old fool*, he told himself.

'When you are running, run, Steven,' he whispered again – trite, but it had the desired effect. Steven seemed to stand a bit taller; the staff glowed a bit brighter.

'When you are fighting, fight!' he shouted; Steven nodded and whirled on Nerak-as-Bellan and the rest of the bone-collectors.

Gilmour looked up at the pretty young girl sitting there on the boulder and smiled. *We've got you, you murdering old horsecock. You're going to lose.*

The attack came from his right as one of the eldritch creatures hunkered down on all its jointed legs, sprang with unholy speed into the low-hanging branches and then leaped for Gilmour. With no time to run, Gilmour crouched, whispered a few words and felt the magic slam into the bone-collector, tumbling it to the ground, where it twitched for a moment and then died.

'Come on, Nerak!' he roared, 'I'm standing right here.'

Bellan held out both hands, a gesture that said *be patient*, and *all in due time*.

Gilmour loosed a devastating blast at the girl, but one of the monsters leaped high into the air, exposing its obsidian underbelly and taking the brunt of the spell. The magic split it in half and as its armoured exoskeleton collapsed in a crumpled pile, its steaming guts spilled into the snow. Immediately another bone-collector crawled from the river, picking its way over the corpse. Gilmour, distracted by the monster's apparent disregard for its dead brother, left himself exposed for an instant; time enough for Bellan to fire a spell at him.

The magic struck him in the stomach, knocking the wind out of him and casting him back across the clearing. As he rolled to a stop, the closest of the bone-collectors skidded in his direction, ready to rip him to pieces. It crouched low, preparing to spring on the incapacitated sorcerer.

'Rutters, that hurt,' Gilmour croaked, curling up. 'Must catch my brea—' He saw his attacker and reached out to summon a spell. He didn't have the strength to kill it now; all he could hope to do was to knock it off balance for a moment, just long enough to get out of the way. It was about to leap; it rolled its bulbous eyes, the pupils shrinking to pinpricks in the light. He couldn't help wondering if the creature was amused as it bent at all its joints and opened a dripping, foetid maw to emit a coarse, high-pitched shriek of laughter.

Thunk.

Thunk.

Two arrows struck the beast almost simultaneously; each shaft buried itself in one of the monster's eyes. The creature wailed, a horrible cry that made Gilmour wince. He caught sight of Garec and Mark, standing side by side on the hill; they both continued to fire into the bone-collector's body. Some of the arrows glanced off the armour-plating, but others found their mark in soft, bleeding tissue: where the neck joined the body, the pliable stalks supporting its eyes, the fleshy area between its hinged jaw and its plated underbelly.

Even blinded, it leaped for the old man, but in vain; the archers had given Gilmour the time he needed and the bone-collector's body blocked out the sun before shattering in midair. Blood, pieces of entrails and bits of chitin showered the clearing.

Garec and Mark had saved his life, but in coming to his aid, they had alerted the remaining monsters to their own position; two immediately made for the forest and clambered through the interconnecting branches towards them.

'Oh no,' Mark groaned, 'here they come.'

'Get out of here, now!' Gilmour shouted. He didn't wait to see what they did, but ran to where Steven was facing off against two of the subterranean monsters – and stopped, frozen in his tracks as Pikan Tettarak waved to him from the water's edge. She was a wraith, but it was her, nonetheless, calling out to him, gesturing, trying to tell him something. Transfixed, Gilmour walked slowly towards her, only vaguely aware of Steven leaping and striking out in an epic battle, the armoured monsters exploding, imploding, or simply dying where they stood. One was hit so hard that it flew up over Pikan's translucent body and into the side of the boulder where Bellan stood, watching the fight with delight.

Now Steven whirled towards the forest, levelled the hickory staff and ignited the trees in a blazing inferno, trapping those bone-collectors that had been stalking his friends. One managed to get out; Gilmour heard it splash into the river somewhere upstream. It would be back. But right now he needed to concentrate on Pikan.

How had Nerak brought her here? Had she really been his slave all these Twinmoons? It didn't seem possible; she had been too strong a sorcerer to have been trapped this long.

'Pikan? Is that you?'

The wraith nodded emphatically.

'Tell me how to free you!' Gilmour took another step forward and reached out as she gestured towards the hillside. She was trying to show him something, maybe some way to free her from Nerak? He turned and watched the trees as Harren Bonn stepped into the meadow.

'Oh northern gods,' Gilmour gasped, 'not you, too – please, not you.' He felt his knees buckle and then give way as guilt over-whelmed him.

'Gilmour!' someone shouted.

'Harren, I'm so sorry, I should have been out there with you. I belonged on those steps with you – I told myself I would be the final defence, inside the spell chamber, but that wasn't true.'

'Gilmour!'

'I locked you in that stairwell because I was too terrified to stand with you, I was afraid to die. Harren, if I could go back—'

'Gilmour, get up!'

A bolt of lighting passed through his body; Steven had struck him with the hickory staff. Shrieking, he sprang to his feet. 'Damnation, Steven Taylor! I *hate* it when you do that!'

'When you are fighting, fight,' Steven growled.

The old sorcerer was suddenly awake and turned back to his former students in time to watch them change from the beautiful young people he had loved to hideous, ghostly killers. Their faces blurred, melted away, and their mouths fell agape beneath empty eye sockets. It was too late to ward himself magically as they attacked together, but Steven was there at his side, and one slash with the glowing hickory staff sent both tortured souls to the depthless abyss of the Fold.

Steven reeled right and incinerated another of the monsters, then strode back to face Gilmour. 'It's all right,' he said, clapping Gilmour on the back. 'We never could have anticipated this.'

'But I don't know how to fight them,' the old man said with a shudder.

'Can't you see it?'

'What?'

'The Fold is open: there, there, and there.' He pointed to three places around the clearing. 'Three tears, just like I saw that morning at the dump. That's where the wraiths are coming through; the bastard's sending people we knew, hoping it will weaken us.'

'I can't see them,' Gilmour said, straining to make out these rips in the fabric of the world.

'Then leave them to me.' Steven swallowed hard. 'We have to turn the tide. We'll never beat him if he keeps us on the defensive, because eventually, one of us will slip.'

But Steven knew Nerak was winning, for the fallen Larion sorcerer was forcing him to fight out of anger and hate, keeping him on his toes, striking out at him again and again. He recognised too many of the wraiths he annihilated, almost weeping as he saw friends and neighbours of Jennifer Sorenson, but having to steel himself as he sent them all into the Fold. There was no compassion here as he ripped through their souls, slicing them open and batting the pieces through the blurry mystical backdrop and into the darkness beyond.

He stood in front of Gilmour, protecting his mentor from the wraiths while the old man blasted away at the bone-collectors until the last of them, one eye blinded and dragging two of its jointed legs, retreated into the river and disappeared with the current.

All the while, Nerak-as-Bellan watched from above, casting a spell down on them from time to time which Steven deflected with ease. The girl watched her ranks of wraiths attack endlessly, enjoying Steven's display of heroism and bravery and marvelling at his determination to live, to protect his mentor and to win the day. Nerak was impressed with the foreigner's decision to be compassionate, an emotion he had nearly forgotten in the past thousand Twinmoons, and he felt Steven weakening every time he rended these otherwise peaceful, departed spirits.

That made Nerak chuckle. With a wave, he summoned the final three wraiths; these would weaken Steven enough that he would be able to sweep him up and cast him into the Fold alongside all those he had slain. But first, he needed the key.

Bellan jumped nimbly from the boulder as Steven hacked through the ghost of the little girl Nerak had killed in Rona when he needed a body for his trip across the Fold into Colorado.

'Well done, Steven,' Nerak said. 'I'm sure that little one will enjoy an eternity of cold, dark emptiness, don't you?'

Steven started towards him. 'I'm—'

'No, wait a moment, I have something for you,' Nerak said, raising Bellan's hand to stop him.

'No,' Steven said as he continued towards the girl. 'No more tricks, no more games, no more keeping us on our heels. It's time to send you back to hell.'

Bellan shrugged, raising both palms to the sky. 'Whatever you say, but here they are anyway.'

Steven stopped as Gabriel O'Reilly, the Seron warrior Lahp and the young mother who had carried her baby onto the plane in Charleston came towards him. In his mind's eye he saw the mother, barely out of girlhood herself, and he heard the baby screaming in his memory, its cries weaving into Nerak's amused laughter; a polyphony that threatened to drive him insane. Gabriel and Lahp: these were more than just friends, he owed them his life; without them he would have died in Eldarn.

There was no way he would be able to battle these ghosts.

'Use the staff, Steven, do,' Nerak chuckled. 'It's quite the most impressive spell Fantus has ever worked. He has my compliments. A silent talisman, really, I am impressed. I look forward to using it myself in the near future – in the *very* near future.'

Steven felt like he had been punched. 'What did you say?'

Bellan's face showed a little surprise at the question. 'I look forward to using your staff when you and old Fantus are gone,' Nerak repeated.

'This staff?'

'That's the only one here, my friend.'

'Mark was right about you,' Steven said, feeling the staff's power rise in burgeoning waves. 'Everything he said was right. I just didn't put it all together until now.'

'Mark Jenkins? The Eldarni prince? Worry not, little sorcerer. I have plans for him too.'

'Shut up,' Steven spat. 'Lessek told us about your weakness, and Mark was right all along: this is it, this is the best that you can do. A few ghosts, an almor here and there, and maybe a big spell from time to time when you need to wipe out a city like Port Denis, but all told, that's all the bullets you have in the gun, Nerak. The evil creature that came through the Fold and took you never knew it, because *you* never knew it. Or if you did know it, you forced yourself to forget.'

Nerak was amused at Steven's bravery. 'I am not sure what you are trying to say, Steven Taylor, but you won't be saying much more—'

'I am saying that you are a hack, and you always *were* a hack. The evil that took you believed what you believed about Eldarn, about the Larion Senate, about the Fold, but especially about a second-rate sorcerer named Nerak.' Now Steven laughed. 'You don't understand power, because as a human, as a sorcerer, you never understood mercy, compassion and love. If you did, you would have been a much more powerful dictator. I am tired of you, Nerak, so now I am speaking to the creature that married you, the creature and the master it serves out there in the Fold somewhere. *You* picked the wrong magician, creature.'

'Enough!' Nerak roared; Steven felt like his head would explode with the noise. 'That was amusing, Steven Taylor, but you are forgetting one thing: I don't have to be the most powerful sorcerer the lands have ever known. I only have to be powerful enough to defeat you and that sorry milksop you've been following these past Twinmoons. With Lessek's key in my possession, I will open the Fold and realise all the glory of its power and I will rule all the worlds in eternity.'

'You still don't get it,' Steven said. 'You can't beat me.' He dropped the hickory staff at Bellan's feet. 'You can't beat me, and I won't fight these wraiths, my friends.'

'Steven, what are you doing?' Gilmour whispered.

To the wraiths, Steven said, 'Gabriel, Lahp, and you, ma'am – I'm sorry I don't know your name – I won't fight you. I am so sorry for what has happened to you, especially to you, ma'am, because your death was partly my fault, but I won't fight you. I won't send you into the Fold. I won't do it.'

'Then you will die, Steven Taylor.' Nerak gestured to the wraiths, who turned together towards Steven, rage sweeping over their features. They swirled about Bellan's head, then swooped down on Steven in a wave of homicidal fury.

THE FLYING BUTTRESS

Hannah reached the atrium and stopped, watching Hoyt and then Alen climb out onto the slanted stone buttress. She didn't want to step through the window until at least one of them had successfully made the jump to the courtyard on the opposite wing of Welstar Palace. She turned back to look for Churn and watched as he slammed the soldier's head into the stone wall.

Why do that now, Churn? she wondered. *Is killing one of them going to make a difference when there are hundreds of thousands of them just outside?*

Behind him, the first soldiers reached the landing and started down the hallway after them. She hoped her uniform would give her an extra few seconds of misdirection, and perhaps it would be enough for her to make the jump to the north wing.

The atrium was a grand chamber; thousands of glass panes were carefully fitted into a sphere-shaped leaded framework; the rounded ceiling, which must have weighed tons, was supported by tall stone buttresses, flying up from the greensward below like a Gothic cathedral. This marvel of Eldarni architecture was like a great glass lens upheld by a circle of stony bones.

Hannah turned back to the window. Alen tossed Milla over to Hoyt.

Foster, Geronimo, Griffey.

The cold wind coupled with the sheer drop stole her breath for a few seconds. She considered stepping back to face whatever awaited her in the prison wing: at least there it was warm half the time, but then she saw Churn come down the hall at a sprint, countless soldiers in pursuit and she climbed quickly onto the buttress and slid carefully down towards a decorative stack of raised stones she hoped would keep her from slipping off the end.

It was much steeper than it had looked from the window, and out here, the wind felt strong enough to knock her off. *I can do this*, she thought. *Just don't look down. It's not far across. It's like a gymnastics competition in Hell.*

A powerful gust blew her clumsy bun undone and she let go with one hand to stuff her hair down inside her collar – and lost her balance …

Shrieking, she tried to tighten her thighs around the buttress, but she had slipped too far round. Reaching wildly, the fingers of her left hand found a strong handhold, but her right slipped across the smooth surface, finding nothing to slow her inexorable slide into the darkness.

Pull yourself up. You have to pull yourself up, because no one is coming to save you. Haul yourself back onto the beam. There are no other options.

Heaving with all her might, Hannah reached for the edge of the buttress, stretching as far up and out as she could without jeopardising the death-like grip she maintained with her left hand. If she could only catch that edge, she knew she could pull herself up far enough to swing a leg onto the lower slant of the beam; it wasn't that far … but it was so cold and so dark. She was out here by herself, and somehow Hannah Sorenson knew she wasn't strong enough to do it.

I can't do it, oh God, I'm going to fall. Geronimo. Geronimo. Cesar Geronimo, played centre field for the '75 Cincinnati Reds. I'm going to fall—

'Up here!' The voice was gruff, impatient and angry.

Ohthankyouthankyouthankyou … The prison, yes, the prison will be fine. Please help me—

'Take my hand.'

'I can't see you,' she shouted, 'I'm going to fall! I can't reach you.'

'I can't come out there.'

'Churn?' Hannah tried to pull herself up, but her arms were failing. 'Is that you, Churn? Did you just—?'

'Hannah, reach up here for me.'

'I can't see you, I can't move – this is all I can— come and get me, Churn, please; I can't hang on here much longer.'

There was an agonising pause, until she heard, 'All right. I'm coming.'

A few seconds later, she felt Churn reach down for her. His hand, dripping something, clamped like a vice around her forearm. He lifted her back onto the buttress with ease.

She hugged him and cried, 'Thank you, oh, thank you, Churn.

I know this must be terrible for—' Her hands came to rest against three arrows protruding from his back. 'You're shot. Oh God, Churn, they shot you!'

'Yes. I'm fine though,' he lied. Hannah could see he was so stricken with vertigo he wouldn't be able to move. She didn't know if he even felt the arrows, because his fear of high places had completely overwhelmed him.

'All right, we'll do this together. Slide with me down—'

A muted thud cut her off; Churn winced and barked, a guttural cry that sent blood spewing from his mouth onto Hannah's tunic. He had taken another arrow in the back, this one at point-blank range from an archer at the window. The Malakasians were firing down on them through the broken panes in the atrium.

'Slide!' she screamed, but Churn, even with four arrows in him, was quicker. He grabbed the small dagger she wore at her waist, turned halfway and threw it back through the window. Hannah watched as the knife buried itself to the hilt in the bowman's chest.

It's light and well-balanced, almost a throwing knife.

It bought them a handful of seconds to get down the buttress and leap to safety.

'Here we go, Churn,' she said calmly, 'slide down, grip the stones and jump. Don't think about it. Just do it. You and me, come on.'

'Hannah, I can't do it.'

'I'm not leaving you up here alone, so let's go.'

A dagger flew past her head in a poor imitation of Churn's killing throw; another followed quickly behind the first. She didn't know if the soldiers were trying to hit them or just to knock them off, but it was clear none of them wanted to step out onto the buttress. They shouted insults and threw more knives; they even made crude jokes while they waited for another archer to push through the crowded ranks.

Hannah took Churn's hands in hers. 'We have to try.' A short sword glanced off her shoulder, slicing a gouge out of her flesh, but she barely noticed it. Behind them, Hoyt and Alen were shouting. Above, the soldiers were crying out and throwing anything they could find. To her right, Hannah heard more glass shatter; that would be the second archer. Their time had run out.

The world diminished in size. The cold dissipated. The wind died and the shouts faded. She and Churn stared into one another's eyes and time slowed. Hannah whispered, 'Please Churn. Please come with me.'

His eyes danced, as if in the glow of ten thousand campfires, and blood dripped from his chin. Hannah could see that at least one of the arrows had pierced his lung: he needed help right away. She wondered what Hoyt would be able to do for his best friend while they tried to make their escape. He would have to decide whether he was a healer or a thief. The irony of it made Hannah smile. 'Come with me, Churn. Let's go.'

He held out his fist. 'One more time.'

'Please Churn.'

'One more time.'

Hannah shook her fist three times and extended two fingers.

Churn's fist bounced three times and remained closed. He smiled, the blood staining his teeth almost black. 'Rock breaks scissors. I win. Take care of Hoyt.' He let go of her and tumbled from the buttress without a sound.

Hannah screamed as the world rushed back to envelop her in darkness, cold and wind. She was scarcely aware of her leap to the courtyard, and completely unaware of the Malakasian bowman who fired and barely missed as she jumped to safety.

And then there was nothing but confusion, turning right and left, running up and down staircases as Hoyt guided her along, his hand clasped firmly over the slash in her neck. Now Alen cast a spell that threw six guards back into the wall, knocking them senseless; there Hoyt used Hannah's blood on his hands and clothes to convince a squad that the partisans were cornered in an empty chamber one flight up. On they went, running, walking, tiptoeing past open doorways and well-lighted windows, until they reached an exit that spilled out into the monsters' encampment.

Hannah, too shocked still to cry at Churn's death, whimpered that she didn't want to go out there.

On the last set of stairs, they met two soldiers. Hoyt took charge. 'Corporal Hannah has been injured fighting the prison fugitives,' he said, pointing back the way they'd come. 'One of them's rutting huge, a monster! I've been ordered to get her to Colonel Strellek's healer, but the main gate's blocked.'

The soldiers nodded agreement. 'You'll need to stay here,' Hoyt said, thinking fast, 'there'll be more wounded coming through: direct them to Colonel Strellek's encampment out along the river. That's the quickest way.'

The soldiers thanked him, held the gate open and wished Hannah well as she passed. Neither of them asked Alen about Milla and once outside, none of them were inclined to linger long enough to wonder why.

Blindly following Hoyt toward the Welstar River, Hannah, confused, bleeding and frightened, tried to remember the gruff timbre of Churn's unused voice. It seemed important that she remember; Hoyt would want to know.

THE STAFF'S SECRET

'Look out, Steven!' Gilmour cried as he rushed forward take the brunt of the wraith attack on himself.

'Steven!' Mark shouted, and ran down into the meadow, followed closely by Garec, Kellin and Brand.

Steven raised a hand to the wraiths sweeping down on him – and Gabriel, Lahp and the young mother halted in midair, their ghostly arms reaching down for him. Steven looked up at them and said, 'I'm sorry. This must be terrible for you. Wait here and I'll do what I can when this is finished.' He gestured towards the boulder at the river's edge and the wraiths, still trying to break free, floated towards it. They hung there, immobile.

For the first time Steven detected a ripple of fear in Nerak and without pausing he lashed out at the dark prince, determined to exploit every weakness he could find. 'You see? Even your slaves can't obey you if I direct them otherwise.' He allowed the magic to flow from both hands and it pounded into Bellan's chest. The girl was hurled backwards through the air and crashed with a grim thud into the boulder. Blood discoloured the stone where her head cracked open.

Apparently unfazed by her fractured skull, Prince Malagon's daughter rose up from where she had fallen and blasted a brutal spell at Steven and Gilmour. The blow sent both men sprawling; Gilmour rolled backwards over what had been one of the bone-collectors. Bellan stood looking down at the hickory staff, then picked it up, brushed the snow from it and held it close to her face.

Steven rolled to his feet and gestured for everyone to stay where they were, willing them to understand: *I have this under control*, he thought. *Let them understand!*

Alone, he crossed to Bellan.

'It was not wise of you to give this up, Steven Taylor,' Nerak said, still considering the staff.

'Nerak's weakness lies elsewhere,' he replied. 'That's what Lessek told Gilmour, and he was right. Do you know where it lies? It lies right there in your hands, and you're just too blazingly stupid to see it. We all were – all of us except Mark, thank Christ – but now it's clear, and you … cannot … win.'

'I already have, Steven Taylor. With this staff, you were the only one who could have stood against me. And with this staff and Lessek's key, my quest is nearly complete.'

'Look closely at it, Nerak.' Steven wanted this conversation done. 'Have you ever seen it before? I'm betting you have.'

Bellan's eyes flared as she raised the staff. 'You have been insulting and tiresome, but now you have crossed into stupidity, Steven Taylor, and I cannot bear stupidity, especially from one whom I have come to respect.'

'Go ahead.' Steven felt his hands begin to tremble; sweat trickled down his temples. 'Kill me with it.'

'Gladly,' Nerak said, 'although in some ways it is a shame. You and I could have been so powerful together.'

Bowstrings thrummed as Garec and Mark fired, but Nerak raised one of Bellan's hands and the shafts fell harmlessly to the ground. Gilmour unleashed a spell to knock Bellan off her feet, stunning Nerak long enough for one of them to retrieve the staff, but Nerak turned it away with a wave; the spell sailed up and over the river and crashed through a riverside willow.

'Come on,' Steven said, 'do it now.'

Nerak reared back and swiped viciously at him.

Garec had to tackle Mark to keep him from diving into the fray. Brand, Kellin and Gilmour all screamed as the dark prince swung the staff at Steven's head. Her eyes aflame, Bellan's entire body heaved with anticipation of feeling the staff's magic rip through the irritating foreigner's body. She screamed as she swung; the staff blurred in the air, a reaper's enchanted scythe.

Effortlessly, Steven reached up and caught the hickory staff in one hand. Pressing forward, he twisted it out of Bellan's grip and shoved it into her face. 'Look again, Nerak. Look closely at it. I think you've seen it before.'

Now Nerak shook as he reached out Bellan's hands to take hold of Steven's throat, to choke the life from him. 'I'll kill you the old-fashioned way!' he roared, but Steven easily batted Bellan's hands away.

'You're not paying attention,' Steven said, backing the girl towards the river. 'I want you to look closely at the staff, and I want you to tell me if you have ever seen it before.' He slapped Bellan hard across the face.

To her great surprise, it hurt; a red welt rose up on her cheek, and a dribble of blood ran from one nostril. It was the first human injury Nerak had sustained in nearly a thousand Twinmoons and it shocked him silent.

'I think you have seen this before.' Steven pressed the end of the staff up into Bellan's face. 'Haven't you?'

The girl's self-assurance began to crumble and she looked over Steven's shoulder to where Gilmour approached warily. 'Fantus?'

'Yes, Nerak?' Gilmour was still confused.

'It's Kantu's staff,' Nerak said, almost wonderingly. 'His walking staff. I hid some things inside it one night, a long time ago.'

'He hid knowledge about himself,' Steven said to Gilmour, 'things Nerak knew about himself.' He turned back to Bellan. 'That's what you hid inside this staff, and that's why you couldn't sense it when I used it – and that's why you couldn't remember it. It's also the reason you can't stop it from reminding you now of just who you really are.'

Steven looked back at Mark, who grinned encouragingly and gestured, *Go on!*

'When you opened the Fold that night,' Steven said, 'the evil creature that claimed you didn't get the all-powerful sorcerer he believed to you be, but a lying fool, one who had convinced himself he was something he wasn't. You hid the truth from yourself inside this staff, and you did it using a deception spell from the second Windscroll. Gilmour told us about it after his conversation with Kantu at Sandcliff,' he added as an aside to Mark, connecting the dots for his friends.

He laughed. 'Nerak, you fooled yourself into believing you could master the Larion spell table, but the spell table was too much for you.

'The evil minion took you hostage; too bad that it believed what you had in your head at the time, because it never knew that you had worked a spell to deceive yourself. I'm almost impressed, Nerak: you couldn't completely erase your memory – your *knowledge* – of your own weaknesses, so you hid it inside this staff. Pretty clever idea, really.'

Now Bellan nodded. 'We were on Larion Isle. Kantu left his walking staff in the common room. I was there alone, experimenting with the deception spell. When I finally managed to get it to work—'

'You hadn't realised you would need a vessel to contain the knowledge,' Gilmour finished for him.

'You changed your own perception of yourself,' Steven went on. 'You lied to yourself – hey, we all do it! But you did it with the help of the Windscrolls, and you made it permanent, in your mind, and, over time, in the minds of those around you. When the evil minion took you, it believed what you believed, because in your mind it was true.'

He motioned across the meadow. 'My friend Mark there lost the woman he loved, you miserable, stinking bastard. She was one of Garec's best friends. Her name was Brynne. You probably don't remember her.' Steven moved and Bellan retreated again. 'I had a friend in Colorado, Myrna Kessler; she planned to go to college this year. You killed her.' Now Bellan was standing ankle-deep in river mud. Steven's voice was soft, almost conversational. 'Mika, Jerond, Versen, Sallax, Rodler – remember them? No? You killed them all. It might have been the Nerak who believed himself to be the most powerful man in Eldarn, or the Nerak standing here now, the one suddenly aware of his own weaknesses, but let me assure you, I don't care. I swore to be compassionate, and I *was* compassionate: I gave you the hickory staff. I gave you the power to save yourself – and you tried to turn it against me. You, the real you, tried to kill me with it.'

The others had to strain to hear Steven whisper, 'Nerak, that was a mistake.'

Bellan trembled. She had gone a cadaverous shade of grey. 'No,' she begged, her lip quivering, 'please don't.'

'I have to,' Steven said simply. 'Goodbye, Nerak.'

He raised one hand above his head and drew a pattern in the air. With the other he grabbed a handful of Bellan's tunic.

'Fantus!' Nerak cried, 'don't let him do this – we were *friends*, Fantus.'

Steven picked Bellan up and heaved her through the tear in the blurry, melted-paraffin backdrop. He stood for a moment in the doorway to the Fold as Nerak's screams echoed back, then faded away.

Now Steven turned to the three rifts Nerak had opened in the Fold that morning and as he gestured at each, it closed and the forested glen around them came slowly back into focus.

The Fold was closed.

Smiling, Steven turned to his friends, who were staring at him in wonder, speechless. Gilmour held the hickory staff reverently in one hand.

'What?' Steven asked. 'Mark figured it out. I just did the dirty work.'

He walked to Gilmour and gave the old sorcerer a great bear-hug. 'Thank you,' he said.

'Thank me? For what?' Gilmour replied. 'Without you, I would now be dead, not once, but ten or twelve times over.'

'And without you, Gilmour, I would be lost.' Steven hugged him again, then walked over to Mark.

'Wait,' Gilmour said, 'here.' He held out the staff.

'Oh, that's just a stick now,' Steven said dismissively. 'You can keep it if you like, or toss it in the river.'

'I don't understand.'

'None of us do,' Garec added.

'I'll explain it all,' Steven said, 'but the short answer is that Mark was right. Nerak never knew what was in the staff because as soon as he put it there, he forgot it.'

'He lied to himself and used magic to make it real?' Brand asked.

'Basically,' Steven replied. 'I began to work it out when Mark and Garec told me I had done magic without using the staff. I was able to do things that should have been child's play for Nerak, but they weren't. He was a master sorcerer who'd studied the Larion system for hundreds of Twinmoons; I was a guy with a stick I found in the woods – but we were sparring with one another as equals. So I figured either he wasn't so powerful after all, or maybe I was a lot more powerful than I appeared. I guess in the end it was a little of both.'

'How did that all become obvious in the past aven?' Garec asked.

Steven chuckled nervously. 'It didn't. Dropping that staff was the hardest thing I've ever done. I was so scared; I thought I was going to piss my pants – but I had to give it to him. I had to give Nerak the chance to save himself.

'Compassion,' Mark said.

'Right,' Steven agreed. 'That's when the staff is at its most powerful, so I had to take the risk.'

'And when he tried to use it against you—' Garec started.

'Nothing,' Steven said.

'Like that night it shattered.'

'Exactly.'

Garec was confused. 'I still don't know how you took down that pine without breaking the staff,' he said.

'Because that wasn't the staff's magic,' Mark said. 'That was the first time we saw across the Fold. It was a different power.'

Steven clapped his hands together to get their attention. 'Right, we still have work to do,' he announced.

'What do you mean?' Garec asked.

'We have to get the table.'

Mark said, 'But I thought you closed the Fold?'

'I closed the *tears*, but I closed those in Idaho Springs, too: that's not *sealing it off* for ever. That's rather more difficult – to do that, I'm afraid we're going to need the spell table, Lessek's key and our Larion Senator here.' He wrapped an arm around Gilmour's shoulders.

'Are you saying he could come back?' Kellin asked, a tremble in her voice.

'No. He's gone for good.' Steven's face darkened a moment. 'So are Myrna and all the others I banished today.'

'But not Lahp and Gabriel,' Garec said.

'Oh my God, you're right—' Steven exclaimed, 'they're still up there. Mark, do me a favour, will you, and get Lessek's key – you remember where I buried it?'

'Sure,' Mark said and trotted towards the tree line, stopping abruptly after a few steps. 'Uh, Steven, can you put out the fire?' The flames from the spells and the staff's incendiary strikes had spread along the riverbank.

'Sure – well, I think so!' He closed his eyes and reached towards the river, feeling the air around his fingertips thicken until it was almost malleable. He imagined a great wave, arising somewhere upstream and rushing down to break over the boulders into a shower of droplets that drenched the surrounding area and helped drown the fire. There was a great crash, and he opened his eyes to see thick clouds of steam billowing down to the riverbank.

'Well, that worked okay,' Mark said, wiping his face dry. 'Remind me never to ask you to pick up milk for breakfast – the stampede would kill us all!'

Steven laughed. 'Sorry – not very subtle, was it? I'll have to work on that. Now I've got to set this lot free.' He crossed to where the wraiths, translucent once again, waited patiently. Lahp and Gabriel were smiling; the Seron and the erstwhile bank manager appreciated Steven's over-the-top display of magical prowess.

Gilmour walked with him. 'So you are—?'

'I must be, Gilmour. I don't know how I could have done those things otherwise. I think Nerak hid more knowledge in that staff than power.'

'So Mark was right on several issues.'

'He must be – we were drawn to Idaho Springs, both of us, just like his father had been. It's the reason I turned down all those job offers, and why we both went to college within spitting distance of the town, and then stayed. Lessek's key was keeping us there.'

'So is it true about Mark as well?'

Steven shrugged. 'That he's Rona's heir, and Eldarn's king? I think it must be, don't you? I can't see him hanging around long enough to lead this place to democracy or anything, though. Still, it'll look good on his CV: history teacher, swimming coach, king of all Eldarn.'

Gilmour laughed. 'You know, something occurred to me today, too: I've always thought I was still alive because I was supposed to battle Nerak, but then I realised I've been around a long time waiting for *you*; I think that supports your theory, doesn't it?'

Steven shook his head and grinned. 'Who could ever have guessed that I would end up here?'

'Someone who knew you were a powerful sorcerer, someone who knew where you were – both you and Mark – and why.'

'Lessek?'

'Lessek.'

'But you're still here, and still alive,' Steven said, trying to puzzle it through. 'If your charge has been met, wouldn't you fade away, or something mystical like that?'

'The Fold is still navigable,' Gilmour reminded him.

'Right. Slipped my mind.' Steven slapped a hand to his forehead. 'I forgot these three again, too.' He turned once again to the imprisoned wraiths.

Steven's heart froze in his chest as he looked at them; Gabriel and Lahp were gesticulating wildly towards the forest, trying to communicate something.

'Oh God,' Steven whispered, 'Mark.' He freed the wraiths with a gesture and grabbed Gilmour's hand.

'Come on!' he shouted, sprinting towards the trees. 'Mark!' he screamed but he was horribly afraid that they were too late.

Mark came down the hill and stepped cautiously beneath the trees.

Water dripped all around as his boots sank into slushy snow made filthy with ash and burned bits of tree. It felt like an acrid cloud of smoke had swallowed him whole, so he covered his eyes and trudged, still coughing, down the trail until he reached the tree with the cross burned into its trunk.

He started digging with the toe of his boot, not really wanting to get either himself or his clothes any more wet than they already were, but after a bit he gave up and crouched down. He dug in with both hands, trying to ignore the freezing slush and icy mud. 'No matter,' he said aloud, 'Steven will dry them out for me.'

He had got down almost far enough when he heard someone say, 'Hello Mark Jenkins.'

Spinning round, he shrieked, 'God! You scared me!'

Mark strained his eyes through the smoke to see who was there. 'Who is that?' he asked loudly and drew his battle-axe.

The disembodied voice came to him through the haze; for a moment Mark thought he could see the outline of a man, but it flickered in the smoke and then was gone.

'Who is that?' he asked again. His voice cracked; his hands were shaking.

'One half of a marriage that went tragically wrong, Mark Jenkins, but I will not make that mistake again.'

An itch began to irritate the back of Mark's left wrist and he rubbed it against the coarse fabric of his tunic while he searched the forest for the steam and smoke visitor. When pain paralysed his forearm, he suddenly realised what had happened – and that it was too late to scream. He flailed about wildly for a moment, gripped the tree in a one-armed hug and then slumped to the ground.

In the instant before he felt himself fade away, Mark was given a glimpse of the entity's vision for the future, Mark's future. Then he did scream, but no one heard him. He slipped into the darkness and was still falling when the entity rubbed a handful of snow across the back of his bloody, pus-covered wrist. He would need gloves. Reaching into the muddy hole beside the tree, Mark retrieved Lessek's key, slipped it inside the pocket of his Gore-tex jacket and jogged north along the path into Falkan.

Follow Steven Taylor's adventures
in the next exciting instalment of

THE ELDARN SEQUENCE:
The Larion Senators, Book 3